OLIVER
TWIST

Charles Dickens

COLLINS
CLASSICS

Harper Press
An imprint of HarperCollins*Publishers*
77–85 Fulham Palace Road
Hammersmith
London W6 8JB

This edition published 2010

Charles Dickens asserts the moral right to be
identified as the author of this work

A catalogue record for this book is available from the British Library

ISBN-13: 978-0-00-735088-9

Printed and bound in Great Britain by Clays Ltd, St Ives plc

MIX
Paper from
responsible sources

FSC
www.fsc.org
FSC° C007454

FSC™ is a non-profit international organisation established to promote
the responsible management of the world's forests. Products carrying the
FSC label are independently certified to assure consumers that they come
from forests that are managed to meet the social, economic and
ecological needs of present and future generations,
and other controlled sources.

Find out more about HarperCollins and the environment at
www.harpercollins.co.uk/green

Life & Times section © HarperCollins*Publishers* Ltd
Gerard Cheshire asserts his moral rights as author of the Life & Times section
Classic Literature: Words and Phrases adapted from
Collins English Dictionary
Typesetting in Kalix by Palimpsest Book Production Limited,
Falkirk, Stirlingshire

History of Collins

In 1819, Millworker William Collins from Glasgow, Scotland, set up a company for printing and publishing pamphlets, sermons, hymn books and prayer books. That company was Collins and was to mark the birth of HarperCollins Publishers as we know it today. The long tradition of Collins dictionary publishing can be traced back to the first dictionary William published in 1824, *Greek and English Lexicon*. Indeed, from 1840 onwards, he began to produce illustrated dictionaries and even obtained a licence to print and publish the Bible.

Soon after, William published the first Collins novel, *Ready Reckoner*, however it was the time of the Long Depression, where harvests were poor, prices were high, potato crops had failed and violence was erupting in Europe. As a result, many factories across the country were forced to close down and William chose to retire in 1846, partly due to the hardships he was facing.

Aged 30, William's son, William II took over the business. A keen humanitarian with a warm heart and a generous spirit, William II was truly 'Victorian' in his outlook. He introduced new, up-to-date steam presses and published affordable editions of Shakespeare's works and *Pilgrim's Progress*, making them available to the masses for the first time. A new demand for educational books meant that success came with the publication of travel books, scientific books, encyclopaedias and dictionaries. This demand to be educated led to the later publication of atlases and Collins also held the monopoly on scripture writing at the time.

In the 1860s Collins began to expand and diversify and the idea of 'books for the millions' was developed. Affordable editions of classical literature were published and in 1903 Collins introduced 10 titles in their Collins Handy Illustrated Pocket Novels. These proved so popular that a few years later this had increased to an output of 50 volumes, selling nearly half a million in their year of publication. In the same year, The Everyman's Library was also instituted, with the idea of publishing an affordable library of the most important classical works, biographies, religious and philosophical treatments, plays, poems, travel and adventure. This series eclipsed all competition at the time and the introduction of paperback books in the 1950s helped to open that market and marked a high point in the industry.

HarperCollins is and has always been a champion of the classics and the current Collins Classics series follows in this tradition – publishing classical literature that is affordable and available to all. Beautifully packaged, highly collectible and intended to be reread and enjoyed at every opportunity.

Life & Times

About the Author

Charles Dickens was born in Portsmouth, England, but had moved to Kent and then to London by the time he was ten years of age. Not long afterwards, his father was arrested and sent to debtors prison for spending beyond his means. This marked a transition in Dickens' early life from one of carefree childhood to one filled with relative uncertainty. Above all, Dickens began to ferment ideas of social injustice and a need for social reform in pre-Victorian Britain. These ideas would become the staple of his literary cannon.

He was first published in 1833 at the age of twenty-one. By the time of his death, in 1870, he had completed nineteen (and a half) novels. His final work, *The Mystery of Edwin Drood*, was only half completed. All of Dickens novels were first published in serialized form, which was the orthodox method in his day.

While other writers tended to complete their books first and then divide them into chapters for serialization, Dickens preferred to write his chapters as and when required. This lent itself to his success, because it meant that his prose was naturally tailored to the format of monthly instalments. Rather than having hiatuses randomly placed in the overall storyline, according to page counts, Dickens was able to deliberately leave the reader wanting more. In essence he had invented the concept of the literary cliff-hanger. Combined with his enhanced characterizations and fabulist allegory this made for a compelling read, so Dickens became the single most popular author in Victorian Britain.

By his forties, Dickens had taken to touring and giving animated readings of his books to captive audiences, who delighted in his ability to bring his characters to life. This was an extension of the storytelling craft he had learnt as a parent, as he had ten children with his wife Catherine, whom he married in 1836.

As well as being a humanistic novelist, Dickens was also a humanitarian in real life. For example, he gave his support to the abolition of slavery in the USA and helped to establish a home of the redemption for 'fallen' women in England, which meant those women who had resorted to crime and prostitution to find their way in life, but had ended up in debtors' prisons, common prisons or workhouses.

A hostel named Urania Cottage was established in London, where these women were given a second chance. They were clothed and fed, provided with education and taught the skills to be able to find domestic employment.

Needless to say, Dickens rubbed shoulders with many extreme characters due to his work with the 'fallen' in society. Due to his celebrity, he also met many people at the other end of the spectrum, so there was no shortage of people upon whom to base his fictitious characters.

In 1865 Dickens was involved in a rail crash at Staplehurst, Kent, in which ten people died and many more were injured. Dickens was not hurt but his efforts to help the injured and dying left him with post traumatic stress disorder for the remaining five years of his life.

On that fateful day he had been travelling with his lover, Ellen Ternan. Dickens had separated from his wife in 1858 when Catherine found out about his affair with the younger woman, who was eighteen years his junior. He managed to keep Ellen a secret from society by never appearing in public with her and keeping her hidden in houses rented under false names. He knew very well that Victorian society would not have held a favourable view of his domestic arrangements. His infidelity would have caused an absolute scandal, especially as he was viewed as a highly virtuous and moralistic man. Falling in love with another was simply not acceptable behaviour, especially as Queen Victoria had remained steadfastly loyal to the memory of her beloved Prince Albert since his demise in 1861 and would continue to do so until her own death in 1901.

Dickens died of a stroke exactly five years following the rail crash at the age of fifty-eight years old. He wished to be buried in a modest and private manner, but his funeral was a rather grand affair at Westminster Abbey.

The Victorian Era

The work of Charles Dickens is rather unusual in that it has become something of a social document of the Victorian era in Britain. That is because his books are a primary point of reference to anyone wondering about what it was like to have lived at that time. Consequently, Dickens' imagined Victorian world is largely perceived by many as a real world, filled with exaggerated characters in extreme circumstances. The result is an odd set of paradoxes. For example, the Victorians are generally understood to have been austere and pious in the extreme, but the truth is that they lived in a highly progressive society where people were pushing the boundaries of behaviour and questioning the role of religion.

Dickens' version of Victorian society came from his requirement for idiosyncratic characters to make his stories work more effectively in evoking emotional responses in the reader. It is fair to assume that they were based on the personalities of people he had met, so there was an element of truth, but Dickens' boiled them down to amplify the traits he was most interested in and remove the traits superfluous to literary requirements. In effect, Dickens' Victorian world is a cartoon, where the more mundane, mediocre and prosaic details serve only as a neutral backdrop, while the colourful characters are allowed to distract the attention.

It can be no coincidence that Dickens himself was an accomplished performer. He was the William Shakespeare of the Victorian age, both writing and taking to the stage as a storyteller. This makes it easy to understand why his characters had such pronounced identities, because Dickens would mentally assume different roles whilst story telling, both on paper and when treading the boards.

As any parent or teacher will attest, it is quite necessary to exaggerate characters with gestures and voices while story telling to capture the imagination of the audience and leave no confusion about who is who. This is exactly what Dickens was doing, so that his version of the Victorian world became one of overblown polarity: villains and do-gooders, the devout and the morally fallen, the wealthy and the poor, the beautiful and the ugly, the selfish and the selfless. Those who fall 'somewhere between' truly are the silent majority in Dickensian Britain.

OLIVER TWIST

CONTENTS

CHAPTER 1

Treats of the place where Oliver Twist was
born, and of the circumstances attending
his birth

Among other public buildings in a certain town, which for many
reasons it will be prudent to refrain from mentioning, and to which
I will assign no fictitious name, there is one anciently common to
most towns, great or small: to wit, a workhouse; and in this workhouse was born; on a day and date which I need not trouble myself
to repeat, inasmuch as it can be of no possible consequence to the
reader, in this stage of the business at all events; the item of mortality
whose name is prefixed to the head of this chapter.

For a long time after it was ushered into this world of sorrow
and trouble, by the parish surgeon, it remained a matter of considerable doubt whether the child would survive to bear any name at all;
in which case it is somewhat more than probable that these memoirs
would never have appeared; or, if they had, that being comprised
within a couple of pages, they would have possessed the inestimable
merit of being the most concise and faithful specimen of biography,
extant in the literature of any age or country.

Although I am not disposed to maintain that the being born
in a workhouse, is in itself the most fortunate and enviable circumstance that can possibly befall a human being, I do mean to say
that in this particular instance, it was the best thing for Oliver
Twist that could by possibility have occurred. The fact is, that
there was considerable difficulty in inducing Oliver to take upon

himself the office of respiration, —a troublesome practice, but one which custom has rendered necessary to our easy existence; and for some time he lay gasping on a little flock mattress, rather unequally poised between this world and the next: the balance being decidedly in favour of the latter. Now, if, during this brief period, Oliver had been surrounded by careful grandmothers, anxious aunts, experienced nurses, and doctors of profound wisdom, he would most inevitably and indubitably have been killed in no time. There being nobody by, however, but a pauper old woman, who was rendered rather misty by an unwonted allowance of beer; and a parish surgeon who did such matters by contract; Oliver and Nature fought out the point between them. The result was, that, after a few struggles, Oliver breathed, sneezed, and proceeded to advertise to the inmates of the workhouse the fact of a new burden having been imposed upon the parish, by setting up as loud a cry as could reasonably have been expected from a male infant who had not been possessed of that very useful appendage, a voice, for a much longer space of time than three minutes and a quarter.

As Oliver gave this first proof of the free and proper action of his lungs, the patchwork coverlet which was carelessly flung over the iron bedstead, rustled; the pale face of a young woman was raised feebly from the pillow; and a faint voice imperfectly articulated the words, 'Let me see the child, and die.'

The surgeon had been sitting with his face turned towards the fire: giving the palms of his hands a warm and a rub alternately. As the young woman spoke, he rose, and advancing to the bed's head, said, with more kindness than might have been expected of him:

'Oh, you must not talk about dying yet.'

'Lor bless her dear heart, no!' interposed the nurse, hastily depositing in her pocket a green glass bottle, the contents of which she had been tasting in a corner with evident satisfaction. 'Lor bless her dear heart, when she has lived as long as I have, sir, and had thirteen children of her own, and all on 'em dead except two, and them in the wurkus with me, she'll know better than to take on in that way, bless her dear heart! Think what it is to be a mother, there's a dear young lamb, do.'

Apparently this consolatory perspective of a mother's prospects failed in producing its due effect. The patient shook her head, and stretched out her hand towards the child.

The surgeon deposited it in her arms. She imprinted her cold white lips passionately on its forehead; passed her hands over her face; gazed wildly round; shuddered; fell back—and died. They chafed her breast, hands, and temples; but the blood had stopped for ever. They talked of hope and comfort. They had been strangers too long.

'It's all over, Mrs. Thingummy!' said the surgeon at last.

'Ah, poor dear, so it is!' said the nurse, picking up the cork of the green bottle, which had fallen out on the pillow, as she stooped to take up the child. 'Poor dear!'

'You needn't mind sending up to me, if the child cries, nurse,' said the surgeon, putting on his gloves with great deliberation. 'It's very likely it *will* be troublesome. Give it a little gruel if it is.' He put on his hat, and, pausing by the bed-side on his way to the door, added, 'She was a good-looking girl, too; where did she come from?'

'She was brought here last night,' replied the old woman, 'by the overseer's order. She was found lying in the street. She had walked some distance, for her shoes were worn to pieces; but where she came from, or where she was going to, nobody knows.'

The surgeon leaned over the body, and raised the left hand. 'The old story,' he said, shaking his head: 'no wedding-ring, I see. Ah! Good night!'

The medical gentleman walked away to dinner; and the nurse, having once more applied herself to the green bottle, sat down on a low chair before the fire, and proceeded to dress the infant.

What an excellent example of the power of dress, young Oliver Twist was! Wrapped in the blanket which had hitherto formed his only covering, he might have been the child of a nobleman or a beggar; it would have been hard for the haughtiest stranger to have assigned him his proper station in society. But now that he was enveloped in the old calico robes which had grown yellow in the same service, he was badged and ticketed, and fell into his place at once—a parish child—the orphan of a workhouse—the humble, half-starved drudge—to be cuffed and buffeted through the world—despised by all, and pitied by none.

Oliver cried lustily. If he could have known that he was an orphan, left to the tender mercies of churchwardens and overseers, perhaps he would have cried the louder.

CHAPTER 2

Treats of Oliver Twist's growth, education,
and board

For the next eight or ten months, Oliver was the victim of a systematic course of treachery and deception. He was brought up by hand. The hungry and destitute situation of the infant orphan was duly reported by the workhouse authorities to the parish authorities. The parish authorities inquired with dignity of the workhouse authorities, whether there was no female then domiciled in 'the house' who was in a situation to impart to Oliver Twist, the consolation and nourishment of which he stood in need. The workhouse authorities replied with humility, that there was not. Upon this, the parish authorities magnanimously and humanely resolved, that Oliver should be 'farmed', or, in other words, that he should be despatched to a branch-workhouse some three miles off, where twenty or thirty other juvenile offenders against the poor-laws, rolled about the floor all day, without the inconvenience of too much food or too much clothing, under the parental superintendence of an elderly female, who received the culprits at and for the consideration of sevenpence-halfpenny per small head per week. Sevenpence-halfpenny's worth per week is a good round diet for a child; a great deal may be got for sevenpence-halfpenny, quite enough to overload its stomach, and make it uncomfortable. The elderly female was a woman of wisdom and experience; she knew what was good for children; and she had a very accurate perception of what was good for herself.

So, she appropriated the greater part of the weekly stipend to her own use, and consigned the rising parochial generation to even a shorter allowance than was originally provided for them. Thereby finding in the lowest depth a deeper still; and proving herself a very great experimental philosopher.

Everybody knows the story of another experimental philosopher who had a great theory about a horse being able to live without eating, and who demonstrated it so well, that he got his own horse down to a straw a day, and would unquestionably have rendered him a very spirited and rampacious animal on nothing at all, if he had not died, four and twenty hours before he was to have had his first comfortable bait of air. Unfortunately for the experimental philosophy of the female to whose protecting care Oliver Twist was delivered over, a similar result usually attended the operation of *her* system; for at the very moment when a child had contrived to exist upon the smallest possible portion of the weakest possible food, it did perversely happen in eight and a half cases out of ten, either that it sickened from want and cold, or fell into the fire from neglect, or got half-smothered by accident; in any one of which cases, the miserable little being was usually summoned into another world, and there gathered to the fathers it had never known in this.

Occasionally, when there was some more than usually interesting inquest upon a parish child who had been overlooked in turning up a bedstead, or inadvertently scalded to death when there happened to be a washing—though the latter accident was very scarce, anything approaching to a washing being of rare occurrence in the farm—the jury would take it into their heads to ask troublesome questions, or the parishioners would rebelliously affix their signatures to a remonstrance. But these impertinences were speedily checked by the evidence of the surgeon, and the testimony of the beadle; the former of whom had always opened the body and found nothing inside (which was very probable indeed), and the latter of whom invariably swore whatever the parish wanted; which was very self-devotional. Besides, the board made periodical pilgrimages to the farm, and always sent the beadle the day before, to say they were going. The children were neat and clean to behold, when *they* went; and what more would the people have!

It cannot be expected that this system of farming would produce any very extraordinary or luxuriant crop. Oliver Twist's ninth birthday found him a pale thin child, somewhat diminutive in stature, and decidedly small in circumference. But nature or inheritance had implanted a good sturdy spirit in Oliver's breast. It had had plenty of room to expand, thanks to the spare diet of the establishment; and perhaps to this circumstance may be attributed his having any ninth birthday at all. Be this as it may, however, it *was* his ninth birthday; and he was keeping it in the coal-cellar with a select party of two other young gentlemen, who, after participating with him in a sound thrashing, had been locked up for atrociously presuming to be hungry, when Mrs. Mann, the good lady of the house, was unexpectedly startled by the apparition of Mr. Bumble, the beadle, striving to undo the wicket of the garden-gate.

'Goodness gracious! Is that you, Mr. Bumble, sir?' said Mrs. Mann, thrusting her head out of the window in well-affected ecstasies of joy. '(Susan, take Oliver and them two brats up stairs, and wash 'em directly.) My heart alive! Mr. Bumble, how glad I am to see you, sure-ly!'

Now, Mr. Bumble was a fat man, and a choleric; so, instead of responding to this open-hearted salutation in a kindred spirit, he gave the little wicket a tremendous shake, and then bestowed upon it a kick which could have emanated from no leg but a beadle's.

'Lor, only think,' said Mrs. Mann, running out, —for the three boys had been removed by this time, —only think of that! That I should have forgotten that the gate was bolted on the inside, on account of them dear children! Walk in, sir; walk in, pray, Mr. Bumble, do, sir.'

Although this invitation was accompanied with a curtsey that might have softened the heart of a churchwarden, it by no means mollified the beadle.

'Do you think this respectful or proper conduct, Mrs. Mann,'

inquired Mr. Bumble, grasping his cane, 'to keep the parish officers a-waiting at your garden-gate, when they come here upon
porochial business connected with the porochial orphans? Are you
aweer, Mrs. Mann, that you are, as I may say, a porochial delegate,
and a stipendiary?'

'I'm sure, Mr. Bumble, that I was only a-telling one or two of
the dear children as is so fond of you, that it was you a-coming,'
replied Mrs. Mann with great humility.

Mr. Bumble had a great idea of his oratorical powers and his
importance. He had displayed the one, and vindicated the other.
He relaxed.

'Well, well, Mrs. Mann,' he replied in a calmer tone; 'it may
be as you say; it may be. Lead the way in, Mrs. Mann, for I come
on business, and have something to say.'

Mrs. Mann ushered the beadle into a small parlour with a
brick floor; placed a seat for him; and officiously deposited his
cocked-hat and cane on the table before him. Mr. Bumble wiped
from his forehead the perspiration which his walk had engendered,
glanced complacently at the cocked-hat, and smiled. Yes, he smiled.
Beadles are but men: and Mr. Bumble smiled.

'Now don't you be offended at what I'm a-going to say,'
observed Mrs. Mann, with captivating sweetness. 'You've had a long
walk, you know, or I wouldn't mention it. Now, will you take a little
drop of somethink, Mr. Bumble?'

'Not a drop. Not a drop,' said Mr. Bumble, waving his right
hand in a dignified, but placid manner.

'I think you will,' said Mrs. Mann, who had noticed the tone
of the refusal, and the gesture that had accompanied it. 'Just a leetle
drop, with a little cold water, and a lump of sugar.'

Mr. Bumble coughed.

'Now, just a leetle drop,' said Mrs. Mann persuasively.

'What is it?' inquired the beadle.

'Why, it's what I'm obliged to keep a little of in the house,
to put into the blessed infants' Daffy, when they ain't well,
Mr. Bumble,' replied Mrs. Mann as she opened a corner cupboard,

and took down a bottle and glass. 'It's gin. I'll not deceive you, Mr. B. It's gin.'

'Do you give the children Daffy, Mrs. Mann?' inquired Bumble, following with his eyes the interesting process of mixing.

'Ah, bless 'em, that I do, dear as it is,' replied the nurse. 'I couldn't see 'em suffer before my very eyes, you know, sir.'

'No,' said Mr. Bumble approvingly; 'no, you could not. You are a humane woman, Mrs. Mann.' (Here she set down the glass.) 'I shall take an early opportunity of mentioning it to the board, Mrs. Mann.' (He drew it towards him.) 'You feel as a mother, Mrs. Mann.' (He stirred the gin-and-water.) 'I—I drink your health with cheerfulness, Mrs. Mann'; and he swallowed half of it.

'And now about business,' said the beadle, taking out a leathern pocket-book. 'The child that was half-baptized Oliver Twist, is nine year old to-day.'

'Bless him!' interposed Mrs. Mann, inflaming her left eye with the corner of her apron.

'And notwithstanding a offered reward of ten pound, which was afterwards increased to twenty pound. Notwithstanding the most superlative, and, I may say, supernat'ral exertions on the part of this parish,' said Bumble, 'we have never been able to discover who is his father, or what was his mother's settlement, name, or condition.'

Mrs. Mann raised her hands in astonishment; but added, after a moment's reflection, 'How comes he to have any name at all, then?'

The beadle drew himself up with great pride, and said, 'I inwented it.'

'You, Mr. Bumble!'

'I, Mrs. Mann. We name our fondlings in alphabetical order. The last was a S, —Swubble, I named him. This was a T, —Twist, I named *him*. The next one as comes will be Unwin, and the next Vilkins. I have got names ready made to the end of the alphabet, and all the way through it again, when we come to Z.'

'Why, you're quite a literary character, sir!' said Mrs. Mann.

'Well, well,' said the beadle, evidently gratified with the compliment; 'perhaps I may be. Perhaps I may be, Mrs. Mann.' He finished the gin-and-water, and added, 'Oliver being now too old to remain here, the board have determined to have him back into the house. I have come out myself to take him there. So let me see him at once.'

'I'll fetch him directly,' said Mrs. Mann, leaving the room for that purpose. Oliver, having had by this time as much of the outer coat of dirt which encrusted his face and hands, removed, as could be scrubbed off in one washing, was led into the room by his benevolent protectress.

'Make a bow to the gentleman, Oliver,' said Mrs. Mann.

Oliver made a bow, which was divided between the beadle on the chair, and the cocked-hat on the table.

'Will you go along with me, Oliver?' said Mr. Bumble, in a majestic voice.

Oliver was about to say that he would go along with anybody with great readiness, when, glancing upward, he caught sight of Mrs. Mann, who had got behind the beadle's chair, and was shaking her fist at him with a furious countenance. He took the hint at once, for the fist had been too often impressed upon his body not to be deeply impressed upon his recollection.

'Will *she* go with me?' inquired poor Oliver.

'No, she can't,' replied Mr. Bumble. 'But she'll come and see you sometimes.'

This was no very great consolation to the child. Young as he was, however, he had sense enough to make a feint of feeling great regret at going away. It was no very difficult matter for the boy to call tears into his eyes. Hunger and recent ill-usage are great assistants if you want to cry; and Oliver cried very naturally indeed. Mrs. Mann gave him a thousand embraces, and, what Oliver wanted a great deal more, a piece of bread and butter, lest he should seem too hungry when he got to the workhouse. With the slice of bread in his hand, and the little brown-cloth parish cap on his head, Oliver was then led away by Mr. Bumble from the wretched home where one kind word or look had never lighted the gloom of his infant years. And yet he burst into an agony of childish grief, as the cottage-gate closed after him. Wretched as were the little companions in misery he was leaving behind, they were the only friends he had ever known; and a sense of his loneliness in the great wide world sank into the child's heart for the first time.

Mr. Bumble walked on with long strides; little Oliver, firmly grasping his gold-laced cuff, trotted beside him, inquiring at the end of every quarter of a mile whether they were 'nearly there.' To these interrogations Mr. Bumble returned very brief and snappish replies; for the temporary blandness which gin-and-water awakens in some bosoms had by this time evaporated; and he was once again a beadle.

Oliver had not been within the walls of the workhouse a quarter of an hour, and had scarcely completed the demolition of a second slice of bread, when Mr. Bumble, who had handed him over to the care of an old woman, returned; and, telling him it was a board night, informed him that the board had said he was to appear before it forthwith.

Not having a very clearly defined notion of what a live board was, Oliver was rather astounded by this intelligence, and was not quite certain whether he ought to laugh or cry. He had no time to think about the matter, however; for Mr. Bumble gave him a tap on the head, with his cane, to wake him up; and another on the back to make him lively; and bidding him follow, conducted him into a large whitewashed room, where eight or ten fat gentlemen were sitting round a table. At the top of the table, seated in an arm-chair rather higher than the rest, was a particularly fat gentleman with a very round, red face.

'Bow to the board,' said Bumble. Oliver brushed away two or three tears that were lingering in his eyes; and seeing no board but the table, fortunately bowed to that.

'What's your name, boy?' said the gentleman in the high chair.

Oliver was frightened at the sight of so many gentlemen, which made him tremble: and the beadle gave him another tap behind, which made him cry. These two causes made him answer in a very low and hesitating voice; whereupon a gentleman in a white waistcoat said he was a fool. Which was a capital way of raising his spirits, and putting him quite at his ease.

'Boy,' said the gentleman in the high chair, 'listen to me. You know you're an orphan, I suppose?'

'What's that, sir?' inquired poor Oliver.

'The boy *is* a fool—I thought he was,' said the gentleman in the white waistcoat.

'Hush!' said the gentleman who had spoken first. 'You know you've got no father or mother, and that you were brought up by the parish, don't you?'

'Yes, sir,' replied Oliver, weeping bitterly.

'What are you crying for?' inquired the gentleman in the white waistcoat. And to be sure it was very extraordinary. What *could* the boy be crying for?

'I hope you say your prayers every night,' said another gentleman in a gruff voice; 'and pray for the people who feed you, and take care of you—like a Christian.'

'Yes, sir,' stammered the boy. The gentleman who spoke last was unconsciously right. It would have been *very* like a Christian, and a marvellously good Christian, too, if Oliver had prayed for the people who fed and took care of *him*. But he hadn't, because nobody had taught him.

'Well! You have come here to be educated, and taught a useful trade,' said the red-faced gentleman in the high chair.

'So you'll begin to pick oakum to-morrow morning at six o'clock,' added the surly one in the white waistcoat.

For the combination of both these blessings in the one simple process of picking oakum, Oliver bowed low by the direction of the beadle, and was then hurried away to a large ward: where, on a rough, hard bed, he sobbed himself to sleep. What a noble illustration of the tender laws of England! They let the paupers go to sleep!

Poor Oliver! He little thought, as he lay sleeping in happy unconsciousness of all around him, that the board had that very day arrived at a decision which would exercise the most material influence over all his future fortunes. But they had. And this was it:

The members of this board were very sage, deep, philosophical men; and when they came to turn their attention to the workhouse, they found out at once, what ordinary folks would never have discovered—the poor people liked it! It was a regular place of public entertainment for the poorer classes; a tavern where there was nothing to pay; a public breakfast, dinner, tea, and supper all the year round; a brick and mortar elysium, where it was all play and no work. 'Oho!' said the board, looking very knowing; 'we are the fellows to set this to rights; we'll stop it all, in no time.' So, they established the rule, that all poor people should have the alternative (for they would compel nobody, not they), of being starved by a gradual process in the house, or by a quick one out of it. With this view, they contracted with the water-works to lay on an unlimited supply of water; and with a corn-factor to supply periodically small quantities of oatmeal; and issued three meals of thin gruel a day, with an onion twice a week, and half a roll on Sundays. They made a great many other wise and humane regulations, having reference to the ladies, which it is not necessary to repeat; kindly undertook to divorce poor married people, in consequence of the great expense of a suit in Doctors' Commons; and, instead of compelling a man to support his family, as they had theretofore done, took his family away from him, and made him a bachelor! There is no saying how many applicants for relief, under these last two heads, might have started up in all classes of society, if it had not been coupled with the workhouse; but the board were long-headed men, and had provided for this difficulty. The relief was inseparable from the workhouse and the gruel; and that frightened people.

For the first six months after Oliver Twist was removed, the system was in full operation. It was rather expensive at first, in consequence of the increase in the undertaker's bill, and the necessity of taking in the clothes of all the paupers, which fluttered loosely on their wasted, shrunken forms, after a week or two's gruel. But the number of workhouse inmates got thin as well as the paupers; and the board were in ecstasies.

The room in which the boys were fed, was a large stone hall, with a copper at one end: out of which the master, dressed in an apron for the purpose, and assisted by one or two women, ladled the gruel at mealtimes. Of this festive composition each boy had one porringer, and no more—except on occasions of great public rejoicing, when he had two ounces and a quarter of bread besides. The bowls never wanted washing. The boys polished them with their spoons till they shone again; and when they had performed this operation (which never took very long, the spoons being nearly as large as the bowls), they would sit staring at the copper, with such eager eyes, as if they could have devoured the very bricks of which it was composed; employing themselves, meanwhile, in sucking their fingers most assiduously, with the view of catching up any stray splashes of gruel that might have been cast thereon. Boys have generally excellent appetites. Oliver Twist and his companions suffered the tortures of slow starvation for three months: at last they got so voracious and wild with hunger, that one boy, who was tall for his age, and hadn't been used to that sort of thing (for his father had kept a small cook-shop), hinted darkly to his companions, that unless he had another basin of gruel *per diem*, he was afraid he might some night happen to eat the boy who slept next him, who happened to be a weakly youth of tender age. He had a wild, hungry eye; and they implicitly believed him. A council was held; lots were cast who should walk up to the master after supper that evening, and ask for more; and it fell to Oliver Twist.

The evening arrived; the boys took their places. The master, in his cook's uniform, stationed himself at the copper; his pauper assistants ranged themselves behind him; the gruel was served out; and a long grace was said over the short commons. The gruel disappeared; the boys whispered each other, and winked at Oliver; while his next neighbours nudged him. Child as he was, he was desperate with hunger, and reckless with misery. He rose from the table; and advancing to the master, basin and spoon in hand, said: somewhat alarmed at his own temerity:

'Please, sir, I want some more.'

The master was a fat, healthy man; but he turned very pale. He gazed in stupefied astonishment on the small rebel for some seconds, and then clung for support to the copper. The assistants were paralysed with wonder; the boys with fear.

'What!' said the master at length, in a faint voice.

'Please, sir,' replied Oliver, 'I want some more.'

The master aimed a blow at Oliver's head with the ladle; pinioned him in his arms; and shrieked aloud for the beadle.

The board were sitting in solemn conclave, when Mr. Bumble rushed into the room in great excitement, and addressing the gentleman in the high chair, said,

'Mr. Limbkins, I beg your pardon, sir! Oliver Twist has asked for more!'

There was a general start. Horror was depicted on every countenance.

'For *more!*' said Mr. Limbkins. 'Compose yourself, Bumble, and answer me distinctly. Do I understand that he asked for more, after he had eaten the supper allotted by the dietary?'

'He did, sir,' replied Bumble.

'That boy will be hung,' said the gentleman in the white waist-coat. 'I know that boy will be hung.'

Nobody controverted the prophetic gentleman's opinion. An animated discussion took place. Oliver was ordered into instant confinement; and a bill was next morning pasted on the outside of the gate, offering a reward of five pounds to anybody who would take Oliver Twist off the hands of the parish. In other words, five pounds and Oliver Twist were offered to any man or woman who wanted an apprentice to any trade, business, or calling.

'I never was more convinced of anything in my life,' said the gentleman in the white waistcoat, as he knocked at the gate and read the bill next morning: 'I never was more convinced of anything in my life, than I am that that boy will come to be hung.'

As I purpose to show in the sequel whether the white-waist-coated gentleman was right or not, I should perhaps mar the interest of this narrative (supposing it to possess any at all), if I ventured to hint just yet, whether the life of Oliver Twist had this violent termination or no.

CHAPTER 3

Relates how Oliver Twist was very near
getting a place, which would not have been
a sinecure

For a week after the commission of the impious and profane offence
of asking for more, Oliver remained a close prisoner in the dark and
solitary room to which he had been consigned by the wisdom and
mercy of the board. It appears, at first sight, not unreasonable to
suppose, that, if he had entertained a becoming feeling of respect
for the prediction of the gentleman in the white waistcoat, he would
have established that sage individual's prophetic character, once and
for ever, by tying one end of his pocket-handkerchief to a hook in
the wall, and attaching himself to the other. To the performance of
this feat, however, there was one obstacle: namely, that pocket-
hand-kerchiefs being decided articles of luxury, had been, for all
future times and ages, removed from the noses of paupers by the
express order of the board, in council assembled: solemnly given
and pronounced under their hands and seals. There was a still
greater obstacle in Oliver's youth and childishness. He only cried
bitterly all day; and, when the long, dismal night came on, spread
his little hands before his eyes to shut out the darkness, and
crouching in the corner, tried to sleep: ever and anon waking with
a start and tremble, and drawing himself closer and closer to the
wall, as if to feel even its cold hard surface were a protection in
the gloom and loneliness which surrounded him.

Let it not be supposed by the enemies of 'the system,' that, during the period of his solitary incarceration, Oliver was denied the benefit of exercise, the pleasure of society, or the advantages of religious consolation. As for exercise, it was nice cold weather, and he was allowed to perform his ablutions every morning under the pump, in a stone yard, in the presence of Mr. Bumble, who prevented his catching cold, and caused a tingling sensation to pervade his frame, by repeated applications of the cane. As for society, he was carried every other day into the hall where the boys dined, and there sociably flogged as a public warning and example. And so far from being denied the advantages of religious consolation, he was kicked into the same apartment every evening at prayer-time, and there permitted to listen to, and console his mind with, a general supplication of the boys, containing a special clause, therein inserted by authority of the board, in which they entreated to be made good, virtuous, contented, and obedient, and to be guarded from the sins and vices of Oliver Twist; whom the supplication distinctly set forth to be under the exclusive patronage and protection of the powers of wickedness, and an article direct from the manufactory of the very Devil himself.

It chanced one morning, while Oliver's affairs were in this auspicious and comfortable state, that Mr. Gamfield, chimney-sweep, went his way down the High Street, deeply cogitating in his mind his ways and means of paying certain arrears of rent, for which his landlord had become rather pressing. Mr. Gamfield's most sanguine estimate of his finances could not raise them within full five pounds of the desired amount; and, in a species of arithmetical desperation, he was alternately cudgelling his brains and his donkey, when, passing the workhouse, his eyes encountered the bill on the gate.

'Wo—o!' said Mr. Gamfield to the donkey.

The donkey was in a state of profound abstraction: wondering, probably, whether he was destined to be regaled with a cabbage-stalk or two when he had disposed of the two sacks of soot with which the little cart was laden; so, without noticing the word of command, he jogged onward.

Mr. Gamfield growled a fierce imprecation on the donkey

generally, but more particularly on his eyes; and, running after him, bestowed a blow on his head, which would inevitably have beaten in any skull but a donkey's. Then, catching hold of the bridle, he gave his jaw a sharp wrench, by way of gentle reminder that he was not his own master; and by these means turned him round. He then gave him another blow on the head, just to stun him till he came back again. Having completed these arrangements, he walked up to the gate, to read the bill.

The gentleman with the white waistcoat was standing at the gate with his hands behind him, after having delivered himself of some profound sentiments in the board-room. Having witnessed the little dispute between Mr. Gamfield and the donkey, he smiled joyously when that person came up to read the bill, for he saw at once that Mr. Gamfield was exactly the sort of master Oliver Twist wanted. Mr. Gamfield smiled, too, as he perused the document; for five pounds was just the sum he had been wishing for; and, as to the boy with which it was encumbered, Mr. Gamfield, knowing what the dietary of the workhouse was, well knew he would be a nice small pattern, just the very thing for register stoves. So, he spelt the bill through again, from beginning to end; and then, touching his fur cap in token of humility, accosted the gentleman in the white waistcoat.

'This here boy, sir, wot the parish wants to 'prentis,' said Mr. Gamfield.

'Ay, my man,' said the gentleman in the white waistcoat, with a condescending smile. 'What of him?'

'If the parish vould like him to learn a right pleasant trade, in a good 'spectable chimbley-sweepin' bisness,' said Mr. Gamfield, 'I wants a 'prentis, and I am ready to take him.'

'Walk in,' said the gentleman in the white waistcoat. Mr. Gamfield having lingered behind, to give the donkey another blow on the head, and another wrench of the jaw, as a caution not to run away in his absence, followed the gentleman with the white waistcoat into the room where Oliver had first seen him.

'It's a nasty trade,' said Mr. Limbkins, when Gamfield had again stated his wish.

'Young boys have been smothered in chimneys before now,' said another gentleman.

'That's acause they damped the straw afore they lit it in the chimbley to make 'em come down agin,' said Gamfield; 'that's all smoke, and no blaze; vereas smoke ain't o' no use at all in making a boy come down, for it only sinds him to sleep, and that's wot he likes. Boys is wery obstinit, and wery lazy, gen'lmen, and there's nothink like a good hot blaze to make 'em come down vith a run. It's humane too, gen'lmen, acause, even if they've stuck in the chimbley, roasting their feet makes 'em struggle to hextricate theirselves.'

The gentleman in the white waistcoat appeared very much amused by this explanation; but his mirth was speedily checked by a look from Mr. Limbkins. The board then proceeded to converse among themselves for a few minutes, but in so low a tone, that the words 'saving of expenditure,' 'looked well in the accounts,' 'have a printed report published,' were alone audible. These only chanced to be heard, indeed, on account of their being very frequently repeated with great emphasis.

At length the whispering ceased; and the members of the board, having resumed their seats and their solemnity, Mr. Limbkins said:

'We have considered your proposition, and we don't approve of it.'

'Not at all,' said the gentleman in the white waistcoat.

'Decidedly not,' added the other members.

As Mr. Gamfield did happen to labour under the slight imputation of having bruised three or four boys to death already, it occurred to him that the board had, perhaps, in some unaccountable freak, taken it into their heads that this extraneous circumstance ought to influence their proceedings. It was very unlike their general mode of doing business, if they had; but still, as he had no particular wish to revive the rumour, he twisted his cap in his hands, and walked slowly from the table.

'So you won't let me have him, gen'lmen?' said Mr. Gamfield, pausing near the door.

'No,' replied Mr. Limbkins; 'at least, as it's a nasty business, we think you ought to take something less than the premium we offered.'

Mr. Gamfield's countenance brightened, as, with a quick step, he returned to the table, and said,

'What'll you give, gen'lmen? Come! Don't be too hard on a poor man. What'll you give?'

'I should say, three pound ten was plenty,' said Mr. Limbkins.

'Ten shillings too much,' said the gentleman in the white waistcoat.

'Come!' said Gamfield; 'say four pound, gen'lmen. Say four pound, and you've got rid on him for good and all. There!'

'Three pound ten,' repeated Mr. Limbkins, firmly.

'Come! I'll split the difference, gen'lmen,' urged Gamfield. 'Three pound fifteen.'

'Not a farthing more,' was the firm reply of Mr. Limbkins.

'You're desperate hard upon me, gen'lmen,' said Gamfield, wavering.

'Pooh! pooh! nonsense!' said the gentleman in the white waistcoat. 'He'd be cheap with nothing at all, as a premium. Take him, you silly fellow! He's just the boy for you. He wants the stick, now and then: it'll do him good; and his board needn't come very expensive, for he hasn't been over-fed since he was born. Ha! ha! ha!'

Mr. Gamfield gave an arch look at the faces round the table, and, observing a smile on all of them, gradually broke into a smile himself. The bargain was made. Mr. Bumble was at once instructed that Oliver Twist and his indentures were to be conveyed before the magistrate, for signature and approval, that very afternoon.

In pursuance of this determination, little Oliver, to his excessive astonishment, was released from bondage, and ordered to put himself into a clean shirt. He had hardly achieved this very unusual gymnastic performance, when Mr. Bumble brought him, with his own hands, a basin of gruel, and the holiday allowance of two ounces and a quarter of bread. At this tremendous sight, Oliver began to cry very piteously: thinking, not unnaturally, that the board must have determined to kill him for some useful purpose, or they never would have begun to fatten him up in that way.

'Don't make your eyes red, Oliver, but eat your food and be thankful,' said Mr. Bumble, in a tone of impressive pomposity. 'You're a-going to be made a 'prentice of, Oliver.'

'A 'prentice, sir!' said the child, trembling.

'Yes, Oliver,' said Mr. Bumble. 'The kind and blessed gentlemen which is so many parents to you, Oliver, when you have none of your own: are a-going to 'prentice you: and to set you up in life, and make a man of you: although the expense to the parish is three pound ten! —three pound ten, Oliver! —seventy shillins— one hundred and forty sixpences! —and all for a naughty orphan which nobody can't love.'

As Mr. Bumble paused to take breath, after delivering this address in an awful voice, the tears rolled down the poor child's face, and he sobbed bitterly.

'Come,' said Mr. Bumble, somewhat less pompously, for it was gratifying to his feelings to observe the effect his eloquence had produced; 'Come, Oliver! Wipe your eyes with the cuffs of your jacket, and don't cry into your gruel; that's a very foolish action, Oliver.' It certainly was, for there was quite enough water in it already.

On their way to the magistrate, Mr. Bumble instructed Oliver that all he would have to do, would be to look very happy, and say, when the gentleman asked him if he wanted to be apprenticed, that he should like it very much indeed; both of which injunctions Oliver promised to obey: the rather as Mr. Bumble threw in a gentle hint, that if he failed in either particular, there was no telling what would be done to him. When they arrived at the office, he was shut up in a little room by himself, and admonished by Mr. Bumble to stay there, until he came back to fetch him.

There the boy remained, with a palpitating heart, for half an hour. At the expiration of which time, Mr. Bumble thrust in his head, unadorned with the cocked-hat, and said aloud:

'Now, Oliver, my dear, come to the gentleman.' As Mr. Bumble said this, he put on a grim and threatening look, and added, in a low voice, 'Mind what I told you, you young rascal!'

Oliver stared innocently in Mr. Bumble's face at this some-what contradictory style of address; but that gentleman prevented his offering any remark thereupon, by leading him at once into an adjoining room: the door of which was open. It was a large room, with a great window. Behind a desk, sat two old gentlemen with powdered heads: one of whom was reading the newspaper; while the other was perusing, with the aid of a pair of tortoise-shell spec-tacles, a small piece of parchment which lay before him. Mr. Limbkins was standing in front of the desk on one side; and Mr. Gamfield, with a partially washed face, on the other; while two or three bluff-looking men, in top-boots, were lounging about.

The old gentleman with the spectacles gradually dozed off, over the little bit of parchment; and there was a short pause, after. Oliver had been stationed by Mr. Bumble in front of the desk.

'This is the boy, your worship,' said Mr. Bumble.

The old gentleman who was reading the newspaper raised his head for a moment, and pulled the other old gentleman by the sleeve; whereupon, the last-mentioned old gentleman woke up.

'Oh, is this the boy?' said the old gentleman.

'This is him, sir,' replied Mr. Bumble. 'Bow to the magistrate, my dear.'

Oliver roused himself, and made his best obeisance. He had been wondering, with his eyes fixed on the magistrates' powder, whether all boards were born with that white stuff on their heads, and were boards from thenceforth on that account.

'Well,' said the old gentleman, 'I suppose he's fond of chimney-sweeping?'

'He doats on it, your worship,' replied Bumble; giving Oliver a sly pinch, to intimate that he had better not say he didn't.

'And he *will* be a sweep, will he?' inquired the old gentleman.

'If we was to bind him to any other trade to-morrow, he'd run away simultaneous, your worship,' replied Bumble.

'And this man that's to be his master—you, sir—you'll treat him well, and feed him, and do all that sort of thing, will you?' said the old gentleman.

'When I says I will, I means I will,' replied Mr. Gamfield doggedly.

'You're a rough speaker, my friend, but you look an honest, open-hearted man,' said the old gentleman: turning his spectacles in the direction of the candidate for Oliver's premium, whose villainous countenance was a regular stamped receipt for cruelty. But the magistrate was half blind and half childish, so he couldn't reasonably be expected to discern what other people did.

'I hope I am, sir,' said Mr. Gamfield, with an ugly leer.

'I have no doubt you are, my friend,' replied the old gentleman: fixing his spectacles more firmly on his nose, and looking about him for the inkstand.

It was the critical moment of Oliver's fate. If the inkstand had been where the old gentleman thought it was, he would have dipped his pen into it, and signed the indentures, and Oliver would have been straightway hurried off. But, as it chanced to be immediately under his nose, it followed, as a matter of course, that he looked all over his desk for it, without finding it; and happening in the course of his search to look straight before him, his gaze encountered the pale and terrified face of Oliver Twist: who, despite all the admonitory looks and pinches of Bumble, was regarding the repulsive countenance of his future master, with a mingled expression of horror and fear, too palpable to be mistaken, even by a half-blind magistrate.

The old gentleman stopped, laid down his pen, and looked from Oliver to Mr. Limbkins; who attempted to take snuff with a cheerful and unconcerned aspect.

'My boy!' said the old gentleman, leaning over the desk. Oliver started at the sound. He might be excused for doing so: for the words were kindly said; and strange sounds frighten one. He trembled violently, and burst into tears.

'My boy!' said the old gentleman, 'you look pale and alarmed. What is the matter?'

'Stand a little away from him, Beadle,' said the other magistrate: laying aside the paper, and leaning forward with an expression of interest. 'Now, boy, tell us what's the matter: don't be afraid.'

Oliver fell on his knees, and clasping his hands together, prayed that they would order him back to the dark room—that they would starve him—beat him—kill him if they pleased—rather than send him away with that dreadful man.

'Well!' said Mr. Bumble, raising his hands and eyes with most impressive solemnity, 'Well! of all the artful and designing orphans that ever I see, Oliver, you are one of the most bare-facedest.'

'Hold your tongue, Beadle,' said the second old gentleman, when Mr. Bumble had given vent to this compound adjective.

'I beg your worship's pardon,' said Mr. Bumble, incredulous of his having heard aright. 'Did your worship speak to me!'

'Yes. Hold your tongue.'

Mr. Bumble was stupefied with astonishment. A beadle ordered to hold his tongue! A moral revolution!

The old gentleman in the tortoise-shell spectacles looked at his companion; he nodded significantly.

'We refuse to sanction these indentures,' said the old gentleman: tossing aside the piece of parchment as he spoke.

'I hope,' stammered Mr. Limbkins: 'I hope the magistrates will not form the opinion that the authorities have been guilty of any improper conduct, on the unsupported testimony of a mere child.'

'The magistrates are not called upon to pronounce any opinion on the matter,' said the second old gentleman sharply. 'Take the boy back to the workhouse, and treat him kindly. He seems to want it.'

That same evening, the gentleman in the white waistcoat most positively and decidedly affirmed, not only that Oliver would be hung, but that he would be drawn and quartered into the bargain. Mr. Bumble shook his head with gloomy mystery, and said he wished he might come to good; whereunto Mr. Gamfield replied, that he wished he might come to him; which, although he agreed with the

beadle in most matters, would seem to be a wish of a totally opposite description.

The next morning, the public were once more informed that
Oliver Twist was again To Let, and that five pounds would be paid
to anybody who would take possession of him.

CHAPTER 4

Oliver, being offered another place, makes
his first entry into public life

In great families, when an advantageous place cannot be obtained,
either in possession, reversion, remainder, or expectancy, for the
young man who is growing up, it is a very general custom to send
him to sea. The board, in imitation of so wise and salutary an
example, took counsel together on the expediency of shipping off
Oliver Twist, in some small trading vessel bound to a good unhealthy
port. This suggested itself as the very best thing that could possibly
be done with him: the probability being, that the skipper would
flog him to death, in a playful mood, some day after dinner, or
would knock his brains out with an iron bar; both pastimes being,
as is pretty generally known, very favourite and common recreations
among gentlemen of that class. The more the case presented itself
to the board, in this point of view, the more manifold the advantages of the step appeared; so, they came to the conclusion that the
only way of providing for Oliver effectually, was to send him to sea
without delay.

Mr. Bumble had been despatched to make various preliminary
inquiries, with the view of finding out some captain or other who
wanted a cabin-boy without any friends; and was returning to the
workhouse to communicate the result of his mission; when he encountered at the gate, no less a person than Mr. Sowerberry, the parochial
undertaker.

Mr. Sowerberry was a tall, gaunt, large-jointed man, attired in a suit of thread-bare black, with darned cotton stockings of the same colour, and shoes to answer. His features were not naturally intended to wear a smiling aspect, but he was in general rather given to professional jocosity. His step was elastic, and his face betokened inward pleasantry, as he advanced to Mr. Bumble, and shook him cordially by the hand.

'I have taken the measure of the two women that died last night, Mr. Bumble,' said the undertaker.

'You'll make your fortune, Mr. Sowerberry,' said the beadle, as he thrust his thumb and forefinger into the proffered snuff-box of the undertaker: which was an ingenious little model of a patent coffin. 'I say you'll make your fortune, Mr. Sowerberry,' repeated Mr. Bumble, tapping the undertaker on the shoulder, in a friendly manner, with his cane.

'Think so?' said the undertaker in a tone which half admitted and half disputed the probability of the event. 'The prices allowed by the board are very small, Mr. Bumble.'

'So are the coffins,' replied the beadle; with precisely as near an approach to a laugh as a great official ought to indulge in.

Mr. Sowerberry was much tickled at this: as of course he ought to be; and laughed a long time without cessation. 'Well, well, Mr. Bumble,' he said at length, 'there's no denying that, since the new system of feeding has come in, the coffins are something narrower and more shallow than they used to be; but we must have some profit, Mr. Bumble. Well-seasoned timber is an expensive article, sir; and all the iron handles come, by canal, from Birmingham.

'Well, well,' said Mr. Bumble, 'every trade has its drawbacks. A fair profit is, of course, allowable.'

'Of course, of course,' replied the undertaker; 'and if I don't get a profit upon this or that particular article, why, I make it up in the long-run, you see—he! he! he!'

'Just so,' said Mr. Bumble.

'Though I must say,' continued the undertaker, resuming the

current of observations which the beadle had interrupted: 'though I must say, Mr. Bumble, that I have to contend against one very great disadvantage: which is, that all the stout people go off the quickest. The people who have been better off, and have paid rates for many years, are the first to sink when they come into the house; and let me tell you, Mr. Bumble, that three or four inches over one's calculation makes a great hole in one's profits: especially when one has a family to provide for, sir.'

As Mr. Sowerberry said this, with the becoming indignation of an ill-used man; and as Mr. Bumble felt that it rather tended to convey a reflection on the honour of the parish; the latter gentleman thought it advisable to change the subject. Oliver Twist being uppermost in his mind, he made him his theme.

'By the bye,' said Mr. Bumble, 'you don't know anybody who wants a boy, do you? A porochial 'prentis, who is at present a deadweight; a millstone, as I may say; round the porochial throat? Liberal terms, Mr. Sowerberry, liberal terms!' As Mr. Bumble spoke, he raised his cane to the bill above him, and gave three distinct raps upon the words 'five pounds': which were printed thereon in Roman capitals of gigantic size.

'Gadso!' said the undertaker: taking Mr. Bumble by the gilt-edged lapel of his official coat; 'that's just the very thing I wanted to speak to you about. You know—dear me, what a very elegant button this is, Mr. Bumble! I never noticed it before.'

'Yes, I think it is rather pretty,' said the beadle, glancing proudly downwards at the large brass buttons which embellished his coat. 'The die is the same as the porochial seal–the Good Samaritan healing the sick and bruised man. The board presented it to me on New-year's morning, Mr. Sowerberry. I put it on, I remember, for the first time, to attend the inquest on that reduced tradesman, who died in a doorway at midnight.'

'I recollect,' said the undertaker. 'The jury brought it in, "Died from exposure to the cold, and want of the common necessaries of life," didn't they?'

Mr. Bumble nodded.

'And they made it a special verdict, I think,' said the undertaker, 'by adding some words to the effect, that if the relieving officer had–'

'Tush! Foolery!' interposed the beadle. 'If the board attended to all the nonsense that ignorant jurymen talk, they'd have enough to do.'

'Very true,' said the undertaker; 'they would indeed.'

'Juries,' said Mr. Bumble, grasping his cane tightly, as was his wont when working into a passion: 'juries is ineddicated, vulgar, grovelling wretches.'

'So they are,' said the undertaker.

'They haven't no more philosophy nor political economy about 'em than that,' said the beadle, snapping his fingers contemptuously.

'No more they have,' acquiesced the undertaker.

'I despise 'em,' said the beadle, growing very red in the face.

'So do I,' rejoined the undertaker.

'And I only wish we'd a jury of the independent sort, in the house for a week or two,' said the beadle; 'the rules and regulations of the board would soon bring their spirit down for 'em.'

'Let 'em alone for that,' replied the undertaker. So saying, he smiled, approvingly: to calm the rising wrath of the indignant parish officer.

Mr. Bumble lifted off his cocked hat; took a handkerchief from the inside of the crown; wiped from his forehead the perspiration which his rage had engendered; fixed the cocked hat on again; and, turning to the undertaker, said in a calmer voice:

'Well; what about the boy?'

'Oh!' replied the undertaker; 'why, you know, Mr. Bumble, I pay a good deal towards the poor's rates.'

'Hem!' said Mr. Bumble. 'Well?'

'Well,' replied the undertaker, 'I was thinking that if I pay so much towards 'em, I've a right to get as much out of 'em as I can, Mr. Bumble; and so—and so—I think I'll take the boy myself.'

Mr. Bumble grasped the undertaker by the arm, and led him into the building. Mr. Sowerberry was closeted with the board for five minutes; and it was arranged that Oliver should go to him that evening 'upon liking' —a phrase which means, in the case of a parish apprentice, that if the master find, upon a short trial, that he can get enough work out of a boy without putting too much food into him, he shall have him for a term of years, to do what he likes with.

When little Oliver was taken before 'the gentlemen' that evening; and informed that he was to go, that night, as general house-lad to a coffin-maker's; and that if he complained of his situation, or ever came back to the parish again, he would be sent to sea, there to be drowned, or knocked on the head, as the case might be, he evinced so little emotion, that they by common consent pronounced him a hardened young rascal, and ordered Mr. Bumble to remove him forthwith.

Now, although it was very natural that the board, of all people in the world, should feel in a great state of virtuous astonishment and horror at the smallest tokens of want of feeling on the part of anybody, they were rather out, in this particular instance. The simple fact was, that Oliver, instead of possessing too little feeling, possessed rather too much; and was in a fair way of being reduced, for life, to a state of brutal stupidity and sullenness by the ill-usage he had received. He heard the news of his destination in perfect silence; and, having had his luggage put into his hand—which was not very difficult to carry, inasmuch as it was all comprised within the limits of a brown paper parcel, about half a foot square by three inches deep—he pulled his cap over his eyes; and once more attaching himself to Mr. Bumble's coat cuff, was led away by that dignitary to a new scene of suffering.

For some time, Mr. Bumble drew Oliver along, without notice or remark; for the beadle carried his head very erect, as a beadle always should: and, it being a windy day, little Oliver was completely enshrouded by the skirts of Mr. Bumble's coat as they blew open, and disclosed to great advantage his flapped waistcoat and drab plush knee-breeches. As they drew near to their destination, however, Mr. Bumble thought it expedient to look down, and see that the boy was in good order for inspection by his new master: which he accordingly did, with a fit and becoming air of gracious patronage.

'Oliver!' said Mr. Bumble.

'Yes, sir,' replied Oliver, in a low, tremulous voice.

'Pull that cap off your eyes, and hold up your head, sir.'

Although Oliver did as he was desired, at once; and passed the back of his unoccupied hand briskly across his eyes, he left a tear in them when he looked up at his conductor. As Mr. Bumble gazed sternly upon him, it rolled down his cheek. It was followed by another, and another. The child made a strong effort, but it was an unsuccessful one. Withdrawing his other hand from Mr. Bumble's, he covered his face with both; and wept until the tears sprung out from between his chin and bony fingers.

'Well!' exclaimed Mr. Bumble, stopping short, and darting at his little charge a look of intense malignity. 'Well! Of *all* the ungratefullest, and worst-disposed boys as ever I see, Oliver, you are the—'

'No, no, sir,' sobbed Oliver, clinging to the hand which held the well-known cane; 'no, no, sir; I will be good indeed; indeed, indeed I will, sir! I am a very little boy, sir; and it is so—so—'

'So what?' inquired Mr. Bumble in amazement.

'So lonely, sir! So very lonely!' cried the child. 'Everybody hates me. Oh! sir, don't, don't pray be cross to me!' The child beat his hand upon his heart; and looked in his companion's face, with tears of real agony.

Mr. Bumble regarded Oliver's piteous and helpless look, with some astonishment, for a few seconds; hemmed three or four times in a husky manner; and, after muttering something about 'that troublesome cough,' bade Oliver dry his eyes and be a good boy. Then once more taking his hand, he walked on with him in silence.

The undertaker, who had just put up the shutters of his shop, was making some entries in his day-book by the light of a most appropriate dismal candle, when Mr. Bumble entered.

'Aha!' said the undertaker: looking up from the book, and pausing in the middle of a word; 'is that you, Bumble?'

'No one else, Mr. Sowerberry,' replied the beadle. 'Here! I've brought the boy.' Oliver made a bow.

'Oh! that's the boy, is it?' said the undertaker: raising the candle above his head, to get a better view of Oliver. 'Mrs. Sowerberry, will you have the goodness to come here a moment, my dear?'

Mrs. Sowerberry emerged from a little room behind the shop, and presented the form of a short, thin, squeezed-up woman, with a vixenish countenance.

'My dear,' said Mr. Sowerberry, deferentially, 'this is the boy from the workhouse that I told you of.' Oliver bowed again.

'Dear me!' said the undertaker's wife, 'He's very small.'

'Why, he *is* rather small,' replied Mr. Bumble: looking at Oliver as if it were his fault that he was no bigger; 'he *is* small. There's no denying it. But he'll grow, Mrs. Sowerberry—he'll grow.'

'Ah! I dare say he will,' replied the lady pettishly, 'on our vict- uals and our drink. I see no saving in parish children, not I; for they always cost more to keep than they're worth. However, men always think they know best. There! Get down stairs, little bag o' bones.' With this, the undertaker's wife opened a side door, and pushed Oliver down a steep flight of stairs into a stone cell, damp and dark: forming the ante-room to the coal-cellar, and denominated 'kitchen': wherein sat a slatternly girl, in shoes down at heel, and blue worsted stockings very much out of repair.

'Here, Charlotte,' said Mrs. Sowerberry, who had followed Oliver down, 'give this boy some of the cold bits that were put by for Trip. He hasn't come home since the morning, so he may go without 'em. I dare say the boy isn't too dainty to eat 'em—are you, boy?'

Oliver, whose eyes had glistened at the mention of meat, and who was trembling with eagerness to devour it, replied in the nega- tive; and a plateful of coarse broken victuals was set before him.

I wish some well-fed philosopher, whose meat and drink turn to gall within him; whose blood is ice, whose heart is iron; could have seen Oliver Twist clutching at the dainty viands that the dog had neglected. I wish he could have witnessed the horrible avidity with which Oliver tore the bits asunder with all the ferocity of famine. There is only one thing I should like better; and that would be to see the Philosopher making the same sort of meal himself, with the same relish.

'Well,' said the undertaker's wife, when Oliver had finished his supper: which she had regarded in silent horror, and with fearful auguries of his future appetite: 'have you done?'

There being nothing eatable within his reach, Oliver replied in the affirmative.

'Then come with me,' said Mrs. Sowerberry: taking up a dim and dirty lamp, and leading the way up stairs; 'your bed's under the counter. You don't mind sleeping among the coffins, I suppose? But it doesn't much matter whether you do or don't, for you can't sleep anywhere else. Come; don't keep me here all night!'

Oliver lingered no longer, but meekly followed his new mistress.

CHAPTER 5

Oliver mingles with new associates. Going to
a funeral for the first time, he forms an
unfavourable notion of his master's business

Oliver, being left to himself in the undertaker's shop, set the lamp
down on a workman's bench, and gazed timidly about him with a
feeling of awe and dread, which many people a good deal older than
he will be at no loss to understand. An unfinished coffin on black
tressels, which stood in the middle of the shop, looked so gloomy
and death-like that a cold tremble came over him, every time his
eyes wandered in the direction of the dismal object: from which he
almost expected to see some frightful form slowly rear its head, to
drive him mad with terror. Against the wall were ranged, in regular
array, a long row of elm boards cut into the same shape: looking in
the dim light, like high-shouldered ghosts with their hands in their
breeches-pockets. Coffin-plates, elm chips, bright-headed nails, and
shreds of black cloth, lay scattered on the floor; and the wall behind
the counter was ornamented with a lively representation of two
mutes in very stiff neckcloths, on duty at a large private door, with
a hearse drawn by four black steeds, approaching in the distance.
The shop was close and hot. The atmosphere seemed tainted with
the smell of coffins. The recess beneath the counter in which his
flock mattress was thrust, looked like a grave.

Nor were these the only dismal feelings which depressed
Oliver. He was alone in a strange place; and we all know how chilled
and desolate the best of us will sometimes feel in such a situation.

The boy had no friends to care for, or to care for him. The regret of no recent separation was fresh in his mind; the absence of no loved and well-remembered face sank heavily into his heart. But his heart *was* heavy, notwithstanding; and he wished, as he crept into his narrow bed, that that were his coffin, and that he could be lain in a calm and lasting sleep in the churchyard ground, with the tall grass waving gently above his head, and the sound of the old deep bell to soothe him in his sleep.

Oliver was awakened in the morning, by a loud kicking at the outside of the shop-door; which, before he could huddle on his clothes, was repeated, in an angry and impetuous manner, about twenty-five times. When he began to undo the chain, the legs desisted, and a voice began.

'Open the door, will yer?' cried the voice which belonged to the legs which had kicked at the door.

'I will, directly, sir,' replied Oliver: undoing the chain, and turning the key.

'I suppose yer the new boy, ain't yer?' said the voice through the key-hole.

'Yes, sir,' replied Oliver.

'How old are yer?' inquired the voice.

'Ten, sir,' replied Oliver.

'Then I'll whop yer when I get in,' said the voice; 'you just see if I don't, that's all, my work'us brat!' and having made this obliging promise, the voice began to whistle.

Oliver had been too often subjected to the process to which the very expressive monosyllable just recorded bears reference, to entertain the smallest doubt that the owner of the voice, whoever he might be, would redeem his pledge, most honourably. He drew back the bolts with a trembling hand, and opened the door.

For a second or two, Oliver glanced up the street, and down the street, and over the way: impressed with the belief that the unknown, who had addressed him through the key-hole, had walked a few paces off, to warm himself; for nobody did he see but a big charity-boy, sitting on a post in front of the house, eating a slice of bread and butter: which he cut into wedges, the size of his mouth, with a clasp knife, and then consumed with great dexterity.

'I beg your pardon, sir,' said Oliver at length: seeing that no other visitor made his appearance; 'did you knock?'

'I kicked,' replied the charity-boy.

'Did you want a coffin, sir?' inquired Oliver, innocently.

At this the charity-boy looked monstrous fierce; and said that Oliver would want one before long, if he cut jokes with his superiors in that way.

'Yer don't know who I am, I suppose, Work'us?' said the charity-boy, in continuation: descending from the top of the post, meanwhile, with edifying gravity.

'No, sir,' rejoined Oliver.

'I'm Mister Noah Claypole,' said the charity-boy, 'and you're under me. Take down the shutters, yer idle young ruffian!' With this, Mr. Claypole administered a kick to Oliver, and entered the shop with a dignified air, which did him great credit. It is difficult for a large-headed, small-eyed youth, of lumbering make and heavy countenance, to look dignified under any circumstances; but it is more especially so, when superadded to these personal attractions are a red nose and yellow smalls.

Oliver, having taken down the shutters, and broken a pane of glass in his efforts to stagger away beneath the weight of the first one to a small court at the side of the house in which they were kept during the day, was graciously assisted by Noah: who having consoled him with the assurance that 'he'd catch it,' condescended to help him. Mr. Sowerberry came down soon after. Shortly afterwards Mrs. Sowerberry appeared. Oliver having 'caught it,' in fulfilment of Noah's prediction, followed that young gentleman down the stairs to breakfast.

'Come near the fire, Noah,' said Charlotte. 'I saved a nice little bit of bacon for you from master's breakfast. Oliver, shut that door at Mister Noah's back, and take them bits that I've put out on the cover of the bread pan. There's your tea; take it away to that box, and drink it there, and make haste, for they'll want you to mind the shop. D'ye hear?'

'D'ye hear, Work'us?' said Noah Claypole.

'Lor, Noah!' said Charlotte, 'what a rum creature you are! Why don't you let the boy alone?'

'Let him alone!' said Noah. 'Why everybody lets him alone enough, for the matter of that. Neither his father nor his mother will ever interfere with him. All his relations let him have his own way pretty well. Eh, Charlotte? He! he! he!'

'Oh, you queer soul!' said Charlotte, bursting into a hearty laugh, in which she was joined by Noah; after which they both looked scornfully at poor Oliver Twist, as he sat shivering on the box in the coldest corner of the room, and ate the stale pieces which had been specially reserved for him.

Noah was a charity-boy, but not a workhouse orphan. No chance-child was he, for he could trace his genealogy all the way back to his parents, who lived hard by; his mother being a washer-woman, and his father a drunken soldier, discharged with a wooden leg, and a diurnal pension of twopence-half-penny and an unstateable fraction. The shop-boys in the neighbourhood had long been in the habit of branding Noah, in the public streets, with the ignominious epithets of 'leathers' 'charity,' and the like; and Noah had borne them without reply. But, now that fortune has cast in his way a nameless orphan, at whom even the meanest could point the finger of scorn, he retorted on him with interest. This affords charming food for contemplation. It shows us what a beautiful thing human nature may be made to be; and how imparti-ally the same amiable qualities are developed in the finest lord and the dirtiest charity-boy.

Oliver had been sojourning at the undertaker's some three weeks or a month. Mr. and Mrs. Sowerberry—the shop being shut up—were taking their supper in the little back-parlour, when Mr. Sowerberry, after several deferential glances at his wife, said,

'My dear—' He was going to say more; but, Mrs. Sowerberry looking up, with a peculiarly unpropitious aspect, he stopped short.

'Well,' said Mrs. Sowerberry, sharply.

'Nothing, my dear, nothing,' said Mr. Sowerberry.

'Ugh, you brute!' said Mrs. Sowerberry.

'Not at all, my dear,' said Mr. Sowerberry humbly. 'I thought you didn't want to hear, my dear. I was only going to say—'

'Oh, don't tell me what you were going to say,' interposed Mrs. Sowerberry. 'I am nobody; don't consult me, pray. *I* don't want to intrude upon your secrets.' As Mrs. Sowerberry said this, she gave an hysterical laugh, which threatened violent consequences.

'But, my dear,' said Sowerberry, 'I want to ask your advice.'

'No, no, don't ask mine,' replied Mrs. Sowerberry, in an affecting manner: 'ask somebody else's.' Here, there was another hysterical laugh, which frightened Mr. Sowerberry very much. This is a very common and much-approved matrimonial course of treatment, which is often very effective. It at once reduced Mr. Sowerberry to begging, as a special favour, to be allowed to say what Mrs. Sowerberry was most curious to hear. After a short altercation of less than three quarters of an hour's duration, the permission was most graciously conceded.

'It's only about young Twist, my dear,' said Mr. Sowerberry. 'A very good-looking boy, that, my dear.'

'He need be, for he eats enough,' observed the lady.

'There's an expression of melancholy in his face, my dear,' resumed Mr. Sowerberry, 'which is very interesting. He would make a delightful mute, my love.'

Mrs. Sowerberry looked up with an expression of considerable wonderment. Mr. Sowerberry remarked it; and, without allowing time for any observation on the good lady's part, proceeded.

'I don't mean a regular mute to attend grown-up people, my dear, but only for children's practice. It would be very new to have a mute in proportion, my dear. You may depend upon it, it would have a superb effect.'

Mrs. Sowerberry, who had a good deal of taste in the under-taking way, was much struck by the novelty of this idea; but, as it would have been compromising her dignity to have said so, under existing circumstances, she merely inquired, with much sharpness, why such an obvious suggestion had not presented itself to her husband's mind before? Mr. Sowerberry rightly construed this, as an acquiescence in his proposition; it was speedily determined, therefore, that Oliver should be at once initiated into the mysteries of the trade; and, with this view, that he should accompany his master on the very next occasion of his services being required.

The occasion was not long in coming. Half an hour after breakfast next morning, Mr. Bumble entered the shop; and supporting his cane against the counter, drew forth his large leathern pocket-book, from which he selected a small scrap of paper, which he handed over to Sowerberry.

'Aha!' said the undertaker, glancing over it with a lively countenance; 'an order for a coffin, eh?'

'For a coffin first, and a porochial funeral afterwards,' replied Mr. Bumble, fastening the strap of the leathern pocket-book, which, like himself, was very corpulent.

'Bayton,' said the undertaker, looking from the scrap of paper to Mr. Bumble. 'I never heard the name before.'

Bumble shook his head, as he replied, 'Obstinate people, Mr. Sowerberry; very obstinate. Proud, too, I'm afraid, sir.'

'Proud, eh?' exclaimed Mr. Sowerberry with a sneer. 'Come, that's too much.'

'Oh, it's sickening,' replied the beadle. 'Antimonial, Mr. Sowerberry!'

'So it is,' acquiesced the undertaker.

'We only heard of the family the night before last,' said the beadle; 'and we shouldn't have known anything about them, then, only a woman who lodges in the same house made an application to the porochial committee for them to send the porochial surgeon to see a woman as was very bad. He had gone out to dinner; but his 'prentice (which is a very clever lad) sent 'em some medicine in a blacking-bottle, off-hand.'

'Ah, there's promptness,' said the undertaker.

'Promptness, indeed!' replied the beadle. 'But what's the

consequence; what's the ungrateful behaviour of these rebels, sir? Why, the husband sends back word that the medicine won't suit his wife's complaint, and so she shan't take it—says she shan't take it, sir! Good, strong, wholesome medicine, as was given with great success to two Irish labourers and a coal-heaver, only a week before—sent 'em for nothing, with a blackin'-bottle in—and he sends back word that she shan't take it, sir!'

As the atrocity presented itself to Mr. Bumble's mind in full force, he struck the counter sharply with his cane, and became flushed with indignation.

'Well,' said the undertaker, 'I ne—ver—did—'

'Never did, sir!' ejaculated the beadle. 'No, nor nobody never did; but, now she's dead, we've got to bury her; and that's the direction, and the sooner it's done, the better.'

Thus saying, Mr. Bumble put on his cocked hat wrong side first, in a fever of parochial excitement, and flounced out of the shop.

'Why, he was so angry, Oliver, that he forgot even to ask after you!' said Mr. Sowerberry, looking after the beadle as he strode down the street.

'Yes, sir,' replied Oliver, who had carefully kept himself out of sight during the interview, and who was shaking from head to foot at the mere recollection of the sound of Mr. Bumble's voice. He needn't have taken the trouble to shrink from Mr. Bumble's glance, however; for that functionary, on whom the prediction of the gentleman in the white waistcoat had made a very strong impression, thought that now the undertaker had got Oliver upon trial the subject was better avoided, until such time as he should be firmly bound for seven years, and all danger of his being returned upon the hands of the parish should be thus effectually and legally overcome.

'Well,' said Mr. Sowerberry, taking up his hat, 'the sooner this job is done, the better. Noah, look after the shop. Oliver, put on your cap, and come with me.' Oliver obeyed, and followed his master on his professional mission.

They walked on, for some time, through the most crowded and densely inhabited part of the town; and then, striking down a narrow street more dirty and miserable than any they had yet passed through, paused to look for the house which was the object of their search. The houses on either side were high and large, but very old, and tenanted by people of the poorest class: as their neglected appearance would have sufficiently denoted, without the concurrent testimony afforded by the squalid looks of the few men and women who, with folded arms and bodies half doubled, occasionally skulked along. A great many of the tenements had shop fronts; but these were fast closed, and mouldering away, only the upper rooms being inhabited. Some houses which had become insecure from age and decay, were prevented from falling into the street, by huge beams of wood reared against the walls, and firmly planted in the road; but even these crazy dens seemed to have been selected as the nightly haunts of some houseless wretches, for many of the rough boards which supplied the place of door and window, were wrenched from their positions, to afford an aperture wide enough for the passage of a human body. The kennel was stagnant and filthy. The very rats, which here and there lay putrefying in its rottenness, were hideous with famine.

There was neither knocker nor bell-handle at the open door where Oliver and his master stopped; so, groping his way cautiously through the dark passage, and bidding Oliver keep close to him and not be afraid, the undertaker mounted to the top of the first flight of stairs. Stumbling against a door on the landing, he rapped at it with his knuckles.

It was opened by a young girl of thirteen or fourteen. The undertaker at once saw enough of what the room contained to know it was the apartment to which he had been directed. He stepped in; Oliver followed him.

There was no fire in the room, but a man was crouching mechanically over the empty stove. An old woman, too, had drawn a low stool to the cold hearth, and was sitting beside him. There were some ragged children in another corner; and in a small recess, opposite the door, there lay upon the ground something covered with an old blanket. Oliver shuddered as he cast his eyes towards the place, and crept involuntarily closer to his master; for though it was covered up, the boy felt that it was a corpse.

The man's face was thin and very pale; his hair and beard were grizzly; his eyes were bloodshot. The old woman's face was wrinkled; her two remaining teeth protruded over her under lip; and her eyes were bright and piercing. Oliver was afraid to look at either her or the man. They seemed so like the rats he had seen outside.

'Nobody shall go near her,' said the man, starting fiercely up, as the undertaker approached the recess. 'Keep back! Damn you, keep back, if you've a life to lose!'

'Nonsense, my good man,' said the undertaker, who was pretty well used to misery in all its shapes. 'Nonsense!'

'I tell you,' said the man: clenching his hands, and stamping furiously on the floor, —'I tell you I won't have her put into the ground. She couldn't rest there. The worms would worry her—not eat her—she is so worn away.'

The undertaker offered no reply to this raving; but producing a tape from his pocket, knelt down for a moment by the side of the body.

'Ah!' said the man: bursting into tears, and sinking on his knees at the feet of the dead woman; 'kneel down, kneel down—kneel round her, every one of you, and mark my words! I say she was starved to death. I never knew how bad she was, till the fever came upon her; and then her bones were starting through the skin. There was neither fire nor candle; she died in the dark—in the dark! She couldn't even see her children's faces, though we heard her gasping out their names. I begged for her in the streets: and they sent me to prison. When I came back, she was dying; and all the blood in my heart has dried up, for they starved her to death. I swear it before the God that saw it! They starved her!' He twined his hands in his hair; and, with a loud scream, rolled grovelling upon the floor: his eyes fixed, and the foam covering his lips.

The terrified children cried bitterly; but the old woman, who had hitherto remained as quiet as if she had been wholly deaf to all that passed, menaced them into silence. Having unloosed the cravat of the man who still remained extended on the ground, she tottered towards the undertaker.

'She was my daughter,' said the old woman, nodding her head in the direction of the corpse; and speaking with an idiotic leer, more ghastly than even the presence of death in such a place. 'Lord, Lord! Well, it *is* strange that I who gave birth to her, and was a woman then, should be alive and merry now, and she lying there: so cold and stiff! Lord, Lord! —to think of it; it's as good as a play—as good as a play!'

As the wretched creature mumbled and chuckled in her hideous merriment, the undertaker turned to go away.

'Stop, stop!' said the old woman in a loud whisper. 'Will she be buried to-morrow, or next day, or to-night? I laid her out; and I must walk, you know. Send me a large cloak: a good warm one: for it is bitter cold. We should have cake and wine, too, before we go! Never mind; send some bread—only a loaf of bread, and a cup of water. Shall we have some bread, dear?' she said eagerly: catching at the undertaker's coat, as he once more moved towards the door.

'Yes, yes,' said the undertaker, 'of course. Anything you like!' He disengaged himself from the old woman's grasp; and, drawing Oliver after him, hurried away.

The next day, (the family having been meanwhile relieved with a half-quartern loaf and a piece of cheese, left with them by Mr. Bumble himself,) Oliver and his master returned to the miserable abode; where Mr. Bumble had already arrived, accompanied by four men from the workhouse, who were to act as bearers. An old black cloak had been thrown over the rags of the old woman and the man; and the bare coffin having been screwed down, was hoisted on the shoulders of the bearers, and carried into the street.

'Now, you must put your best leg foremost, old lady!' whispered Sowerberry in the old woman's ear; 'we are rather late; and it won't do to keep the clergyman waiting. Move on, my men, —as quick as you like!'

Thus directed, the bearers trotted on under their light burden; and the two mourners kept as near them, as they could. Mr. Bumble and Sowerberry walked at a good smart pace in front; and Oliver, whose legs were not so long as his master's, ran by the side.

There was not so great a necessity for hurrying as Mr. Sowerberry had anticipated, however; for when they reached the obscure corner of the churchyard in which the nettles grew, and where the parish graves were made, the clergyman had not arrived; and the clerk, who was sitting by the vestry-room fire, seemed to think it by no means improbable that it might be an hour or so, before he came. So, they put the bier on the brink of the grave; and the two mourners waited patiently in the damp clay, with a cold rain drizzling down, while the ragged boys whom the spectacle had attracted into the church-yard played a noisy game at hide-and-seek among the tombstones, or varied their amusements by jumping backwards and forwards over the coffin. Mr. Sowerberry and Bumble, being personal friends of the clerk, sat by the fire with him, and read the paper.

At length, after a lapse of something more than an hour, Mr. Bumble, and Sowerberry, and the clerk, were seen running towards the grave. Immediately afterwards, the clergyman appeared: putting on his surplice as he came along. Mr. Bumble then thrashed a boy or two, to keep up appearances; and the reverend gentleman, having read as much of the burial service as could be compressed into four minutes, gave his surplice to the clerk, and walked away again.

'Now, Bill!' said Sowerberry to the grave-digger. 'Fill-up!'

It was no very difficult task; for the grave was so full, that the uppermost coffin was within a few feet of the surface. The grave-digger shovelled in the earth; stamped it loosely down with his feet; shouldered his spade; and walked off, followed by the boys, who murmured very loud complaints at the fun being over so soon.

'Come, my good fellow!' said Bumble, tapping the man on the back. 'They want to shut up the yard.'

The man who had never once moved, since he had taken his station by the grave side, started, raised his head, stared at the person who had addressed him, walked forward for a few paces; and fell down in a swoon. The crazy old woman was too much occupied in bewailing the loss of her cloak (which the undertaker had taken off), to pay him any attention; so they threw a can of cold water over him; and when he came to, saw him safely out of the churchyard, locked the gate, and departed on their different ways.

'Well, Oliver,' said Sowerberry, as they walked home, 'how do you like it?'

'Pretty well, thank you, sir,' replied Oliver, with considerable hesitation. 'Not very much, sir.'

'Ah, you'll get used to it in time, Oliver,' said Sowerberry. 'Nothing when you *are* used to it, my boy.'

Oliver wondered, in his own mind, whether it had taken a very long time to get Mr. Sowerberry used to it. But he thought it better not to ask the question; and walked back to the shop: thinking over all he had seen and heard.

CHAPTER 6

Oliver, being goaded by the taunts of Noah,
rouses into action, and rather astonishes him

The month's trial over, Oliver was formally apprenticed. It was a
nice sickly season just at this time. In commercial phrase, coffins
were looking up; and, in the course of a few weeks, Oliver acquired
a great deal of experience. The success of Mr. Sowerberry's ingenious speculation, exceeded even his most sanguine hopes. The oldest
inhabitants recollected no period at which measles had been so
prevalent, or so fatal to infant existence; and many were the mournful
processions which little Oliver headed, in a hat-band reaching down
to his knees, to the indescribable admiration and emotion of all the
mothers in the town. As Oliver accompanied his master in most of
his adult expeditions, too, in order that he might acquire that
equanimity of demeanour and full command of nerve which are
essential to a finished undertaker, he had many opportunities of
observing the beautiful resignation and fortitude with which some
strong-minded people bear their trials and losses.

For instance; when Sowerberry had an order for the burial of
some rich old lady or gentleman, who was surrounded by a great
number of nephews and nieces, who had been perfectly inconsolable
during the previous illness, and whose grief had been wholly irrepressible even on the most public occasions, they would be as happy among
themselves as need be—quite cheerful and contented—conversing
together with as much freedom and gaiety, as if nothing whatever had

happened to disturb them. Husbands, too, bore the loss of their wives with the most heroic calmness. Wives, again, put on weeds for their husbands, as if, so far from grieving in the garb of sorrow, they had made up their minds to render it as becoming and attractive as possible. It was observable, too, that ladies and gentlemen who were in passions of anguish during the ceremony of interment, recovered almost as soon as they reached home, and became quite composed before the tea-drinking was over. All this was very pleasant and improving to see; and Oliver beheld it with great admiration.

That Oliver Twist was moved to resignation by the example of these good people, I cannot, although I am his biographer, undertake to affirm with any degree of confidence; but I can most distinctly say, that for many months he continued meekly to submit to the domination and ill-treatment of Noah Claypole: who used him far worse than before, now that his jealousy was roused by seeing the new boy promoted to the black stick and hatband, while he, the old one, remained stationary in the muffin-cap and leathers. Charlotte treated him ill, because Noah did; and Mrs. Sowerberry was his decided enemy, because Mr. Sowerberry was disposed to be his friend; so, between these three on one side, and a glut of funerals on the other, Oliver was not altogether as comfortable as the hungry pig was, when he was shut up, by mistake, in the grain department of a brewery.

And now, I come to a very important passage in Oliver's history; for I have to record an act, slight and unimportant perhaps in appearance, but which indirectly produced a material change in all his future prospects and proceedings.

One day, Oliver and Noah had descended into the kitchen at the usual dinner-hour, to banquet upon a small joint of mutton—a pound and a half of the worst end of the neck—when Charlotte being called out of the way, there ensued a brief interval of time, which Noah Claypole, being hungry and vicious, considered he could not possibly devote to a worthier purpose than aggravating and tantalising young Oliver Twist.

Intent upon this innocent amusement, Noah put his feet on

the table-cloth; and pulled Oliver's hair; and twitched his ears; and expressed his opinion that he was a 'sneak'; and furthermore announced his intention of coming to see him hanged, whenever that desirable event should take place; and entered upon various other topics of petty annoyance, like a malicious and ill-conditioned charity-boy as he was. But, none of these taunts producing the desired effect of making Oliver cry, Noah attempted to be more facetious still; and in this attempt, did what many small wits, with far greater reputations than Noah, sometimes do to this day, when they want to be funny. He got rather personal.

'Work'us,' said Noah, 'how's your mother?'

'She's dead,' replied Oliver; 'don't you say anything about her to me!'

Oliver's colour rose as he said this; he breathed quickly; and there was a curious working of the mouth and nostrils, which Mr. Claypole thought must be the immediate precursor of a violent fit of crying. Under this impression he returned to the charge.

'What did she die of, Work'us?' said Noah.

'Of a broken heart, some of our old nurses told me,' replied Oliver: more as if he were talking to himself, than answering Noah. 'I think I know what it must be to die of that!'

'Tol de rol lol lol, right fol lairy, Work'us,' said Noah, as a tear rolled down Oliver's cheek. 'What's set you a-snivelling now?'

'Not *you*,' replied Oliver, hastily brushing the tear away. 'Don't think it.'

'Oh, not me, eh!' sneered Noah.

'No, not you,' replied Oliver, sharply. 'There; that's enough. Don't say anything more to me about her; you'd better not!'

'Better not!' exclaimed Noah. 'Well! Better not! Work'us, don't be impudent. *Your* mother, too! She was a nice 'un, she was. Oh, Lor!' And here, Noah nodded his head expressively; and curled up as much of his small red nose as muscular action could collect together, for the occasion.

'Yer know, Work'us,' continued Noah, emboldened by Oliver's silence, and speaking in a jeering tone of affected pity: of all tones the most annoying: 'Yer know, Work'us, it can't be helped now; and of course yer couldn't help it then; and I'm very sorry for it; and I'm sure we all are, and pity yer very much. But yer must know, Work'us, yer mother was a regular right-down bad 'un.'

'What did you say?' inquired Oliver, looking up very quickly.

'A regular right-down bad 'un, Work'us,' replied Noah, coolly. 'And it's a great deal better, Work'us, that she died when she did, or else she'd have been hard labouring in Bridewell, or transported, or hung; which is more likely than either, isn't it?'

Crimson with fury, Oliver started up; overthrew the chair and table; seized Noah by the throat; shook him, in the violence of his rage, till his teeth chattered in his head; and, collecting his whole force into one heavy blow, felled him to the ground.

A minute ago, the boy had looked the quiet, mild, dejected creature that harsh treatment had made him. But his spirit was roused at last; the cruel insult to his dead mother had set his blood on fire. His breast heaved; his attitude was erect; his eye bright and vivid; his whole person changed, as he stood glaring over the cowardly tormentor who now lay crouching at his feet; and defied him with an energy he had never known before.

'He'll murder me!' blubbered Noah. 'Charlotte! missis! Here's the new boy a-murdering of me! Help! help! Oliver's gone mad! Char—lotte!'

Noah's shouts were responded to, by a loud scream from Charlotte, and a louder from Mrs. Sowerberry; the former of whom rushed into the kitchen by a side-door, while the latter paused on the staircase till she was quite certain that it was consistent with the preservation of human life, to come further down.

'Oh, you little wretch!' screamed Charlotte: seizing Oliver with her utmost force, which was about equal to that of a moderately strong man in particularly good training, 'Oh, you little un-grate-ful, mur-de-rous, horrid villain!' And between every syllable, Charlotte gave Oliver a blow with all her might: accompanying it with a scream, for the benefit of society.

Charlotte's fist was by no means a light one; but, lest it should not be effectual in calming Oliver's wrath, Mrs. Sowerberry plunged into the kitchen, and assisted to hold him with one hand, while she scratched his face with the other. In this favourable position of affairs, Noah rose from the ground, and pommelled him behind.

This was rather too violent exercise to last long. When they were all wearied out, and could tear and beat no longer, they dragged Oliver, struggling and shouting, but nothing daunted, into the dust-cellar, and there locked him up. This being done, Mrs. Sowerberry sunk into a chair, and burst into tears.

'Bless her, she's going off!' said Charlotte. 'A glass of water, Noah, dear. Make haste!'

'Oh! Charlotte,' said Mrs. Sowerberry: speaking as well as she could, through a deficiency of breath, and a sufficiency of cold water, which Noah had poured over her head and shoulders. 'Oh! Charlotte, what a mercy we have not all been murdered in our beds!'

'Ah! mercy indeed, ma'am,' was the reply. 'I only hope this'll teach master not to have any more of these dreadful creatures, that are born to be murderers and robbers from their very cradle. Poor Noah! He was all but killed, ma'am, when I come in.'

'Poor fellow!' said Mrs. Sowerberry: looking piteously on the charity-boy.

Noah, whose top waistcoat-button might have been some-where on a level with the crown of Oliver's head, rubbed his eyes with the inside of his wrists while this commiseration was bestowed upon him, and performed some affecting tears and sniffs.

'What's to be done!' exclaimed Mrs. Sowerberry. 'Your master's not at home; there's not a man in the house, and he'll kick that door down in ten minutes.' Oliver's vigorous plunges against the bit of timber in question, rendered this occurrence highly probable.

'Dear, dear! I don't know, ma'am,' said Charlotte, 'unless we send for the police-officers.'

'Or the millingtary,' suggested Mr. Claypole.

'No, no,' said Mrs. Sowerberry: bethinking herself of Oliver's old friend. 'Run to Mr. Bumble, Noah, and tell him to come here directly, and not to lose a minute; never mind your cap! Make haste!

You can hold a knife to that black eye, as you run along. It'll keep the swelling down.'

Noah stopped to make no reply, but started off at his fullest speed; and very much it astonished the people who were out walking, to see a charity-boy tearing through the streets pell-mell, with no cap on his head, and a clasp-knife at his eye.

CHAPTER 7

Oliver continues refractory

Noah Claypole ran along the streets at his swiftest pace, and paused not once for breath, until he reached the workhouse-gate. Having rested here, for a minute or so, to collect a good burst of sobs and an imposing show of tears and terror, he knocked loudly at the wicket; and presented such a rueful face to the aged pauper who opened it, that even he, who saw nothing but rueful faces about him at the best of times, started back in astonishment.

'Why, what's the matter with the boy!' said the old pauper.

'Mr. Bumble! Mr. Bumble!' cried Noah, with well-affected dismay: and in tones so loud and agitated, that they not only caught the ear of Mr. Bumble himself, who happened to be hard by, but alarmed him so much that he rushed into the yard without his cocked hat, —which is a very curious and remarkable circumstance: as showing that even a beadle, acted upon by a sudden and powerful impulse, may be afflicted with a momentary visitation of loss of self-possession, and forgetfulness of personal dignity.

'Oh, Mr. Bumble, sir!' said Noah: 'Oliver, sir, —Oliver has—'

'What? What?' interposed Mr. Bumble: with a gleam of pleasure in his metallic eyes. 'Not run away; he hasn't run away, has he Noah?'

'No, sir, no. Not run away, sir, but he's turned wicious,' replied Noah. 'He tried to murder me, sir; and then he tried to murder Charlotte; and then missis. Oh! what dreadful pain it is! Such agony, please, sir!' And here, Noah writhed and twisted his body into an extensive variety of eel-like positions; thereby giving Mr. Bumble to understand that, from the violent and sanguinary onset of Oliver Twist, he had sustained severe internal injury and damage, from which he was at that moment suffering the acutest torture.

When Noah saw that the intelligence he communicated perfectly paralysed Mr. Bumble, he imparted additional effect thereunto, by bewailing his dreadful wounds ten times louder than before; and when he observed a gentleman in a white waistcoat crossing the yard, he was more tragic in his lamentations than ever: rightly conceiving it highly expedient to attract the notice, and rouse the indignation, of the gentleman aforesaid.

The gentleman's notice was very soon attracted; for he had not walked three paces, when he turned angrily round, and inquired what that young cur was howling for, and why Mr. Bumble did not favour him with something which would render the series of vocular exclamations so designated, an involuntary process?

'It's a poor boy from the free-school, sir,' replied Mr. Bumble, 'who has been nearly murdered—all but murdered, sir, —by young Twist.'

'By Jove!' exclaimed the gentleman in the white waistcoat, stopping short. 'I knew it! I felt a strange presentiment from the very first, that that audacious young savage would come to be hung!'

'He has likewise attempted, sir, to murder the female servant,' said Mr. Bumble, with a face of ashy paleness.

'And his missis,' interposed Mr. Claypole.

'And his master, too, I think you said, Noah?' added Mr. Bumble.

'No! he's out, or he would have murdered him,' replied Noah. 'He said he wanted to.'

'Ah! said he wanted to, did he, my boy?' inquired the gentleman in the white waistcoat.

'Yes, sir,' replied Noah. 'And please, sir, missis wants to know whether Mr. Bumble can spare time to step up there, directly, and flog him—'cause master's out.'

'Certainly, my boy; certainly,' said the gentleman in the white waistcoat: smiling benignly, and patting Noah's head, which was about three inches higher than his own. 'You're a good boy—a very good boy. Here's a penny for you. Bumble, just step up to Sowerberry's with your cane, and see what's best to be done. Don't spare him, Bumble.'

'No, I will not, sir,' replied the beadle: adjusting the wax-end which was twisted round the bottom of his cane, for purposes of parochial flagellation.

'Tell Sowerberry not to spare him either. They'll never do anything with him, without stripes and bruises,' said the gentleman in the white waistcoat.

'I'll take care, sir,' replied the beadle. And the cocked hat and cane having been, by this time, adjusted to their owner's satisfaction, Mr. Bumble and Noah Claypole betook themselves with all speed to the undertaker's shop.

Here the position of affairs had not at all improved. Sowerberry had not yet returned, and Oliver continued to kick, with undiminished vigour, at the cellar-door. The accounts of his ferocity, as related by Mrs. Sowerberry and Charlotte, were of so startling a nature, that Mr. Bumble judged it prudent to parley, before opening the door. With this view he gave a kick at the outside, by way of prelude; and, then, applying his mouth to the keyhole, said, in a deep and impressive tone:

'Oliver!'

'Come; you let me out!' replied Oliver, from the inside.

'Do you know this here voice, Oliver?' said Mr. Bumble.

'Yes,' replied Oliver.

'Ain't you afraid of it, sir? Ain't you a-trembling while I speak, sir?' said Mr. Bumble.

'No!' replied Oliver, boldly.

An answer so different from the one he had expected to elicit, and was in the habit of receiving, staggered Mr. Bumble not a little.

He stepped back from the keyhole; drew himself up to his full height; and looked from one to another of the three bystanders, in mute astonishment.

'Oh, you know, Mr. Bumble, he must be mad,' said Mrs. Sowerberry. 'No boy in half his senses could venture to speak so to you.'

'It's not Madness, ma'am,' replied Mr. Bumble, after a few moments of deep meditation. 'It's Meat.'

'What?' exclaimed Mrs. Sowerberry.

'Meat, ma'am, meat,' replied Bumble, with stern emphasis. 'You've over-fed him, ma'am. You've raised a artificial soul and spirit in him, ma'am, unbecoming a person of his condition: as the board, Mrs. Sowerberry, who are practical philosophers, will tell you. What have paupers to do with soul or spirit? It's quite enough that we let 'em have live bodies. If you had kept the boy on gruel, ma'am, this would never have happened.'

'Dear, dear!' ejaculated Mrs. Sowerberry, piously raising her eyes to the kitchen ceiling: 'this comes of being liberal!'

The liberality of Mrs. Sowerberry to Oliver, had consisted in a profuse bestowal upon him of all the dirty odds and ends which nobody else would eat; so there was a great deal of meekness and self-devotion in her voluntarily remaining under Mr. Bumble's heavy accusation. Of which, to do her justice, she was wholly innocent, in thought, word, or deed.

'Ah!' said Mr. Bumble, when the lady brought her eyes down to earth again; 'the only thing that can be done now, that I know of, is to leave him in the cellar for a day or so, till he's a little starved down; and then to take him out, and keep him on gruel all through his apprenticeship. He comes of a bad family. Excitable natures, Mrs. Sowerberry! Both the nurse and doctor said, that that mother of his made her way here, against difficulties and pain that would have killed any well-disposed woman, weeks before.'

At this point of Mr. Bumble's discourse, Oliver, just hearing enough to know that some new allusion was being made to his mother, recommenced kicking, with a violence that rendered every other sound inaudible. Sowerberry returned at this juncture. Oliver's offence having been explained to him, with such exaggerations as the ladies thought best calculated to rouse his ire, he unlocked the cellar door in a twinkling, and dragged his rebellious apprentice out by the collar.

Oliver's clothes had been torn in the beating he had received; his face was bruised and scratched; and his hair scattered over his forehead. The angry flush had not disappeared, however, and when he was pulled out of his prison, he scowled boldly on Noah, and looked quite undismayed.

'Now, you are a nice young fellow, ain't you?' said Sowerberry; giving Oliver a shake, and a box on the ear.

'He called my mother names,' replied Oliver.

'Well, and what if he did, you little ungrateful wretch?' said Mrs. Sowerberry. 'She deserved what he said, and worse.'

'She didn't,' said Oliver.

'She did,' said Mrs. Sowerberry.

'It's a lie,' said Oliver.

Mrs. Sowerberry burst into a flood of tears.

This flood of tears left Mr. Sowerberry no alternative. If he had hesitated for one instant to punish Oliver most severely, it must be quite clear to every experienced reader that he would have been, according to all precedents in disputes of matrimony established, a brute, an unnatural husband, an insulting creature, a base imitation of a man, and various other agreeable characters too numerous for recital within the limits of this chapter. To do him justice, he was, as far as his power went—it was not very extensive—kindly disposed towards the boy; perhaps, because it was his interest to be so; perhaps, because his wife disliked him. The flood of tears, however, left him no resource; so he at once gave him a drubbing, which satisfied even Mrs. Sowerberry herself, and rendered Mr. Bumble's subsequent application of the parochial cane, rather unnecessary. For the rest of the day, he was shut up in the back kitchen, in company with a pump and a slice of bread, and, at night, Mrs. Sowerberry, after making various remarks outside the door, by no means complimentary to the memory of his mother, looked into the room, and, amidst the jeers and pointings of Noah and Charlotte, ordered him up stairs to his dismal bed.

It was not until he was left alone in the silence and stillness of the gloomy workshop of the undertaker, that Oliver gave way to the feelings which the day's treatment may be supposed likely to have awakened in a mere child. He had listened to their taunts with a look of contempt; he had borne the lash without a cry: for he felt that pride swelling in his heart which would have kept down a shriek to the last, though they had roasted him alive. But now, when there were none to see or hear him, he fell upon his knees on the floor, and, hiding his face in his hands, wept such tears as, God send for the credit of our nature, few so young may ever have cause to pour out before him!

For a long time Oliver remained motionless in this attitude. The candle was burning low in the socket when he rose to his feet. Having gazed cautiously round him, and listened intently, he gently undid the fastenings of the door, and looked abroad.

It was a cold, dark night. The stars seemed, to the boy's eyes, farther from the earth than he had ever seen them before; there was no wind; and the sombre shadows thrown by the trees upon the ground, looked sepulchral and death-like, from being so still. He softly reclosed the door. Having availed himself of the expiring light of the candle to tie up in a handkerchief the few articles of wearing apparel he had, sat himself down upon a bench, to wait for morning.

With the first ray of light that struggled through the crevices in the shutters, Oliver arose, and again unbarred the door. One timid look around—one moment's pause of hesitation—he had closed it behind him, and was in the open street.

He looked to the right and to the left, uncertain whither to fly. He remembered to have seen the waggons, as they went out, toiling up the hill. He took the same route; and arriving at a foot-path across the fields: which he knew, after some distance, led out again into the road: struck into it, and walked quickly on.

Along this same footpath, Oliver well remembered he had trotted beside Mr. Bumble, when he first carried him to the workhouse from the farm. His way lay directly in front of the cottage. His heart beat quickly when he bethought himself of this; and he half resolved to turn back. He had come a long way though, and should lose a great deal of time by doing so. Besides, it was so early that there was very little fear of his being seen; so he walked on.

He reached the house. There was no appearance of its inmates stirring at that early hour. Oliver stopped, and peeped into the garden. A child was weeding one of the little beds; as he stopped, he raised his pale face and disclosed the features of one of his former companions. Oliver felt glad to see him, before he went; for, though younger than himself, he had been his little friend and playmate. They had been beaten and starved, and shut up together, many and many a time.

'Hush, Dick!' said Oliver, as the boy ran to the gate, and thrust his thin arm between the rails to greet him. 'Is any one up?'

'Nobody but me,' replied the child.

'You mustn't say you saw me, Dick,' said Oliver. 'I am running away. They beat and ill-use me, Dick; and I am going to seek my fortune, some long way off. I don't know where. How pale you are!'

'I heard the doctor tell them I was dying,' replied the child with a faint smile. 'I am very glad to see you, dear; but don't stop, don't stop!'

'Yes, yes, I will, to say good-b'ye to you,' replied Oliver. 'I shall see you again, Dick. I know I shall! You will be well and happy!'

'I hope so,' replied the child. 'After I am dead, but not before. I know the doctor must be right, Oliver, because I dream so much of Heaven, and Angels, and kind faces that I never see when I am awake. Kiss me,' said the child, climbing up the low gate, and flinging his little arms round Oliver's neck. 'Good-b'ye, dear! God bless you!'

The blessing was from a young child's lips, but it was the first that Oliver had ever heard invoked upon his head; and through the struggles and sufferings, and troubles and changes, of his after life, he never once forgot it.

CHAPTER 8

Oliver walks to London. He encounters on
the road a strange sort of young gentleman

Oliver reached the stile at which the by-path terminated; and once more gained the high-road. It was eight o'clock now. Though he was nearly five miles away from the town, he ran, and hid behind the hedges, by turns, till noon: fearing that he might be pursued and overtaken. Then he sat down to rest by the side of the mile-stone, and began to think, for the first time, where he had better go and try to live.

The stone by which he was seated, bore, in large characters, an intimation that it was just seventy miles from that spot to London. The name awakened a new train of ideas in the boy's mind. London! —that great large place! —nobody—not even Mr. Bumble—could ever find him there! He had often heard the old men in the workhouse, too, say that no lad of spirit need want in London; and that there were ways of living in that vast city, which those who had been bred up in country parts had no idea of. It was the very place for a homeless boy, who must die in the streets unless some one helped him. As these things passed through his thoughts, he jumped upon his feet, and again walked forward.

He had diminished the distance between himself and London by full four miles more, before he recollected how much he must undergo ere he could hope to reach his place of destination. As this consideration forced itself upon him, he slackened his pace a little, and meditated upon his means of getting there. He had a crust of bread, a coarse shirt, and two pairs of stockings, in his bundle. He had a penny too—a gift of Sowerberry's after some funeral in which he had acquitted himself more than ordinarily well—in his pocket. 'A clean shirt,' thought Oliver, 'is a very comfortable thing; and so are two pairs of darned stockings; and so is a penny; but they are small helps to a sixty-five miles' walk in winter time.' But Oliver's thoughts, like those of most other people, although they were extremely ready and active to point out his difficulties, were wholly at a loss to suggest any feasible mode of surmounting them; so, after a good deal of thinking to no particular purpose, he changed his little bundle over to the other shoulder, and trudged on.

Oliver walked twenty miles that day; and all that time tasted nothing but the crust of dry bread, and a few draughts of water, which he begged at the cottage-doors by the roadside. When the night came, he turned into a meadow; and, creeping close under a hay-rick, determined to lie there, till morning. He felt frightened at first, for the wind moaned dismally over the empty fields: and he was cold and hungry, and more alone than he had ever felt before. Being very tired with his walk, however, he soon fell asleep and forgot his troubles.

He felt cold and stiff, when he got up next morning, and so hungry that he was obliged to exchange the penny for a small loaf, in the very first village through which he passed. He had walked no more than twelve miles, when night closed in again. His feet were sore, and his legs so weak that they trembled beneath him. Another night passed in the bleak damp air made him worse; when he set forward on his journey next morning, he could hardly crawl along.

He waited at the bottom of a steep hill till a stagecoach came up, and then begged of the outside passengers; but there were very few who took any notice of him: and even those told him to wait till they got to the top of the hill, and then let them see how far he could run for a halfpenny. Poor Oliver tried to keep up with the coach a little way, but was unable to do it, by reason of his fatigue and sore feet. When the outsides saw this, they put their halfpence back into their pockets again, declaring that he was an idle young dog, and didn't deserve anything; and the coach rattled away and left only a cloud of dust behind.

In some villages, large painted boards were fixed up: warning all persons who begged within the district, that they would be sent to jail. This frightened Oliver very much, and made him glad to get out of those villages with all possible expedition. In others, he would stand about the inn-yards, and look mournfully at every one who passed: a proceeding which generally terminated in the landlady's ordering one of the post-boys who were lounging about, to drive that strange boy out of the place, for she was sure he had come to steal something. If he begged at a farmer's house, ten to one but they threatened to set the dog on him; and when he showed his nose in a shop, they talked about the beadle—which brought Oliver's heart into his mouth, —very often the only thing he had there, for many hours together.

In fact, if it had not been for a good-hearted turnpike-man, and a benevolent old lady, Oliver's troubles would have been shortened by the very same process which had put an end to his mother's; in other words, he would most assuredly have fallen dead upon the king's highway. But the turnpike-man gave him a meal of bread and cheese; and the old lady, who had a shipwrecked grandson wandering barefoot in some distant part of the earth, took pity upon the poor orphan, and gave him what little she could afford— and more—with such kind and gentle words, and such tears of sympathy and compassion, that they sank deeper into Oliver's soul, than all the sufferings he had ever undergone.

Early on the seventh morning after he had left his native place, Oliver limped slowly into the little town of Barnet. The window-shutters were closed; the street was empty; not a soul had awakened to the business of the day. The sun was rising in all its splendid beauty; but the light only served to show the boy his own lonesomeness and desolation, as he sat, with bleeding feet and covered with dust, upon a door-step.

By degrees, the shutters were opened; the window-blinds were drawn up; and people began passing to and fro. Some few stopped to gaze at Oliver for a moment or two, or turned round to stare at him as they hurried by; but none relieved him, or troubled themselves to inquire how he came there. He had no heart to beg. And there he sat.

He had been crouching on the step for some time: wondering at the great number of public-houses (every other house in Barnet was a tavern, large or small), gazing listlessly at the coaches as they passed through, and thinking how strange it seemed that they could do, with ease, in a few hours, what it had taken him a whole week of courage and determination beyond his years to accomplish: when he was roused by observing that a boy, who had passed him carelessly some minutes before, had returned, and was now surveying him most earnestly from the opposite side of the way. He took little heed of this at first; but the boy remained in the same attitude of close observation so long, that Oliver raised his head, and returned his steady look. Upon this, the boy crossed over; and, walking close up to Oliver, said,

'Hullo, my covey! What's the row?'

The boy who addressed this inquiry to the young wayfarer, was about his own age: but one of the queerest-looking boys that Oliver had ever seen. He was a snub-nosed, flat-browed, common-faced boy enough; and as dirty a juvenile as one would wish to see; but he had about him all the airs and manners of a man. He was short of his age: with rather bow-legs, and little, sharp, ugly eyes. His hat was stuck on the top of his head so lightly, that it threatened to fall off every moment—and would have done so, very often, if the wearer had not had a knack of every now and then giving his head a sudden twitch, which brought it back to its old place again. He wore a man's coat, which reached nearly to his heels. He had turned the cuffs back, half-way up his arm, to get his hands out of the sleeves; apparently with the ultimate view of thrusting them into the pockets of his corduroy trousers; for there he kept them. He was, altogether, as roystering and swaggering a young gentleman as ever stood four feet six, or something less, in his bluchers.

'Hullo, my covey! What's the row?' said this strange young gentleman to Oliver.

'I am very hungry and tired,' replied Oliver: the tears standing in his eyes as he spoke. 'I have walked a long way. I have been walking these seven days.'

'Walking for sivin days!' said the young gentleman. 'Oh, I see. Beak's order, eh? But,' he added, noticing Oliver's look of surprise, 'I suppose you don't know what a beak is, my flash com-pan-i-on.'

Oliver mildly replied, that he had always heard a bird's mouth described by the term in question.

'My eyes, how green!' exclaimed the young gentleman. 'Why, a beak's a madgst'rate; and when you walk by a beak's order, it's not straight forerd, but always a-going up, and nivir a-coming down agin. Was you never on the mill?'

'What mill?' inquired Oliver.

'What mill! Why, *the* mill—the mill as takes up so little room that it'll work inside a Stone Jug; and always goes better when the wind's low with people, than when it's high; acos then they can't get workmen. But come,' said the young gentleman; 'you want grub, and you shall have it. I'm at low-water-mark myself, —only one bob and a magpie; but, *as* far *as* it goes, I'll fork out and stump. Up with you on your pins. There! Now then! Morrice!'

Assisting Oliver to rise, the young gentleman took him to an adjacent chandler's shop, where he purchased a sufficiency of ready-dressed ham and a half-quartern loaf, or, as he himself expressed it, 'a fourpenny bran!' the ham being kept clean and preserved from dust, by the ingenious expedient of making a hole in the loaf by pulling out a portion of the crumb, and stuffing it therein. Taking the bread under his arm, the young gentleman turned into a small public-house, and led the way to a tap-room in the rear of the premises. Here, a pot of beer was brought in, by direction of the mysterious youth; and Oliver, falling to, at his new friend's bidding, made a long and hearty meal, during the progress of which, the strange boy eyed him from time to time with great attention.

'Going to London?' said the strange boy, when Oliver had at length concluded.

'Yes.'

'Got any lodgings?'

'No.'

'Money?'

'No.'

The strange boy whistled; and put his arms into his pockets, as far as the big coat sleeves would let them go.

'Do you live in London?' inquired Oliver.

'Yes. I do, when I'm at home,' replied the boy. 'I suppose you want some place to sleep in to-night, don't you?'

'I do, indeed,' answered Oliver. 'I have not slept under a roof since I left the country.

'Don't fret your eyelids on that score,' said the young gentleman. 'I've got to be in London to-night; and I know a 'spectable old genelman as lives there, wot'll give you lodgings for nothink, and never ask for the change—that is, if any genelman he knows inter-duces you. And don't he know me? Oh, no! Not in the least! By no means. Certainly not!'

The young gentleman smiled, as if to intimate that the latter fragments of discourse were playfully ironical; and finished the beer as he did so.

This unexpected offer of shelter was too tempting to be resisted; especially as it was immediately followed up, by the assurance that the old gentleman referred to, would doubtless provide Oliver with a comfortable place, without loss of time. This led to a more friendly and confidential dialogue; from which Oliver discovered that his friend's name was Jack Dawkins, and that he was a peculiar pet and *protégé* of the elderly gentleman before mentioned.

Mr. Dawkins's appearance did not say a vast deal in favour of the comforts which his patron's interest obtained for those whom he took under his protection; but, as he had a rather flighty and dissolute mode of conversing, and furthermore avowed that among his intimate friends he was better known by the *sobriquet* of 'The artful Dodger,' Oliver concluded that, being of a dissipated and careless turn, the moral precepts of his benefactor had hitherto been thrown away upon him. Under this impression, he secretly resolved to cultivate the good opinion of the old gentleman as quickly as possible; and, if he found the Dodger incorrigible, as he more than half suspected he should, to decline the honour of his farther acquaintance.

As John Dawkins objected to their entering London before nightfall, it was nearly eleven o'clock when they reached the turn-pike at Islington. They crossed from the Angel into St. John's Road; struck down the small street which terminates at Sadler's Wells Theatre; through Exmouth Street and Coppice Row; down the little court by the side of the workhouse; across the classic ground which once bore the name of Hockley-in-the-Hole; thence into Little Saffron Hill; and so into Saffron Hill the Great: along which the Dodger scudded at a rapid pace, directing Oliver to follow close at his heels.

Although Oliver had enough to occupy his attention in keeping sight of his leader, he could not help bestowing a few hasty glances on either side of the way, as he passed along. A dirtier or more wretched place he had never seen. The street was very narrow and muddy, and the air was impregnated with filthy odours. There were a good many small shops; but the only stock in trade appeared to be heaps of children, who, even at that time of night, were crawling in and out at the doors, or screaming from the inside. The sole places that seemed to prosper amid the general blight of the place, were the public-houses; and in them, the lowest orders of Irish were wrangling with might and main. Covered ways and yards, which here and there diverged from the main street, disclosed little knots of houses, where drunken men and women were positively wallowing in filth; and from several of the doorways, great ill-looking fellows were cautiously emerging, bound, to all appearance, on no very well-disposed or harmless errands.

Oliver was just considering whether he hadn't better run away, when they reached the bottom of the hill. His conductor, catching him by the arm, pushed open the door of a house near Field Lane; and, drawing him into the passage, closed it behind them.

'Now, then!' cried a voice from below, in reply to a whistle from the Dodger.

'Plummy and slam!' was the reply.

This seemed to be some watchword or signal that all was right; for the light of a feeble candle gleamed on the wall at the remote end of the passage; and a man's face peeped out, from where a balustrade of the old kitchen staircase had been broken away.

'There's two on you,' said the man, thrusting the candle farther out, and shading his eyes with his hand. 'Who's t'other one?'

'A new pal,' replied Jack Dawkins, pulling Oliver forward.

'Where did he come from?'

'Greenland. Is Fagin up stairs?'

'Yes, he's a-sortin' the wipes. Up with you!' The candle was drawn back, and the face disappeared.

Oliver, groping his way with one hand, and having the other firmly grasped by his companion, ascended with much difficulty the dark and broken stairs: which his conductor mounted with an ease and expedition that showed he was well acquainted with them. He threw open the door of a backroom, and drew Oliver in after him.

The walls and ceiling of the room were perfectly black with age and dirt. There was a deal table before the fire: upon which were a candle, stuck in a ginger-beer bottle, two or three pewter pots, a loaf and butter, and a plate. In a frying-pan, which was on the fire, and which was secured to the mantelshelf by a string, some sausages were cooking; and standing over them, with a toasting-fork in his hand, was a very old shrivelled Jew, whose villainous-looking and repulsive face was obscured by a quantity of matted red hair. He was dressed in a greasy flannel gown, with his throat bare; and seemed to be dividing his attention between the frying-pan and a clothes-horse, over which a great number of silk handkerchiefs were hanging. Several rough beds made of old sacks, were huddled side by side on the floor. Seated round the table were four or five boys, none older than the Dodger, smoking long clay pipes, and drinking spirits with the air of middle-aged men. These all crowded about their associate as he whispered a few words to the Jew; and then turned round and grinned at Oliver. So did the Jew himself, toasting-fork in hand.

'This is him, Fagin,' said Jack Dawkins; 'my friend Oliver Twist.'

The Jew grinned; and, making a low obeisance to Oliver, took him by the hand, and hoped he should have the honour of his intimate acquaintance. Upon this, the young gentlemen with the pipes came round him, and shook both his hands very hard—especially the one in which he held his little bundle. One young gentleman was very anxious to hang up his cap for him; and another was so obliging as to put his hands in his pockets, in order that, as he was very tired, he might not have the trouble of emptying them, himself, when he went to bed. These civilities would probably have been extended much farther, but for a liberal exercise of the Jew's toasting-fork on the heads and shoulders of the affectionate youths who offered them.

'We are very glad to see you, Oliver, very,' said the Jew. 'Dodger, take off the sausages; and draw a tub near the fire for Oliver. Ah! you're a-staring at the pocket-handkerchiefs! eh, my dear! There are a good many of 'em, ain't there? We've just looked 'em out, ready for the wash; that's all, Oliver; that's all. Ha! ha! ha!'

The latter part of this speech, was hailed by a boisterous shout from all the hopeful pupils of the merry old gentleman. In the midst of which, they went to supper.

Oliver ate his share, and the Jew then mixed him a glass of hot gin and water: telling him he must drink it off directly, because another gentleman wanted the tumbler. Oliver did as he was desired. Immediately afterwards he felt himself gently lifted on to one of the sacks; and then he sunk into a deep sleep.

CHAPTER 9

Containing further particulars concerning
the pleasant old gentleman, and his hopeful
pupils

It was late next morning when Oliver awoke, from a sound, long
sleep. There was no other person in the room but the old Jew, who
was boiling some coffee in a saucepan for breakfast, and whistling
softly to himself as he stirred it round and round, with an iron
spoon. He would stop every now and then to listen when there was
the least noise below: and when he had satisfied himself, he would
go on, whistling and stirring again, as before.

Although Oliver had roused himself from sleep, he was not
thoroughly awake. There is a drowsy state, between sleeping and
waking, when you dream more in five minutes with your eyes half
open, and yourself half conscious of everything that is passing around
you, than you would in five nights with your eyes fast closed, and
your senses wrapt in perfect unconsciousness. At such times, a
mortal knows just enough of what his mind is doing, to form some
glimmering conception of its mighty powers, its bounding from earth
and spurning time and space, when freed from the restraint of its
corporeal associate.

Oliver was precisely in this condition. He saw the Jew with his
half-closed eyes; heard his low whistling; and recognised the sound
of the spoon grating against the saucepan's sides; and yet the self-
same senses were mentally engaged, at the same time, in busy action
with almost everybody he had ever known.

When the coffee was done, the Jew drew the saucepan to the hob. Standing, then, in an irresolute attitude for a few minutes, as if he did not well know how to employ himself, he turned round and looked at Oliver, and called him by his name. He did not answer, and was to all appearances asleep.

After satisfying himself upon this head, the Jew stepped gently to the door: which he fastened. He then drew forth: as it seemed to Oliver, from some trap in the floor: a small box, which he placed carefully on the table. His eyes glistened as he raised the lid, and looked in. Dragging an old chair to the table, he sat down; and took from it a magnificent gold watch, sparkling with jewels.

'Aha!' said the Jew, shrugging up his shoulders, and distorting every feature with a hideous grin. 'Clever dogs! Clever dogs! Staunch to the last! Never told the old parson where they were. Never peached upon old Fagin! And why should they? It wouldn't have loosened the knot, or kept the drop up, a minute longer. No, no, no! Fine fellows! Fine fellows!'

With these, and other muttered reflections of the like nature, the Jew once more deposited the watch in its place of safety. At least half a dozen more were severally drawn forth from the same box, and surveyed with equal pleasure; besides rings, brooches, bracelets, and other articles of jewellery, of such magnificent materials, and costly workmanship, that Oliver had no idea, even of their names.

Having replaced these trinkets, the Jew took out another: so small that it lay in the palm of his hand. There seemed to be some very minute inscription on it; for the Jew laid it flat upon the table, and, shading it with his hand, pored over it, long and earnestly. At length he put it down, as if despairing of success; and, leaning back in his chair, muttered:

'What a fine thing capital punishment is! Dead men never repent; dead men never bring awkward stories to light. Ah! it's a fine thing for the trade! Five of 'em strung up in a row, and none left to play booty, or turn white-livered!'

As the Jew uttered these words, his bright dark eyes, which had been staring vacantly before him, fell on Oliver's face; the boy's eyes were fixed on his in mute curiosity; and although the recognition was only for an instant—for the briefest space of time that can possibly be conceived—it was enough to show the old man that he had been observed. He closed the lid of the box with a loud crash; and, laying his hand on a bread knife which was on the table, started furiously up. He trembled very much though; for, even in his terror, Oliver could see that the knife quivered in the air.

'What's that?' said the Jew. 'What do you watch me for? Why are you awake? What have you seen? Speak out, boy! Quick—quick! for your life!'

'I wasn't able to sleep any longer, sir,' replied Oliver, meekly. 'I am very sorry if I have disturbed you, sir.'

'You were not awake an hour ago?' said the Jew, scowling fiercely on the boy.

'No! No, indeed!' replied Oliver.

'Are you sure?' cried the Jew: with a still fiercer look than before: and a threatening attitude.

'Upon my word I was not, sir,' replied Oliver, earnestly. 'I was not, indeed, sir.'

'Tush, tush, my dear!' said the Jew, abruptly resuming his old manner, and playing with the knife a little, before he laid it down; as if to induce the belief that he had caught it up, in mere sport. 'Of course I know that, my dear. I only tried to frighten you. You're a brave boy. Ha! ha! you're a brave boy, Oliver!' The Jew rubbed his hands with a chuckle, but glanced uneasily at the box, notwithstanding.

'Did you see any of these pretty things, my dear?' said the Jew, laying his hand upon it after a short pause.

'Yes, sir,' replied Oliver.

'Ah!' said the Jew, turning rather pale. 'They—they're mine, Oliver; my little property. All I have to live upon, in my old age. The folks call me a miser, my dear. Only a miser; that's all.'

Oliver thought the old gentleman must be a decided miser to live in such a dirty place, with so many watches; but, thinking that perhaps his fondness for the Dodger and the other boys, cost him a good deal of money, he only cast a deferential look at the Jew, and asked if he might get up.

'Certainly, my dear, certainly,' replied the old gentleman. 'Stay. There's a pitcher of water in the corner by the door. Bring it here; and I'll give you a basin to wash in, my dear.'

Oliver got up; walked across the room; and stooped for an instant to raise the pitcher. When he turned his head, the box was gone.

He had scarcely washed himself, and made everything tidy, by emptying the basin out of the window, agreeably to the Jew's directions, when the Dodger returned: accompanied by a very sprightly young friend, whom Oliver had seen smoking on the previous night, and who was now formally introduced to him as Charley Bates. The four sat down, to breakfast, on the coffee, and some hot rolls and ham which the Dodger had brought home in the crown of his hat.

'Well,' said the Jew, glancing slyly at Oliver, and addressing himself to the Dodger, 'I hope you've been at work this morning, my dears?'

'Hard,' replied the Dodger.

'As nails,' added Charley Bates.

'Good boys, good boys!' said the Jew. 'What have *you* got Dodger?'

'A couple of pocket-books,' replied that young gentleman.

'Lined?' inquired the Jew, with eagerness.

'Pretty well,' replied the Dodger, producing two pocket-books; one green, and the other red.

'Not so heavy as they might be,' said the Jew, after looking at the insides carefully; 'but very neat and nicely made. Ingenious workman, ain't he, Oliver?'

'Very, indeed, sir,' said Oliver. At which Mr. Charles Bates laughed uproariously; very much to the amazement of Oliver, who saw nothing to laugh at, in anything that had passed.

'And what have you got, my dear?' said Fagin to Charley Bates.

'Wipes,' replied Master Bates; at the same time producing four pocket-handkerchiefs.

'Well,' said the Jew, inspecting them closely; 'they're very good ones, very. You haven't marked them well, though, Charley; so the marks shall be picked out with a needle, and we'll teach Oliver how to do it. Shall us, Oliver, eh? Ha! ha! ha!'

'If you please, sir,' said Oliver.

'You'd like to be able to make pocket-handkerchiefs as easy as Charley Bates, wouldn't you, my dear?' said the Jew.

'Very much, indeed, if you'll teach me, sir,' replied Oliver.

Master Bates saw something so exquisitely ludicrous in this reply, that he burst into another laugh; which laugh, meeting the coffee he was drinking, and carrying it down some wrong channel, very nearly terminated in his premature suffocation.

'He is so jolly green!' said Charley when he recovered, as an apology to the company for his unpolite behaviour.

The Dodger said nothing, but he smoothed Oliver's hair over his eyes, and said he'd know better, by-and-bye; upon which the old gentleman, observing Oliver's colour mounting, changed the subject by asking whether there had been much of a crowd at the execution that morning? This made him wonder more and more; for it was plain from the replies of the two boys that they had both been there; and Oliver naturally wondered how they could possibly have found time to be so very industrious.

When the breakfast was cleared away, the merry old gentleman and the two boys played at a very curious and uncommon game, which was performed in this way. The merry old gentleman, placing a snuff-box in one pocket of his trousers, a note-case in the other, and a watch in his waistcoat pocket, with a guard-chain round his neck, and sticking a mock diamond pin in his shirt: buttoned his coat tight round him, and putting his spectacle-case and handkerchief in his pockets, trotted up and down the room with a stick, in imitation of the manner in which old gentlemen walk about the streets any hour in the day. Sometimes he stopped at the fireplace, and sometimes at the door, making believe that he was staring with all his might into shop-windows. At such times, he would look constantly round him, for fear of thieves, and would keep slapping all his pockets in turn, to see that he hadn't lost anything, in such a very funny and natural manner, that Oliver laughed till the tears ran down his face. All this time, the two boys followed him closely about: getting out of his sight, so nimbly, every time he turned round, that it was impossible to follow their motions. At last, the Dodger trod upon his toes, or ran upon his boot accidentally, while Charley Bates stumbled up against him behind; and in that one moment they took from him, with the most extraordinary rapidity, snuff-box, note-case, watch-guard, chain, shirt-pin, pocket-handkerchief, even the spectacle-case. If the old gentleman felt a hand in any one of his pockets, he cried out where it was; and then the game began all over again.

When this game had been played a great many times, a couple of young ladies called to see the young gentlemen; one of whom was named Bet, and the other Nancy. They wore a good deal of hair, not very neatly turned up behind, and were rather untidy about the shoes and stockings. They were not exactly pretty, perhaps; but they had a great deal of colour in their faces, and looked quite stout and hearty. Being remarkably free and agreeable in their manners, Oliver thought them very nice girls indeed. As there is no doubt they were.

These visitors stopped a long time. Spirits were produced, in consequence of one of the young ladies complaining of a coldness in her inside; and the conversation took a very convivial and improving turn. At length, Charley Bates expressed his opinion that it was time to pad the hoof. This, it occurred to Oliver, must be French for going out; for, directly afterwards, the Dodger, and Charley, and the two young ladies, went away together, having been kindly furnished by the amiable old Jew with money to spend.

'There, my dear,' said Fagin. 'That's a pleasant life, isn't it? They have gone out for the day.'

'Have they done work, sir?' inquired Oliver.

'Yes,' said the Jew; 'that is, unless they should unexpectedly come across any, when they are out; and they won't neglect it, if they do, my dear, depend upon it. Make 'em your models, my dear.

Make 'em your models,' tapping the fire-shovel on the hearth to add force to his words; 'do everything they bid you, and take their advice in all matters—especially the Dodger's, my dear. He'll be a great man himself, and will make you one too, if you take pattern by him. —Is my handkerchief hanging out of my pocket, my dear?' said the Jew, stopping short.

'Yes, sir,' said Oliver.

'See if you can take it out, without my feeling it: as you saw them do, when we were at play this morning.'

Oliver held up the bottom of the pocket with one hand, as he had seen the Dodger hold it, and drew the handkerchief lightly out of it with the other.

'Is it gone?' cried the Jew.

'Here it is, sir,' said Oliver, showing it in his hand.

'You're a clever boy, my dear,' said the playful old gentleman, patting Oliver on the head approvingly. 'I never saw a sharper lad. Here's a shilling for you. If you go on, in this way, you'll be the greatest man of the time. And now come here, and I'll show you how to take the marks out of the handkerchiefs.'

Oliver wondered what picking the old gentleman's pocket in play, had to do with his chances of being a great man. But, thinking that the Jew, being so much his senior, must know best, he followed him quietly to the table, and was soon deeply involved in his new study.

CHAPTER 10

Oliver becomes better acquainted with the characters of his new associates; and purchases experience at a high price. Being a short, but very important chapter, in this history

For many days, Oliver remained in the Jew's room, picking the marks out of the pocket-handkerchiefs, (of which a great number were brought home), and sometimes taking part in the game already described: which the two boys and the Jew played, regularly, every morning. At length, he began to languish for fresh air, and took many occasions of earnestly entreating the old gentleman to allow him to go out to work, with his two companions.

Oliver was rendered the more anxious to be actively employed, by what he had seen of the stern morality of the old gentleman's character. Whenever the Dodger or Charley Bates came home at night, empty-handed, he would expatiate with great vehemence on the misery of idle and lazy habits; and would enforce upon them the necessity of an active life, by sending them supperless to bed. On one occasion, indeed, he even went so far as to knock them both down a flight of stairs; but this was carrying out his virtuous precepts to an unusual extent.

At length, one morning, Oliver obtained the permission he had so eagerly sought. There had been no handkerchiefs to work upon, for two or three days, and the dinners had been rather meagre. Perhaps these were reasons for the old gentleman's giving his assent; but, whether they were or no, he told Oliver he might go, and placed him under the joint guardianship of Charley Bates, and his friend the Dodger.

The three boys sallied out; the Dodger with his coat-sleeves tucked up, and his hat cocked, as usual; Master Bates sauntering along with his hands in his pockets; and Oliver between them, wondering where they were going, and what branch of manufacture he would be instructed in, first.

The pace at which they went, was such a very lazy, ill-looking saunter, that Oliver soon began to think his companions were going to deceive the old gentleman, by not going to work at all. The Dodger had a vicious propensity, too, of pulling the caps from the heads of small boys and tossing them down areas; while Charley Bates exhibited some very loose notions concerning the rights of property, by pilfering divers apples and onions from the stalls at the kennel sides, and thrusting them into pockets which were so surprisingly capacious, that they seemed to undermine his whole suit of clothes in every direction. These things looked so bad, that Oliver was on the point of declaring his intention of seeking his way back, in the best way he could; when his thoughts were suddenly directed into another channel, by a very mysterious change of behaviour on the part of the Dodger.

They were just emerging from a narrow court not far from the open square in Clerkenwell, which is yet called, by some strange perversion of terms, 'The Green': when the Dodger made a sudden stop; and, laying his finger on his lip, drew his companions back again, with the greatest caution and circumspection.

'What's the matter?' demanded Oliver.

'Hush!' replied the Dodger. 'Do you see that old cove at the book-stall?'

'The old gentleman over the way?' said Oliver. 'Yes, I see him.'

'He'll do,' said the Dodger.

'A prime plant,' observed Master Charley Bates.

Oliver looked from one to the other, with the greatest surprise; but he was not permitted to make any inquiries; for the two boys walked stealthily across the road, and slunk close behind the old gentleman towards whom his attention had been directed. Oliver walked a few paces after them; and, not knowing whether to advance or retire, stood looking on in silent amazement.

The old gentleman was a very respectable-looking personage, with a powdered head and gold spectacles. He was dressed in a bottle-green coat with a black velvet collar; wore white trousers; and carried a smart bamboo cane under his arm. He had taken up a book from the stall, and there he stood, reading away, as hard as if he were in his elbow-chair, in his own study. It is very possible that he fancied himself there, indeed; for it was plain, from his abstraction, that he saw not the book-stall, nor the street, nor the boys, nor, in short, anything but the book itself: which he was reading straight through: turning over the leaf when he got to the bottom of a page, beginning at the top line of the next one, and going regularly on, with the greatest interest and eagerness.

What was Oliver's horror and alarm as he stood a few paces off, looking on with his eyelids as wide open as they would possibly go, to see the Dodger plunge his hand into the old gentleman's pocket, and draw from thence a handkerchief! To see him hand the same to Charley Bates; and finally to behold them, both, running away round the corner at full speed!

In an instant the whole mystery of the handkerchiefs, and the watches, and the jewels, and the Jew, rushed upon the boy's mind. He stood, for a moment, with the blood so tingling through all his veins from terror, that he felt as if he were in a burning fire; then, confused and frightened, he took to his heels; and, not knowing what he did, made off as fast as he could lay his feet to the ground.

This was all done in a minute's space. In the very instant when Oliver began to run, the old gentleman, putting his hand to his pocket, and missing his handkerchief, turned sharp round. Seeing the boy scudding away at such a rapid pace, he very naturally concluded him to be the depredator; and, shouting 'Stop thief!' with all his might, made off after him, book in hand.

But the old gentleman was not the only person who raised the hue-and-cry. The Dodger and Master Bates, unwilling to attract public attention by running down the open street, had merely retired into the very first doorway round the corner. They no sooner heard the cry, and saw Oliver running, than, guessing exactly how the matter stood, they issued forth with great promptitude; and, shouting 'Stop thief!' too, joined in the pursuit like good citizens.

Although Oliver had been brought up by philosophers, he was not theoretically acquainted with the beautiful axiom that self-preservation is the first law of nature. If he had been, perhaps he would have been prepared for this. Not being prepared, however, it alarmed him the more; so away he went like the wind, with the old gentleman and the two boys roaring and shouting behind him.

'Stop thief! Stop thief!' There is a magic in the sound. The tradesman leaves his counter, and the car-man his waggon; the butcher throws down his tray; the baker his basket; the milkman his pail; the errand-boy his parcels; the school-boy his marbles; the paviour his pickaxe; the child his battledore. Away they run, pell-mell, helter-skelter, slap-dash: tearing, yelling, screaming, knocking down the passengers as they turn the corners, rousing up the dogs, and astonishing the fowls: and streets, squares, and courts, re-echo with the sound.

'Stop thief! Stop thief!' The cry is taken up by a hundred voices, and the crowd accumulate at every turning. Away they fly, splashing through the mud, and rattling along the pavements: up go the windows, out run the people, onward bear the mob, a whole audience desert Punch in the very thickest of the plot, and, joining the rushing throng, swell the shout, and lend fresh vigour to the cry, 'Stop thief! Stop thief!'

'Stop thief! Stop thief!' There is a passion *for hunting something* deeply implanted in the human breast. One wretched breathless child, panting with exhaustion; terror in his looks; agony in his eyes; large drops of perspiration streaming down his face; strains every nerve to make head upon his pursuers; and as they follow on his track, and gain upon him every instant, they hail his decreasing strength with still louder shouts, and whoop and scream with joy. 'Stop thief!' Ay, stop him for God's sake, were it only in mercy!

Stopped at last! A clever blow. He is down upon the pavement, and the crowd eagerly gather round him: each newcomer jostling and struggling with the others to catch a glimpse. 'Stand aside!' 'Give him a little air!' 'Nonsense! he don't deserve it.' 'Where's the gentleman?' 'Here he is, coming down the street.' 'Make room there for the gentleman!' 'Is this the boy, sir?' 'Yes.'

Oliver lay, covered with mud and dust, and bleeding from the mouth, looking wildly round upon the heap of faces that surrounded him, when the old gentleman was officiously dragged and pushed into the circle by the foremost of the pursuers.

'Yes,' said the gentleman, 'I am afraid it is the boy.'

'Afraid!' murmured the crowd. 'That's a good 'un!'

'Poor fellow!' said the gentleman, 'he has hurt himself.'

'*I* did that, sir,' said a great lubberly fellow, stepping forward; 'and preciously I cut my knuckle agin' his mouth. *I* stopped him, sir.'

The fellow touched his hat with a grin, expecting something for his pains; but, the old gentleman, eyeing him with an expression of dislike, looked anxiously round, as if he contemplated running away himself: which it is very possible he might have attempted to do, and thus have afforded another chase, had not a police officer (who is generally the last person to arrive in such cases) at that moment made his way through the crowd, and seized Oliver by the collar.

'Come, get up,' said the man, roughly.

'It wasn't me indeed, sir. Indeed, indeed, it was two other boys,' said Oliver, clasping his hands passionately, and looking round. 'They are here somewhere.'

'Oh no, they ain't,' said the officer. He meant this to be ironical, but it was true besides; for the Dodger and Charley Bates had filed off down the first convenient court they came to. 'Come, get up!'

'Don't hurt him,' said the old gentleman, compassionately.

'Oh no, I won't hurt him,' replied the officer, tearing his jacket half off his back, in proof thereof. 'Come, I know you; it won't do. Will you stand upon your legs, you young devil?'

Oliver, who could hardly stand, made a shift to raise himself on his feet, and was at once lugged along the streets by the jacket-collar, at a rapid pace. The gentleman walked on with them by the officer's side; and as many of the crowd as could achieve the feat, got a little ahead, and stared back at Oliver from time to time. The boys shouted in triumph; and on they went.

CHAPTER 11

Treats of Mr. Fang the police magistrate; and
furnishes a slight specimen of his mode of
administering justice

The offence had been committed within the district, and indeed
in the immediate neighbourhood of, a very notorious metropolitan
police office. The crowd had only the satisfaction of accompanying
Oliver through two or three streets, and down a place called Mutton
Hill, when he was led beneath a low archway, and up a dirty court,
into this dispensary of summary justice, by the back way. It was a
small paved yard into which they turned, and here they encountered a stout man with a bunch of whiskers on his face, and a bunch
of keys in his hand.

'What's the matter now?' said the man carelessly.

'A young fogle-hunter,' replied the man who had Oliver in
charge.

'Are you the party that's been robbed, sir?' inquired the man
with the keys.

'Yes, I am,' replied the old gentleman; 'but I am not sure that
this boy actually took the handkerchief. I—I would rather not press
the case.'

'Must go before the magistrate now, sir,' replied the man. 'His
worship will be disengaged in half a minute. Now, young gallows!'

This was an invitation for Oliver to enter through a door which
he unlocked as he spoke, and which led into a stone cell. Here he
was searched; and nothing being found upon him, locked up.

This cell was in shape and size something like an area cellar, only not so light. It was most intolerably dirty; for it was Monday morning; and it had been tenanted by six drunken people, who had been locked up, elsewhere, since Saturday night. But this is little. In our station-houses, men and women are every night confined on the most trivial *charges*—the word is worth noting—in dungeons, compared with which, those in Newgate, occupied by the most atrocious felons, tried, found guilty, and under sentence of death, are palaces. Let any one who doubts this, compare the two.

The old gentleman looked almost as rueful as Oliver when the key grated in the lock. He turned with a sigh to the book, which had been the innocent cause of all this disturbance.

'There is something in that boy's face,' said the old gentleman to himself as he walked slowly away, tapping his chin with the cover of the book, in a thoughtful manner; 'something that touches and interests me. *Can* he be innocent? He looked like. —. By the bye,' exclaimed the old gentleman, halting very abruptly, and staring up into the sky, 'Bless my soul! Where have I seen something like that look before?'

After musing for some minutes, the old gentleman walked, with the same meditative face, into a back anteroom opening from the yard; and there, retiring into a corner, called up before his mind's eye a vast amphitheatre of faces over which a dusky curtain had hung for many years. 'No,' said the old gentleman, shaking his head; 'it must be imagination.'

He wandered over them again. He had called them into view, and it was not easy to replace the shroud that had so long concealed them. There were the faces of friends, and foes, and of many that had been almost strangers peering intrusively from the crowd; there were the faces of young and blooming girls that were now old women; there were faces that the grave had changed and closed upon, but which the mind, superior to its power, still dressed in their old freshness and beauty, calling back the lustre of the eyes, the brightness of the smile, the beaming of the soul through its mask of clay, and whispering of beauty beyond the tomb, changed but to be heightened, and taken from earth only to be set up as a light, to shed a soft and gentle glow upon the path to Heaven.

But the old gentleman could recall no one countenance of which Oliver's features bore a trace. So, he heaved a sigh over the recollections he had awakened; and being, happily for himself, an absent old gentleman, buried them again in the pages of the musty book.

He was roused by a touch on the shoulder, and a request from the man with the keys to follow him into the office. He closed his book hastily; and was at once ushered into the imposing presence of the renowned Mr. Fang.

The office was a front parlour, with a panelled wall. Mr. Fang sat behind a bar, at the upper end; and on one side the door was a sort of wooden pen in which poor little Oliver was already deposited: trembling very much at the awfulness of the scene.

Mr. Fang was a lean, long-backed, stiff-necked, middle-sized man, with no great quantity of hair, and what he had, growing on the back and sides of his head. His face was stern, and much flushed. If he were really not in the habit of drinking rather more than was exactly good for him, he might have brought an action against his countenance for libel, and have recovered heavy damages.

The old gentleman bowed respectfully; and advancing to the magistrate's desk, said, suiting the action to the word, 'That is my name and address, sir.' He then withdrew a pace or two; and, with another polite and gentlemanly inclination of the head, waited to be questioned.

Now, it so happened that Mr. Fang was at that moment perusing a leading article in a newspaper of the morning, adverting to some recent decision of his, and commending him, for the three hundred and fiftieth time, to the special and particular notice of the Secretary of State for the Home Department. He was out of temper; and he looked up with an angry scowl.

'Who are you?' said Mr. Fang.

The old gentleman pointed, with some surprise, to his card.

'Officer!' said Mr. Fang, tossing the card contemptuously away with the newspaper. 'Who is this fellow?'

'My name, sir,' said the old gentleman, speaking *like* a gentleman, 'my name, sir, is Brownlow. Permit me to inquire the name of the magistrate who offers a gratuitous and unprovoked insult to a respectable person, under the protection of the bench.' Saying this, Mr. Brownlow looked round the office as if in search of some person who would afford him the required information.

'Officer!' said Mr. Fang, throwing the paper on one side, 'what's this fellow charged with?'

'He's not charged at all, your worship,' replied the officer. 'He appears against the boy, your worship.'

His worship knew this perfectly well; but it was a good annoyance, and a safe one.

'Appears against the boy, does he?' said Fang, surveying Mr. Brownlow contemptuously from head to foot. 'Swear him!'

'Before I am sworn, I must beg to say one word,' said Mr. Brownlow: 'and that is, that I really never, without actual experience, could have believed—'

'Hold your tongue, sir!' said Mr. Fang, peremptorily.

'I will not, sir!' replied the old gentleman.

'Hold your tongue this instant, or I'll have you turned out of the office!' said Mr. Fang. 'You're an insolent, impertinent fellow. How dare you bully a magistrate!'

'What!' exclaimed the old gentleman, reddening.

'Swear this person!' said Fang to the clerk. 'I'll not hear another word. Swear him.'

Mr. Brownlow's indignation was greatly roused; but reflecting, perhaps, that he might only injure the boy by giving vent to it, he suppressed his feelings and submitted to be sworn at once.

'Now,' said Fang, 'what's the charge against this boy? What have you got to say, sir?'

'I was standing at a book-stall—' Mr. Brownlow began.

'Hold your tongue, sir,' said Mr. Fang. 'Policeman! Where's the policeman? Hear, swear this policeman. Now, policeman, what is this?'

The policeman, with becoming humility, related how he had taken the charge; how he had searched Oliver, and found nothing on his person; and how that was all he knew about it.

'Are there any witnesses?' inquired Mr. Fang.

'None, your worship,' replied the policeman.

Mr. Fang sat silent for some minutes, and then, turning round to the prosecutor, said in a towering passion,

'Do you mean to state what your complaint against this boy is, man, or do you not? You have been sworn. Now, if you stand there, refusing to give evidence, I'll punish you for disrespect to the bench; I will, by—'

By what, or by whom, nobody knows, for the clerk and jailer coughed very loud, just at the right moment; and the former dropped a heavy book upon the floor, thus preventing the word from being heard—accidentally, of course.

With many interruptions and repeated insults, Mr. Brownlow contrived to state his case; observing that, in the surprise of the moment, he had run after the boy because he saw him running away; and expressing his hope that, if the magistrate should believe him, although not actually the thief, to be connected with thieves, he would deal as leniently with him as justice would allow.

'He has been hurt already,' said the old gentleman in conclusion. 'And I fear,' he added, with great energy, looking towards the bar, 'I really fear that he is ill.'

'Oh! yes, I dare say!' said Mr. Fang, with a sneer. 'Come, none of your tricks here, you young vagabond; they won't do. What's your name?'

Oliver tried to reply, but his tongue failed him. He was deadly pale; and the whole place seemed turning round and round.

'What's your name, you hardened scoundrel?' demanded Mr. Fang. 'Officer, what's his name?'

This was addressed to a bluff old fellow, in a striped waistcoat, who was standing by the bar. He bent over Oliver, and repeated the inquiry; but finding him really incapable of understanding the question; and knowing that his not replying would only infuriate the magistrate the more, and add to the severity of his sentence; he hazarded a guess.

'He says his name's Tom White, your worship,' said this kind-hearted thief-taker.

'Oh, he won't speak out, won't he?' said Fang. 'Very well, very well. Where does he live?'

'Where he can, your worship,' replied the officer; again pretending to receive Oliver's answer.

'Has he any parents?' inquired Mr. Fang.

'He says they died in his infancy, your worship,' replied the officer: hazarding the usual reply.

At this point of the inquiry, Oliver raised his head; and, looking round with imploring eyes, murmured a feeble prayer for a draught of water.

'Stuff and nonsense!' said Mr. Fang: 'don't try to make a fool of me.'

'I think he really is ill, your worship,' remonstrated the officer.

'I know better,' said Mr. Fang.

'Take care of him, officer,' said the old gentleman, raising his hands instinctively; 'he'll fall down.'

'Stand away, officer,' cried Fang; 'let him, if he likes.'

Oliver availed himself of the kind permission, and fell to the floor in a fainting fit. The men in the office looked at each other, but no one dared to stir.

'I knew he was shamming,' said Fang, as if this were incontestable proof of the fact. 'Let him lie there; he'll soon be tired of that.'

'How do you propose to deal with the case, sir?' inquired the clerk in a low voice.

'Summarily,' replied Mr. Fang. 'He stands committed for three months—hard labour of course. Clear the office.'

The door was opened for this purpose, and a couple of men were preparing to carry the insensible boy to his cell; when an elderly man of decent but poor appearance, clad in an old suit of black, rushed hastily into the office, and advanced towards the bench.

'Stop, stop! Don't take him away! For Heaven's sake stop a moment!' cried the newcomer, breathless with haste.

Although the presiding Genii in such an office as this, exercise a summary and arbitrary power over the liberties, the good name, the character, almost the lives, of Her Majesty's subjects, especially of the poorer class; and although, within such walls, enough fantastic tricks are daily played to make the angels blind with weeping; they are closed to the public, save through the medium of the daily press.* Mr. Fang was consequently not a little indignant to see an unbidden guest enter in such irreverent disorder.

'What is this? Who is this? Turn this man out. Clear the office!' cried Mr. Fang.

'I *will* speak,' cried the man; 'I will not be turned out. I saw it all. I keep the book-stall. I demand to be sworn. I will not be put down. Mr. Fang, you must hear me. You must not refuse, sir.'

The man was right. His manner was determined; and the matter was growing rather too serious to be hushed up.

'Swear the man,' growled Mr. Fang, with a very ill grace. 'Now, man, what have you got to say?'

'This,' said the man: 'I saw three boys: two others and the prisoner here: loitering on the opposite side of the way, when this gentleman was reading. The robbery was committed by another boy. I saw it done; and I saw that this boy was perfectly amazed and stupefied by it.' Having by this time recovered a little breath, the worthy book-stall keeper proceeded to relate, in a more coherent manner, the exact circumstances of the robbery.

'Why didn't you come here before?' said Fang, after a pause.

'I hadn't a soul to mind the shop,' replied the man. 'Everybody who could have helped me, had joined in the pursuit. I could get nobody till five minutes ago; and I've run here all the way.'

'The prosecutor was reading, was he?' inquired Fang, after another pause.

'Yes,' replied the man. 'The very book he has in his hand.'

---

*Or were virtually, then.

89

'Oh, that book, eh?' said Fang. 'Is it paid for?'

'No, it is not,' replied the man, with a smile.

'Dear me, I forgot all about it!' exclaimed the absent old gentleman, innocently.

'A nice person to prefer a charge against a poor boy!' said Fang, with a comical effort to look humane. 'I consider, sir, that you have obtained possession of that book, under very suspicious and disreputable circumstances; and you may think yourself very fortunate that the owner of the property declines to prosecute. Let this be a lesson to you, my man, or the law will overtake you yet. The boy is discharged. Clear the office.'

'D—n me!' cried the old gentleman, bursting out with the rage he had kept down so long, 'd—n me! I'll—'

'Clear the office!' said the magistrate. 'Officers, do you hear? Clear the office!'

The mandate was obeyed; and the indignant Mr. Brownlow was conveyed out, with the book in one hand, and the bamboo cane in the other: in a perfect phrenzy of rage and defiance. He reached the yard; and his passion vanished in a moment. Little Oliver Twist lay on his back on the pavement, with his shirt unbuttoned, and his temples bathed with water; his face a deadly white; and a cold tremble convulsing his whole frame.

'Poor boy, poor boy!' said Mr. Brownlow, bending over him. 'Call a coach, somebody, pray. Directly!'

A coach was obtained, and Oliver, having been carefully laid on one seat, the old gentleman got in and sat himself on the other.

'May I accompany you?' said the book-stall keeper, looking in.

'Bless me, yes, my dear sir,' said Mr. Brownlow quickly. 'I forgot you. Dear, dear! I have this unhappy book still! Jump in. Poor fellow! There's no time to lose.'

The book-stall keeper got into the coach; and away they drove.

CHAPTER 12

In which Oliver is taken better care of than
he ever was before. And in which the
narrative reverts to the merry old gentleman
and his youthful friends

The coach rattled away, over nearly the same ground as that which
Oliver had traversed when he first entered London in company with
the Dodger; and, turning a different way when it reached the Angel
at Islington, stopped at length before a neat house, in a quiet shady
street near Pentonville. Here, a bed was prepared, without loss of
time, in which Mr. Brownlow saw his young charge carefully and
comfortably deposited; and here, he was tended with a kindness
and solicitude that knew no bounds.

But, for many days, Oliver remained insensible to all the goodness of his new friends. The sun rose and sank, and rose and sank
again, and many times after that; and still the boy lay stretched on
his uneasy bed, dwindling away beneath the dry and wasting heat
of fever. The worm does not his work more surely on the dead body,
than does this slow creeping fire upon the living frame.

Weak, and thin, and pallid, he awoke at last from what seemed
to have been a long and troubled dream. Feebly raising himself in
the bed, with his head resting on his trembling arm, he looked
anxiously around.

'What room is this? Where have I been brought to?' said Oliver.
'This is not the place I went to sleep in.'

He uttered these words in a feeble voice, being very faint and
weak; but they were overheard at once. The curtain at the bed's

head was hastily drawn back, and a motherly old lady, very neatly and precisely dressed, rose as she undrew it, from an arm-chair close by, in which she had been sitting at needle-work.

'Hush, my dear,' said the old lady softly. 'You must be very quiet, or you will be ill again; and you have been very bad, —as bad as bad could be, pretty nigh. Lie down again; there's a dear!' With those words, the old lady very gently placed Oliver's head upon the pillow; and, smoothing back his hair from his forehead, looked so kindly and lovingly in his face, that he could not help placing his little withered hand in hers, and drawing it round his neck.

'Save us!' said the old lady, with tears in her eyes, 'what a grateful little dear it is. Pretty creetur! What would his mother feel if she had sat by him as I have, and could see him now!'

'Perhaps she does see me,' whispered Oliver, folding his hands together; 'perhaps she has sat by me. I almost feel as if she had.'

'That was the fever, my dear,' said the old lady mildly.

'I suppose it was,' replied Oliver, 'because Heaven is a long way off; and they are too happy there, to come down to the bedside of a poor boy. But if she knew I was ill, she must have pitied me, even there; for she was very ill herself before she died. She can't know anything about me though,' added Oliver after a moment's silence. 'If she had seen me hurt, it would have made her sorrowful; and her face has always looked sweet and happy, when I have dreamed of her.'

The old lady made no reply to this; but wiping her eyes first, and her spectacles, which lay on the counterpane, afterwards, as if they were part and parcel of those features, brought some cool stuff for Oliver to drink; and then, patting him on the cheek, told him he must lie very quiet, or he would be ill again.

So, Oliver kept very still; partly because he was anxious to obey the kind old lady in all things; and partly, to tell the truth, because he was completely exhausted with what he had already said. He soon fell into a gentle doze, from which he was awakened by the light of a candle: which, being brought near the bed, showed him a gentleman with a very large and loud-ticking gold watch in his hand, who felt his pulse, and said he was a great deal better.

'You *are* a great deal better, are you not, my dear?' said the gentleman.

'Yes, thank you, sir,' replied Oliver.

'Yes, I know you are,' said the gentleman: 'You're hungry too, a'n't you?'

'No, sir,' answered Oliver.

'Hem!' said the gentleman. 'No, I know you're not. He is not hungry, Mrs. Bedwin,' said the gentleman: looking very wise.

The old lady made a respectful inclination of the head, which seemed to say that she thought the doctor was a very clever man. The doctor appeared much of the same opinion himself.

'You feel sleepy, don't you, my dear?' said the doctor.

'No, sir,' replied Oliver.

'No,' said the doctor, with a very shrewd and satisfied look. 'You're not sleepy. Nor thirsty. Are you?'

'Yes, sir, rather thirsty,' answered Oliver.

'Just as I expected, Mrs. Bedwin,' said the doctor. 'It's very natural that he should be thirsty. You may give him a little tea, ma'am, and some dry toast without any butter. Don't keep him too warm, ma'am; but be careful that you don't let him be too cold; will you have the goodness?'

The old lady dropped a curtsey. The doctor, after tasting the cool stuff, and expressing a qualified approval of it, hurried away: his boots creaking in a very important and wealthy manner as he went down stairs.

Oliver dozed off again, soon after this; when he awoke, it was nearly twelve o'clock. The old lady tenderly bade him good-night shortly afterwards, and left him in charge of a fat old woman who had just come: bringing with her, in a little bundle, a small Prayer Book and a large nightcap. Putting the latter on her head and the former on the table, the old woman, after telling Oliver that she had come to sit up with him, drew her chair close to the fire and went off into a series of short naps, chequered at frequent intervals with sundry tumblings forward, and divers moans and chokings. These, however, had no worse effect than causing her to rub her nose very hard, and then fall asleep again.

And thus the night crept slowly on. Oliver lay awake for some time, counting the little circles of light which the reflection of the rushlight-shade threw upon the ceiling; or tracing with his languid eyes the intricate pattern of the paper on the wall. The darkness and the deep stillness of the room were very solemn; and as they brought into the boy's mind the thought that death had been hovering there, for many days and nights, and might yet fill it with the gloom and dread of his awful presence, he turned his face upon the pillow, and fervently prayed to Heaven.

Gradually, he fell into that deep tranquil sleep which ease from recent suffering alone imparts; that calm and peaceful rest which it is pain to wake from. Who, if this were death, would be roused again to all the struggles and turmoils of life; to all its cares for the present; its anxieties for the future; more than all, its weary recollections of the past!

It had been bright day, for hours, when Oliver opened his eyes; he felt cheerful and happy. The crisis of the disease was safely past. He belonged to the world again.

In three days' time he was able to sit in an easy-chair, well propped up with pillows; and, as he was still too weak to walk, Mrs. Bedwin had him carried down stairs into the little housekeeper's room, which belonged to her. Having him set, here, by the fireside, the good old lady sat herself down too; and, being in a state of considerable delight at seeing him so much better, forthwith began to cry most violently.

'Never mind me, my dear,' said the old lady. 'I'm only having a regular good cry. There; it's all over now; and I'm quite comfortable.'

'You're very, very kind to me, ma'am,' said Oliver.

'Well, never you mind that, my dear,' said the old lady; 'that's got nothing to do with your broth; and it's full time you had it; for the doctor says Mr. Brownlow may come in to see you this morning;

and we must get up our best looks, because the better we look, the more he'll be pleased.' And with this, the old lady applied herself to warming up, in a little saucepan, a basin full of broth: strong enough, Oliver thought, to furnish an ample dinner, when reduced to the regulation strength, for three hundred and fifty paupers, at the lowest computation.

'Are you fond of pictures, dear?' inquired the old lady, seeing that Oliver had fixed his eyes, most intently, on a portrait which hung against the wall; just opposite his chair.

'I don't quite know, ma'am,' said Oliver, without taking his eyes from the canvas; 'I have seen so few that I hardly know. What a beautiful, mild face that lady's is!'

'Ah!' said the old lady, 'painters always make ladies out prettier than they are, or they wouldn't get any custom, child. The man that invented the machine for taking likeness might have known *that* would never succeed; it's a deal too honest. A deal,' said the old lady, laughing very heartily at her own acuteness.

'Is—is that a likeness, ma'am?' said Oliver.

'Yes,' said the old lady, looking up for a moment from the broth; 'that's a portrait.'

'Whose, ma'am?' asked Oliver.

'Why, really, my dear, I don't know,' answered the old lady in a good-humoured manner. 'It's not a likeness of anybody that you or I know, I expect. It seems to strike your fancy, dear.'

'It is so very pretty,' replied Oliver.

'Why, sure you're not afraid of it?' said the old lady: observing, in great surprise, the look of awe with which the child regarded the painting.

'Oh no, no,' returned Oliver quickly; 'but the eyes look so sorrowful; and where I sit, they seem fixed upon me. It makes my heart beat,' added Oliver in a low voice, 'as if it was alive, and wanted to speak to me, but couldn't.'

'Lord save us!' exclaimed the old lady, starting; 'don't talk in that way, child. You're weak and nervous after your illness. Let me wheel your chair round to the other side; and then you won't see it.

There!' said the old lady, suiting the action to the word; 'you don't see it now, at all events.'

Oliver *did* see it in his mind's eye as distinctly as if he had not altered his position; but he thought it better not to worry the kind old lady; so he smiled gently when she looked at him; and Mrs. Bedwin, satisfied that he felt more comfortable, salted and broke bits of toasted bread into the broth, with all the bustle befitting so solemn a preparation. Oliver got through it with extraordinary expedition. He had scarcely swallowed the last spoonful, when there came a soft rap at the door. 'Come in,' said the old lady; and in walked Mr. Brownlow.

Now, the old gentleman came in as brisk as need be; but, he had no sooner raised his spectacles on his forehead, and thrust his hands behind the skirts of his dressing-gown to take a good long look at Oliver, than his countenance underwent a very great variety of odd contortions. Oliver looked very worn and shadowy from sickness, and made an ineffectual attempt to stand up, out of respect to his benefactor, which terminated in his sinking back into the chair again; and the fact is, if the truth must be told, that Mr. Brownlow's heart, being large enough for any six ordinary old gentlemen of humane disposition, forced a supply of tears into his eyes, by some hydraulic process which we are not sufficiently philosophical to be in a condition to explain.

'Poor boy, poor boy!' said Mr. Brownlow, clearing his throat. 'I'm rather hoarse this morning, Mrs. Bedwin. I'm afraid I have caught cold.'

'I hope not, sir,' said Mrs. Bedwin. 'Everything you have had, has been well aired, sir.'

'I don't know, Bedwin. I don't know,' said Mr. Brownlow; 'I rather think I had a damp napkin at dinner-time yesterday; but never mind that. How do you feel, my dear?'

'Very happy, sir,' replied Oliver. 'And very grateful indeed, sir, for your goodness to me.'

'Good boy,' said Mr. Brownlow, stoutly. 'Have you given him any nourishment, Bedwin? Any slops, eh?'

'He has just had a basin of beautiful strong broth, sir,' replied Mrs. Bedwin: drawing herself up slightly, and laying a strong emphasis on the last word: to intimate that between slops, and broth well compounded, there existed no affinity or connection whatsoever.

'Ugh!' said Mr. Brownlow, with a slight shudder; 'a couple of glasses of port wine would have done him a great deal more good. Wouldn't they, Tom White, eh?'

'My name is Oliver, sir,' replied the little invalid: with a look of great astonishment.

'Oliver,' said Mr. Brownlow; 'Oliver what? Oliver White, eh?'

'No sir, Twist, Oliver Twist.'

'Queer name!' said the old gentleman. 'What made you tell the magistrate your name was White?'

'I never told him so, sir,' returned Oliver in amazement.

This sounded so like a falsehood, that the old gentleman looked somewhat sternly in Oliver's face. It was impossible to doubt him; there was truth in every one of its thin and sharpened lineaments.

'Some mistake,' said Mr. Brownlow. But, although his motive for looking steadily at Oliver no longer existed, the old idea of the resemblance between his features and some familiar face came upon him so strongly, that he could not withdraw his gaze.

'I hope you are not angry with me, sir?' said Oliver, raising his eyes beseechingly.

'No, no,' replied the old gentleman. 'Why! what's this? Bedwin, look there!'

As he spoke, he pointed hastily to the picture above Oliver's head, and then to the boy's face. There was its living copy. The eyes, the head, the mouth; every feature was the same. The expression was for the instant, so precisely alike, that the minutest line seemed copied with startling accuracy!

Oliver knew not the cause of this sudden exclamation; for, not being strong enough to bear the start it gave him, he fainted away. A weakness on his part, which affords the narrative an opportunity of relieving the reader from suspense, in behalf of the two young pupils of the Merry Old Gentleman; and of recording—

That when the Dodger, and his accomplished friend Master Bates, joined in the hue-and-cry which was raised at Oliver's heels, in consequence of their executing an illegal conveyance of Mr. Brownlow's personal property, as has been already described, they were actuated by a very laudable and becoming regard for themselves; and forasmuch as the freedom of the subject and the liberty of the individual are among the first and proudest boasts of a true-hearted Englishman, so, I need hardly beg the reader to observe, that this action should tend to exalt them in the opinion of all public and patriotic men, in almost as great a degree as this strong proof of their anxiety for their own preservation and safety goes to corroborate and confirm the little code of laws which certain profound and sound-judging philosophers have laid down as the mainsprings of all Nature's deeds and actions: the said philosophers very wisely reducing the good lady's proceedings to matters of maxim and theory: and, by a very neat and pretty compliment to her exalted wisdom and understanding, putting entirely out of sight any considerations of heart, or generous impulse and feeling. For, these are matters totally beneath a female who is acknowledged by universal admission to be far above the numerous little foibles and weaknesses of her sex.

If I wanted any further proof of the strictly philosophical nature of the conduct of these young gentlemen in their very delicate predicament, I should at once find it in the fact (also recorded in a foregoing part of this narrative), of their quitting the pursuit, when the general attention was fixed upon Oliver; and making immediately for their home by the shortest possible cut. Although I do not mean to assert that it is usually the practice of renowned and learned sages, to shorten the road to any great conclusion (their course indeed being rather to lengthen the distance, by various circumlocutions and discursive staggerings, like unto those in which drunken men under the pressure of a too mighty flow of ideas, are prone to indulge); still, I do mean to say, and do say distinctly, that it is the invariable practice of many mighty philosophers, in carrying out their theories, to evince great wisdom and foresight in providing against every possible contingency which can be supposed at all likely to affect themselves. Thus, to do a great right, you may do a little wrong; and you may take any means which the end to be attained, will justify; the amount of the right, or the amount of the wrong, or indeed the distinction between the two, being left entirely to the philosopher concerned, to be settled and determined by his clear, comprehensive, and impartial view of his own particular case.

It was not until the two boys had scoured, with great rapidity, through a most intricate maze of narrow streets and courts, that they ventured to halt beneath a low and dark archway. Having remained silent here, just long enough to recover breath to speak, Master Bates uttered an exclamation of amusement and delight; and, bursting into an uncontrollable fit of laughter, flung himself upon a door-step, and rolled thereon in a transport of mirth.

'What's the matter?' inquired the Dodger.

'Ha! ha! ha!' roared Charley Bates.

'Hold your noise,' remonstrated the Dodger, looking cautiously round. 'Do you want to be grabbed, stupid?'

'I can't help it,' said Charley, 'I can't help it! To see him splitting away at that pace, and cutting round the corners, and knocking up against the posts, and starting on again as if he was made of iron as well as them, and me with the wipe in my pocket, singing out arter him—oh, my eye!' The vivid imagination of Master Bates, presented the scene before him in too strong colours. As he arrived at this apostrophe, he again rolled upon the door-step, and laughed louder than before.

'What'll Fagin say?' inquired the Dodger; taking advantage of the next interval of breathlessness on the part of his friend to propound the question.

'What?' repeated Charley Bates.

'Ah, what?' said the Dodger.

'Why, what should he say?' inquired Charley: stopping rather suddenly in his merriment; for the Dodger's manner was impressive. 'What should he say?'

Mr. Dawkins whistled for a couple of minutes; then, taking off his hat, scratched his head, and nodded thrice.

'What do you mean?' said Charley.

'Toor rul lol loo, gammon and spinnage, the frog he wouldn't, and high cockolorum,' said the Dodger: with a slight sneer on his intellectual countenance.

This was explanatory, but not satisfactory. Master Bates felt it so; and again said, 'What do you mean?'

The Dodger made no reply; but putting his hat on again, and gathering the skirts of his long-tailed coat under his arm, thrust his tongue into his cheek, slapped the bridge of his nose some half-dozen times in a familiar but expressive manner, and turning on his heel, slunk down the court. Master Bates followed, with a thoughtful countenance.

The noise of footsteps on the creaking stairs, a few minutes after the occurrence of this conversation, roused the merry old gentleman as he sat over the fire with a saveloy and a small loaf in his left hand; a pocket-knife in his right; and a pewter pot on the trivet. There was a rascally smile on his white face as he turned round, and, looking sharply out from under his thick red eyebrows, bent his ear towards the door, and listened.

'Why, how's this?' muttered the Jew: changing countenance; 'only two of 'em? Where's the third? They can't have got into trouble. Hark!'

The footsteps approached nearer; they reached the landing. The door was slowly opened; and the Dodger and Charley Bates entered, closing it behind them.

CHAPTER 13

Some new acquaintances are introduced to
the intelligent reader, connected with whom
various pleasant matters are related,
appertaining to this history

'Where's Oliver?' said the Jew, rising with a menacing look. 'Where's
the boy?'

The young thieves eyed their preceptor as if they were alarmed
at his violence; and looked uneasily at each other. But they made
no reply.

'What's become of the boy?' said the Jew, seizing the Dodger
tightly by the collar, and threatening him with horrid imprecations.
'Speak out, or I'll throttle you!'

Mr. Fagin looked so very much in earnest, that Charley Bates,
who deemed it prudent in all cases to be on the safe side, and who
conceived it by no means improbable that it might be his turn to
be throttled second, dropped upon his knees, and raised a loud,
well-sustained, and continuous roar—something between a mad bull
and a speaking trumpet.

'Will you speak?' thundered the Jew: shaking the Dodger so
much that his keeping in the big coat at all, seemed perfectly
miraculous.

'Why, the traps have got him, and that's all about it,' said the
Dodger, sullenly. 'Come, let go o' me, will you!' And, swinging
himself, at one jerk, clean out of the big coat, which he left in the
Jew's hands, the Dodger snatched up the toasting-fork and made a
pass at the merry old gentleman's waistcoat; which, if it had taken

effect, would have let a little more merriment out, than could have been easily replaced.

The Jew stepped back in this emergency, with more agility than could have been anticipated in a man of his apparent decrepitude; and, seizing up the pot, prepared to hurl it at his assailant's head. But Charley Bates, at this moment, calling his attention by a perfectly terrific howl, he suddenly altered its destination, and flung it full at that young gentleman.

'Why, what the blazes is in the wind now?' growled a deep voice. 'Who pitched that 'ere at me? It's well it's the beer, and not the pot, as hit me, or I'd have settled somebody. I might have know'd, as nobody but an infernal, rich, plundering, thundering old Jew could afford to throw away any drink but water—and not that, unless he done the River Company every quarter. Wot's it all about, Fagin? D— me, if my neck-handkercher ain't lined with beer! Come in you sneaking warmint; wot are you stopping outside for, as if you was ashamed of your master! Come in!'

The man who growled out these words, was a stoutly-built fellow of about five-and-thirty, in a black velveteen coat, very soiled drab breeches, lace-up half boots, and grey cotton stockings, which enclosed a bulky pair of legs, with large swelling calves;—the kind of legs, which in such costume, always look in an unfinished and incomplete state without a set of fetters to garnish them. He had a brown hat on his head, and a dirty belcher handkerchief round his neck: with the long frayed ends of which he smeared the beer from his face as he spoke. He disclosed, when he had done so, a broad heavy countenance with a beard of three days' growth, and two scowling eyes; one of which displayed various parti-coloured symptoms of having been recently damaged by a blow.

'Come in, d'ye hear?' growled this engaging ruffian.

A white shaggy dog, with his face scratched and torn in twenty different places, skulked into the room.

'Why didn't you come in afore?' said the man. 'You're getting too proud to own me afore company, are you? Lie down!'

This command was accompanied with a kick, which sent the

animal to the other end of the room. He appeared well used to it, however; for he coiled himself up in a corner very quietly, without uttering a sound, and winking his very ill-looking eyes twenty times in a minute, appeared to occupy himself in taking a survey of the apartment.

'What are you up to? Ill-treating the boys, you covetous, avaricious, in-sa-ti-a-ble old fence?' said the man, seating himself deliberately. 'I wonder they don't murder you! *I* would if I was them. If I'd been your 'prentice, I'd have done it long ago, and—no I couldn't have sold you afterwards, for you're fit for nothing but keeping as a curiosity of ugliness in a glass bottle, and I suppose they don't blow glass bottles large enough.'

'Hush! hush! Mr. Sikes,' said the Jew, trembling; 'don't speak so loud.'

'None of your mistering,' replied the ruffian; 'you always mean mischief when you come that. You know my name: out with it! I shan't disgrace it when the time comes.'

'Well, well, then—Bill Sikes,' said the Jew, with abject humility. 'You seem out of humour, Bill.'

'Perhaps I am,' replied Sikes; 'I should think *you* was rather out of sorts too, unless you mean as little harm when you throw pewter pots about, as you do when you blab and—'

'Are you mad?' said the Jew, catching the man by the sleeve, and pointing towards the boys.

Mr. Sikes contented himself with tying an imaginary knot under his left ear, and jerking his head over on the right shoulder; a piece of dumb show which the Jew appeared to understand perfectly. He then, in cant terms, with which his whole conversation was plentifully besprinkled, but which would be quite unintelligible if they were recorded here, demanded a glass of liquor.

'And mind you don't poison it,' said Mr. Sikes, laying his hat upon the table.

This was said in jest; but if the speaker could have seen the evil leer with which the Jew bit his pale lip as he turned round to the cupboard, he might have thought the caution not wholly unnecessary, or the wish (at all events) to improve upon the distiller's ingenuity not very far from the old gentleman's merry heart.

After swallowing two or three glasses of spirits, Mr. Sikes condescended to take some notice of the young gentlemen; which gracious act led to a conversation, in which the cause and manner of Oliver's capture were circumstantially detailed, with such alterations and improvements on the truth, as to the Dodger appeared most advisable under the circumstances.

'I'm afraid,' said the Jew, 'that he may say something which will get us into trouble.'

'That's very likely,' returned Sikes with a malicious grin. 'You're blowed upon, Fagin.'

'And I'm afraid, you see,' added the Jew, speaking as if he had not noticed the interruption; and regarding the other closely as he did so,—'I'm afraid that, if the game was up with us, it might be up with a good many more, and that it would come out rather worse for you than it would for me, my dear.'

The man started, and turned round upon the Jew. But the old gentleman's shoulders were shrugged up to his ears; and his eyes were vacantly staring on the opposite wall.

There was a long pause. Every member of the respectable coterie appeared plunged in his own reflections; not excepting the dog, who by a certain malicious licking of his lips seemed to be meditating an attack upon the legs of the first gentleman or lady he might encounter in the streets when he went out.

'Somebody must find out wot's been done at the office,' said Mr. Sikes in a much lower tone than he had taken since he came in.

The Jew nodded assent.

'If he hasn't peached, and is committed, there's no fear till he comes out again,' said Mr. Sikes, 'and then he must be taken care on. You must get hold of him somehow.'

Again the Jew nodded.

The prudence of this line of action, indeed, was obvious; but, unfortunately, there was one very strong objection to its being adopted.

This was, that the Dodger, and Charley Bates, and Fagin, and Mr. William Sikes, happened, one and all, to entertain a violent and deeply rooted antipathy to going near a police-officer on any ground or pretext whatever.

How long they might have sat and looked at each other, in a state of uncertainty not the most pleasant of its kind, it is difficult to guess. It is not necessary to make any guesses on the subject, however; for the sudden entrance of the two young ladies whom Oliver had seen on a former occasion, caused the conversation to flow afresh.

'The very thing!' said the Jew. 'Bet will go; won't you, my dear?'

'Wheres?' inquired the young lady.

'Only just up to the office, my dear,' said the Jew coaxingly.

It is due to the young lady to say that she did not positively affirm that she would not, but that she merely expressed an emphatic and earnest desire to be 'blessed' if she would; a polite and delicate evasion of the request, which shows the young lady to have been possessed of that natural good breeding which cannot bear to inflict upon a fellow-creature, the pain of a direct and pointed refusal.

The Jew's countenance fell. He turned from this young lady, who was gaily, not to say gorgeously attired, in a red gown, green boots, and yellow curl-papers, to the other female.

'Nancy, my dear,' said the Jew in a soothing manner, 'what do *you* say?'

'That it won't do; so it's no use a-trying it on, Fagin,' replied Nancy.

'What do you mean by that?' said Mr. Sikes, looking up in a surly manner.

'What I say, Bill,' replied the lady collectedly.

'Why, you're just the very person for it,' reasoned Mr. Sikes: 'nobody about here knows anything of you.'

'And as I don't want 'em to, neither,' replied Nancy in the same composed manner, 'it's rather more no than yes with me, Bill.'

'She'll go, Fagin,' said Sikes.

'No, she won't, Fagin,' said Nancy.

'Yes she will, Fagin,' said Sikes.

And Mr. Sikes was right. By dint of alternate threats, promises, and bribes, the lady in question was ultimately prevailed upon to undertake the commission. She was not, indeed, withheld by the same considerations as her agreeable friend; for, having recently removed into the neighbourhood of Field Lane from the remote but genteel suburb of Ratcliffe, she was not under the same apprehension of being recognised by any of her numerous acquaintances.

Accordingly, with a clean white apron tied over her gown, and her curl-papers tucked up under a straw bonnet,—both articles of dress being provided from the Jew's inexhaustible stock,—Miss Nancy prepared to issue forth on her errand.

'Stop a minute, my dear,' said the Jew, producing a little covered basket. 'Carry that in one hand. It looks more respectable, my dear.'

'Give her a door-key to carry in her t'other one, Fagin,' said Sikes; 'it looks real and genivine like.'

'Yes, yes, my dear, so it does,' said the Jew, hanging a large street-door key on the forefinger of the young lady's right hand. 'There; very good! Very good indeed, my dear!' said the Jew, rubbing his hands.

'Oh, my brother! My poor, dear, sweet, innocent little brother!' exclaimed Nancy, bursting into tears, and wringing the little basket and the street-door key in an agony of distress. 'What has become of him! Where have they taken him to! Oh, do have pity, and tell me what's been done with the dear boy, gentlemen; do, gentlemen, if you please, gentlemen!'

Having uttered these words in a most lamentable and heartbroken tone: to the immeasurable delight of her hearers: Miss Nancy paused, winked to the company, nodded smilingly round, and disappeared.

'Ah! she's a clever girl, my dears,' said the Jew, turning round to his young friends, and shaking his head gravely, as if in mute admonition to them to follow the bright example they had just beheld.

'She's a honour to her sex,' said Mr. Sikes, filling his glass, and smiting the table with his enormous fist. 'Here's her health, and wishing they was all like her!'

While these, and many other encomiums, were being passed on the accomplished Nancy, that young lady made the best of her way to the police-office; whither, notwithstanding a little natural timidity consequent upon walking through the streets alone and unprotected, she arrived in perfect safety shortly afterwards.

Entering by the back way, she tapped softly with the key at one of the cell-doors, and listened. There was no sound within: so she coughed and listened again. Still there was no reply: so she spoke.

'Nolly, dear?' murmured Nancy in a gentle voice; 'Nolly?'

There was nobody inside but a miserable shoeless criminal, who had been taken up for playing the flute, and who, the offence against society having been clearly proved, had been very properly committed by Mr. Fang to the House of Correction for one month; with the appropriate and amusing remark that since he had so much breath to spare, it would be more wholesomely expended on the treadmill than in a musical instrument. He made no answer: being occupied in mentally bewailing the loss of the flute, which had been confiscated for the use of the county; so Nancy passed on to the next cell, and knocked there.

'Well!' cried a faint and feeble voice.

'Is there a little boy here?' inquired Nancy, with a preliminary sob.

'No,' replied the voice; 'God forbid!'

This was a vagrant of sixty-five, who was going to prison for *not* playing the flute; or, in other words, for begging in the streets, and doing nothing for his livelihood. In the next cell, was another man, who was going to the same prison for hawking tin saucepans without a license; thereby doing something for his living, in defiance of the Stamp-office.

But, as neither of these criminals answered to the name of Oliver, or knew anything about him, Nancy made straight up to the bluff officer in the striped waistcoat; and with the most piteous wailings and lamentations, rendered more piteous by a prompt and efficient use of the street-door key and the little basket, demanded her own dear brother.

'*I* haven't got him, my dear,' said the old man.

'Where is he?' screamed Nancy, in a distracted manner.

'Why, the gentleman's got him,' replied the officer.

'What gentleman? Oh, gracious heavens! What gentleman?' exclaimed Nancy.

In reply to this incoherent questioning, the old man informed the deeply affected sister that Oliver had been taken ill in the office, and discharged in consequence of a witness having proved the robbery to have been committed by another boy, not in custody; and that the prosecutor had carried him away, in an insensible condition, to his own residence: of and concerning which, all the informant knew was, that it was somewhere at Pentonville, he having heard that word mentioned in the directions to the coachman.

In a dreadful state of doubt and uncertainty, the agonised young woman staggered to the gate, and then, exchanging her faltering walk for a swift run, returned by the most devious and complicated route she could think of, to the domicile of the Jew.

Mr. Bill Sikes no sooner heard the account of the expedition delivered, than he very hastily called up the white dog, and, putting on his hat, expeditiously departed: without devoting any time to the formality of wishing the company good-morning.

'We must know where he is, my dears; he must be found,' said the Jew, greatly excited. 'Charley, do nothing but skulk about, till you bring home some news of him! Nancy, my dear, I must have him found. I trust to you, my dear,—to you and the Artful for everything! Stay, stay,' added the Jew, unlocking a drawer with a shaking hand; 'there's money, my dears. I shall shut up this shop to-night. You'll know where to find me! Don't stop here a minute. Not an instant, my dears!'

With these words, he pushed them from the room: and carefully double-locking and barring the door behind them, drew from its place of concealment the box which he had unintentionally disclosed to Oliver. Then, he hastily proceeded to dispose the watches and jewellery beneath his clothing.

A rap at the door startled him in this occupation.

'Who's there?' he cried in a shrill tone.

'Me!' replied the voice of the Dodger, through the keyhole.

'What now?' cried the Jew impatiently.

'Is he to be kidnapped to the other ken, Nancy says?' inquired the Dodger.

'Yes,' replied the Jew, 'wherever she lays hands on him. Find him, find him out, that's all! I shall know what to do next; never fear.'

The boy murmured a reply of intelligence; and hurried down stairs after his companions.

'He has not peached so far,' said the Jew, as he pursued his occupation. 'If he means to blab us among his new friends, we may stop his mouth yet.'

CHAPTER 14

Comprising further particulars of Oliver's stay at Mr. Brownlow's, with the remarkable prediction which one Mr. Grimwig uttered concerning him, when he went out on an errand

Oliver soon recovering from the fainting-fit into which Mr. Brownlow's abrupt exclamation had thrown him, the subject of the picture was carefully avoided, both by the old gentleman and Mrs. Bedwin, in the conversation that ensued: which indeed bore no reference to Oliver's history or prospects, but was confined to such topics as might amuse without exciting him. He was still too weak to get up to breakfast; but, when he came down into the housekeeper's room next day, his first act was to cast an eager glance at the wall, in the hope of again looking on the face of the beautiful lady. His expectations were disappointed, however, for the picture had been removed.

'Ah!' said the housekeeper, watching the direction of Oliver's eyes. 'It is gone, you see.'

'I see it is, ma'am,' replied Oliver. 'Why have they taken it away?'

'It has been taken down, child, because Mr. Brownlow said, that as it seemed to worry you, perhaps it might prevent your getting well, you know,' rejoined the old lady.

'Oh, no, indeed. It didn't worry me, ma'am,' said Oliver. 'I liked to see it. I quite loved it.'

'Well, well!' said the old lady, good-humouredly; 'you get well as fast as ever you can, dear, and it shall be hung up again. There! I promise you that! Now, let us talk about something else.'

This was all the information Oliver could obtain about the picture at that time. As the old lady had been so kind to him in his illness, he endeavoured to think no more of the subject just then; so he listened attentively to a great many stories she told him, about an amiable and handsome daughter of hers, who was married to an amiable and handsome man, and lived in the country; and about a son, who was clerk to a merchant in the West Indies; and who was, also, such a good young man, and wrote such dutiful letters home four times a-year, that it brought the tears into her eyes to talk about them. When the old lady had expatiated, a long time, on the excellences of her children, and the merits of her kind good husband besides, who had been dead and gone, poor dear soul, just six-and-twenty years, it was time to have tea. After tea she began to teach Oliver cribbage: which he learnt as quickly as she could teach; and at which game they played, with great interest and gravity, until it was time for the invalid to have some warm wine and water, with a slice of dry toast, and then to go cosily to bed.

They were happy days, those of Oliver's recovery. Everything was so quiet, and neat, and orderly; everybody was kind and gentle; that after the noise and turbulence in the midst of which he had always lived, it seemed like Heaven itself. He was no sooner strong enough to put his clothes on, properly, than Mr. Brownlow caused a complete new suit, and a new cap, and a new pair of shoes, to be provided for him. As Oliver was told that he might do what he liked with the old clothes, he gave them to a servant who had been very kind to him, and asked her to sell them to a Jew, and keep the money for herself. This she very readily did; and, as Oliver looked out of the parlour window, and saw the Jew roll them up in his bag and walk away, he felt quite delighted to think that they were safely gone, and that there was now no possible danger of his ever being able to wear them again. They were sad rags, to tell the truth; and Oliver had never had a new suit before.

One evening, about a week after the affair of the picture, as he was sitting talking to Mrs. Bedwin, there came a message down from Mr. Brownlow, that if Oliver Twist felt pretty well, he should like to see him in his study, and talk to him a little while.

'Bless us, and save us! Wash your hands, and let me part your hair nicely for you, child,' said Mrs. Bedwin. 'Dear heart alive! If we had known he would have asked for you, we would have put you a clean collar on, and made you as smart as sixpence!'

Oliver did as the old lady bade him; and, although she lamented grievously, meanwhile, that there was not even time to crimp the little frill that bordered his shirt-collar; he looked so delicate and handsome, despite that important personal advantage, that she went so far as to say: looking at him with great complacency from head to foot, that she really didn't think it would have been possible, on the longest notice, to have made much difference in him for the better.

Thus encouraged, Oliver tapped at the study door. On Mr. Brownlow calling to him to come in, he found himself in a little back room, quite full of books, with a window, looking into some pleasant little gardens. There was a table drawn up before the window, at which Mr. Brownlow was seated reading. When he saw Oliver, he pushed the book away from him, and told him to come near the table, and sit down. Oliver complied; marvelling where the people could be found to read such a great number of books as seemed to be written to make the world wiser. Which is still a marvel to more experienced people than Oliver Twist, every day of their lives.

'There are a good many books, are there not, my boy?' said Mr. Brownlow, observing the curiosity with which Oliver surveyed the shelves that reached from the floor to the ceiling.

'A great number, sir,' replied Oliver. 'I never saw so many.'

'You shall read them, if you behave well,' said the old gentleman kindly; 'and you will like that, better than looking at the outsides,—that is, in some cases; because there *are* books of which the backs and covers are by far the best parts.'

'I suppose they are those heavy ones, sir,' said Oliver, pointing to some large quartos, with a good deal of gilding about the binding.

'Not always those,' said the old gentleman, patting Oliver on the head, and smiling as he did so; 'there are other equally heavy ones, though of a much smaller size. How should you like to grow up a clever man, and write books, eh?'

'I think I would rather read them, sir,' replied Oliver.

'What! wouldn't you like to be a book-writer?' said the old gentleman.

Oliver considered a little while; and at last said, he should think it would be a much better thing to be a bookseller; upon which the old gentleman laughed heartily, and declared he had said a very good thing. Which Oliver felt glad to have done, though he by no means knew what it was.

'Well, well,' said the old gentleman, composing his features. 'Don't be afraid! We won't make an author of you, while there's an honest trade to be learnt, or brick making to turn to.'

'Thank you, sir,' said Oliver. At the earnest manner of his reply, the old gentleman laughed again; and said something about a curious instinct, which Oliver, not understanding, paid no very great attention to.

'Now,' said Mr. Brownlow, speaking if possible in a kinder, but at the same time in a much more serious manner, than Oliver had ever known him assume yet, 'I want you to pay great attention, my boy, to what I am going to say. I shall talk to you without any reserve; because I am sure you are as well able to understand me, as many older persons would be.'

'Oh, don't tell me you are going to send me away, sir, pray!' exclaimed Oliver, alarmed at the serious tone of the old gentleman's commencement! 'Don't turn me out of doors to wander in the streets again. Let me stay here, and be a servant. Don't send me back to the wretched place I came from. Have mercy upon a poor boy, sir!'

'My dear child,' said the old gentleman, moved by the warmth of Oliver's sudden appeal; 'you need not be afraid of my deserting you, unless you give me cause.'

'I never, never will, sir,' interposed Oliver.

'I hope not,' rejoined the old gentleman. 'I do not think you ever will. I have been deceived, before, in the objects whom I have endeavoured to benefit; but I feel strongly disposed to trust you, nevertheless; and I am more interested in your behalf than I can well account for, even to myself. The persons on whom I have bestowed my dearest love, lie deep in their graves; but, although the happiness and delight of my life lie buried there too, I have not made a coffin of my heart, and sealed it up, for ever, on my best affections. Deep affliction has but strengthened and refined them.'

As the old gentleman said this in a low voice: more to himself than to his companion: and as he remained silent for a short time afterwards: Oliver sat quite still.

'Well, well,' said the old gentleman at length, in a more cheerful tone, 'I only say this, because you have a young heart; and knowing that I have suffered great pain and sorrow, you will be more careful, perhaps, not to wound me again. You say you are an orphan, without a friend in the world; all the inquiries I have been able to make, confirm the statement. Let me hear your story; where you come from; who brought you up; and how you got into the company in which I found you. Speak the truth, and you shall not be friendless while I live.'

Oliver's sobs checked his utterance for some minutes; when he was on the point of beginning to relate how he had been brought up at the farm, and carried to the workhouse by Mr. Bumble, a peculiarly impatient little double-knock was heard at the street-door: and the servant, running up stairs, announced Mr. Grimwig.

'Is he coming up?' inquired Mr. Brownlow.

'Yes, sir,' replied the servant. 'He asked if there were any muffins in the house; and, when I told him yes, he said he had come to tea.'

Mr. Brownlow smiled; and, turning to Oliver, said that Mr. Grimwig was an old friend of his, and he must not mind his being a little rough in his manners; for he was a worthy creature at bottom, as he had reason to know.

'Shall I go down stairs, sir?' inquired Oliver.

'No,' replied Mr. Brownlow, 'I would rather you remained here.'

At this moment, there walked into the room: supporting himself by a thick stick: a stout old gentleman, rather lame in one leg, who was dressed in a blue coat, striped waistcoat, nankeen breeches and gaiters, and a broad-brimmed white hat, with the sides turned up with green. A very small-plaited shirt frill stuck out from his waistcoat; and a very long steel watch-chain, with nothing but a key at the end, dangled loosely below it. The ends of his white neckerchief were twisted into a ball about the size of an orange; the variety of shapes into which his countenance was twisted, defy description. He had a manner of screwing his head on one side when he spoke; and of looking out of the corners of his eyes at the same time: which irresistibly reminded the beholder of a parrot. In this attitude, he fixed himself, the moment he made his appearance; and, holding out a small piece of orange-peel at arm's length, exclaimed, in a growling, discontented voice.

'Look here! do you see this! Isn't it a most wonderful and extraordinary thing that I can't call at a man's house but I find a piece of this poor surgeon's-friend on the staircase? I've been lamed with orange-peel once, and I know orange-peel will be my death at last. It will, sir: orange-peel will be my death, or I'll be content to eat my own head, sir!'

This was the handsome offer with which Mr. Grimwig backed and confirmed nearly every assertion he made; and it was the more singular in his case, because, even admitting for the sake of argument, the possibility of scientific improvements being ever brought to that pass which will enable a gentleman to eat his own head in the event of his being so disposed, Mr. Grimwig's head was such a particularly large one, that the most sanguine man alive could hardly entertain a hope of being able to get through it at a sitting—to put entirely out of the question, a very thick coating of powder.

'I'll eat my head, sir,' repeated Mr. Grimwig, striking his stick upon the ground. 'Hallo! what's that!' looking at Oliver, and retreating a pace or two.

'This is young Oliver Twist, whom we were speaking about,' said Mr. Brownlow.

Oliver bowed.

'You don't mean to say that's the boy who had the fever, I hope?' said Mr. Grimwig, recoiling a little more. 'Wait a minute! Don't speak! Stop—' continued Mr. Grimwig, abruptly, losing all dread of the fever in his triumph at the discovery; 'that's the boy who had the orange! If that's not the boy, sir, who had the orange, and threw this bit of peel upon the staircase, I'll eat my head, and his too.'

'No, no, he has not had one,' said Mr. Brownlow, laughing. 'Come! Put down your hat; and speak to my young friend.'

'I feel strongly on this subject, sir,' said the irritable old gentleman, drawing off his gloves. 'There's always more or less orange-peel on the pavement in our street; and I *know* it's put there by the surgeon's boy at the corner. A young woman stumbled over a bit last night, and fell against my garden-railings; directly she got up I saw her look towards his infernal red lamp with the pantomime-light. "Don't go to him," I called out of the window, "he's an assassin! A man-trap!" So he is. If he is not—' Here the irascible old gentleman gave a great knock on the ground with his stick; which was always understood, by his friends, to imply the customary offer, whenever it was not expressed in words. Then, still keeping his stick in his hand, he sat down; and, opening a double eyeglass, which he wore attached to a broad black riband, took a view of Oliver: who, seeing that he was the object of inspection, coloured, and bowed again.

'That's the boy, is it?' said Mr. Grimwig, at length.

'That is the boy,' replied Mr. Brownlow.

'How are you, boy?' said Mr. Grimwig.

'A great deal better, thank you, sir,' replied Oliver.

Mr. Brownlow, seeming to apprehend that his singular friend was about to say something disagreeable, asked Oliver to step down stairs and tell Mrs. Bedwin they were ready for tea; which, as he did not half like the visitor's manner, he was very happy to do.

'He is a nice-looking boy, is he not?' inquired Mr. Brownlow.

'I don't know,' replied Mr. Grimwig, pettishly.

'Don't know?'

'No. I don't know. I never see any difference in boys. I only know two sorts of boys. Mealy boys, and beef-faced boys.'

'And which is Oliver?'

'Mealy. I know a friend who has a beef-faced boy; a fine boy, they call him; with a round head, and red cheeks, and glaring eyes; a horrid boy; with a body and limbs that appear to be swelling out of the seams of his blue clothes; with the voice of a pilot, and the appetite of a wolf. I know him! The wretch!'

'Come,' said Mr. Brownlow, 'these are not the characteristics of young Oliver Twist; so he needn't excite your wrath.'

'They are not,' replied Mr. Grimwig. 'He may have worse.'

Here, Mr. Brownlow coughed impatiently; which appeared to afford Mr. Grimwig the most exquisite delight.

'He may have worse, I say,' repeated Mr. Grimwig. 'Where does he come from? Who is he? What is he? He has had a fever. What of that? Fevers are not peculiar to good people; are they? Bad people have fevers sometimes; haven't they, eh? I knew a man who was hung in Jamaica for murdering his master. He had had a fever six times; he wasn't recommended to mercy on that account. Pooh! nonsense!'

Now, the fact was, that in the inmost recesses of his own heart, Mr. Grimwig was strongly disposed to admit that Oliver's appearance and manner were unusually prepossessing; but he had a strong appetite for contradiction, sharpened on this occasion by the finding of the orange-peel; and, inwardly determining that no man should dictate to him whether a boy was well-looking or not, he had resolved, from the first, to oppose his friend. When Mr. Brownlow admitted that on no one point of inquiry could he yet return a satisfactory answer; and that he had postponed any investigation into Oliver's previous history until he thought the boy was strong enough to bear it; Mr. Grimwig chuckled maliciously. And he demanded, with a sneer, whether the housekeeper was in the habit of counting the plate at night; because, if she didn't find a table-spoon or two missing some sunshiny morning, why, he would be content to—and so forth.

All this, Mr. Brownlow, although himself somewhat of an impetuous gentleman: knowing his friend's peculiarities, bore with great good humour; as Mr. Grimwig, at tea, was graciously pleased to express his entire approval of the muffins, matters went on very smoothly; and Oliver, who made one of the party, began to feel more at his ease than he had yet done in the fierce old gentleman's presence.

'And when are you going to hear a full, true, and particular account of the life and adventures of Oliver Twist?' asked Grimwig of Mr. Brownlow, at the conclusion of the meal: looking sideways at Oliver, as he resumed the subject.

'To-morrow morning,' replied Mr. Brownlow. 'I would rather he was alone with me at the time. Come up to me to-morrow morning at ten o'clock, my dear.'

'Yes, sir,' replied Oliver. He answered with some hesitation, because he was confused by Mr. Grimwig's looking so hard at him.

'I'll tell you what,' whispered that gentleman to Mr. Brownlow; 'he won't come up to you to-morrow morning. I saw him hesitate. He is deceiving you, my good friend.'

'I'll swear he is not,' replied Mr. Brownlow, warmly.

'If he is not,' said Mr. Grimwig. 'I'll—' and down went the stick.

'I'll answer for that boy's truth with my life!' said Mr. Brownlow, knocking the table.

'And I for his falsehood with my head!' rejoined Mr. Grimwig, knocking the table also.

'We shall see,' said Mr. Brownlow, checking his rising anger.

'We will,' replied Mr. Grimwig, with a provoking smile; 'we will.'

As fate would have it, Mrs. Bedwin chanced to bring in, at this moment, a small parcel of books, which Mr. Brownlow had that morning purchased of the identical bookstall-keeper, who has already figured in this history; having laid them on the table, she prepared to leave the room.

'Stop the boy, Mrs. Bedwin!' said Mr. Brownlow; 'there is something to go back.'

'He has gone, sir,' replied Mrs. Bedwin.

'Call after him,' said Mr. Brownlow; 'it's particular. He is a poor man, and they are not paid for. There are some books to be taken back, too.'

The street door was opened. Oliver ran one way; and the girl ran another; and Mrs. Bedwin stood on the step and screamed for the boy; but there was no boy in sight. Oliver and the girl returned, in a breathless state, to report that there were no tidings of him.

'Dear me, I am very sorry for that,' exclaimed Mr. Brownlow; 'I particularly wished those books to be returned to-night.'

'Send Oliver with them,' said Mr. Grimwig, with an ironical smile; 'he will be sure to deliver them safely, you know.'

'Yes; do let me take them, if you please, sir,' said Oliver. 'I'll run all the way, sir.'

The old gentleman was just going to say that Oliver should not go out on any account; when a most malicious cough from Mr. Grimwig determined him that he should; and that, by the prompt discharge of the commission, he should prove to him the injustice of his suspicions: on this head at least: at once.

'You *shall* go, my dear,' said the old gentleman. The books are on a chair by my table. Fetch them down.'

Oliver, delighted to be of use, brought down the books under his arm in a great bustle; and waited, cap in hand, to hear what message he was to take.

'You are to say,' said Mr. Brownlow, glancing steadily at Grimwig; 'you are to say that you have brought those books back; and that you have come to pay the four pound ten I owe him. This is a five-pound note, so you will have to bring me back, ten shillings change.'

'I won't be ten minutes, sir,' replied Oliver, eagerly. Having buttoned up the bank-note in his jacket pocket, and placed the books carefully under his arm, he made a respectful bow, and left the room. Mrs. Bedwin followed him to the street door, giving him many directions about the nearest way, and the name of the bookseller, and the name of the street: all of which Oliver said he clearly understood. Having superadded many injunctions to be sure and not take cold, the old lady at length permitted him to depart.

'Bless his sweet face!' said the old lady, looking after him. 'I can't bear, somehow, to let him go out of my sight.'

At this moment, Oliver looked gaily round, and nodded before he turned the corner. The old lady smilingly returned his salutation, and, closing the door, went back to her own room.

'Let me see; he'll be back in twenty minutes, at the longest,' said Mr. Brownlow, pulling out his watch, and placing it on the table. 'It will be dark by that time.'

'Oh! you really expect him to come back, do you?' inquired Mr. Grimwig.

'Don't you?' asked Mr. Brownlow, smiling.

The spirit of contradiction was strong in Mr. Grimwig's breast, at the moment; and it was rendered stronger by his friend's confident smile.

'No,' he said, smiting the table with his fist, 'I do not. The boy has a new suit of clothes on his back, a set of valuable books under his arm, and a five-pound note in his pocket. He'll join his old friends the thieves, and laugh at you. If ever that boy returns to this house, sir, I'll eat my head.'

With these words he drew his chair closer to the table; and there the two friends sat, in silent expectation, with the watch between them.

It is worthy of remark, as illustrating the importance we attach to our own judgments, and the pride with which we put forth our most rash and hasty conclusions, that, although Mr. Grimwig was not by any means a bad-hearted man, and though he would have been unfeignedly sorry to see his respected friend duped and deceived, he really did most earnestly and strongly hope at that moment, that Oliver Twist might not come back.

It grew so dark, that the figures on the dial-plate were scarcely discernible; but there the two old gentlemen continued to sit, in silence, with the watch between them.

CHAPTER 15

Showing how very fond of Oliver Twist, the
merry old Jew and Miss Nancy were

In the obscure parlour of a low public-house, in the filthiest part
of Little Saffron Hill; a dark and gloomy den, where a flaring gas-
light burnt all day in the wintertime; and where no ray of sun ever
shone in the summer: there sat, brooding over a little pewter measure
and a small glass, strongly impregnated with the smell of liquor, a
man in a velveteen coat, drab shorts, half boots and stockings, whom
even by that dim light no experienced agent of police would have
hesitated to recognise as Mr. William Sikes. At his feet, sat a white-
coated, red-eyed dog; who occupied himself, alternately, in winking
at his master with both eyes at the same time; and in licking a large,
fresh cut on one side of his mouth, which appeared to be the result
of some recent conflict.

'Keep quiet, you warmint! Keep quiet!' said Mr. Sikes, suddenly
breaking silence. Whether his meditations were so intense as to be
disturbed by the dog's winking, or whether his feelings were so
wrought upon by his reflections that they required all the relief
derivable from kicking an unoffending animal to allay them, is matter
for argument and consideration. Whatever was the cause, the effect
was a kick and a curse, bestowed upon the dog simultaneously.

Dogs are not generally apt to revenge injuries inflicted upon
them by their masters; but Mr. Sikes's dog, having faults of temper
in common with his owner, and labouring, perhaps, at this moment,

under a powerful sense of injury, made no more ado but at once fixed his teeth in one of the half-boots. Having given it a hearty shake, he retired, growling, under a form; just escaping the pewter measure which Mr. Sikes levelled at his head.

'You would, would you?' said Sikes, seizing the poker in one hand, and deliberately opening with the other a large clasp-knife, which he drew from his pocket. 'Come here, you born devil! Come here! D'ye hear?'

The dog no doubt heard; because Mr. Sikes spoke in the very harshest key of a very harsh voice; but, appearing to entertain some unaccountable objection to having his throat cut, he remained where he was, and growled more fiercely than before: at the same time grasping the end of the poker between his teeth, and biting at it like a wild beast.

This resistance only infuriated Mr. Sikes the more; who, dropping on his knees, began to assail the animal most furiously. The dog jumped from right to left, and from left to right: snapping, growling, barking; the man thrust and swore, and struck and blasphemed; and the struggle was reaching a most critical point for one or other; when, the door suddenly opening, the dog darted out: leaving Bill Sikes with the poker and the clasp-knife in his hands.

There must always be two parties to a quarrel, says the old adage. Mr. Sikes, being disappointed of the dog's participation, at once transferred his share in the quarrel to the newcomer.

'What the devil do you come in between me and my dog for?' said Sikes, with a fierce gesture.

'I didn't know, my dear, I didn't know,' replied Fagin, humbly; for the Jew was the newcomer.

'Didn't know, you white-livered thief!' growled Sikes. 'Couldn't you hear the noise?'

'Not a sound of it, as I'm a living man, Bill,' replied the Jew.

'Oh no! You hear nothing, you don't,' retorted Sikes with a fierce sneer. 'Sneaking in and out, so as nobody hears how you come or go! I wish you had been the dog, Fagin, half a minute ago.'

'Why?' inquired the Jew with a forced smile.

''Cause the government, as cares for the lives of such men as you, as haven't half the pluck of curs, lets a man kill a dog how he likes,' replied Sikes, shutting up the knife with a very expressive look; 'that's why.'

The Jew rubbed his hands; and, sitting down at the table, affected to laugh at the pleasantry of his friend. He was obviously very ill at ease, however.

'Grin away,' said Sikes, replacing the poker, and surveying him with savage contempt; 'grin away. You'll never have the laugh at me, though, unless it's behind a night-cap. I've got the upper hand over you, Fagin; and, d— me, I'll keep it. There! If I go, you go; so take care of me.'

'Well, well, my dear,' said the Jew, 'I know all that; we—we— have a mutual interest, Bill—a mutual interest.'

'Humph,' said Sikes, as if he thought the interest lay rather more on the Jew's side than on his. 'Well, what have you got to say to me?'

'It's all passed safe through the melting-pot,' replied Fagin, 'and this is your share. It's rather more than it ought to be, my dear; but as I know you'll do me a good turn another time, and—'

'Stow that gammon,' interposed the robber, impatiently. 'Where is it? Hand over!'

'Yes, yes, Bill; give me time, give me time,' replied the Jew, soothingly. 'Here it is! All safe!' As he spoke, he drew forth an old cotton handkerchief from his breast; and untying a large knot in one corner, produced a small brown-paper packet. Sikes, snatching it from him, hastily opened it; and proceeded to count the sovereigns it contained.

'This is all, is it?' inquired Sikes.

'All,' replied the Jew.

'You haven't opened the parcel and swallowed one or two as you come along, have you?' inquired Sikes, suspiciously. 'Don't put on an injured look at the question; you've done it many a time. Jerk the tinkler.'

These words, in plain English, conveyed an injunction to ring the bell. It was answered by another Jew: younger than Fagin, but nearly as vile and repulsive in appearance.

Bill Sikes merely pointed to the empty measure. The Jew, perfectly understanding the hint, retired to fill it: previously exchanging a remarkable look with Fagin, who raised his eyes for an instant, as if in expectation of it, and shook his head in reply; so slightly that the action would have been almost imperceptible to an observant third person. It was lost upon Sikes, who was stooping at the moment to tie the boot-lace which the dog had torn. Possibly, if he had observed the brief interchange of signals, he might have thought that it boded no good to him.

'Is anybody here, Barney?' inquired Fagin; speaking, now that Sikes was looking on, without raising his eyes from the ground.

'Dot a shoul,' replied Barney; whose words: whether they came from the heart or not: made their way through the nose.

'Nobody?' inquired Fagin, in a tone of surprise: which perhaps might mean that Barney was at liberty to tell the truth.

'Dobody but Biss Dadsy,' replied Barney.

'Nancy!' exclaimed Sikes. 'Where? Strike me blind, if I don't honour that 'ere girl, for her native talents.'

'She's bid havid a plate of boiled beef id the bar,' replied Barney.

'Send her here,' said Sikes, pouring out a glass of liquor. 'Send her here.'

Barney looked timidly at Fagin, as if for permission; the Jew remaining silent, and not lifting his eyes from the ground, he retired; and presently returned, ushering in Nancy; who was decorated with the bonnet, apron, basket, and street-door key, complete.

'You are on the scent, are you, Nancy?' inquired Sikes, proffering the glass.

'Yes, I am, Bill,' replied the young lady, disposing of its contents; 'and tired enough of it I am, too. The young brat's been ill and confined to the crib; and—'

'Ah, Nancy, dear!' said Fagin, looking up.

Now, whether a peculiar contraction of the Jew's red eyebrows, and a half-closing of his deeply-set eyes, warned Miss Nancy that she was disposed to be too communicative, is not a matter of much importance. The fact is all we need care for here; and the fact is, that she suddenly checked herself, and with several gracious smiles upon Mr. Sikes, turned the conversation to other matters. In about ten minutes' time, Mr. Fagin was seized with a fit of coughing; upon which Nancy pulled her shawl over her shoulders, and declared it was time to go. Mr. Sikes, finding that he was walking a short part of her way himself, expressed his intention of accompanying her; they went away together, followed, at a little distance, by the dog, who slunk out of a backyard as soon as his master was out of sight.

The Jew thrust his head out of the room door when Sikes had left it; looked after him as he walked up the dark passage; shook his clenched fist; muttered a deep curse; and then, with a horrible grin, re-seated himself at the table; where he was soon deeply absorbed in the interesting pages of the Hue-and-Cry.

Meanwhile, Oliver Twist, little dreaming that he was within so very short a distance of the merry old gentleman, was on his way to the book-stall. When he got into Clerkenwell, he accidentally turned down a bye-street which was not exactly in his way; but not discovering his mistake until he had got half-way down it, and knowing it must lead in the right direction, he did not think it worth while to turn back; and so marched on, as quickly as he could, with the books under his arm.

He was walking along, thinking how happy and contented he ought to feel; and how much he would give for only one look at poor little Dick, who, starved and beaten, might be weeping bitterly at that very moment; when he was startled by a young woman screaming out very loud, 'Oh, my dear brother!' And he had hardly looked up, to see what the matter was, when he was stopped by having a pair of arms thrown tight round his neck.

'Don't,' cried Oliver, struggling. 'Let go of me. Who is it? What are you stopping me for?'

The only reply to this, was a great number of loud lamentations from the young woman who had embraced him; and who had a little basket and a street-door key in her hand.

'Oh my gracious!' said the young woman, 'I've found him! Oh! Oliver! Oliver! Oh you naughty boy, to make me suffer such distress on your account! Come home, dear, come. Oh, I've found him. Thank gracious goodness heavins, I've found him!' With these incoherent exclamations, the young woman burst into another fit of crying, and got so dreadfully hysterical, that a couple of women who came up at the moment asked a butcher's boy with a shiny head of hair anointed with suet, who was also looking on, whether he didn't think he had better run for the doctor. To which, the butcher's boy: who appeared of a lounging, not to say indolent disposition: replied, that he thought not.

'Oh, no, no, never mind,' said the young woman, grasping Oliver's hand; 'I'm better now. Come home directly, you cruel boy! Come!'

'What's the matter, ma'am?' inquired one of the women.

'Oh, ma'am,' replied the young woman, 'he ran away, near a month ago, from his parents, who are hardworking and respectable people; and went and joined a set of thieves and bad characters; and almost broke his mother's heart.'

'Young wretch!' said one woman.

'Go home, do, you little brute,' said the other.

'I am not,' replied Oliver, greatly alarmed. 'I don't know her. I haven't any sister, or father and mother either. I'm an orphan; I live at Pentonville.'

'Only hear him, how he braves it out!' cried the young woman.

'Why, it's Nancy!' exclaimed Oliver; who now saw her face for the first time; and started back, in irrepressible astonishment.

'You see he knows me!' cried Nancy, appealing to the bystanders. 'He can't help himself. Make him come home, there's good people, or he'll kill his dear mother and father, and break my heart!'

'What the devil's this?' said a man, bursting out of a beer-shop, with a white dog at his heels; 'young Oliver! Come home to your poor mother, you young dog! Come home directly.'

'I don't belong to them. I don't know them. Help! help!' cried Oliver, struggling in the man's powerful grasp.

'Help!' repeated the man. 'Yes; I'll help you, you young rascal! What books are these? You've been a-stealing 'em, have you? Give 'em here.' With these words, the man tore the volumes from his grasp, and struck him on the head.

'That's right!' cried a looker-on, from a garret-window. 'That's the only way of bringing him to his senses!'

'To be sure!' cried a sleepy-faced carpenter, casting an approving look at the garret-window.

'It'll do him good!' said the two women.

'And he shall have it, too!' rejoined the man, administering another blow, and seizing Oliver by the collar. 'Come on, you young villain! Here, Bull's-eye, mind him, boy! Mind him!'

Weak with recent illness; stupefied by the blows and the suddenness of the attack; terrified by the fierce growling of the dog, and the brutality of the man; overpowered by the conviction of the bystanders that he really was the hardened little wretch he was described to be; what could one poor child do! Darkness had set in; it was a low neighbourhood; no help was near; resistance was useless. In another moment, he was dragged into a labyrinth of dark narrow courts, and was forced along them at a pace which rendered the few cries he dared to give utterance to, unintelligible. It was of little moment, indeed, whether they were intelligible or no; for there was nobody to care for them, had they been ever so plain.

The gas-lamps were lighted; Mrs. Bedwin was waiting anxiously at the open door; the servant had run up the street twenty times to see if there were any traces of Oliver; and still the two old gentlemen sat, perseveringly, in the dark parlour, with the watch between them.

CHAPTER 16

Relates what became of Oliver Twist, after
he had been claimed by Nancy

The narrow streets and courts, at length, terminated in a large open
space; scattered about which, were pens for beasts, and other indications of a cattle-market. Sikes slackened his pace when they reached
this spot: the girl being quite unable to support any longer, the rapid
rate at which they had hitherto walked. Turning to Oliver, he roughly
commanded him to take hold of Nancy's hand.

'Do you hear?' growled Sikes, as Oliver hesitated, and looked
round.

They were in a dark corner, quite out of the track of
passengers. Oliver saw, but too plainly, that resistance would be
of no avail. He held out his hand, which Nancy clasped tight
in hers.

'Give me the other,' said Sikes, seizing Oliver's unoccupied
hand. 'Here, Bull's-eye!'

The dog looked up, and growled.

'See here, boy!' said Sikes, putting his other hand to Oliver's
throat; 'if he speaks ever so soft a word, hold him! D'ye mind!'

The dog growled again; and licking his lips, eyed Oliver as if
he were anxious to attach himself to his windpipe without delay.

'He's as willing as a Christian, strike me blind if he isn't!' said
Sikes, regarding the animal with a kind of grim and ferocious
approval. 'Now, you know what you've got to expect, master, so call

away as quick as you like; the dog will soon stop that game. Get on, young 'un!'

Bull's-eye wagged his tail in acknowledgment of this unusually endearing form of speech; and, giving vent to another admonitory growl for the benefit of Oliver, led the way onward.

It was Smithfield that they were crossing, although it might have been Grosvenor Square, for anything Oliver knew to the contrary. The night was dark and foggy. The lights in the shops could scarcely struggle through the heavy mist, which thickened every moment and shrouded the streets and houses in gloom; rendering the strange place still stranger in Oliver's eyes; and making his uncertainty the more dismal and depressing.

They had hurried on a few paces, when a deep church-bell struck the hour. With its first stroke, his two conductors stopped, and turned their heads in the direction whence the sound proceeded.

'Eight o'clock, Bill,' said Nancy, when the bell ceased.

'What's the good of telling me that; I can hear it, can't I!' replied Sikes.

'I wonder whether *they* can hear it,' said Nancy.

'Of course they can,' replied Sikes. 'It was Bartlemy time when I was shopped; and there warn't a penny trumpet in the fair, as I couldn't hear the squeaking on. Arter I was locked up for the night, the row and din outside made the thundering old jail so silent, that I could almost have beat my brains out against the iron plates of the door.'

'Poor fellows!' said Nancy, who still had her face turned towards the quarter in which the bell had sounded. 'Oh, Bill, such fine young chaps as them!'

'Yes; that's all you women think of,' answered Sikes. 'Fine young chaps! Well, they're as good as dead, so it don't much matter.'

With this consolation, Mr. Sikes appeared to repress a rising tendency to jealousy, and, clasping Oliver's wrist more firmly, told him to step out again.

'Wait a minute!' said the girl: 'I wouldn't hurry by, if it was you that was coming out to be hung, the next time eight o'clock struck, Bill. I'd walk round and round the place till I dropped, if the snow was on the ground, and I hadn't a shawl to cover me.'

'And what good would that do?' inquired the unsentimental Mr. Sikes. 'Unless you could pitch over a file and twenty yards of good stout rope, you might as well be walking fifty mile off, or not walking at all, for all the good it would do me. Come on, and don't stand preaching there.'

The girl burst into a laugh; drew her shawl more closely round her; and they walked away. But Oliver felt her hand tremble, and, looking up in her face as they passed a gas-lamp, saw that it had turned a deadly white.

They walked on, by little-frequented and dirty ways, for a full half-hour: meeting very few people, and those appearing from their looks to hold much the same position in society as Mr. Sikes himself. At length they turned into a very filthy narrow street, nearly full of old-clothes shops; the dog running forward, as if conscious that there was no further occasion for his keeping on guard, stopped before the door of a shop that was closed and apparently untenanted; the house was in a ruinous condition, and on the door was nailed a board, intimating that it was to let: which looked as if it had hung there for many years.

'All right,' cried Sikes, glancing cautiously about.

Nancy stooped below the shutters, and Oliver heard the sound of a bell. They crossed to the opposite side of the street, and stood for a few moments under a lamp. A noise, as if a sash-window were gently raised, was heard; and soon afterwards the door softly opened. Mr. Sikes then seized the terrified boy by the collar with very little ceremony; and all three were quickly inside the house.

The passage was perfectly dark. They waited, while the person who had let them in, chained and barred the door.

'Anybody here?' inquired Sikes.

'No,' replied a voice, which Oliver thought he had heard before.

'Is the old 'un here?' asked the robber.

'Yes,' replied the voice; 'and precious down in the mouth he has been. Won't he be glad to see you? Oh, no!'

The style of this reply, as well as the voice which delivered it, seemed familiar to Oliver's ears; but it was impossible to distinguish even the form of the speaker in the darkness.

'Let's have a glim,' said Sikes, 'or we shall go breaking our necks, or treading on the dog. Look after your legs if you do!'

'Stand still a moment, and I'll get you one,' replied the voice. The receding footsteps of the speaker were heard; and, in another minute, the form of Mr. John Dawkins, otherwise the artful Dodger appeared. He bore in his right hand a tallow candle stuck in the end of a cleft stick.

The young gentleman did not stop to bestow any other mark of recognition upon Oliver than a humorous grin; but, turning away, beckoned the visitors to follow him down a flight of stairs. They crossed an empty kitchen; and, opening the door of a low earthy-smelling room, which seemed to have been built in a small backyard, were received with a shout of laughter.

'Oh, my wig, my wig!' cried Master Charles Bates, from whose lungs the laughter had proceeded; 'here he is! oh, cry, here he is! Oh, Fagin, look at him! Fagin, do look at him! I can't bear it; it is such a jolly game, I can't bear it. Hold me, somebody, while I laugh it out.'

With this irrepressible ebullition of mirth, Master Bates laid himself flat on the floor: and kicked convulsively for five minutes, in an ecstasy of facetious joy. Then jumping to his feet, he snatched the cleft stick from the Dodger; and, advancing to Oliver, viewed him round and round; while the Jew, taking off his night-cap, made a great number of low bows to the bewildered boy. The Artful, meantime, who was of a rather saturnine disposition, and seldom gave way to merriment when it interfered with business, rifled Oliver's pockets with steady assiduity.

'Look at his togs, Fagin!' said Charley, putting the light so close to his new jacket as nearly to set him on fire. 'Look at his togs! Superfine cloth, and the heavy swell cut! Oh, my eye, what a game! And his books, too! Nothing but a gentleman, Fagin!'

'Delighted to see you looking so well, my dear,' said the Jew, bowing with mock humility. 'The Artful shall give you another suit, my dear, for fear you should spoil that Sunday one. Why didn't you write, my dear, and say you were coming? We'd have got something warm for supper.'

At this, Master Bates roared again: so loud, that Fagin himself relaxed, and even the Dodger smiled; but as the Artful drew forth the five-pound note at that instant, it is doubtful whether the sally or the discovery awakened his merriment.

'Hallo! what's that?' inquired Sikes, stepping forward as the Jew seized the note. 'That's mine, Fagin.'

'No, no, my dear,' said the Jew. 'Mine, Bill, mine. You shall have the books.'

'If that ain't mine!' said Bill Sikes, putting on his hat with a determined air; 'mine and Nancy's, that is; I'll take the boy back again.'

The Jew started. Oliver started too, though from a very different cause; for he hoped that the dispute might really end in his being taken back.

'Come! Hand over, will you?' said Sikes.

'This is hardly fair, Bill; hardly fair, is it, Nancy?' inquired the Jew.

'Fair, or not fair,' retorted Sikes, 'hand over, I tell you! Do you think Nancy and me has got nothing else to do with our precious time but to spend it in scouting arter, and kidnapping, every young boy as gets grabbed through you? Give it here, you avaricious old skeleton; give it here!'

With this gentle remonstrance, Mr. Sikes plucked the note from between the Jew's finger and thumb; and looking the old man coolly in the face, folded it up small, and tied it in his neckerchief.

'That's for our share of the trouble,' said Sikes; 'and not half enough, neither. You may keep the books, if you're fond of reading. If you ain't, sell 'em.'

'They're very pretty,' said Charley Bates: who, with sundry grimaces, had been affecting to read one of the volumes in question: 'beautiful writing, isn't it, Oliver?' At sight of the dismayed look with which Oliver regarded his tormentors, Master Bates, who was blessed with a lively sense of the ludicrous, fell into another ecstasy, more boisterous than the first.

'They belong to the old gentleman,' said Oliver, wringing his hands; 'to the good, kind, old gentleman who took me into his house, and had me nursed, when I was near dying of the fever. Oh, pray send them back; send him back the books and money. Keep me here all my life long; but pray, pray send them back. He'll think I stole them; the old lady: all of them who were so kind to me: will think I stole them. Oh, do have mercy upon me, and send them back!'

With these words, which were uttered with all the energy of passionate grief, Oliver fell upon his knees at the Jew's feet; and beat his hands together, in perfect desperation.

'The boy's right,' remarked Fagin, looking covertly round, and knitting his shaggy eyebrows into a hard knot. 'You're right, Oliver, you're right; they *will* think you have stolen 'em. Ha! ha!' chuckled the Jew, rubbing his hands; 'it couldn't have happened better, if we had chosen our time!'

'Of course it couldn't,' replied Sikes; 'I know'd that, directly I see him coming through Clerkenwell, with the books under his arm. It's all right enough. They're soft-hearted psalm singers, or they wouldn't have taken him in at all; and they'll ask no questions after him, fear they should be obliged to prosecute, and so get him lagged. He's safe enough.'

Oliver had looked from one to the other, while these words were being spoken, as if he were bewildered, and could scarcely understand what passed; but when Bill Sikes concluded, he jumped suddenly to his feet, and tore wildly from the room: uttering shrieks for help, which made the bare old house echo to the roof.

'Keep back the dog, Bill!' cried Nancy, springing before the door, and closing it, as the Jew and his two pupils darted out in pursuit. 'Keep back the dog; he'll tear the boy to pieces.'

'Serve him right!' cried Sikes, struggling to disengage himself from the girl's grasp. 'Stand off from me, or I'll split your head against the wall.'

'I don't care for that, Bill, I don't care for that,' screamed the girl, struggling violently with the man: 'the child shan't be torn down by the dog, unless you kill me first.'

'Shan't he!' said Sikes, setting his teeth. 'I'll soon do that, if you don't keep off.'

The housebreaker flung the girl from him to the further end of the room, just as the Jew and the two boys returned, dragging Oliver among them.

'What's the matter here?' said Fagin, looking round.

'The girl's gone mad, I think,' replied Sikes, savagely.

'No, she hasn't,' said Nancy, pale and breathless from the scuffle; 'no, she hasn't, Fagin; don't think it.'

'Then keep quiet, will you?' said the Jew, with a threatening look.

'No, I won't do that, neither,' replied Nancy, speaking very loud. 'Come! What do you think of that?'

Mr. Fagin was sufficiently well acquainted with the manners and customs of that particular species of humanity to which Nancy belonged, to feel tolerably certain that it would be rather unsafe to prolong any conversation with her, at present. With the view of diverting the attention of the company, he turned to Oliver.

'So you wanted to get away, my dear, did you?' said the Jew, taking up a jagged and knotted club which lay in a corner of the fireplace; 'eh?'

Oliver made no reply. But he watched the Jew's motions, and breathed quickly.

'Wanted to get assistance; called for the police; did you?' sneered the Jew, catching the boy by the arm. 'We'll cure you of that, my young master.'

The Jew inflicted a smart blow on Oliver's shoulders with the club; and was raising it for a second, when the girl, rushing forward, wrested it from his hand. She flung it into the fire, with a force that brought some of the glowing coals whirling out into the room.

'I won't stand by and see it done, Fagin,' cried the girl. 'You've got the boy, and what more would you have? —Let him be—let him be—or I shall put that mark on some of you, that will bring me to the gallows before my time.'

The girl stamped her foot violently on the floor as she vented this threat; and with her lips compressed, and her hands clenched, looked alternately at the Jew and the other robber: her face quite colourless from the passion of rage into which she had gradually worked herself.

'Why, Nancy!' said the Jew, in a soothing tone; after a pause, during which he and Mr. Sikes had stared at one another in a disconcerted manner; 'you—you're more clever than ever to-night. Ha! ha! my dear, you are acting beautifully.'

'Am I!' said the girl. 'Take care I don't overdo it. You will be the worse for it, Fagin, if I do; and so I tell you in good time to keep clear of me.'

There is something about a roused woman: especially if she add to all her other strong passions, the fierce impulses of recklessness and despair: which few men like to provoke. The Jew saw that it would be hopeless to affect any further mistake regarding the reality of Miss Nancy's rage; and, shrinking involuntarily back a few paces, cast a glance, half imploring and half cowardly, at Sikes: as if to hint that he was the fittest person to pursue the dialogue.

Mr. Sikes, thus mutely appealed to; and possibly feeling his personal pride and influence interested in the immediate reduction of Miss Nancy to reason; gave utterance to about a couple of score of curses and threats, the rapid production of which reflected great credit on the fertility of his invention. As they produced no visible effect on the object against whom they were discharged, however, he resorted to more tangible arguments.

'What do you mean by this?' said Sikes; backing the inquiry with a very common imprecation concerning the most beautiful of human features: which, if it were heard above, only once out of every fifty thousand times that it is uttered below, would render blindness as common a disorder as measles: 'what do you mean by it? Burn my body! Do you know who you are, and what you are?'

'Oh, yes, I know all about it,' replied the girl, laughing hysterically; and shaking her head from side to side, with a poor assumption of indifference.

'Well, then, keep quiet,' rejoined Sikes, with a growl like that he was accustomed to use when addressing his dog, 'or I'll quiet you for a good long time to come.'

The girl laughed again: even less composedly than before; and, darting a hasty look at Sikes, turned her face aside, and bit her lip till the blood came.

'You're a nice one,' added Sikes, as he surveyed her with a contemptuous air, 'to take up the humane and gen—teel side! A pretty subject for the child, as you call him, to make a friend of!'

'God Almighty help me, I am!' cried the girl passionately; 'and I wish I had been struck dead in the street, or had changed places with them we passed so near to-night, before I had lent a hand in bringing him here. He's a thief, a liar, a devil, all that's bad, from this night forth. Isn't that enough for the old wretch, without blows?'

'Come, come, Sikes,' said the Jew, appealing to him in a remonstratory tone, and motioning towards the boys, who were eagerly attentive to all that passed; 'we must have civil words; civil words, Bill.'

'Civil words!' cried the girl, whose passion was frightful to see. 'Civil words, you villain! Yes, you deserve 'em from me. I thieved for you when I was a child not half as old as this!' pointing to Oliver. 'I have been in the same trade, and in the same service, for twelve years since. Don't you know it? Speak out! Don't you know it?'

'Well, well,' replied the Jew, with an attempt at pacification; 'and, if you have, it's your living!'

'Aye, it is!' returned the girl; not speaking, but pouring out the words in one continuous and vehement scream. 'It is my living; and the cold, wet, dirty streets are my home; and you're the wretch that drove me to them long ago, and that'll keep me there, day and night, day and night, till I die!'

'I shall do you a mischief!' interposed the Jew, goaded by these reproaches; 'a mischief worse than that, if you say much more!'

The girl said nothing more; but, tearing her hair and dress in a transport of passion, made such a rush at the Jew as would probably have left signal marks of her revenge upon him, had not her wrists been seized by Sikes at the right moment; upon which, she made a few ineffectual struggles, and fainted.

'She's all right now,' said Sikes, laying her down in a corner. 'She's uncommon strong in the arms, when she's up in this way.'

The Jew wiped his forehead: and smiled, as if it were a relief to have the disturbance over; but neither he, nor Sikes, nor the dog, nor the boys, seemed to consider it in any other light than a common occurrence incidental to business.

'It's the worst of having to do with women,' said the Jew, replacing his club; 'but they're clever, and we can't get on, in our line, without 'em. Charley, show Oliver to bed.'

'I suppose he'd better not wear his best clothes to-morrow, Fagin, had he?' inquired Charley Bates.

'Certainly not,' replied the Jew, reciprocating the grin with which Charley put the question.

Master Bates, apparently much delighted with his commission, took the cleft stick: and led Oliver into an adjacent kitchen, where there were two or three of the beds on which he had slept before; and here, with many uncontrollable bursts of laughter, he produced the identical old suit of clothes which Oliver had so much congratulated himself upon leaving off at Mr. Brownlow's; and the accidental display of which, to Fagin, by the Jew who purchased them, had been the very first clue received, of his whereabout.

'Pull off the smart ones,' said Charley, 'and I'll give 'em to Fagin to take care of. What fun it is!'

Poor Oliver unwillingly complied. Master Bates rolling up the new clothes under his arm, departed from the room, leaving Oliver in the dark, and locking the door behind him.

The noise of Charley's laughter, and the voice of Miss Betsy, who opportunely arrived to throw water over her friend, and perform other feminine offices for the promotion of her recovery, might have kept many people awake under more happy circumstances than those in which Oliver was placed. But he was sick and weary; and he soon fell sound asleep.

CHAPTER 17

Oliver's destiny continuing unpropitious,
brings a great man to London to injure his
reputation

It is the custom on the stage, in all good murderous melodramas,
to present the tragic and the comic scenes, in as regular alterna-
tion, as the layers of red and white in a side of streaky bacon.
The hero sinks upon his straw bed, weighed down by fetters and
misfortunes; in the next scene, his faithful but unconscious squire
regales the audience with a comic song. We behold, with throb-
bing bosoms, the heroine in the grasp of a proud and ruthless
baron: her virtue and her life alike in danger, drawing forth her
dagger to preserve the one at the cost of the other; and just as
our expectations are wrought up to the highest pitch, a whistle
is heard, and we are straightway transported to the great hall of
the castle: where a grey-headed seneschal sings a funny chorus
with a funnier body of vassals, who are free of all sorts of places,
from church vaults to palaces, and roam about in company,
carolling perpetually.

Such changes appear absurd; but they are not so unnatural as
they would seem at first sight. The transitions in real life from well-
spread boards to death-beds, and from mourning-weeds to holiday
garments, are not a whit less startling; only, there we are busy actors,
instead of passive lookers-on, which makes a vast difference. The
actors in the mimic life of the theatre, are blind to violent transitions and abrupt impulses of passion or feeling, which, presented

before the eyes of mere spectators, are at once condemned as outrageous and preposterous.

As sudden shiftings of the scene, and rapid changes of time and place, are not only sanctioned in books by long usage, but are by many considered as the great art of authorship: an author's skill in his craft being, by such critics, chiefly estimated with relation to the dilemmas in which he leaves his characters at the end of every chapter: this brief introduction to the present one may perhaps be deemed unnecessary. If so, let it be considered a delicate intimation on the part of the historian that he is going back to the town in which Oliver Twist was born; the reader taking it for granted that there are good and substantial reasons for making the journey, or he would not be invited to proceed upon such an expedition.

Mr. Bumble emerged at early morning from the workhouse-gate, and walked with portly carriage and commanding steps, up the High Street. He was in the full bloom and pride of beadlehood; his cocked hat and coat were dazzling in the morning sun; he clutched his cane with the vigorous tenacity of health and power. Mr. Bumble always carried his head high; but this morning it was higher than usual. There was an abstraction in his eye, an elevation in his air, which might have warned an observant stranger that thoughts were passing in the beadle's mind, too great for utterance.

Mr. Bumble stopped not to converse with the small shopkeepers and others who spoke to him, deferentially, as he passed along. He merely returned their salutations with a wave of his hand, and relaxed not in his dignified pace, until he reached the farm where Mrs. Mann tended the infant paupers with parochial care.

'Drat that beadle!' said Mrs. Mann, hearing the well-known shaking at the garden-gate. 'If it isn't him at this time in the morning! Lauk, Mr. Bumble, only think of its being you! Well, dear me, it *is* a pleasure, this is! Come into the parlour, sir, please.'

The first sentence was addressed to Susan; and the exclamations of delight were uttered to Mr. Bumble: as the good lady unlocked the garden-gate: and showed him, with great attention and respect, into the house.

'Mrs. Mann,' said Mr. Bumble; not sitting upon, or dropping himself into a seat, as any common jackanapes would: but letting himself gradually and slowly down into a chair: 'Mrs. Mann, ma'am, good morning.'

'Well, and good morning to *you*, sir,' replied Mrs. Mann, with many smiles; 'and hoping you find yourself well, sir!'

'So-so, Mrs. Mann,' replied the beadle. 'A porochial life is not a bed of roses, Mrs. Mann.'

'Ah, that it isn't indeed, Mr. Bumble,' rejoined the lady. And all the infant paupers might have chorused the rejoinder with great propriety, if they had heard it.

'A porochial life, ma'am,' continued Mr. Bumble, striking the table with his cane, 'is a life of worrit, and vexation, and hardihood; but all public characters, as I may say, must suffer prosecution.'

Mrs. Mann, not very well knowing what the beadle meant, raised her hands with a look of sympathy, and sighed.

'Ah! You may well sigh, Mrs. Mann!' said the beadle.

Finding she had done right, Mrs. Mann sighed again: evidently to the satisfaction of the public character: who, repressing a complacent smile by looking sternly at his cocked hat, said,

'Mrs. Mann, I am a-going to London.'

'Lauk, Mr. Bumble!' cried Mrs. Mann, starting back.

'To London, ma'am,' resumed the inflexible beadle, 'by coach. I and two paupers, Mrs. Mann! A legal action is a-coming on, about a settlement; and the board has appointed me—me, Mrs. Mann—to depose to the matter before the quarter-sessions at Clerkinwell. And I very much question,' added Mr. Bumble, drawing himself up, 'whether the Clerkinwell Sessions will not find themselves in the wrong box before they have done with me.'

'Oh! you mustn't be too hard upon them, sir,' said Mrs. Mann, coaxingly.

'The Clerkinwell Sessions have brought it upon themselves, ma'am,' replied Mr. Bumble; 'and if the Clerkinwell Sessions find that they come off rather worse than they expected, the Clerkinwell Sessions have only themselves to thank.'

There was so much determination and depth of purpose about the menacing manner in which Mr. Bumble delivered himself of these words, that Mrs. Mann appeared quite awed by them. At length she said,

'You're going by coach, sir? I thought it was always usual to send them paupers in carts.'

'That's when they're ill, Mrs. Mann,' said the beadle. 'We put the sick paupers into open carts in the rainy weather, to prevent their taking cold.'

'Oh!' said Mrs. Mann.

'The opposition coach contracts for these two; and takes them cheap,' said Mr. Bumble. 'They are both in a very low state, and we find it would come two pound cheaper to move 'em than to bury 'em—that is, if we can throw 'em upon another parish, which I think we shall be able to do, if they don't die upon the road to spite us. Ha! ha! ha!'

When Mr. Bumble had laughed a little while, his eyes again encountered the cocked hat; and he became grave.

'We are forgetting business, ma'am,' said the beadle; 'here is your porochial stipend for the month.'

Mr. Bumble produced some silver money rolled up in paper, from his pocket-book; and requested a receipt: which Mrs. Mann wrote.

'It's very much blotted, sir,' said the farmer of infants; 'but it's formal enough, I dare say. Thank you, Mr. Bumble, sir, I am very much obliged to you, I'm sure.'

Mr. Bumble nodded, blandly, in acknowledgment of Mrs. Mann's curtsey; and inquired how the children were.

'Bless their dear little hearts!' said Mrs. Mann with emotion, 'they're as well as can be, the dears! Of course, except the two that died last week. And little Dick.'

'Isn't that boy no better?' inquired Mr. Bumble.

Mrs. Mann shook her head.

'He's a ill-conditioned, wicious, bad-disposed porochial child that,' said Mr. Bumble angrily. 'Where is he?'

'I'll bring him to you in one minute, sir,' replied Mrs. Mann. 'Here, you Dick!'

After some calling, Dick was discovered. Having had his face put under the pump, and dried upon Mrs. Mann's gown, he was led into the awful presence of Mr. Bumble, the beadle.

The child was pale and thin; his cheeks were sunken; and his eyes large and bright. The scanty parish dress, the livery of his misery, hung loosely on his feeble body; and his young limbs had wasted away, like those of an old man.

Such was the little being who stood trembling beneath Mr. Bumble's glance; not daring to lift his eyes from the floor; and dreading even to hear the beadle's voice.

'Can't you look at the gentleman, you obstinate boy?' said Mrs. Mann.

The child meekly raised his eyes, and encountered those of Mr. Bumble.

'What's the matter with you, porochial Dick?' inquired Mr. Bumble, with well-timed jocularity.

'Nothing, sir,' replied the child faintly.

'I should think not,' said Mrs. Mann, who had of course laughed very much at Mr. Bumble's humour. 'You want for nothing, I'm sure.'

'I should like—' faltered the child.

'Heyday!' interposed Mrs. Mann, 'I suppose you're going to say that you *do* want for something, now? Why, you little wretch—'

'Stop, Mrs. Mann, stop!' said the beadle, raising his hand with a show of authority. 'Like what, sir, eh?'

'I should like,' faltered the child, 'if somebody that can write, would put a few words down for me on a piece of paper, and fold it up and seal it, and keep it for me, after I am laid in the ground.'

'Why, what does the boy mean?' exclaimed Mr. Bumble, on whom the earnest manner and wan aspect of the child had made some impression: accustomed as he was to such things. 'What do you mean, sir?'

'I should like,' said the child, 'to leave my dear love to poor Oliver Twist; and to let him know how often I have sat by myself and cried to think of his wandering about in the dark nights with nobody to help him. And I should like to tell him,' said the child, pressing his small hands together, and speaking with great fervour, 'that I was glad to die when I was very young; for, perhaps, if I had lived to be a man, and had grown old, my little sister who is in Heaven, might forget me, or be unlike me; and it would be so much happier if we were both children there together.'

Mr. Bumble surveyed the little speaker, from head to foot, with indescribable astonishment; and, turning to his companion, said, 'They're all in one story, Mrs. Mann. That out-dacious Oliver has demogalised them all!'

'I couldn't have believed it, sir!' said Mrs. Mann, holding up her hands, and looking malignantly at Dick. 'I never see such a hardened little wretch!'

'Take him away, ma'am!' said Mr. Bumble imperiously. 'This must be stated to the board, Mrs. Mann.'

'I hope the gentlemen will understand that it isn't my fault, sir?' said Mrs. Mann, whimpering pathetically.

'They shall understand that, ma'am; they shall be acquainted with the true state of the case,' said Mr. Bumble. 'There; take him away, I can't bear the sight on him.'

Dick was immediately taken away, and locked up in the coal-cellar. Mr. Bumble shortly afterwards took himself off, to prepare for his journey.

At six o'clock next morning, Mr. Bumble: having exchanged his cocked hat for a round one, and encased his person in a blue great-coat with a cape to it: took his place on the outside of the coach, accompanied by the criminals whose settlement was disputed; with whom, in due course of time, he arrived in London. He experienced no other crosses on the way, than those which originated in the perverse behaviour of the two paupers, who persisted in shivering, and complaining of the cold, in a manner which, Mr. Bumble declared, caused his teeth to chatter in his head, and made him feel quite uncomfortable; although he had a great-coat on.

Having disposed of these evil-minded persons for the night, Mr. Bumble sat himself down in the house at which the coach stopped; and took a temperate dinner of steaks, oyster sauce, and porter. Putting a glass of hot gin-and-water on the chimney-piece, he drew his chair to the fire; and, with sundry moral reflections on the too-prevalent sin of discontent and complaining, composed himself to read the paper.

The very first paragraph upon which Mr. Bumble's eye rested, was the following advertisement.

five guineas reward

'Whereas a young boy, named Oliver Twist, absconded, or was enticed, on Thursday evening last, from his home at Pentonville; and has not since been heard of. The above reward will be paid to any person who will give such information as will lead to the discovery of the said Oliver Twist, or tend to throw any light upon his previous history, in which the advertiser is, for many reasons, warmly interested.'

And then followed a full description of Oliver's dress, person, appearance, and disappearance: with the name and address of Mr. Brownlow at full length.

Mr. Bumble opened his eyes; read the advertisement, slowly and carefully, three several times; and in something more than five minutes was on his way to Pentonville: having actually, in his excitement, left the glass of hot gin-and-water, untasted.

'Is Mr. Brownlow at home?' inquired Mr. Bumble of the girl who opened the door.

To this inquiry the girl returned the not uncommon, but rather evasive reply of 'I don't know; where do you come from?'

Mr. Bumble no sooner uttered Oliver's name, in explanation of his errand, than Mrs. Bedwin, who had been listening at the parlour door, hastened into the passage in a breathless state.

'Come in, come in,' said the old lady: 'I knew we should hear of him. Poor dear! I knew we should! I was certain of it. Bless his heart! I said so, all along.'

Having said this, the worthy old lady hurried back into the parlour again; and seating herself on a sofa, burst into tears. The girl, who was not quite so susceptible, had run up stairs meanwhile; and now returned with a request that Mr. Bumble would follow her immediately: which he did.

He was shown into the little back study, where sat Mr. Brownlow and his friend Mr. Grimwig, with decanters and glasses before them. The latter gentleman at once burst into the exclamation:

'A beadle! A parish beadle, or I'll eat my head.'

'Pray don't interrupt just now,' said Mr. Brownlow. 'Take a seat, will you?'

Mr. Bumble sat himself down: quite confounded by the oddity of Mr. Grimwig's manner. Mr. Brownlow moved the lamp, so as to obtain an uninterrupted view of the beadle's countenance; and said, with a little impatience,

'Now, sir, you come in consequence of having seen the advertisement?'

'Yes, sir,' said Mr. Bumble.

'And you *are* a beadle, are you not?' inquired Mr. Grimwig.

'I am a porochial beadle, gentlemen,' rejoined Mr. Bumble, proudly.

'Of course,' observed Mr. Grimwig aside to his friend, 'I knew he was. A beadle all over!'

Mr. Brownlow gently shook his head to impose silence on his friend, and resumed:

'Do you know where this poor boy is now?'

'No more than nobody,' replied Mr. Bumble.

'Well, what *do* you know of him?' inquired the old gentleman. 'Speak out, my friend, if you have anything to say. What *do* you know of him?'

'You don't happen to know any good of him, do you?' said Mr. Grimwig, caustically; after an attentive perusal of Mr. Bumble's features.

Mr. Bumble, catching at the inquiry very quickly, shook his head with portentous solemnity.

'You see?' said Mr. Grimwig, looking triumphantly at Mr. Brownlow.

Mr. Brownlow looked apprehensively at Mr. Bumble's pursed-up countenance; and requested him to communicate what he knew regarding Oliver, in as few words as possible.

Mr. Bumble put down his hat; unbuttoned his coat; folded his arms; inclined his head in a retrospective manner; and, after a few moments' reflection, commenced his story.

It would be tedious if given in the beadle's words: occupying, as it did, some twenty minutes in the telling; but the sum and substance of it was, That Oliver was a foundling, born of low and vicious parents. That he had, from his birth, displayed no better qualities than treachery, ingratitude, and malice. That he had terminated his brief career in the place of his birth, by making a sanguinary and cowardly attack on an unoffending lad, and running away in the night-time from his master's house. In proof of his really being the person he represented himself, Mr. Bumble laid upon the table the papers he had brought to town. Folding his arms again, he then awaited Mr. Brownlow's observations.

'I fear it is all too true,' said the old gentleman sorrowfully, after looking over the papers. 'This is not much for your intelligence; but I would gladly have given you treble the money, if it had been favourable to the boy.'

It is not improbable that if Mr. Bumble had been possessed of this information at an earlier period of the interview, he might have imparted a very different colouring to his little history. It was too late to do it now, however; so he shook his head gravely, and, pocketing the five guineas, withdrew.

Mr. Brownlow paced the room to and fro for some minutes; evidently so much disturbed by the beadle's tale, that even Mr. Grimwig forbore to vex him further.

At length he stopped, and rang the bell violently.

'Mrs. Bedwin,' said Mr. Brownlow, when the housekeeper appeared; 'that boy, Oliver, is an impostor.'

'It can't be, sir. It cannot be,' said the old lady energetically.

'I tell you he is,' retorted the old gentleman. 'What do you mean by can't be? We have just heard a full account of him from his birth; and he has been a thorough-paced little villain, all his life.'

'I never will believe it, sir,' replied the old lady, firmly. 'Never!'

'You old women never believe anything but quack-doctors, and lying story-books,' growled Mr. Grimwig. 'I knew it all along. Why didn't you take my advice in the beginning; you would, if he hadn't had a fever, I suppose, eh? He was interesting, wasn't he? Interesting! Bah!' And Mr. Grimwig poked the fire with a flourish.

'He was a dear, grateful, gentle child, sir,' retorted Mrs. Bedwin, indignantly. 'I know what children are, sir; and have done these forty years; and people who can't say the same, shouldn't say anything about them. That's my opinion!'

This was a hard hit at Mr. Grimwig, who was a bachelor. As it extorted nothing from that gentleman but a smile, the old lady tossed her head, and smoothed down her apron preparatory to another speech, when she was stopped by Mr. Brownlow.

'Silence!' said the old gentleman, feigning an anger he was far from feeling. 'Never let me hear the boy's name again. I rang to tell you that. Never. Never, on any pretence, mind! You may leave the room, Mrs. Bedwin. Remember! I am in earnest.'

There were sad hearts at Mr. Brownlow's that night.

Oliver's heart sank within him, when he thought of his good kind friends; it was well for him that he could not know what they had heard, or it might have broken outright.

CHAPTER 18

How Oliver passed his time in the
improving society of his reputable friends

About noon next day, when the Dodger and Master Bates had
gone out to pursue their customary avocations, Mr. Fagin took the
opportunity of reading Oliver a long lecture on the crying sin of
ingratitude: of which he clearly demonstrated he had been guilty,
to no ordinary extent, in wilfully absenting himself from the society
of his anxious friends; and, still more, in endeavouring to escape
from them after so much trouble and expense had been incurred
in his recovery. Mr. Fagin laid great stress on the fact of his having
taken Oliver in, and cherished him, when, without his timely aid,
he might have perished with hunger; and he related the dismal and
affecting history of a young lad whom, in his philanthropy, he had
succoured under parallel circumstances, but who, proving unworthy
of his confidence and evincing a desire to communicate with the
police, had unfortunately come to be hanged at the Old Bailey
one morning. Mr. Fagin did not seek to conceal his share in the
catastrophe, but lamented with tears in his eyes that the wrong-
headed and treacherous behaviour of the young person in question,
had rendered it necessary that he should become the victim of
certain evidence for the crown: which, if it were not precisely true,
was indispensably necessary for the safety of him (Mr. Fagin) and
a few select friends. Mr. Fagin concluded by drawing a rather
disagreeable picture of the discomforts of hanging; and, with great

friendliness and politeness of manner, expressed his anxious hopes that he might never be obliged to submit Oliver Twist to that unpleasant operation.

Little Oliver's blood ran cold, as he listened to the Jew's words, and imperfectly comprehended the dark threats conveyed in them. That it was possible even for justice itself to confound the innocent with the guilty when they were in accidental companionship, he knew already; and that deeply-laid plans for the destruction of inconveniently knowing or over-communicative persons, had been really devised and carried out by the old Jew on more occasions than one, he thought by no means unlikely, when he recollected the general nature of the altercations between that gentleman and Mr. Sikes: which seemed to bear reference to some foregone conspiracy of the kind. As he glanced timidly up, and met the Jew's searching look, he felt that his pale face and trembling limbs were neither unnoticed nor unrelished by that wary old gentleman.

The Jew, smiling hideously, patted Oliver on the head, and said, that if he kept himself quiet, and applied himself to business, he saw they would be very good friends yet. Then, taking his hat, and covering himself with an old patched great-coat, he went out, and locked the room-door behind him.

And so Oliver remained all that day, and for the greater part of many subsequent days, seeing nobody, between early morning and midnight, and left during the long hours to commune with his own thoughts. Which, never failing to revert to his kind friends, and the opinion they must long ago have formed of him, were sad indeed.

After the lapse of a week or so, the Jew left the room-door unlocked; and he was at liberty to wander about the house.

It was a very dirty place. The rooms up stairs had great high wooden chimney-pieces and large doors, with panelled walls and cornices to the ceilings; which, although they were black with neglect and dust, were ornamented in various ways. From all of these tokens Oliver concluded that a long time ago, before the old Jew was born, it had belonged to better people, and had perhaps been quite gay and handsome: dismal and dreary as it looked now.

Spiders had built their webs in the angles of the walls and ceilings; and sometimes, when Oliver walked softly into a room, the mice would scamper across the floor, and run back terrified to their holes. With these exceptions, there was neither sight nor sound of any living thing; and often, when it grew dark, and he was tired of wandering from room to room, he would crouch in the corner of the passage by the street-door, to be as near living people as he could; and would remain there, listening and counting the hours, until the Jew or the boys returned.

In all the rooms, the mouldering shutters were fast closed: the bars which held them were screwed tight into the wood; the only light which was admitted, stealing its way through round holes at the top: which made the rooms more gloomy, and filled them with strange shadows. There was a back-garret window with rusty bars outside, which had no shutter; and out of this, Oliver often gazed with a melancholy face for hours together; but nothing was to be descried from it but a confused and crowded mass of house-tops, blackened chimneys, and gable-ends. Sometimes, indeed, a grizzly head might be seen, peering over the parapet-wall of a distant house: but it was quickly withdrawn again; and as the window of Oliver's observatory was nailed down, and dimmed with the rain and smoke of years, it was as much as he could do to make out the forms of the different objects beyond, without making any attempt to be seen or heard, —which he had as much chance of being, as if he had lived inside the ball of St. Paul's Cathedral.

One afternoon, the Dodger and Master Bates being engaged out that evening, the first-named young gentleman took it into his head to evince some anxiety regarding the decoration of his person (to do him justice, this was by no means an habitual weakness with him); and, with this end and aim, he condescendingly commanded Oliver to assist him in his toilet, straightway.

Oliver was but too glad to make himself useful; too happy to have some faces, however bad, to look upon; too desirous to conciliate those about him when he could honestly do so; to throw any objection in the way of this proposal. So he at once expressed his readiness; and, kneeling on the floor, while the Dodger sat upon the table so that he could take his foot in his lap, he applied himself to a process which Mr. Dawkins designated as 'japanning his trotter-cases'. The phrase, rendered into plain English, signifieth, cleaning his boots.

Whether it was the sense of freedom and independence which a rational animal may be supposed to feel when he sits on a table in an easy attitude smoking a pipe, swinging one leg carelessly to and fro, and having his boots cleaned all the time, without even the past trouble of having taken them off, or the prospective misery of putting them on, to disturb his reflections; or whether it was the goodness of the tobacco that soothed the feelings of the Dodger, or the mildness of the beer that mollified his thoughts; he was evidently tinctured, for the nonce, with a spice of romance and enthusiasm, foreign to his general nature. He looked down on Oliver, with a thoughtful countenance, for a brief space; and then, raising his head, and heaving a gentle sigh, said, half in abstraction, and half to Master Bates:

'What a pity it is he isn't a prig!'

'Ah!' said Master Charles Bates; 'he don't know what's good for him.'

The Dodger sighed again, and resumed his pipe: as did Charley Bates. They both smoked, for some seconds, in silence.

'I suppose you don't even know what a prig is?' said the Dodger mournfully.

'I think I know that,' replied Oliver, looking up. 'It's a th—; you're one, are you not?' inquired Oliver, checking himself.

'I am,' replied the Dodger. 'I'd scorn to be anything else.' Mr. Dawkins gave his hat a ferocious cock, after delivering this senti-ment, and looked at Master Bates, as if to denote that he would feel obliged by his saying anything to the contrary.

'I am,' repeated the Dodger. 'So's Charley. So's Fagin. So's Sikes. So's Nancy. So's Bet. So we all are, down to the dog. And he's the downiest one of the lot!'

'And the least given to peaching,' added Charley Bates.

'He wouldn't so much as bark in a witness-box, for fear of committing himself; no, not if you tied him up in one, and left him there without wittles for a fortnight,' said the Dodger.

'Not a bit of it,' observed Charley.

'He's a rum dog. Don't he look fierce at any strange cove that laughs or sings when he's in company!' pursued the Dodger. 'Won't he growl at all, when he hears a fiddle playing! And don't he hate other dogs as ain't of his breed! Oh, no!'

'He's an out-and-out Christian,' said Charley.

This was merely intended as a tribute to the animal's abilities, but it was an appropriate remark in another sense, if Master Bates had only known it; for there are a good many ladies and gentlemen, claiming to be out-and-out Christians, between whom, and Mr. Sikes' dog, there exist strong and singular points of resemblance.

'Well, well,' said the Dodger, recurring to the point from which they had strayed: with that mindfulness of his profession which influenced all his proceedings. 'This hasn't got anything to do with young Green here.'

'No more it has,' said Charley. 'Why don't you put yourself under Fagin, Oliver?'

'And make your fortun' out of hand?' added the Dodger, with a grin.

'And so be able to retire on your property, and do the genteel: as I mean to, in the very next leap-year but four that ever comes, and the forty-second Tuesday in Trinity-week,' said Charley Bates.

'I don't like it,' rejoined Oliver, timidly; 'I wish they would let me go. I—I—would rather go.'

'And Fagin would *rather* not!' rejoined Charley.

Oliver knew this too well; but thinking it might be dangerous to express his feelings more openly, he only sighed, and went on with his boot-cleaning.

'Go!' exclaimed the Dodger. 'Why, where's your spirit? Don't you take any pride out of yourself? Would you go and be dependent on your friends?'

'Oh, blow that!' said Master Bates: drawing two or three silk handkerchiefs from his pocket, and tossing them into a cupboard, 'that's too mean, that is.'

'*I* couldn't do it,' said the Dodger, with an air of haughty disgust.

'You can leave your friends, though,' said Oliver with a half smile; 'and let them be punished for what you did.'

'That,' rejoined the Dodger, with a wave of his pipe, 'that was all out of consideration for Fagin, 'cause the traps know that we work together, and he might have got into trouble if we hadn't made our lucky; that was the move, wasn't it, Charley?'

Master Bates nodded assent, and would have spoken; but the recollection of Oliver's flight came so suddenly upon him, that the smoke he was inhaling got entangled with a laugh, and went up into his head, and down into his throat: and brought on a fit of coughing and stamping, about five minutes long.

'Look here!' said the Dodger, drawing forth a handful of shillings and half-pence. 'Here's a jolly life! What's the odds where it comes from? Here, catch hold; there's plenty more where they were took from. You won't, won't you? Oh, you precious flat!'

'It's naughty, ain't it, Oliver?' inquired Charley Bates. 'He'll come to be scragged, won't he?'

'I don't know what that means,' replied Oliver.

'Something in this way, old feller,' said Charley. As he said it, Master Bates caught up an end of his neckerchief: and, holding it erect in the air, dropped his head on his shoulder, and jerked a curious sound through his teeth: thereby indicating, by a lively pantomimic representation, that scragging and hanging were one and the same thing.

'That's what it means,' said Charley. 'Look how he stares, Jack! I never did see such prime company as that 'ere boy; he'll be the death of me, I know he will.' Master Charles Bates, having laughed heartily again, resumed his pipe with tears in his eyes.

'You've been brought up bad,' said the Dodger, surveying his boots with much satisfaction when Oliver had polished them. 'Fagin will make something of you, though, or you'll be the first he ever had that turned out unprofitable. You'd better begin at once; for you'll come to the trade long before you think of it; and you're only losing time, Oliver.'

Master Bates backed this advice with sundry moral admonitions of his own: which, being exhausted, he and his friend Mr. Dawkins launched into a glowing description of the numerous pleasures incidental to the life they led, interspersed with a variety of hints to Oliver that the best thing he could do, would be to secure Fagin's favour without more delay, by the means which they themselves had employed to gain it.

'And always put this in your pipe, Nolly,' said the Dodger, as the Jew was heard unlocking the door above, 'if you don't take fogles and tickers—'

'What's the good of talking in that way?' interposed Master Bates: 'he don't know what you mean.'

'If you don't take pocket-handkechers and watches,' said the Dodger, reducing his conversation to the level of Oliver's capacity, 'some other cove will; so that the coves that lose 'em will be all the worse, and you'll be all the worse too, and nobody half a ha'p'orth the better, except the chaps wot gets them—and you've just as good a right to them as they have.'

'To be sure, to be sure!' said the Jew, who had entered, unseen by Oliver. 'It all lies in a nutshell, my dear; in a nutshell, take the Dodger's word for it. Ha! ha! ha! He understands the catechism of his trade.'

The old man rubbed his hands gleefully together, as he corroborated the Dodger's reasoning in these terms; and chuckled with delight at his pupil's proficiency.

The conversation proceeded no farther at this time, for the Jew had returned home accompanied by Miss Betsy, and a gentleman whom Oliver had never seen before, but who was accosted by the Dodger as Tom Chitling; and who, having lingered on the stairs to exchange a few gallantries with the lady, now made his appearance.

Mr. Chitling was older in years than the Dodger: having

perhaps numbered eighteen winters; but there was a degree of deference in his deportment towards that young gentleman which seemed to indicate that he felt himself conscious of a slight inferiority in point of genius and professional acquirements. He had small twinkling eyes, and a pock-marked face; wore a fur cap, a dark corduroy jacket, greasy fustian trousers, and an apron. His wardrobe was, in truth, rather out of repair; but he excused himself to the company by stating that his 'time' was only out an hour before; and that, in consequence of having worn the regimentals for six weeks past, he had not been able to bestow any attention on his private clothes. Mr. Chitling added, with strong marks of irritation, that the new way of fumigating clothes up yonder was infernal unconstitutional, for it burnt holes in them, and there was no remedy against the County. The same remark he considered to apply to the regulation mode of cutting the hair: which he held to be decidedly unlawful. Mr. Chitling wound up his observations by stating that he had not touched a drop of anything for forty-two mortal long hard-working days; and that he 'wished he might be busted if he warn't as dry as a lime-basket.'

'Where do you think this gentleman has come from, Oliver?' inquired the Jew, with a grin, as the other boys put a bottle of spirits on the table.

'I—I—don't know, sir,' replied Oliver.

'Who's that?' inquired Tom Chitling, casting a contemptuous look at Oliver.

'A young friend of mine, my dear,' replied the Jew.

'He's in luck, then,' said the young man, with a meaning look at Fagin. 'Never mind where I came from, young 'un; you'll find your way there, soon enough, I'll bet a crown!'

At this sally, the boys laughed. After some more jokes on the same subject, they exchanged a few short whispers with Fagin; and withdrew.

After some words apart between the last comer and Fagin, they drew their chairs towards the fire; and the Jew, telling Oliver to come and sit by him, led the conversation to the topics most calculated to interest his hearers. These were, the great advantages of the trade, the proficiency of the Dodger, the amiability of Charley Bates, and the liberality of the Jew himself. At length these subjects displayed signs of being thoroughly exhausted; and Mr. Chitling did the same: for the house of correction becomes fatiguing after a week or two. Miss Betsy accordingly withdrew; and left the party to their repose.

From this day, Oliver was seldom left alone; but was placed in almost constant communication with the two boys, who played the old game with the Jew every day: whether for their own improvement or Oliver's, Mr. Fagin best knew. At other times the old man would tell them stories of robberies he had committed in his younger days: mixed up with so much that was droll and curious, that Oliver could not help laughing heartily, and showing that he was amused in spite of all his better feelings.

In short, the wily old Jew had the boy in his toils. Having prepared his mind, by solitude and gloom, to prefer any society to the companionship of his own sad thoughts in such a dreary place, he was now slowly instilling into his soul the poison which he hoped would blacken it, and change its hue for ever.

CHAPTER 19

In which a notable plan is discussed and determined on

It was a chill, damp, windy night, when the Jew: buttoning his great-coat tight round his shrivelled body, and pulling the collar up over his ears so as completely to obscure the lower part of his face: emerged from his den. He paused on the step as the door was locked and chained behind him; and having listened while the boys made all secure, and until their retreating footsteps were no longer audible, slunk down the street as quickly as he could.

The house to which Oliver had been conveyed, was in the neighbourhood of Whitechapel. The Jew stopped for an instant at the corner of the street; and, glancing suspiciously round, crossed the road, and struck off in the direction of Spitalfields.

The mud lay thick upon the stones, and a black mist hung over the streets; the rain fell sluggishly down, and everything felt cold and clammy to the touch. It seemed just the night when it befitted such a being as the Jew to be abroad. As he glided stealthily along, creeping beneath the shelter of the walls and doorways, the hideous old man seemed like some loathsome reptile, engendered in the slime and darkness through which he moved: crawling forth by night, in search of some rich offal for a meal.

He kept on his course, through many winding and narrow ways, until he reached Bethnal Green; then, turning suddenly off to the left, he soon became involved in a maze of the mean and dirty streets which abound in that close and densely-populated quarter.

The Jew was evidently too familiar with the ground he traversed to be at all bewildered, either by the darkness of the night, or the intricacies of the way. He hurried through several alleys and streets, and at length turned into one, lighted only by a single lamp at the farther end. At the door of a house in this street, he knocked; having exchanged a few muttered words with the person who opened it, he walked up stairs.

A dog growled as he touched the handle of a room-door; and a man's voice demanded who was there.

'Only me, Bill; only me, my dear,' said the Jew, looking in.

'Bring in your body then,' said Sikes. 'Lie down, you stupid brute! Don't you know the devil when he's got a great-coat on?'

Apparently, the dog had been somewhat deceived by Mr. Fagin's outer garment; for as the Jew unbuttoned it, and threw it over the back of a chair, he retired to the corner from which he had risen: wagging his tail as he went, to show that he was as well satisfied as it was in his nature to be.

'Well!' said Sikes.

'Well, my dear,' replied the Jew. —'Ah! Nancy.'

The latter recognition was uttered with just enough of embarrassment to imply a doubt of its reception; for Mr. Fagin and his young friend had not met, since she had interfered in behalf of Oliver. All doubts upon the subject, if he had any, were speedily removed by the young lady's behaviour. She took her feet off the fender, pushed back her chair, and bade Fagin draw up his, without saying more about it: for it was a cold night, and no mistake.

'It *is* cold, Nancy dear,' said the Jew, as he warmed his skinny hands over the fire. 'It seems to go right through one,' added the old man, touching his side.

'It must be a piercer, if it finds its way through *your* heart,' said Mr. Sikes. 'Give him something to drink, Nancy. Burn my body, make haste! It's enough to turn a man ill, to see his lean old carcase shivering in that way, like a ugly ghost just rose from the grave.'

Nancy quickly brought a bottle from a cupboard, in which there were many: which, to judge from the diversity of their appearance, were filled with several kinds of liquids. Sikes, pouring out a glass of brandy, bade the Jew drink it off.

'Quite enough, quite, thankye, Bill,' replied the Jew, putting down the glass, after just setting his lips to it.

'What! You're afraid of our getting the better of you, are you?' inquired Sikes, fixing his eyes on the Jew. 'Ugh!'

With a hoarse grunt of contempt, Mr. Sikes seized the glass, and threw the remainder of its contents into the ashes: as a preparatory ceremony to filling it again for himself: which he did at once.

The Jew glanced round the room, as his companion tossed down the second glassful; not in curiosity, for he had seen it often before; but in a restless and suspicious manner habitual to him. It was a meanly-furnished apartment, with nothing but the contents of the closet to induce the belief that its occupier was anything but a working man; and with no more suspicious articles displayed to view than two or three heavy bludgeons which stood in a corner, and a 'life-preserver' that hung over the chimney-piece.

'There,' said Sikes, smacking his lips. 'Now I'm ready.'

'For business?' inquired the Jew.

'For business,' replied Sikes; 'so say what you've got to say.'

'About the crib at Chertsey, Bill?' said the Jew, drawing his chair forward, and speaking in a very low voice.

'Yes. Wot about it?' inquired Sikes.

'Ah! you know what I mean, my dear,' said the Jew. 'He knows what I mean, Nancy, don't he?'

'No, he don't,' sneered Mr. Sikes. 'Or he won't, and that's the same thing. Speak out, and call things by their right names; don't sit there, winking and blinking, and talking to me in hints, as if you warn't the very first that thought about the robbery. Wot d'ye mean?'

'Hush, Bill, hush!' said the Jew who had in vain attempted to stop this burst of indignation; 'somebody will hear us, my dear. Somebody will hear us.'

'Let 'em hear!' said Sikes; 'I don't care.' But as Mr. Sikes *did* care, on reflection, he dropped his voice as he said the words, and grew calmer.

'There, there,' said the Jew, coaxingly, 'It was only my caution, nothing more. Now, my dear, about that crib at Chertsey; when is it to be done, Bill, eh? When is it to be done? Such plate, my dear, such plate!' said the Jew: rubbing his hands, and elevating his eyebrows in a rapture of anticipation.

'Not at all,' replied Sikes coldly.

'Not to be done at all!' echoed the Jew, leaning back in his chair.

'No, not at all,' rejoined Sikes. 'At least it can't be a put-up job, as we expected.'

'Then it hasn't been properly gone about,' said the Jew, turning pale with anger. 'Don't tell me!'

'But I will tell you,' retorted Sikes. 'Who are you that's not to be told? I tell you that Toby Crackit has been hanging about the place for a fortnight, and he can't get one of the servants into a line.'

'Do you mean to tell me, Bill,' said the Jew: softening as the other grew heated: 'that neither of the two men in the house can be got over?'

'Yes, I do mean to tell you so,' replied Sikes. 'The old lady has had 'em these twenty year; and if you were to give 'em five hundred pound, they wouldn't be in it.'

'But do you mean to say, my dear,' remonstrated the Jew, 'that the women can't be got over?'

'Not a bit of it,' replied Sikes.

'Not by flash Toby Crackit?' said the Jew incredulously. 'Think what women, are, Bill.'

'No; not even by flash Toby Crackit,' replied Sikes. 'He says he's worn sham whiskers, and a canary waistcoat, the whole blessed time he's been loitering down there, and it's all of no use.'

'He should have tried mustachios and a pair of military trousers, my dear,' said the Jew.

'So he did,' rejoined Sikes, 'and they warn't of no more use than the other plant.'

The Jew looked blank at this information. After ruminating for some minutes with his chin sunk on his breast, he raised his head and said, with a deep sigh, that if flash Toby Crackit reported aright, he feared the game was up.

'And yet,' said the old man, dropping his hands on his knees, 'it's a sad thing, my dear, to lose so much when we had set our hearts upon it.'

'So it is,' said Mr. Sikes. 'Worse luck!'

A long silence ensued; during which the Jew was plunged in deep thought, with his face wrinkled into an expression of villainy perfectly demoniacal. Sikes eyed him furtively from time to time. Nancy, apparently fearful of irritating the house-breaker, sat with her eyes fixed upon the fire, as if she had been deaf to all that passed.

'Fagin,' said Sikes, abruptly breaking the stillness that prevailed; 'is it worth fifty shiners extra, if it's safely done from the outside?'

'Yes,' said the Jew, as suddenly rousing himself.

'Is it a bargain?' inquired Sikes.

'Yes, my dear, yes,' rejoined the Jew; his eyes glistening, and every muscle in his face working, with the excitement that the inquiry had awakened.

'Then,' said Sikes, thrusting aside the Jew's hand, with some disdain, 'let it come off as soon as you like. Toby and me were over the garden-wall the night afore last, sounding the panels of the door and shutters. The crib's barred up at night like a jail; but there's one part we can crack, safe and softly.'

'Which is that, Bill?' asked the Jew, eagerly.

'Why,' whispered Sikes, 'as you cross the lawn—'

'Yes?' said the Jew, bending his head forward, with his eyes almost starting out of it.

'Umph!' cried Sikes, stopping short, as the girl, scarcely moving her head, looked suddenly round, and pointed for an instant to the Jew's face. 'Never mind which part it is. You can't do it without me, I know; but it's best to be on the safe side when one deals with you.'

'As you like, my dear, as you like,' replied the Jew. 'Is there no help wanted, but yours and Toby's?'

'None,' said Sikes. ''Cept a centre-bit and a boy. The first we've both got; the second you must find us.'

'A boy!' exclaimed the Jew. 'Oh! then it's a panel, eh?'

'Never mind wot it is!' replied Sikes. 'I want a boy, and he mustn't be a big 'un. Lord!' said Mr. Sikes, reflectively, 'if I'd only got that young boy of Ned, the chimbley-sweeper's! He kept him small on purpose, and let him out by the job. But the father gets lagged; and then the Juvenile Delinquent Society comes, and takes the boy away from a trade where he was earning money, teaches him to read and write, and in time makes a 'prentice of him. And so they go on,' said Mr. Sikes, his wrath rising with the recollection of his wrongs, 'so they go on; and, if they'd got money enough (which it's a Providence they haven't), we shouldn't have half-a-dozen boys left in the whole trade, in a year or two.'

'No more we should,' acquiesced the Jew, who had been considering during this speech, and had only caught the last sentence. 'Bill!'

'What now?' inquired Sikes.

The Jew nodded his head towards Nancy, who was still gazing at the fire; and intimated, by a sign, that he would have her told to leave the room. Sikes shrugged his shoulders impatiently, as if he thought the precaution unnecessary; but complied, nevertheless, by requesting Miss Nancy to fetch him a jug of beer.

'You don't want any beer,' said Nancy, folding her arms, and retaining her seat very composedly.

'I tell you I do!' replied Sikes.

'Nonsense,' rejoined the girl coolly. 'Go on, Fagin. I know what he's going to say, Bill; he needn't mind me.'

The Jew still hesitated. Sikes looked from one to the other in some surprise.

'Why, you don't mind the old girl, do you, Fagin?' he asked at length. 'You've known her long enough to trust her, or the Devil's in it. She ain't one to blab. Are you, Nancy?'

'*I* should think not!' replied the young lady: drawing her chair up to the table, and putting her elbows upon it.

'No, no, my dear, I know you're not,' said the Jew; 'but—' and again the old man paused.

'But wot?' inquired Sikes.

'I didn't know whether she mightn't p'r'aps be out of sorts, you know, my dear, as she was the other night,' replied the Jew.

At this confession, Miss Nancy burst into a loud laugh; and, swallowing a glass of brandy, shook her head with an air of defiance, and burst into sundry exclamations of 'Keep the game a-going!' 'Never say die!' and the like. These seemed to have the effect of re-assuring both gentlemen; for the Jew nodded his head with a satisfied air, and resumed his seat; as did Mr. Sikes likewise.

'Now, Fagin,' said Nancy with a laugh. 'Tell Bill at once, about Oliver!'

'Ha! you're a clever one, my dear; the sharpest girl I ever saw!' said the Jew, patting her on the neck. 'It *was* about Oliver I was going to speak, sure enough. Ha! ha! ha!'

'What about him?' demanded Sikes.

'He's the boy for you, my dear,' replied the Jew in a hoarse whisper; laying his finger on the side of his nose, and grinning frightfully.

'He!' exclaimed Sikes.

'Have him, Bill!' said Nancy. 'I would, if I was in your place. He mayn't be so much up, as any of the others; but that's not what you want, if he's only to open a door for you. Depend upon it he's a safe one, Bill.'

'I know he is,' rejoined Fagin. 'He's been in good training these last few weeks, and it's time he began to work for his bread. Besides, the others are all too big.'

'Well, he is just the size I want,' said Mr. Sikes, ruminating.

'And will do everything you want, Bill, my dear,' interposed the Jew; 'he can't help himself. That is, if you frighten him enough.'

'Frighten him!' echoed Sikes. 'It'll be no sham frightening, mind you. If there's anything queer about him when we once get into work; in for a penny, in for a pound. You won't see him alive again, Fagin. Think of that, before you send him. Mark my words!' said the robber, poising a crowbar, which he had drawn from under the bedstead.

'I've thought of it all,' said the Jew with energy. 'I've—I've had my eye upon him, my dears, close—close. Once let him feel that he is one of us; once fill his mind with the idea that he has been a thief; and he's ours! Ours for his life. Oho! It couldn't have come about better!' The old man crossed his arms upon his breast; and, drawing his head and shoulders into a heap, literally hugged himself for joy.

'Ours!' said Sikes. 'Yours, you mean.'

'Perhaps I do, my dear,' said the Jew, with a shrill chuckle. 'Mine, if you like, Bill.'

'And wot,' said Sikes, scowling fiercely on his agreeable friend, 'wot makes you take so much pains about one chalk-faced kid, when you know there are fifty boys snoozing about Common Garden every night, as you might pick and choose from?'

'Because they're of no use to me, my dear,' replied the Jew, with some confusion, 'not worth the taking. Their looks convict 'em when they get into trouble, and I lose 'em all. With this boy, properly managed, my dears, I could do what I couldn't with twenty of them. Besides,' said the Jew, recovering his self-possession, 'he has us now if he could only give us legbail again; and he *must* be in the same boat with us. Never mind how he came there; it's quite enough for my power over him that he was in a robbery; that's all I want. Now, how much better this is, than being obliged to put the poor leetle boy out of the way—which would be dangerous, and we should lose by it besides.'

'When is it to be done?' asked Nancy, stopping some turbulent exclamation on the part of Mr. Sikes, expressive of the disgust with which he received Fagin's affectation of humanity.

'Ah, to be sure,' said the Jew; 'when is it to be done, Bill?'

'I planned with Toby, the night arter to-morrow,' rejoined Sikes in a surly voice, 'if he heerd nothing from me to the contrairy.'

'Good,' said the Jew; 'there's no moon.'

'No,' rejoined Sikes.

'It's all arranged about bringing off the swag, is it?' asked the Jew.

Sikes nodded.

'And about—'

'Oh, ah, it's all planned,' rejoined Sikes, interrupting him. 'Never mind particulars. You'd better bring the boy here tomorrow night. I shall get off the stones an hour arter daybreak. Then you hold your tongue, and keep the melting-pot ready, and that's all you'll have to do.

After some discussion, in which all three took an active part, it was decided that Nancy should repair to the Jew's next evening when the night had set in, and bring Oliver away with her; Fagin craftily observing, that, if he evinced any disinclination to the task, he would be more willing to accompany the girl who had so recently interfered in his behalf, than anybody else. It was also solemnly arranged that poor Oliver should, for the purposes of the contemplated expedition, be unreservedly consigned to the care and custody of Mr. William Sikes; and further, that the said Sikes should deal with him as he thought fit; and should not be held responsible by the Jew for any mischance or evil that might befall him, or any punishment with which it might be necessary to visit him: it being understood that, to render the compact in this respect binding, any representations made by Mr. Sikes on his return should be required to be confirmed and corroborated, in all important particulars, by the testimony of flash Toby Crackit.

These preliminaries adjusted, Mr. Sikes proceeded to drink brandy at a furious rate, and to flourish the crowbar in an alarming manner; yelling forth, at the same time, most unmusical snatches of song, mingled with wild execrations. At length, in a fit of professional enthusiasm, he insisted upon producing his box of housebreaking tools: which he had no sooner stumbled in with, and opened for the purpose of explaining the nature and properties of the various implements it contained, and the peculiar beauties of their construction, than he fell over the box upon the floor, and went to sleep where he fell.

'Good night, Nancy,' said the Jew, muffling himself up as before.

'Good night.'

Their eyes met, and the Jew scrutinised her narrowly. There was no flinching about the girl. She was as true and earnest in the matter as Toby Crackit himself could be.

The Jew again bade her good night, and bestowing a sly kick upon the prostrate form of Mr. Sikes while her back was turned, groped down stairs.

'Always the way!' muttered the Jew to himself as he turned homeward. 'The worst of these women is, that a very little thing serves to call up some long-forgotten feeling; and the best of them is, that it never lasts. Ha! ha! The man against the child, for a bag of gold!'

Beguiling the time with these pleasant reflections, Mr. Fagin wended his way, through mud and mire, to his gloomy abode: where the Dodger was sitting up, impatiently awaiting his return.

'Is Oliver a-bed? I want to speak to him,' was his first remark as they descended the stairs.

'Hours ago,' replied the Dodger, throwing open a door. 'Here he is!'

The boy was lying, fast asleep, on a rude bed upon the floor; so pale with anxiety, and sadness, and the closeness of his prison, that he looked like death; not death as it shows in shroud and coffin, but in the guise it wears when life has just departed; when a young and gentle spirit has, but an instant, fled to Heaven, and the gross air of the world has not had time to breathe upon the changing dust it hallowed.

'Not now,' said the Jew, turning softly away. 'To-morrow. To-morrow.'

CHAPTER 20

Wherein Oliver is delivered over to
Mr. William Sikes

When Oliver awoke in the morning, he was a good deal surprised to find that a new pair of shoes, with strong thick soles, had been placed at his bedside; and that his old shoes had been removed. At first, he was pleased with the discovery: hoping that it might be the forerunner of his release; but such thoughts were quickly dispelled, on his sitting down to breakfast along with the Jew, who told him, in a tone and manner which increased his alarm, that he was to be taken to the residence of Bill Sikes that night.

'To—to—stop there, sir?' asked Oliver, anxiously.

'No, no, my dear. Not to stop there,' replied the Jew. 'We shouldn't like to lose you. Don't be afraid, Oliver, you shall come back to us again. Ha! ha! ha! We won't be so cruel as to send you away, my dear. Oh no, no!'

The old man, who was stooping over the fire toasting a piece of bread, looked round as he bantered Oliver thus; and chuckled as if to show that he knew he would still be very glad to get away if he could.

'I suppose,' said the Jew, fixing his eyes on Oliver, 'you want to know what you're going to Bill's for—eh, my dear?'

Oliver coloured, involuntarily, to find that the old thief had been reading his thoughts; but boldly said, Yes, he did want to know.

'Why, do you think?' inquired Fagin, parrying the question.

'Indeed I don't know, sir,' replied Oliver.

'Bah!' said the Jew, turning away with a disappointed countenance from a close perusal of the boy's face. 'Wait till Bill tells you, then.'

The Jew seemed much vexed by Oliver's not expressing any greater curiosity on the subject; but the truth is, that, although Oliver felt very anxious, he was too much confused by the earnest cunning of Fagin's looks, and his own speculations, to make any further inquiries just then. He had no other opportunity; for the Jew remained very surly and silent till night: when he prepared to go abroad.

'You may burn a candle,' said the Jew, putting one upon the table. 'And here's a book for you to read, till they come to fetch you. Good night!'

'Good night!' replied Oliver, softly.

The Jew walked to the door: looking over his shoulder at the boy as he went. Suddenly stopping, he called him by his name.

Oliver looked up; the Jew, pointing to the candle, motioned him to light it. He did so; and, as he placed the candlestick upon the table, saw that the Jew was gazing fixedly at him, with lowering and contracted brows, from the dark end of the room.

'Take heed, Oliver! take heed!' said the old man, shaking his right hand before him in a warning manner. 'He's a rough man, and thinks nothing of blood when his own is up. Whatever falls out, say nothing; and do what he bids you. Mind!' Placing a strong emphasis on the last word, he suffered his features gradually to resolve themselves into a ghastly grin, and, nodding his head, left the room.

Oliver leaned his head upon his hand when the old man disappeared, and pondered, with a trembling heart, on the words he had just heard. The more he thought of the Jew's admonition, the more he was at a loss to divine its real purpose and meaning. He could think of no bad object to be attained by sending him to Sikes, which would not be equally well answered by his remaining with Fagin; and after meditating for a long time, concluded that he had been selected to perform some ordinary menial offices for the house-breaker, until another boy, better suited for his purpose, could be engaged. He was too well accustomed to suffering, and had suffered too much where he was, to bewail the prospect of change very severely. He remained lost in thought for some minutes; and then, with a heavy sigh, snuffed the candle, and taking up the book which the Jew had left with him, began to read.

He turned over the leaves. Carelessly at first; but, lighting on a passage which attracted his attention, he soon became intent upon the volume. It was a history of the lives and trials of great criminals; and the pages were soiled and thumbed with use. Here, he read of dreadful crimes that made the blood run cold; of secret murders that had been committed by the lonely wayside; of bodies hidden from the eye of man in deep pits and wells; which would not keep them down, deep as they were, but had yielded them up at last, after many years, and so maddened the murderers with their sight, that in their horror they had confessed their guilt, and yelled for the gibbet to end their agony. Here, too, he read of men who, lying in their beds at dead of night, had been tempted (so they said) and led on, by their own bad thoughts, to such dreadful bloodshed as it made the flesh creep, and the limbs quail, to think of. The terrible descriptions were so real and vivid, that the sallow pages seemed to turn red with gore; and the words upon them, to be sounded in his ears, as if they were whispered, in hollow murmurs, by the spirits of the dead.

In a paroxysm of fear, the boy closed the book, and thrust it from him. Then, falling upon his knees, he prayed Heaven to spare him from such deeds; and rather to will that he should die at once, than be reserved for crimes, so fearful and appalling. By degrees, he grew more calm, and besought, in a low and broken voice, that he might be rescued from his present dangers; and that if any aid were to be raised up for a poor outcast boy who had never known the love of friends or kindred, it might come to him now, when, desolate and deserted, he stood alone in the midst of wickedness and guilt.

He had concluded his prayer, but still remained with his head buried in his hands, when a rustling noise aroused him.

'What's that!' he cried, starting up, and catching sight of a figure standing by the door. 'Who's there?'

'Me. Only me,' replied a tremulous voice.

Oliver raised the candle above his head: and looked towards the door. It was Nancy.

'Put down the light,' said the girl, turning away her head. 'It hurts my eyes.'

Oliver saw that she was very pale, and gently inquired if she were ill. The girl threw herself into a chair, with her back towards him: and wrung her hands; but made no reply.

'God forgive me!' she cried after a while. 'I never thought of this.'

'Has anything happened?' asked Oliver. 'Can I help you? I will if I can. I will, indeed.'

She rocked herself to and fro; caught her throat; and, uttering a gurgling sound, gasped for breath.

'Nancy!' cried Oliver, 'What is it?'

The girl beat her hands upon her knees, and her feet upon the ground; and, suddenly stopping, drew her shawl close round her: and shivered with cold.

Oliver stirred the fire. Drawing her chair close to it, she sat there, for a little time, without speaking; but at length she raised her head, and looked round.

'I don't know what comes over me sometimes,' said she, affecting to busy herself in arranging her dress; 'it's this damp, dirty room. I think. Now, Nolly, dear, are you ready?'

'Am I to go with you?' asked Oliver.

'Yes; I have come from Bill,' replied the girl. 'You are to go with me.'

'What for?' asked Oliver, recoiling.

'What for?' echoed the girl, raising her eyes, and averting them again, the moment they encountered the boy's face. 'Oh! For no harm.'

'I don't believe it,' said Oliver: who had watched her closely.

'Have it your own way,' rejoined the girl, affecting to laugh. 'For no good, then.'

Oliver could see that he had some power over the girl's better feelings, and, for an instant, thought of appealing to her compassion for his helpless state. But, then, the thought darted across his mind that it was barely eleven o'clock; and that many people were still in the streets: of whom surely some might be found to give credence to his tale. As the reflection occurred to him, he stepped forward: and said, somewhat hastily, that he was ready.

Neither his brief consideration, nor its purport, was lost on his companion. She eyed him narrowly, while he spoke; and cast upon him a look of intelligence which sufficiently showed that she guessed what had been passing in his thoughts.

'Hush!' said the girl, stooping over him, and pointing to the door as she looked cautiously round. 'You can't help yourself. I have tried hard for you, but all to no purpose. You are hedged round and round. If ever you are to get loose from here, this is not the time.'

Struck by the energy of her manner, Oliver looked up in her face with great surprise. She seemed to speak the truth; her countenance was white and agitated; and she trembled with very earnestness.

'I have saved you from being ill-used once, and I will again, and I do now,' continued the girl aloud; 'for those who would have fetched you, if I had not, would have been far more rough than me. I have promised for your being quiet and silent; if you are not, you will only do harm to yourself and me too, and perhaps be my death. See here! I have borne all this for you already, as true as God sees me show it.'

She pointed, hastily, to some livid bruises on her neck and arms; and continued, with great rapidity:

'Remember this! And don't let me suffer more for you, just now. If I could help you, I would; but I have not the power. They don't mean to harm you; whatever they make you do, is no fault of yours. Hush! Every word from you is a blow for me. Give me your hand. Make haste! Your hand!'

She caught the hand which Oliver instinctively placed in hers, and, blowing out the light, drew him after her up the stairs. The door was opened, quickly, by some one shrouded in the darkness, and was as quickly closed, when they had passed out. A hackney-cabriolet was in waiting; with the same vehemence which she had exhibited in addressing Oliver, the girl pulled him in with her, and drew the curtains close. The driver wanted no directions, but lashed his horse into full speed, without the delay of an instant.

The girl still held Oliver fast by the hand, and continued to pour into his ear, the warnings and assurances she had already imparted. All was so quick and hurried, that he had scarcely time to recollect where he was, or how he came there, when the carriage stopped at the house to which the Jew's steps had been directed on the previous evening.

For one brief moment, Oliver cast a hurried glance along the empty street, and a cry for help hung upon his lips. But the girl's voice was in his ear, beseeching him in such tones of agony to remember her, that he had not the heart to utter it. While he hesitated, the opportunity was gone; he was already in the house, and the door was shut.

'This way,' said the girl, releasing her hold for the first time. 'Bill!'

'Hallo!' replied Sikes: appearing at the head of the stairs, with a candle. 'Oh! That's the time of day. Come on!'

This was a very strong expression of approbation, an uncommonly hearty welcome, from a person of Mr. Sikes' temperament. Nancy, appearing much gratified thereby, saluted him cordially.

'Bull's-eye's gone home with Tom,' observed Sikes, as he lighted them up. 'He'd have been in the way.'

'That's right,' rejoined Nancy.

'So you've got the kid,' said Sikes, when they had all reached the room: closing the door as he spoke.

'Yes, here he is,' replied Nancy.

'Did he come quiet?' inquired Sikes.

'Like a lamb,' rejoined Nancy.

'I'm glad to hear it,' said Sikes, looking grimly at Oliver; 'for the sake of his young carcase: as would otherways have suffered for it. Come here, young un; and let me read you a lectur', which is as well got over at once.'

Thus addressing his new pupil, Mr. Sikes pulled off Oliver's cap and threw it into a corner; and then, taking him by the shoulder, sat himself down by the table, and stood the boy in front of him.

'Now, first: do you know wot this is?' inquired Sikes, taking up a pocket-pistol which lay on the table.

Oliver replied in the affirmative.

'Well, then, look here,' continued Sikes. 'This is powder; that 'ere's a bullet; and this is a little bit of a old hat for waddin.'

Oliver murmured his comprehension of the different bodies referred to; and Mr. Sikes proceeded to load the pistol, with great nicety and deliberation.

'Now it's loaded,' said Mr. Sikes, when he had finished.

'Yes, I see it is, sir,' replied Oliver.

'Well,' said the robber, grasping Oliver's wrist, and putting the barrel so close to his temple that they touched; at which moment the boy could not repress a start; 'if you speak a word when you're out o' doors with me, except when I speak to you, that loading will be in your head without notice. So, if you *do* make up your mind to speak without leave, say your prayers first.'

Having bestowed a scowl upon the object of this warning, to increase its effect, Mr. Sikes continued.

'As near as I know, there isn't anybody as would be asking very partickler arter you, if you *was* disposed of; so I needn't take this devil-and-all of trouble to explain matters to you, if it warn't for your own good. D'ye hear me?'

'The short and the long of what you mean,' said Nancy: speaking very emphatically, and slightly frowning at Oliver as if to bespeak his serious attention to her words: 'is, that if you're crossed by him in this job you have on hand, you'll prevent his ever telling tales afterwards, by shooting him through the head, and will take your chance of swinging for it, as you do for a great many other things in the way of business, every month of your life.'

'That's it!' observed Mr. Sikes, approvingly; 'women can always put things in fewest words.—Except when it's blowing up; and then they lengthens it out. And now that he's thoroughly up to it, let's have some supper, and get a snooze before starting.'

In pursuance of this request, Nancy quickly laid the cloth; disappearing for a few minutes, she presently returned with a pot of porter and a dish of sheep's heads: which gave occasion to several pleasant witticisms on the part of Mr. Sikes, founded upon the singular coincidence of 'jemmies' being a cant name, common to them, and also to an ingenious implement much used in his profession. Indeed, the worthy gentleman, stimulated perhaps by the immediate prospect of being on active service, was in great spirits and good humour; in proof whereof, it may be here remarked, that he humorously drank all the beer at a draught, and did not utter, on a rough calculation, more than four-score oaths during the whole progress of the meal.

Supper being ended—it may be easily conceived that Oliver had no great appetite for it—Mr. Sikes disposed of a couple of glasses of spirits and water, and threw himself on the bed; ordering Nancy, with many imprecations in case of failure, to call him at five precisely. Oliver stretched himself in his clothes, by command of the same authority, on a mattress upon the floor; and the girl, mending the fire, sat before it, in readiness to rouse them at the appointed time.

For a long time Oliver lay awake, thinking it not impossible that Nancy might seek that opportunity of whispering some further advice; but the girl sat brooding over the fire, without moving, save now and then to trim the light. Weary with watching and anxiety, he at length fell asleep.

When he awoke, the table was covered with tea-things, and Sikes was thrusting various articles into the pockets of his great-coat, which hung over the back of a chair. Nancy was busily engaged in preparing breakfast. It was not yet daylight; for the candle was still burning, and it was quite dark outside. A sharp rain, too, was beating against the window-panes; and the sky looked black and cloudy.

'Now, then!' growled Sikes, as Oliver started up; 'half-past five! Look sharp, or you'll get no breakfast; for it's late as it is.'

Oliver was not long in making his toilet; having taken some breakfast, he replied to a surly inquiry from Sikes, by saying that he was quite ready.

Nancy, scarcely looking at the boy, threw him a handkerchief to tie round his throat; Sikes gave him a large rough cape to button over his shoulders. Thus attired, he gave his hand to the robber, who, merely pausing to show him with a menacing gesture, that he had that same pistol in a side-pocket of his great-coat, clasped it firmly in his, and, exchanging a farewell with Nancy, led him away.

Oliver turned, for an instant, when they reached the door, in the hope of meeting a look from the girl. But she had resumed her old seat in front of the fire, and sat, perfectly motionless, before it.

CHAPTER 21

The Expedition

It was a cheerless morning when they got into the street; blowing and raining hard; and the clouds looking dull and stormy. The night had been very wet: large pools of water had collected in the road: and the kennels were overflowing. There was a faint glimmering of the coming day in the sky; but it rather aggravated than relieved the gloom of the scene: the sombre light only serving to pale that which the street lamps afforded, without shedding any warmer or brighter tints upon the wet house-tops, and dreary streets. There appeared to be nobody stirring in that quarter of the town; the windows of the houses were all closely shut; and the streets through which they passed, were noiseless and empty.

By the time they had turned into the Bethnal Green Road, the day had fairly begun to break. Many of the lamps were already extinguished; a few country waggons were slowly toiling on, towards London; now and then, a stage-coach, covered with mud, rattled briskly by: the driver bestowing, as he passed, an admonitory lash upon the heavy waggoner who, by keeping on the wrong side of the road, had endangered his arriving at the office, a quarter of a minute after his time. The public-houses, with gas-lights burning inside, were already open. By degrees, other shops began to be unclosed, and a few scattered people were met with. Then, came straggling groups of labourers going to their work; then, men and women with fish-baskets on their heads; donkey-carts laden with vegetables; chaise-carts filled with live-stock or whole carcasses of meat; milk-women with pails; an unbroken concourse of people, trudging out with various supplies to the eastern suburbs of the town. As they approached the City, the noise and traffic gradually increased; when they threaded the streets between Shoreditch and Smithfield, it had swelled into a roar of sound and bustle. It was as light as it was likely to be, till night came on again, and the busy morning of half the London population had begun.

Turning down Sun Street and Crown Street, and crossing Finsbury Square, Mr. Sikes struck, by way of Chiswell Street, into Barbican: thence into Long Lane, and so into Smithfield; from which latter place arose a tumult of discordant sounds that filled Oliver Twist with amazement.

It was market-morning. The ground was covered, nearly ankle-deep, with filth and mire; a thick steam, perpetually rising from the reeking bodies of the cattle, and mingling with the fog, which seemed to rest upon the chimney-tops, hung heavily above. All the pens in the centre of the large area, and as many temporary pens as could be crowded into the vacant space, were filled with sheep; tied up to posts by the gutter side were long lines of beasts and oxen, three or four deep. Countrymen, butchers, drovers, hawkers, boys, thieves, idlers, and vagabonds of every low grade, were mingled together in a mass; the whistling of drovers, the barking of dogs, the bellowing and plunging of oxen, the bleating of sheep, the grunting and squeaking of pigs, the cries of hawkers, the shouts, oaths, and quar-relling on all sides; the ringing of bells and roar of voices, that issued from every public-house; the crowding, pushing, driving, beating, whooping, and yelling; the hideous and discordant din that resounded from every corner of the market; and the unwashed, unshaven, squalid, and dirty figures constantly running to and fro, and bursting in and out of the throng; rendered it a stunning and bewildering scene, which quite confounded the senses.

Mr. Sikes, dragging Oliver after him, elbowed his way through the thickest of the crowd, and bestowed very little attention on the numerous sights and sounds, which so astonished the boy. He nodded, twice or thrice, to a passing friend; and, resisting as many invitations to take a morning dram, pressed steadily onward, until they were clear of the turmoil, and had made their way through Hosier Lane into Holborn.

'Now, young un!' said Sikes, looking up at the clock of St. Andrew's Church, 'hard upon seven! you must step out. Come, don't lag behind already, Lazy-legs!'

Mr. Sikes accompanied this speech with a jerk at his little companion's wrist; Oliver, quickening his pace into a kind of trot, between a fast walk and a run, kept up with the rapid strides of the housebreaker as well as he could.

They held their course at this rate, until they had passed Hyde Park corner, and were on their way to Kensington: when Sikes relaxed his pace, until an empty cart, which was at some little distance behind, came up. Seeing 'Hounslow' written on it, he asked the driver with as much civility as he could assume, if he would give them a lift as far as Isleworth.

'Jump up,' said the man. 'Is that your boy?'

'Yes; he's my boy,' replied Sikes, looking hard at Oliver, and putting his hand abstractedly into the pocket where the pistol was.

'Your father walks rather too quick for you, don't he, my man?' inquired the driver: seeing that Oliver was out of breath.

'Not a bit of it,' replied Sikes, interposing. 'He's used to it. Here, take hold of my hand, Ned. In with you!'

Thus addressing Oliver, he helped him into the cart; and the driver, pointing to a heap of sacks, told him to lie down there, and rest himself.

As they passed the different mile-stones, Oliver wondered, more and more, where his companion meant to take him. Kensington, Hammersmith, Chiswick, Kew Bridge, Brentford, were all passed; and yet they went on as steadily as if they had only just begun their journey. At length, they came to a public-house called the Coach and Horses: a little way beyond which, another road appeared to turn off. And here, the cart stopped.

Sikes dismounted with great precipitation, holding Oliver by the hand all the while; and lifting him down directly, bestowed a furious look upon him, and rapped the side-pocket with his fist, in a significant manner.

'Good-bye, boy,' said the man.

'He's sulky,' replied Sikes, giving him a shake; 'he's sulky. A young dog! Don't mind him.'

'Not I!' rejoined the other, getting into his cart. 'It's a fine day, after all.' And he drove away.

Sikes waited until he had fairly gone; and then, telling Oliver he might look about him if he wanted, once again led him onward on his journey.

They turned round to the left, a short way past the public-house; and then, taking a right-hand road, walked on for a long time: passing many large gardens and gentlemen's houses on both sides of the way, and stopping for nothing but a little beer, until they reached a town. Here against the wall of a house, Oliver saw written up in pretty large letters, 'Hampton.' They lingered about, in the fields, for some hours. At length, they came back into the town; and, turning into an old public-house with a defaced sign-board, ordered some dinner by the kitchen fire.

The kitchen was an old, low-roofed room; with a great beam across the middle of the ceiling, and benches, with high backs to them, by the fire; on which were seated several rough men in smock-frocks, drinking and smoking. They took no notice of Oliver; and very little of Sikes; and, as Sikes took very little notice of them, he and his young comrade sat in a corner by themselves, without being much troubled by their company.

They had some cold meat for dinner, and sat so long after it, while Mr. Sikes indulged himself with three or four pipes, that Oliver began to feel quite certain they were not going any further. Being much tired with the walk, and getting up so early, he dozed a little at first; then, quite overpowered by fatigue and the fumes of the tobacco, fell asleep.

It was quite dark when he was awakened by a push from Sikes.

Rousing himself sufficiently to sit up and look about him, he found that worthy in close fellowship and communication with a labouring man, over a pint of ale.

'So, you're going on to Lower Halliford, are you?' inquired Sikes.

'Yes, I am,' replied the man, who seemed a little the worse— or better, as the case might be—for drinking; 'and not slow about it neither. My horse hasn't got a load behind him going back, as he had coming up in the mornin'; and he won't be long a-doing of it. Here's luck to him! Ecod! he's a good un!'

'Gould you give my boy and me a lift as far as there?' demanded Sikes, pushing the ale towards his new friend.

'If you're going directly, I can,' replied the man, looking out of the pot. 'Are you going to Halliford?'

'Going on to Shepperton,' replied Sikes.

'I'm your man, as far as I go,' replied the other. 'Is all paid, Becky?'

'Yes, the other gentleman's paid,' replied the girl.

'I say!' said the man, with tipsy gravity; 'that won't do, you know.'

'Why not?' rejoined Sikes. 'You're a-going to accommodate us, and wot's to prevent my standing treat for a pint or so, in return?'

The stranger reflected upon this argument, with a very profound face; having done so, he seized Sikes by the hand: and declared he was a real good fellow. To which Mr. Sikes replied, he was joking; as, if he had been sober, there would have been strong reason to suppose he was.

After the exchange of a few more compliments, they bade the company good night, and went out; the girl gathering up the pots and glasses as they did so, and lounging out to the door, with her hands full, to see the party start.

The horse, whose health had been drunk in his absence, was standing outside: ready harnessed to the cart. Oliver and Sikes got in without any further ceremony; and the man to whom he belonged, having lingered for a minute or two 'to bear him up,' and to defy the hostler and the world to produce his equal, mounted also. Then, the hostler was told to give the horse his head: and, his head being given him, he made a very unpleasant use of it: tossing it into the air with great disdain, and running into the parlour windows over the way; after performing those feats, and supporting himself for a short time on his hind legs, he started off at great speed, and rattled out of the town right gallantly.

The night was very dark. A damp mist rose from the river, and the marshy ground about; and spread itself over the dreary fields. It was piercing cold, too; all was gloomy and black. Not a word was spoken; for the driver had grown sleepy; and Sikes was in no mood to lead him into conversation. Oliver sat huddled together, in a corner of the cart; bewildered with alarm and apprehension; and figuring strange objects in the gaunt trees, whose branches waved grimly to and fro, as if in some fantastic joy at the desolation of the scene.

As they passed Sunbury Church, the clock struck seven. There was a light in the ferry-house window opposite: which streamed across the road, and threw into more sombre shadow a dark yew-tree with graves beneath it. There was a dull sound of falling water not far off; and the leaves of the old tree stirred gently in the night wind. It seemed like quiet music for the repose of the dead.

Sunbury was passed through, and they came again into the lonely road. Two or three miles more, and the cart stopped. Sikes alighted, took Oliver by the hand, and they once again walked on.

They turned into no house at Shepperton, as the weary boy had expected; but still kept walking on, in mud and darkness, through gloomy lanes and over cold open wastes, until they came within sight of the lights of a town at no great distance. On looking intently forward, Oliver saw that the water was just below them, and that they were coming to the foot of a bridge.

Sikes kept straight on, until they were close upon the bridge; then turned suddenly down a bank upon the left.

'The water!' thought Oliver, turning sick with fear. 'He has brought me to this lonely place to murder me!'

He was about to throw himself on the ground, and make one struggle for his young life, when he saw that they stood before a solitary house: all ruinous and decayed. There was a window on each side of the dilapidated entrance; and one story above; but no light was visible. The house was dark, dismantled: and, to all appearance, uninhabited.

Sikes, with Oliver's hand still in his, softly approached the low porch, and raised the latch. The door yielded to the pressure, and they passed in together.

CHAPTER 22

The Burglary

'Hallo!' cried a loud, hoarse voice, as soon as they set foot in the passage.

'Don't make such a row,' said Sikes, bolting the door. 'Show a glim, Toby.'

'Aha! my pal!' cried the same voice. 'A glim, Barney, a glim! Show the gentleman in, Barney; wake up first, if convenient.'

The speaker appeared to throw a boot-jack, or some such article, at the person he addressed, to rouse him from his slumbers: for the noise of a wooden body, falling violently, was heard; and then an indistinct muttering, as of a man between asleep and awake.

'Do you hear?' cried the same voice. 'There's Bill Sikes in the passage with nobody to do the civil to him; and you sleeping there, as if you took laudanum with your meals, and nothing stronger. Are you any fresher now, or do you want the iron candlestick to wake you thoroughly?'

A pair of slipshod feet shuffled, hastily, across the bare floor of the room, as this interrogatory was put; and there issued, from a door on the right hand: first, a feeble candle: and next, the form of the same individual who has been heretofore described as labouring under the infirmity of speaking through his nose, and officiating as waiter at the public-house on Saffron Hill.

'Bister Sikes!' exclaimed Barney, with real or counterfeit joy; 'cub id, sir; cub id.'

'Here! you get on first,' said Sikes, putting Oliver in front of him. 'Quicker! or I shall tread upon your heels.'

Muttering a curse upon his tardiness, Sikes pushed Oliver before him; and they entered a low dark room with a smoky fire, two or three broken chairs, a table, and a very old couch: on which, with his legs much higher than his head, a man was reposing at full length, smoking a long clay pipe. He was dressed in a smartly-cut snuff-coloured coat, with large brass buttons; an orange neckerchief; a coarse, staring, shawl-pattern waistcoat; and drab breeches. Mr. Crackit (for he it was) had no very great quantity of hair, either upon his head or face; but what he had, was of a reddish dye, and tortured into long corkscrew curls, through which he occasionally thrust some very dirty fingers, ornamented with large common rings. He was a trifle above the middle size, and apparently rather weak in the legs; but this circumstance by no means detracted from his own admiration of his top-boots, which he contemplated, in their elevated situation, with lively satisfaction.

'Bill, my boy!' said this figure, turning his head towards the door, 'I'm glad to see you. I was almost afraid you'd given it up: in which case I should have made a personal wentur. Hallo!'

Uttering this exclamation in a tone of great surprise, as his eye rested on Oliver, Mr. Toby Crackit brought himself into a sitting posture, and demanded who that was.

'The boy. Only the boy!' replied Sikes, drawing a chair towards the fire.

'Wud of Bister Fagid's lads,' exclaimed Barney, with a grin.

'Fagin's, eh!' exclaimed Toby, looking at Oliver. 'Wot an inwalable boy that'll make, for the old ladies' pockets in chapels! His mug is a fortun' to him.'

'There—there's enough of that,' interposed Sikes, impatiently; and stooping over his recumbent friend, he whispered a few words in his ear: at which Mr. Crackit laughed immensely, and honoured Oliver with a long stare of astonishment.

'Now,' said Sikes, as he resumed his seat, 'if you'll give us something to eat and drink while we're waiting, you'll put some heart in us; or in me, at all events. Sit down by the fire, younker, and rest yourself; for you'll have to go out with us again to-night, though not very far off.'

Oliver looked at Sikes, in mute and timid wonder; and drawing a stool to the fire, sat with his aching head upon his hands, scarcely knowing where he was, or what was passing around him.

'Here,' said Toby, as the young Jew placed some fragments of food, and a bottle, upon the table, 'Success to the crack!' He rose to honour the toast; and, carefully depositing his empty pipe in a corner, advanced to the table, filled a glass with spirits, and drank off its contents. Mr. Sikes did the same.

'A drain for the boy,' said Toby, half-filling a wine glass. 'Down with it, innocence.'

'Indeed,' said Oliver, looking piteously up into the man's face; 'indeed, I—'

'Down with it!' echoed Toby. 'Do you think I don't know what's good for you? Tell him to drink it, Bill.'

'He had better!' said Sikes, clapping his hand upon his pocket. 'Burn my body, if he isn't more trouble than a whole family of Dodgers. Drink it, you perwerse imp; drink it!'

Frightened by the menacing gestures of the two men, Oliver hastily swallowed the contents of the glass, and immediately fell into a violent fit of coughing: which delighted Toby Crackit and Barney, and even drew a smile from the surly Mr. Sikes.

This done, and Sikes having satisfied his appetite (Oliver could eat nothing but a small crust of bread which they made him swallow), the two men laid themselves down on chairs for a short nap. Oliver retained his stool by the fire; Barney, wrapped in a blanket, stretched himself on the floor: close outside the fender.

They slept, or appeared to sleep, for some time; nobody stirring but Barney, who rose once or twice to throw coals upon the fire. Oliver fell into a heavy doze: imagining himself straying along the gloomy lanes, or wandering about the dark churchyard, or retracing some one or other of the scenes of the past day: when he was roused by Toby Crackit jumping up and declaring it was half-past one.

In an instant, the other two were on their legs, and all were actively engaged in busy preparation. Sikes and his companion enveloped their necks and chins in large dark shawls, and drew on their great-coats; Barney, opening a cupboard, brought forth several articles, which he hastily crammed into the pockets.

'Barkers for me, Barney,' said Toby Crackit.

'Here they are,' replied Barney, producing a pair of pistols. 'You loaded them yourself.'

'All right!' replied Toby, stowing them away. 'The persuaders?'

'I've got 'em,' replied Sikes.

'Crape, keys, centre-bits, darkies—nothing forgotten?' inquired Toby: fastening a small crowbar to a loop inside the skirt of his coat.

'All right,' rejoined his companion. 'Bring them bits of timber, Barney. That's the time of day.'

With these words, he took a thick stick from Barney's hands, who, having delivered another to Toby, busied himself in fastening on Oliver's cape.

'Now then!' said Sikes, holding out his hand.

Oliver: who was completely stupefied by the unwonted exercise, and the air, and the drink which had been forced upon him: put his hand mechanically into that which Sikes extended for the purpose.

'Take his other hand, Toby,' said Sikes. 'Look out, Barney.'

The man went to the door, and returned to announce that all was quiet. The two robbers issued forth with Oliver between them. Barney, having made all fast, rolled himself up as before, and was soon asleep again.

It was now intensely dark. The fog was much heavier than it had been in the early part of the night; and the atmosphere was so damp, that, although no rain fell, Oliver's hair and eyebrows, within a few minutes after leaving the house, had become stiff with the half-frozen moisture that was floating about. They crossed the bridge, and kept on towards the lights which he had seen before. They were at no great distance off; and, as they walked pretty briskly, they soon arrived at Chertsey.

'Slap through the town,' whispered Sikes; 'there'll be nobody in the way, to-night, to see us.'

Toby acquiesced; and they hurried through the main street of the little town, which at that late hour was wholly deserted. A dim light shone at intervals from some bed-room window; and the hoarse barking of dogs occasionally broke the silence of the night. But there was nobody abroad. They had cleared the town, as the church-bell struck two.

Quickening their pace, they turned up a road upon the left hand. After walking about a quarter of a mile, they stopped before a detached house surrounded by a wall: to the top of which, Toby Crackit, scarcely pausing to take breath, climbed in a twinkling.

'The boy next,' said Toby. 'Hoist him up; I'll catch hold of him.'

Before Oliver had time to look round, Sikes had caught him under the arms; and in three or four seconds he and Toby were lying on the grass on the other side. Sikes followed directly. And they stole cautiously towards the house.

And now, for the first time, Oliver, well-nigh mad with grief and terror, saw that housebreaking and robbery, if not murder, were the objects of the expedition. He clasped his hands together, and involuntarily uttered a subdued exclamation of horror. A mist came before his eyes; the cold sweat stood upon his ashy face; his limbs failed him; and he sank upon his knees.

'Get up!' murmured Sikes, trembling with rage, and drawing the pistol from his pocket; 'Get up, or I'll strew your brains upon the grass.'

'Oh! for God's sake let me go!' cried Oliver; 'let me run away and die in the fields. I will never come near London; never, never! Oh! pray have mercy on me, and do not make me steal. For the love of all the bright angels that rest in Heaven, have mercy upon me!'

The man to whom this appeal was made, swore a dreadful

oath, and had cocked the pistol, when Toby, striking it from his grasp, placed his hand upon the boy's mouth, and dragged him to the house.

'Hush!' cried the man; 'it won't answer here. Say another word, and I'll do your business myself with a crack on the head. That makes no noise, and is quite as certain, and more genteel. Here, Bill, wrench the shutter open. He's game enough now, I'll engage. I've seen older hands of his age took the same way, for a minute or two, on a cold night.'

Sikes, invoking terrific imprecations upon Fagin's head for sending Oliver on such an errand, plied the crowbar vigorously, but with little noise. After some delay, and some assistance from Toby, the shutter to which he had referred, swung open on its hinges.

It was a little lattice window, about five feet and a half above the ground, at the back of the house: which belonged to a scullery, or small brewing-place, at the end of the passage. The aperture was so small, that the inmates had probably not thought it worth while to defend it more securely; but it was large enough to admit a boy of Oliver's size, nevertheless. A very brief exercise of Mr. Sikes's art, sufficed to overcome the fastening of the lattice; and it soon stood wide open also.

'Now listen, you young limb,' whispered Sikes, drawing a dark lantern from his pocket, and throwing the glare full on Oliver's face; 'I'm a-going to put you through there. Take this light; go softly up the steps straight afore you, and along the little hall, to the street door; unfasten it, and let us in.'

'There's a bolt at the top, you won't be able to reach,' interposed Toby. 'Stand upon one of the hall chairs. There are three there, Bill, with a jolly large blue unicorn and gold pitchfork on 'em: which is the old lady's arms.'

'Keep quiet, can't you?' replied Sikes, with a threatening look. 'The room-door is open, is it?'

'Wide,' replied Toby, after peeping in to satisfy himself. 'The game of that is, that they always leave it open with a catch, so that the dog, who's got a bed in here, may walk up and down the passage when he feels wakeful. Ha! ha! Barney 'ticed him away to-night. So neat!'

Although Mr. Crackit spoke in a scarcely audible whisper, and laughed without noise, Sikes imperiously commanded him to be silent, and to get to work. Toby complied, by first producing his lantern, and placing it on the ground; then by planting himself firmly with his head against the wall beneath the window, and his hands upon his knees, so as to make a step of his back. This was no sooner done, than Sikes, mounting upon him, put Oliver gently through the window with his feet first; and, without leaving hold of his collar, planted him safely on the floor inside.

'Take this lantern,' said Sikes, looking into the room. 'You see the stairs afore you?'

Oliver, more dead than alive, gasped out, 'Yes.' Sikes, pointing to the street-door with the pistol-barrel, briefly advised him to take notice that he was within shot all the way; and that if he faltered, he would fall dead that instant.

'It's done in a minute,' said Sikes, in the same low whisper. 'Directly I leave go of you, do your work. Hark!'

'What's that?' whispered the other man.

They listened intently.

'Nothing,' said Sikes, releasing his hold of Oliver. 'Now!'

In the short time he had had to collect his senses, the boy had firmly resolved that, whether he died in the attempt or not, he would make one effort to dart up stairs from the hall, and alarm the family. Filled with this idea, he advanced at once, but stealthily.

'Come back!' suddenly cried Sikes aloud. 'Back! back!'

Scared by the sudden breaking of the dead stillness of the place, and by a loud cry which followed it, Oliver let his lantern fall, and knew not whether to advance or fly.

The cry was repeated—a light appeared—a vision of two terrified half-dressed men at the top of the stairs swam before his eyes—a flash—a loud noise—a smoke—a crash somewhere, but where he knew not,—and he staggered back.

Sikes had disappeared for an instant; but he was up again,

and had him by the collar before the smoke had cleared away. He fired his own pistol after the men, who were already retreating; and dragged the boy up.

'Clasp your arm tighter,' said Sikes, as he drew him through the window. 'Give me a shawl here. They've hit him. Quick! How the boy bleeds!'

Then came the loud ringing of a bell, mingled with the noise of fire-arms, and the shouts of men, and the sensation of being carried over uneven ground at a rapid pace. And then, the noises grew confused in the distance; and a cold deadly feeling crept over the boy's heart; and he saw or heard no more.

CHAPTER 23

Which contains the substance of a pleasant conversation between Mr. Bumble and a lady; and shows that even a beadle may be susceptible on some points

The night was bitter cold. The snow lay on the ground, frozen into a hard thick crust, so that only the heaps that had drifted into byways and corners were affected by the sharp wind that howled abroad: which, as if expending increased fury on such prey as it found, caught it savagely up in clouds, and, whirling it into a thousand misty eddies, scattered it in air. Bleak, dark, and piercing cold, it was a night for the well-housed and fed to draw round the bright fire and thank God they were at home; and for the homeless, starving wretch to lay him down and die. Many hunger-worn outcasts close their eyes in our bare streets, at such times, who, let their crimes have been what they may, can hardly open them in a more bitter world.

Such was the aspect of out-of-doors affairs, when Mrs. Corney, the matron of the workhouse to which our readers have been already introduced as the birthplace of Oliver Twist, sat herself down before a cheerful fire in her own little room, and glanced, with no small degree of complacency, at a small round table: on which stood a tray of corresponding size, furnished with all necessary materials for the most grateful meal that matrons enjoy. In fact, Mrs. Corney was about to solace herself with a cup of tea. As she glanced from the table to the fireplace, where the smallest of all possible kettles was singing a small song in a small voice, her inward satisfaction evidently increased,—so much so, indeed, that Mrs. Corney smiled.

'Well!' said the matron, leaning her elbow on the table, and looking reflectively at the fire; 'I'm sure we have all on us a great deal to be grateful for! A great deal, if we did but know it. Ah!'

Mrs. Corney shook her head mournfully, as if deploring the mental blindness of those paupers who did not know it; and thrusting a silver spoon (private property) into the inmost recesses of a two-ounce tin tea-caddy, proceeded to make the tea.

How slight a thing will disturb the equanimity of our frail minds! The black teapot, being very small and easily filled, ran over while Mrs. Corney was moralising; and the water slightly scalded Mrs. Corney's hand.

'Drat the pot!' said the worthy matron, setting it down very hastily on the hob; 'a little stupid thing, that only holds a couple of cups! What use is it of, to anybody! Except,' said Mrs. Corney, pausing, 'except to a poor desolate creature like me. Oh dear!'

With these words, the matron dropped into her chair, and, once more resting her elbow on the table, thought of her solitary fate. The small teapot, and the single cup, had awakened in her mind sad recollections of Mr. Corney (who had not been dead more than five-and-twenty years); and she was overpowered.

'I shall never get another!' said Mrs. Corney, pettishly; 'I shall never get another—like him.'

Whether this remark bore reference to the husband, or the teapot, is uncertain. It might have been the latter; for Mrs. Corney looked at it as she spoke; and took it up afterwards. She had just tasted her first cup, when she was disturbed by a soft tap at the room-door.

'Oh, come in with you!' said Mrs. Corney, sharply. 'Some of the old women dying, I suppose. They always die when I'm at meals. Don't stand there, letting the cold air in, don't. What's amiss now, eh?'

'Nothing, ma'am, nothing,' replied a man's voice.

'Dear me!' exclaimed the matron, in a much sweeter tone, 'is that Mr. Bumble?'

'At your service, ma'am,' said Mr. Bumble, who had been stopping outside to rub his shoes clean, and to shake the snow off his coat; and who now made his appearance, bearing the cocked-hat in one hand, and a bundle in the other. 'Shall I shut the door, ma'am?'

The lady modestly hesitated to reply, lest there should be any impropriety in holding an interview with Mr. Bumble, with closed doors. Mr. Bumble taking advantage of the hesitation, and being very cold himself, shut it without permission.

'Hard weather, Mr. Bumble,' said the matron.

'Hard, indeed, ma'am.' replied the beadle. 'Antiporochial weather this, ma'am. We have given away. Mrs. Corney, we have given away a matter of twenty quartern loaves and a cheese and a half, this very blessed afternoon; and yet them paupers are not contented.'

'Of course not. When would they be, Mr. Bumble?' said the matron, sipping her tea.

'When, indeed, ma'am!' rejoined Mr. Bumble. 'Why here's one man that, in consideration of his wife and large family, has a quartern loaf and a good pound of cheese, full weight. Is he grateful, ma'am? Is he grateful? Not a copper farthing's worth of it! What does he do, ma'am, but ask for a few coals; if it's only a pocket handkerchief full, he says! Coals! What would he do with coals? Toast his cheese with 'em, and then come back for more. That's the way with these people, ma'am; give 'em a apron full of coals to-day, and they'll come back for another, the day after to-morrow, as brazen as alabaster.'

The matron expressed her entire concurrence in this intelligible simile; and the beadle went on.

'I never,' said Mr. Bumble, 'see anything like the pitch it's got to. The day afore yesterday, a man—you have been a married woman, ma'am, and I may mention it to you—a man, with hardly a rag upon his back (here Mrs. Corney looked at the floor), goes to our overseer's door when he has got company coming to dinner; and says, he must be relieved, Mrs. Corney. As he wouldn't go away, and shocked the company very much, our overseer sent him out a pound of potatoes and half a pint of oatmeal. "My heart!" says the ungrateful villain, "what's the use of *this* to me? You might as well give me a pair of iron spectacles!" "Very good," says our overseer, taking 'em away again, "you won't get anything else here." "Then I'll die in the streets!" says the vagrant. "Oh no, you won't," says our overseer.'

'Ha! ha! That was very good! So like Mr. Grannett, wasn't it?' interposed the matron. 'Well, Mr. Bumble?'

'Well, ma'am,' rejoined the beadle, 'he went away; and he *did* die in the streets. There's a obstinate pauper for you!'

'It beats anything I could have believed,' observed the matron emphatically. 'But don't you think out-of-door relief a very bad thing, any way, Mr. Bumble? You're a gentleman of experience, and ought to know. Come.'

'Mrs. Corney,' said the beadle, smiling as men smile who are conscious of superior information, 'out-of-door relief, properly managed: properly managed, ma'am: is the porochial safeguard. The great principle of out-of-door relief is, to give the paupers exactly what they don't want; and then they get tired of coming.'

'Dear me!' exclaimed Mrs. Corney. 'Well, that is a good one, too!'

'Yes. Betwixt you and me, ma'am,' returned Mr. Bumble, 'that's the great principle; and that's the reason why, if you look at any cases that get into them owdacious newspapers, you'll always observe that sick families have been relieved with slices of cheese. That's the rule now, Mrs. Corney, all over the country. But, however,' said the beadle, stopping to unpack his bundle, 'these are official secrets, ma'am; not to be spoken of; except, as I may say, among the porochial officers, such as ourselves. This is the port wine, ma'am, that the board ordered for the infirmary; real, fresh, genuine port wine; only out of the cask this forenoon; clear as a bell; and no sediment!'

Having held the first bottle up to the light, and shaken it well to test its excellence, Mr. Bumble placed them both on the top of a chest of drawers; folded the handkerchief in which they had been wrapped; put it carefully in his pocket; and took up his hat, as if to go.

'You'll have a very cold walk, Mr. Bumble,' said the matron.

'It blows, ma'am,' replied Mr. Bumble, turning up his coat-collar, 'enough to cut one's ears off.'

The matron looked, from the little kettle, to the beadle, who was moving towards the door; and as the beadle coughed, preparatory to bidding her good night, bashfully inquired whether—whether he wouldn't take a cup of tea?

Mr. Bumble instantaneously turned back his collar again; laid his hat and stick upon a chair; and drew another chair up to the table. As he slowly seated himself, he looked at the lady. She fixed her eyes upon the little tea-pot. Mr. Bumble coughed again, and slightly smiled.

Mrs. Corney rose to get another cup and saucer from the closet. As she sat down, her eyes once again encountered those of the gallant beadle; she coloured, and applied herself to the task of making his tea. Again Mr. Bumble coughed,—louder this time than he had coughed yet.

'Sweet, Mr. Bumble?' inquired the matron, taking up the sugar-basin.

'Very sweet, indeed, ma'am,' replied Mr. Bumble. He fixed his eyes on Mrs. Corney as he said this; and if ever a beadle looked tender, Mr. Bumble was that beadle at that moment.

The tea was made, and handed in silence. Mr. Bumble, having spread a handkerchief over his knees to prevent the crumbs from sullying the splendour of his shorts, began to eat and drink; varying these amusements, occasionally, by fetching a deep sigh; which, however, had no injurious effect upon his appetite, but, on the contrary, rather seemed to facilitate his operations in the tea and toast department.

'You have a cat, ma'am, I see,' said Mr. Bumble, glancing at one who, in the centre of her family, was basking before the fire; 'and kittens too, I declare!'

'I am so fond of them, Mr. Bumble, you can't think,' replied the matron. 'They're *so* happy, *so* frolicsome, and *so* cheerful, that they are quite companions for me.'

'Very nice animals, ma'am,' replied Mr. Bumble, approvingly; 'so very domestic.'

'Oh, yes!' rejoined the matron with enthusiasm; 'so fond of their home too, that it's quite a pleasure, I'm sure.'

'Mrs. Corney, ma'am,' said Mr. Bumble, slowly, and marking the time with his teaspoon, 'I mean to say this, ma'am; that any cat, or kitten, that could live with you, ma'am, and *not* be fond of its home, must be a ass, ma'am.'

'Oh, Mr. Bumble!' remonstrated Mrs. Corney.

'It's of no use disguising facts, ma'am,' said Mr. Bumble, slowly flourishing the teaspoon with a kind of amorous dignity which made him doubly impressive; 'I would drown it myself, with pleasure.'

'Then you're a cruel man,' said the matron vivaciously, as she held out her hand for the beadle's cup; 'and a very hard-hearted man besides.'

'Hard-hearted, ma'am?' said Mr. Bumble. 'Hard?' Mr. Bumble resigned his cup without another word; squeezed Mrs. Corney's little finger as she took it; and inflicting two open-handed slaps upon his laced waistcoat, gave a mighty sigh, and hitched his chair a very little morsel farther from the fire.

It was a round table; and as Mrs. Corney and Mr. Bumble had been sitting opposite each other, with no great space between them, and fronting the fire, it will be seen that Mr. Bumble, in receding from the fire, and still keeping at the table, increased the distance between himself and Mrs. Corney; which proceeding, some prudent readers will doubtless be disposed to admire, and to consider an act of great heroism on Mr. Bumble's part: he being in some sort tempted by time, place, and opportunity, to give utterance to certain soft nothings, which however well they may become the lips of the light and thoughtless, do seem immeasurably beneath the dignity of judges of the land, members of parliament, ministers of state, lord mayors, and other great public functionaries, but more particularly beneath the stateliness and gravity of a beadle: who (as is well known) should be the sternest and most inflexible among them all.

Whatever were Mr. Bumble's intentions, however (and no

doubt they were of the best): it unfortunately happened, as has been twice before remarked, that the table was a round one; consequently Mr. Bumble, moving his chair by little and little, soon began to diminish the distance between himself and the matron; and, continuing to travel round the outer edge of the circle, brought his chair, in time, close to that in which the matron was seated. Indeed, the two chairs touched; and when they did so, Mr. Bumble stopped.

Now, if the matron had moved her chair to the right, she would have been scorched by the fire; and if to the left, she must have fallen into Mr. Bumble's arms; so (being a discreet matron, and no doubt foreseeing these consequences at a glance) she remained where she was, and handed Mr. Bumble another cup of tea.

'Hard-hearted, Mrs. Corney?' said Mr. Bumble, stirring his tea, and looking up into the matron's face; 'are *you* hard-hearted, Mrs. Corney?'

'Dear me!' exclaimed the matron, 'what a very curious question from a single man. What can you want to know for, Mr. Bumble?'

The beadle drank his tea to the last drop; finished a piece of toast; whisked the crumbs off his knees; wiped his lips; and deliberately kissed the matron.

'Mr. Bumble!' cried that discreet lady in a whisper; for the fright was so great, that she had quite lost her voice, 'Mr. Bumble, I shall scream!' Mr. Bumble made no reply; but, in a slow and dignified manner, put his arm round the matron's waist.

As the lady had stated her intention of screaming, of course she would have screamed at this additional boldness, but that the exertion was rendered unnecessary by a hasty knocking at the door: which was no sooner heard, than Mr. Bumble darted, with much agility, to the wine bottles, and began dusting them with great violence: while the matron sharply demanded who was there. It is worthy of remark, as a curious physical instance of the efficacy of a sudden surprise in counteracting the effects of extreme fear, that her voice had quite recovered all its official asperity.

'If you please, mistress,' said a withered old female pauper, hideously ugly: putting her head in at the door, 'Old Sally is a-going fast.'

'Well, what's that to me?' angrily demanded the matron. 'I can't keep her alive, can I?'

'No, no, mistress,' replied the old woman, 'nobody can; she's far beyond the reach of help. I've seen a many people die; little babes and great strong men; and I know when death's a-coming, well enough. But she's troubled in her mind: and when the fits are not on her,—and that's not often, for she is dying very hard,—she says she has got something to tell, which you must hear. She'll never die quiet till you come, mistress.'

At this intelligence, the worthy Mrs. Corney muttered a variety of invectives against old women who couldn't even die without purposely annoying their betters; and, muffling herself in a thick shawl which she hastily caught up, briefly requested Mr. Bumble to stay till she came back, lest anything particular should occur. Bidding the messenger walk fast, and not be all night hobbling up the stairs, she followed her from the room with a very ill grace, scolding all the way.

Mr. Bumble's conduct on being left to himself was rather inexplicable. He opened the closet, counted the teaspoons, weighed the sugar-tongs, closely inspected a silver milk-pot to ascertain that it was of the genuine metal, and, having satisfied his curiosity on these points, put on his cocked-hat cornerwise, and danced with much gravity four distinct times round the table. Having gone through this very extraordinary performance, he took off his cocked-hat again, and, spreading himself before the fire with his back towards it, seemed to be mentally engaged in taking an exact inventory of the furniture.

CHAPTER 24

Treats of a very poor subject. But it is a short one, and may be found of importance in this history

It was no unfit messenger of death, who had disturbed the quiet of the matron's room. Her body was bent by age; her limbs trembled with palsy; her face, distorted into a mumbling leer, resembled more the grotesque shaping of some wild pencil, than the work of Nature's hand.

Alas! How few of Nature's faces are left alone to gladden us with their beauty! The cares, and sorrows, and hungerings, of the world, change them as they change hearts; and it is only when those passions sleep, and have lost their hold for ever, that the troubled clouds pass off, and leave Heaven's surface clear. It is a common thing for the countenances of the dead, even in that fixed and rigid state, to subside into the long-forgotten expression of sleeping infancy, and settle into the very look of early life; so calm, so peaceful, do they grow again, that those who knew them in their happy childhood, kneel by the coffin's side in awe, and see the Angel even upon earth.

The old crone tottered along the passages, and up the stairs, muttering some indistinct answers to the chidings of her companion; being at length compelled to pause for breath, she gave the light into her hand, and remained behind to follow as she might: while the more nimble superior made her way to the room where the sick woman lay.

It was a bare garret-room, with a dim light burning at the farther end. There was another old woman watching by the bed; the parish apothecary's apprentice was standing by the fire, making a toothpick out of a quill.

'Cold night, Mrs. Corney,' said this young gentleman, as the matron entered.

'Very cold, indeed, sir,' replied the mistress, in her most civil tones, and dropping a curtsey as she spoke.

'You should get better coals out of your contractors,' said the apothecary's deputy, breaking a lump on the top of the fire with the rusty poker; 'these are not at all the sort of thing for a cold night.'

'They're the board's choosing, sir,' returned the matron. 'The least they could do, would be to keep us pretty warm: for our places are hard enough.'

The conversation was here interrupted by a moan from the sick woman.

'Oh!' said the young man, turning his face towards the bed, as if he had previously quite forgotten the patient, 'it's all U. P. there, Mrs. Corney.'

'It is, is it, sir?' asked the matron.

'If she lasts a couple of hours, I shall be surprised,' said the apothecary's apprentice, intent upon the toothpick's point. 'It's a break-up of the system altogether. Is she dozing, old lady?'

The attendant stooped over the bed, to ascertain; and nodded in the affirmative.

'Then perhaps she'll go off in that way, if you don't make a row,' said the young man. 'Put the light on the floor. She won't see it there.'

The attendant did as she was told: shaking her head meanwhile, to intimate that the woman would not die so easily; having done so, she resumed her seat by the side of the other nurse, who had by this time returned. The mistress, with an expression of impatience, wrapped herself in her shawl, and sat at the foot of the bed.

The apothecary's apprentice, having completed the manufacture of the toothpick, planted himself in front of the fire, and made good use of it for ten minutes or so: when apparently growing rather dull, he wished Mrs. Corney joy of her job, and took himself off on tiptoe.

When they had sat in silence for some time, the two old women rose from the bed, and crouching over the fire, held out their withered hands to catch the heat. The flame threw a ghastly look on their shrivelled faces, and made their ugliness appear terrible, as, in this position, they began to converse in a low voice.

'Did she say any more, Anny dear, while I was gone?' inquired the messenger.

'Not a word,' replied the other. 'She plucked and tore at her arms for a little time; but I held her hands, and she soon dropped off. She hasn't much strength in her, so I easily kept her quiet. I ain't so weak for an old woman, although I am on parish allowance; no, no!'

'Did she drink the hot wine the doctor said she was to have?' demanded the first.

'I tried to get it down,' rejoined the other. 'But her teeth were tight set, and she clenched the mug so hard that it was as much as I could do to get it back again. So *I* drank it; and it did me good!'

Looking cautiously round, to ascertain that they were not overheard, the two hags cowered nearer to the fire, and chuckled heartily.

'I mind the time,' said the first speaker, 'when she would have done the same, and made rare fun of it afterwards.'

'Ay, that she would,' rejoined the other; 'she had a merry heart. A many, many, beautiful corpses she laid out, as nice and neat as wax-work. My old eyes have seen them—ay, and those old hands touched them too; for I have helped her, scores of times.'

Stretching forth her trembling fingers as she spoke, the old creature shook them exultingly before her face, and fumbling in her pocket, brought out an old time-discoloured tin snuffbox, from which she shook a few grains into the outstretched palm of her companion, and a few more into her own. While they were thus employed, the matron, who had been impatiently watching until the dying woman should awaken from her stupor, joined them by the fire, and sharply asked how long she was to wait.

'Not long, mistress,' replied the second woman, looking up into her face. 'We have none of us long to wait for Death. Patience, patience! He'll be here soon enough for us all.'

'Hold your tongue, you doting idiot!' said the matron, sternly. 'You, Martha, tell me; has she been in this way before?'

'Often,' answered the first woman.

'But will never be again,' added the second one; 'that is, she'll never wake again but once—and mind, mistress, that won't be for long!'

'Long or short,' said the matron, snappishly, 'she won't find me here when she does wake; take care, both of you, how you worry me again for nothing. It's no part of my duty to see all the old women in the house die, and I won't—that's more. Mind that, you impudent old harridans. If you make a fool of me again, I'll soon cure you, I warrant you!'

She was bouncing away, when a cry from the two women, who had turned towards the bed, caused her to look round. The patient had raised herself upright, and was stretching her arms towards them.

'Who's that?' she cried, in a hollow voice.

'Hush, hush!' said one of the women, stooping over her. 'Lie down, lie down!'

'I'll never lie down again alive!' said the woman, struggling. 'I *will* tell her! Come here! Nearer! Let me whisper in your ear.'

She clutched the matron by the arm, and forcing her into a chair by the bed-side, was about to speak, when looking round, she caught sight of the two old women bending forward in the attitude of eager listeners.

'Turn them away,' said the woman, drowsily; 'make haste! make haste!'

The two old crones, chiming in together, began pouring out many piteous lamentations that the poor dear was too far gone to know her best friends; and were uttering sundry protestations that they would never leave her, when the superior pushed them from the room, closed the door, and returned to the bed-side. On being excluded, the old ladies changed their tone, and cried through the keyhole that old Sally was drunk; which, indeed, was not unlikely; since, in addition to a moderate dose of opium prescribed by the apothecary, she was labouring under the effects of a final taste of gin-and-water which had been privily administered, in the openness of their hearts, by the worthy old ladies themselves.

'Now listen to me,' said the dying woman aloud, as if making a great effort to revive one latent spark of energy. 'In this very room—in this very bed—I once nursed a pretty young creetur', that was brought into the house with her feet cut and bruised with walking, and all soiled with dust and blood. She gave birth to a boy, and died. Let me think—what was the year again?'

'Never mind the year,' said the impatient auditor; 'what about her?'

'Ay,' murmured the sick woman, relapsing into her former drowsy state, 'what about her?—what about—I know!' she cried, jumping fiercely up: her face flushed, and her eyes starting from her head—'I robbed her, so I did! She wasn't cold—I tell you she wasn't cold, when I stole it!'

'Stole what, for God's sake?' cried the matron, with a gesture as if she would call for help.

'*It!*' replied the woman, laying her hand over the other's mouth. 'The only thing she had. She wanted clothes to keep her warm, and food to eat; but she had kept it safe, and had it in her bosom. It was gold, I tell you! Rich gold, that might have saved her life!'

'Gold!' echoed the matron, bending eagerly over the woman as she fell back. 'Go on, go on—yes—what of it? Who was the mother? When was it?'

'She charged me to keep it safe,' replied the woman with a groan, 'and trusted me as the only woman about her. I stole it in my heart when she first showed it me hanging round her neck; and the child's death, perhaps, is on me besides! They would have treated him better, if they had known it all!'

'Known what?' asked the other. 'Speak!'

'The boy grew so like his mother,' said the woman, rambling on, and not heeding the question, 'that I could never forget it when I saw his face. Poor girl! poor girl! She was so young, too! Such a gentle lamb! Wait; there's more to tell. I have not told you all, have I?'

'No, no,' replied the matron, inclining her head to catch the words, as they came more faintly from the dying woman. 'Be quick, or it may be too late!'

'The mother,' said the woman, making a more violent effort than before; 'the mother, when the pains of death first came upon her, whispered in my ear that if her baby was born alive, and thrived, the day might come when it would not feel so much disgraced to hear its poor young mother named. "And oh, kind Heaven!" she said, folding her thin hands together, "whether it be boy or girl, raise up some friends for it in this troubled world, and take pity upon a lonely desolate child, abandoned to its mercy!"'

'The boy's name?' demanded the matron.

'They *called* him Oliver,' replied the woman, feebly. 'The gold I stole was—'

'Yes, yes—what?' cried the other.

She was bending eagerly over the woman to hear her reply; but drew back, instinctively, as she once again rose, slowly and stiffly, into a sitting posture; then, clutching the coverlid with both hands, muttered some indistinct sounds in her throat, and fell lifeless on the bed.

'Stone dead!' said one of the old women, hurrying in as soon as the door was opened.

'And nothing to tell, after all,' rejoined the matron, walking carelessly away.

The two crones, to all appearance, too busily occupied in the preparations for their dreadful duties to make any reply, were left alone, hovering about the body.

CHAPTER 25

Wherein this history reverts to Mr. Fagin and company

While these things were passing in the country workhouse, Mr. Fagin sat in the old den—the same from which Oliver had been removed by the girl—brooding over a dull, smoky fire. He held a pair of bellows upon his knee, with which he had apparently been endeavouring to rouse it into more cheerful action; but he had fallen into deep thought; and with his arms folded on them, and his chin resting on his thumbs, fixed his eyes, abstractedly, on the rusty bars.

At a table behind him sat the Artful Dodger, Master Charles Bates, and Mr. Chitling: all intent upon a game of whist; the Artful taking dummy against Master Bates and Mr. Chitling. The countenance of the first-named gentleman, peculiarly intelligent at all times, acquired great additional interest from his close observance of the game, and his attentive perusal of Mr. Chitling's hand; upon which, from time to time, as occasion served, he bestowed a variety of earnest glances: wisely regulating his own play by the result of his observations upon his neighbour's cards. It being a cold night, the Dodger wore his hat, as, indeed, was often his custom within doors. He also sustained a clay pipe between his teeth, which he only removed for a brief space when he deemed it necessary to apply for refreshment to a quart pot upon the table, which stood ready filled with gin-and-water for the accommodation of the company.

Master Bates was also attentive to the play; but being of a

more excitable nature than his accomplished friend, it was observable that he more frequently applied himself to the gin-and-water, and moreover indulged in many jests and irrelevant remarks, all highly unbecoming a scientific rubber. Indeed, the Artful, presuming upon their close attachment, more than once took occasion to reason gravely with his companion upon these improprieties: all of which remonstrances, Master Bates received in extremely good part; merely requesting his friend to be 'blowed,' or to insert his head in a sack, or replying with some other neatly-turned witticism of a similar kind, the happy application of which, excited considerable admiration in the mind of Mr. Chitling. It was remarkable that the latter gentleman and his partner invariably lost; and that the circumstance, so far from angering Master Bates, appeared to afford him the highest amusement, inasmuch as he laughed most uproariously at the end of every deal, and protested that he had never seen such a jolly game in all his born days.

'That's two doubles and the rub,' said Mr. Chitling, with a very long face, as he drew half-a-crown from his waistcoat-pocket. 'I never see such a feller as you, Jack; you win everything. Even when we've good cards, Charley and I can't make nothing of 'em.'

Either the matter or the manner of this remark, which was made very ruefully, delighted Charley Bates so much, that his consequent shout of laughter roused the Jew from his reverie, and induced him to inquire what was the matter.

'Matter, Fagin!' cried Charley. 'I wish you had watched the play. Tommy Chitling hasn't won a point; and I went partners with him against the Artful and dum.'

'Ay, ay!' said the Jew, with a grin, which sufficiently demonstrated that he was at no loss to understand the reason. 'Try 'em again, Tom; try 'em again.'

'No more of it for me, thankee, Fagin,' replied Mr. Chitling; 'I've had enough. That 'ere Dodger has such a run of luck that there's no standing again' him.'

'Ha! ha! my dear,' replied the Jew, 'you must get up very early in the morning, to win against the Dodger.'

'Morning!' said Charley Bates; 'you must put your boots on overnight, and have a telescope at each eye, and a opera-glass between your shoulders, if you want to come over *him*.'

Mr. Dawkins received these handsome compliments with much philosophy, and offered to cut any gentleman in company, for the first picture-card, at a shilling a time. Nobody accepting the challenge, and his pipe being by this time smoked out, he proceeded to amuse himself by sketching a ground-plan of Newgate on the table with the piece of chalk which had served him in lieu of counters; whistling, meantime, with peculiar shrillness.

'How precious dull you are, Tommy!' said the Dodger, stopping short when there had been a long silence; and addressing Mr. Chitling. 'What do you think he's thinking of, Fagin?'

'How should I know, my dear?' replied the Jew, looking round as he plied the bellows. 'About his losses, maybe; or the little retirement in the country that he's just left, eh? Ha! ha! Is that it, my dear?'

'Not a bit of it,' replied the Dodger, stopping the subject of discourse as Mr. Chitling was about to reply. 'What do *you* say, Charley?'

'*I* should say,' replied Master Bates, with a grin, 'that he was uncommon sweet upon Betsy. See how he's a-blushing! Oh, my eye! here's a merry-go-rounder! Tommy Chitling's in love! Oh, Fagin, Fagin! what a spree!'

Thoroughly overpowered with the notion of Mr. Chitling being the victim of the tender passion, Master Bates threw himself back in his chair with such violence, that he lost his balance, and pitched over upon the floor; where (the accident abating nothing of his merriment) he lay at full length until his laugh was over, when he resumed his former position, and began another laugh.

'Never mind him, my dear,' said the Jew, winking at Mr. Dawkins, and giving Master Bates a reproving tap with the nozzle of the bellows. 'Betsy's a fine girl. Stick up to her, Tom. Stick up to her.'

'What I mean to say, Fagin,' replied Mr. Chitling, very red in the face, 'is, that that isn't anything to anybody here.'

'No more it is,' replied the Jew; 'Charley will talk. Don't mind him, my dear; don't mind him. Betsy's a fine girl. Do as she bids you, Tom, and you will make your fortune.'

'So I *do* do as she bids me,' replied Mr. Chitling; 'I shouldn't have been milled, if it hadn't been for her advice. But it turned out a good job for you; didn't it, Fagin! And what's six weeks of it? It must come, some time or another, and why not in the winter time when you don't want to go out a-walking so much; eh, Fagin?'

'Ah, to be sure, my dear,' replied the Jew.

'You wouldn't mind it again, Tom, would you,' asked the Dodger, winking upon Charley and the Jew, 'if Bet was all right?'

'I mean to say that I shouldn't,' replied Tom, angrily. 'There, now. Ah! Who'll say as much as that, I should like to know; eh, Fagin?'

'Nobody, my dear,' replied the Jew; 'not a soul, Tom. I don't know one of 'em that would do it besides you; not one of 'em, my dear.'

'I might have got clear off, if I'd split upon her; mightn't I, Fagin?' angrily pursued the poor half-witted dupe. 'A word from me would have done it; wouldn't it, Fagin?'

'To be sure it would, my dear,' replied the Jew.

'But I didn't blab it; did I, Fagin?' demanded Tom, pouring question upon question with great volubility.

'No, no, to be sure,' replied the Jew; 'you were too stout-hearted for that. A deal too stout, my dear!'

'Perhaps I was,' rejoined Tom, looking round; 'and if I was, what's to laugh at, in that; eh, Fagin?'

The Jew, perceiving that Mr. Chitling was considerably roused, hastened to assure him that nobody was laughing; and to prove the gravity of the company, appealed to Master Bates, the principal offender. But, unfortunately, Charley, in opening his mouth to reply that he was never more serious in his life, was unable to prevent the escape of such a violent roar, that the abused Mr. Chitling, without any preliminary ceremonies, rushed across the room and aimed a blow at the offender; who, being skilful in evading pursuit, ducked to avoid it, and chose his time so well that it lighted on the chest of the merry old gentleman, and caused him to stagger to the wall, where he stood panting for breath, while Mr. Chitling looked on in intense dismay.

'Hark!' cried the Dodger at this moment, 'I heard the tinkler.' Catching up the light, he crept softly up stairs.

The bell was rung again, with some impatience, while the party were in darkness. After a short pause, the Dodger reappeared, and whispered Fagin mysteriously.

'What!' cried the Jew, 'alone?'

The Dodger nodded in the affirmative, and, shading the flame of the candle with his hand, gave Charley Bates a private intimation, in dumb show, that he had better not be funny just then. Having performed this friendly office, he fixed his eyes on the Jew's face, and awaited his directions.

The old man bit his yellow fingers, and meditated for some seconds; his face working with agitation the while, as if he dreaded something, and feared to know the worst. At length he raised his head.

'Where is he?' he asked.

The Dodger pointed to the floor above, and made a gesture, as if to leave the room.

'Yes,' said the Jew, answering the mute inquiry; 'bring him down. Hush! Quiet, Charley! Gently, Tom! Scarce, scarce!'

This brief direction to Charley Bates, and his recent antagonist, was softly and immediately obeyed. There was no sound of their whereabout, when the Dodger descended the stairs, bearing the light in his hand, and followed by a man in a coarse smock-frock; who, after casting a hurried glance round the room, pulled off a large wrapper which had concealed the lower portion of his face, and disclosed: all haggard, unwashed, and unshorn: the features of flash Toby Crackit.

'How are you, Faguey?' said this worthy, nodding to the Jew. 'Pop that shawl away in my castor, Dodger, so that I may know where to find it when I cut; that's the time of day! You'll be a fine young cracksman afore the old file now.'

With these words he pulled up the smock-frock; and, winding it round his middle, drew a chair to the fire, and placed his feet upon the hob.

'See there, Faguey,' he said, pointing disconsolately to his top-boots; 'not a drop of Day and Martin since you know when; not a bubble of blacking, by Jove! But don't look at me in that way, man. All in good time. I can't talk about business till I've eat and drank; so produce the sustenance, and let's have a quiet fill-out for the first time these three days!'

The Jew motioned to the Dodger to place what eatables there were, upon the table; and, seating himself opposite the housebreaker, waited his leisure.

To judge from appearances, Toby was by no means in a hurry to open the conversation. At first, the Jew contented himself with patiently watching his countenance, as if to gain from its expression some clue to the intelligence he brought; but in vain. He looked tired and worn, but there was the same complacent repose upon his features that they always wore: and through dirt, and beard, and whisker, there still shone, unimpaired, the self-satisfied smirk of flash Toby Crackit. Then, the Jew, in an agony of impatience, watched every morsel he put into his mouth; pacing up and down the room, meanwhile, in irrepressible excitement. It was all of no use. Toby continued to eat with the utmost outward indifference, until he could eat no more; then, ordering the Dodger out, he closed the door, mixed a glass of spirits and water, and composed himself for talking.

'First and foremost, Faguey,' said Toby.

'Yes, yes!' interposed the Jew, drawing up his chair.

Mr. Crackit stopped to take a draught of spirits and water, and to declare that the gin was excellent; then placing his feet against the low mantelpiece, so as to bring his boots to about the level of his eye, he quietly resumed—

'First and foremost, Faguey,' said the housebreaker, 'how's Bill?'

'What!' screamed the Jew, starting from his seat.

'Why, you don't mean to say—' began Toby, turning pale.

'Mean!' cried the Jew, stamping furiously on the ground. 'Where are they? Sikes and the boy! Where are they? Where have they been? Where are they hiding? Why have they not been here?'

'The crack failed,' said Toby, faintly.

'I know it,' replied the Jew, tearing a newspaper from his pocket and pointing to it. 'What more?'

'They fired and hit the boy. We cut over the fields at the back, with him between us—straight as the crow flies—through hedge and ditch. They gave chase. Damme! the whole country was awake, and the dogs upon us.'

'The boy!'

'Bill had him on his back, and scudded like the wind. We stopped to take him between us; his head hung down, and he was cold. They were close upon our heels; every man for himself, and each from the gallows! We parted company, and left the youngster lying in a ditch. Alive or dead, that's all I know about him.'

The Jew stopped to hear no more; but uttering a loud yell, and twining his hands in his hair, rushed from the room, and from the house.

CHAPTER 26

In which a mysterious character appears
upon the scene; and many things,
inseparable from this history, are done and
performed

The old man had gained the street corner, before he began to
recover the effect of Toby Crackit's intelligence. He had relaxed
nothing of his unusual speed; but was still pressing onward, in the
same wild and disordered manner, when the sudden dashing past
of a carriage: and a boisterous cry from the foot passengers, who
saw his danger: drove him back upon the pavement. Avoiding, as
much as possible, all the main streets, and skulking only through
the byways and alleys, he at length emerged on Snow Hill. Here he
walked even faster than before; nor did he linger until he had again
turned into a court; when, as if conscious that he was now in his
proper element, he fell into his usual shuffling pace, and seemed
to breathe more freely.

Near to the spot on which Snow Hill and Holborn Hill meet,
there opens upon the right hand as you come out of the City, a
narrow and dismal alley leading to Saffron Hill. In its filthy shops
are exposed for sale huge bunches of second-hand silk handkerchiefs, of all sizes and patterns; for here reside the traders who
purchase them from pickpockets. Hundreds of these handkerchiefs
hang dangling from pegs outside the windows or flaunting from the
door-posts; and the shelves, within, are piled with them. Confined
as the limits of Field Lane are, it has its barber, its coffee-shop, its
beer-shop, and its fried-fish warehouse. It is a commercial colony

of itself: the emporium of petty larceny: visited at early morning, and setting-in of dusk, by silent merchants, who traffic in dark back-parlours, and who go as strangely as they come. Here, the clothesman, the shoe-vamper, and the rag merchant, display their goods, as sign-boards to the petty thief; here, stores of old iron and bones, and heaps of mildewy fragments of woollen-stuff and linen, rust and rot in the grimy cellars.

It was into this place that the Jew turned. He was well known to the sallow denizens of the lane; for such of them as were on the look-out to buy or sell, nodded, familiarly, as he passed along. He replied to their salutations in the same way; but bestowed no closer recognition until he reached the further end of the alley; when he stopped, to address a salesman of small stature, who had squeezed as much of his person into a child's chair as the chair would hold, and was smoking a pipe at his warehouse door.

'Why, the sight of you, Mr. Fagin, would cure the hoptalmy!' said this respectable trader, in acknowledgment of the Jew's inquiry after his health.

'The neighbourhood was a little too hot, Lively,' said Fagin elevating his eyebrows, and crossing his hands upon his shoulders.

'Well, I've heerd that complaint of it, once or twice before,' replied the trader; 'but it soon cools down again; don't you find it so?'

Fagin nodded in the affirmative. Pointing in the direction of Saffron Hill, he inquired whether any one was up yonder to-night.

'At the Cripples?' inquired the man.

The Jew nodded.

'Let me see,' pursued the merchant, reflecting. 'Yes, there's some half dozen of 'em gone in, that I knows. I don't think your friend's there.'

'Sikes is not, I suppose?' inquired the Jew, with a disappointed countenance.

'*Non istwentus,* as the lawyers say,' replied the little man, shaking his head, and looking amazingly sly. 'Have you got anything in my line to-night?'

'Nothing to-night,' said the Jew, turning away.

'Are you going up to the Cripples, Fagin?' cried the little man, calling after him. 'Stop! I don't mind if I have a drop there with you!'

But as the Jew, looking back, waved his hand to intimate that he preferred being alone; and, moreover, as the little man could not very easily disengage himself from the chair; the sign of the Cripples was, for a time, bereft of the advantage of Mr. Lively's presence. By the time he had got upon his legs, the Jew had disappeared; so Mr. Lively, after ineffectually standing on tiptoe, in the hope of catching sight of him, again forced himself into the little chair, and, exchanging a shake of the head with a lady in the opposite shop, in which doubt and mistrust were plainly mingled, resumed his pipe with a grave demeanour.

The Three Cripples, or rather the Cripples: which was the sign by which the establishment was familiarly known to its patrons: was the public-house in which Mr. Sikes and his dog have already figured. Merely making a sign to a man at the bar, Fagin walked straight up stairs, and opening the door of a room, and softly insinuating himself into the chamber, looked anxiously about: shading his eyes with his hand, as if in search of some particular person.

The room was illuminated by two gas-lights; the glare of which was prevented by the barred shutters, and closely-drawn curtains of faded red, from being visible outside. The ceiling was blackened, to prevent its colour from being injured by the flaring of the lamps; and the place was so full of dense tobacco smoke, that at first it was scarcely possible to discern anything more. By degrees, however, as some of it cleared away through the open door, an assemblage of heads, as confused as the noises that greeted the ear, might be made out; and as the eye grew more accustomed to the scene, the spectator gradually became aware of the presence of a numerous company, male and female, crowded round a long table: at the upper end of which, sat a chairman with a hammer of office in his hand; while a professional gentleman, with a bluish nose, and his face tied up for the benefit of a toothache, presided at a jingling piano in a remote corner.

As Fagin stepped softly in, the professional gentleman, running over the keys by way of prelude, occasioned a general cry of order for a song; which, having subsided, a young lady proceeded to entertain the company with a ballad in four verses, between each of which the accompanyist played the melody all through, as loud as he could. When this was over, the chairman gave a sentiment, after which, the professional gentlemen on the chairman's right and left volunteered a duet, and sang it, with great applause.

It was curious to observe some faces which stood out prominently from among the group. There was the chairman himself (the landlord of the house), a coarse, rough, heavy built fellow, who, while the songs were proceeding, rolled his eyes hither and thither, and, seeming to give himself up to joviality, had an eye for everything that was done, and an ear for everything that was said—and sharp ones, too. Near him were the singers: receiving, with professional indifference, the compliments of the company, and applying themselves, in turn, to a dozen proffered glasses of spirits and water, tendered by their more boisterous admirers; whose countenances, expressive of almost every vice in almost every grade, irresistibly attracted the attention, by their very repulsiveness. Cunning, ferocity, and drunkenness in all its stages, were there, in their strongest aspects; and women: some with the last lingering tinge of their early freshness almost fading as you looked: others with every mark and stamp of their sex utterly beaten out, and presenting but one loathsome blank of profligacy and crime; some mere girls, others but young women, and none past the prime of life; formed the darkest and saddest portion of this dreary picture.

Fagin, troubled by no grave emotions, looked eagerly from face to face while these proceedings were in progress; but apparently without meeting that of which he was in search. Succeeding, at length, in catching the eye of the man who occupied the chair, he beckoned to him slightly, and left the room, as quietly as he had entered it.

'What can I do for you, Mr. Fagin?' inquired the man, as he followed him out to the landing. 'Won't you join us? They'll be delighted, every one of 'em.'

The Jew shook his head impatiently, and said in a whisper, 'Is *he* here?'

'No,' replied the man.

'And no news of Barney?' inquired Fagin.

'None,' replied the landlord of the Cripples; for it was he. 'He won't stir till it's all safe. Depend on it, they're on the scent down there; and that if he moved, he'd blow upon the thing at once. He's all right enough, Barney is, else I should have heard of him. I'll pound it, that Barney's managing properly. Let him alone for that.'

'Will *he* be here to-night?' asked the Jew, laying the same emphasis on the pronoun as before.

'Monks, do you mean?' inquired the landlord, hesitating.

'Hush!' said the Jew. 'Yes.'

'Certain,' replied the man, drawing a gold watch from his fob; 'I expected him here before now. If you'll wait ten minutes, he'll be—'

'No, no,' said the Jew, hastily; as though, however desirous he might be to see the person in question, he was nevertheless relieved by his absence. 'Tell him I came here to see him; and that he must come to me to-night. No, say to-morrow. As he is not here, to-morrow will be time enough.'

'Good!' said the man. 'Nothing more?'

'Not a word now,' said the Jew, descending the stairs.

'I say,' said the other, looking over the rails, and speaking in a hoarse whisper; 'what a time this would be for a sell! I've got Phil Barker here: so drunk, that a boy might take him.'

'Aha! But it's not Phil Barker's time,' said the Jew, looking up. 'Phil has something more to do, before we can afford to part with him; so go back to the company, my dear, and tell them to lead merry lives—*while they last.* Ha! ha! ha!'

The landlord reciprocated the old man's laugh; and returned to his guests. The Jew was no sooner alone, than his countenance resumed its former expression of anxiety and thought. After a brief reflection, he called a hack cabriolet, and bade the man drive towards Bethnal Green. He dismissed him within some quarter of a mile of Mr. Sikes's residence, and performed the short remainder of the distance, on foot.

'Now,' muttered the Jew, as he knocked at the door, 'if there is any deep play here, I shall have it out of you, my girl, cunning as you are.'

She was in her room, the woman said. Fagin crept softly up stairs, and entered it without any previous ceremony. The girl was alone; lying with her head upon the table, and her hair straggling over it.

'She has been drinking,' thought the Jew, coolly, 'or perhaps she is only miserable.'

The old man turned to close the door, as he made this reflection; the noise thus occasioned, roused the girl. She eyed his crafty face narrowly, as she inquired whether there was any news, and as she listened to his recital of Toby Crackit's story. When it was concluded, she sank into her former attitude, but spoke not a word. She pushed the candle impatiently away; and once or twice as she feverishly changed her position, shuffled her feet upon the ground; but this was all.

During the silence, the Jew looked restlessly about the room, as if to assure himself that there were no appearances of Sikes having covertly returned. Apparently satisfied with his inspection, he coughed twice or thrice, and made as many efforts to open a conversation; but the girl heeded him no more than if he had been made of stone. At length he made another attempt; and rubbing his hands together, said, in his most conciliatory tone—

'And where should you think Bill was now, my dear?'

The girl moaned out some half intelligible reply, that she could not tell; and seemed, from the smothered noise that escaped her, to be crying.

'And the boy, too,' said the Jew, straining his eyes to catch a glimpse at her face. 'Poor leetle child! Left in a ditch, Nance; only think!'

'The child,' said the girl, suddenly looking up, 'is better where he is, than among us; and if no harm comes to Bill from it, I hope he lies dead in the ditch, and that his young bones may rot there.'

'What!' cried the Jew, in amazement.

'Ay, I do,' returned the girl, meeting his gaze. 'I shall be glad to have him away from my eyes, and to know that the worst is over. I can't bear to have him about me. The sight of him turns me against myself, and all of you.'

'Pooh!' said the Jew, scornfully. 'You're drunk.'

'Am I?' cried the girl, bitterly. 'It's no fault of yours, if I am not! You'd never have me anything else, if you had your will, except now;—the humour doesn't suit you, doesn't it?'

'No!' rejoined the Jew, furiously. 'It does not.'

'Change it, then!' responded the girl, with a laugh.

'Change it!' exclaimed the Jew, exasperated beyond all bounds by his companion's unexpected obstinacy, and the vexation of the night, 'I will change it! Listen to me, you drab. Listen to me, who, with six words, can strangle Sikes as surely as if I had his bull's throat between my fingers now. If he comes back, and leaves the boy behind him; if he gets off free, and dead or alive, fails to restore him to me; murder him yourself if you would have him escape Jack Ketch. And do it the moment he sets foot in this room, or mind me, it will be too late!'

'What is all this?' cried the girl, involuntarily.

'What is it?' pursued Fagin, mad with rage. 'When the boy's worth hundreds of pounds to me, am I to lose what chance threw me in the way of getting safely, through the whims of a drunken gang that I could whistle away the lives of! And me bound, too, to a born devil that only wants the will, and has the power to, to—'

Panting for breath, the old man stammered for a word; and in that instant checked the torrent of his wrath, and changed his whole demeanour. A moment before, his clenched hands had grasped the air; his eyes had dilated; and his face grown livid with passion; but now, he shrunk into a chair, and, cowering together, trembled with the apprehension of having himself disclosed some hidden villainy. After a short silence, he ventured to look round at his companion. He appeared somewhat reassured, on beholding her in the same listless attitude from which he had first roused her.

'Nancy, dear!' croaked the Jew, in his usual voice. 'Did you mind me, dear?'

'Don't worry me now, Fagin!' replied the girl, raising her head languidly. 'If Bill has not done it this time, he will another. He has done many a good job for you, and will do many more when he can; and when he can't he won't; so no more about that.'

'Regarding this boy, my dear?' said the Jew, rubbing the palms of his hands nervously together.

'The boy must take his chance with the rest,' interrupted Nancy, hastily; 'and I say again, I hope he is dead, and out of harm's way, and out of yours,—that is, if Bill comes to no harm. And if Toby got clear, Bill's pretty sure to be safe; for Bill's worth two of Toby any time.'

'And about what was I saying, my dear?' observed the Jew, keeping his glistening eye steadily upon her.

'You must say it all over again, if it's anything you want me to do,' rejoined Nancy; 'and if it is, you had better wait till to-morrow. You put me up for a minute; but now I'm stupid again.'

Fagin put several other questions: all with the same drift of ascertaining whether the girl had profited by his unguarded hints; but, she answered them so readily, and was withal so utterly unmoved by his searching looks, that his original impression of her being more than a trifle in liquor, was confirmed. Nancy, indeed, was not exempt from a failing which was very common among the Jew's female pupils; and in which, in their tenderer years, they were rather encouraged than checked. Her disordered appearance, and a wholesale perfume of Geneva which pervaded the apartment, afforded strong confirmatory evidence of the justice of the Jew's supposition; and when, after indulging in the temporary display of violence above described, she subsided, first into dulness, and afterwards into a compound of feelings: under the influence of which she shed tears one minute, and in the next gave utterance to various exclamations of 'Never say die!' and divers calculations as to what might be the amount of the odds so long as a lady or gentleman was happy, Mr. Fagin, who had had considerable experience of such matters in his time, saw, with great satisfaction, that she was very far gone indeed.

Having eased his mind by this discovery; and having accomplished his twofold object of imparting to the girl what he had, that night, heard, and of ascertaining, with his own eyes, that Sikes had not returned, Mr. Fagin again turned his face homeward: leaving his young friend asleep, with her head upon the table.

It was within an hour of midnight. The weather being dark, and piercing cold, he had no great temptation to loiter. The sharp wind that scoured the streets, seemed to have cleared them of passengers, as of dust and mud, for few people were abroad, and they were to all appearance hastening fast home. It blew from the right quarter for the Jew, however, and straight before it he went: trembling, and shivering, as every fresh gust drove him rudely on his way.

He had reached the corner of his own street, and was already fumbling in his pocket for the door-key, when a dark figure emerged from a projecting entrance which lay in deep shadow, and, crossing the road, glided up to him unperceived.

'Fagin!' whispered a voice close to his ear.

'Ah!' said the Jew, turning quickly round, 'is that—'

'Yes!' interrupted the stranger. 'I have been lingering here these two hours. Where the devil have you been?'

'On your business, my dear,' replied the Jew, glancing uneasily at his companion, and slackening his pace as he spoke. 'On your business all night.'

'Oh, of course!' said the stranger, with a sneer. 'Well; and what's come of it?'

'Nothing good,' said the Jew.

'Nothing bad, I hope?' said the stranger, stopping short, and turning a startled look on his companion.

The Jew shook his head, and was about to reply, when the stranger, interrupting him, motioned to the house, before which they had by this time arrived: remarking, that he had better say what he had got to say, under cover: for his blood was chilled with standing about so long, and the wind blew through him.

Fagin looked as if he could have willingly excused himself from taking home a visitor at that unseasonable hour; and, indeed, muttered something about having no fire; but his companion repeating his request in a peremptory manner, he unlocked the door, and requested him to close it softly, while he got a light.

'It's as dark as the grave,' said the man, groping forward a few steps. 'Make haste!'

'Shut the door,' whispered Fagin from the end of the passage. As he spoke, it closed with a loud noise.

'That wasn't my doing,' said the other man, feeling his way. 'The wind blew it to, or it shut of its own accord: one or the other. Look sharp with the light, or I shall knock my brains out against something in this confounded hole.'

Fagin stealthily descended the kitchen stairs. After a short absence, he returned with a lighted candle, and the intelligence that Toby Crackit was asleep in the back room below, and that the boys were in the front one. Beckoning the man to follow him, he led the way up stairs.

'We can say the few words we've got to say in here, my dear,' said the Jew, throwing open a door on the first floor; 'and as there are holes in the shutters, and we never show lights to our neighbours, we'll set the candle on the stairs. There!'

With those words, the Jew, stooping down, placed the candle on an upper flight of stairs, exactly opposite to the room door. This done, he led the way into the apartment; which was destitute of all moveables save a broken arm-chair, and an old couch or sofa without covering, which stood behind the door. Upon this piece of furniture, the stranger sat himself with the air of a weary man; and the Jew, drawing up the arm-chair opposite, they sat face to face. It was not quite dark; the door was partially open; and the candle outside threw a feeble reflection on the opposite wall.

They conversed for some time in whispers. Though nothing

of the conversation was distinguishable beyond a few disjointed words here and there, a listener might easily have perceived that Fagin appeared to be defending himself against some remarks of the stranger; and that the latter was in a state of considerable irritation. They might have been talking, thus, for a quarter of an hour or more, when Monks—by which name the Jew had designated the strange man several times in the course of their colloquy—said, raising his voice a little—

'I tell you again, it was badly planned. Why not have kept him here among the rest, and made a sneaking, snivelling pickpocket of him at once?'

'Only hear him!' exclaimed the Jew, shrugging his shoulders.

'Why, do you mean to say you couldn't have done it, if you had chosen?' demanded Monks, sternly. 'Haven't you done it, with other boys, scores of times? If you had had patience for a twelve-month, at most, couldn't you have got him convicted, and sent safely out of the kingdom; perhaps for life?'

'Whose turn would that have served, my dear?' inquired the Jew, humbly.

'Mine,' replied Monks.

'But not mine,' said the Jew, submissively. 'He might have become of use to me. When there are two parties to a bargain, it is only reasonable that the interests of both should be consulted; is it, my good friend?'

'What then?' demanded Monks.

'I saw it was not easy to train him to the business,' replied the Jew; 'he was not like other boys in the same circumstances.'

'Curse him, no!' muttered the man, 'or he would have been a thief, long ago.'

'I had no hold upon him to make him worse,' pursued the Jew, anxiously watching the countenance of his companion. 'His hand was not in. I had nothing to frighten him with; which we always must have in the beginning, or we labour in vain. What could I do? Send him out with the Dodger and Charley? We had enough of that, at first, my dear; I trembled for us all.'

'*That* was not my doing,' observed Monks.

'No, no, my dear!' renewed the Jew. 'And I don't quarrel with it now; because, if it had never happened, you might never have clapped eyes upon the boy to notice him, and so led to the discovery that it was him you were looking for. Well! I got him back for you by means of the girl; and then *she* begins to favour him.'

'Throttle the girl!' said Monks, impatiently.

'Why, we can't afford to do that just now, my dear,' replied the Jew, smiling; 'and, besides, that sort of thing is not in our way; or, one of these days, I might be glad to have it done. I know what these girls are, Monks, well. As soon as the boy begins to harden, she'll care no more for him, than for a block of wood. You want him made a thief. If he is alive, I can make him one from this time; and if—if—' said the Jew, drawing nearer to the other, —'it's not likely, mind, —but if the worst comes to the worst, and he is dead—'

'It's no fault of mine if he is!' interposed the other man, with a look of terror, and clasping the Jew's arm with trembling hands. 'Mind that, Fagin! I had no hand in it. Anything but his death, I told you from the first. I won't shed blood; it's always found out, and haunts a man besides. If they shot him dead, I was not the cause; do you hear me? Fire this infernal den! What's that?'

'What!' cried the Jew, grasping the coward round the body, with both arms, as he sprung to his feet. 'Where?'

'Yonder!' replied the man, glaring at the opposite wall. 'The shadow! I saw the shadow of a woman, in a cloak and bonnet, pass along the wainscot like a breath!'

The Jew released his hold, and they rushed tumultuously from the room. The candle, wasted by the draught, was standing where it had been placed. It showed them only the empty staircase, and their own white faces. They listened intently: a profound silence reigned throughout the house.

'It's your fancy,' said the Jew, taking up the light and turning to his companion.

'I'll swear I saw it!' replied Monks, trembling. 'It was bending forward when I saw it first; and when I spoke, it darted away.'

The Jew glanced contemptuously at the pale face of his associate, and, telling him he could follow, if he pleased, ascended the
stairs. They looked into all the rooms; they were cold, bare, and
empty. They descended into the passage, and thence into the cellars
below. The green damp hung upon the low walls; the tracks of the
snail and slug glistened in the light of the candle; but all was still
as death.

'What do you think now?' said the Jew, when they had regained
the passage. 'Besides ourselves, there's not a creature in the house
except Toby and the boys; and they're safe enough. See here!'

As a proof of the fact, the Jew drew forth two keys from his
pocket; and explained, that when he first went down stairs, he had
locked them in, to prevent any intrusion on the conference.

This accumulated testimony effectually staggered Mr. Monks.
His protestations had gradually become less and less vehement as
they proceeded in their search without making any discovery; and,
now, he gave vent to several very grim laughs, and confessed it could
only have been his excited imagination. He declined any renewal
of the conversation, however, for that night: suddenly remembering
that it was past one o'clock. And so the amiable couple parted.

CHAPTER 27

Atones for the unpoliteness of a former chapter; which deserted a lady, most unceremoniously

As it would be, by no means, seemly in a humble author to keep so mighty a personage as a beadle waiting, with his back to the fire, and the skirts of his coat gathered up under his arms, until such time as it might suit his pleasure to relieve him; and as it would still less become his station, or his gallantry to involve in the same neglect a lady on whom that beadle had looked with an eye of tenderness and affection, and in whose ear he had whispered sweet words, which, coming from such a quarter, might well thrill the bosom of maid or matron of whatsoever degree; the historian whose pen traces these words—trusting that he knows his place, and that he entertains a becoming reverence for those upon earth to whom high and import-ant authority is delegated—hastens to pay them that respect which their position demands, and to treat them with all that duteous cere-mony which their exalted rank, and (by consequence) great virtues, imperatively claim at his hands. Towards this end, indeed, he had purposed to introduce, in this place, a dissertation touching the divine right of beadles, and elucidative of the position, that a beadle can do no wrong: which could not fail to have been both pleasurable and profitable to the right-minded reader, but which he is unfortu-nately compelled, by want of time and space, to postpone to some more convenient and fitting opportunity; on the arrival of which, he will be prepared to show, that a beadle properly constituted: that is to say, a parochial beadle, attached to a parochial workhouse, and attending in his official capacity the parochial church: is, in right and virtue of his office, possessed of all the excellences and best qualities of humanity; and that to none of those excellences, can mere companies' beadles, or court-of-law beadles, or even chapel-of-ease beadles (save the last, and they in a very lowly and inferior degree), lay the remotest sustainable claim.

Mr. Bumble had re-counted the tea-spoons, re-weighed the sugar-tongs, made a closer inspection of the milk-pot, and ascertained to a nicety the exact condition of the furniture, down to the very horse-hair seats of the chairs; and had repeated each process full half-a-dozen times; before he began to think that it was time for Mrs. Corney to return. Thinking begets thinking; as there were no sounds of Mrs. Corney's approach, it occurred to Mr. Bumble that it would be an innocent and virtuous way of spending the time, if he were further to allay his curiosity by a cursory glance at the interior of Mrs. Corney's chest of drawers.

Having listened at the keyhole, to assure himself that nobody was approaching the chamber, Mr. Bumble, beginning at the bottom, proceeded to make himself acquainted with the contents of the three long drawers: which, being filled with various garments of good fashion and texture, carefully preserved between two layers of old newspapers, speckled with dried lavender: seemed to yield him exceeding satisfaction. Arriving, in course of time, at the right-hand corner drawer (in which was the key), and beholding therein a small padlocked box, which, being shaken, gave forth a pleasant sound, as of the chinking of coin, Mr. Bumble returned with a stately walk to the fireplace; and, resuming his old attitude, said, with a grave and determined air, 'I'll do it!' He followed up this remarkable declaration, by shaking his head in a waggish manner for ten minutes, as though he were remonstrating with himself for being such a pleasant dog; and then, he took a view of his legs in profile, with much seeming pleasure and interest.

He was still placidly engaged in this latter survey, when Mrs. Corney, hurrying into the room, threw herself, in a breathless state, on a chair by the fireside, and covering her eyes with one hand, placed the other over her heart, and gasped for breath.

'Mrs. Corney,' said Mr. Bumble, stooping over the matron, 'what is this, ma'am? Has anything happened, ma'am? Pray answer me; I'm on—on—' Mr. Bumble, in his alarm, could not immediately think of the word 'tenter-hooks,' so he said 'broken bottles.'

'Oh, Mr. Bumble!' cried the lady, 'I have been so dreadfully put out!'

'Put out, ma'am!' exclaimed Mr. Bumble; 'who has dared to—? I know!' said Mr. Bumble, checking himself, with native majesty, 'this is them wicious paupers!'

'It's dreadful to think of!' said the lady, shuddering.

'Then *don't* think of it, ma'am,' rejoined Mr. Bumble.

'I can't help it,' whimpered the lady.

'Then take something, ma'am,' said Mr. Bumble, soothingly. 'A little of the wine?'

'Not for the world!' replied Mrs. Corney. 'I couldn't, —oh! The top shelf in the right-hand corner—oh!' Uttering these words, the good lady pointed, distractedly, to the cupboard, and underwent a convulsion from internal spasms. Mr. Bumble rushed to the closet; and, snatching a pint green-glass bottle from the shelf thus incoherently indicated, filled a tea-cup with its contents, and held it to the lady's lips.

'I'm better now,' said Mrs. Corney, falling back, after drinking half of it.

Mr. Bumble raised his eyes piously to the ceiling in thankfulness; and, bringing them down again to the brim of the cup, lifted it to his nose.

'Peppermint,' exclaimed Mrs. Corney, in a faint voice, smiling gently on the beadle as she spoke. 'Try it! There's a little—a little something else in it.'

Mr. Bumble tasted the medicine with a doubtful look; smacked his lips; took another taste; and put the cup down empty.

'It's very comforting,' said Mrs. Corney.

'Very much so indeed, ma'am,' said the beadle. As he spoke,

he drew a chair beside the matron, and tenderly inquired what had happened to distress her.

'Nothing,' replied Mrs. Corney. 'I am a foolish, excitable, weak creetur.'

'Not weak, ma'am,' retorted Mr. Bumble, drawing his chair a little closer. 'Are you a weak creetur, Mrs. Corney?'

'We are all weak creeturs,' said Mrs. Corney, laying down a general principle.

'So we are,' said the beadle.

Nothing was said, on either side, for a minute or two afterwards. By the expiration of that time, Mr. Bumble had illustrated the position by removing his left arm from the back of Mrs. Corney's chair, where it had previously rested, to Mrs. Corney's apron-string, round which it gradually became entwined.

'We are all weak creeturs,' said Mr. Bumble.

Mrs. Corney sighed.

'Don't sigh, Mrs. Corney,' said Mr. Bumble.

'I can't help it,' said Mrs. Corney. And she sighed again.

'This is a very comfortable room, ma'am,' said Mr. Bumble, looking round. 'Another room, and this, ma'am, would be a complete thing.'

'It would be too much for one,' murmured the lady.

'But not for two, ma'am,' rejoined Mr. Bumble, in soft accents. 'Eh, Mrs. Corney?'

Mrs. Corney drooped her head, when the beadle said this; the beadle drooped his, to get a view of Mrs. Corney's face. Mrs. Corney, with great propriety, turned her head away, and released her hand to get at her pocket-handkerchief; but insensibly replaced it in that of Mr. Bumble.

'The board allow you coals, don't they, Mrs. Corney?' inquired the beadle, affectionately pressing her hand.

'And candles,' replied Mrs. Corney, slightly returning the pressure.

'Coals, candles, and house-rent free,' said Mr. Bumble. 'Oh, Mrs. Corney, what a Angel you are!'

The lady was not proof against this burst of feeling. She sank into Mr. Bumble's arms; and that gentleman, in his agitation, imprinted a passionate kiss upon her chaste nose.

'Such porochial perfection!' exclaimed Mr. Bumble, rapturously. 'You know that Mr. Slout is worse to-night, my fascinator?'

'Yes,' replied Mrs. Corney, bashfully.

'He can't live a week, the doctor says,' pursued Mr. Bumble. 'He is the master of this establishment; his death will cause a vacancy; that vacancy must be filled up. Oh, Mrs. Corney, what a prospect this opens! What a opportunity for a joining of hearts and housekeepings!'

Mrs. Corney sobbed.

'The little word?' said Mr. Bumble, bending over the bashful beauty. 'The one little, little, little word, my blessed Corney?'

'Ye—ye—yes!' sighed out the matron.

'One more,' pursued the beadle; 'compose your darling feelings for only one more. When is it to come off?'

Mrs. Corney twice essayed to speak; and twice failed. At length summoning up courage, she threw her arms round Mr. Bumble's neck, and said, it might be as soon as ever he pleased, and that he was 'a irresistible duck.'

Matters being thus amicably and satisfactorily arranged, the contract was solemnly ratified in another tea-cupful of the peppermint mixture; which was rendered the more necessary, by the flutter and agitation of the lady's spirits. While it was being disposed of, she acquainted Mr. Bumble with the old woman's decease.

'Very good,' said that gentleman, sipping his peppermint; 'I'll call at Sowerberry's as I go home, and tell him to send to-morrow morning. Was it that as frightened you, love?'

'It wasn't anything particular, dear,' said the lady, evasively.

'It must have been something, love,' urged Mr. Bumble. 'Won't you tell your own B.?'

'Not now,' rejoined the lady; 'one of these days. After we're married, dear.'

'After we're married!' exclaimed Mr. Bumble. 'It wasn't any impudence from any of them male paupers as—'

'No, no, love!' interposed the lady, hastily.

'If I thought it was,' continued Mr. Bumble; 'if I thought as any one of 'em had dared to lift his wulgar eyes to that lovely countenance—'

'They wouldn't have dared to do it, love,' responded the lady.

'They had better not!' said Mr. Bumble, clenching his fist. 'Let me see any man, porochial or extra-porochial, as would presume to do it; and I can tell him that he wouldn't do it a second time!'

Unembellished by any violence of gesticulation, this might have seemed no very high compliment to the lady's charms; but, as Mr. Bumble accompanied the threat with many warlike gestures, she was much touched with this proof of his devotion, and protested, with great admiration, that he was indeed a dove.

The dove then turned up his coat-collar, and put on his cocked-hat; and, having exchanged a long and affectionate embrace with his future partner, once again braved the cold wind of the night: merely pausing, for a few minutes, in the male pauper's ward, to abuse them a little, with the view of satisfying himself that he could fill the office of workhouse-master with needful acerbity. Assured of his qualifications, Mr. Bumble left the building with a light heart, and bright visions of his future promotion: which served to occupy his mind until he reached the shop of the undertaker.

Now, Mr. and Mrs. Sowerberry having gone out to tea and supper: and Noah Claypole not being at any time disposed to take upon himself a greater amount of physical exertion than is necessary to a convenient performance of the two functions of eating and drinking, the shop was not closed, although it was past the usual hour of shutting-up. Mr. Bumble tapped with his cane on the counter several times; but, attracting no attention, and beholding a light shining through the glass-window of the little parlour at the back of the shop, he made bold to peep in and see what was going forward; and when he saw what *was* going forward, he was not a little surprised.

The cloth was laid for supper; the table was covered with bread and butter, plates and glasses; a porter-pot and a wine-bottle. At the upper end of the table, Mr. Noah Claypole lolled negligently in an easy-chair, with his legs thrown over one of the arms: an open clasp-knife in one hand, and a mass of buttered bread in the other. Close beside him stood Charlotte, opening oysters from a barrel: which Mr. Claypole condescended to swallow, with remarkable avidity. A more than ordinary redness in the region of the young gentleman's nose, and a kind of fixed wink in his right eye, denoted that he was in a slight degree intoxicated; these symptoms were confirmed by the intense relish with which he took his oysters, for which nothing but a strong appreciation of their cooling properties, in cases of internal fever, could have sufficiently accounted.

'Here's a delicious fat one, Noah, dear!' said Charlotte; 'try him, do; only this one.'

'What a delicious thing is a oyster!' remarked Mr. Claypole, after he had swallowed it. 'What a pity it is, a number of 'em should ever make you feel uncomfortable; isn't it, Charlotte?'

'It's quite a cruelty,' said Charlotte.

'So it is,' acquiesced Mr. Claypole. 'A'nt yer fond of oysters?'

'Not overmuch,' replied Charlotte. 'I like to see you eat 'em, Noah dear, better than eating 'em myself.'

'Lor'!' said Noah, reflectively; 'how queer!'

'Have another,' said Charlotte. 'Here's one with such a beautiful, delicate beard!'

'I can't manage any more,' said Noah. 'I'm very sorry. Come here, Charlotte, and I'll kiss yer.'

'What!' said Mr. Bumble, bursting into the room. 'Say that again, sir.'

Charlotte uttered a scream, and hid her face in her apron. Mr. Claypole, without making any further change in his position than suffering his legs to reach the ground, gazed at the beadle in drunken terror.

'Say it again, you wile, owdacious fellow!' said Mr. Bumble. 'How dare you mention such a thing, sir? And how dare you encourage him, you insolent minx? Kiss her!' exclaimed Mr. Bumble, in strong indignation. 'Faugh!'

'I didn't mean to do it!' said Noah, blubbering. 'She's always a-kissing of me, whether I like it, or not.'

'Oh, Noah!' cried Charlotte, reproachfully.

'Yer are; yer know yer are!' retorted Noah. 'She's always a-doing of it, Mr. Bumble, sir; she chucks me under the chin, please, sir; and makes all manner of love!'

'Silence!' cried Mr. Bumble, sternly. 'Take yourself down stairs, ma'am. Noah, you shut up the shop; say another word till your master comes home, at your peril; and, when he does come home, tell him that Mr. Bumble said he was to send a old woman's shell after breakfast to-morrow morning. Do you hear, sir? Kissing!' cried Mr. Bumble, holding up his hands. 'The sin and wickedness of the lower orders in this porochial district is frightful! If parliament don't take their abominable courses under consideration, this country's ruined, and the character of the peasantry gone for ever!' With these words, the beadle strode, with a lofty and gloomy air, from the undertaker's premises.

And now that we have accompanied him so far on his road home, and have made all necessary preparations for the old woman's funeral, let us set on foot a few inquiries after young Oliver Twist, and ascertain whether he be still lying in the ditch where Toby Crackit left him.

CHAPTER 28

Looks after Oliver, and proceeds with his adventures

'Wolves tear your throats!' muttered Sikes, grinding his teeth. 'I wish I was among some of you; you'd howl the hoarser for it.'

As Sikes growled forth this imprecation, with the most desperate ferocity that his desperate nature was capable of, he rested the body of the wounded boy across his bended knee; and turned his head, for an instant, to look back at his pursuers.

There was little to be made out, in the mist and darkness; but the loud shouting of men vibrated through the air, and the barking of the neighbouring dogs, roused by the sound of the alarm bell, resounded in every direction.

'Stop, you white-livered hound!' cried the robber, shouting after Toby Crackit, who, making the best use of his long legs, was already ahead. 'Stop!'

The repetition of the word, brought Toby to a dead stand-still. For he was not quite satisfied that he was beyond the range of pistol-shot; and Sikes was in no mood to be played with.

'Bear a hand with the boy,' cried Sikes, beckoning furiously to his confederate. 'Come back!'

Toby made a show of returning; but ventured, in a low voice, broken for want of breath, to intimate considerable reluctance as he came slowly along.

'Quicker!' cried Sikes, laying the boy in a dry ditch at his feet, and drawing a pistol from his pocket. 'Don't play booty with me.'

At this moment the noise grew louder. Sikes, again looking round, could discern that the men who had given chase were already climbing the gate of the field in which he stood; and that a couple of dogs were some paces in advance of them.

'It's all up, Bill!' cried Toby; 'drop the kid, and show 'em your heels.' With this parting advice, Mr. Crackit, preferring the chance of being shot by his friend, to the certainty of being taken by his enemies, fairly turned tail, and darted off at full speed. Sikes clenched his teeth; took one look around; threw over the prostrate form of Oliver, the cape in which he had been hurriedly muffled; ran along the front of the hedge, as if to distract the attention of those behind, from the spot where the boy lay; paused, for a second, before another hedge which met it at right angles; and whirling his pistol high into the air, cleared it at a bound, and was gone.

'Ho, ho, there!' cried a tremulous voice in the rear. 'Pincher! Neptune! Come here, come here!'

The dogs, who, in common with their masters, seemed to have no particular relish for the sport in which they were engaged, readily answered to the command. Three men, who had by this time advanced some distance into the field, stopped to take counsel together.

'My advice, or, leastways, I should say, my *orders*, is,' said the fattest man of the party, 'that we 'mediately go home again.'

'I am agreeable to anything which is agreeable to Mr. Giles,' said a shorter man; who was by no means of a slim figure, and who was very pale in the face, and very polite: as frightened men frequently are.

'I shouldn't wish to appear ill-mannered, gentlemen,' said the third, who had called the dogs back, 'Mr. Giles ought to know.'

'Certainly,' replied the shorter man; 'and whatever Mr. Giles says, it isn't our place to contradict him. No, no, I know my sitiwation! Thank my stars, I know my sitiwation.' To tell the truth, the little man *did* seem to know his situation, and to know perfectly well that it was by no means a desirable one; for his teeth chattered in his head as he spoke.

'You are afraid, Brittles,' said Mr. Giles.

'I a'n't,' said Brittles.

'You are,' said Giles.

'You're a falsehood, Mr. Giles,' said Brittles.

'You're a lie, Brittles,' said Mr. Giles.

Now, these four retorts arose from Mr. Giles's taunt; and Mr. Giles's taunt had arisen from his indignation at having the responsibility of going home again, imposed upon himself under cover of a compliment. The third man brought the dispute to a close, most philosophically.

'I'll tell you what it is, gentlemen,' said he, 'we're all afraid.'

'Speak for yourself, sir,' said Mr. Giles, who was the palest of the party.

'So I do,' replied the man. 'It's natural and proper to be afraid under such circumstances. *I* am.'

'So am I,' said Brittles; 'only there's no call to tell a man he is, so bounceably.'

These frank admissions softened Mr. Giles, who at once owned that *he* was afraid; upon which, they all three faced about, and ran back again with the completest unanimity, until Mr. Giles (who had the shortest wind of the party, and was encumbered with a pitchfork) most handsomely insisted on stopping, to make an apology for his hastiness of speech.

'But it's wonderful,' said Mr. Giles, when he had explained, 'what a man will do, when his blood is up. I should have committed murder—I know I should—if we'd caught one of them rascals.'

As the other two were impressed with a similar presentiment; and as their blood, like his, had all gone down again; some speculation ensued upon the cause of this sudden change in their temperament.

'I know what it was,' said Mr. Giles; 'it was the gate.'

'I shouldn't wonder if it was,' exclaimed Brittles, catching at the idea.

'You may depend upon it,' said Giles, 'that that gate stopped the flow of excitement. I felt all mine suddenly going away, as I was climbing over it.'

By a remarkable coincidence, the other two had been visited with the same unpleasant sensation at that precise moment. It was quite obvious, therefore, that it was the gate; especially as there was no doubt regarding the time at which the change had taken place, because all three remembered that they had come in sight of the robbers at the instant of its occurrence.

This dialogue was held between the two men who had surprised the burglars, and a travelling tinker who had been sleeping in an outhouse, and who had been roused, together with his two mongrel curs, to join in the pursuit. Mr. Giles acted in the double capacity of butler and steward to the old lady of the mansion; Brittles was a lad of all work: who, having entered her service a mere child, was treated as a promising young boy still, though he was something past thirty.

Encouraging each other with such converse as this; but, keeping very close together, notwithstanding, and looking apprehensively round, whenever a fresh gust rattled through the boughs; the three men hurried back to a tree, behind which they had left their lantern, lest its light should inform the thieves in what direction to fire. Catching up the light, they made the best of their way home, at a good round trot; and long after their dusky forms had ceased to be discernible, the light might have been seen twinkling and dancing in the distance, like some exhalation of the damp and gloomy atmosphere through which it was swiftly borne.

The air grew colder, as day came slowly on; and the mist rolled along the ground like a dense cloud of smoke. The grass was wet; the pathways, and low places were all mire and water; the damp breath of an unwholesome wind went languidly by, with a hollow moaning. Still, Oliver lay motionless and insensible on the spot where Sikes had left him.

Morning drew on apace. The air became more sharp and piercing, as its first dull hue—the death of night, rather than the birth of day—glimmered faintly in the sky. The objects which had looked dim and terrible in the darkness, grew more and more defined, and gradually resolved into their familiar shapes. The rain came down, thick and fast, and pattered noisily among the leafless bushes. But, Oliver felt it not, as it beat against him; for he still lay stretched, helpless and unconscious, on his bed of clay.

At length, a low cry of pain broke the stillness that prevailed; and uttering it, the boy awoke. His left arm, rudely bandaged in a shawl, hung heavy and useless at his side: the bandage was saturated with blood. He was so weak, that he could scarcely raise himself into a sitting posture; when he had done so, he looked feebly round for help, and groaned with pain. Trembling in every joint, from cold and exhaustion, he made an effort to stand upright; but, shuddering from head to foot, fell prostrate on the ground.

After a short return of the stupor in which he had been so long plunged, Oliver: urged by a creeping sickness at his heart, which seemed to warn him that if he lay there, he must surely die: got upon his feet, and essayed to walk. His head was dizzy, and he staggered to and fro like a drunken man. But he kept up, nevertheless, and, with his head drooping languidly on his breast, went stumbling onward, he knew not whither.

And now, hosts of bewildering and confused ideas came crowding on his mind. He seemed to be still walking between Sikes and Crackit, who were angrily disputing—for the very words they said, sounded in his ears; and when he caught his own attention, as it were, by making some violent effort to save himself from falling, he found that he was talking to them. Then, he was alone with Sikes, plodding on as on the previous day; and as shadowy people passed them, he felt the robber's grasp upon his wrist. Suddenly, he started back at the report of fire-arms; there rose into the air, loud cries and shouts; lights gleamed before his eyes; all was noise and tumult, as some unseen hand bore him hurriedly away. Through all these rapid visions, there ran an undefined, uneasy consciousness of pain, which wearied and tormented him incessantly.

Thus he staggered on, creeping, almost mechanically, between the bars of gates, or through hedge-gaps as they came in his way, until he reached a road. Here the rain began to fall so heavily, that it roused him.

He looked about, and saw that at no great distance there was a house, which perhaps he could reach. Pitying his condition, they might have compassion on him; and if they did not, it would be better, he thought, to die near human beings, than in the lonely open fields. He summoned up all his strength for one last trial, and bent his faltering steps towards it.

As he drew nearer to this house, a feeling came over him that he had seen it before. He remembered nothing of its details; but the shape and aspect of the building seemed familiar to him.

That garden wall! On the grass inside, he had fallen on his knees last night, and prayed the two men's mercy. It was the very house they had attempted to rob.

Oliver felt such fear come over him when he recognised the place, that, for the instant, he forgot the agony of his wound, and thought only of flight. Flight! He could scarcely stand: and if he were in full possession of all the best powers of his slight and youthful frame, whither could he fly? He pushed against the garden-gate; it was unlocked, and swung open on its hinges. He tottered across the lawn; climbed the steps; knocked faintly at the door; and, his whole strength failing him, sunk down against one of the pillars of the little portico.

It happened that about this time, Mr. Giles, Brittles, and the tinker, were recruiting themselves, after the fatigues and terrors of the night, with tea and sundries, in the kitchen. Not that it was Mr. Giles's habit to admit to too great familiarity the humbler servants: towards whom it was rather his wont to deport himself with a lofty affability, which, while it gratified, could not fail to remind them of his superior position in society. But, death, fires, and burglary, make all men equals; so Mr. Giles sat with his legs stretched out before the kitchen fender, leaning his left arm on the table, while, with his right, he illustrated a circumstantial and minute account of the robbery, to which his hearers (but especially the cook and housemaid, who were of the party) listened with breathless interest.

'It was about half-past two,' said Mr. Giles, 'or I wouldn't swear that it mightn't have been a little nearer three, when I woke up, and, turning round in my bed, as it might be so (here Mr. Giles turned round in his chair, and pulled the corner of the tablecloth over him to imitate bed-clothes), I fancied I heerd a noise.'

At this point of the narrative the cook turned pale, and asked the housemaid to shut the door: who asked Brittles, who asked the tinker, who pretended not to hear.

'—Heerd a noise,' continued Mr. Giles. 'I says, at first, "This is illusion;" and was composing myself off to sleep, when I heerd the noise again, distinct.'

'What sort of a noise?' asked the cook.

'A kind of a busting noise,' replied Mr. Giles, looking round him.

'More like the noise of powdering a iron bar on a nutmeg-grater,' suggested Brittles.

'It was, when *you* heerd it, sir,' rejoined Mr. Giles; 'but, at this time, it had a busting sound. I turned down the clothes;' continued Giles, rolling back the tablecloth, 'sat up in bed; and listened.'

The cook and housemaid simultaneously ejaculated 'Lor!' and drew their chairs closer together.

'I heerd it now, quite apparent,' resumed Mr. Giles. '"Somebody," I says, "is forcing of a door, or window; what's to be done? I'll call up that poor lad, Brittles, and save him from being murdered in his bed; or his throat," I says, "may be cut from his right ear to his left, without his ever knowing it."'

Here, all eyes were turned upon Brittles, who fixed his upon the speaker, and stared at him, with his mouth wide open, and his face expressive of the most unmitigated horror.

'I tossed off the clothes,' said Giles, throwing away the table-cloth, and looking very hard at the cook and housemaid, 'got softly out of bed; drew on a pair of—'

'Ladies present, Mr. Giles,' murmured the tinker.

'—Of *shoes*, sir,' said Giles, turning upon him, and laying great emphasis on the word; 'seized the loaded pistol that always goes up stairs with the plate-basket; and walked on tiptoes to his room. "Brittles," I says, when I had woke him, "don't be frightened!"'

'So you did,' observed Brittles, in a low voice.

'"We're dead men, I think, Brittles," I says,' continued Giles; '"but don't be frightened."'

'*Was* he frightened?' asked the cook.

'Not a bit of it,' replied Mr. Giles. 'He was as firm—ah! pretty near as firm as I was.'

'I should have died at once, I'm sure, if it had been me,' observed the housemaid.

'You're a woman,' retorted Brittles, plucking up a little.

'Brittles is right,' said Mr. Giles, nodding his head, approvingly; 'from a woman, nothing else was to be expected. We, being men, took a dark lantern that was standing on Brittles's hob, and groped our way down stairs in the pitch dark, —as it might be so.'

Mr. Giles had risen from his seat, and taken two steps with his eyes shut, to accompany his description with appropriate action, when he started violently, in common with the rest of the company, and hurried back to his chair. The cook and housemaid screamed.

'It was a knock,' said Mr. Giles, assuming perfect serenity. 'Open the door, somebody.'

Nobody moved.

'It seems a strange sort of thing, a knock coming at such a time in the morning,' said Mr. Giles, surveying the pale faces which surrounded him, and looking very blank himself; 'but the door must be opened. Do you hear, somebody?'

Mr. Giles, as he spoke, looked at Brittles; but that young man, being naturally modest, probably considered himself nobody, and so held that the inquiry could not have any application to him; at all events, he tendered no reply. Mr. Giles directed an appealing glance at the tinker; but he had suddenly fallen asleep. The women were out of the question.

'If Brittles would rather open the door, in the presence

of witnesses,' said Mr. Giles, after a short silence, 'I am ready to make one.'

'So am I,' said the tinker, waking up, as suddenly as he had fallen asleep.

Brittles capitulated on these terms; and the party being somewhat re-assured by the discovery (made on throwing open the shutters) that it was now broad day, took their way up stairs; with the dogs in front. The two women, who were afraid to stay below, brought up the rear. By the advice of Mr. Giles, they all talked very loud, to warn any evil-disposed person outside, that they were strong in numbers; and by a master-stroke of policy, originating in the brain of the same ingenious gentleman, the dogs' tails were well pinched, in the hall, to make them bark savagely.

These precautions having been taken, Mr. Giles held on fast by the tinker's arm (to prevent his running away, as he pleasantly said), and gave the word of command to open the door. Brittles obeyed; the group, peeping timorously over each other's shoulders, beheld no more formidable object than poor little Oliver Twist, speechless and exhausted, who raised his heavy eyes, and mutely solicited their compassion.

'A boy!' exclaimed Mr. Giles, valiantly pushing the tinker into the background. 'What's the matter with the—eh? —Why— Brittles—look here—don't you know?'

Brittles, who had got behind the door to open it, no sooner saw Oliver, than he uttered a loud cry. Mr. Giles, seizing the boy by one leg and one arm (fortunately not the broken limb) lugged him straight into the hall, and deposited him at full length on the floor thereof.

'Here he is!' bawled Giles, calling, in a state of great excitement, up the staircase; 'here's one of the thieves, ma'am! Here's a thief, miss! Wounded, miss! I shot him, miss; and Brittles held the light.'

'—In a lantern, miss' cried Brittles, applying one hand to the side of his mouth, so that his voice might travel the better.

The two women-servants ran up stairs to carry the intelligence that Mr. Giles had captured a robber; and the tinker busied himself in endeavouring to restore Oliver, lest he should die before he could be hanged. In the midst of all this noise and commotion, there was heard a sweet female voice, which quelled it in an instant.

'Giles!' whispered the voice from the stair-head.

'I'm here, miss,' replied Mr. Giles. 'Don't be frightened, miss; I ain't much injured. He didn't make a very desperate resistance, miss! I was soon too many for him.'

'Hush!' replied the young lady; 'you frighten my aunt as much as the thieves did. Is the poor creature much hurt?'

'Wounded desperate, miss,' replied Giles, with indescribable complacency.

'He looks as if he was a-going, miss,' bawled Brittles, in the same manner as before. 'Wouldn't you like to come and look at him, miss, in case he should?'

'Hush, pray; there's a good man!' rejoined the lady. 'Wait quietly only one instant, while I speak to aunt.'

With a footstep as soft and gentle as the voice, the speaker tripped away. She soon returned, with the direction that the wounded person was to be carried, carefully, up stairs to Mr. Giles's room; and that Brittles was to saddle the pony and betake himself instantly to Chertsey: from which place, he was to despatch, with all speed, a constable and doctor.

'But won't you take one look at him, first, miss?' asked Mr. Giles, with as much pride as if Oliver were some bird of rare plumage, that he had skilfully brought down. 'Not one little peep, miss?'

'Not now, for the world,' replied the young lady. 'Poor fellow! Oh! treat him kindly, Giles, for my sake!'

The old servant looked up at the speaker, as she turned away, with a glance as proud and admiring as if she had been his own child. Then, bending over Oliver, he helped to carry him up stairs, with the care and solicitude of a woman.

CHAPTER 29

Has an introductory account of the inmates of the house, to which Oliver resorted

In a handsome room: though its furniture had rather the air of old-fashioned comfort, than of modern elegance: there sat two ladies at a well-spread breakfast-table. Mr. Giles, dressed with scrupulous care in a full suit of black, was in attendance upon them. He had taken his station some half-way between the sideboard and the breakfast-table; and, with his body drawn up to its full height, his head thrown back, and inclined the merest trifle on one side, his left leg advanced, and his right hand thrust into his waistcoat, while his left hung down by his side, grasping a waiter, looked like one who laboured under a very agreeable sense of his own merits and importance.

Of the two ladies, one was well advanced in years; but the high-backed oaken chair in which she sat, was not more upright than she. Dressed with the utmost nicety and precision, in a quaint mixture of by-gone costume, with some slight concessions to the prevailing taste, which rather served to point the old style pleasantly than to impair its effect, she sat, in a stately manner, with her hands folded on the table before her. Her eyes (and age had dimmed but little of their brightness) were attentively fixed upon her young companion.

The younger lady was in the lovely bloom and springtime of womanhood; at that age, when, if ever angels be for God's good purposes enthroned in mortal forms, they may be, without impiety, supposed to abide in such as hers.

She was not past seventeen. Cast in so slight and exquisite a mould; so mild and gentle; so pure and beautiful; that earth seemed not her element, nor its rough creatures her fit companions. The very intelligence that shone in her deep blue eye, and was stamped upon her noble head, seemed scarcely of her age, or of the world; and yet the changing expression of sweetness and good humour, the thousand lights that played about the face, and left no shadow there; above all, the smile, the cheerful, happy smile, were made for Home, and fireside peace and happiness.

She was busily engaged in the little offices of the table. Chancing to raise her eyes as the elder lady was regarding her, she playfully put back her hair, which was simply braided on her forehead; and threw into her beaming look, such an expression of affection and artless loveliness, that blessed spirits might have smiled to look upon her.

'And Brittles has been gone upwards of an hour, has he?' asked the old lady, after a pause.

'An hour and twelve minutes, ma'am,' replied Mr. Giles, referring to a silver watch, which he drew forth by a black ribbon.

'He is always slow,' remarked the old lady.

'Brittles always was a slow boy, ma'am,' replied the attendant. And seeing, by-the-by, that Brittles had been a slow boy for upwards of thirty years, there appeared no great probability of his ever being a fast one.

'He gets worse instead of better, I think,' said the elder lady.

'It is very inexcusable in him if he stops to play with any other boys,' said the young lady, smiling.

Mr. Giles was apparently considering the propriety of indulging in a respectful smile himself, when a gig drove up to the garden gate: out of which there jumped a fat gentleman, who ran straight up to the door: and who, getting quickly into the house by some mysterious process, burst into the room, and nearly overturned Mr. Giles and the breakfast-table together.

'I never heard of such a thing!' exclaimed the fat gentleman. 'My dear Mrs. Maylie—bless my soul—in the silence of the night, too—I *never* heard of such a thing!'

With these expressions of condolence, the fat gentleman shook hands with both ladies, and drawing up a chair, inquired how they found themselves.

'You ought to be dead; positively dead with the fright,' said the fat gentleman. 'Why didn't you send? Bless me, my man should have come in a minute; and so would I; and my assistant would have been delighted; or anybody, I'm sure, under such circumstances. Dear, dear! So unexpected! In the silence of night, too!'

The doctor seemed especially troubled by the fact of the robbery having been unexpected, and attempted in the night-time; as if it were the established custom of gentlemen in the housebreaking way to transact business at noon, and to make an appointment, by post, a day or two previous.

'And you, Miss Rose,' said the doctor, turning to the young lady, 'I—'

'Oh! very much so, indeed,' said Rose, interrupting him; 'but there is a poor creature up stairs, whom aunt wishes you to see.'

'Ah! to be sure,' replied the doctor, 'so there is. That was your handiwork, Giles, I understand.'

Mr. Giles, who had been feverishly putting the teacups to rights, blushed very red, and said that he had had that honour.

'Honour, eh?' said the doctor; 'well, I don't know; perhaps it's as honourable to hit a thief in a back kitchen, as to hit your man at twelve paces. Fancy that he fired in the air, and you've fought a duel, Giles.'

Mr. Giles, who thought this light treatment of the matter an unjust attempt at diminishing his glory, answered respectfully, that it was not for the like of him to judge about that; but he rather thought it was no joke to the opposite party.

'Gad, that's true!' said the doctor. 'Where is he? Show me the way. I'll look in again, as I come down, Mrs. Maylie. That's the little window that he got in at, eh? Well, I couldn't have believed it!'

Talking all the way, he followed Mr. Giles up stairs; and while he is going up stairs, the reader may be informed, that Mr. Losberne, a surgeon in the neighbourhood, known through a circuit of ten miles round as 'the doctor,' had grown fat, more from good-humour than from good living: and was as kind and hearty, and withal as eccentric an old bachelor, as will be found in five times that space, by any explorer alive.

The doctor was absent, much longer than either he or the ladies had anticipated. A large flat box was fetched out of the gig; and a bedroom bell was rung very often; and the servants ran up and down stairs perpetually; from which tokens it was justly concluded that something important was going on above. At length he returned; and in reply to an anxious inquiry after his patient, looked very mysterious, and closed the door, carefully.

'This is a very extraordinary thing, Mrs. Maylie,' said the doctor, standing with his back to the door, as if to keep it shut.

'He is not in danger, I hope?' said the old lady.

'Why, that would *not* be an extraordinary thing, under the circumstances,' replied the doctor; 'though I don't think he is. Have you seen this thief?'

'No,' rejoined the old lady.

'Nor heard anything about him?'

'No.'

'I beg your pardon, ma'am,' interposed Mr. Giles; 'but I was going to tell you about him when Dr. Losberne came in.'

The fact was, that Mr. Giles had not, at first, been able to bring his mind to the avowal, that he had only shot a boy. Such commendations had been bestowed upon his bravery, that he could not, for the life of him, help postponing the explanation for a few delicious minutes; during which he had flourished, in the very zenith of a brief reputation for undaunted courage.

'Rose wished to see the man,' said Mrs. Maylie, 'but I wouldn't hear of it.'

'Humph!' rejoined the doctor. 'There is nothing very alarming in his appearance. Have you any objection to see him in my presence?'

'If it be necessary,' replied the old lady, 'certainly not.'

'Then I think it is necessary,' said the doctor; 'at all events, I am quite sure that you would deeply regret not having done so, if you postponed it. He is perfectly quiet and comfortable now. Allow me—Miss Rose, will you permit me? Not the slightest fear, I pledge you my honour!'

CHAPTER 30

Relates what Oliver's new visitors thought of him

With many loquacious assurances that they would be agreeably surprised in the aspect of the criminal, the doctor drew the young lady's arm through one of his; and offering his disengaged hand to Mrs. Maylie, led them, with much ceremony and stateliness, up stairs.

'Now,' said the doctor, in a whisper, as he softly turned the handle of a bedroom door, 'let us hear what you think of him. He has not been shaved very recently, but he don't look at all ferocious notwithstanding. Stop, though! Let me first see that he is in visiting order.'

Stepping before them, he looked into the room. Motioning them to advance, he closed the door when they had entered; and gently drew back the curtains of the bed. Upon it, in lieu of the dogged, black-visaged ruffian they had expected to behold, there lay a mere child: worn with pain and exhaustion, and sunk into a deep sleep. His wounded arm, bound and splintered up, was crossed upon his breast; his head reclined upon the other arm, which was half hidden by his long hair, as it streamed over the pillow.

The honest gentleman held the curtain in his hand, and looked on for a minute or so, in silence. Whilst he was watching the patient thus, the younger lady glided softly past, and seating herself in a chair by the bedside, gathered Oliver's hair from his face. As she stooped over him, her tears fell upon his forehead.

The boy stirred, and smiled in his sleep, as though these marks of pity and compassion had awakened some pleasant dream of a love and affection he had never known. Thus, a strain of gentle music, or the rippling of water in a silent place, or the odour of a flower, or the mention of a familiar word, will sometimes call up sudden dim remembrances of scenes that never were, in this life; which vanish like a breath; which some brief memory of a happier existence, long gone by, would seem to have awakened; which no voluntary exertion of the mind can ever recall.

'What can this mean?' exclaimed the elder lady. 'This poor child can never have been the pupil of robbers!'

'Vice,' sighed the surgeon, replacing the curtain, 'takes up her abode in many temples; and who can say that a fair outside shall not enshrine her?'

'But at so early an age!' urged Rose.

'My dear young lady,' rejoined the surgeon, mournfully shaking his head; 'crime, like death, is not confined to the old and withered alone. The youngest and fairest are too often its chosen victims.'

'But, can you—oh! can you really believe that this delicate boy has been the voluntary associate of the worst outcasts of society?' said Rose.

The surgeon shook his head, in a manner which intimated that he feared it was very possible; and observing that they might disturb the patient, led the way into an adjoining apartment.

'But even if he has been wicked,' pursued Rose, 'think how young he is; think that he may never have known a mother's love, or the comfort of a home; that ill-usage and blows, or the want of bread, may have driven him to herd with men who have forced him to guilt. Aunt, dear aunt, for mercy's sake, think of this, before you let them drag this sick child to a prison, which in any case must be the grave of all his chances of amendment. Oh! as you love me, and know that I have never felt the want of parents in your goodness and affection, but that I might have done so, and might have been equally helpless and unprotected with this poor child, have pity upon him before it is too late!'

'My dear love,' said the elder lady, as she folded the weeping girl to her bosom, 'do you think I would harm a hair of his head?'

'Oh, no!' replied Rose, eagerly.

'No, surely,' said the old lady; 'my days are drawing to their close; and may mercy be shown to me as I show it to others! What can I do to save him, sir?'

'Let me think, ma'am,' said the doctor; 'let me think.'

Mr. Losberne thrust his hands into his pockets, and took several turns up and down the room; often stopping, and balancing himself on his toes, and frowning frightfully. After various exclamations of 'I've got it now' and 'no, I haven't,' and as many renewals of the walking and frowning, he at length made a dead halt, and spoke as follows:

'I think if you give me a full and unlimited commission to bully Giles, and that little boy, Brittles, I can manage it. Giles is a faithful fellow and an old servant, I know; but you can make it up to him in a thousand ways, and reward him for being such a good shot besides. You don't object to that?'

'Unless there is some other way of preserving the child,' replied Mrs. Maylie.

'There is no other,' said the doctor. 'No other, take my word for it.'

'Then my aunt invests you with full power,' said Rose, smiling through her tears; 'but pray don't be harder upon the poor fellows than is indispensably necessary.'

'You seem to think,' retorted the doctor, 'that everybody is disposed to be hard-hearted to-day, except yourself, Miss Rose. I only hope, for the sake of the rising male sex generally, that you may be found in as vulnerable and soft-hearted a mood by the first eligible young fellow who appeals to your compassion; and I wish I were a young fellow, that I might avail myself, on the spot, of such a favourable opportunity for doing so, as the present.'

'You are as great a boy as poor Brittles himself,' returned Rose, blushing.

'Well,' said the doctor, laughing heartily, 'that is no very difficult matter. But to return to this boy. The great point of our agreement is yet to come. He will wake in an hour or so, I dare say; and although I have told that thick-headed constable-fellow down stairs that he mustn't be moved or spoken to, on peril of his life, I think we may converse with him without danger. Now I make this stipulation—that I shall examine him in your presence, and that, if, from what he says, we judge, and I can show to the satisfaction of your cool reason, that he is a real and thorough bad one (which is more than possible), he shall be left to his fate, without any further interference on my part, at all events.'

'Oh no, aunt!' entreated Rose.

'Oh yes, aunt!' said the doctor. 'Is it a bargain?'

'He cannot be hardened in vice,' said Rose; 'it is impossible.'

'Very good,' retorted the doctor; 'then so much the more reason for acceding to my proposition.'

Finally the treaty was entered into; and the parties thereunto sat down to wait, with some impatience, until Oliver should awake.

The patience of the two ladies was destined to undergo a longer trial than Mr. Losberne had led them to expect; for hour after hour passed on, and still Oliver slumbered heavily. It was evening, indeed, before the kind-hearted doctor brought them the intelligence, that he was at length sufficiently restored to be spoken to. The boy was very ill, he said, and weak from the loss of blood; but his mind was so troubled with anxiety to disclose something, that he deemed it better to give him the opportunity, than to insist upon his remaining quiet until next morning: which he should otherwise have done.

The conference was a long one. Oliver told them all his simple history, and was often compelled to stop, by pain and want of strength. It was a solemn thing, to hear, in the darkened room, the feeble voice of the sick child recounting a weary catalogue of evils and calamities which hard men had brought upon him. Oh! if when we oppress and grind our fellow-creatures, we bestowed but one thought on the dark evidences of human error, which, like dense and heavy clouds, are rising, slowly it is true, but not less surely, to Heaven, to pour their after-vengeance on our heads; if we heard but one instant, in imagination, the deep testimony of dead men's voices, which no power can stifle, and no pride shut out; where would be the injury and injustice, the suffering, misery, cruelty, and wrong, that each day's life brings with it?

Oliver's pillow was smoothed by gentle hands that night; and loveliness and virtue watched him as he slept. He felt calm and happy, and could have died without a murmur.

The momentous interview was no sooner concluded, and Oliver composed to rest again, than the doctor, after wiping his eyes, and condemning them for being weak all at once, betook himself down stairs to open upon Mr. Giles. And finding nobody about the parlours, it occurred to him, that he could perhaps originate the proceedings with better effect in the kitchen; so into the kitchen he went.

There were assembled, in that lower house of the domestic parliament, the women-servants, Mr. Brittles, Mr. Giles, the tinker (who had received a special invitation to regale himself for the remainder of the day, in consideration of his services), and the constable. The latter gentleman had a large staff, a large head, large features, and large half-boots; and he looked as if he had been taking a proportionate allowance of ale—as indeed he had.

The adventures of the previous night were still under discussion; for Mr. Giles was expatiating upon his presence of mind, when the doctor entered; Mr. Brittles, with a mug of ale in his hand, was corroborating everything, before his superior said it.

'Sit still!' said the doctor, waving his hand.

'Thank you, sir,' said Mr. Giles. 'Misses wished some ale to be given out, sir; and as I felt no ways inclined for my own little room, sir, and was disposed for company, I am taking mine among 'em here.'

Brittles headed a low murmur, by which the ladies and gentlemen generally were understood to express the gratification they derived from Mr. Giles's condescension. Mr. Giles looked round with a patronising air, as much as to say that so long as they behaved properly, he would never desert them.

'How is the patient to-night, sir?' asked Giles.

'So-so;' returned the doctor. 'I am afraid you have got your-self into a scrape there, Mr. Giles.'

'I hope you don't mean to say, sir,' said Mr. Giles, trembling, 'that he's going to die. If I thought it, I should never be happy again. I wouldn't cut a boy off: no, not even Brittles here: not for all the plate in the county, sir.'

'That's not the point,' said the doctor, mysteriously. 'Mr. Giles, are you a Protestant?'

'Yes, sir, I hope so,' faltered Mr. Giles, who had turned very pale.

'And what are *you*, boy?' said the doctor, turning sharply upon Brittles.

'Lord bless me, sir!' replied Brittles, starting violently; 'I'm— the same as Mr. Giles, sir.'

'Then tell me this,' said the doctor, 'both of you, both of you! Are you going to take upon yourselves to swear, that that boy up stairs is the boy that was put through the little window last night? Out with it! Come! We are prepared for you!'

The doctor, who was universally considered one of the best-tempered creatures on earth, made this demand in such a dreadful tone of anger, that Giles and Brittles, who were considerably muddled by ale and excitement, stared at each other in a state of stupefaction.

'Pay attention to the reply, constable, will you?' said the doctor, shaking his forefinger with great solemnity of manner, and tapping the bridge of his nose with it, to bespeak the exercise of that worthy's utmost acuteness. 'Something may come of this before long.'

The constable looked as wise as he could, and took up his staff of office: which had been reclining indolently in the chimney-corner.

'It's a simple question of identity, you will observe,' said the doctor.

'That's what it is, sir,' replied the constable, coughing with great violence; for he had finished his ale in a hurry, and some of it had gone the wrong way.

'Here's a house broken into,' said the doctor, 'and a couple of men catch one moment's glimpse of a boy, in the midst of gunpowder-smoke, and in all the distraction of alarm and darkness. Here's a boy comes to that very same house, next morning, and because he happens to have his arm tied up, these men lay violent hands upon him—by doing which, they place his life in great danger—and swear he is the thief. Now, the question is, whether these men are justified by the fact; if not, in what situation do they place themselves?

The constable nodded profoundly. He said, if that wasn't law, he would be glad to know what was.

'I ask you again,' thundered the doctor, 'are you, on your solemn oaths, able to identify that boy?'

Brittles looked doubtfully at Mr. Giles; Mr. Giles looked doubtfully at Brittles; the constable put his hand behind his ear, to catch the reply; the two women and the tinker leaned forward to listen; the doctor glanced keenly round; when a ring was heard at the gate, and at the same moment, the sound of wheels.

'It's the runners!' cried Brittles, to all appearance much relieved.

'The what?' exclaimed the doctor, aghast in his turn.

'The Bow Street officers, sir,' replied Brittles, taking up a candle; 'me and Mr. Giles sent for 'em this morning.'

'What?' cried the doctor.

'Yes,' replied Brittles; 'I sent a message up by the coachman, and I only wonder they weren't here before, sir.'

'You did, did you? Then confound your—slow coaches down here; that's all,' said the doctor, walking away.

CHAPTER 31

Involves a critical position

'Who's that?' inquired Brittles, opening the door a little way, with the chain up, and peeping out, shading the candle with his hand.

'Open the door,' replied a man outside; 'it's the officers from Bow Street, as was sent to, to-day.'

Much comforted by this assurance, Brittles opened the door to its full width, and confronted a portly man in a great-coat; who walked in, without saying anything more, and wiped his shoes on the mat, as coolly as if he lived there.

'Just send somebody out to relieve my mate, will you, young man?' said the officer; 'he's in the gig, a-minding the prad. Have you got a coach-'us here, that you could put it up in, for five or ten minutes?'

Brittles replying in the affirmative, and pointing out the building, the portly man stepped back to the garden-gate, and helped his companion to put up the gig: while Brittles lighted them, in a state of great admiration. This done, they returned to the house, and, being shown into a parlour, took off their great-coats and hats, and showed like what they were.

The man who had knocked at the door, was a stout personage of middle height, aged about fifty: with shiny black hair, cropped pretty close; half-whiskers, a round face, and sharp eyes. The other was a red-headed, bony man, in top-boots; with a rather ill-favoured countenance, and a turned-up, sinister-looking nose.

'Tell your governor that Blathers and Duff is here, will you?' said the stouter man, smoothing down his hair, and laying a pair of hand-cuffs on the table. 'Oh! Good evening, master. Can I have a word or two with you in private, if you please?'

This was addressed to Mr. Losberne, who now made his appearance; that gentleman, motioning Brittles to retire, brought in the two ladies, and shut the door.

'This is the lady of the house,' said Mr. Losberne, motioning towards Mrs. Maylie.

Mr. Blathers made a bow. Being desired to sit down, he put his hat on the floor, and taking a chair, motioned Duff to do the same. The latter gentleman, who did not appear quite so much accustomed to good society, or quite so much at his ease in it—one of the two—seated himself, after undergoing several muscular affections of the limbs, and forced the head of his stick into his mouth, with some embarrassment.

'Now, with regard to this here robbery, master,' said Blathers. 'What are the circumstances?'

Mr. Losberne, who appeared desirous of gaining time, recounted them at great length, and with much circumlocution. Messrs. Blathers and Duff looked very knowing meanwhile, and occasionally exchanged a nod.

'I can't say, for certain, till I see the work, of course,' said Blathers; 'but my opinion at once is,—I don't mind committing myself to that extent,—that this wasn't done by a yokel; eh, Duff?'

'Certainly not,' replied Duff.

'And, translating the word yokel for the benefit of the ladies, I apprehend your meaning to be, that this attempt was not made by a countryman?' said Mr. Losberne, with a smile.

'That's it, master,' replied Blathers. 'This is all about the robbery, is it?'

'All,' replied the doctor.

'Now, what is this, about this here boy that the servants are a-talking on?' said Blathers.

'Nothing at all,' replied the doctor. 'One of the frightened servants chose to take it into his head, that he had something to do with this attempt to break into the house; but it's nonsense: sheer absurdity.'

'Wery easy disposed of, if it is,' remarked Duff.

'What he says is quite correct,' observed Blathers, nodding his head in a confirmatory way, and playing carelessly with the hand-cuffs, as if they were a pair of castanets. 'Who is the boy? What account does he give of himself? Where did he come from? He didn't drop out of the clouds, did he, master?'

'Of course not,' replied the doctor, with a nervous glance at the two ladies. 'I know his whole history: but we can talk about that presently. You would like, first, to see the place where the thieves made their attempt, I suppose?'

'Certainly,' rejoined Mr. Blathers. 'We had better inspect the premises first, and examine the servants afterwards. That's the usual way of doing business.'

Lights were then procured; and Messrs. Blathers and Duff, attended by the native constable, Brittles, Giles, and everybody else in short, went into the little room at the end of the passage and looked out at the window; and afterwards went round by way of the lawn, and looked in at the window; and after that, had a candle handed out to inspect the shutter with; and after that, a lantern to trace the footsteps with; and after that, a pitchfork to poke the bushes with. This done, amidst the breathless interest of all beholders, they came in again; and Mr. Giles and Brittles were put through a melodramatic representation of their share in the previous night's adventures: which they performed some six times over: contradicting each other, in not more than one important respect, the first time, and in not more than a dozen the last. This consummation being arrived at, Blathers and Duff cleared the room, and held a long council together, compared with which, for secrecy and solemnity, a consultation of great doctors on the knottiest point in medicine, would be mere child's play.

Meanwhile, the doctor walked up and down the next room in a very uneasy state; and Mrs. Maylie and Rose looked on, with anxious faces.

'Upon my word,' he said, making a halt, after a great number of very rapid turns, 'I hardly know what to do.'

'Surely,' said Rose, 'the poor child's story, faithfully repeated to these men, will be sufficient to exonerate him.'

'I doubt it, my dear young lady,' said the doctor, shaking his head. 'I don't think it would exonerate him, either with them, or with legal functionaries of a higher grade. What is he, after all, they would say? A runaway. Judged by mere worldly considerations and probabilities, his story is a very doubtful one.'

'You believe it, surely?' interrupted Rose.

'*I* believe it, strange as it is; and perhaps I may be an old fool for doing so,' rejoined the doctor; 'but I don't think it is exactly the tale for a practised police-officer, nevertheless.'

'Why not?' demanded Rose.

'Because, my pretty cross-examiner,' replied the doctor: 'because, viewed with their eyes, there are many ugly points about it; he can only prove the parts that look ill, and none of those that look well. Confound the fellows, they *will* have the why and the wherefore, and will take nothing for granted. On his own showing, you see, he has been the companion of thieves for some time past; he has been carried to a police-office, on a charge of picking a gentleman's pocket; he has been taken away, forcibly, from that gentleman's house, to a place which he cannot describe or point out, and of the situation of which he has not the remotest idea. He is brought down to Chertsey, by men who seem to have taken a violent fancy to him, whether he will or no; and is put through a window to rob a house; and then, just at the very moment when he is going to alarm the inmates, and so do the very thing that would set him all to rights, there rushes into the way, a blundering dog of a half-bred butler, and shoots him! As if on purpose to prevent his doing any good for himself! Don't you see all this?'

'I see it, of course,' replied Rose, smiling at the doctor's impetuosity; 'but still I do not see anything in it, to criminate the poor child.'

'No,' replied the doctor; 'of course not! Bless the bright eyes of your sex! They never see, whether for good or bad, more than one side of any question; and that is, always, the one which first presents itself to them.'

Having given vent to this result of experience, the doctor put his hands into his pockets, and walked up and down the room with even greater rapidity than before.

'The more I think of it,' said the doctor, 'the more I see that it will occasion endless trouble and difficulty if we put these men in possession of the boy's real story. I am certain it will not be believed; and even if they can do nothing to him in the end, still the dragging it forward, and giving publicity to all the doubts that will be cast upon it, must interfere, materially, with your benevolent plan of rescuing him from misery.'

'Oh! what is to be done?' cried Rose. 'Dear, dear! why did they send for these people?'

'Why, indeed!' exclaimed Mrs. Maylie. 'I would not have had them here, for the world.'

'All I know is,' said Mr. Losberne, at last: sitting down with a kind of desperate calmness, 'that we must try and carry it off with a bold face. The object is a good one, and that must be our excuse. The boy has strong symptoms of fever upon him, and is in no condition to be talked to any more; that's one comfort. We must make the best of it; and if bad be the best, it is no fault of ours. Come in!'

'Well, master,' said Blathers, entering the room followed by his colleague, and making the door fast, before he said any more. 'This warn't a put-up thing.'

'And what the devil's a put-up thing?' demanded the doctor, impatiently.

'We call it a put-up robbery, ladies,' said Blathers, turning to them, as if he pitied their ignorance, but had a contempt for the doctor's, 'when the servants is in it.'

'Nobody suspected them, in this case,' said Mrs. Maylie.

'Wery likely not, ma'am,' replied Blathers; 'but they might have been in it, for all that.'

'More likely on that wery account,' said Duff.

'We find it was a town hand,' said Blathers, continuing his report; 'for the style of work is first-rate.'

'Wery pretty indeed it is,' remarked Duff, in an undertone.

'There was two of 'em in it,' continued Blathers; 'and they had a boy with 'em; that's plain from the size of the window. That's all to be said at present. We'll see this lad that you've got up stairs at once, if you please.'

'Perhaps they will take something to drink first, Mrs. Maylie?' said the doctor: his face brightening, as if some new thought had occurred to him.

'Oh! to be sure!' exclaimed Rose, eagerly. 'You shall have it immediately, if you will.'

'Why, thank you, miss!' said Blathers, drawing his coat-sleeve across his mouth; 'it's dry work, this sort of duty. Anythink that's handy, miss; don't put yourself out of the way, on our accounts.'

'What shall it be?' asked the doctor, following the young lady to the sideboard.

'A little drop of spirits, master, if it's all the same,' replied Blathers. 'It's a cold ride from London, ma'am; and I always find that spirits comes home warmer to the feelings.'

This interesting communication was addressed to Mrs. Maylie, who received it very graciously. While it was being conveyed to her, the doctor slipped out of the room.

'Ah!' said Mr. Blathers: not holding his wine-glass by the stem, but grasping the bottom between the thumb and forefinger of his left hand: and placing it in front of his chest; 'I have seen a good many pieces of business like this, in my time, ladies.'

'That crack down in the back lane at Edmonton, Blathers,' said Mr. Duff, assisting his colleague's memory.

'That was something in this way, warn't it?' rejoined Mr. Blathers; 'that was done by Conkey Chickweed, that was.'

'You always gave that to him,' replied Duff. 'It was the Family Pet, I tell you. Conkey hadn't any more to do with it than I had.'

'Get out!' retorted Mr. Blathers; 'I know better. Do you mind that time when Conkey was robbed of his money, though? What a start that was! Better than any novel-book *I* ever see!'

'What was that?' inquired Rose: anxious to encourage any symptoms of good-humour in the unwelcome visitors.

'It was a robbery, miss, that hardly anybody would have been down upon,' said Blathers. 'This here Conkey Chickweed—'

'Conkey means Nosey, ma'am,' interposed Duff.

'Of course the lady knows that, don't she?' demanded Mr. Blathers. 'Always interrupting, you are, partner! This here Conkey Chickweed, miss, kept a public-house over Battle-bridge way, and he had a cellar, where a good many young lords went to see cock-fighting, and badger-drawing, and that; and a wery intellectual manner the sports was conducted in, for I've seen 'em off'en. He warn't one of the family, at that time; and one night he was robbed of three hundred and twenty-seven guineas in a canvas bag, that was stole out of his bedroom in the dead of night, by a tall man with a black patch over his eye, who had concealed himself under the bed, and after committing the robbery, jumped slap out of window: which was only a story high. He was wery quick about it. But Conkey was quick, too; for he was woke by the noise, and darting out of bed, he fired a blunderbuss arter him, and roused the neighbourhood. They set up a hue-and-cry, directly, and when they came to look about 'em, found that Conkey had hit the robber; for there was traces of blood, all the way to some palings a good distance off; and there they lost 'em. However he had made off with the blunt; and, consequently, the name of Mr. Chickweed, licensed witler, appeared in the Gazette among the other bankrupts; and all manner of benefits and subscriptions, and I don't know what all, was got up for the poor man, who was in a wery low state of mind about his loss, and went up and down the streets, for three or four days, a-pulling his hair off in such a desperate manner that many people was afraid he might be going to make away with himself. One day he came up to the office, all in a hurry, and had a private interview with the magistrate, who, after a deal of talk, rings the bell, and orders Jem Spyers in (Jem was a active officer), and tells him to go and assist Mr. Chickweed in apprehending the man as robbed his house. "I see him, Spyers," said Chickweed, "pass my house yesterday morning." "Why didn't you up, and collar him?" says Spyers. "I was so struck all of a heap, that you might have fractured my skull with a tooth-pick," says the poor man; "but we're sure to have him; for between ten and eleven o'clock at night he passed again." Spyers no sooner heard this, than he put some clean linen and a comb, in his pocket, in case he should have to stop a day or two; and away he goes, and sets himself down at one of the public-house windows behind the little red curtain, with his hat on, all ready to bolt out, at a moment's notice. He was smoking his pipe here, late at night, when all of a sudden Chickweed roars out "Here he is! Stop thief! Murder!" Jem Spyers dashes out; and there he sees Chickweed, a-tearing down the street full cry. Away goes Spyers; on goes Chickweed; round turns the people; everybody roars out, "Thieves!" and Chickweed himself keeps on shouting, all the time, like mad. Spyers loses sight of him a minute as he turns a corner; shoots round; sees a little crowd; dives in; "Which is the man?" "D—me!" says Chickweed, "I've lost him again!" It was a remarkable occurrence, but he warn't to be seen nowhere, so they went back to the public-house. Next morning, Spyers took his old place, and looked out, from behind the curtain, for a tall man with a black patch over his eye, till his own two eyes ached again. At last, he couldn't help shutting 'em, to ease 'em a minute; and the very moment he did so, he hears Chickweed a-roaring out, "Here he is!" Off he starts once more, with Chickweed half-way down the street ahead of him; and after twice as long a run as the yesterday's one, the man's lost again! This was done, once or twice more, till one-half the neighbours gave out that Mr. Chickweed had been robbed by the devil, who was playing tricks with him arterwards; and the other half, that poor Mr. Chickweed had gone mad with grief.'

'What did Jem Spyers say?' inquired the doctor: who had returned to the room shortly after the commencement of the story.

'Jem Spyers,' resumed the officer, 'for a long time said nothing at all, and listened to everything without seeming to, which showed he understood his business. But, one morning, he walked into the bar, and taking out his snuff-box, says, "Chickweed, I've found out who done this here robbery." "Have you?" said Chickweed. "Oh, my dear Spyers, only let me have wengeance, and I shall die contented! Oh, my dear Spyers, where is the villain?" "Come!" said Spyers, offering him a pinch of snuff, "none of that gammon! You did it yourself." So he had; and a good bit of money he had made by it, too; and nobody would never have found it out, if he hadn't been so precious anxious to keep up appearances!' said Mr. Blathers, putting down his wine-glass, and clinking the hand-cuffs together.

'Very curious, indeed,' observed the doctor. 'Now, if you please, you can walk up stairs.'

'If *you* please, sir,' returned Mr. Blathers. Closely following Mr. Losberne, the two officers ascended to Oliver's bedroom; Mr. Giles preceding the party, with a lighted candle.

Oliver had been dozing; but looked worse, and was more feverish than he had appeared yet. Being assisted by the doctor, he managed to sit up in bed for a minute or so; and looked at the strangers without at all understanding what was going forward—in fact, without seeming to recollect where he was, or what had been passing.

'This,' said Mr. Losberne, speaking softly, but with great vehemence notwithstanding, 'this is the lad, who, being accidentally wounded by a spring-gun in some boyish trespass on Mr. What-d'ye-call-him's grounds, at the back here, comes to the house for assistance this morning, and is immediately laid hold of and maltreated, by that ingenious gentleman with the candle in his hand, who has placed his life in considerable danger, as I can professionally certify.'

Messrs. Blathers and Duff looked at Mr. Giles, as he was thus recommended to their notice. The bewildered butler gazed from them towards Oliver, and from Oliver towards Mr. Losberne, with a most ludicrous mixture of fear and perplexity.

'You don't mean to deny that, I suppose?' said the doctor, laying Oliver gently down again.

'It was all done for the—for the best, sir!' answered Giles. 'I am sure I thought it was the boy, or I wouldn't have meddled with him. I am not of an inhuman disposition, sir.'

'Thought it was what boy?' inquired the senior officer.

'The housebreaker's boy, sir!' replied Giles. 'They—they certainly had a boy.'

'Well? Do you think so now?' inquired Blathers.

'Think what, now?' replied Giles, looking vacantly at his questioner.

'Think it's the same boy, Stupid-head?' rejoined Blathers, impatiently.

'I don't know; I really don't know,' said Giles, with a rueful countenance. 'I couldn't swear to him.'

'What do you think?' asked Mr. Blathers.

'I don't know what to think,' replied poor Giles. 'I don't think it is the boy; indeed, I'm almost certain that it isn't. You know it can't be.'

'Has this man been a-drinking, sir?' inquired Blathers, turning to the doctor.

'What a precious muddle-headed chap you are!' said Duff, addressing Mr. Giles, with supreme contempt.

Mr. Losberne had been feeling the patient's pulse during this short dialogue; but he now rose from the chair by the bedside, and remarked, that if the officers had any doubts upon the subject, they would perhaps like to step into the next room, and have Brittles before them.

Acting upon this suggestion, they adjourned to a neighbouring apartment, where Mr. Brittles, being called in, involved himself and his respected superior in such a wonderful maze of fresh contradictions and impossibilities, as tended to throw no particular light on anything, but the fact of his own strong mystification; except, indeed, his declarations that he shouldn't know the real boy, if he were put before him that instant; that he had only taken Oliver to be he, because Mr. Giles had said he was; and that Mr. Giles had, five minutes previously, admitted in the kitchen, that he began to be very much afraid he had been a little too hasty.

Among other ingenious surmises, the question was then raised, whether Mr. Giles had really hit anybody; and upon examination of the fellow pistol to that which he had fired, it turned out to have no more destructive loading than gunpowder and brown paper: a discovery which made a considerable impression on everybody but the doctor, who had drawn the ball about ten minutes before. Upon no one, however, did it make a greater impression than on Mr. Giles himself; who, after labouring, for some hours, under the fear of having mortally wounded a fellow-creature, eagerly caught at this new idea, and favoured it to the utmost. Finally, the officers, without troubling themselves very much about Oliver, left the Chertsey constable in the house, and took up their rest for that night in the town; promising to return next morning.

With the next morning, there came a rumour, that two men and a boy were in the cage at Kingston, who had been apprehended over night under suspicious circumstances; and to Kingston Messrs. Blathers and Duff journeyed accordingly. The suspicious circumstances, however, resolving themselves, on investigation, into the one fact, that they had been discovered sleeping under a haystack; which, although a great crime, is only punishable by imprisonment, and is, in the merciful eye of the English law, and its comprehensive love of all the king's subjects, held to be no satisfactory proof, in the absence of all other evidence, that the sleeper, or sleepers, have committed burglary accompanied with violence, and have therefore rendered themselves liable to the punishment of death; Messrs. Blathers and Duff came back again, as wise as they went.

In short, after some more examination, and a great deal more conversation, a neighbouring magistrate was readily induced to take the joint bail of Mrs. Maylie and Mr. Losberne for Oliver's appearance if he should ever be called upon; and Blathers and Duff, being rewarded with a couple of guineas, returned to town with divided opinions on the subject of their expedition: the latter gentleman on a mature consideration of all the circumstances, inclining to the belief that the burglarious attempt had originated with the Family Pet; and the former being equally disposed to concede the full merit of it to the great Mr. Gonkey Chickweed.

Meanwhile, Oliver gradually throve and prospered under the united care of Mrs. Maylie, Rose, and the kind-hearted Mr. Losberne. If fervent prayers, gushing from hearts overcharged with gratitude, be heard in heaven—and if they be not, what prayers are!—the blessings which the orphan child called down upon them, sunk into their souls, diffusing peace and happiness.

CHAPTER 32

Of the happy life Oliver began to lead with his kind friends

Oliver's ailings were neither slight nor few. In addition to the pain and delay attendant on a broken limb, his exposure to the wet and cold had brought on fever and ague: which hung about him for many weeks, and reduced him sadly. But, at length, he began, by slow degrees, to get better, and to be able to say sometimes, in a few tearful words, how deeply he felt the goodness of the two sweet ladies, and how ardently he hoped that when he grew strong and well again, he could do something to show his gratitude; only something which would let them see the love and duty with which his breast was full; something, however slight, which would prove to them that their gentle kindness had not been cast away; but that the poor boy whom their charity had rescued from misery, or death, was eager to serve them with his whole heart and soul.

'Poor fellow!' said Rose, when Oliver had been one day feebly endeavouring to utter the words of thankfulness that rose to his pale lips: 'you shall have many opportunities of serving us, if you will. We are going into the country, and my aunt intends that you shall accompany us. The quiet place, the pure air, and all the pleasures and beauties of spring, will restore you in a few days. We will employ you in a hundred ways, when you can bear the trouble.'

'The trouble!' cried Oliver. 'Oh! dear lady, if I could but work for you; if I could only give you pleasure by watering your flowers, or watching your birds, or running up and down the whole day long, to make you happy; what would I give to do it!'

'You shall give nothing at all,' said Miss Maylie, smiling; 'for, as I told you before, we shall employ you in a hundred ways; and if you only take half the trouble to please us, that you promise now, you will make me very happy indeed.'

'Happy, ma'am!' cried Oliver; 'how kind of you to say so!'

'You will make me happier than I can tell you,' replied the young lady. 'To think that my dear good aunt should have been the means of rescuing any one from such sad misery as you have described to us, would be an unspeakable pleasure to me; but to know that the object of her goodness and compassion was sincerely grateful and attached, in consequence, would delight me, more than you can well imagine. Do you understand me?' she inquired, watching Oliver's thoughtful face.

'Oh yes, ma'am, yes!' replied Oliver, eagerly; 'but I was thinking that I am ungrateful now.'

'To whom?' inquired the young lady.

'To the kind gentleman, and the dear old nurse, who took so much care of me before,' rejoined Oliver. 'If they knew how happy I am, they would be pleased, I am sure.'

'I am sure they would,' rejoined Oliver's benefactress; 'and Mr. Losberne has already been kind enough to promise that when you are well enough to bear the journey, he will carry you to see them.'

'Has he, ma'am?' cried Oliver, his face brightening with pleasure. 'I don't know what I shall do for joy when I see their kind faces once again!'

In a short time Oliver was sufficiently recovered to undergo the fatigue of this expedition. One morning he and Mr. Losberne set out, accordingly, in a little carriage which belonged to Mrs. Maylie. When they came to Chertsey Bridge, Oliver turned very pale, and uttered a loud exclamation.

'What's the matter with the boy?' cried the doctor, as usual, all in a bustle. 'Do you see anything—hear anything—feel anything—eh?'

'That, sir,' cried Oliver, pointing out of the carriage window. 'That house!'

'Yes; well, what of it? Stop, coachman. Pull up here,' cried the doctor. 'What of the house, my man; eh?'

'The thieves—the house they took me to!' whispered Oliver.

'The devil it is!' cried the doctor. 'Halloa, there! let me out!'

But, before the coachman could dismount from his box, he had tumbled out of the coach, by some means or other; and, running down to the deserted tenement, began kicking at the door like a madman.

'Halloa?' said a little ugly hump-backed man: opening the door so suddenly, that the doctor, from the very impetus of his last kick, nearly fell forward into the passage. 'What's the matter here?'

'Matter!' exclaimed the other, collaring him, without a moment's reflection. 'A good deal. Robbery is the matter.'

'There'll be murder the matter, too,' replied the humpbacked man, coolly, 'if you don't take your hands off. Do you hear me?'

'I hear you,' said the doctor, giving his captive a hearty shake. 'Where's—confound the fellow, what's his rascally name—Sikes; that's it. Where's Sikes, you thief?'

The hump-backed man stared, as if in excess of amazement and indignation; then, twisting himself, dexterously, from the doctor's grasp, growled forth a volley of horrid oaths, and retired into the house. Before he could shut the door, however, the doctor had passed into the parlour, without a word of parley. He looked anxiously round; not an article of furniture; not a vestige of anything, animate or inanimate; not even the position of the cupboards; answered Oliver's description!

'Now!' said the hump-backed man, who had watched him keenly, 'what do you mean by coming into my house, in this violent way? Do you want to rob me, or to murder me? Which is it?'

'Did you ever know a man come out to do either, in a chariot and pair, you ridiculous old vampire?' said the irritable doctor.

'What do you want, then?' demanded the hunchback. 'Will you take yourself off, before I do you a mischief? Curse you!'

'As soon as I think proper,' said Mr. Losberne, looking into the other parlour; which, like the first, bore no resemblance whatever to Oliver's account of it. 'I shall find you out, some day, my friend.'

'Will you?' sneered the ill-favoured cripple. 'If you ever want me, I'm here. I haven't lived here mad and all alone, for five-and-twenty years, to be scared by you. You shall pay for this; you shall pay for this.' And so saying, the misshapen little demon set up a yell, and danced upon the ground, as if wild with rage.

'Stupid enough, this,' muttered the doctor to himself; 'the boy must have made a mistake. Here! Put that in your pocket, and shut yourself up again.' With these words he flung the hunchback a piece of money, and returned to the carriage.

The man followed to the chariot door, uttering the wildest imprecations and curses all the way; but as Mr. Losberne turned to speak to the driver, he looked into the carriage, and eyed Oliver for an instant with a glance so sharp and fierce and at the same time so furious and vindictive, that, waking or sleeping, he could not forget it for months afterwards. He continued to utter the most fearful imprecations, until the driver had resumed his seat; and when they were once more on their way, they could see him some distance behind: beating his feet upon the ground, and tearing his hair, in transports of real or pretended rage.

'I am an ass!' said the doctor, after a long silence. 'Did you know that before, Oliver?'

'No, sir.'

'Then don't forget it another time.'

'An ass,' said the doctor again, after a further silence of some minutes. 'Even if it had been the right place, and the right fellows had been there, what could I have done, single-handed? And if I had had assistance, I see no good that I should have done, except leading to my own exposure, and an unavoidable statement of the manner in which I have hushed up this business. That would have served me right, though. I am always involving myself in some scrape or other, by acting on impulse. It might have done me good.'

Now, the fact was that the excellent doctor had never acted upon anything but impulse all through his life, and it was no bad compliment to the nature of the impulses which governed him, that so far from being involved in any peculiar troubles or misfortunes, he had the warmest respect and esteem of all who knew him. If the truth must be told, he was a little out of temper, for a minute or two, at being disappointed in procuring corroborative evidence of Oliver's story, on the very first occasion on which he had a chance of obtaining any. He soon came round again, however; and finding that Oliver's replies to his questions, were still as straightforward and consistent, and still delivered with as much apparent sincerity and truth, as they had ever been, he made up his mind to attach full credence to them, from that time forth.

As Oliver knew the name of the street in which Mr. Brownlow resided, they were enabled to drive straight thither. When the coach turned into it, his heart beat so violently, that he could scarcely draw his breath.

'Now, my boy, which house is it?' inquired Mr. Losberne.

'That! That!' replied Oliver, pointing eagerly out of the window. 'The white house. Oh! make haste! Pray make haste! I feel as if I should die; it makes me tremble so.'

'Come, come!' said the good doctor, patting him on the shoulder. 'You will see them directly, and they will be overjoyed to find you safe and well.'

'Oh! I hope so!' cried Oliver. 'They were so good to me; so very, very good to me.'

The coach rolled on. It stopped. No; that was the wrong house; the next door. It went on a few paces, and stopped again. Oliver looked up at the windows, with tears of happy expectation coursing down his face.

Alas! the white house was empty, and there was a bill in the window. 'To Let.'

'Knock at the next door,' cried Mr. Losberne, taking Oliver's arm in his. 'What has become of Mr. Brownlow, who used to live in the adjoining house, do you know?'

The servant did not know; but would go and inquire. She presently returned, and said, that Mr. Brownlow had sold off his goods, and gone to the West Indies, six weeks before. Oliver clasped his hands, and sank feebly backward.

'Has his housekeeper gone, too?' inquired Mr. Losberne, after a moment's pause.

'Yes, sir,' replied the servant. 'The old gentleman, the house-keeper, and a gentleman who was a friend of Mr. Brownlow's, all went together.'

'Then turn towards home again,' said Mr. Losberne to the driver; 'and don't stop to bait the horses, till you get out of this confounded London!'

'The book-stall keeper, sir?' said Oliver. 'I know the way there. See him, pray, sir! Do see him!'

'My poor boy, this is disappointment enough for one day,' said the doctor. 'Quite enough for both of us. If we go to the book-stall keeper's, we shall certainly find that he is dead, or has set his house on fire, or run away. No; home again straight!' And in obedience to the doctor's impulse, home they went.

This bitter disappointment caused Oliver much sorrow and grief, even in the midst of his happiness; for he had pleased himself, many times during his illness, with thinking of all that Mr. Brownlow and Mrs. Bedwin would say to him: and what delight it would be to tell them how many long days and nights he had passed in reflecting on what they had done for him, and in bewailing his cruel separation from them. The hope of eventually clearing himself with them, too, and explaining how he had been forced away, had buoyed him up, and sustained him, under many of his recent trials; and now, the idea that they should have gone so far, and carried with them the belief that he was an impostor and a robber—a belief which might remain uncontradicted to his dying day—was almost more than he could bear.

The circumstance occasioned no alteration, however, in the behaviour of his benefactors. After another fortnight, when the fine warm weather had fairly begun, and every tree and flower was putting forth its young leaves and rich blossoms, they made preparations for quitting the house at Chertsey, for some months. Sending the plate, which had so excited Fagin's cupidity, to the banker's; and leaving Giles and another servant in care of the house, they departed to a cottage at some distance in the country, and took Oliver with them.

Who can describe the pleasure and delight, the peace of mind and soft tranquillity, the sickly boy felt in the balmy air, and among the green hills and rich woods, of an inland village! Who can tell how scenes of peace and quietude sink into the minds of pain-worn dwellers in close and noisy places, and carry their own freshness, deep into their jaded hearts! Men who have lived in crowded, pent-up streets, through lives of toil, and who have never wished for change; men, to whom custom has indeed been second nature, and who have come almost to love each brick and stone that formed the narrow boundaries of their daily walks; even they, with the hand of death upon them, have been known to yearn at last for one short glimpse of Nature's face; and, carried far from the scenes of their old pains and pleasures, have seemed to pass at once into a new state of being. Crawling forth, from day to day, to some green sunny spot, they have had such memories wakened up within them by the sight of sky, and hill and plain, and glistening water, that a foretaste of heaven itself has soothed their quick decline, and they have sunk into their tombs, as peacefully as the sun whose setting they watched from their lonely chamber window but a few hours before, faded from their dim and feeble sight! The memories which peaceful country scenes call up, are not of this world, nor of its thoughts and hopes. Their gentle influence may teach us how to weave fresh garlands for the graves of those we loved: may purify our thoughts, and bear down before it old enmity and hatred; but beneath all this, there lingers, in the least reflective mind, a vague and half-formed consciousness of having held such feelings long before, in some remote and distant time, which calls up solemn thoughts of distant times to come, and bends down pride and worldliness beneath it.

It was a lovely spot to which they repaired. Oliver, whose days had been spent among squalid crowds, and in the midst of noise and brawling, seemed to enter on a new existence there. The rose and honeysuckle clung to the cottage walls; the ivy crept round the trunks of the trees; and the garden-flowers perfumed the air with delicious odours. Hard by, was a little churchyard; not crowded with tall unsightly gravestones, but full of humble mounds, covered with fresh turf and moss: beneath which, the old people of the village lay at rest. Oliver often wandered here; and, thinking of the wretched grave in which his mother lay, would sometimes sit him down and sob unseen; but, when he raised his eyes to the deep sky overhead, he would cease to think of her as lying in the ground, and would weep for her, sadly, but without pain.

It was a happy time. The days were peaceful and serene; the nights brought with them neither fear nor care; no languishing in a wretched prison, or associating with wretched men; nothing but pleasant and happy thoughts. Every morning he went to a white-headed old gentleman, who lived near the little church: who taught him to read better, and to write: and who spoke so kindly, and took such pains, that Oliver could never try enough to please him. Then, he would walk with Mrs. Maylie and Rose, and hear them talk of books; or perhaps sit near them, in some shady place, and listen while the young lady read: which he could have done, until it grew too dark to see the letters. Then, he had his own lesson for the next day to prepare; and at this, he would work hard, in a little room which looked into the garden, till evening came slowly on, when the ladies would walk out again, and he with them: listening with such pleasure to all they said: and so happy if they wanted a flower that he could climb to reach, or had forgotten anything he could run to fetch: that he could never be quick enough about it. When it became quite dark, and they returned home, the young lady would sit down to the piano, and play some pleasant air, or sing, in a low and gentle voice, some old song which it pleased her aunt to hear. There would be no candles lighted at such times as these; and Oliver would sit by one of the windows, listening to the sweet music, in a perfect rapture.

And when Sunday came, how differently the day was spent, from any way in which he had ever spent it yet! and how happily too; like all the other days in that most happy time! There was the little church, in the morning, with the green leaves fluttering at the windows: the birds singing without: and the sweet-smelling air stealing in at the low porch, and filling the homely building with its fragrance. The poor people were so neat and clean, and knelt so reverently in prayer, that it seemed a pleasure, not a tedious duty, their assembling there together; and though the singing might be rude, it was real, and sounded more musical (to Oliver's ears at least) than any he had ever heard in church before. Then, there were the walks as usual, and many calls at the clean houses of the labouring men; and at night, Oliver read a chapter or two from the Bible, which he had been studying all the week, and in the performance of which duty he felt more proud and pleased, than if he had been the clergyman himself.

In the morning, Oliver would be a-foot by six o'clock, roaming the fields, and plundering the hedges, far and wide, for nosegays of wild flowers, with which he would return laden, home; and which it took great care and consideration to arrange, to the best advantage, for the embellishment of the breakfast-table. There was fresh groundsel, too, for Miss Maylie's birds, with which Oliver, who had been studying the subject under the able tuition of the village clerk, would decorate the cages, in the most approved taste. When the birds were made all spruce and smart for the day, there was usually some little commission of charity to execute in the village; or, failing that, there was rare cricket-playing, sometimes, on the green; or, failing that, there was always something to do in the garden, or about the plants, to which Oliver (who had studied this science also, under the same master, who was a gardener by trade) applied himself with hearty goodwill, until Miss Rose made her appearance: when there were a thousand commendations to be bestowed on all he had done.

So three months glided away; three months which, in the life of the most blessed and favoured of mortals, might have been unmingled happiness, and which, in Oliver's, were true felicity. With the purest and most amiable generosity on one side; and the truest, warmest, soul-felt gratitude on the other; it is no wonder that, by the end of that short time, Oliver Twist had become completely domesticated with the old lady and her niece, and that the fervent attachment of his young and sensitive heart, was repaid by their pride in, and attachment to, himself.

CHAPTER 33

Wherein the happiness of Oliver and his
friends, experiences a sudden check

Spring flew swiftly by, and summer came. If the village had been
beautiful at first, it was now in the full glow and luxuriance of its
richness. The great trees, which had looked shrunken and bare in
the earlier months, had now burst into strong life and health; and
stretching forth their green arms over the thirsty ground, converted
open and naked spots into choice nooks, where was a deep and
pleasant shade from which to look upon the wide prospect, steeped
in sunshine, which lay stretched beyond. The earth had donned her
mantle of brightest green; and shed her richest perfumes abroad. It
was the prime and vigour of the year; all things were glad and
flourishing.

Still, the same quiet life went on at the little cottage, and the
same cheerful serenity prevailed among its inmates. Oliver had long
since grown stout and healthy; but health or sickness made no difference in his warm feelings to those about him, though they do in
the feelings of a great many people. He was still the same gentle,
attached, affectionate creature that he had been when pain and
suffering had wasted his strength, and when he was dependent for
every slight attention and comfort on those who tended him.

One beautiful night, they had taken a longer walk than was
customary with them: for the day had been unusually warm, and
there was a brilliant moon, and a light wind had sprung up, which

was unusually refreshing. Rose had been in high spirits, too, and they had walked on, in merry conversation, till they had far exceeded their ordinary bounds. Mrs. Maylie being fatigued, they returned more slowly home. The young lady merely throwing off her simple bonnet, sat down to the piano as usual. After running abstractedly over the keys for a few minutes, she fell into a low and very solemn air; and as she played it, they heard a sound as if she were weeping.

'Rose, my dear!' said the elder lady.

Rose made no reply, but played a little quicker, as though the words had roused her from some painful thoughts.

'Rose, my love!' cried Mrs. Maylie, rising hastily and bending over her. 'What is this? In tears! My dear child, what distresses you?'

'Nothing, aunt; nothing,' replied the young lady. 'I don't know what it is; I can't describe it; but I feel—'

'Not ill, my love?' interposed Mrs. Maylie.

'No, no! Oh, not ill!' replied Rose: shuddering as though some deadly chillness were passing over her, while she spoke; 'I shall be better presently. Close the window, pray!'

Oliver hastened to comply with her request. The young lady, making an effort to recover her cheerfulness, strove to play some livelier tune; but her fingers dropped powerless on the keys. Covering her face with her hands, she sank upon a sofa, and gave vent to the tears which she was now unable to repress.

'My child!' said the elderly lady, folding her arms about her, 'I never saw you so before.'

'I would not alarm you if I could avoid it,' rejoined Rose; 'but indeed I have tried, very hard, and cannot help this. I fear I *am* ill, aunt.'

She was, indeed; for, when candles were brought, they saw that in the very short time which had elapsed since their return home, the hue of her countenance had changed to a marble whiteness. Its expression had lost nothing of its beauty; but it was changed; and there was an anxious, haggard look about the gentle face, which it had never worn before. Another minute, and it was suffused with a crimson flush: and a heavy wildness came over the soft blue eye. Again this disappeared, like the shadow thrown by a passing cloud; and she was once more deadly pale.

Oliver, who watched the old lady anxiously, observed that she was alarmed by these appearances; and so in truth, was he; but seeing that she affected to make light of them, he endeavoured to do the same, and they so far succeeded, that when Rose was persuaded by her aunt to retire for the night, she was in better spirits; and appeared even in better health; assuring them that she felt certain she should rise in the morning, quite well.

'I hope,' said Oliver, when Mrs. Maylie returned, 'that nothing is the matter? She don't look well tonight, but—'

The old lady motioned to him not to speak; and sitting herself down in a dark corner of the room, remained silent for some time. At length, she said, in a trembling voice:

'I hope not, Oliver. I have been very happy with her for some years: too happy, perhaps. It may be time that I should meet with some misfortune; but I hope it is not this.'

'What?' inquired Oliver.

'The heavy blow,' said the old lady, 'of losing the dear girl who has so long been my comfort and happiness.'

'Oh! God forbid!' exclaimed Oliver, hastily.

'Amen to that, my child!' said the old lady, wringing her hands.

'Surely there is no danger of anything so dreadful?' said Oliver. 'Two hours ago, she was quite well.'

'She is very ill now,' rejoined Mrs. Maylie; 'and will be worse, I am sure. My dear, dear Rose! Oh, what should I do without her!'

She gave way to such great grief, that Oliver, suppressing his own emotion, ventured to remonstrate with her; and to beg, earnestly, that, for the sake of the dear young lady herself, she would be more calm.

'And consider, ma'am,' said Oliver, as the tears forced themselves into his eyes, despite of his efforts to the contrary. 'Oh! consider how young and good she is, and what pleasure and comfort she gives to all about her. I am sure—certain—quite certain—that, for your sake, who are so good yourself; and for her own; and for the sake of all she makes so happy; she will not die. Heaven will never let her die so young.'

'Hush!' said Mrs. Maylie, laying her hand on Oliver's head. 'You think like a child, poor boy. But you teach me my duty, notwithstanding. I had forgotten it for a moment, Oliver, but I hope I may be pardoned, for I am old, and have seen enough of illness and death to know the agony of separation from the objects of our love. I have seen enough, too, to know that it is not always the youngest and best who are spared to those that love them; but this should give us comfort in our sorrow; for Heaven is just; and such things teach us, impressively, that there is a brighter world than this; and that the passage to it is speedy. God's will be done! I love her; and He knows how well!'

Oliver was surprised to see that as Mrs. Maylie said these words, she checked her lamentations as though by one effort; and drawing herself up as she spoke, became composed and firm. He was still more astonished to find that this firmness lasted; and that, under all the care and watching which ensued, Mrs. Maylie was ever ready and collected: performing all the duties which devolved upon her, steadily, and, to all external appearance, even cheerfully. But he was young, and did not know what strong minds are capable of, under trying circumstances. How should he, when their possessors so seldom know themselves?

An anxious night ensued. When morning came, Mrs. Maylie's predictions were but too well verified. Rose was in the first stage of a high and dangerous fever.

'We must be active, Oliver, and not give way to useless grief,' said Mrs. Maylie, laying her finger on her lip, as she looked steadily into his face; 'this letter must be sent, with all possible expedition, to Mr. Losberne. It must be carried to the market-town: which is not more than four miles off, by the footpath across the fields: and thence dispatched, by an express on horseback, straight to Chertsey. The people at the inn will undertake to do this; and I can trust to you to see it done, I know.'

Oliver could make no reply, but looked his anxiety to be gone at once.

'Here is another letter,' said Mrs. Maylie, pausing to reflect; 'but whether to send it now, or wait until I see how Rose goes on, I scarcely know. I would not forward it, unless I feared the worst.'

'Is it for Chertsey, too, ma'am?' inquired Oliver: impatient to execute his commission, and holding out his trembling hand for the letter.

'No,' replied the old lady, giving it to him mechanically. Oliver glanced at it, and saw that it was directed to Harry Maylie, Esquire, at some great lord's house in the country; where, he could not make out.

'Shall it go, ma'am?' asked Oliver, looking up, impatiently.

'I think not,' replied Mrs. Maylie, taking it back. 'I will wait until to-morrow.'

With these words, she gave Oliver her purse, and he started off, without more delay, at the greatest speed he could muster.

Swiftly he ran across the fields, and down the little lanes which sometimes divided them: now almost hidden by the high corn on either side, and now emerging on an open field, where the mowers and hay-makers were busy at their work: nor did he stop once, save now and then, for a few seconds, to recover breath, until he came, in a great heat, and covered with dust, on the little market-place of the market-town.

Here he paused, and looked about for the inn. There were a white bank, and a red brewery, and a yellow town-hall; and in one corner there was a large house, with all the wood about it painted green: before which was the sign of 'The George.' To this he hastened, as soon as it caught his eye.

He spoke to a post boy who was dozing under the gateway; and who, after hearing what he wanted, referred him to the ostler; who after hearing all he had to say again, referred him to the landlord; who was a tall gentleman in a blue neckcloth, a white hat, drab breeches, and boots with tops to match, leaning against a pump by the stable-door, picking his teeth with a silver toothpick.

This gentleman walked with much deliberation into the bar to make out the bill: which took a long time making out: and after it was ready, and paid, a horse had to be saddled, and a man to be dressed, which took up ten good minutes more. Meanwhile Oliver was in such a desperate state of impatience and anxiety, that he felt as if he could have jumped upon the horse himself, and galloped away, full tear, to the next stage. At length, all was ready; and the little parcel having been handed up, with many injunctions and entreaties for its speedy delivery, the man set spurs to his horse, and rattling over the uneven paving of the market-place, was out of the town, and galloping along the turnpike-road, in a couple of minutes.

As it was something to feel certain that assistance was sent for, and that no time had been lost, Oliver hurried up the inn-yard, with a somewhat lighter heart. He was turning out of the gateway when he accidentally stumbled against a tall man wrapped in a cloak, who was at that moment coming out of the inn door.

'Hah!' cried the man, fixing his eyes on Oliver, and suddenly recoiling. 'What the devil's this?'

'I beg your pardon, sir,' said Oliver; 'I was in a great hurry to get home, and didn't see you were coming.'

'Death!' muttered the man to himself, glaring at the boy with his large dark eyes. 'Who would have thought it! Grind him to ashes! He'd start up from a stone coffin, to come in my way!'

'I am sorry,' stammered Oliver, confused by the strange man's wild look. 'I hope I have not hurt you!'

'Rot you!' murmured the man, in a horrible passion; between his clenched teeth; 'if I had only had the courage to say the word, I might have been free of you in a night. Curses on your head, and black death on your heart, you imp! What are you doing here?'

The man shook his fist, as he uttered these words incoherently. He advanced towards Oliver, as if with the intention of aiming a blow at him, but fell violently on the ground: writhing and foaming, in a fit.

Oliver gazed, for a moment, at the struggles of the madman (for such he supposed him to be); and then darted into the house for help. Having seen him safely carried into the hotel, he turned his face homewards, running as fast as he could, to make up for lost time: and recalling with a great deal of astonishment and some fear, the extraordinary behaviour of the person from whom he had just parted.

The circumstance did not dwell in his recollection long, however; for when he reached the cottage, there was enough to occupy his mind, and to drive all considerations of self completely from his memory.

Rose Maylie had rapidly grown worse; before midnight she was delirious. A medical practitioner, who resided on the spot, was in constant attendance upon her; and after first seeing the patient, he had taken Mrs. Maylie aside, and pronounced her disorder to be one of a most alarming nature. 'In fact,' he said, 'it would be little short of a miracle, if she recovered.'

How often did Oliver start from his bed that night, and stealing out, with noiseless footstep, to the staircase, listen for the slightest sound from the sick chamber! How often did a tremble shake his frame, and cold drops of terror start upon his brow, when a sudden trampling of feet caused him to fear that something too dreadful to think of, had even then occurred! And what had been the fervency of all the prayers he had ever uttered, compared with those he poured forth, now, in the agony and passion of his supplication for the life and health of the gentle creature, who was tottering on the deep grave's verge!

Oh! the suspense, the fearful, acute suspense, of standing idly by while the life of one we dearly love, is trembling in the balance! Oh! the racking thoughts that crowd upon the mind, and make the heart beat violently, and the breath come thick, by the force of the images they conjure up before it; the desperate anxiety *to be doing something* to relieve the pain, or lessen the danger, which we have no power to alleviate; the sinking of soul and spirit, which the sad remembrance of our helplessness produces; what tortures can equal these; what reflections or endeavours can, in the full tide and fever of the time, allay them!

Morning came; and the little cottage was lonely and still. People spoke in whispers; anxious faces appeared at the gate, from time to time; women and children went away in tears. All the livelong day, and for hours after it had grown dark, Oliver paced softly up and down the garden, raising his eyes every instant to the sick chamber, and shuddering to see the darkened window, looking as if death lay stretched inside. Late at night, Mr. Losberne arrived. 'It is hard,' said the good doctor, turning away as he spoke; 'so young; so much beloved; but there is very little hope.'

Another morning. The sun shone brightly: as brightly as if it looked upon no misery or care; and, with every leaf and flower in full bloom about her: with life, and health, and sounds and sights of joy, surrounding her on every side: the fair young creature lay, wasting fast. Oliver crept away to the old church-yard, and sitting down on one of the green mounds, wept, and prayed for her, in silence.

There was such peace and beauty in the scene; so much of brightness and mirth in the sunny landscape; such blithesome music in the songs of the summer birds; such freedom in the rapid flight of the rook, careering overhead; so much of life and joyousness in all; that, when the boy raised his aching eyes, and looked about, the thought instinctively occurred to him, that this was not a time for death; that Rose could surely never die when humbler things were all so glad and gay; that graves were for cold and cheerless winter: not for sunlight and fragrance. He almost thought that shrouds were for the old and shrunken; and that they never wrapped the young and graceful form in their ghastly folds.

A knell from the church bell broke harshly on these youthful thoughts. Another! Again! It was tolling for the funeral service. A group of humble mourners entered the gate: wearing white favours; for the corpse was young. They stood uncovered by a grave; and there was a mother—a mother once—among the weeping train. But the sun shone brightly, and the birds sang on.

Oliver turned homeward, thinking on the many kindnesses he had received from the young lady, and wishing that the time could come over again, that he might never cease showing her how grateful and attached he was. He had no cause for self-reproach on the score of neglect, or want of thought, for he had been devoted to her service; and yet a hundred little occasions rose up before him, on which he fancied he might have been more zealous, and more earnest, and wished he had been. We need be careful how we deal with those about us, when every death carries to some small circle of survivors, thoughts of so much omitted, and so little done—of so many things forgotten, and so many more which might have been repaired! There is no remorse so deep as that which is unavailing; if we would be spared its tortures, let us remember this, in time.

When he reached home Mrs. Maylie was sitting in the little parlour. Oliver's heart sank at sight of her; for she had never left the bedside of her niece; and he trembled to think what change could have driven her away. He learnt that she had fallen into a deep sleep, from which she would waken, either to recovery and life, or to bid them farewell, and die.

They sat, listening, and afraid to speak, for hours. The untasted meal was removed. With looks which showed that their thoughts were elsewhere, they watched the sun as he sank lower and lower, and, at length, cast over sky and earth those brilliant hues which herald his departure. Their quick ears caught the sound of an approaching footstep. They both involuntarily darted to the door, as Mr. Losberne entered.

'What of Rose?' cried the old lady. 'Tell me at once! I can bear it; anything but suspense! Oh, tell me! in the name of Heaven!'

'You must compose yourself,' said the doctor, supporting her. 'Be calm, my dear ma'am, pray.'

'Let me go, in God's name! My dear child! She is dead! She is dying!'

'No!' cried the doctor, passionately. 'As He is good and merciful, she will live to bless us all, for years to come.'

The lady fell upon her knees, and tried to fold her hands together; but the energy which had supported her so long, fled up to Heaven with her first thanksgiving; and she sank into the friendly arms which were extended to receive her.

CHAPTER 34

Contains some introductory particulars
relative to a young gentleman who now
arrives upon the scene; and a new adventure
which happened to Oliver

It was almost too much happiness to bear. Oliver felt stunned and
stupefied by the unexpected intelligence; he could not weep, or
speak, or rest. He had scarcely the power of understanding anything
that had passed, until, after a long ramble in the quiet evening air,
a burst of tears came to his relief, and he seemed to awaken, all at
once, to a full sense of the joyful change that had occurred, and the
almost insupportable load of anguish which had been taken from
his breast.

The night was fast closing in, when he returned homeward: laden
with flowers which he had culled, with peculiar care, for the adorn-
ment of the sick chamber. As he walked briskly along the road, he
heard behind him, the noise of some vehicle, approaching at a furious
pace. Looking round, he saw that it was a post-chaise, driven at great
speed; and as the horses were galloping, and the road was narrow, he
stood leaning against a gate until it should have passed him.

As it dashed on, Oliver caught a glimpse of a man in a white
nightcap, whose face seemed familiar to him, although his view was
so brief that he could not identify the person. In another second or
two, the nightcap was thrust out of the chaise-window, and a stento-
rian voice bellowed to the driver to stop: which he did, as soon as he
could pull up his horses. Then, the nightcap once again appeared: and
the same voice called Oliver by his name.

'Here!' cried the voice. 'Oliver, what's the news? Miss Rose! Master O-li-ver!'

'Is it you, Giles?' cried Oliver, running up to the chaise-door.

Giles popped out his nightcap again, preparatory to making some reply, when he was suddenly pulled back by a young gentleman who occupied the other corner of the chaise, and who eagerly demanded what was the news.

'In a word!' cried the gentleman. 'Better or worse?'

'Better—much better!' replied Oliver, hastily.

'Thank heaven!' exclaimed the gentleman. 'You are sure?'

'Quite, sir,' replied Oliver. 'The change took place only a few hours ago; and Mr. Losberne says, that all danger is at an end.'

The gentleman said not another word, but, opening the chaise-door, leaped out, and taking Oliver hurriedly by the arm, led him aside.

'You are quite certain? There is no possibility of any mistake on your part, my boy, is there?' demanded the gentleman in a tremulous voice. 'Do not deceive me, by awakening hopes that are not to be fulfilled.'

'I would not for the world, sir,' replied Oliver. 'Indeed you may believe me. Mr. Losberne's words were, that she would live to bless us all for many years to come. I heard him say so.'

The tears stood in Oliver's eyes as he recalled the scene which was the beginning of so much happiness; and the gentleman turned his face away, and remained silent, for some minutes. Oliver thought he heard him sob, more than once; but he feared to interrupt him by any fresh remark—for he could well guess what his feelings were—and so stood apart, feigning to be occupied with his nosegay.

All this time, Mr. Giles, with the white nightcap on, had been sitting on the steps of the chaise, supporting an elbow on each knee, and wiping his eyes with a blue cotton pocket-handkerchief dotted with white spots. That the honest fellow had not been feigning emotion, was abundantly demonstrated by the very red eyes with which he regarded the young gentleman, when he turned round and addressed him.

'I think you had better go on to my mother's in the chaise, Giles,' said he. 'I would rather walk slowly on, so as to gain a little time before I see her. You can say I am coming.'

'I beg your pardon, Mr. Harry,' said Giles: giving a final polish to his ruffled countenance with the handkerchief; 'but if you would leave the postboy to say that, I should be very much obliged to you. It wouldn't be proper for the maids to see me in this state, sir; I should never have any more authority with them if they did.'

'Well,' rejoined Harry Maylie, smiling, 'you can do as you like. Let him go on with the luggage, if you wish it, and do you follow with us. Only first exchange that nightcap for some more appropriate covering, or we shall be taken for madmen.'

Mr. Giles, reminded of his unbecoming costume, snatched off and pocketed his nightcap; and substituted a hat, of grave and sober shape, which he took out of the chaise. This done, the postboy drove off; Giles, Mr. Maylie, and Oliver, followed at their leisure.

As they walked along, Oliver glanced from time to time with much interest and curiosity at the new-comer. He seemed about five-and-twenty years of age, and was of the middle height; his countenance was frank and handsome; and his demeanour easy and prepossessing. Notwithstanding the difference between youth and age, he bore so strong a likeness to the old lady, that Oliver would have had no great difficulty in imagining their relationship, if he had not already spoken of her as his mother.

Mrs. Maylie was anxiously waiting to receive her son when he reached the cottage. The meeting did not take place without great emotion on both sides.

'Mother!' whispered the young man; 'why did you not write before?'

'I did,' replied Mrs. Maylie; 'but, on reflection, I determined to keep back the letter until I had heard Mr. Losberne's opinion.'

'But why,' said the young man, 'why run the chance of that occurring which so nearly happened? If Rose had—I cannot utter that word now—if this illness had terminated differently, how could you ever have forgiven yourself! How could I ever have known happiness again!'

'If that *had* been the case, Harry,' said Mrs. Maylie, 'I fear your happiness would have been effectually blighted, and that your arrival here, a day sooner or a day later, would have been of very, very little import.'

'And who can wonder if it be so, mother?' rejoined the young man; 'or why should I say *if*?—It is—it is—you know it, mother—you must know it!'

'I know that she deserves the best and purest love the heart of man can offer,' said Mrs. Maylie; 'I know that the devotion and affection of her nature require no ordinary return, but one that shall be deep and lasting. If I did not feel this, and know, besides, that a changed behaviour in one she loved would break her heart, I should not feel my task so difficult of performance, or have to encounter so many struggles in my own bosom, when I take what seems to me to be the strict line of duty.'

'This is unkind, mother,' said Harry. 'Do you still suppose that I am a boy ignorant of my own mind, and mistaking the impulses of my own soul?'

'I think, my dear son,' returned Mrs. Maylie, laying her hand upon his shoulder, 'that youth has many generous impulses which do not last; and that among them are some, which, being gratified, become only the more fleeting. Above all, I think,' said the lady, fixing her eyes on her son's face, 'that if an enthusiastic, ardent, and ambitious man marry a wife on whose name there is a stain, which, though it originate in no fault of hers, may be visited by cold and sordid people upon her, and upon his children also: and, in exact proportion to his success in the world, be cast in his teeth, and made the subject of sneers against him: he may, no matter how generous and good his nature, one day repent of the connexion he formed in early life. And she may have the pain of knowing that he does so.'

'Mother,' said the young man, impatiently, 'he would be a selfish brute, unworthy alike of the name of man and of the woman you describe, who acted thus.'

'You think so now, Harry,' replied his mother.

'And ever will!' said the young man. 'The mental agony I have suffered, during the last two days, wrings from me the avowal to you of a passion which, as you well know, is not one of yesterday, nor one I have lightly formed. On Rose, sweet, gentle girl! my heart is set, as firmly as ever heart of man was set on woman. I have no thought, no view, no hope in life, beyond her; and if you oppose me in this great stake, you take my peace and happiness in your hands, and cast them to the wind. Mother, think better of this, and of me, and do not disregard the happiness of which you seem to think so little.'

'Harry,' said Mrs. Maylie, 'it is because I think so much of warm and sensitive hearts, that I would spare them from being wounded. But we have said enough, and more than enough, on this matter, just now.'

'Let it rest with Rose, then,' interposed Harry. 'You will not press these overstrained opinions of yours, so far, as to throw any obstacle in my way?'

'I will not,' rejoined Mrs. Maylie; 'but I would have you consider—'

'I *have* considered!' was the impatient reply; 'Mother, I have considered, years and years. I have considered, ever since I have been capable of serious reflection. My feelings remain unchanged, as they ever will; and why should I suffer the pain of a delay in giving them vent, which can be productive of no earthly good? No! Before I leave this place, Rose shall hear me.'

'She shall,' said Mrs. Maylie.

'There is something in your manner, which would almost imply that she will hear me coldly, mother,' said the young man.

'Not coldly,' rejoined the old lady; 'far from it.'

'How then?' urged the young man. 'She has formed no other attachment?'

'No, indeed,' replied his mother; 'you have, or I mistake, too strong a hold on her affections already. What I would say,' resumed the old lady, stopping her son as he was about to speak, 'is this.

Before you stake your all on this chance; before you suffer yourself to be carried to the highest point of hope; reflect for a few moments, my dear child, on Rose's history, and consider what effect the knowledge of her doubtful birth may have on her decision: devoted as she is to us, with all the intensity of her noble mind, and with that perfect sacrifice of self which, in all matters, great or trifling, has always been her characteristic.'

'What do you mean?'

'That I leave you to discover,' replied Mrs. Maylie. 'I must go back to her. God bless you!'

'I shall see you again to-night?' said the young man, eagerly.

'By and by,' replied the lady; 'when I leave Rose.'

'You will tell her I am here?' said Harry.

'Of course,' replied Mrs. Maylie.

'And say how anxious I have been, and how much I have suffered, and how I long to see her. You will not refuse to do this, mother?'

'No,' said the old lady; 'I will tell her all.' And pressing her son's hand, affectionately, she hastened from the room.

Mr. Losberne and Oliver had remained at another end of the apartment while this hurried conversation was proceeding. The former now held out his hand to Harry Maylie; and hearty salutations were exchanged between them. The doctor then communicated, in reply to multifarious questions from his young friend, a precise account of his patient's situation; which was quite as consolatory and full of promise, as Oliver's statement had encouraged him to hope; and to the whole of which, Mr. Giles, who affected to be busy about the luggage, listened with greedy ears.

'Have you shot anything particular, lately, Giles?' inquired the doctor, when he had concluded.

'Nothing particular, sir,' replied Mr. Giles, colouring up to the eyes.

'Nor catching any thieves, nor identifying any housebreakers?' said the doctor.

'None at all, sir,' replied Mr. Giles, with much gravity.

'Well,' said the doctor, 'I am sorry to hear it, because you do that sort of thing admirably. Pray, how is Brittles?'

'The boy is very well, sir,' said Mr. Giles, recovering his usual tone of patronage; 'and sends his respectful duty, sir.'

'That's well,' said the doctor. 'Seeing you here, reminds me, Mr. Giles, that on the day before that on which I was called away so hurriedly, I executed, at the request of your good mistress, a small commission in your favour. Just step into this corner a moment, will you?'

Mr. Giles walked into the corner with much importance, and some wonder, and was honoured with a short whispering conference with the doctor, on the termination of which, he made a great many bows, and retired with steps of unusual stateliness. The subject matter of this conference was not disclosed in the parlour, but the kitchen was speedily enlightened concerning it; for Mr. Giles walked straight thither, and having called for a mug of ale, announced, with an air of majesty, which was highly effective, that it had pleased his mistress, in consideration of his gallant behaviour on the occasion of that attempted robbery, to deposit, in the local savings-bank, the sum of five and twenty pounds, for his sole use and benefit. At this, the two women-servants lifted up their hands and eyes, and supposed that Mr. Giles would begin to be quite proud now; whereunto Mr. Giles, pulling out his shirt-frill, replied, 'No, no;' and that if they observed that he was at all haughty to his inferiors, he would thank them to tell him so. And then he made a great many other remarks, no less illustrative of his humility, which were received with equal favour and applause, and were, withal, as original and as much to the purpose, as the remarks of great men commonly are.

Above stairs, the remainder of the evening passed cheerfully away; for the doctor was in high spirits; and however fatigued or thoughtful Harry Maylie might have been at first, he was not proof against the worthy gentleman's good humour, which displayed itself in a great variety of sallies and professional recollections, and an abundance of small jokes, which struck Oliver as being the drollest things he had ever heard, and caused him to laugh proportionately:

to the evident satisfaction of the doctor, who laughed immoderately at himself, and made Harry laugh almost as heartily, by the very force of sympathy. So, they were as pleasant a party as, under the circumstances, they could well have been; and it was late before they retired, with light and thankful hearts, to take that rest of which, after the doubt and suspense they had recently undergone, they stood much in need.

Oliver rose next morning, in better heart, and went about his usual early occupations, with more hope and pleasure than he had known for many days. The birds were once more hung out, to sing, in their old places; and the sweetest wild flowers that could be found, were once more gathered to gladden Rose with their beauty. The melancholy which had seemed to the sad eyes of the anxious boy to hang, for days past, over every object, beautiful as all were, was dispelled by magic. The dew seemed to sparkle more brightly on the green leaves; the air to rustle among them with a sweeter music; and the sky itself to look more blue and bright. Such is the influence which the condition of our own thoughts, exercises, even over the appearance of external objects. Men who look on nature, and their fellow-men, and cry that all is dark and gloomy, are in the right; but the sombre colours are reflections from their own jaundiced eyes and hearts. The real hues are delicate, and need a clearer vision.

It is worthy of remark, and Oliver did not fail to note it at the time, that his morning expeditions were no longer made alone. Harry Maylie, after the very first morning when he met Oliver coming laden home, was seized with such a passion for flowers, and displayed such a taste in their arrangement, as left his young companion far behind. If Oliver were behindhand in these respects, however, he knew where the best were to be found; and morning after morning they scoured the country together, and brought home the fairest that blossomed. The window of the young lady's chamber was opened now; for she loved to feel the rich summer air stream in, and revive her with its freshness; but there always stood in water, just inside the lattice, one particular little bunch, which was made up with great care, every morning. Oliver could not help noticing that the withered flowers were never thrown away, although the little vase was regularly replenished; nor, could he help observing, that whenever the doctor came into the garden, he invariably cast his eyes up to that particular corner, and nodded his head most expressively, as he set forth on his morning's walk. Pending these observations, the days were flying by; and Rose was rapidly recovering.

Nor did Oliver's time hang heavy on his hands, although the young lady had not yet left her chamber, and there were no evening walks, save now and then, for a short distance, with Mrs. Maylie. He applied himself, with redoubled assiduity, to the instructions of the white-headed old gentleman, and laboured so hard that his quick progress surprised even himself. It was while he was engaged in this pursuit, that he was greatly startled and distressed by a most unexpected occurrence.

The little room in which he was accustomed to sit, when busy at his books, was on the ground-floor, at the back of the house. It was quite a cottage-room, with a lattice-window: around which were clusters of jessamine and honeysuckle, that crept over the case-ment, and filled the place with their delicious perfume. It looked into a garden, whence a wicket-gate opened into a small paddock; all beyond, was fine meadowland and wood. There was no other dwelling near, in that direction; and the prospect it commanded was very extensive.

One beautiful evening, when the first shades of twilight were beginning to settle upon the earth, Oliver sat at this window, intent upon his books. He had been poring over them for some time; and, as the day had been uncommonly sultry, and he had exerted himself a great deal, it is no disparagement to the authors, whoever they may have been, to say, that gradually and by slow degrees, he fell asleep.

There is a kind of sleep that steals upon us sometimes, which, while it holds the body prisoner, does not free the mind from a sense of things about it, and enable it to ramble at its pleasure.

So far as an overpowering heaviness, a prostration of strength, and an utter inability to control our thoughts or power of motion, can be called sleep, this is it; and yet, we have a consciousness of all that is going on about us, and, if we dream at such a time, words which are really spoken, or sounds which really exist at the moment, accommodate themselves with surprising readiness to our visions, until reality and imagination become so strangely blended that it is afterwards almost matter of impossibility to separate the two. Nor is this, the most striking phenomenon incidental to such a state. It is an undoubted fact, that although our senses of touch and sight be for the time dead, yet our sleeping thoughts, and the visionary scenes that pass before us, will be influenced, and materially influenced, by the *mere silent presence* of some external object; which may not have been near us when we closed our eyes: and of whose vicinity we have had no waking consciousness.

Oliver knew, perfectly well, that he was in his own little room; that his books were lying on the table before him; that the sweet air was stirring among the creeping plants outside. And yet he was asleep. Suddenly, the scene changed; the air became close and confined; and he thought, with a glow of terror, that he was in the Jew's house again. There sat the hideous old man, in his accustomed corner, pointing at him, and whispering to another man, with his face averted, who sat beside him.

'Hush, my dear!' he thought he heard the Jew say; 'it is he, sure enough. Come away.'

'He!' the other man seemed to answer; 'could I mistake him, think you? If a crowd of ghosts were to put themselves into his exact shape, and he stood amongst them, there is something that would tell me how to point him out. If you buried him fifty feet deep, and took me across his grave, I fancy I should know, if there wasn't a mark above it, that he lay buried there!'

The man seemed to say this, with such dreadful hatred, that Oliver awoke with the fear, and started up.

Good Heaven! what was that, which sent the blood tingling to his heart, and deprived him of his voice, and of power to move!

There—there—at the window—close before him—so close, that he could have almost touched him before he started back: with his eyes peering into the room, and meeting his: there stood the Jew! And beside him, white with rage or fear, or both, were the scowling features of the very man who had accosted him in the inn-yard.

It was but an instant, a glance, a flash, before his eyes; and they were gone. But they had recognised him, and he them; and their look was as firmly impressed upon his memory, as if it had been deeply carved in stone, and set before him from his birth. He stood transfixed for a moment; then, leaping from the window into the garden, called loudly for help.

CHAPTER 35

Containing the unsatisfactory result of Oliver's adventure; and a conversation of some importance between Harry Maylie and Rose

When the inmates of the house, attracted by Oliver's cries, hurried to the spot from which they proceeded, they found him, pale and agitated, pointing in the direction of the meadows behind the house, and scarcely able to articulate the words, 'The Jew! the Jew!'

Mr. Giles was at a loss to comprehend what this outcry meant; but Harry Maylie, whose perceptions were something quicker, and who had heard Oliver's history from his mother, understood it at once.

'What direction did he take?' he asked, catching up a heavy stick which was standing in a corner.

'That,' replied Oliver, pointing out the course the men had taken; 'I missed them in an instant.'

'Then, they are in the ditch!' said Harry. 'Follow! And keep as near me, as you can.' So saying, he sprang over the hedge, and darted off with a speed which rendered it matter of exceeding difficulty for the others to keep near him.

Giles followed as well as he could; and Oliver followed too; and in the course of a minute or two, Mr. Losberne, who had been out walking, and just then returned, tumbled over the hedge after them, and picking himself up with more agility than he could have been supposed to possess, struck into the same course at no contemptible speed, shouting all the while, most prodigiously, to know what was the matter.

On they all went; nor stopped they once to breathe, until the leader, striking off into an angle of the field indicated by Oliver, began to search, narrowly, the ditch and hedge adjoining; which afforded time for the remainder of the party to come up; and for Oliver to communicate to Mr. Losberne the circumstances that had led to so vigorous a pursuit.

The search was all in vain. There were not even the traces of recent footsteps, to be seen. They stood now, on the summit of a little hill, commanding the open fields in every direction for three or four miles. There was the village in the hollow on the left; but, in order to gain that, after pursuing the track Oliver had pointed out, the men must have made a circuit of open ground, which it was impossible they could have accomplished in so short a time. A thick wood skirted the meadowland in another direction; but they could not have gained that covert for the same reason.

'It must have been a dream, Oliver,' said Harry Maylie.

'Oh no, indeed, sir,' replied Oliver, shuddering at the very recollection of the old wretch's countenance; 'I saw him too plainly for that. I saw them both, as plainly as I see you now.'

'Who was the other?' inquired Harry and Mr. Losberne together.

'The very same man I told you of, who came so suddenly upon me at the inn,' said Oliver. 'We had our eyes fixed full upon each other; and I could swear to him.'

'They took this way?' demanded Harry: 'are you sure?'

'As I am that the men were at the window,' replied Oliver, pointing down, as he spoke, to the hedge which divided the cottage-garden from the meadow. 'The tall man leaped over, just there; and the Jew, running a few paces to the right, crept through that gap.'

The two gentlemen watched Oliver's earnest face, as he spoke, and looking from him to each other, seemed to feel satisfied of the accuracy of what he said. Still, in no direction were there any appearances of the trampling of men in hurried flight. The grass was long; but it was trodden down nowhere, save where their own feet had crushed it. The sides and brinks of the ditches were of damp clay;

but in no one place could they discern the print of men's shoes, or the slightest mark which would indicate that any feet had pressed the ground for hours before.

'This is strange!' said Harry.

'Strange?' echoed the doctor. 'Blathers and Duff, themselves, could make nothing of it.'

Notwithstanding the evidently useless nature of their search, they did not desist until the coming on of night rendered its further prosecution hopeless; and even then, they gave it up with reluctance. Giles was despatched to the different ale-houses in the village, furnished with the best description Oliver could give of the appearance and dress of the strangers. Of these, the Jew was, at all events, sufficiently remarkable to be remembered, supposing he had been seen drinking, or loitering about; but Giles returned without any intelligence, calculated to dispel or lessen the mystery.

On the next day, fresh search was made, and the inquiries renewed; but with no better success. On the day following, Oliver and Mr. Maylie repaired to the market-town, in the hope of seeing or hearing something of the men there; but this effort was equally fruitless. After a few days, the affair began to be forgotten, as most affairs are, when wonder, having no fresh food to support it, dies away of itself.

Meanwhile, Rose was rapidly recovering. She had left her room: was able to go out; and mixing once more with the family, carried joy into the hearts of all.

But, although this happy change had a visible effect on the little circle; and although cheerful voices and merry laughter were once more heard in the cottage; there was at times, an unwonted restraint upon some there: even upon Rose herself: which Oliver could not fail to remark. Mrs. Maylie and her son were often closeted together for a long time; and more than once Rose appeared with traces of tears upon her face. After Mr. Losberne had fixed a day for his departure to Chertsey, these symptoms increased; and it became evident that something was in progress which affected the peace of the young lady, and of somebody else besides.

At length, one morning, when Rose was alone in the break-fast-parlour, Harry Maylie entered; and, with some hesitation, begged permission to speak with her for a few moments.

'A few—a very few—will suffice, Rose,' said the young man, drawing his chair towards her. 'What I shall have to say, has already presented itself to your mind; the most cherished hopes of my heart are not unknown to you, though from my lips you have not yet heard them stated.'

Rose had been very pale from the moment of his entrance; but that might have been the effect of her recent illness. She merely bowed; and bending over some plants that stood near, waited in silence for him to proceed.

'I—I—ought to have left here, before,' said Harry.

'You should, indeed,' replied Rose. 'Forgive me for saying so, but I wish you had.'

'I was brought here, by the most dreadful and agonising of all apprehensions,' said the young man; 'the fear of losing the one dear being on whom my every wish and hope are fixed. You had been dying: trembling between earth and heaven. We know that when the young, the beautiful, and good, are visited with sickness, their pure spirits insensibly turn towards their bright home of lasting rest; we know, Heaven help us! that the best and fairest of our kind, too often fade in blooming.'

There were tears in the eyes of the gentle girl, as these words were spoken; and when one fell upon the flower over which she bent, and glistened brightly in its cup, making it more beautiful, it seemed as though the outpouring of her fresh young heart, claimed kindred naturally with the loveliest things in nature.

'A creature,' continued the young man, passionately, 'a creature as fair and innocent of guile as one of God's own angels, fluttered between life and death. Oh! who could hope, when the distant world to which she was akin, half opened to her view, that she would return to the sorrow and calamity of this! Rose, Rose, to know that you were passing away like some soft shadow, which a light from above, casts upon the earth; to have no hope that you would be spared to those who linger here; hardly to know a reason why you should be; to feel that you belonged to that bright sphere whither so many of the fairest and the best have winged their early flight; and yet to pray, amid all these consolations, that you might be restored to those who loved you—these were distractions almost too great to bear. They were mine, by day and night; and with them, came such a rushing torrent of fears, and apprehensions, and selfish regrets, lest you should die, and never know how devotedly I loved you, as almost bore down sense and reason in its course. You recovered. Day by day, and almost hour by hour, some drop of health came back, and mingling with the spent and feeble stream of life which circulated languidly within you, swelled it again to a high and rushing tide. I have watched you change almost from death to life, with eyes that turned blind with their eagerness and deep affection. Do not tell me that you wish I had lost this; for it has softened my heart to all mankind.'

'I did not mean that,' said Rose, weeping; 'I only wish you had left here, that you might have turned to high and noble pursuits again; to pursuits well worthy of you.'

'There is no pursuit more worthy of me: more worthy of the highest nature that exists: than the struggle to win such a heart as yours,' said the young man, taking her hand. 'Rose, my own dear Rose! For years—for years—I have loved you; hoping to win my way to fame, and then come proudly home and tell you it had been pursued only for you to share; thinking, in my day-dreams, how I would remind you, in that happy moment, of the many silent tokens I had given of a boy's attachment, and claim your hand, as in redemption of some old mute contract that had been sealed between us! That time has not arrived; but here, with no fame won, and no young vision realised, I offer you the heart so long your own, and stake my all upon the words with which you greet the offer.'

'Your behaviour has ever been kind and noble,' said Rose, mastering the emotions by which she was agitated. 'As you believe that I am not insensible or ungrateful, so hear my answer.'

'It is, that I may endeavour to deserve you; it is, dear Rose?'

'It is,' replied Rose, 'that you must endeavour to forget me; not as your old and dearly-attached companion, for that would wound me deeply; but, as the object of your love. Look into the world; think how many hearts you would be proud to gain, are there. Confide some other passion to me, if you will; I will be the truest, warmest, and most faithful friend you have.'

There was a pause, during which, Rose, who had covered her face with one hand, gave free vent to her tears. Harry still retained the other.

'And your reasons, Rose,' he said, at length, in a low voice; 'your reasons for this decision?'

'You have a right to know them,' rejoined Rose. 'You can say nothing to alter my resolution. It is a duty that I must perform. I owe it, alike to others, and to myself.'

'To yourself?'

'Yes, Harry. I owe it to myself that I, a friendless, portionless girl, with a blight upon my name, should not give your friends reason to suspect that I had sordidly yielded to your first passion, and fastened myself, a clog, on all your hopes and projects. I owe it to you and yours, to prevent you from opposing, in the warmth of your generous nature, this great obstacle to your progress in the world.'

'If your inclinations chime with your sense of duty—' Harry began.

'They do not,' replied Rose, colouring deeply.

'Then you return my love?' said Harry. 'Say but that, dear Rose; say but that; and soften the bitterness of this hard disappointment!'

'If I could have done so, without doing heavy wrong to him I loved,' rejoined Rose, 'I could have—'

'Have received this declaration very differently?' said Harry. 'Do not conceal that from me, at least, Rose.'

'I could,' said Rose. 'Stay!' she added, disengaging her hand, 'why should we prolong this painful interview? Most painful to me, and yet productive of lasting happiness, notwithstanding; for it *will* be happiness to know that I once held the high place in your regard which I now occupy, and every triumph you achieve in life will animate me with new fortitude and firmness. Farewell, Harry! As we have met to-day, we meet no more; but in other relations than those in which this conversation would have placed us, we may be long and happily entwined; and may every blessing that the prayers of a true and earnest heart can call down from the source of all truth and sincerity, cheer and prosper you!'

'Another word, Rose,' said Harry. 'Your reason in your own words. From your own lips, let me hear it!'

'The prospect before you,' answered Rose, firmly, 'is a brilliant one. All the honours to which great talents and powerful connexions can help men in public life, are in store for you. But those connexions are proud; and I will neither mingle with such as may hold in scorn the mother who gave me life; nor bring disgrace or failure on the son of her who has so well supplied that mother's place. In a word,' said the young lady, turning away, as her temporary firmness forsook her, 'there is a stain upon my name, which the world visits on innocent heads. I will carry it into no blood but my own; and the reproach shall rest alone on me.'

'One word more, Rose. Dearest Rose! one more!' cried Harry, throwing himself before her. 'If I had been less—less fortunate, the world would call it—if some obscure and peaceful life had been my destiny—if I had been poor, sick, helpless—would you have turned from me then? Or has my probable advancement to riches and honour, given this scruple birth?'

'Do not press me to reply,' answered Rose. 'The question does not arise, and never will. It is unfair, almost unkind, to urge it.'

'If your answer be what I almost dare to hope it is,' retorted Harry, 'it will shed a gleam of happiness upon my lonely way, and light the path before me. It is not an idle thing to do so much, by the utterance of a few brief words, for one who loves you beyond all else. Oh, Rose! in the name of my ardent and enduring attachment; in the name of all I have suffered for you, and all you doom me to undergo; answer me this one question!'

'Then, if your lot had been differently cast,' rejoined Rose; 'if you had been even a little, but not so far, above me; if I could have been a help and comfort to you in any humble scene of peace and retirement, and not a blot and drawback in ambitious and distinguished crowds; I should have been spared this trial. I have every reason to be happy, very happy, now; but then, Harry, I own I should have been happier.'

Busy recollections of old hopes, cherished as a girl, long ago, crowded into the mind of Rose, while making this avowal; but they brought tears with them, as old hopes will when they come back withered; and they relieved her.

'I cannot help this weakness, and it makes my purpose stronger,' said Rose, extending her hand. 'I must leave you now, indeed.'

'I ask one promise,' said Harry. 'Once, and only once more, — say within a year, but it may be much sooner, —I may speak to you again on this subject, for the last time.'

'Not to press me to alter my right determination,' replied Rose, with a melancholy smile; 'it will be useless.'

'No,' said Harry; 'to hear you repeat it, if you will—finally repeat it! I will lay at your feet, whatever of station or fortune I may possess; and if you still adhere to your present resolution, will not seek, by word or act, to change it.'

'Then let it be so,' rejoined Rose; 'it is but one pang the more, and by that time I may be enabled to bear it better.'

She extended her hand again. But the young man caught her to his bosom; and imprinting one kiss on her beautiful forehead, hurried from the room.

CHAPTER 36

Is a very short one, and may appear of no great importance in its place, but it should be read notwithstanding, as a sequel to the last, and a key to one that will follow when its time arrives

'And so you are resolved to be my travelling companion this morning; eh?' said the doctor, as Harry Maylie joined him and Oliver at the breakfast-table. 'Why, you are not in the same mind or intention two half-hours together!'

'You will tell me a different tale one of these days,' said Harry, colouring without any perceptible reason.

'I hope I may have good cause to do so,' replied Mr. Losberne; 'though I confess I don't think I shall. But yesterday morning you had made up your mind, in a great hurry, to stay here, and to accompany your mother, like a dutiful son, to the sea-side. Before noon, you announce that you are going to do me the honour of accompanying me as far as I go, on your road to London. And at night, you urge me, with great mystery, to start before the ladies are stirring; the consequence of which is, that young Oliver here is pinned down to his breakfast when he ought to be ranging the meadows after botanical phenomena of all kinds. Too bad, isn't it, Oliver?'

'I should have been very sorry not to have been at home when you and Mr. Maylie went away, sir,' rejoined Oliver.

'That's a fine fellow,' said the doctor; 'you shall come and see me when you return. But, to speak seriously, Harry; has any communication from the great nobs produced this sudden anxiety on your part to be gone?'

'The great nobs,' replied Harry, 'under which designation, I presume, you include my most stately uncle, have not communicated with me at all, since I have been here; nor, at this time of the year, is it likely that anything would occur to render necessary my immediate attendance among them.'

'Well,' said the doctor, 'you are a queer fellow. But of course they will get you into parliament at the election before Christmas, and these sudden shiftings and changes are no bad preparation for political life. There's something in that. Good training is always desirable, whether the race be for place, cup, or sweepstakes.'

Harry Maylie looked as if he could have followed up this short dialogue by one or two remarks that would have staggered the doctor not a little; but he contented himself with saying, 'We shall see,' and pursued the subject no farther. The post-chaise drove up to the door shortly afterwards; and Giles coming in for the luggage, the good doctor bustled out, to see it packed.

'Oliver,' said Harry Maylie, in a low voice, 'let me speak a word with you.'

Oliver walked into the window-recess to which Mr. Maylie beckoned him; much surprised at the mixture of sadness and boisterous spirits, which his whole behaviour displayed.

'You can write well now?' said Harry, laying his hand upon his arm.

'I hope so, sir,' replied Oliver.

'I shall not be at home again, perhaps for some time; I wish you would write to me—say once a fortnight: every alternate Monday: to the General Post Office in London. Will you?'

'Oh! certainly, sir; I shall be proud to do it,' exclaimed Oliver, greatly delighted with the commission.

'I should like to know how—how my mother and Miss Maylie are,' said the young man; 'and you can fill up a sheet by telling me what walks you take, and what you talk about, and whether she—they, I mean—seem happy and quite well. You understand me?'

'Oh! quite, sir, quite,' replied Oliver.

'I would rather you did not mention it to them,' said Harry, hurrying over his words; 'because it might make my mother anxious to write to me oftener, and it is a trouble and worry to her. Let it be a secret between you and me; and mind you tell me everything. I depend upon you.'

Oliver, quite elated and honoured by a sense of his importance, faithfully promised to be secret and explicit in his communications. Mr. Maylie took leave of him, with many assurances of his regard and protection.

The doctor was in the chaise; Giles (who, it had been arranged, should be left behind) held the door open in his hand; and the women-servants were in the garden, looking on. Harry cast one slight glance at the latticed window, and jumped into the carriage.

'Drive on!' he cried, 'hard, fast, full gallop! Nothing short of flying will keep pace with me to-day.'

'Halloa!' cried the doctor, letting down the front glass in a great hurry, and shouting to the postilion; 'something very short of flying will keep pace with *me*. Do you hear?'

Jingling and clattering, till distance rendered its noise inaudible, and its rapid progress only perceptible to the eye, the vehicle wound its way along the road, almost hidden in a cloud of dust: now wholly disappearing, and now becoming visible again, as intervening objects, or the intricacies of the way, permitted. It was not until even the dusty cloud was no longer to be seen, that the gazers dispersed.

And there was one looker-on, who remained with eyes fixed upon the spot where the carriage had disappeared, long after it was many miles away; for, behind the white curtain which had shrouded her from view when Harry raised his eyes towards the window, sat Rose herself.

'He seems in high spirits and happy,' she said, at length. 'I feared for a time he might be otherwise. I was mistaken. I am very, very glad.'

Tears are signs of gladness as well as grief; but those which coursed down Rose's face, as she sat pensively at the window, still gazing in the same direction, seemed to tell more of sorrow than of joy.

CHAPTER 37

In which the reader may perceive a contrast, not uncommon in matrimonial cases

Mr. Bumble sat in the workhouse parlour with his eyes moodily fixed on the cheerless grate, whence, as it was summer time, no brighter gleam proceeded, than the reflection of certain sickly rays of the sun, which were sent back from its cold and shining surface. A paper fly cage dangled from the ceiling, to which he occasionally raised his eyes in gloomy thought; and, as the heedless insects hovered round the gaudy network, Mr. Bumble would heave a deep sigh, while a more gloomy shadow overspread his countenance. Mr. Bumble was meditating; it might be that the insects brought to mind, some painful passage in his own past life.

Nor was Mr. Bumble's gloom the only thing calculated to awaken a pleasing melancholy in the bosom of a spectator. There were not wanting other appearances, and those closely connected with his own person, which announced that a great change had taken place in the position of his affairs. The laced coat, and the cocked-hat; where were they? He still wore knee-breeches, and dark cotton stockings on his nether limbs; but they were not *the* breeches. The coat was wide-skirted; and in that respect like *the* coat, but, oh, how different! The mighty cocked-hat was replaced by a modest round one. Mr. Bumble was no longer a beadle.

There are some promotions in life, which, independent of the more substantial rewards they offer, acquire peculiar value and dignity from the coats and waistcoats connected with them. A field-marshal has his uniform; a bishop his silk apron; a counsellor his silk gown; a beadle his cocked-hat. Strip the bishop of his apron, or the beadle of his hat and lace; what are they? Men. Mere men. Dignity, and even holiness too, sometimes, are more questions of coat and waistcoat than some people imagine.

Mr. Bumble had married Mrs. Corney, and was master of the workhouse. Another beadle had come into power. On him the cocked-hat, gold-laced coat, and staff, had all three descended.

'And to-morrow two months it was done!' said Mr. Bumble, with a sigh. 'It seems a age.'

Mr. Bumble might have meant that he had concentrated a whole existence of happiness into the short space of eight weeks; but the sigh—there was a vast deal of meaning in the sigh.

'I sold myself,' said Mr. Bumble, pursuing the same train of reflection, 'for six teaspoons, a pair of sugar-tongs, and a milk-pot; with a small quantity of second-hand furniture, and twenty pound in money. I went very reasonable. Cheap, dirt cheap!'

'Cheap!' cried a shrill voice in Mr. Bumble's ear: 'you would have been dear at any price; and dear enough I paid for you, Lord above knows that!'

Mr. Bumble turned, and encountered the face of his inter-esting consort, who, imperfectly comprehending the few words she had overheard of his complaint, had hazarded the foregoing remark at a venture.

'Mrs. Bumble, ma'am!' said Mr. Bumble, with sentimental stern-ness.

'Well!' cried the lady.

'Have the goodness to look at me,' said Mr. Bumble, fixing his eyes upon her. ('If she stands such a eye as that,' said Mr. Bumble to himself, 'she can stand anything. It is a eye I never knew to fail with paupers. If it fails with her, my power is gone.')

Whether an exceedingly small expansion of eye be sufficient to quell paupers, who, being lightly fed, are in no very high condi-tion; or whether the late Mrs. Corney was particularly proof against eagle glances; are matters of opinion. The matter of fact, is, that the matron was in no way overpowered by Mr. Bumble's scowl, but, on the contrary, treated it with great disdain, and even raised a laugh thereat, which sounded as though it were genuine.

On hearing this most unexpected sound, Mr. Bumble looked first incredulous, and afterwards amazed. He then relapsed into his former state; nor did he rouse himself until his attention was again awakened by the voice of his partner.

'Are you going to sit snoring there, all day?' inquired Mrs. Bumble.

'I am going to sit here, as long as I think proper, ma'am,' rejoined Mr. Bumble; 'and although I was *not* snoring, I shall snore, gape, sneeze, laugh, or cry, as the humour strikes me; such being my prerogative.'

'*Your* prerogative!' sneered Mrs. Bumble, with ineffable contempt.

'I said the word, ma'am,' said Mr. Bumble. 'The prerogative of a man is to command.'

'And what's the prerogative of a woman, in the name of Goodness?' cried the relict of Mr. Corney deceased.

'To obey, ma'am,' thundered Mr. Bumble. 'Your late unfortunate husband should have taught it you; and then, perhaps, he might have been alive now. I wish he was, poor man!'

Mrs. Bumble, seeing at a glance, that the decisive moment had now arrived, and that a blow struck for the mastership on one side or other, must necessarily be final and conclusive, no sooner heard this allusion to the dead and gone, than she dropped into a chair, and with a loud scream that Mr. Bumble was a hard-hearted brute, fell into a paroxysm of tears.

But, tears were not the things to find their way to Mr. Bumble's soul; his heart was waterproof. Like washable beaver hats that improve with rain, his nerves were rendered stouter and more vigorous, by showers of tears, which, being tokens of weakness, and so far tacit admissions of his own power, pleased and exalted him. He eyed his good lady with looks of great satisfaction, and begged, in an encouraging manner, that she should cry her hardest:

the exercise being looked upon, by the faculty, as strongly conducive to health.

'It opens the lungs, washes the countenance, exercises the eyes, and softens down the temper,' said Mr. Bumble. 'So cry away.'

As he discharged himself of this pleasantry, Mr. Bumble took his hat from a peg, and putting it on, rather rakishly, on one side, as a man might, who felt he had asserted his superiority in a becoming manner, thrust his hands into his pockets, and sauntered towards the door, with much ease and waggishness depicted in his whole appearance.

Now, Mrs. Corney that was, had tried the tears, because they were less troublesome than a manual assault; but she was quite prepared to make trial of the latter mode of proceeding, as Mr. Bumble was not long in discovering.

The first proof he experienced of the fact, was conveyed in a hollow sound, immediately succeeded by the sudden flying off of his hat to the opposite end of the room. This preliminary proceeding laying bare his head, the expert lady, clasping him tightly round the throat with one hand, inflicted a shower of blows (dealt with singular vigour and dexterity) upon it with the other. This done, she created a little variety by scratching his face, and tearing his hair; and, having, by this time, inflicted as much punishment as she deemed necessary for the offence, she pushed him over a chair, which was luckily well situated for the purpose: and defied him to talk about his prerogative again, if he dared.

'Get up!' said Mrs. Bumble, in a voice of command. 'And take yourself away from here, unless you want me to do something desperate.'

Mr. Bumble rose with a very rueful countenance: wondering much what something desperate might be. Picking up his hat, he looked towards the door.

'Are you going?' demanded Mrs. Bumble.

'Certainly, my dear, certainly,' rejoined Mr. Bumble, making a quicker motion towards the door. 'I didn't intend to—I'm going, my dear! You are so very violent, that really I—'

At this instant, Mrs. Bumble stepped hastily forward to replace the carpet, which had been kicked up in the scuffle. Mr. Bumble immediately darted out of the room, without bestowing another thought on his unfinished sentence: leaving the late Mrs. Corney in full possession of the field.

Mr. Bumble was fairly taken by surprise, and fairly beaten. He had a decided propensity for bullying; derived no inconsiderable pleasure from the exercise of petty cruelty; and, consequently, was (it is needless to say) a coward. This is by no means a disparagement to his character; for many official personages, who are held in high respect and admiration, are the victims of similar infirmities. The remark is made, indeed, rather in his favour than otherwise, and with a view of impressing the reader with a just sense of his qualifications for office.

But, the measure of his degradation was not yet full. After making a tour of the house, and thinking, for the first time, that the poor-laws really were too hard on people; and that men who ran away from their wives, leaving them chargeable to the parish, ought, in justice, to be visited with no punishment at all, but rather rewarded as meritorious individuals who had suffered much; Mr. Bumble came to a room where some of the female paupers were usually employed in washing the parish linen: whence the sound of voices in conversation, now proceeded.

'Hem!' said Mr. Bumble, summoning up all his native dignity. 'These women at least shall continue to respect the prerogative. Hallo! hallo there! What do you mean by this noise, you hussies?'

With these words, Mr. Bumble opened the door, and walked in with a very fierce and angry manner: which was at once exchanged for a most humiliated and cowering air, as his eyes unexpectedly rested on the form of his lady wife.

'My dear,' said Mr. Bumble, 'I didn't know you were here.'

'Didn't know I was here!' repeated Mrs. Bumble. 'What do *you* do here?'

'I thought they were talking rather too much to be doing their work properly, my dear,' replied Mr. Bumble: glancing distractedly at a couple of old women at the wash-tub, who were comparing notes of admiration at the workhouse-master's humility.

'*You* thought they were talking too much?' said Mrs. Bumble. 'What business is it of yours?'

'Why, my dear—' urged Mr. Bumble, submissively.

'What business is it of yours?' demanded Mrs. Bumble, again.

'It's very true, you're matron here, my dear,' submitted Mr. Bumble; 'but I thought you mightn't be in the way just then.'

'I'll tell you what, Mr. Bumble,' returned his lady. 'We don't want any of your interference. You're a great deal too fond of poking your nose into things that don't concern you, making everybody in the house laugh, the moment your back is turned, and making yourself look like a fool every hour in the day. Be off; come!'

Mr. Bumble, seeing with excruciating feelings, the delight of the two old paupers, who were tittering together most rapturously, hesitated for an instant. Mrs. Bumble, whose patience brooked no delay, caught up a bowl of soap-suds, and motioning him towards the door, ordered him instantly to depart, on pain of receiving the contents upon his portly person.

What could Mr. Bumble do? He looked dejectedly round, and slunk away; and as he reached the door, the titterings of the paupers broke into a shrill chuckle of irrepressible delight. It wanted but this. He was degraded in their eyes; he had lost caste and station before the very paupers; he had fallen from all the height and pomp of beadleship, to the lowest depth of the most snubbed hen-peckery.

'All in two months!' said Mr. Bumble, filled with dismal thoughts. 'Two months! No more than two months ago, I was not only my own master, but everybody else's, so far as the porochial workhouse was concerned, and now!—'

It was too much. Mr. Bumble boxed the ears of the boy who opened the gate for him (for he had reached the portal in his reverie); and walked, distractedly, into the street.

He walked up one street, and down another, until exercise had abated the first passion of his grief; and then the revulsion of feeling made him thirsty. He passed a great many public-houses; but at length paused before one in a by-way, whose parlour, as he gathered from a hasty peep over the blinds, was deserted, save by one solitary customer. It began to rain, heavily, at the moment. This determined him. Mr. Bumble stepped in; and ordering something to drink, as he passed the bar, entered the apartment into which he had looked from the street.

The man who was seated there, was tall and dark, and wore a large cloak. He had the air of a stranger; and seemed, by a certain haggardness in his look, as well as by the dusty soils on his dress, to have travelled some distance. He eyed Bumble askance, as he entered, but scarcely deigned to nod his head in acknowledgment of his salutation.

Mr. Bumble had quite dignity enough for two: supposing even that the stranger had been more familiar: so he drank his gin-and-water in silence, and read the paper with great show of pomp and circumstance.

It so happened, however: as it will happen very often, when men fall into company under such circumstances: that Mr. Bumble felt, every now and then, a powerful inducement, which he could not resist, to steal a look at the stranger; and that whenever he did so, he withdrew his eyes, in some confusion, to find that the stranger was at that moment stealing a look at him. Mr. Bumble's awkwardness was enhanced by the very remarkable expression of the stranger's eye, which was keen and bright, but shadowed by a scowl of distrust and suspicion, unlike anything he had ever observed before, and repulsive to behold.

When they had encountered each other's glance several times in this way, the stranger, in a harsh, deep voice, broke silence.

'Were you looking for me,' he said, 'when you peered in at the window?'

'Not that I am aware of, unless you're Mr. —' Here Mr. Bumble stopped short; for he was curious to know the stranger's name, and thought, in his impatience, he might supply the blank.

'I see you were not,' said the stranger; an expression of quiet sarcasm playing about his mouth; 'or you would have known my name. You don't know it. I would recommend you not to ask for it.'

'I meant no harm, young man,' observed Mr. Bumble, majestically.

'And have done none,' said the stranger.

Another silence succeeded this short dialogue: which was again broken by the stranger.

'I have seen you before, I think?' said he. 'You were differently dressed at that time, and I only passed you in the street, but I should know you again. You were beadle here, once; were you not?'

'I was,' said Mr. Bumble, in some surprise; 'porochial beadle.'

'Just so,' rejoined the other, nodding his head. 'It was in that character I saw you. What are you now?'

'Master of the workhouse,' rejoined Mr. Bumble, slowly and impressively, to check any undue familiarity the stranger might otherwise assume. 'Master of the workhouse, young man!'

'You have the same eye to your own interest, that you always had, I doubt not?' resumed the stranger, looking keenly into Mr. Bumble's eyes, as he raised them in astonishment at the question. 'Don't scruple to answer freely, man. I know you pretty well, you see.'

'I suppose, a married man,' replied Mr. Bumble, shading his eyes with his hand, and surveying the stranger, from head to foot, in evident perplexity, 'is not more averse to turning an honest penny when he can, than a single one. Porochial officers are not so well paid that they can afford to refuse any little extra fee, when it comes to them in a civil and proper manner.'

The stranger smiled, and nodded his head again: as much as to say, he had not mistaken his man; then rang the bell.

'Fill this glass again,' he said, handing Mr. Bumble's empty tumbler to the landlord. 'Let it be strong and hot. You like it so, I suppose?'

'Not too strong,' replied Mr. Bumble, with a delicate cough.

'You understand what that means, landlord!' said the stranger, drily.

The host smiled, disappeared, and shortly afterwards returned with a steaming jorum: of which, the first gulp brought the water into Mr. Bumble's eyes.

'Now listen to me,' said the stranger, after closing the door and window. 'I came down to this place, to-day, to find you out; and, by one of those chances which the devil throws in the way of his friends sometimes, you walked into the very room I was sitting in, while you were uppermost in my mind. I want some information from you. I don't ask you to give it for nothing, slight as it is. Put up that, to begin with.'

As he spoke, he pushed a couple of sovereigns across the table to his companion, carefully, as though unwilling that the chinking of money should be heard without. When Mr. Bumble had scrupulously examined the coins, to see that they were genuine, and had put them up, with much satisfaction, in his waistcoat-pocket, he went on:

'Carry your memory back—let me see—twelve years, last winter.'

'It's a long time,' said Mr. Bumble. 'Very good. I've done it.'

'The scene, the workhouse.'

'Good!'

'And the time, night.'

'Yes.'

'And the place, the crazy hole, wherever it was, in which miserable drabs brought forth the life and health so often denied to themselves—gave birth to puling children for the parish to rear; and hid their shame, rot 'em, in the grave!'

'The lying-in room, I suppose?' said Mr. Bumble, not quite following the stranger's excited description.

'Yes,' said the stranger. 'A boy was born there.'

'A many boys,' observed Mr. Bumble, shaking his head, despondingly.

'A murrain on the young devils!' cried the stranger; 'I speak of one; a meek-looking, pale-faced boy, who was apprenticed down here, to a coffin-maker: I wish he had made his coffin, and screwed his body in it: and who afterwards ran away to London, as it was supposed.'

'Why, you mean Oliver! Young Twist!' said Mr. Bumble; 'I remember him, of course. There wasn't a obstinater young rascal—'

'It's not of him I want to hear; I've heard enough of him,' said the stranger, stopping Mr. Bumble in the outset of a tirade on the subject of poor Oliver's vices. 'It's of a woman; the hag that nursed his mother. Where is she?'

'Where is she?' said Mr. Bumble, whom the gin-and-water had rendered facetious. 'It would be hard to tell. There's no midwifery there, whichever place she's gone to; so I suppose she's out of employment, any way.'

'What do you mean?' demanded the stranger, sternly.

'That she died last winter,' rejoined Mr. Bumble.

The man looked fixedly at him when he had given this information, and although he did not withdraw his eyes for some time afterwards, his gaze gradually became vacant and abstracted, and he seemed lost in thought. For some time, he appeared doubtful whether he ought to be relieved or disappointed by the intelligence; but at length he breathed more freely; and withdrawing his eyes, observed that it was no great matter. With that he rose, as if to depart.

But Mr. Bumble was cunning enough; and he at once saw that an opportunity was opened, for the lucrative disposal of some secret in the possession of his better half. He well remembered the night of old Sally's death, which the occurrences of that day had given him good reason to recollect, as the occasion on which he had proposed to Mrs. Corney; and although that lady had never confided to him the disclosure of which she had been the solitary witness, he had heard enough to know that it related to something that had occurred in the old woman's attendance, as workhouse nurse, upon the young mother of Oliver Twist. Hastily calling this circumstance to mind, he informed the stranger, with an air of mystery, that one woman had been closeted with the old harridan shortly before she died; and that she could, as he had reason to believe, throw some light on the subject of his inquiry.

'How can I find her?' said the stranger, thrown off his guard; and plainly showing that all his fears (whatever they were) were aroused afresh by the intelligence.

'Only through me,' rejoined Mr. Bumble.

'When?' cried the stranger, hastily.

'To-morrow,' rejoined Bumble.

'At nine in the evening,' said the stranger, producing a scrap of paper, and writing down upon it, an obscure address by the water-side, in characters that betrayed his agitation; 'at nine in the evening, bring her to me there. I needn't tell you to be secret. It's your interest.'

With these words, he led the way to the door, after stopping to pay for the liquor that had been drunk. Shortly remarking that their roads were different, he departed, without more ceremony than an emphatic repetition of the hour of appointment for the following night.

On glancing at the address, the parochial functionary observed that it contained no name. The stranger had not gone far, so he made after him to ask it.

'What do you want?' cried the man, turning quickly round, as Bumble touched him on the arm. 'Following me?'

'Only to ask a question,' said the other, pointing to the scrap of paper. 'What name am I to ask for?'

'Monks!' rejoined the man; and strode, hastily, away.

CHAPTER 38

Containing an account of what passed between Mr. and Mrs. Bumble, and Mr. Monks, at their nocturnal interview

It was a dull, close, overcast summer evening. The clouds, which had been threatening all day, spread out in a dense and sluggish mass of vapour, already yielded large drops of rain, and seemed to presage a violent thunderstorm, when Mr. and Mrs. Bumble, turning out of the main street of the town, directed their course towards a scattered little colony of ruinous houses, distant from it some mile and a half, or thereabouts, and erected on a low unwholesome swamp, bordering upon the river.

They were both wrapped in old and shabby outer garments, which might, perhaps, serve the double purpose of protecting their persons from the rain, and sheltering them from observation. The husband carried a lantern, from which, however, no light yet shone; and trudged on, a few paces in front, as though—the way being dirty—to give his wife the benefit of treading in his heavy footprints. They went on, in profound silence; every now and then, Mr. Bumble relaxed his pace, and turned his head as if to make sure that his helpmate was following; then, discovering that she was close at his heels, he mended his rate of walking, and proceeded, at a considerable increase of speed, towards their place of destination.

This was far from being a place of doubtful character; for it had long been known as the residence of none but low ruffians, who, under various pretences of living by their labour, subsisted chiefly on plunder and crime. It was a collection of mere hovels: some, hastily built with loose bricks: others, of old worm-eaten ship-timber: jumbled together without any attempt at order or arrangement, and planted, for the most part, within a few feet of the river's bank. A few leaky boats drawn up on the mud, and made fast to the dwarf wall which skirted it: and here and there an oar or coil of rope: appeared, at first, to indicate that the inhabitants of these miserable cottages pursued some avocation on the river; but a glance at the shattered and useless condition of the articles thus displayed, would have led a passer-by, without much difficulty, to the conjecture that they were disposed there, rather for the preservation of appearances, than with any view to their being actually employed.

In the heart of this cluster of huts; and skirting the river, which its upper stories overhung; stood a large building, formerly used as a manufactory of some kind. It had, in its day, probably furnished employment to the inhabitants of the surrounding tenements. But it had long since gone to ruin. The rat, the worm, and the action of the damp, had weakened and rotted the piles on which it stood; and a considerable portion of the building had already sunk down into the water; while the remainder, tottering and bending over the dark stream, seemed to wait a favourable opportunity of following its old companion, and involving itself in the same fate.

It was before this ruinous building that the worthy couple paused, as the first peal of distant thunder reverberated in the air, and the rain commenced pouring violently down.

'The place should be somewhere here,' said Bumble, consulting a scrap of paper he held in his hand.

'Halloa there!' cried a voice from above.

Following the sound, Mr. Bumble raised his head, and descried a man looking out of a door, breast-high, on the second story.

'Stand still, a minute,' cried the voice; 'I'll be with you directly.' With which the head disappeared, and the door closed.

'Is that the man?' asked Mr. Bumble's good lady.

Mr. Bumble nodded in the affirmative.

'Then, mind what I told you,' said the matron: 'and be careful to say as little as you can, or you'll betray us at once.'

Mr. Bumble, who had eyed the building with very rueful looks, was apparently about to express some doubts relative to the advisability of proceeding any further with the enterprise just then, when he was prevented by the appearance of Monks: who opened a small door, near which they stood, and beckoned them inwards.

'Come in!' he cried impatiently, stamping his foot upon the ground. 'Don't keep me here!'

The woman, who had hesitated at first, walked boldly in, without any other invitation. Mr. Bumble, who was ashamed or afraid to lag behind, followed: obviously very ill at ease and with scarcely any of that remarkable dignity which was usually his chief characteristic.

'What the devil made you stand lingering there, in the wet?' said Monks, turning round, and addressing Bumble, after he had bolted the door behind them.

'We—we were only cooling ourselves,' stammered Bumble, looking apprehensively about him.

'Cooling yourselves!' retorted Monks. 'Not all the rain that ever fell, or ever will fall, will put as much of hell's fire out, as a man can carry about with him. You won't cool yourselves so easily; don't think it!'

With this agreeable speech, Monks turned short upon the matron, and bent his gaze upon her, till even she, who was not easily cowed, was fain to withdraw her eyes, and turn them towards the ground.

'This is the woman, is it?' demanded Monks.

'Hem! That is the woman,' replied Mr. Bumble, mindful of his wife's caution.

'You think women never can keep secrets, I suppose?' said the matron, interposing, and returning, as she spoke, the searching look of Monks.

'I know they will always keep *one* till it's found out,' said Monks.

'And what may that be?' asked the matron.

'The loss of their own good name,' replied Monks. 'So, by the same rule, if a woman's a party to a secret that might hang or transport her, I'm not afraid of her telling it to anybody; not I! Do you understand, mistress?'

'No,' rejoined the matron, slightly colouring as she spoke.

'Of course you don't!' said Monks. 'How should you?'

Bestowing something half-way between a smile and a frown upon his two companions, and again beckoning them to follow him, the man hastened across the apartment, which was of considerable extent, but low in the roof. He was preparing to ascend a steep staircase, or rather ladder, leading to another floor of warehouses above: when a bright flash of lightning streamed down the aperture, and a peal of thunder followed, which shook the crazy building to its centre.

'Hear it!' he cried, shrinking back. 'Hear it! Rolling and crashing on as if it echoed through a thousand caverns where the devils were hiding from it. I hate the sound!'

He remained silent for a few moments; and then, removing his hands suddenly from his face, showed, to the unspeakable discomposure of Mr. Bumble, that it was much distorted, and discoloured.

'These fits come over me, now and then,' said Monks, observing his alarm; 'and thunder sometimes brings them on. Don't mind me now; it's all over for this once.'

Thus speaking, he led the way up the ladder; and hastily closing the window-shutter of the room into which it led, lowered a lantern which hung at the end of a rope and pulley passed through one of the heavy beams in the ceiling: and which cast a dim light upon an old table and three chairs that were placed beneath it.

'Now,' said Monks, when they had all three seated themselves, 'the sooner we come to our business, the better for all. The woman knows what it is, does she?'

The question was addressed to Bumble; but his wife anticipated the reply, by intimating that she was perfectly acquainted with it.

'He is right in saying that you were with this hag the night she died; and that she told you something—'

'About the mother of the boy you named,' replied the matron, interrupting him. 'Yes.'

'The first question is, of what nature was her communication?' said Monks.

'That's the second,' observed the woman with much deliberation. 'The first is, what may the communication be worth?'

'Who the devil can tell that, without knowing of what kind it is?' asked Monks.

'Nobody better than you, I am persuaded,' answered Mrs. Bumble: who did not want for spirit, as her yokefellow could abundantly testify.

'Humph!' said Monks significantly, and with a look of eager inquiry; 'there may be money's worth to get, eh?'

'Perhaps there may,' was the composed reply.

'Something that was taken from her,' said Monks. 'Something that she wore. Something that—'

'You had better bid,' interrupted Mrs. Bumble. 'I have heard enough, already, to assure me that you are the man I ought to talk to.'

Mr. Bumble, who had not yet been admitted by his better half into any greater share of the secret than he had originally possessed, listened to this dialogue with outstretched neck and distended eyes: which he directed towards his wife and Monks, by turns, in undisguised astonishment; increased, if possible, when the latter sternly demanded what sum was required for the disclosure.

'What's it worth to you?' asked the woman, as collectedly as before.

'It may be nothing; it may be twenty pounds,' replied Monks. 'Speak out, and let me know which.'

'Add five pounds to the sum you have named; give me five-and-twenty pounds in gold,' said the woman; 'and I'll tell you all I know. Not before.'

'Five-and-twenty pounds!' exclaimed Monks, drawing back.

'I spoke as plainly as I could,' replied Mrs. Bumble. 'It's not a large sum, either.'

'Not a large sum for a paltry secret, that may be nothing when it's told!' cried Monks impatiently; 'and which has been lying dead for twelve years past or more!'

'Such matters keep well, and, like good wine, often double their value in course of time,' answered the matron, still preserving the resolute indifference she had assumed. 'As to lying dead, there are those who will lie dead for twelve thousand years to come, or twelve million, for anything you or I know, who will tell strange tales at last!'

'What if I pay it for nothing?' asked Monks, hesitating.

'You can easily take it away again,' replied the matron. 'I am but a woman; alone here; and unprotected.'

'Not alone, my dear, nor unprotected neither,' submitted Mr. Bumble, in a voice tremulous with fear: '*I* am here, my dear. And besides,' said Mr. Bumble, his teeth chattering as he spoke, 'Mr. Monks is too much of a gentleman to attempt any violence on porochial persons. Mr. Monks is aware that I am not a young man, my dear, and also that I am a little run to seed, as I may say; but he has heerd: I say I have no doubt Mr. Monks has heerd, my dear: that I am a very determined officer, with very uncommon strength, if I'm once roused. I only want a little rousing; that's all.'

As Mr. Bumble spoke, he made a melancholy feint of grasping his lantern with fierce determination; and plainly showed, by the alarmed expression of every feature, that he *did* want a little rousing, and not a little, prior to making any very warlike demonstration: unless, indeed, against paupers, or other person or persons trained down for the purpose.

'You are a fool,' said Mrs. Bumble, in reply; 'and had better hold your tongue.'

'He had better have cut it out, before he came, if he can't speak in a lower tone,' said Monks, grimly. 'So! He's your husband, eh?'

'He my husband!' tittered the matron, parrying the question.

'I thought as much, when you came in,' rejoined Monks,

marking the angry glance which the lady darted at her spouse as she spoke. 'So much the better; I have less hesitation in dealing with two people, when I find that there's only one will between them. I'm in earnest. See here!'

He thrust his hand into a side-pocket; and producing a canvas bag, told out twenty-five sovereigns on the table, and pushed them over to the woman.

'Now,' he said, 'gather them up; and when this cursed peal of thunder, which I feel is coming up to break over the housetop, is gone, let's hear your story.'

The thunder, which seemed in fact much nearer, and to shiver and break almost over their heads, having subsided, Monks, raising his face from the table, bent forward to listen to what the woman should say. The faces of the three nearly touched, as the two men leant over the small table in their eagerness to hear, and the woman also leant forward to render her whisper audible. The sickly rays of the suspended lantern falling directly upon them, aggravated the paleness and anxiety of their countenances: which, encircled by the deepest gloom and darkness, looked ghastly in the extreme.

'When this woman, that we called old Sally, died,' the matron began, 'she and I were alone.'

'Was there no one by?' asked Monks, in the same hollow whisper; 'no sick wretch or idiot in some other bed? No one who could hear, and might, by possibility, understand?'

'Not a soul,' replied the woman; 'we were alone. *I* stood alone beside the body when death came over it.'

'Good,' said Monks, regarding her attentively. 'Go on.'

'She spoke of a young creature,' resumed the matron, 'who had brought a child into the world some years before; not merely in the same room, but in the same bed, in which she then lay dying.'

'Ay?' said Monks, with quivering lip, and glancing over his shoulder. 'Blood! How things come about!'

'The child was the one you named to him last night,' said the matron, nodding carelessly towards her husband; 'the mother this nurse had robbed.'

'In life?' asked Monks.

'In death,' replied the woman, with something like a shudder. 'She stole from the corpse, when it had hardly turned to one, that which the dead mother had prayed her, with her last breath, to keep for the infant's sake.'

'She sold it?' cried Monks, with desperate eagerness; 'did she sell it? Where? When? To whom? How long before?'

'As she told me, with great difficulty, that she had done this,' said the matron, 'she fell back and died.'

'Without saying more?' cried Monks, in a voice which, from its very suppression, seemed only the more furious. 'It's a lie! I'll not be played with. She said more. I'll tear the life out of you both, but I'll know what it was.'

'She didn't utter another word,' said the woman, to all appearance unmoved (as Mr. Bumble was very far from being) by the strange man's violence; 'but she clutched my gown violently, with one hand, which was partly closed; and when I saw that she was dead, and so removed the hand by force, I found it clasped a scrap of dirty paper.'

'Which contained—' interposed Monks, stretching forward.

'Nothing.' replied the woman; 'it was a pawnbroker's duplicate.'

'For what?' demanded Monks.

'In good time I'll tell you,' said the woman. 'I judge that she had kept the trinket, for some time, in the hope of turning it to better account; and then had pawned it; and had saved or scraped together money to pay the pawnbroker's interest year by year, and prevent its running out; so that if anything came of it, it could still be redeemed. Nothing had come of it; and, as I tell you, she died with the scrap of paper, all worn and tattered, in her hand. The time was out in two days; I thought something might one day come of it too; and so redeemed the pledge.'

'Where is it now?' asked Monks quickly.

'*There*,' replied the woman. And, as if glad to be relieved of it, she hastily threw upon the table a small kid bag scarcely large enough for a French watch, which Monks pouncing upon, tore open with trembling hands. It contained a little gold locket; in which were two locks of hair, and a plain gold wedding-ring.

It has the word "Agnes" engraved on the inside,' said the woman. 'There is a blank left for the surname; and then follows the date; which is within a year before the child was born. I found out that.'

'And this is all?' said Monks, after a close and eager scrutiny of the contents of the little packet.

'All,' replied the woman.

Mr. Bumble drew a long breath, as if he were glad to find that the story was over, and no mention made of taking the five-and-twenty pounds back again; and now he took courage to wipe off the perspiration which had been trickling over his nose, unchecked, during the whole of the previous dialogue.

'I know nothing of the story, beyond what I can guess at,' said his wife, addressing Monks, after a short silence; 'and I want to know nothing; for it's safer not. But I may ask you two questions, may I?'

'You may ask,' said Monks, with some show of surprise; 'but whether I answer or not is another question.'

'—Which makes three,' observed Mr. Bumble, essaying a stroke of facetiousness.

'Is that what you expected to get from me?' demanded the matron.

'It is,' replied Monks. 'The other question?'

'What you propose to do with it? Can it be used against me?'

'Never,' rejoined Monks; 'nor against me either. See here! But don't move a step forward, or your life is not worth a bulrush.'

With these words, he suddenly wheeled the table aside, and pulling an iron ring in the boarding, threw back a large trap-door which opened close at Mr. Bumble's feet, and caused that gentleman to retire several paces backward, with great precipitation.

'Look down,' said Monks, lowering the lantern into the gulf. 'Don't fear me. I could have let you down, quietly enough, when you were seated over it, if that had been my game.'

Thus encouraged the matron drew near to the brink; and even Mr. Bumble himself, impelled by curiosity, ventured to do the same. The turbid water, swollen by the heavy rain, was rushing rapidly on below; and all other sounds were lost in the noise of its plashing and eddying against the green and slimy piles. There had once been a water-mill beneath; the tide foaming and chafing round the few rotten stakes, and fragments of machinery that yet remained, seemed to dart onward, with a new impulse, when freed from the obstacles which had unavailingly attempted to stem its headlong course.

'If you flung a man's body down there, where would it be to-morrow morning?' said Monks, swinging the lantern to and fro in the dark well.

'Twelve miles down the river, and cut to pieces besides,' replied Bumble, recoiling at the thought.

Monks drew the little packet from his breast, where he had hurriedly thrust it; and tying it to a leaden weight, which had formed a part of some pulley, and was lying on the floor, dropped it into the stream. It fell straight, and true as a die; clove the water with a scarcely audible splash; and was gone.

The three looking into each other's faces, seemed to breathe more freely.

'There!' said Monks, closing the trap-door, which fell heavily back into its former position. 'If the sea ever gives up its dead, as books say it will, it will keep its gold and silver to itself, and that trash among it. We have nothing more to say, and may break up our pleasant party.'

'By all means,' observed Mr. Bumble, with great alacrity.

'You'll keep a quiet tongue in your head, will you?' said Monks, with a threatening look. 'I am not afraid of your wife.'

'You may depend upon me, young man,' answered Mr. Bumble, bowing himself gradually towards the ladder, with excessive politeness. 'On everybody's account, young man; on my own, you know, Mr. Monks.'

'I am glad, for your sake, to hear it,' remarked Monks. 'Light your lantern! And get away from here as fast as you can.'

It was fortunate that the conversation terminated at this point, or Mr. Bumble, who had bowed himself to within six inches of the ladder, would infallibly have pitched headlong into the room below. He lighted his lantern from that which Monks had detached from the rope, and now carried in his hand; and making no effort to prolong the discourse, descended in silence, followed by his wife. Monks brought up the rear, after pausing on the steps to satisfy himself that there were no other sounds to be heard than the beating of the rain without, and the rushing of the water.

They traversed the lower room, slowly, and with caution; for Monks started at every shadow; and Mr. Bumble, holding his lantern a foot above the ground, walked not only with remarkable care, but with a marvellously light step for a gentleman of his figure: looking nervously about him for hidden trap-doors. The gate at which they had entered, was softly unfastened and opened by Monks; merely exchanging a nod with their mysterious acquaintance, the married couple emerged into the wet and darkness outside.

They were no sooner gone, than Monks, who appeared to entertain an invincible repugnance to being left alone, called to a boy who had been hidden somewhere below. Bidding him go first, and bear the light, he returned to the chamber he had just quitted.

CHAPTER 39

Introduces some respectable characters with
whom the reader is already acquainted, and
shows how Monks and the Jew laid their
worthy heads together

On the evening following that upon which the three worthies
mentioned in the last chapter, disposed of their little matter of business as therein narrated, Mr. William Sikes, awakening from a nap,
drowsily growled forth an inquiry what time of night it was.

The room in which Mr. Sikes propounded this question, was
not one of those he had tenanted, previous to the Chertsey expedition, although it was in the same quarter of the town, and was
situated at no great distance from his former lodgings. It was not,
in appearance, so desirable a habitation as his old quarters: being a
mean and badly-furnished apartment, of very limited size; lighted
only by one small window in the shelving roof, and abutting on a
close and dirty lane. Nor were there wanting other indications of the
good gentleman's having gone down in the world of late; for a great
scarcity of furniture, and total absence of comfort, together with the
disappearance of all such small moveables as spare clothes and linen,
bespoke a state of extreme poverty; while the meagre and attenu-
ated condition of Mr. Sikes himself would have fully confirmed these
symptoms, if they had stood in any need of corroboration.

The housebreaker was lying on the bed, wrapped in his white
great-coat, by way of dressing-gown, and displaying a set of features
in no degree improved by the cadaverous hue of illness, and the
addition of a soiled nightcap, and a stiff, black beard of a week's

growth. The dog sat at the bedside: now eyeing his master with a wistful look, and now pricking his ears, and uttering a low growl as some noise in the street, or in the lower part of the house, attracted his attention. Seated by the window, busily engaged in patching an old waistcoat which formed a portion of the robber's ordinary dress, was a female: so pale and reduced with watching and privation, that there would have been considerable difficulty in recognising her as the same Nancy who has already figured in this tale, but for the voice in which she replied to Mr. Sikes's question.

'Not long gone seven,' said the girl. 'How do you feel tonight, Bill?'

'As weak as water,' replied Mr. Sikes, with an imprecation on his eyes and limbs. 'Here; lend us a hand, and let me get off this thundering bed anyhow.'

Illness had not improved Mr. Sikes's temper; for, as the girl raised him up and led him to a chair, he muttered various curses on her awkwardness, and struck her.

'Whining, are you?' said Sikes. 'Come! Don't stand snivelling there. If you can't do anything better than that, cut off altogether. D'ye hear me?'

'I hear you,' replied the girl, turning her face aside, and forcing a laugh. 'What fancy have you got in your head now?'

'Oh! you've thought better of it, have you?' growled Sikes, marking the tear which trembled in her eye. 'All the better for you, you have.'

'Why, you don't mean to say, you'd be hard upon me tonight, Bill,' said the girl, laying her hand upon his shoulder.

'No!' cried Mr. Sikes. 'Why not?'

'Such a number of nights,' said the girl, with a touch of woman's tenderness, which communicated something like sweetness of tone, even to her voice: 'such a number of nights as I've been patient with you, nursing and caring for you, as if you had been a child: and this the first that I've seen you like yourself; you wouldn't have served me as you did just now, if you'd thought of that, would you? Come, come; say you wouldn't.'

'Well, then,' rejoined Mr. Sikes, 'I wouldn't. Why, damme, now, the girl's whining again!'

'It's nothing,' said the girl, throwing herself into a chair. 'Don't you seem to mind me. It'll soon be over.'

'What'll be over?' demanded Mr. Sikes in a savage voice. 'What foolery are you up to, now, again? Get up and bustle about, and don't come over me with your woman's nonsense.'

At any other time, this remonstrance, and the tone in which it was delivered, would have had the desired effect; but the girl being really weak and exhausted, dropped her head over the back of the chair, and fainted, before Mr. Sikes could get out a few of the appropriate oaths with which, on similar occasions, he was accustomed to garnish his threats. Not knowing, very well, what to do, in this uncommon emergency; for Miss Nancy's hysterics were usually of that violent kind which the patient fights and struggles out of, without much assistance; Mr. Sikes tried a little blasphemy: and finding that mode of treatment wholly ineffectual, called for assistance.

'What's the matter here, my dear?' said Fagin, looking in.

'Lend a hand to the girl, can't you?' replied Sikes impatiently. 'Don't stand chattering and grinning at me!'

With an exclamation of surprise, Fagin hastened to the girl's assistance, while Mr. John Dawkins (otherwise the Artful Dodger), who had followed his venerable friend into the room, hastily deposited on the floor a bundle with which he was laden; and snatching a bottle from the grasp of Master Charles Bates who came close at his heels, uncorked it in a twinkling with his teeth, and poured a portion of its contents down the patient's throat: previously taking a taste, himself, to prevent mistakes.

'Give her a whiff of fresh air with the bellows, Charley,' said Mr. Dawkins; 'and you slap her hands, Fagin, while Bill undoes the petticuts.'

These united restoratives, administered with great energy: especially that department consigned to Master Bates, who appeared to consider his share in the proceedings, a piece of unexampled pleasantry: were not long in producing the desired effect. The girl gradually recovered her senses; and, staggering to a chair by the bedside, hid her face upon the pillow: leaving Mr. Sikes to confront the new-comers, in some astonishment at their unlooked-for appearance.

'Why, what evil wind has blowed you here?' he asked Fagin.

'No evil wind at all, my dear, for evil winds blow nobody any good; and I've brought something good with me, that you'll be glad to see. Dodger, my dear, open the bundle; and give Bill the little trifles that we spent all our money on, this morning.'

In compliance with Mr. Fagin's request, the Artful untied his bundle, which was of large size, and formed of an old tablecloth; and handed the articles it contained, one by one, to Charley Bates: who placed them on the table, with various encomiums on their rarity and excellence.

'Sitch a rabbit pie, Bill,' exclaimed that young gentleman, disclosing to view a huge pasty; 'sitch delicate creeturs, with sitch tender limbs, Bill, that the wery bones melt in your mouth, and there's no occasion to pick 'em; half a pound of seven and sixpenny green, so precious strong that if you mix it with biling water, it'll go nigh to blow the lid of the teapot off; a pound and a half of moist sugar that the niggers didn't work at all at, afore they got it up to sitch a pitch of goodness, —oh no! Two half-quartern brans; pound of best fresh; piece of double Glo'ster; and, to wind up all, some of the richest sort you ever lushed!'

Uttering this last panegyric, Master Bates produced, from one of his extensive pockets, a full-sized wine bottle, carefully corked; while Mr. Dawkins, at the same instant, poured out a wine-glassful of raw spirits from the bottle he carried: which the invalid tossed down his throat without a moment's hesitation.

'Ah!' said Fagin, rubbing his hands with great satisfaction. 'You'll do, Bill; you'll do now.'

'Do!' exclaimed Mr. Sikes; 'I might have been done for, twenty times over, afore you'd have done anything to help me. What do mean by leaving a man in this state, three weeks and more, you false-hearted wagabond?'

'Only hear him, boys!' said Fagin, shrugging his shoulders. 'And us come to bring him all these beautiful things.'

'The things is well enough in their way,' observed Mr. Sikes: a little soothed as he glanced over the table; 'but what have you got to say for yourself, why you should leave me here, down in the mouth, health, blunt, and everything else; and take no more notice of me, all this mortal time, than if I was that 'ere dog.—Drive him down, Charley!'

'I never see such a jolly dog as that,' cried Master Bates, doing as he was desired. 'Smelling the grub like a old lady a-going to market! He'd make his fortun on the stage that dog would, and rewive the drayma besides.'

'Hold your din,' cried Sikes, as the dog retreated under the bed: still growling angrily. 'What have you got to say for yourself, you withered old fence, eh?'

'I was away from London, a week and more, my dear, on a plant,' replied the Jew.

'And what about the other fortnight?' demanded Sikes. 'What about the other fortnight that you've left me lying here, like a sick rat in his hole?'

'I couldn't help it, Bill. I can't go into a long explanation before company; but I couldn't help it, upon my honour.'

'Upon your what?' growled Sikes, with excessive disgust. 'Here! Cut me off a piece of that pie, one of you boys, to take the taste of that out of my mouth, or it'll choke me dead.'

'Don't be out of temper, my dear,' urged Fagin, submissively. 'I have never forgot you, Bill; never once.'

'No! I'll pound it that you han't,' replied Sikes, with a bitter grin. 'You've been scheming and plotting away, every hour that I have laid shivering and burning here; and Bill was to do this; and Bill was to do that; and Bill was to do it all, dirt cheap, as soon as he got well: and was quite poor enough for your work. If it hadn't been for the girl, I might have died.'

'There now, Bill,' remonstrated Fagin, eagerly catching at the word. 'If it hadn't been for the girl! Who but poor ould Fagin was the means of your having such a handy girl about you?'

'He says true enough there!' said Nancy, coming hastily forward. 'Let him be; let him be.'

Nancy's appearance gave a new turn to the conversation; for the boys, receiving a sly wink from the wary old Jew, began to ply her with liquor: of which, however, she took very sparingly; while Fagin, assuming an unusual flow of spirits, gradually brought Mr. Sikes into a better temper, by affecting to regard his threats as a little pleasant banter; and, moreover, by laughing very heartily at one or two rough jokes, which, after repeated applications to the spirit-bottle, he condescended to make.

'It's all very well,' said Mr. Sikes; 'but I must have some blunt from you to-night.'

'I haven't a piece of coin about me,' replied the Jew.

'Then you've got lots at home,' retorted Sikes; 'and I must have some from there.'

'Lots!' cried Fagin, holding up his hands. 'I haven't so much as would—'

'I don't know how much you've got, and I dare say you hardly know yourself, as it would take a pretty long time to count it,' said Sikes; 'but I must have some to-night; and that's flat.'

'Well, well,' said Fagin, with a sigh, 'I'll send the Artful round presently.'

'You won't do nothing of the kind,' rejoined Mr. Sikes. 'The Artful's a deal too artful, and would forget to come, or lose his way, or get dodged by traps and so be perwented, or anything for an excuse, if you put him up to it. Nancy shall go to the ken and fetch it, to make all sure; and I'll lie down and have a snooze while she's gone.'

After a great deal of haggling and squabbling, Fagin beat down the amount of the required advance from five pounds to three pounds four and sixpence: protesting with many solemn asseverations that that would only leave him eighteenpence to keep house with; Mr. Sikes sullenly remarking that if he couldn't get any more he must be content with that, Nancy prepared to accompany him home; while the Dodger and Master Bates put the eatables in the cupboard. The Jew then, taking leave of his affectionate friend, returned homeward, attended by Nancy and the boys: Mr. Sikes, meanwhile, flinging himself on the bed, and composing himself to sleep away the time until the young lady's return.

In due course, they arrived at Fagin's abode, where they found Toby Crackit and Mr. Chitling intent upon their fifteenth game at cribbage, which it is scarcely necessary to say the latter gentleman lost, and with it, his fifteenth and last sixpence: much to the amusement of his young friends. Mr. Crackit, apparently somewhat ashamed at being found relaxing himself with a gentleman so much his inferior in station and mental endowments, yawned, and inquiring after Sikes, took up his hat to go.

'Has nobody been, Toby?' asked Fagin.

'Not a living leg,' answered Mr. Crackit, pulling up his collar; 'it's been as dull as swipes. You ought to stand something handsome, Fagin, to recompense me for keeping house so long. Damme, I'm as flat as a juryman; and should have gone to sleep, as fast as Newgate, if I hadn't had the good natur' to amuse this youngster. Horrid dull, I'm blessed if I an't.'

With these and other ejaculations of the same kind, Mr. Toby Crackit swept up his winnings, and crammed them into his waistcoat pocket with a haughty air, as though such small pieces of silver were wholly beneath the consideration of a man of his figure; this done, he swaggered out of the room, with so much elegance and gentility, that Mr. Chitling, bestowing numerous admiring glances on his legs and boots till they were out of sight, assured the company that he considered his acquaintance cheap at fifteen sixpences an interview, and that he didn't value his losses the snap of his little finger.

'Wot a rum chap you are, Tom!' said Master Bates, highly amused by this declaration.

'Not a bit of it,' replied Mr. Chitling. 'Am I, Fagin?'

'A very clever fellow, my dear,' said Fagin, patting him on the shoulder, and winking to his other pupils.

'And Mr. Crackit *is* a heavy swell; an't he, Fagin?' asked Tom.

'No doubt at all of that, my dear.'

'And it *is* a creditable thing to have his acquaintance; an't it, Fagin?' pursued Tom.

'Very much so, indeed, my dear. They're only jealous, Tom, because he won't give it to them.'

'Ah!' cried Tom triumphantly, 'that's where it is! He has cleaned me out. But I can go and earn some more, when I like; can't I, Fagin?'

'To be sure you can, and the sooner you go the better, Tom; so make up your loss at once, and don't lose any more time. Dodger! Charley! It's time you were on the lay. Come! It's near ten, and nothing done yet.'

In obedience to this hint, the boys, nodding to Nancy, took up their hats, and left the room; the Dodger and his vivacious friend indulging, as they went, in many witticisms at the expense of Mr. Chitling; in whose conduct, it is but justice to say, there was nothing very conspicuous or peculiar: inasmuch as there are a great number of spirited young bloods upon town, who pay a much higher price than Mr. Chitling for being seen in good society: and a great number of fine gentlemen (composing the good society aforesaid) who establish their reputation upon very much the same footing as flash Toby Crackit.

'Now,' said Fagin, when they had left the room, 'I'll go and get you that cash, Nancy. This is only the key of a little cupboard where I keep a few odd things the boys get, my dear. I never lock up my money, for I've got none to lock up, my dear—ha! ha! ha!— none to lock up. It's a poor trade, Nancy, and no thanks; but I'm fond of seeing the young people about me; and I bear it all, I bear it all. Hush!' he said, hastily concealing the key in his breast; 'who's that? Listen!'

The girl, who was sitting at the table with her arms folded, appeared in no way interested in the arrival: or to care whether the person, whoever he was, came or went: until the murmur of a man's voice reached her ears. The instant she caught the sound, she tore off her bonnet and shawl, with the rapidity of lightning, and thrust them under the table. The Jew, turning round immediately afterwards, she muttered a complaint of the heat: in a tone of languor that contrasted, very remarkably, with the extreme haste and violence of this action: which, however, had been unobserved by Fagin, who had his back towards her at the time.

'Bah!' he whispered, as though nettled by the interruption; 'it's the man I expected before; he's coming down stairs. Not a word about the money while he's here, Nance. He won't stop long. Not ten minutes, my dear.'

Laying his skinny forefinger upon his lip, the Jew carried a candle to the door, as a man's step was heard upon the stairs without. He reached it, at the same moment as the visitor, who, coming hastily into the room, was close upon the girl before he observed her.

It was Monks.

'Only one of my young people,' said Fagin, observing that Monks drew back, on beholding a stranger. 'Don't move, Nancy.'

The girl drew closer to the table, and glancing at Monks with an air of careless levity, withdrew her eyes; but as he turned his towards Fagin, she stole another look: so keen and searching, and full of purpose, that if there had been any bystander to observe the change, he could hardly have believed the two looks to have proceeded from the same person.

'Any news?' inquired Fagin.

'Great.'

'And—and—good?' asked Fagin, hesitating as though he feared to vex the other man by being too sanguine.

'Not bad, any way,' replied Monks with a smile. 'I have been prompt enough this time. Let me have a word with you.'

The girl drew closer to the table, and made no offer to leave the room, although she could see that Monks was pointing to her. The Jew: perhaps fearing she might say something aloud about the money, if he endeavoured to get rid of her: pointed upwards, and took Monks out of the room.

'Not that infernal hole we were in before,' she could hear the man say as they went up stairs. Fagin laughed; and making some reply which did not reach her, seemed, by the creaking of the boards, to lead his companion to the second story.

Before the sound of their footsteps had ceased to echo through the house, the girl had slipped off her shoes; and drawing her gown loosely over her head, and muffling her arms in it, stood at the door, listening with breathless interest. The moment the noise ceased, she glided from the room; ascended the stairs with incredible softness and silence; and was lost in the gloom above.

The room remained deserted for a quarter of an hour or more; the girl glided back with the same unearthly tread; and, immediately afterwards, the two men were heard descending. Monks went at once into the street; and the Jew crawled up stairs again for the money. When he returned, the girl was adjusting her shawl and bonnet, as if preparing to be gone.

'Why, Nance,' exclaimed the Jew, starting back as he put down the candle, 'how pale you are!'

'Pale!' echoed the girl, shading her eyes with her hands, as if to look steadily at him.

'Quite horrible. What have you been doing to yourself?'

'Nothing that I know of, except sitting in this close place for I don't know how long and all,' replied the girl carelessly. 'Come! Let me get back; that's a dear.'

With a sigh for every piece of money, Fagin told the amount into her hand. They parted without more conversation, merely interchanging a 'good night.'

When the girl got into the open street, she sat down upon a doorstep; and seemed, for a few moments, wholly bewildered and unable to pursue her way. Suddenly she arose; and hurrying on, in a direction quite opposite to that in which Sikes was awaiting her return, quickened her pace, until it gradually resolved into a violent run. After completely exhausting herself, she stopped to take breath: and, as if suddenly recollecting herself, and deploring her inability to do something she was bent upon, wrung her hands, and burst into tears.

It might be that her tears relieved her, or that she felt the full hopelessness of her condition; but she turned back; and hurrying with nearly as great rapidity in the contrary direction: partly to recover lost time, and partly to keep pace with the violent current of her own thoughts: soon reached the dwelling where she had left the housebreaker.

If she betrayed any agitation, when she presented herself to Mr. Sikes, he did not observe it; for merely inquiring if she had brought the money, and receiving a reply in the affirmative, he uttered a growl of satisfaction, and replacing his head upon the pillow, resumed the slumbers which her arrival had interrupted.

It was fortunate for her that the possession of money occasioned him so much employment next day in the way of eating and drinking; and withal had so beneficial an effect in smoothing down the asperities of his temper; that he had neither time nor inclination to be very critical upon her behaviour and deportment. That she had all the abstracted and nervous manner of one who is on the eve of some bold and hazardous step, which it has required no common struggle to resolve upon, would have been obvious to the lynx-eyed Fagin, who would most probably have taken the alarm at once; but Mr. Sikes lacking the niceties of discrimination, and being troubled with no more subtle misgivings than those which resolve themselves into a dogged roughness of behaviour towards everybody; and being, furthermore, in an unusually amiable condition, as has been already observed; saw nothing unusual in her demeanour, and indeed, troubled himself so little about her, that, had her agitation been far more perceptible than it was, it would have been very unlikely to have awakened his suspicions.

As that day closed in, the girl's excitement increased; and, when night came on, and she sat by, watching until the housebreaker should drink himself asleep, there was an unusual paleness in her cheek, and a fire in her eye, that even Sikes observed with astonishment.

Mr. Sikes being weak from the fever, was lying in bed, taking hot water with his gin to render it less inflammatory; and had pushed his glass towards Nancy to be replenished for the third or fourth time, when these symptoms first struck him.

'Why, burn my body!' said the man, raising himself on his hands as he stared the girl in the face. 'You look like a corpse come to life again. What's the matter?'

'Matter!' replied the girl. 'Nothing. What do you look at me so hard for?'

'What foolery is this?' demanded Sikes, grasping her by the arm, and shaking her roughly. 'What is it? What do you mean? What are you thinking of?'

'Of many things, Bill,' replied the girl, shivering, and as she did so, pressing her hands upon her eyes. 'But, Lord! What odds in that?'

The tone of forced gaiety in which the last words were spoken, seemed to produce a deeper impression on Sikes than the wild and rigid look which had preceded them.

'I tell you wot it is,' said Sikes; 'if you haven't caught the fever, and got it comin' on, now, there's something more than usual in the wind, and something dangerous too. You're not a-going to—. No, damme! you wouldn't do that!'

'Do what?' asked the girl.

'There ain't,' said Sikes, fixing his eyes upon her, and muttering the words to himself; 'there ain't a stauncher-hearted gal going, or I'd have cut her throat three months ago. She's got the fever coming on; that's it.'

Fortifying himself with this assurance, Sikes drained the glass to the bottom, and then, with many grumbling oaths, called for his physic. The girl jumped up, with great alacrity; poured it quickly out, but with her back towards him; and held the vessel to his lips, while he drank off the contents.

'Now,' said the robber, 'come and sit aside of me, and put on your own face; or I'll alter it so, that you won't know it again when you *do* want it.'

The girl obeyed. Sikes, locking her hand in his, fell back upon the pillow: turning his eyes upon her face. They closed; opened again; closed once more; again opened. He shifted his position restlessly; and, after dozing again, and again, for two or three minutes, and as often springing up with a look of terror, and gazing vacantly about him, was suddenly stricken, as it were, while in the very attitude of rising, into a deep and heavy sleep. The grasp of his hand relaxed; the uparised arm fell languidly by his side; and he lay like one in a profound trance.

'The laudanum has taken effect at last,' murmured the girl, as she rose from the bedside. 'I may be too late, even now.'

She hastily dressed herself in her bonnet and shawl: looking fearfully round, from time to time, as if, despite the sleeping draught, she expected every moment to feel the pressure of Sikes's heavy hand upon her shoulder, then, stooping softly over the bed, she kissed the robber's lips; and then opening and closing the room-door with noiseless touch, hurried from the house.

A watchman was crying half-past nine, down a dark passage through which she had to pass, in gaining the main thorough-fare.

'Has it long gone the half-hour?' asked the girl.

'It'll strike the hour in another quarter,' said the man: raising his lantern to her face.

'And I cannot get there in less than an hour or more,' muttered Nancy: brushing swiftly past him, and gliding rapidly down the street.

Many of the shops were already closing in the back lanes and avenues through which she tracked her way, in making from Spitalfields towards the West-End of London. The clock struck ten, increasing her impatience. She tore along the narrow pavement: elbowing the passengers from side to side; and darting almost under the horses' heads, crossed crowded streets, where clusters of persons were eagerly watching their opportunity to do the like.

'The woman is mad!' said the people, turning to look after her as she rushed away.

When she reached the more wealthy quarter of the town, the streets were comparatively deserted; and here her head-long progress excited a still greater curiosity in the stragglers whom she hurried past. Some quickened their pace behind, as though to see whither she was hastening at such an unusual rate; and a few made head upon her, and looked back surprised at her undiminished speed; but they fell off one by one; and when she neared her place of destination, she was alone.

It was a family hotel in a quiet but handsome street near Hyde Park. As the brilliant light of the lamp which burnt before its door, guided her to the spot, the clock struck eleven. She had loitered for a few paces as though irresolute, and making up her mind to advance; but the sound determined her, and she stepped into the hall. The porter's seat was vacant. She looked round with an air of incertitude, and advanced towards the stairs.

'Now, young woman!' said a smartly-dressed female, looking out from a door behind her, 'who do you want here?'

'A lady who is stopping in this house,' answered the girl.

'A lady!' was the reply, accompanied with a scornful look. 'What lady?'

'Miss Maylie,' said Nancy.

The young woman, who had, by this time, noted her appearance, replied only by a look of virtuous disdain; and summoned a man to answer her. To him, Nancy repeated her request.

'What name am I to say?' asked the waiter.

'It's of no use saying any,' replied Nancy.

'Nor business?' said the man.

'No, nor that neither,' rejoined the girl. 'I must see the lady.'

'Come!' said the man, pushing her towards the door. 'None of this. Take yourself off.'

'I shall be carried out, if I go!' said the girl violently; 'and I can make that a job that two of you won't like to do. Isn't there anybody here,' she said, looking round, 'that will see a simple message carried for a poor wretch like me?'

This appeal produced an effect on a good-tempered-faced man-cook, who with some other of the servants was looking on, and who stepped forward to interfere.

'Take it up for her, Joe; can't you?' said this person.

'What's the good?' replied the man. 'You don't suppose the young lady will see such as her; do you?'

This allusion to Nancy's doubtful character, raised a vast quantity of chaste wrath in the bosoms of four housemaids, who remarked with great fervour, that the creature was a disgrace to her sex; and strongly advocated her being thrown, ruthlessly, into the kennel.

'Do what you like with me,' said the girl, turning to the men again; 'but do what I ask you first, and I ask you to give this message for God Almighty's sake.'

The soft-hearted cook added his intercession, and the result was that the man who had first appeared undertook its delivery.

'What's it to be?' said the man, with one foot on the stairs.

'That a young woman earnestly asks to speak to Miss Maylie alone,' said Nancy; 'and that if the lady will only hear the first word she has to say, she will know whether to hear her business, or to have her turned out of doors as an impostor.'

'I say,' said the man, 'you're coming it strong!'

'You give the message,' said the girl firmly; 'and let me hear the answer.'

The man ran up stairs. Nancy remained, pale and almost breathless, listening with quivering lip to the very audible expressions of scorn, of which the chaste housemaids were very prolific; and of which they became still more so, when the man returned, and said the young woman was to walk up stairs.

'It's no good being proper in this world,' said the first housemaid.

'Brass can do better than the gold what has stood the fire,' said the second.

The third contented herself with wondering 'what ladies was made of;' and the fourth took the first in a quartette of 'Shameful!' with which the Dianas concluded.

Regardless of all this: for she had weightier matters at heart: Nancy followed the man, with trembling limbs, to a small antechamber, lighted by a lamp from the ceiling. Here he left her, and retired.

CHAPTER 40

A strange interview, which is a sequel to the last chapter

The girl's life had been squandered in the streets, and among the most noisome of the stews and dens of London, but there was something of the woman's original nature left in her still; and when she heard a light step approaching the door opposite to that by which she had entered, and thought of the wide contrast which the small room would in another moment contain, she felt burdened with the sense of her own deep shame, and shrunk as though she could scarcely bear the presence of her with whom she had sought this interview.

But struggling with these better feelings was pride, —the vice of the lowest and most debased creatures no less than of the high and self-assured. The miserable companion of thieves and ruffians, the fallen outcast of low haunts, the associate of the scourings of the jails and hulks, living within the shadow of the gallows itself, —even this degraded being felt too proud to betray a feeble gleam of the womanly feeling which she thought a weakness, but which alone connected her with that humanity, of which her wasting life had obliterated so many, many traces when a very child.

She raised her eyes sufficiently to observe that the figure which presented itself was that of a slight and beautiful girl; then, bending them on the ground, she tossed her head with affected carelessness as she said:

'It's a hard matter to get to see you, lady. If I had taken offence, and gone away, as many would have done, you'd have been sorry for it one day, and not without reason either.'

'I am very sorry if any one has behaved harshly to you,' replied Rose. 'Do not think of that. Tell me why you wished to see me. I am the person you inquired for.'

The kind tone of this answer, the sweet voice, the gentle manner, the absence of any accent of haughtiness or displeasure, took the girl completely by surprise, and she burst into tears.

'Oh, lady, lady!' she said, clasping her hands passionately before her face, 'if there was more like you, there would be fewer like me, —there would—there would!'

'Sit down,' said Rose, earnestly, 'If you are in poverty or affliction I shall be truly glad to relieve you if I can, —I shall indeed. Sit down.'

'Let me stand, lady,' said the girl, still weeping, 'and do not speak to me so kindly till you know me better. It is growing late. Is—is—that door shut?'

'Yes,' said Rose, recoiling a few steps, as if to be nearer assistance in case she should require it. 'Why?'

'Because,' said the girl, 'I am about to put my life, and the lives of others in your hands. I am the girl that dragged little Oliver back to old Fagin's, on the night he went out from the house in Pentonville.'

'You!' said Rose Maylie.

'I, lady!' replied the girl. 'I am the infamous creature you have heard of, that lives among the thieves, and that never from the first moment I can recollect my eyes and senses opening on London streets have known any better life, or kinder words than they have given me, so help me God! Do not mind shrinking openly from me, lady. I am younger than you would think, to look at me, but I am well used to it. The poorest women fall back, as I make my way along the crowded pavement.'

'What dreadful things are these!' said Rose, involuntarily falling from her strange companion.

'Thank Heaven upon your knees, dear lady,' cried the girl,

'that you had friends to care for and keep you in your childhood, and that you were never in the midst of cold and hunger, and riot and drunkenness, and—and—something worse than all—as I have been from my cradle. I may use the word, for the alley and the gutter were mine, as they will be my deathbed.'

'I pity you!' said Rose, in a broken voice. 'It wrings my heart to hear you!'

'Heaven bless you for your goodness!' rejoined the girl. 'If you knew what I am sometimes, you would pity me, indeed. But I have stolen away from those who would surely murder me, if they knew I had been here, to tell you what I have over-heard. Do you know a man named Monks?'

'No,' said Rose.

'He knows you,' replied the girl; 'and knew you were here, for it was by hearing him tell the place that I found you out.'

'I never heard the name,' said Rose.

'Then he goes by some other amongst us,' rejoined the girl, 'which I more than thought before. Some time ago, and soon after Oliver was put into your house on the night of the robbery, I—suspecting this man—listened to a conversation held between him and Fagin in the dark. I found out, from what I heard, that Monks—the man I asked you about, you know—'

'Yes,' said Rose, 'I understand.'

'—That Monks,' pursued the girl, 'had seen him accidentally with two of our boys on the day we first lost him, and had known him directly to be the same child that he was watching for, though I couldn't make out why. A bargain was struck with Fagin, that if Oliver was got back he should have a certain sum; and he was to have more for making him a thief, which this Monks wanted for some purpose of his own.'

'For what purpose?' asked Rose.

'He caught sight of my shadow on the wall as I listened, in the hope of finding out,' said the girl; 'and there are not many people besides me that could have got out of their way in time to escape discovery. But I did; and I saw him no more till last night.'

'And what occurred then?'

'I'll tell you, lady. Last night he came again. Again they went up stairs, and I, wrapping myself up so that my shadow should not betray me, again listened at the door. The first words I heard Monks say were these: "So the only proofs of the boy's identity lie at the bottom of the river, and the old hag that received them from the mother is rotting in her coffin." They laughed, and talked of his success in doing this; and Monks, talking on about the boy, and getting very wild, said that though he had got the young devil's money safely now, he'd rather have had it the other way; for, what a game it would have been to have brought down the boast of the father's will, by driving him through every jail in town, and then hauling him up for some capital felony which Fagin could easily manage, after having made a good profit of him besides.'

'What is all this!' said Rose.

'The truth, lady, though it comes from my lips,' replied the girl. 'Then, he said, with oaths common enough in my ears, but strange to yours, that if he could gratify his hatred by taking the boy's life without bringing his own neck in danger, he would; but, as he couldn't, he'd be upon the watch to meet him at every turn in life; and if he took advantage of his birth and history, he might harm him yet. "In short, Fagin," he says, "Jew as you are, you never laid such snares as I'll contrive for my young brother, Oliver."'

'His brother!' exclaimed Rose.

'Those were his words,' said Nancy, glancing uneasily round, as she had scarcely ceased to do, since she began to speak, for a vision of Sikes haunted her perpetually. 'And more. When he spoke of you and the other lady, and said it seemed contrived by Heaven, or the devil, against him, that Oliver should come into your hands, he laughed, and said there was some comfort in that too, for how many thousands and hundreds of thousands of pounds would you not give, if you had them, to know who your two-legged spaniel was.'

'You do not mean,' said Rose, turning very pale, 'to tell me that this was said in earnest?'

'He spoke in hard and angry earnest, if a man ever did,' replied the girl, shaking her head. 'He is an earnest man when his hatred is up. I know many who do worse things; but I'd rather listen to them all a dozen times, than to that Monks once. It is growing late, and I have to reach home without suspicion of having been on such an errand as this. I must get back quickly.'

'But what can I do?' said Rose. 'To what use can I turn this communication without you? Back! Why do you wish to return to companions you paint in such terrible colours? If you repeat this information to a gentleman whom I can summon in an instant from the next room, you can be consigned to some place of safety without half an hour's delay.'

'I wish to go back,' said the girl. 'I must go back, because— how can I tell such things to an innocent lady like you? —because among the men I have told you of, there is one: the most desperate among them all: that I can't leave; no, not even to be saved from the life I am leading now.'

'Your having interfered in this dear boy's behalf before,' said Rose; 'your coming here, at so great a risk, to tell me what you have heard; your manner, which convinces me of the truth of what you say; your evident contrition, and sense of shame; all lead me to believe that you might be yet reclaimed. Oh!' said the earnest girl, folding her hands as the tears coursed down her face, 'do not turn a deaf ear to the entreaties of one of your own sex; the first—the first, I do believe, who ever appealed to you in the voice of pity and compassion. Do hear my words, and let me save you yet, for better things.'

'Lady,' cried the girl, sinking on her knees, 'dear, sweet, angel lady, you *are* the first that ever blessed me with such words as these, and if I had heard them years ago, they might have turned me from a life of sin and sorrow; but it is too late, it is too late!'

'It is never too late,' said Rose, 'for penitence and atonement.'

'It is,' cried the girl, writhing in the agony of her mind; 'I cannot leave him now! I could not be his death.'

'Why should you be?' asked Rose.

'Nothing could save him,' cried the girl. 'If I told others what I have told you, and led to their being taken, he would be sure to die. He is the boldest, and has been so cruel!'

'Is it possible,' cried Rose, 'that for such a man as this, you can resign every future hope, and the certainty of immediate rescue? It is madness.'

'I don't know what it is,' answered the girl; 'I only know that it is so, and not with me alone, but with hundreds of others as bad and wretched as myself. I must go back. Whether it is God's wrath for the wrong I have done, I do not know; but I am drawn back to him through every suffering and ill usage; and I should be, I believe, if I knew that I was to die by his hand at last.'

'What am I to do?' said Rose. 'I should not let you depart from me thus.'

'You should, lady, and I know you will,' rejoined the girl, rising. 'You will not stop my going because I have trusted in your goodness, and forced no promise from you, as I might have done.'

'Of what use, then, is the communication you have made?' said Rose. 'This mystery must be investigated, or how will its disclosure to me, benefit Oliver, whom you are anxious to serve?'

'You must have some kind gentleman about you that will hear it as a secret, and advise you what to do,' rejoined the girl.

'But where can I find you again when it is necessary?' asked Rose. 'I do not seek to know where these dreadful people live, but where will you be walking or passing at any settled period from this time?'

'Will you promise me that you will have my secret strictly kept, and come alone, or with the only other person that knows it; and that I shall not be watched or followed?' asked the girl.

'I promise you solemnly,' answered Rose.

'Every Sunday night, from eleven until the clock strikes twelve,' said the girl without hesitation, 'I will walk on London Bridge if I am alive.'

'Stay another moment,' interposed Rose, as the girl moved hurriedly towards the door. 'Think once again on your own condition, and the opportunity you have of escaping from it. You have a claim on me: not only as the voluntary bearer of this intelligence, but as a woman lost almost beyond redemption. Will you return to this gang of robbers, and to this man, when a word can save you? What fascination is it that can take you back, and make you cling to wickedness and misery? Oh! is there no chord in your heart that I can touch! Is there nothing left, to which I can appeal against this terrible infatuation!'

'When ladies as young, and good, and beautiful as you are,' replied the girl steadily, 'give away your hearts, love will carry you all lengths—even such as you, who have home, friends, other admirers, everything, to fill them. When such as I, who have no certain roof but the coffin-lid, and no friend in sickness or death but the hospital nurse, set our rotten hearts on any man, and let him fill the place that has been a blank through all our wretched lives, who can hope to cure us? Pity us, lady—pity us for having only one feeling of the woman left, and for having that turned, by a heavy judgment, from a comfort and a pride, into a new means of violence and suffering.'

'You will,' said Rose, after a pause, 'take some money from me, which may enable you to live without dishonesty—at all events until we meet again?'

'Not a penny,' replied the girl, waving her hand.

'Do not close your heart against all my efforts to help you,' said Rose, stepping gently forward. 'I wish to serve you indeed.'

'You would serve me best, lady,' replied the girl, wringing her hands, 'if you could take my life at once; for I have felt more grief to think of what I am, to-night, than I ever did before, and it would be something not to die in the hell in which I have lived. God bless you, sweet lady, and send as much happiness on your head as I have brought shame on mine!'

Thus speaking, and sobbing aloud, the unhappy creature

turned away; while Rose Maylie, overpowered by this extraordinary interview, which had more the semblance of a rapid dream than an actual occurrence, sank into a chair, and endeavoured to collect her wandering thoughts.

CHAPTER 41

Containing fresh discoveries, and showing
that surprises, like misfortunes, seldom
come alone

Her situation was, indeed, one of no common trial and difficulty.
While she felt the most eager and burning desire to penetrate the
mystery in which Oliver's history was enveloped, she could not but
hold sacred the confidence which the miserable woman with whom
she had just conversed, had reposed in her, as a young and guileless girl. Her words and manner had touched Rose Maylie's heart;
and, mingled with her love for her young charge, and scarcely less
intense in its truth and fervour, was her fond wish to win the outcast
back to repentance and hope.

They purposed remaining in London only three days, prior
to departing for some weeks to a distant part of the coast. It was
now midnight of the first day. What course of action could she
determine upon, which could be adopted in eight-and-forty
hours? Or how could she postpone the journey without exciting
suspicion?

Mr. Losberne was with them, and would be for the next two
days; but Rose was too well acquainted with the excellent
gentleman's impetuosity, and foresaw too clearly the wrath with
which, in the first explosion of his indignation, he would regard the
instrument of Oliver's re-capture, to trust him with the secret, when
her representations in the girl's behalf could be seconded by no
experienced person. These were all reasons for the greatest caution

and most circumspect behaviour in communicating it to Mrs. Maylie, whose first impulse would infallibly be to hold a conference with the worthy doctor on the subject. As to resorting to any legal adviser, even if she had known how to do so, it was scarcely to be thought of, for the same reasons. Once the thought occurred to her of seeking assistance from Harry; but this awakened the recollection of their last parting, and it seemed unworthy of her to call him back, when— the tears rose to her eyes as she pursued this train of reflection—he might have by this time learnt to forget her, and to be happier away.

Disturbed by these different reflections; inclining now to one course and then to another, and again recoiling from all, as each successive consideration presented itself to her mind; Rose passed a sleepless and anxious night. After more communing with herself next day, she arrived at the desperate conclusion of consulting Harry.

'If it be painful to him,' she thought, 'to come back here, how painful it will be to me! But perhaps he will not come; he may write, or he may come himself, and studiously abstain from meeting me— he did when he went away. I hardly thought he would, but it was better for us both.' And here Rose dropped the pen and turned away, as though the very paper which was to be her messenger should not see her weep.

She had taken up the same pen, and laid it down again fifty times, and had considered and reconsidered the first line of her letter without writing the first word, when Oliver, who had been walking in the streets, with Mr. Giles for a bodyguard, entered the room in such breathless haste and violent agitation, as seemed to betoken some new cause of alarm.

'What makes you look so flurried?' asked Rose, advancing to meet him.

'I hardly know how; I feel as if I should be choked,' replied the boy. 'Oh dear! To think that I should see him at last, and you should be able to know that I have told you all the truth!'

'I never thought you had told us anything but the truth,' said Rose, soothing him. 'But what is this? —of whom do you speak?'

'I have seen the gentleman,' replied Oliver, scarcely able to articulate, 'the gentleman who was so good to me—Mr. Brownlow, that we have so often talked about.'

'Where?' asked Rose.

'Getting out of a coach,' replied Oliver, shedding tears of delight, 'and going into a house. I didn't speak to him—I couldn't speak to him, for he didn't see me, and I trembled so, that I was not able to go up to him. But Giles asked, for me, whether he lived there, and they said he did. Look here,' said Oliver, opening a scrap of paper, 'here it is; here's where he lives—I'm going there directly! Oh, dear me, dear me! What shall I do when I come to see him and hear him speak again!'

With her attention not a little distracted by these and a great many other incoherent exclamations of joy, Rose read the address, which was Craven Street, in the Strand. She very soon determined upon turning the discovery to account.

'Quick!' she said. 'Tell them to fetch a hackney coach, and be ready to go with me. I will take you there directly, without a minute's loss of time. I will only tell my aunt that we are going out for an hour, and be ready as soon as you are.'

Oliver needed no prompting to despatch, and in little more than five minutes they were on their way to Craven Street. When they arrived there, Rose left Oliver in the coach, under pretence of preparing the old gentleman to receive him; and sending up her card by the servant, requested to see Mr. Brownlow on very pressing business. The servant soon returned, to beg that she would walk up stairs; and following him into an upper room, Miss Maylie was presented to an elderly gentleman of benevolent appearance, in a bottle-green coat. At no great distance from whom, was seated another old gentleman, in nankeen breeches and gaiters; who did not look particularly benevolent, and who was sitting with his hands clasped on the top of a thick stick, and his chin propped there upon.

'Dear me,' said the gentleman, in the bottle-green coat, hastily rising with great politeness, 'I beg your pardon, young lady—I imagined it was some importunate person who—I beg you will excuse me. Be seated, pray.'

'Mr. Brownlow, I believe, sir?' said Rose, glancing from the other gentleman to the one who had spoken.

'That is my name,' said the old gentleman. 'This is my friend, Mr. Grimwig. Grimwig, will you leave us for a few minutes?'

'I believe,' interposed Miss Maylie, 'that at this period of our interview, I need not give that gentleman the trouble of going away. If I am correctly informed, he is cognizant of the business on which I wish to speak to you.'

Mr. Brownlow inclined his head. Mr. Grimwig, who had made one very stiff bow, and risen from his chair, made another very stiff bow, and dropped into it again.

'I shall surprise you very much, I have no doubt,' said Rose, naturally embarrassed; 'but you once showed great benevolence and goodness to a very dear young friend of mine, and I am sure you will take an interest in hearing of him again.'

'Indeed!' said Mr. Brownlow.

'Oliver Twist you knew him as,' replied Rose.

The words no sooner escaped her lips, than Mr. Grimwig, who had been affecting to dip into a large book that lay on the table, upset it with a great crash, and falling back in his chair, discharged from his features every expression but one of unmitigated wonder, and indulged in a prolonged and vacant stare; then, as if ashamed of having betrayed so much emotion, he jerked himself, as it were, by a convulsion into his former attitude, and looking out straight before him emitted a long deep whistle, which seemed, at last, not to be discharged on empty air, but to die away in the innermost recesses of his stomach.

Mr. Brownlow was no less surprised, although his astonishment was not expressed in the same eccentric manner. He drew his chair nearer to Miss Maylie's, and said,

'Do me the favour, my dear young lady, to leave entirely out of the question that goodness and benevolence of which you speak, and of which nobody else knows anything; and if you have it in your power to produce any evidence which will alter the unfavourable opinion I was once induced to entertain of that poor child, in Heaven's name put me in possession of it.'

'A bad one! I'll eat my head if he is not a bad one,' growled Mr. Grimwig, speaking by some ventriloquial power, without moving a muscle of his face.

'He is a child of a noble nature and a warm heart,' said Rose, colouring; 'and that Power which has thought fit to try him beyond his years, has planted in his breast affections and feelings which would do honour to many who have numbered his days six times over.'

'I'm only sixty-one,' said Mr. Grimwig, with the same rigid face. 'And, as the devil's in it if this Oliver is not twelve years old at least, I don't see the application of that remark.'

'Do not heed my friend, Miss Maylie,' said Mr. Brownlow; 'he does not mean what he says.'

'Yes, he does,' growled Mr. Grimwig.

'No, he does not,' said Mr. Brownlow, obviously rising in wrath as he spoke.

'He'll eat his head, if he doesn't,' growled Mr. Grimwig.

'He would deserve to have it knocked off, if he does,' said Mr. Brownlow.

'And he'd uncommonly like to see any man offer to do it,' responded Mr. Grimwig, knocking his stick upon the floor.

Having gone thus far, the two old gentlemen severally took snuff, and afterwards shook hands, according to their invariable custom.

'Now, Miss Maylie,' said Mr. Brownlow, 'to return to the subject in which your humanity is so much interested. Will you let me know what intelligence you have of this poor child: allowing me to premise that I exhausted every means in my power of discovering him, and that since I have been absent from this country, my first impression that he had imposed upon me, and had been persuaded by his former associates to rob me, has been considerably shaken.'

Rose, who had had time to collect her thoughts, at once related, in a few natural words, all that had befallen Oliver since he left Mr. Brownlow's house; reserving Nancy's information for that gentleman's private ear, and concluding with the assurance that his only sorrow, for some months past, had been the not being able to meet with his former benefactor and friend.

'Thank God!' said the old gentleman. 'This is great happiness to me, great happiness. But you have not told me where he is now, Miss Maylie. You must pardon my finding fault with you, —but why not have brought him?'

'He is waiting in a coach at the door,' replied Rose.

'At this door!' cried the old gentleman. With which he hurried out of the room, down the stairs, up the coach-steps, and into the coach, without another word.

When the room-door closed behind him, Mr. Grimwig lifted up his head, and converting one of the hind legs of his chair into a pivot, described three distinct circles with the assistance of his stick and the table: sitting in it all the time. After performing this evolution, he rose and limped as fast as he could up and down the room at least a dozen times, and then stopping suddenly before Rose, kissed her without the slightest preface.

'Hush!' he said, as the young lady rose in some alarm at this unusual proceeding. 'Don't be afraid. I'm old enough to be your grandfather. You're a sweet girl. I like you. Here they are!'

In fact, as he threw himself at one dexterous dive into his former seat, Mr. Brownlow returned, accompanied by Oliver, whom Mr. Grimwig received very graciously; and if the gratification of that moment had been the only reward for all her anxiety and care in Oliver's behalf, Rose Maylie would have been well repaid.

'There is somebody else who should not be forgotten, by the by,' said Mr. Brownlow, ringing the bell. 'Send Mrs. Bedwin here, if you please.'

The old housekeeper answered the summons with all dispatch; and dropping a curtsey at the door, waited for orders.

'Why, you get blinder every day, Bedwin,' said Mr. Brownlow, rather testily.

'Well, that I do, sir,' replied the old lady. 'People's eyes, at my time of life, don't improve with age, sir.'

'I could have told you that,' rejoined Mr. Brownlow; 'but put on your glasses, and see if you can't find out what you were wanted for, will you?'

The old lady began to rummage in her pocket for her spectacles. But Oliver's patience was not proof against this new trial; and yielding to his first impulse, he sprang into her arms.

'God be good to me!' cried the old lady, embracing him; 'it is my innocent boy!'

'My dear old nurse!' cried Oliver.

'He would come back—I knew he would,' said the old lady, holding him in her arms. 'How well he looks, and how like a gentleman's son he is dressed again! Where have you been, this long, long while? Ah! the same sweet face, but not so pale; the same soft eye, but not so sad. I have never forgotten them or his quiet smile, but have seen them every day, side by side with those of my own dear children, dead and gone since I was a lightsome young creature.' Running on thus, and now holding Oliver from her to mark how he had grown, now clasping him to her and passing her fingers fondly through his hair, the good soul laughed and wept upon his neck by turns.

Leaving her and Oliver to compare notes at leisure, Mr. Brownlow led the way into another room; and there, heard from Rose a full narration of her interview with Nancy, which occasioned him no little surprise and perplexity. Rose also explained her reasons for not confiding in her friend Mr. Losberne in the first instance. The old gentleman considered that she had acted prudently, and readily undertook to hold solemn conference with the worthy doctor himself. To afford him an early opportunity for the execution of this design, it was arranged that he should call at the hotel at eight o'clock that evening, and that in the meantime Mrs. Maylie should be cautiously informed of all that had occurred. These preliminaries adjusted, Rose and Oliver returned home.

Rose had by no means overrated the measure of the good doctor's wrath. Nancy's history was no sooner unfolded to him, than he poured forth a shower of mingled threats and execrations; threatened to make her the first victim of the combined ingenuity of Messrs. Blathers and Duff; and actually put on his hat preparatory to sallying forth to obtain the assistance of those worthies. And, doubtless, he would, in this first outbreak, have carried the intention into effect without a moment's consideration of the consequences, if he had not been restrained, in part, by corresponding violence on the side of Mr. Brownlow, who was himself of an irascible temperament, and partly by such arguments and representations as seemed best calculated to dissuade him from his hotbrained purpose.

'Then what the devil is to be done?' said the impetuous doctor, when they had rejoined the two ladies. 'Are we to pass a vote of thanks to all these vagabonds, male and female, and beg them to accept a hundred pounds, or so, apiece, as a trifling mark of our esteem, and some slight acknowledgment of their kindness to Oliver?'

'Not exactly that,' rejoined Mr. Brownlow, laughing; 'but we must proceed gently and with great care.'

'Gentleness and care,' exclaimed the doctor. 'I'd send them one and all to—'

'Never mind where,' interposed Mr. Brownlow. 'But reflect whether sending them anywhere is likely to attain the object we have in view.'

'What object?' asked the doctor.

'Simply, the discovery of Oliver's parentage, and regaining for him the inheritance of which, if this story be true, he has been fraudulently deprived.'

'Ah!' said Mr. Losberne, cooling himself with his pocket-handkerchief; 'I almost forgot that.'

'You see,' pursued Mr. Brownlow; 'placing this poor girl entirely out of the question, and supposing it were possible to bring these scoundrels to justice without compromising her safety, what good should we bring about?'

'Hanging a few of them at least, in all probability,' suggested the doctor, 'and transporting the rest.'

'Very good,' replied Mr. Brownlow, smiling; 'but no doubt

they will bring that about for themselves in the fulness of time, and if we step in to forestall them, it seems to me that we shall be performing a very Quixotic act, in direct opposition to our own interest—or at least to Oliver's, which is the same thing.'

'How?' inquired the doctor.

'Thus. It is quite clear that we shall have extreme difficulty in getting to the bottom of this mystery, unless we can bring this man, Monks, upon his knees. That can only be done by stratagem, and by catching him when he is not surrounded by these people. For, suppose he were apprehended, we have no proof against him. He is not even (so far as we know, or as the facts appear to us) concerned with the gang in any of their robberies. If he were not discharged, it is very unlikely that he could receive any further punishment than being committed to prison as a rogue and vagabond; and of course ever afterwards his mouth would be so obstinately closed that he might as well, for our purposes, be deaf, dumb, blind, and an idiot.'

'Then,' said the doctor impetuously, 'I put it to you again, whether you think it reasonable that this promise to the girl should be considered binding; a promise made with the best and kindest intentions, but really—'

'Do not discuss the point, my dear young lady, pray,' said Mr. Brownlow, interrupting Rose as she was about to speak. 'The promise shall be kept. I don't think it will, in the slightest degree, interfere with our proceedings. But, before we can resolve upon any precise course of action, it will be necessary to see the girl; to ascertain from her whether she will point out this Monks, on the understanding that he is to be dealt with by us, and not by the law; or, if she will not, or cannot do that, to procure from her such an account of his haunts and description of his person, as will enable us to identify him. She cannot be seen until next Sunday night; this is Tuesday. I would suggest that in the meantime, we remain perfectly quiet, and keep these matters secret even from Oliver himself.'

Although Mr. Losberne received with many wry faces a proposal involving a delay of five whole days, he was fain to admit that no better course occurred to him just then; and as both Rose and Mrs. Maylie sided very strongly with Mr. Brownlow, that gentleman's proposition was carried unanimously.

'I should like,' he said, 'to call in the aid of my friend Grimwig. He is a strange creature, but a shrewd one, and might prove of material assistance to us; I should say that he was bred a lawyer, and quitted the Bar in disgust because he had only one brief and a motion of course, in twenty years, though whether that is a recommendation or not, you must determine for yourselves.'

'I have no objection to your calling in your friend if I may call in mine,' said the doctor.

'We must put it to the vote,' replied Mr. Brownlow, 'who may he be?'

'That lady's son, and this young lady's—very old friend,' said the doctor, motioning towards Mrs. Maylie, and concluding with an expressive glance at her niece.

Rose blushed deeply, but she did not make any audible objection to this motion (possibly she felt in a hopeless minority); and Harry Maylie and Mr. Grimwig were accordingly added to the committee.

'We stay in town, of course,' said Mrs. Maylie, 'while there remains the slightest prospect of prosecuting this inquiry with a chance of success. I will spare neither trouble nor expense in behalf of the object in which we are all so deeply interested, and I am content to remain here, if it be for twelve months, so long as you assure me that any hope remains.'

'Good!' rejoined Mr. Brownlow. 'And as I see on the faces about me, a disposition to inquire how it happened that I was not in the way to corroborate Oliver's tale, and had so suddenly left the kingdom, let me stipulate that I shall be asked no questions until such time as I may deem it expedient to forestall them by telling my own story. Believe me, I make this request with good reason, for I might otherwise excite hopes destined never to be realised, and only increase difficulties and disappointments already quite numerous enough. Come! Supper has been announced, and young

Oliver, who is all alone in the next room, will have begun to think, by this time, that we have wearied of his company, and entered into some dark conspiracy to thrust him forth upon the world.'

With these words, the old gentleman gave his hand to Mrs. Maylie, and escorted her into the supper-room. Mr. Losberne followed, leading Rose; and the council was, for the present, effectually broken up.

CHAPTER 42

An old acquaintance of Oliver's, exhibiting
decided marks of genius, becomes a public
character in the metropolis

Upon the night when Nancy, having lulled Mr. Sikes to sleep, hurried
on her self-imposed mission to Rose Maylie, there advanced towards
London, by the Great North Road, two persons, upon whom it is
expedient that this history should bestow some attention.

They were a man and a woman; or perhaps they would be
better described as a male and female: for the former was one of
those long-limbed, knock-kneed, shambling, bony people, to whom
it is difficult to assign any precise age, —looking as they do, when
they are yet boys, like undergrown men, and when they are almost
men, like overgrown boys. The woman was young, but of a robust
and hardy make, as she need have been to bear the weight of the
heavy bundle which was strapped to her back. Her companion was
not encumbered with much luggage as, there merely dangled from
a stick which he carried over his shoulder, a small parcel wrapped
in a common handkerchief, and apparently light enough. This
circumstance, added to the length of his legs which were of unusual
extent, enabled him with much ease to keep some half-dozen paces
in advance of his companion, to whom he occasionally turned with
an impatient jerk of the head: as if reproaching her tardiness, and
urging her to greater exertion.

Thus, they had toiled along the dusty road, taking little heed
of any object within sight, save when they stepped aside to allow a

wider passage for the mail-coaches which were whirling out of town, until they passed through Highgate archway; when the foremost traveller stopped and called impatiently to his companion.

'Come on, can't yer? What a lazybones yer are, Charlotte.'

'It's a heavy load, I can tell you,' said the female, coming up, almost breathless with fatigue.

'Heavy! What are yer talking about? What are yer made for?' rejoined the male traveller, changing his own little bundle, as he spoke, to the other shoulder. 'Oh, there yer are, resting again! Well, if yer ain't enough to tire any body's patience out, I don't know what is!'

'Is it much farther?' asked the woman, resting herself against a bank, and looking up with the perspiration streaming from her face.

'Much farther! Yer as good as there,' said the long-legged tramper pointing out before him. 'Look there! Those are the lights of London.'

'They're a good two mile off, at least,' said the woman despondingly.

'Never mind whether they're two mile off, or twenty,' said Noah Claypole; for he it was; 'but get up and come on, or I'll kick yer, and so I give yer notice.'

As Noah's red nose grew redder with anger, and as he crossed the road while speaking, as if fully prepared to put his threat into execution, the woman rose without any further remark, and trudged onward by his side.

'Where do you mean to stop for the night, Noah?' she asked, after they had walked a few hundred yards.

'How should I know?' replied Noah, whose temper had been considerably impaired by walking.

'Near, I hope,' said Charlotte.

'No, not near,' replied Mr. Claypole. 'There! Not near; so don't think it.'

'Why not?'

'When I tell yer that I don't mean to do a thing, that's enough, without any why or because either,' replied Mr. Claypole with dignity.

'Well, you needn't be so cross,' said his companion.

'A pretty thing it would be, wouldn't it, to go and stop at the very first public-house outside the town, so that Sowerberry, if he come up after us, might poke in his old nose, and have us taken back in a cart with hand-cuffs on,' said Mr. Claypole in a jeering tone. 'No! I shall go and lose myself among the narrowest streets I can find, and not stop till we come to the very out-of-the-wayest house I can set eyes on. 'Cod, yer may thank yer stars I've got a head; for if we hadn't gone, at first, the wrong road a purpose, and come back across country, yer'd have been locked up hard and fast a week ago, my lady. And serve yer right for being a fool.'

'I know I ain't as cunning as you are,' replied Charlotte; 'but don't put all the blame on me, and say I should have been locked up. You would have been if I had been, any way.'

'Yer took the money from the till, yer know yer did,' said Mr. Claypole.

'I took it for you, Noah, dear,' rejoined Charlotte.

'Did I keep it?' asked Mr. Claypole.

'No; you trusted in me, and let me carry it like a dear, and so you are,' said the lady, chucking him under the chin, and drawing her arm through his.

This was indeed the case; but as it was not Mr. Claypole's habit to repose a blind and foolish confidence in anybody, it should be observed, in justice to that gentleman, that he had trusted Charlotte to this extent, in order that, if they were pursued, the money might be found on her: which would leave him an opportunity of asserting his innocence of any theft, and would greatly facilitate his chances of escape. Of course, he entered at this juncture, into no explanation of his motives, and they walked on very lovingly together.

In pursuance of this cautious plan, Mr. Claypole went on, without halting, until he arrived at the Angel at Islington, where he wisely judged, from the crowd of passengers and number of vehicles, that London began in earnest. Just pausing to observe which appeared the most crowded streets, and consequently the most to be avoided, he crossed into St. John's Road, and was soon deep in the obscurity of the intricate and dirty ways, which, lying between Gray's Inn Lane and Smithfield, render that part of the town one of the lowest and worst that improvement has left in the midst of London.

Through these streets, Noah Claypole walked, dragging Charlotte after him; now stepping into the kennel to embrace at a glance the whole external character of some small public-house; now jogging on again, as some fancied appearance induced him to believe it too public for his purpose. At length, he stopped in front of one, more humble in appearance and more dirty than any he had yet seen; and, having crossed over and surveyed it from the opposite pavement, graciously announced his intention of putting up there, for the night.

'So give us the bundle,' said Noah, unstrapping it from the woman's shoulders, and slinging it over his own; 'and don't yer speak, except when yer spoke to. What's the name of the house—t-h-r—three what?'

'Cripples,' said Charlotte.

'Three Cripples,' repeated Noah, 'and a very good sign too. Now, then! Keep close at my heels, and come along.' With these injunctions, he pushed the rattling door with his shoulder, and entered the house, followed by his companion.

There was nobody at the bar but a young Jew, who, with his two elbows on the counter, was reading a dirty newspaper. He stared very hard at Noah, and Noah stared very hard at him.

If Noah had been attired in his charity-boy's dress, there might have been some reason for the Jew opening his eyes so wide; but as he had discarded the coat and badge, and wore a short smock-frock over his leathers, there seemed no particular reason for his appearance exciting so much attention in a public-house.

'Is this the Three Cripples?' asked Noah.

'That is the dabe of this ouse,' replied the Jew.

'A gentleman we met on the road, coming up from the country, recommended us here,' said Noah, nudging Charlotte, perhaps to call her attention to this most ingenious device for attracting respect, and perhaps to warn her to betray no surprise. 'We want to sleep here to-night.'

'I'b dot certaid you cad,' said Barney, who was the attendant sprite; 'but I'll idquire.'

'Show us the tap, and give us a bit of cold meat and a drop of beer while yer inquiring, will yer?' said Noah.

Barney complied by ushering them into a small backroom, and setting the required viands before them; having done which, he informed the travellers that they could be lodged that night, and left the amiable couple to their refreshment.

Now, this back-room was immediately behind the bar, and some steps lower, so that any person connected with the house, undrawing a small curtain which concealed a single pane of glass fixed in the wall of the last-named apartment, about five feet from its flooring, could not only look down upon any guests in the back-room without any great hazard of being observed (the glass being in a dark angle of the wall, between which and a large upright beam the observer had to thrust himself), but could, by applying his ear to the partition, ascertain with tolerable distinctness, their subject of conversation. The landlord of the house had not withdrawn his eye from this place of espial for five minutes, and Barney had only just returned from making the communication above related, when Fagin, in the course of his evening's business, came into the bar to inquire after some of his young pupils.

'Hush!' said Barney: 'stradegers id the next roob.'

'Strangers!' repeated the old man in a whisper.

'Ah! Ad rub uds too,' added Barney. 'Frob the cuttry, but subthig in your way, or I'b bistaked.'

Fagin appeared to receive this communication with great interest. Mounting a stool, he cautiously applied his eye to the pane of glass, from which secret post he could see Mr. Claypole taking cold beef from the dish, and porter from the pot, and administering homoeopathic doses of both to Charlotte, who sat patiently by, eating and drinking at his pleasure.

'Aha!' he whispered, looking round to Barney. 'I like that fellow's looks. He'd be of use to us; he knows how to train the girl already. Don't make as much noise as a mouse, my dear, and let me hear 'em talk—let me hear 'em.'

He again applied his eye to the glass, and turning his ear to the partition, listened attentively: with a subtle and eager look upon his face, that might have appertained to some old goblin.

'So I mean to be a gentleman,' said Mr. Claypole, kicking out his legs, and continuing a conversation, the commencement of which Fagin had arrived too late to hear. 'No more jolly old coffins, Charlotte, but a gentleman's life for me: and, if yer like yer shall be a lady.'

'I should like that well enough, dear,' replied Charlotte; 'but tills ain't to be emptied every day, and people to get clear off after it.'

'Tills be blowed!' said Mr. Claypole; 'there's more things besides tills to be emptied.'

'What do you mean?' asked his companion.

'Pockets, women's ridicules, houses, mail-coaches, banks!' said Mr. Claypole, rising with the porter.

'But you can't do all that, dear,' said Charlotte.

'I shall look out to get into company with them as can,' replied Noah. 'They'll be able to make us useful some way or another. Why, you yourself are worth fifty women; I never see such a precious sly and deceitful creetur as yer can be when I let yer.'

'Lor, how nice it is to hear you say so!' exclaimed Charlotte, imprinting a kiss upon his ugly face.

'There, that'll do: don't yer be too affectionate, in case I'm cross with yer,' said Noah, disengaging himself with great gravity. 'I should like to be the captain of some band, and have the whopping of 'em, and follering 'em about, unbeknown to themselves. That would suit me, if there was good profit; and if we could only get in with some gentlemen of this sort, I say it would be cheap at that twenty-pound note you've got,—especially as we don't very well know how to get rid of it ourselves.'

After expressing this opinion, Mr. Claypole looked into the porter-pot with an aspect of deep wisdom; and having well shaken its contents, nodded condescendingly to Charlotte, and took a draught, wherewith he appeared greatly refreshed. He was meditating another, when the sudden opening of the door, and the appearance of a stranger, interrupted him.

The stranger was Mr. Fagin. And very amiable he looked, and a very low bow he made, as he advanced, and setting himself down at the nearest table, ordered something to drink of the grinning Barney.

'A pleasant night, sir, but cool for the time of year,' said Fagin, rubbing his hands. 'From the country, I see, sir?'

'How do yer see that?' asked Noah Claypole.

'We have not so much dust as that in London,' replied Fagin, pointing from Noah's shoes to those of his companion, and from them to the two bundles.

'Yer a sharp feller,' said Noah. 'Ha! ha! only hear that, Charlotte!'

'Why, one need be sharp in this town, my dear,' replied the Jew, sinking his voice to a confidential whisper; 'and that's the truth.'

Fagin followed up this remark by striking the side of his nose with his right forefinger,—a gesture which Noah attempted to imitate, though not with complete success, in consequence of his own nose not being large enough for the purpose. However, Mr. Fagin seemed to interpret the endeavour as expressing a perfect coincidence with his opinion, and put about the liquor which Barney reappeared with, in a very friendly manner.

'Good stuff that,' observed Mr. Claypole, smacking his lips.

'Dear!' said Fagin. 'A man need be always emptying a till, or a pocket, or a woman's reticule, or a house, or a mail-coach, or a bank, if he drinks it regularly.'

Mr. Claypole no sooner heard this extract from his own remarks than he fell back in his chair, and looked from the Jew to Charlotte with a countenance of ashy paleness and excessive terror.

'Don't mind me, my dear,' said Fagin, drawing his chair closer. 'Ha! ha! it was lucky it was only me that heard you by chance. It was very lucky it was only me.'

'I didn't take it,' stammered Noah, no longer stretching out his legs like an independent gentleman, but coiling them, up as well as he could under his chair; 'it was all her doing: yer've got it now, Charlotte, yer know yer have.'

'No matter who's got it, or who did it, my dear!' replied Fagin, glancing, nevertheless, with a hawk's eye at the girl and the two bundles. 'I'm in that way myself, and I like you for it.'

'In what way?' asked Mr. Claypole, a little recovering.

'In that way of business,' rejoined Fagin; 'and so are the people of the house. You've hit the right nail upon the head, and are as safe here as you could be. There is not a safer place in all this town than is the Cripples; that is, when I like to make it so. And I have taken a fancy to you and the young woman; so I've said the word, and you may make your minds easy.'

Noah Claypole's mind might have been at ease after this assurance, but his body certainly was not; for he shuffled and writhed about, into various uncouth positions: eyeing his new friend meanwhile with mingled fear and suspicion.

'I'll tell you more,' said Fagin, after he had reassured the girl, by dint of friendly nods and muttered encouragements. 'I have got a friend that I think can gratify your darling wish, and put you in the right way, where you can take whatever department of the business you think will suit you best at first, and be taught all the others.'

'Yer speak as if yer were in earnest,' replied Noah.

'What advantage would it be to me to be anything else?' inquired Fagin, shrugging his shoulders. 'Here! Let me have a word with you outside.'

'There's no occasion to trouble ourselves to move,' said Noah, getting his legs by gradual degrees abroad again. 'She'll take the luggage up stairs the while. Charlotte, see to them bundles!'

This mandate, which had been delivered with great majesty, was obeyed without the slightest demur; and Charlotte made the best of her way off with the packages while Noah held the door open and watched her out.

'She's kept tolerably well under, ain't she?' he asked as he resumed his seat: in the tone of a keeper who has tamed some wild animal.

'Quite perfect,' rejoined Fagin, clapping him on the shoulder. 'You're a genius, my dear.'

'Why, I suppose if I wasn't, I shouldn't be here,' replied Noah. 'But, I say, she'll be back if yer lose time.'

'Now, what do you think?' said Fagin. 'If you was to like my friend, could you do better than join him?'

'Is he in a good way of business; that's where it is!' responded Noah, winking one of his little eyes.

'The top of the tree; employs a power of hands; has the very best society in the profession.'

'Regular town-maders?' asked Mr. Claypole.

'Not a countryman among 'em; and I don't think he'd take you, even on my recommendation, if he didn't run rather short of assistants just now,' replied Fagin.

'Should I have to hand over?' said Noah, slapping his breeches-pocket.

'It couldn't possibly be done without,' replied Fagin, in a most decided manner.

'Twenty pound, though,—it's a lot of money!'

'Not when it's in a note you can't get rid of,' retorted Fagin. 'Number and date taken, I suppose? Payment stopped at the Bank? Ah! It's not worth much to him. It'll have to go abroad, and he couldn't sell it for a great deal in the market.'

'When could I see him?' asked Noah doubtfully.

'To-morrow morning.'

'Where?'

'Here.'

'Um!' said Noah. 'What's the wages?'

'Live like a gentleman—board and lodging, pipes and spirits free—half of all you earn, and half of all the young woman earns,' replied Mr. Fagin.

Whether Noah Claypole, whose rapacity was none of the least comprehensive, would have acceded even to these glowing terms, had he been a perfectly free agent, is very doubtful; but as he recollected that, in the event of his refusal it was in the power of his new acquaintance to give him up to justice immediately (and more unlikely things had come to pass), he gradually relented, and said he thought that would suit him.

'But, yer see,' observed Noah, 'as she will be able to do a good deal, I should like to take something very light.'

'A little fancy work?' suggested Fagin.

'Ah! something of that sort,' replied Noah. 'What do you think would suit me now? Something not too trying for the strength, and not very dangerous, you know. That's the sort of thing!'

'I heard you talk of something in the spy way upon the others, my dear,' said Fagin. 'My friend wants somebody who would do that well, very much.'

'Why, I did mention that, and I shouldn't mind turning my hand to it sometimes,' rejoined Mr. Claypole slowly; 'but it wouldn't pay by itself, you know.'

'That's true!' observed the Jew, ruminating or pretending to ruminate. 'No, it might not.'

'What do you think, then?' asked Noah, anxiously regarding him. 'Something in the sneaking way, where it was pretty sure work, and not much more risk than being at home.'

'What do you think of the old ladies?' asked Fagin. 'There's a good deal of money made in snatching their bags and parcels, and running round the corner.'

'Don't they holler out a good deal, and scratch sometimes?' asked Noah, shaking his head. 'I don't think that would answer my purpose. Ain't there any other line open?'

'Stop!' said Fagin, laying his hand on Noah's knee. 'The kinchin lay.'

'What's that?' demanded Mr. Claypole.

'The kinchins, my dear,' said Fagin, 'is the young children that's sent on errands by their mothers, with sixpences and shillings;

and the lay is just to take their money away—they've always got it ready in their hands,—then knock 'em into the kennel, and walk off very slow, as if there was nothing else the matter but a child fallen down and hurt itself. Ha! ha! ha!'

'Ha! ha!' roared Mr. Claypole, kicking up his legs in an ecstasy. 'Lord, that's the very thing!'

'To be sure it is,' replied Fagin; 'and you can have a few good beats chalked out in Camden Town, and Battle Bridge, and neighbourhoods like that, where they're always going errands; and you can upset as many kinchins as you want, any hour in the day. Ha! ha! ha!'

With this, Fagin poked Mr. Claypole in the side, and they joined in a burst of laughter both long and loud.

'Well, that's all right!' said Noah, when he had recovered himself, and Charlotte had returned. 'What time to-morrow shall we say?'

'Will ten do?' asked Fagin, adding, as Mr. Claypole nodded assent, 'What name shall I tell my good friend?'

'Mr. Bolter,' replied Noah, who had prepared himself for such an emergency. 'Mr. Morris Bolter. This is Mrs. Bolter.'

'Mrs. Bolter's humble servant,' said Fagin, bowing with grotesque politeness. 'I hope I shall know her better very shortly.'

'Do you hear the gentleman, Charlotte?' thundered Mr. Claypole.

'Yes, Noah, dear!' replied Mrs. Bolter, extending her hand.

'She calls me Noah, as a sort of fond way of talking,' said Mr. Morris Bolter, late Claypole, turning to Fagin. 'You understand?'

'Oh yes, I understand—perfectly,' replied Fagin, telling the truth for once. 'Good night! Good night!'

With many adieus and good wishes, Mr. Fagin went his way. Noah Claypole, bespeaking his good lady's attention, proceeded to enlighten her relative to the arrangement he had made, with all that haughtiness and air of superiority, becoming, not only a member of the sterner sex, but a gentleman who appreciated the dignity of a special appointment on the kinchin lay, in London and its vicinity.

CHAPTER 43

Wherein is shown how the Artful Dodger got into trouble

'And so it was you that was your own friend, was it?' asked Mr. Claypole, otherwise Bolter, when, by virtue of the compact entered into between them, he had removed next day to Fagin's house. 'Cod, I thought as much last night!'

'Every man's his own friend, my dear,' replied Fagin, with his most insinuating grin. 'He hasn't as good a one as himself anywhere.'

'Except sometimes,' replied Morris Bolter, assuming the air of a man of the world. 'Some people are nobody's enemies but their own, yer know.'

'Don't believe that,' said Fagin. 'When a man's his own enemy, it's only because he's too much his own friend; not because he's careful for everybody but himself. Pooh! pooh! There ain't such a thing in nature.'

'There oughtn't to be, if there is,' replied Mr. Bolter.

'That stands to reason. Some conjurers say that number three is the magic number, and some say number seven. It's neither, my friend, neither. It's number one.'

'Ha! ha!' cried Mr. Bolter. 'Number one for ever.'

'In a little community like ours, my dear,' said Fagin, who felt it necessary to qualify this position, 'we have a general number one; that is, you can't consider yourself as number one, without considering me too as the same, and all the other young people.'

'Oh, the devil!' exclaimed Mr. Bolter.

'You see,' pursued Fagin, affecting to disregard this interruption, we are so mixed up together, and identified in our interests, that it must be so. For instance, it's your object to take care of number one—meaning yourself.'

'Certainly,' replied Mr. Bolter. 'Yer about right there.'

'Well! You can't take care of yourself, number one, without taking care of me, number one.'

'Number two, you mean,' said Mr. Bolter, who was largely endowed with the quality of selfishness.

'No, I don't!' retorted Fagin. 'I'm of the same importance to you, as you are to yourself.'

'I say,' interrupted Mr. Bolter, 'yer a very nice man, and I'm very fond of yer; but we ain't quite so thick together, as all that comes to.'

'Only think,' said Fagin, shrugging his shoulders, and stretching out his hands; 'only consider. You've done what's a very pretty thing, and what I love you for doing; but what at the same time would put the cravat round your throat, that's so very easily tied and so very difficult to unloose—in plain English, the halter!'

Mr. Bolter put his hand to his neckerchief, as if he felt it inconveniently tight; and murmured an assent, qualified in tone but not in substance.

'The gallows,' continued Fagin, 'the gallows, my dear, is an ugly finger-post, which points out a very short and sharp turning that has stopped many a bold fellow's career on the broad highway. To keep in the easy road, and keep it at a distance, is object number one with you.'

'Of course it is,' replied Mr. Bolter. 'What do yer talk about such things for?'

'Only to show you my meaning clearly,' said the Jew, raising his eyebrows. 'To be able to do that, you depend upon me. To keep my little business all snug, I depend upon you. The first is your number one, the second my number one. The more you value your number one, the more careful you must be of mine; so we come at last to what I told you at first—that a regard for number one holds us all together, and must do so, unless we would all go to pieces in company.'

'That's true,' rejoined Mr. Bolter, thoughtfully. 'Oh! yer a cunning old codger!'

Mr. Fagin saw, with delight, that this tribute to his powers was no mere compliment, but that he had really impressed his recruit with a sense of his wily genius, which it was most important that he should entertain in the outset of their acquaintance. To strengthen an impression so desirable and useful, he followed up the blow by acquainting him, in some detail, with the magnitude and extent of his operations; blending truth and fiction together, as best served his purpose; and bringing both to bear, with so much art, that Mr. Bolter's respect visibly increased, and became tempered, at the same time, with a degree of wholesome fear, which it was highly desirable to awaken.

'It's this mutual trust we have in each other that consoles me under heavy losses,' said Fagin. 'My best hand was taken from me, yesterday morning.'

'You don't mean to say he died?' cried Mr. Bolter.

'No, no,' replied Fagin, 'not so bad as that. Not quite so bad.'

'What, I suppose he was—'

'Wanted,' interposed Fagin. 'Yes, he was wanted.'

'Very particular?' inquired Mr. Bolter.

'No,' replied Fagin, 'not very. He was charged with attempting to pick a pocket, and they found a silver snuff-box on him,—his own, my dear, his own, for he took snuff himself, and was very fond of it. They remanded him till to-day, for they thought they knew the owner. Ah! he was worth fifty boxes, and I'd give the price of as many to have him back. You should have known the Dodger, my dear; you should have known the Dodger.'

'Well, but I shall know him, I hope; don't yer think so?' said Mr. Bolter.

'I'm doubtful about it,' replied Fagin, with a sigh. 'If they don't get any fresh evidence, it'll only be a summary conviction, and we shall have him back again after six weeks or so; but, if they do, it's a case of lagging. They know what a clever lad he is; he'll be a lifer. They'll make the Artful nothing less than a lifer.'

'What do yer mean by lagging and a lifer?' demanded Mr. Bolter. 'What's the good of talking in that way to me; why don't yer speak so as I can understand yer?'

Fagin was about to translate these mysterious expressions into the vulgar tongue; and, being interpreted, Mr. Bolter would have been informed that they represented that combination of words, 'transportation for life,' when the dialogue was cut short by the entry of Master Bates, with his hands in his breeches-pockets, and his face twisted into a look of semi-comical woe.

'It's all up, Fagin,' said Charley, when he and his new companion had been made known to each other.

'What do you mean?'

'They've found the gentleman as owns the box; two or three more's a-coming to 'dentify him; and the Artful's booked for a passage out,' replied Master Bates. 'I must have a full suit of mourning, Fagin, and a hatband, to wisit him in, afore he sets out upon his travels. To think of Jack Dawkins—lummy Jack—the Dodger—the Artful Dodger—going abroad for a common two-penny-halfpenny sneeze-box! I never thought he'd a done it under a gold watch, chain, and seals, at the lowest. Oh, why didn't he rob some rich old gentleman of all his walables, and go out *as* a gentleman, and not like a common prig, without no honour nor glory!'

With this expression of feeling for his unfortunate friend, Master Bates sat himself on the nearest chair with an aspect of chagrin and despondency.

'What do you talk about his having neither honour nor glory for!' exclaimed Fagin, darting an angry look at his pupil. 'Wasn't he always top-sawyer among you all! Is there one of you that could touch him or come near him on any scent! Eh?'

'Not one,' replied Master Bates, in a voice rendered husky by regret; 'not one.'

'Then what do you talk of?' replied Fagin angrily; 'what are you blubbering for?'

''Cause it isn't on the rec-ord, is it?' said Charley, chafed into perfect defiance of his venerable friend by the current of his regrets; ''cause it can't come out in the 'dictment; 'cause nobody will never know half of what he was. How will he stand in the Newgate Calendar? P'raps not be there at all. Oh, my eye, my eye, wot a blow it is!'

'Ha! ha!' cried Fagin, extending his right hand, and turning to Mr. Bolter in a fit of chuckling which shook him as though he had the palsy; 'see what a pride they take in their profession, my dear. Ain't it beautiful?'

Mr. Bolter nodded assent; and Fagin, after contemplating the grief of Charley Bates for some seconds with evident satisfaction, stepped up to that young gentleman and patted him on the shoulder.

'Never mind, Charley,' said Fagin soothingly; 'it'll come out, it'll be sure to come out. They'll all know what a clever fellow he was; he'll show it himself, and not disgrace his old pals and teachers. Think how young he is too! What a distinction, Charley, to be lagged at his time of life!'

'Well, it is a honour that is!' said Charley, a little consoled.

'He shall have all he wants,' continued the Jew. 'He shall be kept in the Stone Jug, Charley, like a gentleman. Like a gentleman! With his beer every day, and money in his pocket to pitch and toss with, if he can't spend it.'

'No, shall he though?' cried Charley Bates.

'Ay, that he shall,' replied Fagin, 'and we'll have a big-wig, Charley: one that's got the greatest gift of the gab: to carry on his defence; and he shall make a speech for himself too, if he likes; and we'll read it all in the papers—"Artful Dodger—shrieks of laughter—here the court was convulsed"—eh, Charley, eh?'

'Ha! ha!' laughed Master Bates, 'what a lark that would be, wouldn't it, Fagin? I say, how the Artful would bother 'em, wouldn't he?'

'Would!' cried Fagin. 'He shall—he will!'

'Ah, to be sure, so he will,' repeated Charley, rubbing his hands.

'I think I see him now,' cried the Jew, bending his eyes upon his pupil.

'So do I,' cried Charley Bates. 'Ha! ha! ha! so do I. I see it all afore me, upon my soul I do, Fagin. What a game! What a regular game! All the big-wigs trying to look solemn, and Jack Dawkins addressing of 'em as intimate and comfortable as if he was the judge's own son making a speech arter dinner—ha! ha! ha!'

In fact, Mr. Fagin had so well humoured his young friend's eccentric disposition, that Master Bates, who had at first been disposed to consider the imprisoned Dodger rather in the light of a victim, now looked upon him as the chief actor in a scene of most uncommon and exquisite humour, and felt quite impatient for the arrival of the time when his old companion should have so favourable an opportunity of displaying his abilities.

'We must know how he gets on to-day, by some handy means or other,' said Fagin. 'Let me think.'

'Shall I go?' asked Charley.

'Not for the world,' replied Fagin. 'Are you mad, my dear, stark mad, that you'd walk into the very place where—No, Charley, no. One is enough to lose at a time.'

'You don't mean to go yourself, I suppose?' said Charley, with a humorous leer.

'That wouldn't quite fit,' replied Fagin, shaking his head.

'Then why don't you send this new cove?' asked Master Bates, laying his hand on Noah's arm. 'Nobody knows him.'

'Why, if he didn't mind—' observed Fagin.

'Mind!' interposed Charley. 'What should *he* have to mind?'

'Really nothing, my dear,' said Fagin, turning to Mr. Bolter, 'really nothing.'

'Oh, I dare say about that, yer know,' observed Noah, backing towards the door, and shaking his head with a kind of sober alarm. 'No, no—none of that. It's not in my department, that ain't.'

'Wot department has he got, Fagin?' inquired Master Bates, surveying Noah's lank form with much disgust. 'The cutting away when there's anything wrong, and the eating all the wittles when there's everything right; is that his branch?'

'Never mind,' retorted Mr. Bolter; 'and don't yer take liberties with yer superiors, little boy, or yer'll find yerself in the wrong shop.'

Master Bates laughed so vehemently at this magnificent threat, that it was some time before Fagin could interpose, and represent to Mr. Bolter that he incurred no possible danger in visiting the police-office; that, inasmuch as no account of the little affair in which he had been engaged, nor any description of his person, had yet been forwarded to the metropolis, it was very probable that he was not even suspected of having resorted to it for shelter; and that, if he were properly disguised, it would be as safe a spot for him to visit as any in London, inasmuch as it would be, of all places, the very last, to which he could be supposed likely to resort of his own free will.

Persuaded in part, by these representations, but overborne in a much greater degree by his fear of Fagin, Mr. Bolter at length consented, with a very bad grace, to undertake the expedition. By Fagin's directions, he immediately substituted for his own attire, a waggoner's frock, velveteen breeches, and leather leggings: all of which articles the Jew had at hand. He was likewise furnished with a felt hat well garnished with turnpike tickets; and a carter's whip. Thus equipped, he was to saunter into the office, as some country fellow from Covent Garden market might be supposed to do for the gratification of his curiosity; and as he was as awkward, ungainly, and raw-boned a fellow as need be, Mr. Fagin had no fear but that he would look the part to perfection.

These arrangements completed, he was informed of the necessary signs and tokens by which to recognise the Artful Dodger, and was conveyed by Master Bates through dark and winding ways to within a very short distance of Bow Street. Having described the precise situation of the office, and accompanied it with copious directions how he was to walk straight up the passage, and when he got into the yard take the door up the steps on the right-hand side, and pull off his hat as he went into the room, Charley Bates bade him hurry on alone, and promised to bide his return on the spot of their parting.

Noah Claypole, or Morris Bolter as the reader pleases, punctually followed the directions he had received, which—Master Bates being pretty well acquainted with the locality—were so exact that he was enabled to gain the magisterial presence without asking any question, or meeting with any interruption by the way. He found himself jostled among a crowd of people, chiefly women, who were huddled together in a dirty frowsy room, at the upper end of which was a raised platform railed off from the rest, with a dock for the prisoners on the left hand against the wall, a box for the witnesses in the middle, and a desk for the magistrates on the right; the awful locality last named, being screened off by a partition which concealed the bench from the common gaze, and left the vulgar to imagine (if they could) the full majesty of justice.

There were only a couple of women in the dock, who were nodding to their admiring friends, while the clerk read some depositions to a couple of policemen and a man in plain clothes who leant over the table. A jailer stood reclining against the dock-rail, tapping his nose listlessly with a large key, except when he repressed an undue tendency to conversation among the idlers, by proclaiming silence; or looked sternly up to bid some woman 'Take that baby out,' when the gravity of justice was disturbed by feeble cries, half-smothered in the mother's shawl, from some meagre infant. The room smelt close and unwholesome; the walls were dirt-discoloured; and the ceiling blackened. There was an old smoky bust over the mantel-shelf, and a dusty clock above the dock—the only thing present, that seemed to go on as it ought; for depravity, or poverty, or an habitual acquaintance with both, had left a taint on all the animate matter, hardly less unpleasant than the thick greasy scum on every inanimate object that frowned upon it.

Noah looked eagerly about him for the Dodger; but although there were several women who would have done very well for that distinguished character's mother or sister, and more than one man who might be supposed to bear a strong resemblance to his father, nobody at all answering the description given him of Mr. Dawkins was to be seen. He waited in a state of much suspense and uncertainty until the women, being committed for trial, went flaunting out; and then was quickly relieved by the appearance of another prisoner who he felt at once could be no other than the object of his visit.

It was indeed Mr. Dawkins, who, shuffling into the office with the big coat sleeves tucked up as usual, his left hand in his pocket, and his hat in his right hand, preceded the jailer, with a rolling gait altogether indescribable, and, taking his place in the dock, requested in an audible voice to know what he was placed in that 'ere disgraceful sitivation for.

'Hold you tongue, will you?' said the jailer.

'I'm an Englishman, ain't I?' rejoined the Dodger. 'Where are my priwileges?'

'You'll get your privileges soon enough,' retorted the jailer, 'and pepper with 'em.'

'We'll see wot the Secretary of State for the Home Affairs has got to say to the beaks, if I don't,' replied Mr. Dawkins. 'Now then! Wot is this here business? I shall thank the madg'strates to dispose of this here little affair, and not to keep me while they read the paper, for I've got an appointment with a genelman in the City, and as I'm a man of my word and wery punctual in business matters, he'll go away if I ain't there to my time, and then pr'aps there won't be an action for damage against them as kep me away. Oh no, certainly not!'

At this point, the Dodger, with a show of being very particular with a view to proceedings to be had thereafter, desired the jailer to communicate 'the names of them two files as was on the bench.' Which so tickled the spectators, that they laughed almost as heartily as Master Bates could have done if he had heard the request.

'Silence there!' cried the jailer.

'What is this?' inquired one of the magistrates.

'A pick-pocketing case, your worship.'

'Has the boy ever been here before?'

'He ought to have been, a many times,' replied the jailer. 'He has been pretty well everywhere else. *I* know him well, your worship.'

'Oh! you know me, do you?' cried the Artful, making a note of the statement. 'Wery good. That's a case of deformation of character, any way.'

Here there was another laugh, and another cry of silence.

'Now then, where are the witnesses?' said the clerk.

'Ah! that's right,' added the Dodger. 'Where are they? I should like to see 'em.'

This wish was immediately gratified, for a policeman stepped forward who had seen the prisoner attempt the pocket of an unknown gentleman in a crowd, and indeed take a handkerchief therefrom, which, being a very old one, he deliberately put back again, after trying it on his own countenance. For this reason, he took the Dodger into custody as soon as he could get near him, and the said Dodger, being searched, had upon his person a silver snuff-box, with the owner's name engraved upon the lid. This gentleman had been discovered on reference to the Court Guide, and being then and there present, swore that the snuff-box was his, and that he had missed it on the previous day, the moment he had disengaged himself from the crowd before referred to. He had also remarked a young gentleman in the throng, particularly active in making his way about, and that young gentleman was the prisoner before him.

'Have you anything to ask this witness, boy?' said the magistrate.

'I wouldn't abase myself by descending to hold no conversation with him,' replied the Dodger.

'Have you anything to say at all?'

'Do you hear his worship ask if you've anything to say?' inquired the jailer, nudging the silent Dodger with his elbow.

'I beg your pardon,' said the Dodger, looking up with an air of abstraction. 'Did you redress yourself to me, my man?'

'I never see such an out-and-out young wagabond, your worship,' observed the officer with a grin. 'Do you mean to say anything, you young shaver?'

'No,' replied the Dodger, 'not here, for this ain't the shop for justice; besides which, my attorney is a-break-fasting this morning with the Wice President of the House of Commons; but I shall have something to say elsewhere, and so will he, and so will a wery numerous and 'spectable circle of acquaintance as'll make them beaks wish they'd never been born, or that they'd got their footmen to hang 'em up to their own hat-pegs, 'afore they let 'em come out this morning to try it on upon me. I'll—'

'There! He's fully committed!' interposed the clerk. 'Take him away.'

'Come on,' said the jailer.

'Oh ah! I'll come on,' replied the Dodger, brushing his hat with the palm of his hand. 'Ah! (to the Bench) it's no use your looking frightened; I won't show you no mercy, not a ha'porth of it. *You'll* pay for this, my fine fellers. I wouldn't be you for something! I wouldn't go free, now, if you was to fall down on your knees and ask me. Here, carry me off to prison! Take me away!'

With these last words, the Dodger suffered himself to be led off by the collar; threatening, till he got into the yard, to make a parliamentary business of it; and then grinning in the officer's face, with great glee and self-approval.

Having seen him locked up by himself in a little cell, Noah made the best of his way back to where he had left Master Bates. After waiting here some time, he was joined by that young gentleman, who had prudently abstained from showing himself until he had looked carefully abroad from a snug retreat, and ascertained that his new friend had not been followed by any impertinent person.

The two hastened back together, to bear to Mr. Fagin the animating news that the Dodger was doing full justice to his bringing-up, and establishing for himself a glorious reputation.

CHAPTER 44

The time arrives for Nancy to redeem her pledge to Rose Maylie. She fails

Adept as she was, in all the arts of cunning and dissimulation, the girl Nancy could not wholly conceal the effect which the knowledge of the step she had taken, wrought upon her mind. She remembered that both the crafty Jew and the brutal Sikes had confided to her schemes, which had been hidden from all others: in the full confidence that she was trustworthy and beyond the reach of their suspicion. Vile as those schemes were, desperate as were their originators, and bitter as were her feelings towards Fagin, who had led her, step by step, deeper and deeper down into an abyss of crime and misery, whence was no escape; still, there were times when, even towards him, she felt some relenting, lest her disclosure should bring him within the iron grasp he had so long eluded, and he should fall at last—richly as he merited such a fate—by her hand.

But, these were the mere wanderings of a mind unable wholly to detach itself from old companions and associations, though enabled to fix itself steadily on one object, and resolved not to be turned aside by any consideration. Her fears for Sikes would have been more powerful inducements to recoil while there was yet time; but she had stipulated that her secret should be rigidly kept, she had dropped no clue which could lead to his discovery, she had refused, even for his sake, a refuge from all the guilt and wretchedness that encompassed her—and what more could she do! She was resolved.

Though all her mental struggles terminated in this conclusion, they forced themselves upon her, again and again, and left their traces too. She grew pale and thin, even within a few days. At times, she took no heed of what was passing before her, or no part in conversations where once, she would have been the loudest. At other times, she laughed without merriment, and was noisy without cause or meaning. At others—often within a moment afterwards—she sat silent and dejected, brooding with her head upon her hands, while the very effort by which she roused herself, told, more forcibly than even these indications, that she was ill at ease, and that her thoughts were occupied with matters very different and distant from those in course of discussion by her companions.

It was Sunday night, and the bell of the nearest church struck the hour. Sikes and the Jew were talking, but they paused to listen. The girl looked up from the low seat on which she crouched, and listened too. Eleven.

'An hour this side of midnight,' said Sikes, raising the blind to look out and returning to his seat. 'Dark and heavy it is too. A good night for business this.'

'Ah!' replied Fagin. 'What a pity, Bill, my dear, that there's none quite ready to be done.'

'You're right for once,' replied Sikes gruffly. 'It is a pity, for I'm in the humour too.'

Fagin sighed, and shook his head despondingly.

'We must make up for lost time when we've got things into a good train. That's all I know,' said Sikes.

'That's the way to talk, my dear,' replied Fagin, venturing to pat him on the shoulder. 'It does me good to hear you.'

'Does you good does it!' cried Sikes. 'Well, so be it.'

'Ha! ha! ha!' laughed Fagin, as if he were relieved by even this concession. 'You're like yourself to-night, Bill! Quite like yourself.'

'I don't feel like myself when you lay that withered old claw on my shoulder, so take it away,' said Sikes, casting off the Jew's hand.

'It makes you nervous, Bill,—reminds you of being nabbed, does it?' said Fagin, determined not to be offended.

'Reminds me of being nabbed by the devil,' returned Sikes. 'There never was another man with such a face as yours, unless it was your father, and I suppose *he* is singeing his grizzled red beard by this time, unless you came straight from the old 'un without any father at all betwixt you; which I shouldn't wonder at, a bit.'

Fagin offered no reply to this compliment; but, pulling Sikes by the sleeve, pointed his finger towards Nancy, who had taken advantage of the foregoing conversation to put on her bonnet, and was now leaving the room.

'Hallo!' cried Sikes. 'Nance. Where's the gal going to at this time of night?'

'Not far.'

'What answer's that?' returned Sikes. 'Where are you going?'

'I say, not far.'

'And I say where?' retorted Sikes. 'Do you hear me?'

'I don't know where,' replied the girl.

'Then I do,' said Sikes, more in the spirit of obstinacy than because he had any real objection to the girl going where she listed. 'Nowhere. Sit down.'

'I'm not well. I told you that before,' rejoined the girl. 'I want a breath of air.'

'Put your head out of the winder,' replied Sikes.

'There's not enough there,' said the girl. 'I want it in the street.'

'Then you won't have it,' replied Sikes. With which assurance he rose, locked the door, took the key out, and pulling her bonnet from her head, flung it up to the top of an old press. 'There,' said the robber. 'Now stop quietly where you are, will you?'

'It's not such a matter as a bonnet would keep me,' said the girl turning very pale. 'What do you mean, Bill? Do you know what you're doing?'

'Know what I'm—Oh!' cried Sikes turning to Fagin, 'she's out of her senses, you know, or she daren't talk to me in that way.'

'You'll drive me on to something desperate,' muttered the girl placing both hands upon her breast, as though to keep down by force some violent outbreak. 'Let me go, will you,—this minute—this instant.'

'No!' said Sikes.

'Tell him to let me go, Fagin. He had better. It'll be better for him. Do you hear me?' cried Nancy, stamping her foot upon the ground.

'Hear you!' repeated Sikes turning round in his chair to confront her. 'Aye! And if I hear you for half a minute longer, the dog shall have such a grip on your throat as'll tear some of that screaming voice out. Wot has come over you, you jade! Wot is it?'

'Let me go,' said the girl with great earnestness; then sitting herself down on the floor, before the door, she said, 'Bill, let me go; you don't know what you are doing. You don't, indeed. For only one hour—do—do!'

'Cut my limbs off one by one!' cried Sikes, seizing her roughly by the arm, 'if I don't think the gal's stark raving mad. Get up.'

'Not till you let me go—not till you let me go—Never—never!' screamed the girl. Sikes looked on, for a minute, watching his opportunity, and suddenly pinioning her hands dragged her, struggling and wrestling with him by the way, into a small room adjoining, where he sat himself on a bench, and thrusting her into a chair, held her down by force. She struggled and implored by turns until twelve o'clock had struck, and then, wearied and exhausted, ceased to contest the point any further. With a caution, backed by many oaths, to make no more efforts to go out that night, Sikes left her to recover at leisure and rejoined Fagin.

'Whew!' said the housebreaker, wiping the perspiration from his face. 'Wot a precious strange gal that is!'

'You may say that, Bill,' replied Fagin thoughtfully. 'You may say that.'

'Wot did she take it into her head to go out to-night for,

do you think?' asked Sikes. 'Come; you should know her better than me. Wot does it mean?'

'Obstinacy; woman's obstinacy, I suppose, my dear.'

'Well, I suppose it is,' growled Sikes. 'I thought I had tamed her, but she's as bad as ever.'

'Worse,' said Fagin thoughtfully. 'I never knew her like this, for such a little cause.'

'Nor I,' said Sikes. 'I think she's got a touch of that fever in her blood yet, and it won't come out—eh?'

'Like enough.'

'I'll let her a little blood, without troubling the doctor, if she's took that way again,' said Sikes.

Fagin nodded an expressive approval of this mode of treatment.

'She was hanging about me all day, and night too, when I was stretched on my back; and you, like a black-hearted wolf as you are, kept yourself aloof,' said Sikes. 'We was very poor too, all the time, and I think, one way or other, it's worried and fretted her; and that being shut up here so long has made her restless—eh?'

'That's it, my dear,' replied the Jew in a whisper. 'Hush!'

As he uttered these words, the girl herself appeared and resumed her former seat. Her eyes were swollen and red; she rocked herself to and fro; tossed her head; and, after a little time, burst out laughing.

'Why, now she's on the other tack!' exclaimed Sikes, turning a look of excessive surprise on his companion.

Fagin nodded to him to take no further notice just then; and, in a few minutes, the girl subsided into her accustomed demeanour. Whispering Sikes that there was no fear of her relapsing, Fagin took up his hat and bade him good night. He paused when he reached the room-door, and looking round, asked if somebody would light him down the dark stairs.

'Light him down,' said Sikes, who was filling his pipe. 'It's a pity he should break his neck himself, and disappoint the sight-seers. Show him a light.'

Nancy followed the old man down stairs, with a candle. When

they reached the passage, he laid his finger on his lip, and drawing close to the girl, said, in a whisper,

'What is it, Nancy, dear?'

'What do you mean?' replied the girl, in the same tone.

'The reason of all this,' replied Fagin. 'If *he*'—he pointed with his skinny fore-finger up the stairs—'is so hard with you (he's a brute, Nance, a brute-beast), why don't you—'

'Well!' said the girl, as Fagin paused, with his mouth almost touching her ear, and his eyes looking into hers.

'No matter just now. We'll talk of this again. You have a friend in me, Nance; a staunch friend. I have the means at hand, quiet and close. If you want revenge on those that treat you like a dog—like a dog! worse than his dog, for he humours him sometimes—come to me. I say, come to me. He is the mere hound of a day, but you know me of old, Nance.'

'I know you well,' replied the girl, without manifesting the least emotion. 'Good night.'

She shrank back, as Fagin offered to lay his hand on hers, but said good night again, in a steady voice, and, answering his parting look with a nod of intelligence, closed the door between them.

Fagin walked towards his own home, intent upon the thoughts that were working within his brain. He had conceived the idea—not from what had just passed, though that had tended to confirm him, but slowly and by degrees—that Nancy, wearied of the housebreaker's brutality, had conceived an attachment for some new friend. Her altered manner, her repeated absences from home alone, her comparative indifference to the interests of the gang for which she had once been so zealous, and, added to these, her desperate impatience to leave home that night at a particular hour, all favoured the supposition, and rendered it, to him at least, almost matter of certainty. The object of this new liking was not among his myrmidons. He would be a valuable acquisition with such an assistant as Nancy, and must (thus Fagin argued) be secured without delay.

There was another, and a darker object, to be gained. Sikes

knew too much, and his ruffian taunts had not galled Fagin the less, because the wounds were hidden. The girl must know, well, that if she shook him off, she could never be safe from his fury, and that it would be surely wreaked—to the maiming of limbs, or perhaps the loss of life—on the object of her more recent fancy. 'With a little persuasion,' thought Fagin, 'what more likely than that she would consent to poison him? Women have done such things, and worse, to secure the same object before now. There would be the dangerous villain: the man I hate: gone; another secured in his place; and my influence over the girl, with a knowledge of this crime to back it, unlimited.'

These things passed through the mind of Fagin, during the short time he sat alone, in the housebreaker's room; and with them uppermost in his thoughts, he had taken the opportunity afterwards afforded him, of sounding the girl in the broken hints he threw out at parting. There was no expression of surprise, no assumption of an inability to understand his meaning. The girl clearly comprehended it. Her glance at parting showed *that.*

But perhaps she would recoil from a plot to take the life of Sikes, and that was one of the chief ends to be attained. 'How,' thought Fagin, as he crept homeward, 'can I increase my influence with her? what new power can I acquire?'

Such brains are fertile in expedients. If, without extracting a confession from herself, he laid a watch, discovered the object of her altered regard, and threatened to reveal the whole history to Sikes (of whom she stood in no common fear) unless she entered into his designs, could he not secure her compliance?

'I can,' said Fagin, almost aloud. 'She durst not refuse me then, Not for her life, not for her life! I have it all. The means are ready, and shall be set to work. I shall have you yet!'

He cast back a dark look, and a threatening motion of the hand, towards the spot where he had left the bolder villain; and went on his way: busying his bony hands in the folds of his tattered garment, which he wrenched tightly in his grasp, as though there were a hated enemy crushed with every motion of his fingers.

CHAPTER 45

Noah Claypole is employed by Fagin on a secret mission

The old man was up, betimes, next morning, and waited impatiently for the appearance of his new associate, who after a delay that seemed interminable, at length presented himself, and commenced a voracious assault on the breakfast.

'Bolter,' said Fagin, drawing up a chair and seating himself opposite Morris Bolter.

'Well, here I am,' returned Noah. 'What's the matter? Don't yer ask me to do anything till I have done eating. That's a great fault in this place. Yer never get time enough over yer meals.'

'You can talk as you eat, can't you?' said Fagin, cursing his dear young friend's greediness from the very bottom of his heart.

'Oh yes, I can talk. I get on better when I talk,' said Noah, cutting a monstrous slice of bread. 'Where's Charlotte?'

'Out,' said Fagin. 'I sent her out this morning with the other young woman, because I wanted us to be alone.'

'Oh!' said Noah. 'I wish yer'd ordered her to make some buttered toast first. Well. Talk away. Yer won't interrupt me.'

There seemed, indeed, no great fear of anything interrupting him, as he had evidently sat down with a determination to do a great deal of business.

'You did well yesterday, my dear,' said Fagin. 'Beautiful! Six shillings and ninepence halfpenny on the very first day! The kinchin lay will be a fortune to you.'

'Don't you forget to add three pint-pots and a milk can,' said Mr. Bolter.

'No, no, my dear. The pint-pots were great strokes of genius: but the milk-can was a perfect masterpiece.'

'Pretty well, I think, for a beginner,' remarked Mr. Bolter complacently. 'The pots I took off airy railings, and the milk can was standing by itself outside a public-house. I thought it might get rusty with the rain, or catch cold, yer know. Eh? Ha! ha! ha!'

Fagin affected to laugh very heartily; and Mr. Bolter having had his laugh out, took a series of large bites, which finished his first hunk of bread and butter, and assisted himself to a second.

'I want you, Bolter,' said Fagin, leaning over the table, 'to do a piece of work for me, my dear, that needs great care and caution.'

'I say,' rejoined Bolter, 'don't yer go shoving me into danger, or sending me to any more o' yer police-offices. That don't suit me, that don't; and so I tell yer.'

'There's not the smallest danger in it—not the very smallest,' said the Jew; 'it's only to dodge a woman.'

'An old woman?' demanded Mr. Bolter.

'A young one,' replied Fagin.

'I can do that pretty well, I know,' said Bolter. 'I was a regular cunning sneak when I was at school. What am I to dodge her for? Not to—'

'Not to do anything, but to tell me where she goes, who she sees, and, if possible, what she says; to remember the street, if it is a street, or the house, if it is a house; and to bring me back all the information you can.'

'What'll yer give me?' asked Noah, setting down his cup, and looking his employer, eagerly, in the face.

'If you do it well, a pound, my dear. One pound,' said Fagin, wishing to interest him in the scent as much as possible. 'And that's what I never gave yet, for any job of work where there wasn't valuable consideration to be gained.'

'Who is she?' inquired Noah.

'One of us.'

'Oh Lor!' cried Noah, curling up his nose. 'Yer doubtful of her, are yer?'

'She has found out some new friends, my dear, and I must know who they are,' replied Fagin.

'I see,' said Noah. 'Just to have the pleasure of knowing them, if they're respectable people, eh? Ha! ha! ha! I'm your man.'

'I knew you would be,' cried Fagin, elated by the success of his proposal.

'Of course, of course,' replied Noah. 'Where is she? Where am I to wait for her? Where am I to go?'

'All that, my dear, you shall hear from me. I'll point her out at the proper time,' said Fagin. 'You keep ready, and leave the rest to me.'

That night, and the next, and the next again, the spy sat booted and equipped in his carter's dress: ready to turn out at a word from Fagin. Six nights passed—six long weary nights—and on each, Fagin came home with a disappointed face, and briefly intimated that it was not yet time. On the seventh, he returned earlier, and with an exultation he could not conceal. It was Sunday.

'She goes abroad to-night,' said Fagin, 'and on the right errand, I'm sure; for she has been alone all day, and the man she is afraid of, will not be back much before daybreak. Come with me. Quick!'

Noah started up without saying a word; for the Jew was in a state of such intense excitement that it infected him. They left the house stealthily, and, hurrying through a labyrinth of streets, arrived at length before a public-house, which Noah recognised as the same in which he had slept, on the night of his arrival in London.

It was past eleven o'clock, and the door was closed. It opened softly on its hinges as Fagin gave a low whistle. They entered, without noise; and the door was closed behind them.

Scarcely venturing to whisper, but substituting dumb show for words, Fagin, and the young Jew who had admitted them, pointed out the pane of glass to Noah, and signed to him to climb up and observe the person in the adjoining room.

'Is that the woman?' he asked, scarcely above his breath.

Fagin nodded yes.

'I can't see her face well,' whispered Noah. 'She is looking down, and the candle is behind her.'

'Stay there,' whispered Fagin. He signed to Barney, who withdrew. In an instant, the lad entered the room adjoining, and, under pretence of snuffing the candle, moved it in the required position, and, speaking to the girl, caused her to raise her face.

'I see her now,' cried the spy.

'Plainly?'

'I should know her among a thousand.'

He hastily descended, as the room-door opened, and the girl came out. Fagin drew him behind a small partition which was curtained off, and they held their breaths as she passed within a few feet of their place of concealment, and emerged by the door at which they had entered.

'Hist!' cried the lad who held the door. 'Dow.'

Noah exchanged a look with Fagin, and darted out.

'To the left,' whispered the lad; 'take the left had, and keep od the other side.'

He did so; and, by the light of the lamps, saw the girl's retreating figure, already at some distance before him. He advanced as near as he considered prudent, and kept on the opposite side of the street, the better to observe her motions. She looked nervously round, twice or thrice, and once stopped to let two men who were following close behind her, pass on. She seemed to gather courage as she advanced, and to walk with a steadier and firmer step. The spy preserved the same relative distance between them, and followed: with his eye upon her.

CHAPTER 46

The appointment kept

The church clocks chimed three quarters past eleven, as two figures emerged on London Bridge. One, which advanced with a swift and rapid step, was that of a woman who looked eagerly about her as though in quest of some expected object; the other figure was that of a man, who slunk along in the deepest shadow he could find, and, at some distance, accommodated his pace to hers: stopping when she stopped: and as she moved again, creeping stealthily on: but never allowing himself, in the ardour of his pursuit, to gain upon her footsteps. Thus, they crossed the bridge, from the Middlesex to the Surrey shore, when the woman, apparently disappointed in her anxious scrutiny of the foot-passengers, turned back. The movement was sudden; but he who watched her, was not thrown off his guard by it; for, shrinking into one of the recesses which surmount the piers of the bridge, and leaning over the parapet the better to conceal his figure, he suffered her to pass on the opposite pavement. When she was about the same distance in advance as she had been before, he slipped quietly down, and followed her again. At nearly the centre of the bridge, she stopped. The man stopped too.

It was a very dark night. The day had been unfavourable, and at that hour and place there were few people stirring. Such as there were, hurried quickly past: very possibly without seeing, but certainly without noticing, either the woman, or the man who kept her in view. Their appearance was not calculated to attract the importunate regards of such of London's destitute population, as chanced to take their way over the bridge that night in search of some cold arch or doorless hovel wherein to lay their heads; they stood there in silence: neither speaking nor spoken to, by any one who passed.

A mist hung over the river, deepening the red glare of the fires that burnt upon the small craft moored off the different wharfs, and rendering darker and more indistinct the murky buildings on the banks. The old smoke-stained storehouses on either side, rose heavy and dull from the dense mass of roofs and gables, and frowned sternly upon water too black to reflect even their lumbering shapes. The tower of old Saint Saviour's Church, and the spire of Saint Magnus, so long the giantwarders of the ancient bridge, were visible in the gloom; but the forest of shipping below bridge, and the thickly scattered spires of churches above, were nearly all hidden from the sight.

The girl had taken a few restless turns to and fro—closely watched meanwhile by her hidden observer—when the heavy bell of St. Paul's tolled for the death of another day. Midnight had come upon the crowded city. The palace, the night-cellar, the jail, the madhouse: the chambers of birth and death, of health and sickness, the rigid face of the corpse and the calm sleep of the child: midnight was upon them all.

The hour had not struck two minutes, when a young lady, accompanied by a grey-haired gentleman, alighted from a hackney-carriage within a short distance of the bridge, and, having dismissed the vehicle, walked straight towards it. They had scarcely set foot upon its pavement, when the girl started, and immediately made towards them.

They walked onward, looking about them with the air of persons who entertained some very slight expectation which had little chance of being realised, when they were suddenly joined by this new associate. They halted with an exclamation of surprise, but suppressed it immediately; for a man in the garments of a countryman came close up—brushed against them, indeed—at that precise moment.

'Not here,' said Nancy hurriedly, 'I am afraid to speak to you here. Come away—out of the public road—down the steps yonder!'

As she uttered these words, and indicated, with her hand, the direction in which she wished them to proceed, the countryman looked round, and roughly asking what they took up the whole pavement for, passed on.

The steps to which the girl had pointed, were those which, on the Surrey bank, and on the same side of the bridge as Saint Saviour's Church, form a landing-stairs from the river. To this spot, the man bearing the appearance of a countryman, hastened unobserved; and after a moment's survey of the place, he began to descend.

These stairs are a part of the bridge; they consist of three flights. Just below the end of the second, going down, the stone wall on the left terminates in an ornamental pilaster facing towards the Thames. At this point the lower steps widen: so that a person turning that angle of the wall, is necessarily unseen by any others on the stairs who chance to be above him, if only a step. The countryman looked hastily round, when he reached this point; and as there seemed no better place of concealment, and, the tide being out, there was plenty of room, he slipped aside, with his back to the pilaster, and there waited: pretty certain that they would come no lower, and that even if he could not hear what was said, he could follow them again, with safety.

So tardily stole the time in this lonely place, and so eager was the spy to penetrate the motives of an interview so different from what he had been led to expect, that he more than once gave the matter up for lost, and persuaded himself, either that they had stopped far above, or had resorted to some entirely different spot to hold their mysterious conversation. He was on the point of emerging from his hiding-place, and regaining the road above, when he heard the sound of footsteps, and directly afterwards of voices almost close at his ear.

He drew himself straight upright against the wall, and, scarcely breathing, listened attentively.

'This is far enough,' said a voice, which was evidently that of the gentleman. 'I will not suffer the young lady to go any farther. Many people would have distrusted you too much to have come even so far, but you see I am willing to humour you.

'To humour me!' cried the voice of the girl whom he had followed. 'You're considerate, indeed, sir. To humour me! Well, well, it's no matter.'

'Why, for what,' said the gentleman in a kinder tone, 'for what purpose can you have brought us to this strange place? Why not have let me speak to you, above there, where it is light, and there is something stirring, instead of bringing us to this dark and dismal hole?'

'I told you before,' replied Nancy, 'that I was afraid to speak to you there. I don't know why it is,' said the girl, shuddering, 'but I have such a fear and dread upon me to-night that I can hardly stand.'

'A fear of what?' asked the gentleman, who seemed to pity her.

'I scarcely know of what,' replied the girl. 'I wish I did. Horrible thoughts of death, and shrouds with blood upon them, and a fear that has made me burn as if I was on fire, have been upon me all day. I was reading a book to-night, to wile the time away, and the same things came into the print.'

'Imagination,' said the gentleman, soothing her.

'No imagination,' replied the girl in a hoarse voice. 'I'll swear I saw "coffin" written in every page of the book in large black letters, —aye, and they carried one close to me, in the streets to-night.'

'There is nothing unusual in that,' said the gentleman. 'They have passed me often.'

'*Real ones,*' rejoined the girl. 'This was not.'

There was something so uncommon in her manner, that the flesh of the concealed listener crept as he heard the girl utter these words, and the blood chilled within him. He had never experienced a greater relief than in hearing the sweet voice of the young lady as she begged her to be calm, and not allow herself to become the prey of such fearful fancies.

'Speak to her kindly,' said the young lady to her companion. 'Poor creature! she seems to need it.'

'Your haughty religious people would have held their heads up to see me as I am to-night, and preached of flames and vengeance,' cried the girl. 'Oh, dear lady, why ar'n't those who claim to be God's own folks as gentle and as kind to us poor wretches as you, who, having youth, and beauty, and all that they have lost, might be a little proud instead of so much humbler?'

'Ah!' said the gentleman. 'A Turk turns his face, after washing it well, to the East, when he says his prayers; these good people, after giving their faces such a rub against the World as to take the smiles off, turn with no less regularity, to the darkest side of Heaven. Between the Mussulman and the Pharisee, commend me to the first!'

These words appeared to be addressed to the young lady, and were perhaps uttered with the view of affording Nancy time to recover herself. The gentleman, shortly afterwards, addressed himself to her.

'You were not here last Sunday night,' he said.

'I couldn't come,' replied Nancy; 'I was kept by force.'

'By whom?'

'Him that I told the young lady of before.'

'You were not suspected of holding any communication with anybody on the subject which has brought us here to-night, I hope?' asked the old gentleman.

'No,' replied the girl, shaking her head. 'It's not very easy for me to leave him unless he knows why; I couldn't have seen the lady when I did, but that I gave him a drink of laudanum before I came away.'

'Did he awake before you returned?' inquired the gentleman.

'No; and neither he nor any of them suspect me.'

'Good,' said the gentleman. 'Now listen to me.'

'I am ready,' replied the girl, as he paused for a moment.

'This young lady,' the gentleman began, 'has communicated to me, and to some other friends who can be safely trusted, what you told her nearly a fortnight since. I confess to you that I had doubts, at first, whether you were to be implicitly relied upon, but now I firmly believe you are.'

'I am,' said the girl earnestly.

'I repeat that I firmly believe it. To prove to you that I am disposed to trust you, I tell you without reserve, that we propose to extort the secret, whatever it may be, from the fears of this man Monks. But if—if—' said the gentleman, 'he cannot be secured, or, if secured, cannot be acted upon as we wish, you must deliver up the Jew.'

'Fagin,' cried the girl, recoiling.

'That man must be delivered up by you,' said the gentleman.

'I will not do it! I will never do it!' replied the girl. 'Devil that he is, and worse than devil as he has been to me, I will never do that.'

'You will not?' said the gentleman, who seemed fully prepared for this answer.

'Never!' returned the girl.

'Tell me why?'

'For one reason,' rejoined the girl firmly, 'for one reason, that the lady knows and will stand by me in, I know she will, for I have her promise; and for this other reason, besides, that, bad life as he has led, I have led a bad life too; there are many of us who have kept the same courses together, and I'll not turn upon them, who might—any of them—have turned upon me, but didn't, bad as they are.'

'Then,' said the gentleman, quickly, as if this had been the point he had been aiming to attain; 'put Monks into my hands, and leave him to me to deal with.'

'What if he turns against the others?'

'I promise you that in that case, if the truth is forced from him, there the matter will rest; there must be circumstances in Oliver's little history which it would be painful to drag before the public eye, and if the truth is once elicited, they shall go scot free.'

'And if it is not?' suggested the girl.

'Then,' pursued the gentleman, 'this Fagin shall not be brought to justice without your consent. In such a case I could show you reasons, I think, which would induce you to yield it.'

'Have I the lady's promise for that?' asked the girl.

'You have,' replied Rose. 'My true and faithful pledge.'

'Monks would never learn how you knew what you do?' said the girl, after a short pause.

'Never,' replied the gentleman. 'The intelligence should be so brought to bear upon him, that he could never even guess.'

'I have been a liar, and among liars from a little child,' said the girl after another interval of silence, 'but I will take your words.'

After receiving an assurance from both, that she might safely do so, she proceeded in a voice so low that it was often difficult for the listener to discover even the purport of what she said, to describe, by name and situation, the public-house whence she had been followed that night. From the manner in which she occasionally paused, it appeared as if the gentleman were making some hasty notes of the information she communicated. When she had thoroughly explained the localities of the place, the best position from which to watch it without exciting observation, and the night and hour on which Monks was most in the habit of frequenting it, she seemed to consider for a few moments, for the purpose of recalling his features and appearance more forcibly to her recollection.

'He is tall,' said the girl, 'and a strongly made man, but not stout; he has a lurking walk; and as he walks, constantly looks over his shoulder, first on one side, and then on the other. Don't forget that, for his eyes are sunk in his head so much deeper than any other man's, that you might almost tell him by that alone. His face is dark, like his hair and eyes; and, although he can't be more than six or eight and twenty, withered and haggard. His lips are often discoloured and disfigured with the marks of teeth; for he has desperate fits, and sometimes even bites his hands and covers them with wounds—why did you start?' said the girl, stopping suddenly.

The gentleman replied, in a hurried manner, that he was not conscious of having done so, and begged her to proceed.

'Part of this,' said the girl, 'I've drawn out from other people at the house I tell you of, for I have only seen him twice, and both times he was covered up in a large cloak. I think that's all I can give you to know him by. Stay though,' she added. 'Upon his throat: so high that you can see a part of it below his neckerchief when he turns his face: there is—'

'A broad red mark, like a burn or scald?' cried the gentleman.

'How's this?' said the girl. 'You know him!'

The young lady uttered a cry of surprise, and for a few moments they were so still that the listener could distinctly hear them breathe.

'I think I do,' said the gentleman, breaking silence. 'I should by your description. We shall see. Many people are singularly like each other. It may not be the same.'

As he expressed himself to this effect, with assumed careless-ness, he took a step or two nearer the concealed spy, as the latter could tell from the distinctness with which he heard him mutter, 'It must be he!'

'Now,' he said, returning: so it seemed by the sound: to the spot where he had stood before, 'you have given us most valuable assistance, young woman, and I wish you to be the better for it. What can I do to serve you?'

'Nothing,' replied Nancy.

'You will not persist in saying that,' rejoined the gentleman, with a voice and emphasis of kindness that might have touched a much harder and more obdurate heart. 'Think now. Tell me.'

'Nothing, sir,' rejoined the girl, weeping. 'You can do nothing to help me. I am past all hope, indeed.'

'You put yourself beyond its pale,' said the gentleman. 'The past has been a dreary waste with you, of youthful energies mis-spent, and such priceless treasures lavished, as the Creator bestows but once and never grants again, but, for the future, you may hope. I do not say that it is in our power to offer you peace of heart and mind, for that must come as you seek it; but a quiet asylum, either in England, or, if you fear to remain here, in some foreign country, it is not only within the compass of our ability but our most anxious wish to secure you. Before the dawn of morning, before this river wakes to the first glimpse of daylight, you shall be placed as entirely beyond the reach of your former associates, and leave as utter an absence of all trace behind you, as if you were to disappear from the earth this moment. Come! I would not have you go back to exchange one word with any old companion, or take one look at any old haunt, or breathe the very air which is pestilence and death to you. Quit them all, while there is time and opportunity!'

'She will be persuaded now,' cried the young lady. 'She hesitates, I am sure.'

'I fear not, my dear,' said the gentleman.

'No, sir, I do not,' replied the girl, after a short struggle. 'I am chained to my old life. I loathe and hate it now, but I cannot leave it. I must have gone too far to turn back, —and yet I don't know, for if you had spoken to me so, some time ago, I should have laughed it off. But,' she said, looking hastily round, 'this fear comes over me again. I must go home.'

'Home!' repeated the young lady, with great stress upon the word.

'Home, lady,' rejoined the girl. 'To such a home as I have raised for myself with the work of my whole life. Let us part. I shall be watched or seen. Go! Go! If I have done you any service, all I ask is, that you leave me, and let me go my way alone.'

'It is useless,' said the gentleman, with a sigh. 'We compromise her safety, perhaps, by staying here. We may have detained her longer than she expected already.'

'Yes, yes,' urged the girl. 'You have.'

'What,' cried the young lady, 'can be the end of this poor creature's life!'

'What!' repeated the girl. 'Look before you, lady. Look at that dark water. How many times do you read of such as I who spring into the tide, and leave no living thing, to care for, or bewail them.

It may be years hence, or it may be only months, but I shall come to that at last.'

'Do not speak thus, pray,' returned the young lady, sobbing.

'It will never reach your ears, dear lady, and God forbid such horrors should!' replied the girl. 'Good night, good night!'

The gentleman turned away.

'This purse,' cried the young lady. 'Take it for my sake, that you may have some resource in an hour of need and trouble.'

'No!' replied the girl. 'I have not done this for money. Let me have that to think of. And yet—give me something that you have worn: I should like to have something—no, no, not a ring—your gloves or handkerchief—anything that I can keep, as having belonged to you, sweet lady. There. Bless you! God bless you! Good night, good night!'

The violent agitation of the girl, and the apprehension of some discovery which would subject her to ill-usage and violence, seemed to determine the gentleman to leave her, as she requested. The sound of retreating footsteps were audible, and the voices ceased.

The two figures of the young lady and her companion soon afterwards appeared upon the bridge. They stopped at the summit of the stairs.

'Hark!' cried the young lady, listening. 'Did she call! I thought I heard her voice.'

'No, my love,' replied Mr. Brownlow, looking sadly back. 'She has not moved, and will not till we are gone.'

Rose Maylie lingered, but the old gentleman drew her arm through his, and led her, with gentle force, away. As they disappeared, the girl sank down nearly at her full length upon one of the stone stairs, and vented the anguish of her heart in bitter tears.

After a time she arose, and with feeble and tottering steps ascended to the street. The astonished listener remained motionless on his post for some minutes afterwards, and having ascertained, with many cautious glances round him, that he was again alone, crept slowly from his hiding-place, and returned, stealthily and in the shade of the wall, in the same manner as he had descended.

Peeping out, more than once, when he reached the top, to make sure that he was unobserved, Noah Claypole darted away at his utmost speed, and made for the Jew's house as fast as his legs would carry him.

CHAPTER 47

Fatal consequences

It was nearly two hours before day-break; that time which, in the autumn of the year, may be truly called the dead of night; when the streets are silent and deserted; when even sounds appear to slumber, and profligacy and riot have staggered home to dream; it was at this still and silent hour, that Fagin sat watching in his old lair, with face so distorted and pale, and eyes so red and bloodshot, that he looked less like a man, than like some hideous phantom, moist from the grave, and worried by an evil spirit.

He sat crouching over a cold hearth, wrapped in an old torn coverlet, with his face turned towards a wasting candle that stood upon a table by his side. His right hand was raised to his lips, and as, absorbed in thought, he bit his long black nails, he disclosed among his toothless gums a few such fangs as should have been a dog's or rat's.

Stretched upon a mattress on the floor, lay Noah Claypole, fast asleep. Towards him the old man sometimes directed his eyes for an instant, and then brought them back again to the candle; which with a long-burnt wick drooping almost double, and hot grease falling down in clots upon the table, plainly showed that his thoughts were busy elsewhere.

Indeed they were. Mortification at the overthrow of his notable scheme; hatred of the girl who had dared to palter with strangers;

an utter distrust of the sincerity of her refusal to yield him up; bitter disappointment at the loss of his revenge on Sikes; the fear of detection, and ruin, and death; and a fierce and deadly rage kindled by all; these were the passionate considerations which, following close upon each other with rapid and ceaseless whirl, shot through the brain of Fagin, as every evil thought and blackest purpose lay working at his heart.

He sat without changing his attitude in the least, or appearing to take the smallest heed of time, until his quick ear seemed to be attracted by a footstep in the street.

'At last,' he muttered, wiping his dry and fevered mouth. 'At last!'

The bell rang gently as he spoke. He crept up stairs to the door, and presently returned accompanied by a man muffled to the chin, who carried a bundle under one arm. Sitting down and throwing back his outer coat, the man displayed the burly frame of Sikes.

'There!' he said, laying the bundle on the table. 'Take care of that, and do the most you can with it. It's been trouble enough to get; I thought I should have been here, three hours ago.'

Fagin laid his hand upon the bundle, and locking it in the cupboard, sat down again without speaking. But he did not take his eyes off the robber, for an instant, during this action; and now that they sat over against each other, face to face, he looked fixedly at him, with his lips quivering so violently, and his face so altered by the emotions which had mastered him, that the housebreaker involuntarily drew back his chair, and surveyed him with a look of real affright.

'Wot now?' cried Sikes. 'Wot do you look at a man so for?'

Fagin raised his right hand, and shook his trembling forefinger in the air; but his passion was so great, that the power of speech was for the moment gone.

'Damme!' said Sikes, feeling in his breast with a look of alarm. 'He's gone mad. I must look to myself here.'

'No, no,' rejoined Fagin, finding his voice. 'It's not—you're not the person, Bill. I've no—no fault to find with you.'

'Oh, you haven't, haven't you?' said Sikes, looking sternly at him, and ostentatiously passing a pistol into a more convenient pocket. 'That's lucky—for one of us. Which one that is, don't matter.'

'I've got that to tell you, Bill,' said Fagin, drawing his chair nearer, 'will make you worse than me.'

'Aye?' returned the robber with an incredulous air. 'Tell away! Look sharp, or Nance will think I'm lost.'

'Lost!' cried Fagin. 'She has pretty well settled that, in her own mind, already.'

Sikes looked with an aspect of great perplexity into the Jew's face, and reading no satisfactory explanation of the riddle there, clenched his coat collar in his huge hand and shook him soundly.

'Speak, will you!' he said; 'or if you don't, it shall be for want of breath. Open your mouth and say wot you've got to say in plain words. Out with it, you thundering old cur, out with it!'

'Suppose that lad that's lying there—' Fagin began.

Sikes turned round to where Noah was sleeping, as if he had not previously observed him. 'Well!' he said, resuming his former position.

'Suppose that lad,' pursued Fagin, 'was to peach—to blow upon us all—first seeking out the right folks for the purpose, and then having a meeting with 'em in the street to paint our likenesses, describe every mark that they might know us by, and the crib where we might be most easily taken. Suppose he was to do all this, and besides to blow upon a plant we've all been in, more or less—of his own fancy; not grabbed, trapped, tried, ear wigged by the parson and brought to it on bread and water, —but of his own fancy; to please his own taste; stealing out at nights to find those most inter-ested against us, and peaching to them. Do you hear me?' cried the Jew, his eyes flashing with rage. 'Suppose he did all this, what then?'

'What then!' replied Sikes; with a tremendous oath. 'If he was left alive till I came, I'd grind his skull under the iron heel of my boot into as many grains as there are hairs upon his head.'

'What if *I* did it!' cried Fagin almost in a yell. '*I*, that know so much, and could hang so many besides myself!'

'I don't know,' replied Sikes, clenching his teeth and turning white at the mere suggestion. 'I'd do something in the jail that 'ud get me put in irons; and if I was tried along with you, I'd fall upon you with them in the open court, and beat your brains out afore the people. I should have such strength,' muttered the robber, poising his brawny arm, 'that I could smash your head as if a loaded waggon had gone over it.'

'You would?'

'Would I!' said the housebreaker. 'Try me.'

'If it was Charley, or the Dodger, or Bet, or—'

'I don't care who,' replied Sikes impatiently. 'Whoever it was, I'd serve them the same.'

Fagin looked hard at the robber; and, motioning him to be silent, stooped over the bed upon the floor, and shook the sleeper to rouse him. Sikes leant forward in his chair: looking on with his hands upon his knees, as if wondering much what all this questioning and preparation was to end in.

'Bolter, Bolter! Poor lad!' said Fagin, looking up with an expression of devilish anticipation, and speaking slowly and with marked emphasis. 'He's tired—tired with watching for *her* so long, —watching for *her*, Bill.'

'Wot d'ye mean?' asked Sikes, drawing back.

Fagin made no answer, but bending over the sleeper again, hauled him into a sitting posture. When his assumed name had been repeated several times, Noah rubbed his eyes, and, giving a heavy yawn, looked sleepily about him.

'Tell me that again—once again, just for him to hear,' said the Jew, pointing to Sikes as he spoke.

'Tell yer what?' asked the sleepy Noah, shaking himself pettishly.

'That about—Nancy,' said Fagin, clutching Sikes by the wrist, as if to prevent his leaving the house before he had heard enough. 'You followed her?'

'Yes.'

'To London Bridge?'

'Yes.'

'Where she met two people?'

'So she did.'

'A gentleman and a lady that she had gone to of her own accord before, who asked her to give up all her pals, and Monks first, which she did—and to describe him, which she did—and to tell her what house it was that we meet at, and go to, which she did—and where it could be best watched from, which she did—and what time the people went there, which she did. She did all this. She told it all every word without a threat, without a murmur—she did—did she not?' cried Fagin, half mad with fury.

'All right,' replied Noah, scratching his head. 'That's just what it was!'

'What did they say, about last Sunday?'

'About last Sunday!' replied Noah, considering. 'Why, I told yer that before.'

'Again. Tell it again!' cried Fagin, tightening his grasp on Sikes, and brandishing his other hand aloft, as the foam flew from his lips.

'They asked her,' said Noah, who, as he grew more wakeful, seemed to have a dawning perception who Sikes was, 'they asked her why she didn't come, last Sunday, as she promised. She said she couldn't.'

'Why—why? Tell him that.'

'Because she was forcibly kept at home by Bill, the man she had told them of before,' replied Noah.

'What more of him?' cried Fagin. 'What more of the man she had told them of before? Tell him that, tell him that.'

'Why, that she couldn't very easily get out of doors unless he knew where she was going to,' said Noah; 'and so the first time she went to see the lady, she—ha! ha! ha! it made me laugh when she said it, that it did—she gave him a drink of laudanum.'

'Hell's fire!' cried Sikes, breaking fiercely from the Jew. 'Let me go!'

Flinging the old man from him, he rushed from the room, and darted, wildly and furiously, up the stairs.

'Bill, Bill!' cried Fagin, following him hastily. 'A word. Only a word.'

The word would not have been exchanged, but that the house-breaker was unable to open the door: on which he was expending fruitless oaths and violence, when the Jew came panting up.

'Let me out,' said Sikes. 'Don't speak to me; it's not safe. Let me out, I say!'

'Here me speak a word,' rejoined Fagin, laying his hand upon the lock. 'You won't be—'

'Well,' replied the other.

'You won't be—too—violent, Bill?'

The day was breaking, and there was light enough for the men to see each other's faces. They exchanged one brief glance; there was a fire in the eyes of both, which could not be mistaken.

'I mean,' said Fagin, showing that he felt all disguise was now useless, 'not too violent for safety. Be crafty, Bill, and not too bold.'

Sikes made no reply; but, pulling open the door, of which Fagin had turned the lock, dashed into the silent streets.

Without one pause, or moment's consideration; without once turning his head to the right or left, or raising his eyes to the sky, or lowering them to the ground, but looking straight before him with savage resolution: his teeth so tightly compressed that the strained jaw seemed starting through his skin; the robber held on his headlong course, nor muttered a word, nor relaxed a muscle, until he reached his own door. He opened it, softly, with a key; strode lightly up the stairs; and entering his own room, double-locked the door, and lifting a heavy table against it, drew back the curtain of the bed.

The girl was lying, half-dressed, upon it. He had roused her from her sleep, for she raised herself with a hurried and startled look.

'Get up!' said the man.

'It *is* you, Bill!' said the girl, with an expression of pleasure at his return.

'It is,' was the reply. 'Get up.'

There was a candle burning, but the man hastily drew it from the candlestick, and hurled it under the grate. Seeing the faint light of early day without, the girl rose to undraw the curtain.

'Let it be,' said Sikes, thrusting his hand before her. 'There's light enough for wot I've got to do.'

'Bill,' said the girl, in the low voice of alarm, 'why do you look like that at me!'

The robber sat regarding her, for a few seconds, with dilated nostrils and heaving breast; and then, grasping her by the head and throat, dragged her into the middle of the room, and looking once towards the door, placed his heavy hand upon her mouth.

'Bill, Bill!' gasped the girl, wrestling with the strength of mortal fear,—'I—I won't scream or cry—not once—hear me—speak to me—tell me what I have done!'

'You know, you she devil!' returned the robber, suppressing his breath. 'You were watched to-night; every word you said was heard.'

'Then spare my life for the love of Heaven, as I spared yours,' rejoined the girl, clinging to him. 'Bill, dear Bill, you cannot have the heart to kill me. Oh! think of all I have given up, only this one night, for you. You *shall* have time to think, and save yourself this crime; I will not loose my hold, you cannot throw me off. Bill, Bill, for dear God's sake, for your own, for mine, stop before you spill my blood! I have been true to you, upon my guilty soul I have!'

The man struggled violently, to release his arms; but those of the girl were clasped round his, and tear her as he would, he could not tear them away.

'Bill,' cried the girl, striving to lay her head upon his breast, 'the gentleman and that dear lady, told me tonight of a home in some foreign country where I could end my days in solitude and peace. Let me see them again, and beg them, on my knees, to show the same mercy and goodness to you; and let us both leave this dreadful place, and far apart lead better lives, and forget how we have lived, except in prayers, and never see each other more. It is never too late to repent. They told me so—I feel it now—but we must have time—a little, little time!'

The housebreaker freed one arm, and grasped his pistol. The certainty of immediate detection if he fired, flashed across his mind even in the midst of his fury; and he beat it twice with all the force he could summon, upon the upturned face that almost touched his own.

She staggered and fell: nearly blinded with the blood that rained down from a deep gash in her forehead; but raising herself, with difficulty, on her knees, drew from her bosom a white handkerchief—Rose Maylie's own—and holding it up, in her folded hands, as high towards Heaven as her feeble strength would allow, breathed one prayer for mercy to her Maker.

It was a ghastly figure to look upon. The murderer staggering backward to the wall, and shutting out the sight with his hand, seized a heavy club and struck her down.

CHAPTER 48

The flight of Sikes

Of all bad deeds that, under cover of the darkness, had been committed within wide London's bounds since night hung over it, that was the worst. Of all the horrors that rose with an ill scent upon the morning air, that was the foulest and most cruel.

The sun—the bright sun, that brings back, not light alone, but new life, and hope, and freshness to man—burst upon the crowded city in clear and radiant glory. Through costly-coloured glass and paper-mended window, through cathedral dome and rotten crevice, it shed its equal ray. It lighted up the room where the murdered woman lay. It did. He tried to shut it out, but it would stream in. If the sight had been a ghastly one in the dull morning, what was it, now, in all that brilliant light!

He had not moved; he had been afraid to stir. There had been a moan and motion of the hand; and, with terror added to rage, he had struck and struck again. Once he threw a rug over it; but it was worse to fancy the eyes, and imagine them moving towards him, than to see them glaring upward, as if watching the reflection of the pool of gore that quivered and danced in the sunlight on the ceiling. He had plucked it off again. And there was the body—mere flesh and blood, no more—but such flesh, and so much blood!

He struck a light, kindled a fire, and thrust the club into it. There was hair upon the end, which blazed and shrunk into a light cinder, and, caught by the air, whirled up the chimney. Even that frightened him, sturdy as he was; but he held the weapon till it broke, and then piled it on the coals to burn away, and smoulder into ashes. He washed himself, and rubbed his clothes; there were spots that would not be removed, but he cut the pieces out, and burnt them. How those stains were dispersed about the room! The very feet of the dog were bloody.

All this time he had, never once, turned his back upon the corpse; no, not for a moment. Such preparations completed, he moved, backward, towards the door: dragging the dog with him, lest he should soil his feet anew and carry out new evidences of the crime into the streets. He shut the door softly, locked it, took the key, and left the house.

He crossed over, and glanced up at the window, to be sure that nothing was visible from the outside. There was the curtain still drawn, which she would have opened to admit the light she never saw again. It lay nearly under there. *He* knew that. God, how the sun poured down upon the very spot!

The glance was instantaneous. It was a relief to have got free of the room. He whistled on the dog, and walked rapidly away.

He went through Islington; strode up the hill at Highgate on which stands the stone in honour of Whittington; turned down to Highgate Hill, unsteady of purpose, and uncertain where to go; struck off to the right again, almost as soon as he began to descend it; and taking the foot-path across the fields, skirted Caen Wood, and so came out on Hampstead Heath. Traversing the hollow by the Vale of Health, he mounted the opposite bank, and crossing the road which joins the villages of Hampstead and Highgate, made along the remaining portion of the heath to the fields at North End, in one of which he laid himself down under a hedge, and slept.

Soon he was up again, and away—not far into the country, but back towards London by the high-road—then back again—then over another part of the same ground as he already traversed—then wandering up and down in fields, and lying on ditches' brinks to rest, and starting up to make for some other spot, and do the same, and ramble on again.

Where could he go, that was near and not too public, to get some meat and drink? Hendon. That was a good place, not far off, and out of most people's way. Thither he directed his steps,—running sometimes, and sometimes, with a strange perversity, loitering at a snail's pace, or stopping altogether and idly breaking the hedges with his stick. But when he got there, all the people he met—the very children at the doors—seemed to view him with suspicion. Back he turned again, without the courage to purchase bit or drop, though he had tasted no food for many hours; and once more he lingered on the Heath, uncertain where to go.

He wandered over miles and miles of ground, and still came back to the old place. Morning and noon had passed, and the day was on the wane, and still he rambled to and fro, and up and down, and round and round, and still lingered about the same spot. At last he got away, and shaped his course for Hatfield.

It was nine o'clock at night, when the man, quite tired out, and the dog, limping and lame from the unaccustomed exercise, turned down the hill by the church of the quiet village, and plodding along the little street, crept into a small public-house, whose scanty light had guided them to the spot. There was a fire in the taproom, and some country-labourers were drinking before it. They made room for the stranger, but he sat down in the furthest corner, and ate and drank alone, or rather with his dog: to whom he cast a morsel of food from time to time.

The conversation of the men assembled here, turned upon the neighbouring land, and farmers; and when those topics were exhausted, upon the age of some old man who had been buried on the previous Sunday: the young men present considering him very old, and the old men present declaring him to have been quite young—not older, one white-haired grandfather said, than he was—with ten or fifteen year of life in him at least—if he had taken care; if he had taken care.

There was nothing to attract attention, or excite alarm in this.

The robber, after paying his reckoning, sat silent and unnoticed in his corner, and had almost dropped asleep, when he was half wakened by the noisy entrance of a new-comer.

This was an antic fellow, half pedlar and half mountebank, who travelled about the country on foot to vend hones, strops, razors, wash-balls, harness-paste, medicine for dogs and horses, cheap perfumery, cosmetics, and such-like wares, which he carried in a case slung to his back. His entrance was the signal for various homely jokes with the countrymen, which slackened not until he had made his supper, and opened his box of treasures, when he ingeniously contrived to unite business with amusement.

'And what be that stoof? Good to eat, Harry?' asked a grinning countryman, pointing to some composition-cakes in one corner.

'This,' said the fellow, producing one, 'this is the infallible and invaluable composition for removing all sorts of stain, rust, dirt, mildew, spick, speck, spot, or spatter, from silk, satin, linen, cambric, cloth, crape, stuff, carpet, merino, muslin, bombazeen, or woollen stuff. Wine-stains, fruit-stains, beer-stains, water-stains, paint-stains, pitch-stains, any stains, all come out at one rub with the infallible and invaluable composition. If a lady stains her honour, she has only need to swallow one cake and she's cured at once—for it's poison. If a gentleman wants to prove this, he has only need to bolt one little square, and he has put it beyond question—for it's quite as satisfactory as a pistol-bullet, and a great deal nastier in the flavour, consequently the more credit in taking it. One penny a square. With all these virtues, one penny a square!'

There were two buyers directly, and more of the listeners plainly hesitated. The vendor observing this, increased in loquacity.

'It's all bought up as fast as it can be made,' said the fellow. 'There are fourteen water-mills, six steam-engines, and a galvanic battery, always a-working upon it, and they can't make it fast enough, though the men work so hard that they die off, and the widows is pensioned directly, with twenty pound a-year for each of the children, and a premium of fifty for twins. One penny a square! Two halfpence is all the same, and four farthings is received with joy.

One penny a square! Wine-stains, fruit-stains, beer-stains, water-stains, paint-stains, pitch-stains, mud-stains, blood-stains! Here is a stain upon the hat of a gentleman in company, that I'll take clean out, before he can order me a pint of ale.'

'Hah!' cried Sikes starting up. 'Give that back.'

'I'll take it clean out, sir,' replied the man, winking to the company, 'before you can come across the room to get it. Gentlemen all, observe the dark stain upon this gentleman's hat, no wider than a shilling, but thicker than a half-crown. Whether it is a wine-stain, fruit-stain, beer-stain, water-stain, paint-stain, pitch-stain, mud-stain, or blood-stain—'

The man got no further, for Sikes with a hideous imprecation overthrew the table, and tearing the hat from him, burst out of the house.

With the same perversity of feeling and irresolution that had fastened upon him, despite himself, all day, the murderer, finding that he was not followed, and that they most probably considered him some drunken sullen fellow, turned back up the town, and getting out of the glare of the lamps of a stage-coach that was standing in the street, was walking past, when he recognised the mail from London, and saw that it was standing at the little post-office. He almost knew what was to come; but he crossed over, and listened.

The guard was standing at the door, waiting for the letter-bag. A man, dressed like a gamekeeper, came up at the moment, and he handed him a basket which lay ready on the pavement.

'That's for your people,' said the guard. 'Now, look alive in there, will you. Damn that 'ere bag, it warn't ready night afore last; this won't do, you know!'

'Anything new up in town, Ben?' asked the gamekeeper, drawing back to the window-shutters, the better to admire the horses.

'No, nothing that I knows on,' replied the man, pulling on his gloves. 'Corn's up a little. I heerd talk of a murder, too, down Spitalfields way, but I don't reckon much upon it.'

'Oh, that's quite true,' said a gentleman inside, who was looking out of the window. 'And a dreadful murder it was.'

'Was it, sir?' rejoined the guard, touching his hat. 'Man or woman, pray, sir?'

'A woman,' replied the gentleman. 'It is supposed—'

'Now, Ben,' replied the coachman impatiently.

'Damn that 'ere bag,' said the guard; 'are you gone to sleep in there?'

'Coming!' cried the office-keeper, running out.

'Coming,' growled the guard. 'Ah, and so's the young 'ooman of property that's going to take a fancy to me, but I don't know when. Here, give hold. All ri—ight!'

The horn sounded a few cheerful notes, and the coach was gone.

Sikes remained standing in the street, apparently unmoved by what he had just heard, and agitated by no stronger feeling than a doubt where to go. At length he went back again, and took the road which leads from Hatfield to St. Albans.

He went on doggedly; but as he left the town behind him, and plunged into the solitude and darkness of the road, he felt a dread and awe creeping upon him which shook him to the core. Every object before him, substance or shadow, still or moving, took the semblance of some fearful thing; but these fears were nothing compared to the sense that haunted him of that morning's ghastly figure following at his heels. He could trace its shadow in the gloom, supply the smallest item of the outline, and note how stiff and solemn it seemed to stalk along. He could hear its garments rustling in the leaves, and every breath of wind came laden with that last low cry. If he stopped it did the same. If he ran, it followed—not running too: that would have been a relief: but like a corpse endowed with the mere machinery of life, and borne on one slow melancholy wind that never rose or fell.

At times, he turned, with desperate determination, resolved to beat this phantom off, though it should look him dead; but the hair rose on his head, and his blood stood still, for it had turned with him and was behind him then. He had kept it before him that morning, but it was behind now—always. He leaned his back against a bank, and felt that it stood above him, visibly out against the cold night-sky. He threw himself upon the road—on his back upon the road. At his head it stood, silent, erect, and still—a living grave-stone, with its epitaph in blood.

Let no man talk of murderers escaping justice, and hint that Providence must sleep. There were twenty score of violent deaths in one long minute of that agony of fear.

There was a shed in a field he passed, that offered shelter for the night. Before the door, were three tall poplar trees, which made it very dark within; and the wind moaned through them with a dismal wail. He *could not* walk on, till daylight came again; and here he stretched himself close to the wall—to undergo new torture.

For now, a vision came before him, as constant and more terrible than that from which he had escaped. Those widely staring eyes, so lustreless and so glassy, that he had better borne to see them than think upon them, appeared in the midst of the darkness: light in themselves, but giving light to nothing. There were but two, but they were everywhere. If he shut out the sight, there came the room with every well-known object—some, indeed, that he would have forgotten, if he had gone over its contents from memory—each in its accustomed place. The body was in *its* place, and its eyes were as he saw them when he stole away. He got up, and rushed into the field without. The figure was behind him. He re-entered the shed, and shrunk down once more. The eyes were there, before he had laid himself along.

And here he remained in such terror as none but he can know, trembling in every limb, and the cold sweat starting from every pore, when suddenly there arose upon the night-wind the noise of distant shouting, and the roar of voices mingled in alarm and wonder. Any sound of men in that lonely place, even though it conveyed a real cause of alarm, was something to him. He regained his strength and energy at the prospect of personal danger; and springing to his feet, rushed into the open air.

The broad sky seemed on fire. Rising into the air with showers of sparks, and rolling one above the other, were sheets of flame, lighting the atmosphere for miles round, and driving clouds of smoke in the direction where he stood. The shouts grew louder as new voices swelled the roar, and he could hear the cry of Fire! mingled with the ringing of an alarm-bell, the fall of heavy bodies, and the crackling of flames as they twined round some new obstacle, and shot aloft as though refreshed by food. The noise increased as he looked. There were people there—men and women—light, bustle. It was like new life to him. He darted onward—straight, headlong—dashing through brier and brake, and leaping gate and fence as madly as his dog, who careered with loud and sounding bark before him.

He came upon the spot. There were half-dressed figures tearing to and fro, some endeavouring to drag the frightened horses from the stables, others driving the cattle from the yard and out-houses, and others coming laden from the burning pile, amidst a shower of falling sparks, and the tumbling down of red-hot beams. The apertures, where doors and windows stood an hour ago, disclosed a mass of raging fire; walls rocked and crumbled into the burning well; the molten lead and iron poured down, white hot, upon the ground. Women and children shrieked, and men encouraged each other with noisy shouts and cheers. The clanking of the engine-pumps, and the spirting and hissing of the water as it fell upon the blazing wood, added to the tremendous roar. He shouted, too, till he was hoarse; and flying from memory and himself, plunged into the thickest of the throng.

Hither and thither he dived that night: now working at the pumps, and now hurrying through the smoke and flame, but never ceasing to engage himself wherever noise and men were thickest. Up and down the ladders, upon the roofs of buildings, over floors that quaked and trembled with his weight, under the lee of falling bricks and stones, in every part of that great fire was he; but he bore a charmed life, and had neither scratch nor bruise, nor weariness nor thought, till morning dawned again, and only smoke and blackened ruins remained.

This mad excitement over, there returned, with tenfold force, the dreadful consciousness of his crime. He looked suspiciously about him, for the men were conversing in groups, and he feared to be the subject of their talk. The dog obeyed the significant beck of his finger, and they drew off, stealthily, together. He passed near an engine where some men were seated, and they called to him to share in their refreshment. He took some bread and meat; and as he drank a draught of beer, heard the firemen, who were from London, talking about the murder. 'He has gone to Birmingham, they say,' said one: 'but they'll have him yet, for the scouts are out, and by tomorrow night there'll be a cry all through the country.'

He hurried off, and walked till he almost dropped upon the ground; then lay down in a lane, and had a long, but broken and uneasy sleep. He wandered on again, irresolute and undecided, and oppressed with the fear of another solitary night.

Suddenly, he took the desperate resolution of going back to London.

'There's somebody to speak to there, at all events,' he thought. 'A good hiding-place, too. They'll never expect to nab me there, after this country scent. Why can't I lie by for a week or so, and, forcing blunt from Fagin, get abroad to France? Damme, I'll risk it.'

He acted upon this impulse without delay, and choosing the least frequented roads began his journey back, resolved to lie concealed within a short distance of the metropolis, and, entering it at dusk by a circuitous route, to proceed straight to that part of it which he had fixed on for his destination.

The dog, though. If any descriptions of him were out, it would not be forgotten that the dog was missing, and had probably gone with him. This might lead to his apprehension as he passed along the streets. He resolved to drown him, and walked on, looking about for a pond: picking up a heavy stone and tying it to his handkerchief as he went.

The animal looked up into his master's face while these preparations were making; whether his instinct apprehended something of their purpose, or the robber's sidelong look at him was sterner than ordinary, he skulked a little farther in the rear than usual, and cowered as he came more slowly along. When his master halted at the brink of a pool, and looked round to call him, he stopped outright.

'Do you hear me call? Come here!' cried Sikes.

The animal came up from the very force of habit; but as Sikes stooped to attach the handkerchief to his throat, he uttered a low growl and started back.

'Come back!' said the robber.

The dog wagged his tail, but moved not. Sikes made a running noose and called him again.

The dog advanced, retreated, paused an instant, turned, and scoured away at his hardest speed.

The man whistled again and again, and sat down and waited in the expectation that he would return. But no dog appeared, and at length he resumed his journey.

CHAPTER 49

Monks and Mr. Brownlow at length meet.
Thir conversation, and the intelligence that
interrupts it

The twilight was beginning to close in, when Mr. Brownlow alighted
from a hackney-coach at his own door, and knocked softly. The door
being opened, a sturdy man got out of the coach and stationed
himself on one side of the steps, while another man, who had been
seated on the box, dismounted too, and stood upon the other side.
At a sign from Mr. Brownlow, they helped out a third man, and
taking him between them, hurried him into the house. This man
was Monks.

They walked in the same manner up the stairs without
speaking, and Mr. Brownlow, preceding them, led the way into a
back-room. At the door of this apartment. Monks, who had ascended
with evident reluctance, stopped. The two men looked to the old
gentleman as if for instructions.

'He knows the alternative,' said Mr. Brownlow. 'If he hesitates or moves a finger but as you bid him, drag him into the street,
call for the aid of the police, and impeach him as a felon in my
name.'

'How dare you say this of me?' asked Monks.

'How dare you urge me to it, young man?' replied Mr. Brownlow,
confronting him with a steady look. 'Are you mad enough to leave
this house? Unhand him. There, sir. You are free to go, and we to
follow. But I warn you, by all I hold most solemn and most sacred,

that the instant you set foot in the street, that instant will I have you apprehended on a charge of fraud and robbery. I am resolute and immoveable. If you are determined to be the same, your blood be upon your own head!'

'By what authority am I kidnapped in the street, and brought here by these dogs?' asked Monks, looking from one to the other of the men who stood beside him.

'By mine,' replied Mr. Brownlow. 'Those persons are indemnified by me. If you complain of being deprived of your liberty—you had power and opportunity to retrieve it as you came along, but you deemed it advisable to remain quiet—I say again, throw yourself for protection on the law. I will appeal to the law too; but when you have gone too far to recede, do not sue to me for leniency, when the power will have passed into other hands; and do not say I plunged you down the gulf into which you rushed yourself.'

Monks was plainly disconcerted, and alarmed besides. He hesitated.

'You will decide quickly,' said Mr. Brownlow, with perfect firmness and composure. 'If you wish me to prefer my charges publicly, and consign you to a punishment the extent of which, although I can, with a shudder, foresee, I cannot control, once more, I say, you know the way. If not, and you appeal to my forbearance, and the mercy of those you have deeply injured, seat yourself, without a word, in that chair. It has waited for you two whole days.'

Monks muttered some unintelligible words, but wavered still.

'You will be prompt,' said Mr. Brownlow. 'A word from me, and the alternative has gone for ever.'

Still the man hesitated.

'I have not the inclination to parley,' said Mr. Brownlow, 'and, as I advocate the dearest interests of others, I have not the right.'

'Is there—' demanded Monks with a faltering tongue,—'is there—no middle course?'

'None.'

Monks looked at the old gentleman, with an anxious eye; but, reading in his countenance nothing but severity and determination, walked into the room, and, shrugging his shoulders, sat down.

'Lock the door on the outside,' said Mr. Brownlow to the attendants, 'and come when I ring.'

The men obeyed, and the two were left alone together.

'This is pretty treatment, sir,' said Monks, throwing down his hat and cloak, 'from my father's oldest friend.'

'It is because I was your father's oldest friend, young man,' returned Mr. Brownlow; 'it is because the hopes and wishes of young and happy years were bound up with him, and that fair creature of his blood and kindred who rejoined her God in youth, and left me here a solitary, lonely man: it is because he knelt with me beside his only sister's death-bed when he was yet a boy, on the morning that would—but Heaven willed otherwise—have made her my young wife; it is because my seared heart clung to him, from that time forth, through all his trials and errors, till he died; it is because old recollections and associations filled my heart, and even the sight of you brings with it old thoughts of him; it is because of all these things that I am moved to treat you gently now—yes, Edward Leeford, even now—and blush for your unworthiness who bear the name.'

'What has the name to do with it?' asked the other, after contemplating, half in silence, and half in dogged wonder, the agitation of his companion. 'What is the name to me?'

'Nothing,' replied Mr. Brownlow, 'nothing to you. But it was *hers,* and even at this distance of time brings back to me, an old man, the glow and thrill which I once felt, only to hear it repeated by a stranger. I am very glad you have changed it—very—very.'

'This is all mighty fine,' said Monks (to retain his assumed designation) after a long silence, during which he had jerked himself in sullen defiance to and fro, and Mr. Brownlow had sat, shading his face with his hand. 'But what do you want with me?'

'You have a brother,' said Mr. Brownlow, rousing himself: 'a brother, the whisper of whose name in your ear when I came behind you in the street, was, in itself, almost enough to make you accompany me hither, in wonder and alarm.'

'I have no brother,' replied Monks. 'You know I was an only child. Why do you talk to me of brothers? You know that, as well as I.'

'Attend to what I do know, and you may not,' said Mr. Brownlow. 'I shall interest you by and by. I know that of the wretched marriage, into which family pride, and the most sordid and narrowest of all ambition, forced your unhappy father when a mere boy, you were the sole and most unnatural issue.'

'I don't care for hard names,' interrupted Monks with a jeering laugh. 'You know the fact, and that's enough for me.'

'But I also know,' pursued the old gentleman, 'the misery, the slow torture, the protracted anguish of that ill-assorted union. I know how listlessly and wearily each of that wretched pair dragged on their heavy chain through a world that was poisoned to them both. I know how cold formalities were succeeded by open taunts; how indifference gave place to dislike, dislike to hate, and hate to loathing, until at last they wrenched the clanking bond asunder, and retiring a wide space apart, carried each a galling fragment, of which nothing but death could break the rivets, to hide it in new society beneath the gayest looks they could assume. Your mother succeeded; she forgot it soon. But it rusted and cankered at your father's heart for years.'

'Well, they were separated,' said Monks, 'and what of that?'

'When they had been separated for some time,' returned Mr. Brownlow, 'and your mother, wholly given up to continental frivolities, had utterly forgotten the young husband ten good years her junior, who, with prospects blighted, lingered on at home, he fell among new friends. *This* circumstance, at least, you know already.'

'Not I,' said Monks, turning away his eyes and beating his foot upon the ground, as a man who is determined to deny everything. 'Not I.'

'Your manner, no less than your actions, assures me that you have never forgotten it, or ceased to think of it with bitterness,' returned Mr. Brownlow. 'I speak of fifteen years ago, when you were not more than eleven years old, and your father but one-and-thirty—for he was,

I repeat, a boy, when *his* father ordered him to marry. Must I go back to events which cast a shade upon the memory of your parent, or will you spare it, and disclose to me the truth?'

'I have nothing to disclose,' rejoined Monks. 'You must talk on if you will.'

'These new friends, then,' said Mr. Brownlow, 'were a naval officer retired from active service, whose wife had died some half-a-year before, and left him with two children —there had been more, but, of all their family, happily but two survived. They were both daughters; one a beautiful creature of nineteen, and the other a mere child of two or three years old.'

'What's this to me?' asked Monks.

'They resided,' said Mr. Brownlow, without seeming to hear the interruption, 'in a part of the country to which your father in his wandering had repaired, and where he had taken up his abode. Acquaintance, intimacy, friendship, fast followed on each other. Your father was gifted as few men are. He had his sister's soul and person. As the old officer knew him more and more, he grew to love him. I would that it had ended there. His daughter did the same.'

The old gentleman paused; Monks was biting his lips, with his eyes fixed upon the floor; seeing this, he immediately resumed:

'The end of a year found him contracted, solemnly contracted, to that daughter; the object of the first, true, ardent, only passion of a guileless girl.'

'Your tale is of the longest,' observed Monks, moving restlessly in his chair.

'It is a true tale of grief and trial, and sorrow, young man,' returned Mr. Brownlow, 'and such tales usually are; if it were one of unmixed joy and happiness, it would be very brief. At length one of those rich relations to strengthen whose interest and importance your father had been sacrificed, as others are often—it is no uncommon case—died, and to repair the misery he had been instrumental in occasioning, left him *his* panacea for all griefs—Money. It was necessary that he should immediately repair to Rome, whither this man had sped for health, and where he had died, leaving his affairs in great confusion. He went; was seized with mortal illness there; was followed, the moment the intelligence reached Paris, by your mother who carried you with her; he died the day after her arrival, leaving no will—*no will*—so that the whole property fell to her and you.'

At this part of the recital Monks held his breath, and listened with a face of intense eagerness, though his eyes were not directed towards the speaker. As Mr. Brownlow paused, he changed his position with the air of one who has experienced a sudden relief, and wiped his hot face and hands.

'Before he went abroad, and as he passed through London on his way,' said Mr. Brownlow, slowly, and fixing his eyes upon the other's face, 'he came to me.'

'I never heard of that,' interrupted Monks in a tone intended to appear incredulous, but savouring more of disagreeable surprise.

'He came to me, and left with me, among some other things, a picture—a portrait painted by himself—a likeness of this poor girl—which he did not wish to leave behind, and could not carry forward on his hasty journey. He was worn by anxiety and remorse almost to a shadow; talked in a wild, distracted way, of ruin and dishonour worked by himself; confided to me his intention to convert his whole property, at any loss, into money, and, having settled on his wife and you a portion of his recent acquisition, to fly the country—I guessed too well he would not fly alone—and never see it more. Even from me, his old and early friend, whose strong attachment had taken root in the earth that covered one most clear to both —even from me he withheld any more particular confession, promising to write and tell me all, and after that to see me once again, for the last time on earth. Alas! *That* was the last time. I had no letter, and I never saw him more.

'I went,' said Mr. Brownlow, after a short pause, 'I went, when all was over, to the scene of his—I will use the term the world would freely use, for worldly harshness or favour are now alike to him—of his guilty love, resolved that if my fears were realised that erring child should find one heart and home to shelter and compassionate her. The family had left that part a week before; they had called in such trifling debts as were outstanding, discharged them, and left the place by night. Why, or whither, none can tell.'

Monks drew his breath yet more freely, and looked round with a smile of triumph.

'When your brother,' said Mr. Brownlow, drawing nearer to the other's chair, 'when your brother: a feeble, ragged, neglected child: was cast in my way by a stronger hand than chance, and rescued by me from a life of vice and infamy—'

'What?' cried Monks.

'By me,' said Mr. Brownlow. 'I told you I should interest you before long. I say by me—I see that your cunning associate suppressed my name, although for aught he knew, it would be quite strange to your ears. When he was rescued by me, then, and lay recovering from sickness in my house, his strong resemblance to this picture I have spoken of, struck me with astonishment. Even when I first saw him in all his dirt and misery, there was a lingering expression in his face that came upon me like a glimpse of some old friend flashing on one in a vivid dream. I need not tell you he was snared away before I knew his history—'

'Why not?' asked Monks hastily.

'Because you know it well.'

'I!'

'Denial to me is vain,' replied Mr. Brownlow. 'I shall show you that I know more than that.'

'You—you—can't prove anything against me,' stammered Monks. 'I defy you to do it!'

'We shall see,' returned the old gentleman with a searching glance. 'I lost the boy, and no efforts of mine could recover him. Your mother being dead, I knew that you alone could solve the mystery if anybody could, and as when I had last heard of you you were on your own estate in the West Indies—whither, as you well know, you retired upon your mother's death to escape the conse- quences of vicious courses here—I made the voyage. You had left it, months before, and were supposed to be in London, but no one could tell where. I returned. Your agents had no clue to your residence. You came and went, they said, as strangely as you had ever done: sometimes for days together and sometimes not for months: keeping to all appearance the same low haunts and mingling with the same infamous herd who had been your associates when a fierce ungovernable boy. I wearied them with new applications. I paced the streets by night and day, but until two hours ago all my efforts were fruitless, and I never saw you for an instant.'

'And now you do see me,' said Monks, rising boldly, 'what then? Fraud, and robbery are high-sounding words—justified, you think, by a fancied resemblance in some young imp to an idle daub of a dead man's. Brother! You don't even know that a child was born of this maudlin pair; you don't even know that.'

'*I did not*,' replied Mr. Brownlow, rising too; 'but within the last fortnight I have learnt it all. You have a brother; you know it, and him. There was a will, which your mother destroyed, leaving the secret and the gain to you at her own death. It contained a reference to some child likely to be the result of this sad connection, which child was born, and accidentally encountered by you, when your suspicions were first awakened by his resemblance to his father. You repaired to the place of his birth. There existed proofs—proofs long suppressed—of his birth and parentage. Those proofs were destroyed by you, and now, in your own words to your accomplice the Jew, *"the only proofs of the boy's identity lie at the bottom of the river, and the old hag that received them from the mother is rotting in her coffin."* Unworthy son, coward, liar,—you, who hold your councils with thieves and murderers in dark rooms at night,—you, whose plots and wiles have brought a violent death upon the head of one worth millions such as you,—you, who from your cradle were gall and bitterness to your own father's heart, and in whom all evil passions, vice, and profligacy, festered, till they found a vent in a hideous disease which has made your face an index even to your mind—you, Edward Leeford, do you still brave me!'

'No, no, no!' returned the coward, overwhelmed by these accumulated charges.

'Every word!' cried the old gentleman, 'every word that has passed between you and this detested villain, is known to me. Shadows on the wall have caught your whispers, and brought them to my ear; the sight of the persecuted child has turned vice itself, and given it the courage and almost the attribute of virtue. Murder has been done, to which you were morally if not really a party.'

'No, no,' interposed Monks. 'I—I—know nothing of that; I was going to inquire the truth of the story when you overtook me. I didn't know the cause. I thought it was a common quarrel.'

'It was the partial disclosure of your secrets,' replied Mr. Brownlow. 'Will you disclose the whole?'

'Yes, I will.'

'Set your hand to a statement of truth and facts, and repeat it before witnesses?'

'That I promise too.'

'Remain quietly here, until such a document is drawn up, and proceed with me to such a place as I may deem most advisable, for the purpose of attesting it?'

'If you insist upon that, I'll do that also,' replied Monks.

'You must do more than that,' said Mr. Brownlow. 'Make restitution to an innocent and unoffending child, for such he is, although the offspring of a guilty and most miserable love. You have not forgotten the provisions of the will. Carry them into execution so far as your brother is concerned, and then go where you please. In this world you need meet no more.'

While Monks was pacing up and down, meditating with dark and evil looks on this proposal and the possibilities of evading it: torn by his fears on the one hand and his hatred on the other: the door was hurriedly unlocked, and a gentleman (Mr. Losberne) entered the room in violent agitation.

'The man will be taken,' he cried. 'He will be taken tonight!'

'The murderer?' asked Mr. Brownlow.

'Yes, yes,' replied the other. 'His dog has been seen lurking about some old haunt, and there seems little doubt that his master either is, or will be, there, under cover of the darkness. Spies are hovering about in every direction. I have spoken to the men who are charged with his capture, and they tell me he cannot escape. A reward of a hundred pounds is proclaimed by Government to-night.'

'I will give fifty more,' said Mr. Brownlow, 'and proclaim it with my own lips upon the spot, if I can reach it. Where is Mr. Maylie?'

'Harry? As soon as he had seen your friend here, safe in a coach with you, he hurried off to where he heard this,' replied the doctor, 'and mounting his horse sallied forth to join the first party at some place in the outskirts agreed upon between them.'

'Fagin,' said Mr. Brownlow; 'what of him?'

'When I last heard, he had not been taken, but he will be, or is, by this time. They're sure of him.'

'Have you made up your mind?' asked Mr. Brownlow, in a low voice, of Monks.

'Yes,' he replied. 'You—you—will be secret with me?'

'I will. Remain here till I return. It is your only hope of safety.'

They left the room, and the door was again locked.

'What have you done?' asked the doctor in a whisper.

'All that I could hope to do, and even more. Coupling the poor girl's intelligence with my previous knowledge, and the result of our good friend's inquiries on the spot, I left him no loophole of escape, and laid bare the whole villainy which by these lights became plain as day. Write and appoint the evening after to-morrow, at seven, for the meeting. We shall be down there, a few hours before, but shall require rest: especially the young lady, who *may* have greater need of firmness than either you or I can quite foresee just now. But my blood boils to avenge this poor murdered creature. Which way have they taken?'

'Drive straight to the office and you will be in time,' replied Mr. Losberne. 'I will remain here.'

The two gentlemen hastily separated; each in a fever of excitement wholly uncontrollable.

CHAPTER 50

The pursuit and escape

Near to that part of the Thames on which the church at Rotherhithe abuts, where the buildings on the banks are dirtiest and the vessels on the river blackest with the dust of colliers and the smoke of close-built low-roofed houses, there exists the filthiest, the strangest, the most extraordinary of the many localities that are hidden in London, wholly unknown, even by name, to the great mass of its inhabitants.

To reach this place, the visitor has to penetrate through a maze of close, narrow, and muddy streets, thronged by the roughest and poorest of waterside people, and devoted to the traffic they may be supposed to occasion. The cheapest and least delicate provisions are heaped in the shops; the coarsest and commonest articles of wearing apparel dangle at the salesman's door, and stream from the house-parapet and windows. Jostling with unemployed labourers of the lowest class, ballast-heavers, coal-whippers, brazen women, ragged children, and the raff and refuse of the river, he makes his way with difficulty along, assailed by offensive sights and smells from the narrow alleys which branch off on the right and left, and deafened by the clash of ponderous waggons that bear great piles of merchandise from the stacks of warehouses that rise from every corner. Arriving, at length, in streets remoter and less-frequented than those through which he has passed, he walks beneath tottering house fronts, projecting over the pavement, dismantled walls that seem to totter as he passes, chimneys half crushed half hesitating to fall, windows guarded by rusty iron bars that time and dirt have almost eaten away, every imaginable sign of desolation and neglect.

In such a neighbourhood, beyond Dockhead in the Borough of Southwark, stands Jacob's Island, surrounded by a muddy ditch, six or eight feet deep and fifteen or twenty wide when the tide is in, once called Mill Pond, but known in the days of this story as Folly Ditch. It is a creek or inlet from the Thames, and can always be filled at high water by opening the sluices at the Lead Mills from which it took its old name. At such times, a stranger, looking from one of the wooden bridges thrown across it at Mill Lane, will see the inhabitants of the houses on either side lowering from their back doors and windows, buckets, pails, domestic utensils of all kinds, in which to haul the water up; and when his eye is turned from these operations to the houses themselves, his utmost astonishment will be excited by the scene before him. Crazy wooden galleries common to the backs of half-a-dozen houses, with holes from which to look upon the slime beneath; windows, broken and patched, with poles thrust out, on which to dry the linen that is never there; rooms so small, so filthy, so confined, that the air would seem too tainted even for the dirt and squalor which they shelter; wooden chambers thrusting themselves out above the mud, and threatening to fall into it—as some have done; dirt-besmeared walls and decaying foundations; every repulsive lineament of poverty, every loathsome indication of filth, rot, and garbage; all these ornament the banks of Folly Ditch.

In Jacob's Island, the warehouses are roofless and empty; the walls are crumbling down; the windows are windows no more; the doors are falling into the streets; the chimneys are blackened, but they yield no smoke. Thirty or forty years ago, before losses and chancery suits came upon it, it was a thriving place; but now it is a desolate island indeed. The houses have no owners; they are broken open, and entered upon by those who have the courage; and there they live, and there they die. They must have powerful motives for a secret residence, or be reduced to a destitute condition indeed, who seek a refuge in Jacob's Island.

In an upper room of one of these houses—a detached house of fair size, ruinous in other respects, but strongly defended at door and window: of which house the back commanded the ditch in manner already described—there were assembled three men, who, regarding each other every now and then with looks expressive of perplexity and expectation, sat for some time in profound and gloomy silence. One of these was Toby Crackit, another Mr. Chitling, and the third a robber of fifty years, whose nose had been almost beaten in, in some old scuffle, and whose face bore a frightful scar which might probably be traced to the same occasion. This man was a returned transport, and his name was Kags.

'I wish,' said Toby turning to Mr. Chitling, 'that you had picked out some other crib when the two old ones got too warm, and had not come here, my fine feller.'

'Why didn't you, blunder-head?' said Kags.

'Well, I thought you'd have been a little more glad to see me than this,' replied Mr. Chitling, with a melancholy air.

'Why look'e, young gentleman,' said Toby, 'when a man keeps himself so very exclusive as I have done, and by that means has a snug house over his head with nobody a-prying and smelling about it, it's rather a startling thing to have the honour of a wisit from a young gentleman (however respectable and pleasant a person he may be to play cards with at conweniency) circumstanced as you are.'

'Especially, when the exclusive young man has got a friend stopping with him, that's arrived sooner than was expected from foreign parts, and is too modest to want to be presented to the Judges on his return,' added Mr. Kags.

There was a short silence, after which Toby Crackit, seeming to abandon as hopeless any further effort to maintain his usual devil-may-care swagger, turned to Chitling and said,

'When was Fagin took then?'

'Just at dinner-time—two o'clock this afternoon. Charley and

I made our lucky up the wash'us chimney, and Bolter got into the empty water-butt, head downwards; but his legs were so precious long that they stuck out at the top, and so they took him too.'

'And Bet?'

'Poor Bet! She went to see the body, to speak to who it was,' replied Chitling, his countenance falling more and more, 'and went off mad, screaming and raving, and beating her head against the boards; so they put a strait-weskut on her and took her to the hospital—and there she is.'

'Wot's come of young Bates?' demanded Kags.

'He hung about, not to come over here afore dark, but he'll be here soon,' replied Chitling. 'There's nowhere else to go to now, for the people at the Cripples are all in custody, and the bar of the ken—I went up there and see it with my own eyes—is filled with traps.'

'This is a smash,' observed Toby biting his lips. 'There's more than one will go with this.'

'The sessions are on,' said Kags: 'if they get the inquest over, and Bolter turns King's evidence: as of course he will, from what he's said already: they can prove Fagin an accessory before the fact, and get the trial on on Friday, and he'll swing in six days from this, by G—'

'You should have heard the people groan,' said Chitling; 'the officers fought like devils, or they'd have torn him away. He was down once, but they made a ring round him, and fought their way along. You should have seen how he looked about him, all muddy and bleeding, and clung to them as if they were his dearest friends. I can see 'em now, not able to stand upright with the pressing of the mob, and dragging him along amongst 'em; I can see the people jumping up, one behind another, and snarling with their teeth and making at him; I can see the blood upon his hair and beard, and hear the cries with which the women worked themselves into the centre of the crowd at the street corner, and swore they'd tear his heart out!'

The horror-stricken witness of this scene pressed his hands

upon his ears, and with his eyes closed got up and paced violently to and fro, like one distracted.

While he was thus engaged, and the two men sat by in silence with their eyes fixed upon the floor, a pattering noise was heard upon the stairs, and Sikes's dog bounded into the room. They ran to the window, down stairs, and into the street. The dog had jumped in at an open window; he made no attempt to follow them, nor was his master to be seen.

'What's the meaning of this?' said Toby when they had returned. 'He can't be coming here. I——hope not.'

'If he was coming here, he'd have come with the dog,' said Kags, stooping down to examine the animal, who lay panting on the floor. 'Here! Give us some water for him; he has run himself faint.'

'He's drunk it all up, every drop,' said Chitling after watching the dog some time in silence. 'Covered with mud—lame—half-blind—he must have come a long way.'

'Where can he have come from!' exclaimed Toby. 'He's been to the other kens of course, and finding them filled with strangers come on here, where he's been many a time and often. But where can he have come from first, and how comes he here alone without the other!'

'He'—(none of them called the murderer by his old name)—'He can't have made away with himself. What do you think?' said Chitling.

Toby shook his head.

'If he had,' said Kags, 'the dog 'ud want to lead us away to where he did it. No. I think he's got out of the country, and left the dog behind. He must have given him the slip somehow, or he wouldn't be so easy.'

This solution, appearing the most probable one, was adopted as the right; the dog, creeping under a chair, coiled himself up to sleep, without more notice from anybody.

It being now dark, the shutter was closed, and a candle lighted and placed upon the table. The terrible events of the last two days had made a deep impression on all three, increased by the danger and uncertainty of their own position. They drew their chairs closer together, starting at every sound. They spoke little, and that in whispers, and were as silent and awe-stricken as if the remains of the murdered woman lay in the next room.

They had sat thus, some time, when suddenly was heard a hurried knocking at the door below.

'Young Bates,' said Kags, looking angrily round, to check the fear he felt himself.

The knocking came again. No, it wasn't he. He never knocked like that.

Crackit went to the window, and shaking all over, drew in his head. There was no need to tell them who it was; his pale face was enough. The dog too was on the alert in an instant, and ran whining to the door.

'We must let him in,' he said, taking up the candle.

'Isn't there any help for it?' asked the other man in a hoarse voice.

'None. He *must* come in.'

'Don't leave us in the dark,' said Kags, taking down a candle from the chimney-piece, and lighting it, with such a trembling hand that the knocking was twice repeated before he had finished.

Crackit went down to the door, and returned followed by a man with the lower part of his face buried in a handkerchief, and another tied over his head under his hat. He drew them slowly off. Blanched face, sunken eyes, hollow cheeks, beard of three days' growth, wasted flesh, short thick breath; it was the very ghost of Sikes.

He laid his hand upon a chair which stood in the middle of the room, but shuddering as he was about to drop into it, and seeming to glance over his shoulder, dragged it back close to the wall—as close as it would go—ground it against it—and sat down.

Not a word had been exchanged. He looked from one to another in silence. If an eye were furtively raised and met his, it was instantly averted. When his hollow voice broke silence, they all three started. They seemed never to have heard its tones before.

'How came that dog here?' he asked.

'Alone. Three hours ago.'

'To-night's paper says that Fagin's took. Is it true, or a lie?'

'True.'

They were silent again.

'Damn you all!' said Sikes, passing his hand across his forehead. 'Have you nothing to say to me?'

There was an uneasy movement among them, but nobody spoke.

'You that keep this house,' said Sikes, turning his face to Crackit, 'do you mean to sell me, or to let me lie here till this hunt is over?'

'You may stop here, if you think it safe,' returned the person addressed, after some hesitation.

Sikes carried his eyes slowly up the wall behind him: rather trying to turn his head than actually doing it: and said, 'Is—it—the body—is it buried?'

They shook their heads.

'Why isn't it!' he retorted with the same glance behind him. 'Wot do they keep such ugly things above the ground for? — Who's that knocking?'

Crackit intimated, by a motion of his hand as he left the room, that there was nothing to fear; and directly came back with Charley Bates behind him. Sikes sat opposite the door, so that the moment the boy entered the room he encountered his figure.

'Toby,' said the boy falling back, as Sikes turned his eyes towards him, 'why didn't you tell me this, down stairs?'

There had been something so tremendous in the shrinking off of the three, that the wretched man was willing to propitiate even this lad. Accordingly he nodded, and made as though he would shake hands with him.

'Let me go into some other room,' said the boy, retreating still farther.

'Charley!' said Sikes, stepping forward. 'Don't you—don't you know me?'

'Don't come nearer me,' answered the boy, still retreating, and looking, with horror in his eyes, upon the murderer's face. 'You monster!'

The man stopped half-way, and they looked at each other; but Sikes's eyes sunk gradually to the ground.

'Witness you three,' cried the boy shaking his clenched fist, and becoming more and more excited as he spoke. 'Witness you three—I'm not afraid of him—if they come here after him, I'll give him up; I will. I tell you out at once. He may kill me for it if he likes, or if he dares, but if I am here I'll give him up. I'd give him up if he was to be boiled alive. Murder! Help! If there's the pluck of a man among you three, you'll help me. Murder! Help! Down with him!'

Pouring out these cries, and accompanying them with violent gesticulation, the boy actually threw himself, single-handed, upon the strong man, and in the intensity of his energy and the suddenness of his surprise, brought him heavily to the ground.

The three spectators seemed quite stupefied. They offered no interference, and the boy and man rolled on the ground together; the former, heedless of the blows that showered upon him, wrenching his hands tighter and tighter in the garments about the murderer's breast, and never ceasing to call for help with all his might.

The contest, however, was too unequal to last long. Sikes had him down, and his knee was on his throat, when Crackit pulled him back with a look of alarm, and pointed to the window. There were lights gleaming below, voices in loud and earnest conversation, the tramp of hurried footsteps—endless they seemed in number—crossing the nearest wooden bridge. One man on horseback seemed to be among the crowd; for there was the noise of hoofs rattling on the uneven pavement. The gleam of lights increased; the footsteps came more thickly and noisily on. Then, came a loud knocking at the door, and then a hoarse murmur from such a multitude of angry voices as would have made the boldest quail.

'Help!' shrieked the boy in a voice that rent the air. 'He's here! Break down the door!'

'In the King's name,' cried the voices without; and the hoarse cry arose again, but louder.

'Break down the door!' screamed the boy. 'I tell you they'll never open it. Run straight to the room where the light is. Break down the door!'

Strokes, thick and heavy, rattled upon the door and lower window-shutters as he ceased to speak, and a loud huzzah burst from the crowd; giving the listener, for the first time, some adequate idea of its immense extent.

'Open the door of some place where I can lock this screeching Hell-babe,' cried Sikes fiercely; running to and fro, and dragging the boy, now, as easily as if he were an empty sack. 'That door. Quick!' He flung him in, bolted it, and turned the key. 'Is the downstairs door fast?'

'Double-locked and chained,' replied Crackit, who, with the other two men, still remained quite helpless and bewildered.

'The panels—are they strong?'

'Lined with sheet-iron.'

'And the windows too?'

'Yes, and the windows.'

'Damn you!' cried the desperate ruffian, throwing up the sash and menacing the crowd. 'Do your worst! I'll cheat you yet!'

Of all the terrific yells that ever fell on mortal ears, none could exceed the cry of the infuriated throng. Some shouted to those who were nearest to set the house on fire; others roared to the officers to shoot him dead. Among them all, none showed such fury as the man on horseback, who, throwing himself out of the saddle, and bursting through the crowd as if he were parting water, cried, beneath the window, in a voice that rose above all others, 'Twenty guineas to the man who brings a ladder!'

The nearest voices took up the cry, and hundreds echoed it. Some called for ladders, some for sledgehammers; some ran with torches to and fro as if to seek them, and still came back and roared again; some spent their breath in impotent curses and execrations; some pressed forward with the ecstasy of madmen, and thus impeded the progress of those below; some among the boldest attempted to climb up by the water-spout and crevices in the wall; and all waved to and fro, in the darkness beneath, like a field of corn moved by an angry wind: and joined from time to time in one loud furious roar.

'The tide,' cried the murderer, as he staggered back into the room, and shut the faces out, 'the tide was in as I came up. Give me a rope, a long rope. They're all in front. I may drop into the Folly Ditch, and clear off that way. Give me a rope, or I shall do three more murders and kill myself.'

The panic-stricken men pointed to where such articles were kept; the murderer, hastily selecting the longest and strongest cord, hurried up to the house-top.

All the windows in the rear of the house had been long ago bricked up, except one small trap in the room where the boy was locked, and that was too small even for the passage of his body. But, from this aperture, he had never ceased to call on those without, to guard the back; and thus, when the murderer emerged at last on the house-top by the door in the roof, a loud shout proclaimed the fact to those in front, who immediately began to pour round, pressing upon each other in an unbroken stream.

He planted a board, which he had carried up with him for the purpose, so firmly against the door that it must be matter of great difficulty to open it from the inside; and creeping over the tiles, looked over the low parapet.

The water was out, and the ditch a bed of mud.

The crowd had been hushed during these few moments, watching his motions and doubtful of his purpose, but the instant they perceived it and knew it was defeated, they raised a cry of triumphant execration to which all their previous shouting had been whispers. Again and again it rose. Those who were at too great a distance to know its meaning, took up the sound; it echoed and re-echoed; it seemed as though the whole city had poured its population out to curse him.

On pressed the people from the front—on, on, on, in a strong struggling current of angry faces, with here and there a glaring torch to light them up, and show them out in all their wrath and passion. The houses on the opposite side of the ditch had been entered by the mob; sashes were thrown up, or torn bodily out; there were tiers and tiers of faces in every window; cluster upon cluster of people clinging to every house-top. Each little bridge (and there were three in sight) bent beneath the weight of the crowd upon it. Still the current poured on to find some nook or hole from which to vent their shouts, and only for an instant see the wretch.

'They have him now,' cried a man on the nearest bridge. 'Hurrah!'

The crowd grew light with uncovered heads; and again the shout uprose.

'I will give fifty pounds,' cried an old gentleman from the same quarter, 'to the man who takes him alive. I will remain here, till he comes to ask me for it.'

There was another roar. At this moment the word was passed among the crowd that the door was forced at last, and that he who had first called for the ladder had mounted into the room. The stream abruptly turned, as this intelligence ran from mouth to mouth; and the people at the windows, seeing those upon the bridges pouring back, quitted their stations, and running into the street, joined the concourse that now thronged pell-mell to the spot they had left: each man crushing and striving with his neighbour, and all panting with impatience to get near the door, and look upon the criminal as the officers brought him out. The cries and shrieks of those who were pressed almost to suffocation, or trampled down and trodden under foot in the confusion, were dreadful; the narrow ways were completely blocked up; and at this time, between the rush of some to regain the space in front of the house, and the unavailing struggles of others to extricate themselves from the mass, the immediate attention was distracted from the murderer, although the universal eagerness for his capture was, if possible, increased.

The man had shrunk down, thoroughly quelled by the ferocity of the crowd, and the impossibility of escape; but seeing this sudden change with no less rapidity than it had occurred, he sprang upon his feet, determined to make one last effort for his life by dropping into the ditch, and, at the risk of being stifled, endeavouring to creep away in the darkness and confusion.

Roused into new strength and energy, and stimulated by the noise within the house which announced that an entrance had really been effected, he set his foot against the stack of chimneys, fastened one end of the rope tightly and firmly round it, and with the other made a strong running noose by the aid of his hands and teeth almost in a second. He could let himself down by the cord to within a less distance of the ground than his own height, and had his knife ready in his hand to cut it then and drop.

At the very instant when he brought the loop over his head previous to slipping it beneath his arm-pits, and when the old gentleman before-mentioned (who had clung so tight to the railing of the bridge as to resist the force of the crowd, and retain his position) earnestly warned those about him that the man was about to lower himself down—at that very instant the murderer, looking behind him on the roof, threw his arms above his head, and uttered a yell of terror.

'The eyes again!' he cried in an unearthly screech.

Staggering as if struck by lightning, he lost his balance and tumbled over the parapet. The noose was on his neck. It ran up with his weight, tight as a bowstring, and swift as the arrow it speeds. He fell for five-and-thirty feet. There was a sudden jerk, a terrific convulsion of the limbs; and there he hung, with the open knife clenched in his stiffening hand.

The old chimney quivered with the shock, but stood it bravely. The murderer swung lifeless against the wall; and the boy, thrusting aside the dangling body which obscured his view, called to the people to come and take him out, for God's sake.

A dog, which had lain concealed till now, ran backwards and

forwards on the parapet with a dismal howl, and collecting himself for a spring, jumped for the dead man's shoulders. Missing his aim, he fell into the ditch, turning completely over as he went; and striking his head against a stone, dashed out his brains.

CHAPTER 51

Affording an explanation of more mysteries
than one, and comprehending a proposal of
marriage with no word of settlement or
pin-money

The events narrated in the last chapter were yet but two days old,
when Oliver found himself, at three o'clock in the afternoon, in a
travelling-carriage rolling fast towards his native town. Mrs. Maylie,
and Rose, and Mrs. Bedwin, and the good doctor, were with him:
and Mr. Brownlow followed in a post-chaise, accompanied by one
other person whose name had not been mentioned.

They had not talked much upon the way; for Oliver was in a
flutter of agitation and uncertainty which deprived him of the power
of collecting his thoughts, and almost of speech, and appeared to
have scarcely less effect on his companions, who shared it, in at
least an equal degree. He and the two ladies had been very carefully made acquainted by Mr. Brownlow with the nature of the
admissions which had been forced from Monks; and although they
knew that the object of their present journey was to complete the
work which had been so well begun, still the whole matter was
enveloped in enough of doubt and mystery to leave them in
endurance of the most intense suspense.

The same kind friend had, with Mr. Losberne's assistance,
cautiously stopped all channels of communication through which
they could receive intelligence of the dreadful occurrences that had
so recently taken place. 'It was quite true,' he said, 'that they must
know them before long, but it might be at a better time than the

present, and it could not be at a worse.' So, they travelled on in silence: each busied with reflections on the object which had brought them together: and no one disposed to give utterance to the thoughts which crowded upon all.

But if Oliver, under these influences, had remained silent while they journeyed towards his birth-place by a road he had never seen, how the whole current of his recollections ran back to old times, and what a crowd of emotions were wakened up in his breast, when they turned into that which he had traversed on foot: a poor, house-less, wandering boy, without a friend to help him, or a roof to shelter his head.

'See there, there!' cried Oliver, eagerly clasping the hand of Rose, and pointing out at the carriage window; 'that's the stile I came over; there are the hedges I crept behind, for fear any one should overtake me and force me back! Yonder is the path across the fields, leading to the old house where I was a little child! Oh, Dick, Dick, my dear old friend, if I could only see you now!'

'You will see him soon,' replied Rose, gently taking his folded hands between her own. 'You shall tell him how happy you are, and how rich you have grown, and that in all your happiness you have none so great as the coming back to make him happy too.'

'Yes, yes,' said Oliver, 'and we'll—we'll take him away from here, and have him clothed and taught, and send him to some quiet country place where he may grow strong and well, —shall we?'

Rose nodded 'yes,' for the boy was smiling through such happy tears that she could not speak.

'You will be kind and good to him, for you are to every one,' said Oliver. 'It will make you cry, I know, to hear what he can tell; but never mind, never mind, it will be all over, and you will smile again—I know that too—to think how changed he is; you did the same with me. He said "God bless you" to me when I ran away,' cried the boy with a burst of affectionate emotion; 'and I will say "God bless *you*" now, and show him how I love him for it!'

As they approached the town, and at length drove through its narrow streets, it became matter of no small difficulty to restrain the boy within reasonable bounds. There was Sowerberry's the undertaker's just as it used to be, only smaller and less imposing in appearance than he remembered it—there were all the well-known shops and houses, with almost every one of which he had some slight incident connected—there was Gamfield's cart, the very cart he used to have, standing at the old public-house door—there was the workhouse, the dreary prison of his youthful days, with its dismal windows frowning on the street—there was the same lean porter standing at the gate, at sight of whom Oliver involuntarily shrunk back, and then laughed at himself for being so foolish, then cried, then laughed again—there were scores of faces at the doors and windows that he knew quite well—there was nearly everything as if he had left it but yesterday, and all his recent life had been but a happy dream.

But it was pure, earnest, joyful reality. They drove straight to the door of the chief hotel (which Oliver used to stare up at, with awe, and think a mighty palace, but which had somehow fallen off in grandeur and size); and here was Mr. Grimwig all ready to receive them, kissing the young lady, and the old one too, when they got out of the coach, as if he were the grandfather of the whole party, all smiles and kindness, and not offering to eat his head—no, not once; not even when he contradicted a very old postboy about the nearest road to London, and maintained he knew it best, though he had only come that way once, and that time fast asleep. There was dinner prepared, and there were bedrooms ready, and everything was arranged as if by magic.

Notwithstanding all this, when the hurry of the first half-hour was over, the same silence and constraint prevailed that had marked their journey down. Mr. Brownlow did not join them at dinner, but remained in a separate room. The two other gentlemen hurried in and out with anxious faces, and, during the short intervals when they were present, conversed apart. Once, Mrs. Maylie was called away, and after being absent for nearly an hour, returned with eyes swollen with weeping. All these things made Rose and Oliver, who were not in any new secrets, nervous and uncomfortable. They sat wondering, in silence; or, if they exchanged a few words, spoke in whispers, as if they were afraid to hear the sound of their own voices.

At length, when nine o'clock had come, and they began to think they were to hear no more that night, Mr. Losberne and Mr. Grimwig entered the room, followed by Mr. Brownlow and a man whom Oliver almost shrieked with surprise to see; for they told him it was his brother, and it was the same man he had met at the market-town, and seen looking in with Fagin at the window of his little room. Monks cast a look of hate, which, even then, he could not dissemble, at the astonished boy, and sat down near the door. Mr. Brownlow, who had papers in his hand, walked to a table near which Rose and Oliver were seated.

'This is a painful task,' said he, 'but these declarations, which have been signed in London before many gentlemen, must be in substance repeated here. I would have spared you the degradation, but we must hear them from your own lips before we part, and you know why.'

'Go on,' said the person addressed, turning away his face. 'Quick. I have almost done enough, I think. Don't keep me here.'

'This child,' said Mr. Brownlow, drawing Oliver to him, and laying his hand upon his head, 'is your half-brother; the illegitimate son of your father, my dear friend Edwin Leeford, by poor young Agnes Fleming, who died in giving him birth.'

'Yes,' said Monks, scowling at the trembling boy: the beating of whose heart he might have heard. 'That is their bastard child.'

'The term you use,' said Mr. Brownlow, sternly, 'is a reproach to those who long since passed beyond the feeble censure of the world. It reflects disgrace on no one living, except you who use it. Let that pass. He was born in this town.'

'In the workhouse of this town,' was the sullen reply. 'You have the story there.' He pointed impatiently to the papers as he spoke.

'I must have it here, too,' said Mr. Brownlow, looking round upon the listeners.

'Listen then! You!' returned Monks. 'His father being taken

ill at Rome, was joined by his wife, my mother, from whom he had been long separated, who went from Paris and took me with her—to look after his property, for what I know, for she had no great affection for him, nor he for her. He knew nothing of us, for his senses were gone, and he slumbered on till next day, when he died. Among the papers in his desk, were two, dated on the night his illness first came on, directed to yourself;' he addressed himself to Mr. Brownlow; 'and enclosed in a few short lines to you, with an intimation on the cover of the package that it was not to be forwarded till after he was dead. One of these papers was a letter to this girl Agnes; the other a will.'

'What of the letter?' asked Mr. Brownlow.

'The letter? —A sheet of paper crossed and crossed again, with a penitent confession, and prayers to God to help her. He had palmed a tale on the girl that some secret mystery—to be explained one day—prevented his marrying her just then; and so she had gone on, trusting patiently to him, until she trusted too far, and lost what none could ever give her back. She was, at that time, within a few months of her confinement. He told her all he had meant to do, to hide her shame, if he had lived, and prayed her, if he died, not to curse his memory, or think the consequences of their sin would be visited on her or their young child; for all the guilt was his. He reminded her of the day he had given her the little locket and the ring with her Christian name engraved upon it, and a blank left for that which he hoped one day to have bestowed on her—prayed her yet to keep it, and wear it next her heart, as she had done before—and then ran on, wildly, in the same words, over and over again, as if he had gone distracted. I believe he had.'

'The will,' said Mr. Brownlow, as Oliver's tears fell fast.

Monks was silent.

'The will,' said Mr. Brownlow, speaking for him, 'was in the same spirit as the letter. He talked of miseries which his wife had brought upon him; of the rebellious disposition, vice, malice, and premature bad passions of you his only son, who had been trained to hate him; and left you, and your mother, each an annuity of eight hundred pounds. The bulk of his property he divided into two equal portions—one for Agnes Fleming, and the other for their child, if it should be born alive, and ever come of age. If it were a girl, it was to inherit the money unconditionally; but if a boy, only on the stipulation that in his minority he should never have stained his name with any public act of dishonour, meanness, cowardice, or wrong. He did this, he said, to mark his confidence in the mother, and his conviction—only strengthened by approaching death—that the child would share her gentle heart, and noble nature. If he were disappointed in this expectation, then the money was to come to you: for then, and not till then, when both children were equal, would he recognise your prior claim upon his purse, who had none upon his heart, but had, from an infant, repulsed him with coldness and aversion.'

'My mother,' said Monks, in a louder tone, 'did what a woman should have done. She burnt this will. The letter never reached its destination; but that, and other proofs, she kept, in case they ever tried to lie away the blot. The girl's father had the truth from her with every aggravation that her violent hate—I love her for it now— could add. Goaded by shame and dishonour he fled with his children into a remote corner of Wales, changing his very name that his friends might never know of his retreat; and here, no great while afterwards, he was found dead in his bed. The girl had left her home, in secret, some weeks before; he had searched for her, on foot, in every town and village near; it was on the night when he returned home, assured that she had destroyed herself, to hide her shame and his, that his old heart broke.'

There was a short silence here, until Mr. Brownlow took up the thread of the narrative.

'Years after this,' he said, 'this man's—Edward Leeford's— mother came to me. He had left her, when only eighteen; robbed her of jewels and money; gambled, squandered, forged, and fled to London: where for two years he had associated with the lowest outcasts. She was sinking under a painful and incurable disease, and wished to recover him before she died. Inquiries were set on foot, and strict searches made. They were unavailing for a long time, but ultimately successful; and he went back with her to France.

'There she died,' said Monks, 'after a lingering illness; and, on her deathbed, she bequeathed these secrets to me, together with her unquenchable and deadly hatred of all whom they involved—though she need not have left me that, for I had inherited it long before. She would not believe that the girl had destroyed herself, and the child too, but was filled with the impression that a male child had been born, and was alive. I swore to her, if ever it crossed my path, to hunt it down; never to let it rest; to pursue it with the bitterest and most unrelenting animosity; to vent upon it the hatred that I deeply felt, and to spit upon the empty vaunt of that insulting will by dragging it, if I could, to the very gallows-foot. She was right. He came in my way at last. I began well: and, but for babbling drabs, I would have finished as I began!'

As the villain folded his arms tight together, and muttered curses on himself in the impotence of baffled malice, Mr. Brownlow turned to the terrified group beside him, and explained that the Jew, who had been his old accomplice and confidant, had a large reward for keeping Oliver ensnared: of which some part was to be given up, in the event of his being rescued: and that a dispute on this head had led to their visit to the country house for the purpose of identifying him.

'The locket and ring?' said Mr. Brownlow, turning to Monks.

'I bought them from the man and woman I told you of, who stole them from the nurse, who stole them from the corpse,' answered Monks without raising his eyes. 'You know what became of them.'

Mr. Brownlow merely nodded to Mr. Grimwig, who, disappearing with great alacrity, shortly returned, pushing in Mrs. Bumble, and dragging her unwilling consort after him.

'Do my hi's deceive me!' cried Mr. Bumble, with ill-feigned enthusiasm, 'or is that little Oliver? Oh O-li-ver, if you know'd how I've been a-grieving for you—'

'Hold your tongue, fool,' murmured Mrs. Bumble.

'Isn't natur, natur, Mrs. Bumble?' remonstrated the work-house master. 'Can't I be supposed to feel—*I* as brought him up porochially—when I see him a-setting here, among ladies and gentlemen of the very affablest description! I always loved that boy as if he'd been my—my—my own grandfather,' said Mr. Bumble, halting for an appropriate comparison. 'Master Oliver, my dear, you remember the blessed gentleman in the white waistcoat? Ah! he went to heaven last week, in a oak coffin with plated handles, Oliver.'

'Come, sir,' said Mr. Grimwig, tartly; 'suppress your feelings.'

'I will do my endeavours, sir,' replied Mr. Bumble. 'How do you do, sir? I hope you are very well.'

This salutation was addressed to Mr. Brownlow, who had stepped up to within a short distance of the respectable couple. He inquired, as he pointed to Monks,

'Do you know that person?'

'No,' replied Mrs. Bumble flatly.

'Perhaps *you* don't?' said Mr. Brownlow, addressing her spouse.

'I never saw him in all my life,' said Mr. Bumble.

'Nor sold him anything, perhaps?'

'No,' replied Mrs. Bumble.

'You never had, perhaps, a certain gold locket and ring?' said Mr. Brownlow.

'Certainly not,' replied the matron. 'Why are we brought here to answer to such nonsense as this?'

Again Mr. Brownlow nodded to Mr. Grimwig; and again that gentleman limped away with extraordinary readiness. But not again did he return with a stout man and wife; for this time, he led in two palsied women, who shook and tottered as they walked.

'You shut the door the night old Sally died,' said the foremost one, raising her shrivelled hand, 'but you couldn't shut out the sound, nor stop the chinks.'

'No, no,' said the other, looking round her and wagging her toothless jaws. 'No, no, no.'

'We heard her try to tell you what she'd done, and saw you

take a paper from her hand, and watched you too, next day, to the pawnbroker's shop,' said the first.

'Yes,' added the second, 'and it was a "locket and gold ring". We found out that, and saw it given you. We were by. Oh! we were by.'

'And we know more than that,' resumed the first, 'for she told us often, long ago, that the young mother had told her that, feeling she should never get over it, she was on her way, at the time that she was taken ill, to die near the grave of the father of the child.'

'Would you like to see the pawnbroker himself?' asked Mr. Grimwig with a motion towards the door.

'No,' replied the woman; 'if he'—she pointed to Monks—'has been coward enough to confess, as I see he has, and you have sounded all these hags till you have found the right ones, I have nothing more to say. I *did* sell them, and they're where you'll never get them. What then?'

'Nothing,' replied Mr. Brownlow, 'except that it remains for us to take care that neither of you is employed in a situation of trust again. You may leave the room.'

'I hope,' said Mr. Bumble, looking about him with great ruefulness, as Mr. Grimwig disappeared with the two old women: 'I hope that this unfortunate little circumstance will not deprive me of my porochial office?'

'Indeed it will,' replied Mr. Brownlow. 'You may make up your mind to that, and think yourself well off besides.'

'It was all Mrs. Bumble. She *would* do it,' urged Mr. Bumble; first looking round to ascertain that his partner had left the room.

'That is no excuse,' replied Mr. Brownlow. 'You were present on the occasion of the destruction of these trinkets, and indeed are the more guilty of the two, in the eye of the law; for the law supposes that your wife acts under your direction.'

'If the law supposes that,' said Mr. Bumble, squeezing his hat emphatically in both hands, 'the law is a ass—a idiot. If that's the eye of the law, the law is a bachelor; and the worst I wish the law is, that his eye may be opened by experience—by experience.'

Laying great stress on the repetition of these two words, Mr. Bumble fixed his hat on very tight, and putting his hands in his pockets, followed his helpmate down stairs.

'Young lady,' said Mr. Brownlow, turning to Rose, 'give me your hand. Do not tremble. You need not fear to hear the few remaining words we have to say.'

'If they have—I do not know how they can, but if they have— any reference to me,' said Rose, 'pray let me hear them at some other time. I have not strength or spirits now.'

'Nay,' returned the old gentleman, drawing her arm through his; 'you have more fortitude than this, I am sure. Do you know this young lady, sir?'

'Yes,' replied Monks.

'I never saw you before,' said Rose faintly.

'I have seen you often,' returned Monks.

'The father of the unhappy Agnes had *two* daughters,' said Mr. Brownlow. 'What was the fate of the other—the child?'

'The child,' replied Monks, 'when her father died in a strange place, in a strange name, without a letter, book, or scrap of paper that yielded the faintest clue by which his friends or relatives could be traced—the child was taken by some wretched cottagers, who reared it as their own.'

'Go on,' said Mr. Brownlow, signing to Mrs. Maylie to approach. 'Go on!'

'You couldn't find the spot to which these people had repaired,' said Monks, 'but where friendship fails, hatred will often force a way. My mother found it, after a year of cunning search—ay, and found the child.'

'She took it, did she?'

'No. The people were poor and began to sicken—at least the man did—of their fine humanity; so she left it with them, giving them a small present of money which would not last long, and promised more, which she never meant to send. She didn't quite rely, however, on their discontent and poverty for the child's unhappiness, but told the history of the sister's shame, with such alterations as suited her; bade them take good heed of the child, for she came of bad blood; and told them she was illegitimate, and sure to go wrong at one time or other. The circumstances countenanced all this; the people believed it; and there the child dragged on an existence, miserable enough even to satisfy us, until a widow lady, residing, then, at Chester, saw the girl by chance, pitied her, and took her home. There was some cursed spell, I think, against us; for in spite of all our efforts she remained there and was happy. I lost sight of her, two or three years ago, and saw her no more until a few months back.'

'Do you see her now?'

'Yes. Leaning on your arm.'

'But not the less my niece,' cried Mrs. Maylie, folding the fainting girl in her arms; 'not the less my dearest child. I would not lose her now, for all the treasures of the world. My sweet companion, my own dear girl!'

'The only friend I ever had,' cried Rose, clinging to her. 'The kindest, best of friends. My heart will burst. I cannot bear all this.'

'You have borne more, and have been, through all, the best and gentlest creature that ever shed happiness on every one she knew,' said Mrs. Maylie, embracing her tenderly. 'Come, come, my love, remember who this is who waits to clasp you in his arms, poor child! See here—look, look, my dear!'

'Not aunt,' cried Oliver, throwing his arms about her neck; 'I'll never call her aunt—sister, my own dear sister, that something taught my heart to love so dearly from the first! Rose, dear, darling Rose!'

Let the tears which fell, and the broken words which were exchanged in the long close embrace between the orphans, be sacred. A father, sister, and mother, were gained, and lost in that one moment. Joy and grief were mingled in the cup; but there were no bitter tears: for even grief itself arose so softened, and clothed in such sweet and tender recollections, that it became a solemn pleasure, and lost all character of pain.

They were a long, long time alone. A soft tap at the door,

at length announced that some one was without. Oliver opened it, glided away, and gave place to Harry Maylie.

'I know it all,' he said, taking a seat beside the lovely girl. 'Dear Rose, I know it all.

'I am not here by accident,' he added after a lengthened silence; 'nor have I heard all this to-night, for I knew it yesterday—only yesterday. Do you guess that I have come to remind you of a promise?'

'Stay,' said Rose. 'You *do* know all.'

'All. You gave me leave, at any time within a year, to renew the subject of our last discourse.'

'I did.'

'Not to press you to alter your determination,' pursued the young man, 'but to hear you repeat it, if you would. I was to lay whatever of station or fortune I might possess at your feet, and if you still adhered to your former determination, I pledged myself, by no word or act, to seek to change it.'

'The same reasons which influenced me then, will influence me now,' said Rose firmly. 'If I ever owed a strict and rigid duty to her, whose goodness saved me from a life of indigence and suffering, when should I ever feel it, as I should to-night? It is a struggle,' said Rose, 'but one I am proud to make; it is a pang, but one my heart shall bear.'

'The disclosure of to-night, —' Harry began.

'The disclosure of to-night,' replied Rose softly, 'leaves me in the same position, with reference to you, as that in which I stood before.'

'You harden your heart against me, Rose,' urged her lover.

'Oh, Harry, Harry,' said the young lady, bursting into tears; 'I wish I could, and spare myself this pain.'

'Then why inflict it on yourself?' said Harry, taking her hand. 'Think, dear Rose, think what you have heard to-night.'

'And what have I heard! What have I heard!' cried Rose. 'That a sense of his deep disgrace so worked upon my own father that he shunned all—there, we have said enough, Harry, we have said enough.'

'Not yet, not yet,' said the young man, detaining her as she rose. 'My hopes, my wishes, prospects, feeling: every thought in life except my love for you: have undergone a change. I offer you, now, no distinction among a bustling crowd; no mingling with a world of malice and detraction, where the blood is called into honest cheeks by aught but real disgrace and shame; but a home—a heart and home— yes, dearest Rose, and those, and those alone, are all I have to offer.'

'What do you mean!' she faltered.

'I mean but this—that when I left you last, I left you with a firm determination to level all fancied barriers between yourself and me; resolved that if my world could not be yours, I would make yours mine; that no pride of birth should curl the lip at you, for I would turn from it. This I have done. Those who have shrunk from me because of this, have shrunk from you, and proved you so far right. Such power and patronage: such relatives of influence and rank: as smiled upon me then, look coldly now; but there are smiling fields and waving trees in England's richest country; and by one village church—mine, Rose, my own! —there stands a rustic dwelling which you can make me prouder of, than all the hopes I have renounced, measured a thousandfold. This is *my* rank and station now, and here I lay it down!'

'It's a trying thing waiting supper for lovers,' said Mr. Grimwig, waking up, and pulling his pocket-handkerchief from over his head.

Truth to tell, the supper had been waiting a most unreasonable time. Neither Mrs. Maylie, nor Harry, nor Rose (who all came in together), could offer a word in extenuation.

'I had serious thoughts of eating my head to-night,' said Mr. Grimwig, 'for I began to think I should get nothing else. I'll take the liberty, if you'll allow me, of saluting the bride that is to be.'

Mr. Grimwig lost no time in carrying this notice into effect upon the blushing girl; and the example, being contagious, was followed both by the doctor and Mr. Brownlow: some people affirm that Harry Maylie had been observed to set it, originally, in a dark room adjoining; but the best authorities consider this downright scandal: he being young and a clergyman.

'Oliver, my child,' said Mrs. Maylie, 'where have you been, and why do you look so sad? There are tears stealing down your face at this moment. What is the matter?'

It is a world of disappointment: often to the hopes we most cherish, and hopes that do our nature the greatest honour.

Poor Dick was dead!

CHAPTER 52

Fagin's last night alive

The court was paved, from floor to roof, with human faces. Inquisitive and eager eyes peered from every inch of space. From the rail before the dock, away into the sharpest angle of the smallest corner in the galleries, all looks were fixed upon one man—Fagin. Before him and behind: above, below, on the right and on the left: he seemed to stand surrounded by a firmament, all bright with gleaming eyes.

He stood there, in all this glare of living light, with one hand resting on the wooden slab before him, the other held to his ear, and his head thrust forward to enable him to catch with greater distinctness every word that fell from the presiding judge, who was delivering his charge to the jury. At times, he turned his eyes sharply upon them to observe the effect of the slightest featherweight in his favour; and when the points against him were stated with terrible distinctness, looked towards his counsel, in mute appeal that he would, even then, urge something in his behalf. Beyond these manifestations of anxiety, he stirred not hand or foot. He had scarcely moved since the trial began; and now that the judge ceased to speak, he still remained in the same strained attitude of close attention, with his gaze bent on him, as though he listened still.

A slight bustle in the court, recalled him to himself. Looking round, he saw that the jurymen had turned together, to consider of their verdict. As his eyes wandered to the gallery, he could see the people rising above each other to see his face: some hastily applying their glasses to their eyes: and others whispering their neighbours with looks expressive of abhorrence. A few there were, who seemed unmindful of him, and looked only to the jury, in impatient wonder how they could delay. But in no one face—not even among the women, of whom there were many there—could he read the faintest sympathy with himself, or any feeling but one of all-absorbing interest that he should be condemned.

As he saw all this in one bewildered glance, the deathlike stillness came again, and looking back, he saw that the jurymen had turned towards the judge. Hush!

They only sought permission to retire.

He looked, wistfully, into their faces, one by one, when they passed out, as though to see which way the greater number leant; but that was fruitless. The jailer touched him on the shoulder. He followed mechanically to the end of the dock, and sat down on a chair. The man pointed it out, or he would not have seen it.

He looked up into the gallery again. Some of the people were eating, and some fanning themselves with handkerchiefs; for the crowded place was very hot. There was one young man sketching his face in a little note-book. He wondered whether it was like, and looked on when the artist broke his pencil-point, and made another with his knife, as any idle spectator might have done.

In the same way, when he turned his eyes towards the judge, his mind began to busy itself with the fashion of his dress, and what it cost, and how he put it on. There was an old fat gentleman on the bench, too, who had gone out, some half an hour before, and now come back. He wondered within himself whether this man had been to get his dinner, what he had had, and where he had had it; and pursued this train of careless thought until some new object caught his eye and roused another.

Not that, all this time, his mind was, for an instant, free from one oppressive overwhelming sense of the grave that opened at his feet; it was ever present to him, but in a vague and general way, and he could not fix his thoughts upon it. Thus, even while he trembled, and turned burning hot at the idea of speedy death, he fell to counting the iron spikes before him, and wondering how the head of one had been broken off, and whether they would mend it, or leave it as it was. Then, he thought of all the horrors of the gallows and the scaffold—and stopped to watch a man sprinkling the floor to cool it—and then went on to think again.

At length there was a cry of silence, and a breathless look from all towards the door. The jury returned, and passed him close. He could glean nothing from their faces; they might as well have been of stone. Perfect stillness ensued—not a rustle—not a breath—Guilty.

The building rang with a tremendous shout, and another, and another, and then it echoed loud groans, that gathered strength as they swelled out, like angry thunder. It was a peal of joy from the populace outside, greeting the news that he would die on Monday.

The noise subsided, and he was asked if he had anything to say why sentence of death should not be passed upon him. He had resumed his listening attitude, and looked intently at his questioner while the demand was made; but it was twice repeated before he seemed to hear it, and then he only muttered that he was an old man—an old man—an old man—and so, dropping into a whisper, was silent again.

The judge assumed the black cap, and the prisoner still stood with the same air and gesture. A woman in the gallery uttered some exclamation, called forth by this dread solemnity; he looked hastily up as if angry at the interruption, and bent forward yet more attentively. The address was solemn and impressive; the sentence fearful to hear. But he stood, like a marble figure, without the motion of a nerve. His haggard face was still thrust forward, his under-jaw hanging down, and his eyes staring out before him, when the jailer put his hand upon his arm, and beckoned him away. He gazed stupidly about him for an instant, and obeyed.

They led him through a paved room under the court, where some prisoners were waiting till their turns came, and others were talking to their friends, who crowded round a grate which looked into the open yard. There was nobody there, to speak to *him;* but, as he passed, the prisoners fell back to render him more visible to the people who were clinging to the bars: and they assailed him with opprobrious names, and screeched and hissed. He shook his fist, and would have spat upon them; but his conductors hurried him on, through a gloomy passage lighted by a few dim lamps, into the interior of the prison.

Here, he was searched, that he might not have about him the means of anticipating the law; this ceremony performed, they led him to one of the condemned cells, and left him there—alone.

He sat down on a stone bench opposite the door, which served for seat and bedstead; and casting his blood-shot eyes upon the ground, tried to collect his thoughts. After awhile, he began to remember a few disjointed fragments of what the judge had said: though it had seemed to him, at the time, that he could not hear a word. These gradually fell into their proper places, and by degrees suggested more: so that in a little time he had the whole, almost as it was delivered. To be hanged by the neck, till he was dead—that was the end. To be hanged by the neck till he was dead.

As it came on very dark, he began to think of all the men he had known who had died upon the scaffold; some of them through his means. They rose up, in such quick succession, that he could hardly count them. He had seen some of them die,—and had joked too, because they died with prayers upon their lips. With what a rattling noise the drop went down; and how suddenly they changed, from strong and vigorous men to dangling heaps of clothes!

Some of them might have inhabited that very cell—sat upon that very spot. It was very dark; why didn't they bring a light? The cell had been built for many years. Scores of men must have passed their last hours there. It was like sitting in a vault strewn with dead bodies—the cap, the noose, the pinioned arms, the faces that he knew, even beneath that hideous veil.—Light, light!

At length, when his hands were raw with beating against the heavy door and walls, two men appeared: one bearing a candle, which he thrust into an iron candlestick fixed against the wall: the other dragging in a mattress on which to pass the night; for the prisoner was to be left alone no more.

Then came night—dark, dismal, silent night. Other watchers are glad to hear this church-clock strike, for they tell of life and coming day. To him they brought despair. The boom of every iron bell came laden with the one, deep, hollow sound—Death. What availed the noise and bustle of cheerful morning, which penetrated even there, to him? It was another form of knell, with mockery added to the warning.

The day passed off. Day? There was no day; it was gone as soon as come—and night came on again; night so long, and yet so short; long in its dreadful silence, and short in its fleeting hours. At one time he raved and blasphemed; and at another howled and tore his hair. Venerable men of his own persuasion had come to pray beside him, but he had driven them away with curses. They renewed their charitable efforts, and he beat them off.

Saturday night. He had only one night more to live. And as he thought of this, the day broke—Sunday.

It was not until the night of this last awful day, that a withering sense of his helpless, desperate state came in its full intensity upon his blighted soul; not that he had ever held any defined or positive hope of mercy, but that he had never been able to consider more than the dim probability of dying so soon. He had spoken little to either of the two men, who relieved each other in their attendance upon him; and they, for their parts, made no effort to rouse his attention. He had sat there, awake, but dreaming. Now, he started up, every minute, and with gasping mouth and burning skin, hurried to and fro, in such a paroxysm of fear and wrath that even they—used to such sights—recoiled from him with horror. He grew so terrible, at last, in all the tortures of his evil conscience, that one man could not bear to sit there, eyeing him alone; and so the two kept watch together.

He cowered down upon his stone bed, and thought of the past. He had been wounded with some missiles from the crowd on the day of his capture, and his head was bandaged with a linen cloth.

His red hair hung down upon his bloodless face; his beard was torn, and twisted into knots; his eyes shone with a terrible light; his unwashed flesh crackled with the fever that burnt him up. Eight—nine—ten. If it was not a trick to frighten him, and those were the real hours treading on each other's heels, where would he be, when they came round again! Eleven! Another struck, before the voice of the previous hour had ceased to vibrate. At eight, he would be the only mourner in his own funeral train; at eleven—

Those dreadful walls of Newgate, which have hidden so much misery and such unspeakable anguish, not only from the eyes, but, too often, and too long, from the thoughts, of men, never held so dread a spectacle as that. The few who lingered as they passed, and wondered what the man was doing who was to be hanged tomorrow, would have slept but ill that night, if they could have seen him.

From early in the evening until nearly midnight, little groups of two and three presented themselves at the lodge-gate, and inquired, with anxious faces, whether any reprieve had been received. These being answered in the negative, communicated the welcome intelligence to clusters in the street, who pointed out to one another the door from which he must come out, and showed where the scaffold would be built, and, walking with unwilling steps away, turned back to conjure up the scene. By degrees they fell off, one by one; and, for an hour, in the dead of night, the street was left to solitude and darkness.

The space before the prison was cleared, and a few strong barriers, painted black, had been already thrown across the road to break the pressure of the expected crowd, when Mr. Brownlow and Oliver appeared at the wicket, and presented an order of admission to the prisoner, signed by one of the sheriffs. They were immediately admitted into the lodge.

'Is the young gentleman to come too, sir?' said the man whose duty it was to conduct them. 'It's not a sight for children, sir.'

'It is not indeed, my friend,' rejoined Mr. Brownlow; 'but my business with this man is intimately connected with him; and as this child has seen him in the full career of his success and villainy,

I think it as well—even at the cost of some pain and fear—that he should see him now.'

These few words had been said apart, so as to be inaudible to Oliver. The man touched his hat; and glancing at Oliver with some curiosity, opened another gate, opposite to that by which they had entered, and led them on, through dark and winding ways, towards the cells.

'This,' said the man, stopping in a gloomy passage where a couple of workmen were making some preparations in profound silence—'this is the place he passes through. If you step this way, you can see the door he goes out at.'

He led them into a stone kitchen, fitted with coppers for dressing the prison food, and pointed to a door. There was an open grating above it, through which came the sound of men's voices, mingled with the noise of hammering, and the throwing down of boards. They were putting up the scaffold.

From this place, they passed through several strong gates, opened by other turnkeys from the inner side; and, having entered an open yard, ascended a flight of narrow steps, and came into a passage with a row of strong doors on the left hand. Motioning them to remain where they were, the turnkey knocked at one of these with his bunch of keys. The two attendants, after a little whispering, came out into the passage, stretching themselves as if glad of the temporary relief, and motioned the visitors to follow the jailer into the cell. They did so.

The condemned criminal was seated on his bed, rocking himself from side to side, with a countenance more like that of a snared beast than the face of a man. His mind was evidently wandering to his old life, for he continued to mutter, without appearing conscious of their presence otherwise than as part of his vision.

'Good boy, Charley—well done—' he mumbled. 'Oliver, too, ha! ha! ha! Oliver too—quite the gentleman now—quite the—take that boy away to bed!'

The jailer took the disengaged hand of Oliver; and, whispering him not to be alarmed, looked on without speaking.

'Take him away to bed!' cried Fagin. 'Do you hear me, some of you? He has been the—the—somehow the cause of all this. It's worth the money to bring him up to it—Bolter's throat, Bill; never mind the girl—Bolter's throat as deep as you can cut. Saw his head off!'

'Fagin,' said the jailer.

'That's me!' cried the Jew, falling, instantly, into the attitude of listening he had assumed upon his trial. 'An old man, my Lord; a very old, old man!'

'Here,' said the turnkey, laying his hand upon his breast to keep him down. 'Here's somebody wants to see you, to ask you some questions, I suppose. Fagin, Fagin! Are you a man?'

'I shan't be one long,' he replied, looking up with a face retaining no human expression but rage and terror. 'Strike them all dead! What right have they to butcher me?'

As he spoke he caught sight of Oliver and Mr. Brownlow. Shrinking to the furthest corner of the seat, he demanded to know what they wanted there.

'Steady,' said the turnkey, still holding him down. 'Now, sir, tell him what you want. Quick, if you please, for he grows worse as the time gets on.'

'You have some papers,' said Mr. Brownlow advancing, 'which were placed in your hands, for better security, by a man called Monks.'

'It's all a lie together,' replied Fagin. 'I haven't one—not one.'

'For the love of God,' said Mr. Brownlow solemnly, 'do not say that now, upon the very verge of death; but tell me where they are. You know that Sikes is dead; that Monks has confessed; that there is no hope of any further gain. Where are those papers?'

'Oliver,' cried Fagin, beckoning to him. 'Here, here! Let me whisper to you.'

'I am not afraid,' said Oliver in a low voice, as he relinquished Mr. Brownlow's hand.

'The papers,' said Fagin, drawing Oliver towards him, 'are in a canvas bag, in a hole a little way up the chimney in the top front-room. I want to talk to you, my dear. I want to talk to you.'

'Yes, yes,' returned Oliver. 'Let me say a prayer. Do! Let me say one prayer. Say only one, upon your knees, with me, and we will talk till morning.'

'Outside, outside,' replied Fagin, pushing the boy before him towards the door, and looking vacantly over his head. 'Say I've gone to sleep—they'll believe *you*. You can get me out, if you take me so. Now then, now then!'

'Oh! God forgive this wretched man!' cried the boy with a burst of tears.

'That's right, that's right,' said Fagin. 'That'll help us on. This door first. If I shake and tremble, as we pass the gallows, don't you mind, but hurry on. Now, now, now!'

'Have you nothing else to ask him, sir?' inquired the turnkey.

'No other question,' replied Mr. Brownlow. 'If I hoped we could recall him to a sense of his position—'

'Nothing will do that, sir,' replied the man, shaking his head. 'You had better leave him.'

The door of the cell opened, and the attendants returned.

'Press on, press on,' cried Fagin. 'Softly, but not so slow. Faster, faster!'

The men laid hands upon him, and disengaging Oliver from his grasp, held him back. He struggled with the power of desperation, for an instant; and, then sent up cry upon cry that penetrated even those massive walls, and rang in their ears until they reached the open yard.

It was some time before they left the prison. Oliver nearly swooned after this frightful scene, and was so weak that for an hour or more, he had not the strength to walk.

Day was dawning when they again emerged. A great multitude had already assembled; the windows were filled with people, smoking and playing cards to beguile the time; the crowd were pushing, quarrelling, joking. Everything told of life and animation, but one dark cluster of objects in the centre of all—the black stage, the cross-beam, the rope, and all the hideous apparatus of death.

CHAPTER 53

And last

The fortunes of those who have figured in this tale are nearly closed. The little that remains to their historian to relate, is told in few and simple words.

Before three months had passed, Rose Fleming and Harry Maylie were married in the village church which was henceforth to be the scene of the young clergyman's labours; on the same day they entered into possession of their new and happy home.

Mrs. Maylie took up her abode with her son and daughter-in-law, to enjoy, during the tranquil remainder of her days, the greatest felicity that age and worth can know—the contemplation of the happiness of those on whom the warmest affections and tenderest cares of a well-spent life, have been unceasingly bestowed.

It appeared, on full and careful investigation, that if the wreck of property remaining in the custody of Monks (which had never prospered either in his hands or in those of his mother) were equally divided between himself and Oliver, it would yield, to each, little more than three thousand pounds. By the provisions of his father's will, Oliver would have been entitled to the whole; but Mr. Brownlow, unwilling to deprive the elder son of the opportunity of retrieving his former vices and pursuing an honest career, proposed this mode of distribution, to which his young charge joyfully acceded.

Monks, still bearing that assumed name, retired with his

portion to a distant part of the New World; where, having quickly squandered it, he once more fell into his old courses, and, after undergoing a long confinement for some fresh act of fraud and knavery, at length sunk under an attack of his old disorder, and died in prison. As far from home, died the chief remaining members of his friend Fagin's gang.

Mr. Brownlow adopted Oliver as his son. Removing with him and the old housekeeper to within a mile of the parsonage-house, where his dear friends resided, he gratified the only remaining wish of Oliver's warm and earnest heart, and thus linked together a little society, whose condition approached as nearly to one of perfect happiness as can ever be known in this changing world.

Soon after the marriage of the young people, the worthy doctor returned to Chertsey, where, bereft of the presence of his old friends, he would have been discontented if his temperament had admitted of such a feeling; and would have turned quite peevish if he had known how. For two or three months, he contented himself with hinting that he feared the air began to disagree with him; then, finding that the place really no longer was, to him, what it had been, he settled his business on his assistant, took a bachelor's cottage outside the village of which his young friend was pastor, and instantaneously recovered. Here, he took to gardening, planting, fishing, carpentering, and various other pursuits of a similar kind: all undertaken with his characteristic impetuosity. In each and all, he has since become famous throughout the neighbourhood, as a most profound authority.

Before his removal, he had managed to contract a strong friendship for Mr. Grimwig, which that eccentric gentleman cordially reciprocated. He is accordingly visited by Mr. Grimwig a great many times in the course of the year. On all such occasions, Mr. Grimwig plants, fishes, and carpenters, with great ardour; doing everything in a very singular and unprecedented manner, but always maintaining, with his favourite asseveration, that his mode is the right one. On Sundays, he never fails to criticise the sermon to the young clergyman's face: always informing Mr. Losberne, in strict confidence afterwards, that he considers it an excellent performance, but deems it as well not to say so. It is a standing and very favourite joke, for Mr. Brownlow to rally him on his old prophecy concerning Oliver, and to remind him of the night on which they sat with the watch between them, waiting his return; but Mr. Grimwig contends that he was right in the main, and, in proof thereof, remarks that Oliver *did not come back*, after all; which always calls forth a laugh on his side, and increases his good humour.

Mr. Noah Claypole: receiving a free pardon from the Crown in consequence of being admitted approver against Fagin: and considering his profession not altogether as safe a one as he could wish: was, for some little time, at a loss for the means of a livelihood, not burthened with too much work. After some consideration, he went into business as an Informer, in which calling he realises a genteel subsistence. His plan is, to walk out once a week during church time attended by Charlotte in respectable attire. The lady faints away at the doors of charitable publicans, and the gentleman being accommodated with threepenny-worth of brandy to restore her, lays an information next day, and pockets half the penalty. Sometimes Mr. Claypole faints himself, but the result is the same.

Mr. and Mrs. Bumble, deprived of their situations, were gradually reduced to great indigence and misery, and finally became paupers in that very same workhouse in which they had once lorded it over others. Mr. Bumble has been heard to say, that in this reverse and degradation, he has not even spirits to be thankful for being separated from his wife.

As to Mr. Giles and Brittles, they still remain in their old posts, although the former is bald, and the last-named boy quite grey. They sleep at the parsonage, but divide their attentions so equally among its inmates, and Oliver, and Mr. Brownlow, and Mr. Losberne, that to this day the villagers have never been able to discover to which establishment they properly belong.

Master Charles Bates, appalled by Sikes's crime, fell into a train of reflection whether an honest life was not, after all, the best. Arriving at the conclusion that it certainly was, he turned his back upon the scenes of the past, resolved to amend it in some new sphere of action. He struggled hard, and suffered much, for some time; but, having a contented disposition, and a good purpose, succeeded in the end; and, from being a farmer's drudge, and a carrier's lad, he is now the merriest young grazier in all Northamptonshire.

And now, the hand that traces these words, falters, as it approaches the conclusion of its task; and would weave, for a little longer space, the thread of these adventures.

I would fain linger yet with a few of those among whom I have so long moved, and share their happiness by endeavouring to depict it. I would show Rose Maylie in all the bloom and grace of early womanhood, shedding on her secluded path in life soft and gentle light, that fell on all who trod it with her, and shone into their hearts. I would paint her the life and joy of the fire-side circle and the lively summer group; I would follow her through the sultry fields at noon, and hear the low tones of her sweet voice in the moonlit evening walk; I would watch her in all her goodness and charity abroad, and the smiling untiring discharge of domestic duties at home; I would paint her and her dead sister's child happy in their love for one another, and passing whole hours together in picturing the friends whom they had so sadly lost; I would summon before me, once again, those joyous little faces that clustered round her knee, and listen to their merry prattle; I would recall the tones of that clear laugh, and conjure up the sympathising tear that glistened in the soft blue eye. These, and a thousand looks and smiles, and turns of thought and speech—I would fain recall them every one.

How Mr. Brownlow went on, from day to day, filling the mind of his adopted child with stores of knowledge, and becoming attached to him, more and more, as his nature developed itself, and showed the thriving seeds of all he wished him to become—how he traced in him new traits of his early friend, that awakened in his own bosom old remembrances, melancholy and yet sweet and soothing—how the two orphans, tried by adversity, remembered its lessons in mercy to others, and mutual love, and fervent thanks to Him who had protected and preserved them—these are all matters which need not to be told. I have said that they were truly happy; and without strong affection and humanity of heart, and gratitude to that Being whose code is Mercy, and whose great attribute is Benevolence to all things that breathe, happiness can never be attained.

Within the altar of the old village church there stands a white marble tablet, which bears as yet but one word: 'Agnes.' There is no coffin in that tomb; and may it be many, many years, before another name is placed above it! But, if the spirits of the Dead ever come back to earth, to visit spots hallowed by the love—the love beyond the grave—of those whom they knew in life, I believe that the shade of Agnes sometimes hovers round that solemn nook. I believe it none the less because that nook is in a Church, and she was weak and erring.

CLASSIC LITERATURE: WORDS AND PHRASES
adapted from the Collins English Dictionary

Accoucheur NOUN a male midwife or doctor ❑ *I think my sister must have had some general idea that I was a young offender whom an Accoucheur Policemen had taken up (on my birthday) and delivered over to her* (*Great Expectations* by Charles Dickens)

addled ADJ confused and unable to think properly ❑ *But she counted and counted till she got that addled* (*The Adventures of Huckleberry Finn* by Mark Twain)

admiration NOUN amazement or wonder ❑ *lifting up his hands and eyes by way of admiration* (*Gulliver's Travels* by Jonathan Swift)

afeard ADJ afeard means afraid ❑ *shake it – and don't be afeard* (*The Adventures of Huckleberry Finn* by Mark Twain)

affected VERB affected means followed ❑ *Hadst thou affected sweet divinity* (*Doctor Faustus 5.2* by Christopher Marlowe)

aground ADV when a boat runs aground, it touches the ground in a shallow part of the water and gets stuck ❑ *what kep' you? – boat get aground?* (*The Adventures of Huckleberry Finn* by Mark Twain)

ague NOUN a fever in which the patient has alternate hot and cold shivering fits ❑ *his exposure to the wet and cold had brought on fever and ague* (*Oliver Twist* by Charles Dickens)

alchemy ADJ false or worthless ❑ *all wealth alchemy* (*The Sun Rising* by John Donne)

all alike phrase the same all the time ❑ *Love, all alike* (*The Sun Rising* by John Donne)

alow and aloft phrase alow means in the lower part or bottom, and aloft means on the top, so alow and aloft means on the top and in the bottom or throughout ❑ *Someone's turned the chest out alow and aloft* (*Treasure Island* by Robert Louis Stevenson)

ambuscade NOUN ambuscade is not a proper word. Tom means an ambush, which is when a group of people attack their enemies, after hiding and waiting for them ❑ *and so we would lie in ambuscade, as he called it* (*The Adventures of Huckleberry Finn* by Mark Twain)

amiable ADJ likeable or pleasant ❑ *Such amiable qualities must speak for themselves* (*Pride and Prejudice* by Jane Austen)

amulet NOUN an amulet is a charm thought to drive away evil spirits. ❑ *uttered phrases at once occult and familiar, like the amulet worn on the heart* (*Silas Marner* by George Eliot)

amusement NOUN here amusement means a strange and disturbing puzzle ❑ *this was an amusement the other way* (*Robinson Crusoe* by Daniel Defoe)

ancient NOUN an ancient was the flag displayed on a ship to show which country it belongs to. It is also called the ensign ❑ *her ancient and pendants out* (*Robinson Crusoe* by Daniel Defoe)

antic ADJ here antic means horrible or grotesque ❑ *armed and dressed after a very antic manner* (*Gulliver's Travels* by Jonathan Swift)

antics NOUN antics is an old word meaning clowns, or people who do silly things to make other people laugh ❑ *And point like antics at his triple crown* (*Doctor Faustus 3.2* by Christopher Marlowe)

appanage NOUN an appanage is a living allowance ❑ *As if loveliness were not the special prerogative of woman*

481

– her legitimate appanage and heritage! (*Jane Eyre* by Charlotte Brontë)

appended VERB appended means attached or added to ❏ *and these words appended* (*Treasure Island* by Robert Louis Stevenson)

approver NOUN an approver is someone who gives evidence against someone he used to work with ❏ *Mr. Noah Claypole: receiving a free pardon from the Crown in consequence of being admitted approver against Fagin* (*Oliver Twist* by Charles Dickens)

areas NOUN the areas is the space, below street level, in front of the basement of a house ❏ *The Dodger had a vicious propensity, too, of pulling the caps from the heads of small boys and tossing them down areas* (Oliver Twist by Charles Dickens)

argument NOUN theme or important idea or subject which runs through a piece of writing ❏ *Thrice needful to the argument which now* (*The Prelude* by William Wordsworth)

artificially ADJ artfully or cleverly ❏ *and he with a sharp flint sharpened very artificially* (*Gulliver's Travels* by Jonathan Swift)

artist NOUN here artist means a skilled workman ❏ *This man was a most ingenious artist* (*Gulliver's Travels* by Jonathan Swift)

assizes NOUN assizes were regular court sessions which a visiting judge was in charge of ❏ *you shall hang at the next assizes* (*Treasure Island* by Robert Louis Stevenson)

attraction NOUN gravitation, or Newton's theory of gravitation ❏ *he predicted the same fate to attraction* (*Gulliver's Travels* by Jonathan Swift)

aver VERB to aver is to claim something strongly ❏ *for Jem Rodney, the mole catcher, averred that one evening as he was returning homeward* (*Silas Marner* by George Eliot)

baby NOUN here baby means doll, which is a child's toy that looks like a small person ❏ *and skilful dressing her baby* (*Gulliver's Travels* by Jonathan Swift)

bagatelle NOUN bagatelle is a game rather like billiards and pool ❏ *Breakfast had been ordered at a pleasant little tavern, a mile or so away upon the rising ground beyond the green; and there was a bagatelle board in the room, in case we should desire to unbend our minds after the solemnity.* (*Great Expectations* by Charles Dickens)

bah exclam Bah is an exclamation of frustration or anger ❏ *"Bah," said Scrooge.* (*A Christmas Carol* by Charles Dickens)

bairn NOUN a northern word for child ❏ *Who has taught you those fine words, my bairn?* (*Wuthering Heights* by Emily Brontë)

bait VERB to bait means to stop on a journey to take refreshment ❏ *So, when they stopped to bait the horse, and ate and drank and enjoyed themselves, I could touch nothing that they touched, but kept my fast unbroken.* (*David Copperfield* by Charles Dickens)

balustrade NOUN a balustrade is a row of vertical columns that form railings ❏ *but I mean to say you might have got a hearse up that staircase, and taken it broadwise, with the splinter-bar towards the wall, and the door towards the balustrades: and done it easy* (*A Christmas Carol* by Charles Dickens)

bandbox NOUN a large lightweight box for carrying bonnets or hats ❏ *I am glad I bought my bonnet, if it is only for the fun of having another bandbox* (*Pride and Prejudice* by Jane Austen)

barren NOUN a barren here is a stretch or expanse of barren land ❏ *a line of upright stones, continued the length of the barren* (*Wuthering Heights* by Emily Brontë)

basin NOUN a basin was a cup without a handle ❏ *who is drinking his tea* *out of a basin* (*Wuthering Heights* by Emily Brontë)

battalia NOUN the order of battle ❏ *till I saw part of his army in battalia* (*Gulliver's Travels* by Jonathan Swift)

battery NOUN a Battery is a fort or a place where guns are positioned ❏ *You bring the lot to me, at that old Battery over yonder* (*Great Expectations* by Charles Dickens)

battledore and shuttlecock NOUN The game battledore and shuttlecock was an early version of the game now known as badminton. The aim of the early game was simply to keep the shuttlecock from hitting the ground. ❏ *Battledore and shuttlecock's a wery good game vhen you an't the shuttlecock and two lawyers the battledores, in which case it gets too excitin' to be pleasant* (*Pickwick Papers* by Charles Dickens)

beadle NOUN a beadle was a local official who had power over the poor ❏ *But these impertinences were speedily checked by the evidence of the surgeon, and the testimony of the beadle* (*Oliver Twist* by Charles Dickens)

bearings NOUN the bearings of a place are the measurements or directions that are used to find or locate it ❏ *the bearings of the island* (*Treasure Island* by Robert Louis Stevenson)

beaufet NOUN a beaufet was a sideboard ❏ *and sweet-cake from the beaufet* (*Emma* by Jane Austen)

beck NOUN a beck is a small stream ❏ *a beck which follows the bend of the glen* (*Wuthering Heights* by Emily Brontë)

bedight VERB decorated ❏ *and bedight with Christmas holly stuck into the top.* (*A Christmas Carol* by Charles Dickens)

Bedlam NOUN Bedlam was a lunatic asylum in London which had statues carved by Caius Gabriel Cibber at its entrance ❏ *Bedlam, and those carved maniacs at the gates* (*The Prelude* by William Wordsworth)

beeves NOUN oxen or castrated bulls which are animals used for pulling vehicles or carrying things ❏ *to deliver in every morning six beeves* (*Gulliver's Travels* by Jonathan Swift)

begot VERB created or caused ❏ *Begot in thee* (*On His Mistress* by John Donne)

behoof NOUN behoof means benefit ❏ *"Yes, young man," said he, releasing the handle of the article in question, retiring a step or two from my table, and speaking for the behoof of the landlord and waiter at the door* (*Great Expectations* by Charles Dickens)

berth NOUN a berth is a bed on a boat ❏ *this is the berth for me* (*Treasure Island* by Robert Louis Stevenson)

bevers NOUN a bever was a snack, or small portion of food, eaten between main meals ❏ *that buys me thirty meals a day and ten bevers* (*Doctor Faustus 2.1* by Christopher Marlowe)

bilge water NOUN the bilge is the widest part of a ship's bottom, and the bilge water is the dirty water that collects there ❏ *no gush of bilge-water had turned it to fetid puddle* (*Jane Eyre* by Charlotte Brontë)

bills NOUN bills is an old term meaning prescription. A prescription is the piece of paper on which your doctor writes an order for medicine and which you give to a chemist to get the medicine ❏ *Are not thy bills hung up as monuments* (*Doctor Faustus 1.1* by Christopher Marlowe)

black cap NOUN a judge wore a black cap when he was about to sentence a prisoner to death ❏ *The judge assumed the black cap, and the prisoner still stood with the same air and gesture.* (*Oliver Twist* by Charles Dickens)

black gentleman NOUN this was another word for the devil ❏ *for she is as impatient as the black gentleman* (*Emma* by Jane Austen)

boot-jack NOUN a wooden device to help take boots off ❑ *The speaker appeared to throw a boot-jack, or some such article, at the person he addressed* (*Oliver Twist* by Charles Dickens)

booty NOUN booty means treasure or prizes ❑ *would be inclined to give up their booty in payment of the dead man's debts* (*Treasure Island* by Robert Louis Stevenson)

Bow Street runner phrase Bow Street runners were the first British police force, set up by the author Henry Fielding in the eighteenth century ❑ *as would have convinced a judge or a Bow Street runner* (*Treasure Island* by Robert Louis Stevenson)

brawn NOUN brawn is a dish of meat which is set in jelly ❑ *Heaped up upon the floor, to form a kind of throne, were turkeys, geese, game, poultry, brawn, great joints of meat, sucking-pigs* (*A Christmas Carol* by Charles Dickens)

bray VERB when a donkey brays, it makes a loud, harsh sound ❑ *and she doesn't bray like a jackass* (*The Adventures of Huckleberry Finn* by Mark Twain)

break VERB in order to train a horse you first have to break it ❑*"If a high-mettled creature like this," said he, "can't be broken by fair means, she will never be good for anything"* (*Black Beauty* by Anna Sewell)

bullyragging VERB bullyragging is an old word which means bullying. To bullyrag someone is to threaten or force someone to do something they don't want to do ❑ *and a lot of loafers bullyragging him for sport* (*The Adventures of Huckleberry Finn* by Mark Twain)

but prep except for (this) ❑ *but this, all pleasures fancies be* (*The Good-Morrow* by John Donne)

by hand phrase by hand was a common expression of the time meaning that baby had been fed either using a spoon or a bottle rather than by breast-feeding ❑ *My sister, Mrs. Joe Gargery, was more than twenty years older than I, and had established a great reputation with herself . . . because she had bought me up 'by hand'* (*Great Expectations* by Charles Dickens)

bye-spots NOUN bye-spots are lonely places ❑ *and bye-spots of tales rich with indigenous produce* (*The Prelude* by William Wordsworth)

calico NOUN calico is plain white fabric made from cotton ❑ *There was two old dirty calico dresses* (*The Adventures of Huckleberry Finn* by Mark Twain)

camp-fever NOUN camp-fever was another word for the disease typhus ❑ *during a severe camp-fever* (*Emma* by Jane Austen)

cant NOUN cant is insincere or empty talk ❑ *"Man," said the Ghost, "if man you be in heart, not adamant, forbear that wicked cant until you have discovered What the surplus is, and Where it is."* (*A Christmas Carol* by Charles Dickens)

canty ADJ canty means lively, full of life ❑ *My mother lived til eighty, a canty dame to the last* (*Wuthering Heights* by Emily Brontë)

canvas VERB to canvas is to discuss ❑ *We think so very differently on this point Mr Knightley, that there can be no use in canvassing it* (*Emma* by Jane Austen)

capital ADJ capital means excellent or extremely good ❑ *for it's capital, so shady, light, and big* (*Little Women* by Louisa May Alcott)

capstan NOUN a capstan is a device used on a ship to lift sails and anchors ❑ *capstans going, ships going out to sea, and unintelligible sea creatures roaring curses over the bulwarks at respondent lightermen* (*Great Expectations* by Charles Dickens)

case-bottle NOUN a square bottle designed to fit with others into a case ❑ *The spirit being set before him in a huge case-bottle, which had originally come out of some* ship's locker (*The Old Curiosity Shop* by Charles Dickens)

casement NOUN casement is a word meaning window. The teacher in Nicholas Nickleby misspells window showing what a bad teacher he is ❑ *W-i-n, win, d-e-r, der, winder, a casement.'* (*Nicholas Nickleby* by Charles Dickens)

cataleptic ADJ a cataleptic fit is one in which the victim goes into a trancelike state and remains still for a long time ❑ *It was at this point in their history that Silas's cataleptic fit occurred during the prayer-meeting* (*Silas Marner* by George Eliot)

cauldron NOUN a cauldron is a large cooking pot made of metal ❑ *stirring a large cauldron which seemed to be full of soup* (*Alice's Adventures in Wonderland* by Lewis Carroll)

cephalic ADJ cephalic means to do with the head ❑ *with ink composed of a cephalic tincture* (*Gulliver's Travels* by Jonathan Swift)

chaise and four NOUN a closed four-wheel carriage pulled by four horses ❑ *he came down on Monday in a chaise and four to see the place* (*Pride and Prejudice* by Jane Austen)

chamberlain NOUN the main servant in a household ❑ *In those times a bed was always to be got there at any hour of the night, and the chamberlain, letting me in at his ready wicket, lighted the candle next in order on his shelf* (*Great Expectations* by Charles Dickens)

characters NOUN distinguishing marks ❑ *Impressed upon all forms the characters* (*The Prelude* by William Wordsworth)

chary ADJ cautious ❑ *I should have been chary of discussing my guardian too freely even with her* (*Great Expectations* by Charles Dickens)

cherishes VERB here cherishes means cheers or brightens ❑ *some*

philosophic song of Truth that cherishes our daily life* (*The Prelude* by William Wordsworth)

chickens' meat phrase chickens' meat is an old term which means chickens' feed or food ❑ *I had shook a bag of chickens' meat out in that place* (*Robinson Crusoe* by Daniel Defoe)

chimeras NOUN a chimera is an unrealistic idea or a wish which is unlikely to be fulfilled ❑ *with many other wild impossible chimeras* (*Gulliver's Travels* by Jonathan Swift)

chines NOUN chine is a cut of meat that includes part or all of the backbone of the animal ❑ *and they found hams and chines uncut* (*Silas Marner* by George Eliot)

chits NOUN chits is a slang word which means girls ❑ *I hate affected, niminy-piminy chits!* (*Little Women* by Louisa May Alcott)

chopped VERB chopped means come suddenly or accidentally ❑ *if I had chopped upon them* (*Robinson Crusoe* by Daniel Defoe)

chute NOUN a narrow channel ❑ *One morning about day-break, I found a canoe and crossed over a chute to the main shore* (*The Adventures of Huckleberry Finn* by Mark Twain)

circumspection NOUN careful observation of events and circumstances; caution ❑ *I honour your circumspection* (*Pride and Prejudice* by Jane Austen)

clambered VERB clambered means to climb somewhere with difficulty, usually using your hands and your feet ❑ *he clambered up and down stairs* (*Treasure Island* by Robert Louis Stevenson)

clime NOUN climate ❑ *no season knows nor clime* (*The Sun Rising* by John Donne)

clinched VERB clenched ❑ *the tops whereof I could but just reach with my fist clinched* (*Gulliver's Travels* by Jonathan Swift)

close chair NOUN a close chair is a sedan chair, which is a covered chair which has room for one person. The sedan chair is carried on two poles by two men, one in front and one behind ❑ *persuaded even the Empress herself to let me hold her in her close chair* (*Gulliver's Travels* by Jonathan Swift)

clown NOUN clown here means peasant or person who lives off the land ❑ *In ancient days by emperor and clown* (*Ode on a Nightingale* by John Keats)

coalheaver NOUN a coalheaver loaded coal onto ships using a spade ❑ *Good, strong, wholesome medicine, as was given with great success to two Irish labourers and a coalheaver* (*Oliver Twist* by Charles Dickens)

coal-whippers NOUN men who worked at docks using machines to load coal onto ships ❑ *here, were colliers by the score and score, with the coal-whippers plunging off stages on deck* (*Great Expectations* by Charles Dickens)

cobweb NOUN a cobweb is the net which a spider makes for catching insects ❑ *the walls and ceilings were all hung round with cobwebs* (*Gulliver's Travels* by Jonathan Swift)

coddling VERB coddling means to treat someone too kindly or protect them too much ❑ *and I've been coddling the fellow as if I'd been his grandmother* (*Little Women* by Louisa May Alcott)

coil NOUN coil means noise or fuss or disturbance ❑ *What a coil is there?* (*Doctor Faustus 4.7* by Christopher Marlowe)

collared VERB to collar something is a slang term which means to capture. In this sentence, it means he stole it [the money] ❑ *he collared it* (*The Adventures of Huckleberry Finn* by Mark Twain)

colling VERB colling is an old word which means to embrace and kiss ❑ *and no clasping and colling at all* (*Tess of the D'Urbervilles* by Thomas Hardy)

colloquies NOUN colloquy is a formal conversation or dialogue ❑ *Such colloquies have occupied many a pair of pale-faced weavers* (*Silas Marner* by George Eliot)

comfit NOUN sugar-covered pieces of fruit or nut eaten as sweets ❑ *and pulled out a box of comfits* (*Alice's Adventures in Wonderland* by Lewis Carroll)

coming out VERB when a girl came out in society it meant she was of marriageable age. In order to 'come out' girls were expecting to attend balls and other parties during a season ❑ *The younger girls formed hopes of coming out a year or two sooner than they might otherwise have done* (*Pride and Prejudice* by Jane Austen)

commit VERB commit means arrest or stop ❑ *Commit the rascals* (*Doctor Faustus 4.7* by Christopher Marlowe)

commodious ADJ commodious means convenient ❑ *the most commodious and effectual ways* (*Gulliver's Travels* by Jonathan Swift)

commons NOUN commons is an old term meaning food shared with others ❑ *his pauper assistants ranged themselves behind him; the gruel was served out; and a long grace was said over the short commons.* (*Oliver Twist* by Charles Dickens)

complacency NOUN here complacency means a desire to please others. Today complacency means feeling pleased with oneself without good reason. ❑ *Twas thy power that raised the first complacency in me* (*The Prelude* by William Wordsworth)

complaisance NOUN complaisance was eagerness to please ❑ *we cannot wonder at his complaisance* (*Pride and Prejudice* by Jane Austen)

complaisant ADJ complaisant means polite ❑ *extremely cheerful and* complaisant to their guest (*Gulliver's Travels* by Jonathan Swift)

conning VERB conning means learning by heart ❑ *Or conning more* (*The Prelude* by William Wordsworth)

consequent NOUN consequence ❑ *as avarice is the necessary consequent of old age* (*Gulliver's Travels* by Jonathan Swift)

consorts NOUN concerts ❑ *The King, who delighted in music, had frequent consorts at Court* (*Gulliver's Travels* by Jonathan Swift)

conversible ADJ conversible meant easy to talk to, companionable ❑ *He can be a conversible companion* (*Pride and Prejudice* by Jane Austen)

copper NOUN a copper is a large pot than can be heated directly over a fire ❑ *He gazed in stupefied astonishment on the small rebel for some seconds, and then clung for support to the copper* (*Oliver Twist* by Charles Dickens)

copper-stick NOUN a copper-stick is the long piece of wood used to stir washing in the copper (or boiler) which was usually the biggest cooking pot in the house ❑ *It was Christmas Eve, and I had to stir the pudding for next day, with a copper-stick, from seven to eight by the Dutch clock* (*Great Expectations* by Charles Dickens)

counting-house NOUN a counting house is a place where accountants work ❑ *Once upon a time – of all the good days in the year, on Christmas Eve – old Scrooge sat busy in his countinghouse* (*A Christmas Carol* by Charles Dickens)

courtier NOUN a courtier is someone who attends the king or queen – a member of the court ❑ *next the ten courtiers;* (*Alice's Adventures in Wonderland* by Lewis Carroll)

covies NOUN covies were flocks of partridges ❑ *and will save all of the best covies for you* (*Pride and Prejudice* by Jane Austen)

cowed VERB cowed means frightened or intimidated ❑ *it cowed me more than the pain* (*Treasure Island* by Robert Louis Stevenson)

cozened VERB cozened means tricked or deceived ❑ *Do you remember, sir, how you cozened me* (*Doctor Faustus 4.7* by Christopher Marlowe)

cravats NOUN a cravat is a folded cloth that a man wears wrapped around his neck as a decorative item of clothing ❑ *we'd a' slept in our cravats to-night* (*The Adventures of Huckleberry Finn* by Mark Twain)

crock and dirt phrase crock and dirt is an old expression meaning soot and dirt ❑ *and the mare catching cold at the door, and the boy grimed with crock and dirt* (*Great Expectations* by Charles Dickens)

crockery NOUN here crockery means pottery ❑ *By one of the parrots was a cat made of crockery* (*The Adventures of Huckleberry Finn* by Mark Twain)

crooked sixpence phrase it was considered unlucky to have a bent sixpence ❑ *You've got the beauty, you see, and I've got the luck, so you must keep me by you for your crooked sixpence* (*Silas Marner* by George Eliot)

croquet NOUN croquet is a traditional English summer game in which players try to hit wooden balls through hoops ❑ *and once she remembered trying to box her own ears for having cheated herself in a game of croquet* (*Alice's Adventures in Wonderland* by Lewis Carroll)

cross prep across ❑ *The two great streets, which run cross and divide it into four quarters* (*Gulliver's Travels* by Jonathan Swift)

culpable ADJ if you are culpable for something it means you are to blame ❑ *deep are the sorrows that spring from false ideas for which no man is culpable.* (*Silas Marner* by George Eliot)

cultured ADJ cultivated ❑ *Nor less when spring had warmed the cultured Vale* (*The Prelude* by William Wordsworth)

cupidity NOUN cupidity is greed ❑ *These people hated me with the hatred of cupidity and disappointment.* (*Great Expectations* by Charles Dickens)

curricle NOUN an open two-wheeled carriage with one seat for the driver and space for a single passenger ❑ *and they saw a lady and a gentleman in a curricle* (*Pride and Prejudice* by Jane Austen)

cynosure NOUN a cynosure is something that strongly attracts attention or admiration ❑ *Then I thought of Eliza and Georgiana; I beheld one the cynosure of a ballroom, the other the inmate of a convent cell* (*Jane Eyre* by Charlotte Brontë)

dalliance NOUN someone's dalliance with something is a brief involvement with it ❑ *nor sporting in the dalliance of love* (*Doctor Faustus Chorus* by Christopher Marlowe)

darkling ADV darkling is an archaic way of saying in the dark ❑ *Darkling I listen* (*Ode on a Nightingale* by John Keats)

delf-case NOUN a sideboard for holding dishes and crockery ❑ *at the pewter dishes and delf-case* (*Wuthering Heights* by Emily Brontë)

determined ■ VERB here determined means ended ❑ *and be out of vogue when that was determined* (*Gulliver's Travels* by Jonathan Swift) ■ VERB determined can mean to have been learned or found especially by investigation or experience ❑ *All the sensitive feelings it wounded so cruelly, all the shame and misery it kept alive within my breast, became more poignant as I thought of this; and I determined that the life was unendurable* (*David Copperfield* by Charles Dickens)

Deuce NOUN a slang term for the Devil ❑ *Ah, I dare say I did. Deuce take me, he added suddenly, I know I did. I find I am not quite unscrewed yet.* (*Great Expectations* by Charles Dickens)

diabolical ADJ diabolical means devilish or evil ❑ *and with a thousand diabolical expressions* (*Treasure Island* by Robert Louis Stevenson)

direction NOUN here direction means address ❑ *Elizabeth was not surprised at it, as Jane had written the direction remarkably ill* (*Pride and Prejudice* by Jane Austen)

discover VERB to make known or announce ❑ *the Emperor would discover the secret while I was out of his power* (*Gulliver's Travels* by Jonathan Swift)

dissemble VERB hide or conceal ❑ *Dissemble nothing* (*On His Mistress* by John Donne)

dissolve VERB dissolve here means to release from life, to die ❑ *Fade far away, dissolve, and quite forget* (*Ode on a Nightingale* by John Keats)

distrain VERB to distrain is to seize the property of someone who is in debt in compensation for the money owed ❑ *for he's threatening to distrain for it* (*Silas Marner* by George Eliot)

Divan NOUN a Divan was originally a Turkish council of state – the name was transferred to the couches they sat on and is used to mean this in English ❑ *Mr Brass applauded this picture very much, and the bed being soft and comfortable, Mr Quilp determined to use it, both as a sleeping place by night and as a kind of Divan by day.* (*The Old Curiosity Shop* by Charles Dickens)

divorcement NOUN separation ❑ *By all pains which want and divorcement hath* (*On His Mistress* by John Donne)

dog in the manger, a phrase this phrase describes someone who prevents you from enjoying something that they themselves have no need for ❏ *You are a dog in the manger, Cathy, and desire no one to be loved but yourself* (*Wuthering Heights* by Emily Brontë)

dolorifuge NOUN dolorifuge is a word which Thomas Hardy invented. It means pain-killer or comfort ❏ *as a species of dolorifuge* (*Tess of the D'Urbervilles* by Thomas Hardy)

dome NOUN building ❏ *that river and that mouldering dome* (*The Prelude* by William Wordsworth)

domestic phrase here domestic means a person's management of the house ❏ *to give some account of my domestic* (*Gulliver's Travels* by Jonathan Swift)

dunce a dunce is another word for idiot ❏ *Do you take me for a dunce? Go on?* (*Alice's Adventures in Wonderland* by Lewis Carroll)

Ecod exclam a slang exclamation meaning 'oh God!' ❏ *"Ecod," replied Wemmick, shaking his head, "that's not my trade."* (*Great Expectations* by Charles Dickens)

egg-hot NOUN an egg-hot (see also 'flip' and 'negus') was a hot drink made from beer and eggs, sweetened with nutmeg ❏ *She fainted when she saw me return, and made a little jug of egg-hot afterwards to console us while we talked it over.* (*David Copperfield* by Charles Dickens)

encores NOUN an encore is a short extra performance at the end of a longer one, which the entertainer gives because the audience has enthusiastically asked for it ❏ *we want a little something to answer encores with, anyway* (*The Adventures of Huckleberry Finn* by Mark Twain)

equipage NOUN an elegant and impressive carriage ❏ *and besides, the equipage did not answer to any of their neighbours* (*Pride and Prejudice* by Jane Austen)

exordium NOUN an exordium is the opening part of a speech ❏ *"Now, Handel," as if it were the grave beginning of a portentous business exordium, he had suddenly given up that tone* (*Great Expectations* by Charles Dickens)

expect VERB here expect means to wait for ❏ *to expect his farther commands* (*Gulliver's Travels* by Jonathan Swift)

familiars NOUN familiars means spirits or devils who come to someone when they are called ❏ *I'll turn all the lice about thee into familiars* (*Doctor Faustus 1.4* by Christopher Marlowe)

fantods NOUN a fantod is a person who fidgets or can't stop moving nervously ❏ *It most give me the fantods* (*The Adventures of Huckleberry Finn* by Mark Twain)

farthing NOUN a farthing is an old unit of British currency which was worth a quarter of a penny ❏ *Not a farthing less. A great many back-payments are included in it, I assure you.* (*A Christmas Carol* by Charles Dickens)

farthingale NOUN a hoop worn under a skirt to extend it ❏ *A bell with an old voice – which I dare say in its time had often said to the house, Here is the green farthingale* (*Great Expectations* by Charles Dickens)

favours NOUN here favours is an old word which means ribbons ❏ *A group of humble mourners entered the gate: wearing white favours* (*Oliver Twist* by Charles Dickens)

feigned VERB pretend or pretending ❏ *not my feigned page* (*On His Mistress* by John Donne)

fence ◼ NOUN a fence is someone who receives and sells stolen goods ❏ *What are you up to? Ill-treating the boys, you covetous, avaricious, in-sa-ti-a-ble old fence?* (*Oliver Twist* by Charles Dickens) ◻ NOUN defence or protection ❏ *but honesty hath no fence against superior cunning* (*Gulliver's Travels* by Jonathan Swift)

fess ADJ fess is an old word which means pleased or proud ❏ *You'll be* *fess enough, my poppet* (*Tess of the D'Urbervilles* by Thomas Hardy)

fettered ADJ fettered means bound in chains or chained ❑ *"You are fettered," said Scrooge, trembling. "Tell me why?"* (*A Christmas Carol* by Charles Dickens)

fidges VERB fidges means fidgets, which is to keep moving your hands slightly because you are nervous or excited ❑ *Look, Jim, how my fingers fidges* (*Treasure Island* by Robert Louis Stevenson)

finger-post NOUN a finger-post is a sign-post showing the direction to different places ❑ *"The gallows," continued Fagin, "the gallows, my dear, is an ugly finger-post, which points out a very short and sharp turning that has stopped many a bold fellow's career on the broad highway."* (*Oliver Twist* by Charles Dickens)

fire-irons NOUN fire-irons are tools kept by the side of the fire to either cook with or look after the fire ❑ *the fire-irons came first* (*Alice's Adventures in Wonderland* by Lewis Carroll)

fire-plug NOUN a fire-plug is another word for a fire hydrant ❑ *The pony looked with great attention into a fire-plug, which was near him, and appeared to be quite absorbed in contemplating it* (*The Old Curiosity Shop* by Charles Dickens)

flank NOUN flank is the side of an animal ❑ *And all her silken flanks with garlands dressed* (*Ode on a Grecian Urn* by John Keats)

flip NOUN a flip is a drink made from warmed ale, sugar, spice and beaten egg ❑ *The events of the day, in combination with the twins, if not with the flip, had made Mrs. Micawber hysterical, and she shed tears as she replied* (*David Copperfield* by Charles Dickens)

flit VERB flit means to move quickly ❑ *and if he had meant to flit to Thrushcross Grange* (*Wuthering Heights* by Emily Brontë)

floorcloth NOUN a floorcloth was a hard-wearing piece of canvas used instead of carpet ❑ *This avenging phantom was ordered to be on duty at eight on Tuesday morning in the hall (it was two feet square, as charged for floorcloth)* (*Great Expectations* by Charles Dickens)

fly-driver NOUN a fly-driver is a carriage drawn by a single horse ❑ *The fly-drivers, among whom I inquired next, were equally jocose and equally disrespectful* (*David Copperfield* by Charles Dickens)

fob NOUN a small pocket in which a watch is kept ❑ *"Certain," replied the man, drawing a gold watch from his fob* (*Oliver Twist* by Charles Dickens)

folly NOUN folly means foolishness or stupidity ❑ *the folly of beginning a work* (*Robinson Crusoe* by Daniel Defoe)

fond ADJ fond means foolish ❑ *Fond worldling* (*Doctor Faustus 5.2* by Christopher Marlowe)

fondness NOUN silly or foolish affection ❑ *They have no fondness for their colts or foals* (*Gulliver's Travels* by Jonathan Swift)

for his fancy phrase for his fancy means for his liking or as he wanted ❑ *and as I did not obey quick enough for his fancy* (*Treasure Island* by Robert Louis Stevenson)

forlorn ADJ lost or very upset ❑ *you are from that day forlorn* (*Gulliver's Travels* by Jonathan Swift)

foster-sister NOUN a foster-sister was someone brought up by the same nurse or in the same household ❑ *I had been his foster-sister* (*Wuthering Heights* by Emily Brontë)

fox-fire NOUN fox-fire is a weak glow that is given off by decaying, rotten wood ❑ *what we must have was a lot of them rotten chunks that's called fox-fire* (*The Adventures of Huckleberry Finn* by Mark Twain)

frozen sea phrase the Arctic Ocean ❑ *into the frozen sea* (*Gulliver's Travels* by Jonathan Swift)

gainsay VERB to gainsay something is to say it isn't true or to deny it ❏ *"So she had," cried Scrooge. "You're right. I'll not gainsay it, Spirit. God forbid!" (A Christmas Carol* by Charles Dickens)

gaiters NOUN gaiters were leggings made of a cloth or piece of leather which covered the leg from the knee to the ankle ❏ *Mr Knightley was hard at work upon the lower buttons of his thick leather gaiters (Emma* by Jane Austen)

galluses NOUN galluses is an old spelling of gallows, and here means suspenders. Suspenders are straps worn over someone's shoulders and fastened to their trousers to prevent the trousers falling down ❏ *and home-knit galluses (The Adventures of Huckleberry Finn* by Mark Twain)

galoot NOUN a sailor but also a clumsy person ❏ *and maybe a galoot on it chopping (The Adventures of Huckleberry Finn* by Mark Twain)

gayest ADJ gayest means the most lively and bright or merry ❏ *Beth played her gayest march (Little Women* by Louisa May Alcott)

gem NOUN here gem means jewellery ❏ *the mountain shook off turf and flower, had only heath for raiment and crag for gem (Jane Eyre* by Charlotte Brontë)

giddy ADJ giddy means dizzy ❏ *and I wish you wouldn't keep appearing and vanishing so suddenly; you make one quite giddy. (Alice's Adventures in Wonderland* by Lewis Carroll)

gig NOUN a light two-wheeled carriage ❏ *when a gig drove up to the garden gate: out of which there jumped a fat gentleman (Oliver Twist* by Charles Dickens)

gladsome ADJ gladsome is an old word meaning glad or happy ❏ *Nobody ever stopped him in the street to say, with gladsome looks (A Christmas Carol* by Charles Dickens)

glen NOUN a glen is a small valley; the word is used commonly in Scotland ❏ *a beck which follows the bend of the glen (Wuthering Heights* by Emily Brontë)

gravelled VERB gravelled is an old term which means to baffle or defeat someone ❏ *Gravelled the pastors of the German Church (Doctor Faustus 1.1* by Christopher Marlowe)

grinder NOUN a grinder was a private tutor ❏ *but that when he had had the happiness of marrying Mrs Pocket very early in his life, he had impaired his prospects and taken up the calling of a Grinder (Great Expectations* by Charles Dickens)

gruel NOUN gruel is a thin, watery cornmeal or oatmeal soup ❏ *and the little saucepan of gruel (Scrooge had a cold in his head) upon the hob. (A Christmas Carol* by Charles Dickens)

guinea, half a NOUN a half guinea was ten shillings and sixpence ❏ *but lay out half a guinea at Ford's (Emma* by Jane Austen)

gull VERB gull is an old term which means to fool or deceive someone ❏ *Hush, I'll gull him supernaturally (Doctor Faustus 3.4* by Christopher Marlowe)

gunnel NOUN the gunnel, or gunwhale, is the upper edge of a boat's side ❏ *But he put his foot on the gunnel and rocked her (The Adventures of Huckleberry Finn* by Mark Twain)

gunwale NOUN the side of a ship ❏ *He dipped his hand in the water over the boat's gunwale (Great Expectations* by Charles Dickens)

Gytrash NOUN a Gytrash is an omen of misfortune to the superstitious, usually taking the form of a hound ❏ *I remembered certain of Bessie's tales, wherein figured a North-of-England spirit, called a 'Gytrash' (Jane Eyre* by Charlotte Brontë)

hackney-cabriolet NOUN a two-wheeled carriage with four seats for hire and pulled by a horse ❑ *A hackney-cabriolet was in waiting; with the same vehemence which she had exhibited in addressing Oliver, the girl pulled him in with her, and drew the curtains close.* (*Oliver Twist* by Charles Dickens)

hackney-coach NOUN a four-wheeled horse-drawn vehicle for hire ❑ *The twilight was beginning to close in, when Mr. Brownlow alighted from a hackney-coach at his own door, and knocked softly.* (*Oliver Twist* by Charles Dickens)

haggler NOUN a haggler is someone who travels from place to place selling small goods and items ❑ *when I be plain Jack Durbeyfield, the haggler* (*Tess of the D'Urbervilles* by Thomas Hardy)

halter NOUN a halter is a rope or strap used to lead an animal or to tie it up ❑ *I had of course long been used to a halter and a headstall* (*Black Beauty* by Anna Sewell)

hamlet NOUN a hamlet is a small village or a group of houses in the countryside ❑ *down from the hamlet* (*Treasure Island* by Robert Louis Stevenson)

hand-barrow NOUN a hand-barrow is a device for carrying heavy objects. It is like a wheelbarrow except that it has handles, rather than wheels, for moving the barrow ❑ *his sea chest following behind him in a hand-barrow* (*Treasure Island* by Robert Louis Stevenson)

handspike NOUN a handspike was a stick which was used as a lever ❑ *a bit of stick like a handspike* (*Treasure Island* by Robert Louis Stevenson)

haply ADV haply means by chance or perhaps ❑ *And haply the Queen-Moon is on her throne* (*Ode on a Nightingale* by John Keats)

harem NOUN the harem was the part of the house where the women lived ❑ *mostly they hang round the harem* (*The Adventures of Huckleberry Finn* by Mark Twain)

hautboys NOUN hautboys are oboes ❑ *sausages and puddings resembling flutes and hautboys* (*Gulliver's Travels* by Jonathan Swift)

hawker NOUN a hawker is someone who sells goods to people as he travels rather than from a fixed place like a shop ❑ *to buy some stockings from a hawker* (*Treasure Island* by Robert Louis Stevenson)

hawser NOUN a hawser is a rope used to tie up or tow a ship or boat ❑ *Again among the tiers of shipping, in and out, avoiding rusty chain-cables, frayed hempen hawsers* (*Great Expectations* by Charles Dickens)

headstall NOUN the headstall is the part of the bridle or halter that goes around a horse's head ❑ *I had of course long been used to a halter and a headstall* (*Black Beauty* by Anna Sewell)

hearken VERB hearken means to listen ❑ *though we sometimes stopped to lay hold of each other and hearken* (*Treasure Island* by Robert Louis Stevenson)

heartless ADJ here heartless means without heart or dejected ❑ *I am not heartless* (*The Prelude* by William Wordsworth)

hebdomadal ADJ hebdomadal means weekly ❑ *It was the hebdomadal treat to which we all looked forward from Sabbath to Sabbath* (*Jane Eyre* by Charlotte Brontë)

highwaymen NOUN highwaymen were people who stopped travellers and robbed them ❑ *We are highwaymen* (*The Adventures of Huckleberry Finn* by Mark Twain)

hinds NOUN hinds means farm hands, or people who work on a farm ❑ *He called his hinds about him* (*Gulliver's Travels* by Jonathan Swift)

histrionic ADJ if you refer to someone's behaviour as histrionic, you are being critical of it because it is dramatic and exaggerated

❑ *But the histrionic muse is the darling* (*The Adventures of Huckleberry Finn* by Mark Twain)

hogs NOUN hogs is another word for pigs ❑ *Tom called the hogs 'ingots'* (*The Adventures of Huckleberry Finn* by Mark Twain)

horrors NOUN the horrors are a fit, called delirium tremens, which is caused by drinking too much alcohol ❑ *I'll have the horrors* (*Treasure Island* by Robert Louis Stevenson)

huffy ADJ huffy means to be obviously annoyed or offended about something ❑ *They will feel that more than angry speeches or huffy actions* (*Little Women* by Louisa May Alcott)

hulks NOUN hulks were prison-ships ❑ *The miserable companion of thieves and ruffians, the fallen outcast of low haunts, the associate of the scourings of the jails and hulks* (*Oliver Twist* by Charles Dickens)

humbug NOUN humbug means nonsense or rubbish ❑ *"Bah," said Scrooge. "Humbug!"* (*A Christmas Carol* by Charles Dickens)

humours NOUN it was believed that there were four fluids in the body called humours which decided the temperament of a person depending on how much of each fluid was present ❑ *other peccant humours* (*Gulliver's Travels* by Jonathan Swift)

husbandry NOUN husbandry is farming animals ❑ *bad husbandry were plentifully anointing their wheels* (*Silas Marner* by George Eliot)

huswife NOUN a huswife was a small sewing kit ❑ *but I had put my huswife on it* (*Emma* by Jane Austen)

ideal ADJ ideal in this context means imaginary ❑ *I discovered the yell was not ideal* (*Wuthering Heights* by Emily Brontë)

If our two phrase if both our ❑ *If our*

two loves be one (*The Good-Morrow* by John Donne)

ignis-fatuus NOUN ignis-fatuus is the light given out by burning marsh gases, which lead careless travellers into danger ❑ *it is madness in all women to let a secret love kindle within them, which, if unreturned and unknown, must devour the life that feeds it; and, if discovered and responded to, must lead ignis-fatuus-like, into miry wilds whence there is no extrication.* (*Jane Eyre* by Charlotte Brontë)

imaginations NOUN here imaginations means schemes or plans ❑ *soon drove out those imaginations* (*Gulliver's Travels* by Jonathan Swift)

impressible ADJ impressible means open or impressionable ❑ *for Marner had one of those impressible, self-doubting natures* (*Silas Marner* by George Eliot)

in good intelligence phrase friendly with each other ❑ *that these two persons were in good intelligence with each other* (*Gulliver's Travels* by Jonathan Swift)

inanity NOUN inanity is sillyness or dull stupidity ❑ *Do we not wile away moments of inanity* (*Silas Marner* by George Eliot)

incivility NOUN incivility means rudeness or impoliteness ❑ *if it's only for a piece of incivility like to-night's* (*Treasure Island* by Robert Louis Stevenson)

indigenae NOUN indigenae means natives or people from that area ❑ *an exotic that the surly indigenae will not recognise for kin* (*Wuthering Heights* by Emily Brontë)

indocible ADJ unteachable ❑ *so they were the most restive and indocible* (*Gulliver's Travels* by Jonathan Swift)

ingenuity NOUN inventiveness ❑ *entreated me to give him something as an encouragement to ingenuity* (*Gulliver's Travels* by Jonathan Swift)

ingots NOUN an ingot is a lump of a valuable metal like gold, usually shaped like a brick ❏ *Tom called the hogs 'ingots'* (*The Adventures of Huckleberry Finn* by Mark Twain)

inkstand NOUN an inkstand is a pot which was put on a desk to contain either ink or pencils and pens ❏ *throwing an inkstand at the Lizard as she spoke* (*Alice's Adventures in Wonderland* by Lewis Carroll)

inordinate ADJ without order. Today inordinate means 'excessive'. ❏ *Though yet untutored and inordinate* (*The Prelude* by William Wordsworth)

intellectuals NOUN here intellectuals means the minds (of the workmen) ❏ *those instructions they give being too refined for the intellectuals of their workmen* (*Gulliver's Travels* by Jonathan Swift)

interview NOUN meeting ❏ *By our first strange and fatal interview* (*On His Mistress* by John Donne)

jacks NOUN jacks are rods for turning a spit over a fire ❏ *It was a small bit of pork suspended from the kettle hanger by a string passed through a large door key, in a way known to primitive housekeepers unpossessed of jacks* (*Silas Marner* by George Eliot)

jews-harp NOUN a jews-harp is a small, metal, musical instrument that is played by the mouth ❏ *A jews-harp's plenty good enough for a rat* (*The Adventures of Huckleberry Finn* by Mark Twain)

jorum NOUN a large bowl ❏ *while Miss Skiffins brewed such a jorum of tea, that the pig in the back premises became strongly excited* (*Great Expectations* by Charles Dickens)

jostled VERB jostled means bumped or pushed by someone or some people ❏ *being jostled into the kennel* (*Gulliver's Travels* by Jonathan Swift)

keepsake NOUN a keepsake is a gift which reminds someone of an event or of the person who gave it to them. ❏ *books and ornaments they had in their boudoirs at home: keepsakes that different relations had presented to them* (*Jane Eyre* by Charlotte Brontë)

kenned VERB kenned means knew ❏ *though little kenned the lamplighter that he had any company but Christmas!* (*A Christmas Carol* by Charles Dickens)

kennel NOUN kennel means gutter, which is the edge of a road next to the pavement, where rain water collects and flows away ❏ *being jostled himself into the kennel* (*Gulliver's Travels* by Jonathan Swift)

knock-knee ADJ knock-knee means slanted, at an angle. ❏ *LOT 1 was marked in whitewashed knock-knee letters on the brewhouse* (*Great Expectations* by Charles Dickens)

ladylike ADJ to be ladylike is to behave in a polite, dignified and graceful way ❏ *No, winking isn't ladylike* (*Little Women* by Louisa May Alcott)

lapse NOUN flow ❏ *Stealing with silent lapse to join the brook* (*The Prelude* by William Wordsworth)

larry NOUN larry is an old word which means commotion or noisy celebration ❏ *That was all a part of the larry!* (*Tess of the D'Urbervilles* by Thomas Hardy)

laths NOUN laths are strips of wood ❏ *The panels shrunk, the windows cracked; fragments of plaster fell out of the ceiling, and the naked laths were shown instead* (*A Christmas Carol* by Charles Dickens)

leer NOUN a leer is an unpleasant smile ❏ *with a kind of leer* (*Treasure Island* by Robert Louis Stevenson)

lenitives NOUN these are different kinds of drugs or medicines: lenitives and palliatives were pain relievers; aperitives were laxatives; abstersives caused vomiting; corrosives destroyed human tissue; restringents caused constipation; cephalalgics stopped headaches;

icterics were used as medicine for jaundice; apophlegmatics were cough medicine, and acoustics were cures for the loss of hearing ❑ *lenitives, aperitives, abstersives, corrosives, restringents, palliatives, laxatives, cephalalgics, icterics, apophlegmatics, acoustics* (*Gulliver's Travels* by Jonathan Swift)

lest CONJ in case. If you do something lest something (usually) unpleasant happens you do it to try to prevent it happening ❑ *She went in without knocking, and hurried upstairs, in great fear lest she should meet the real Mary Ann* (*Alice's Adventures in Wonderland* by Lewis Carroll)

levee NOUN a levee is an old term for a meeting held in the morning, shortly after the person holding the meeting has got out of bed ❑ *I used to attend the King's levee once or twice a week* (*Gulliver's Travels* by Jonathan Swift)

life-preserver NOUN a club which had lead inside it to make it heavier and therefore more dangerous ❑ *and with no more suspicious articles displayed to view than two or three heavy bludgeons which stood in a corner, and a 'life-preserver' that hung over the chimney-piece.* (*Oliver Twist* by Charles Dickens)

lighterman NOUN a lighterman is another word for sailor ❑ *in and out, hammers going in ship-builders' yards, saws going at timber, clashing engines going at things unknown, pumps going in leaky ships, capstans going, ships going out to sea, and unintelligible sea creatures roaring curses over the bulwarks at respondent lightermen* (*Great Expectations* by Charles Dickens)

livery NOUN servants often wore a uniform known as a livery ❑ *suddenly a footman in livery came running out of the wood* (*Alice's Adventures in Wonderland* by Lewis Carroll)

livid ADJ livid means pale or ash coloured. Livid also means very angry ❑ *a dirty, livid white*

(*Treasure Island* by Robert Louis Stevenson)

lottery-tickets NOUN a popular card game ❑ *and Mrs. Philips protested that they would have a nice comfortable noisy game of lottery tickets* (*Pride and Prejudice* by Jane Austen)

lower and upper world phrase the earth and the heavens are the lower and upper worlds ❑ *the changes in the lower and upper world* (*Gulliver's Travels* by Jonathan Swift)

lustres NOUN lustres are chandeliers. A chandelier is a large, decorative frame which holds light bulbs or candles and hangs from the ceiling ❑ *the lustres, lights, the carving and the guilding* (*The Prelude* by William Wordsworth)

lynched VERB killed without a criminal trial by a crowd of people ❑ *He'll never know how nigh he come to getting lynched* (*The Adventures of Huckleberry Finn* by Mark Twain)

malingering VERB if someone is malingering they are pretending to be ill to avoid working ❑ *And you stand there malingering* (*Treasure Island* by Robert Louis Stevenson)

managing phrase treating with consideration ❑ *to think the honour of my own kind not worth managing* (*Gulliver's Travels* by Jonathan Swift)

manhood phrase manhood means human nature ❑ *concerning the nature of manhood* (*Gulliver's Travels* by Jonathan Swift)

man-trap NOUN a man-trap is a set of steel jaws that snap shut when trodden on and trap a person's leg ❑ *"Don't go to him," I called out of the window, "he's an assassin! A man-trap!"* (*Oliver Twist* by Charles Dickens)

maps NOUN charts of the night sky ❑ *Let maps to others, worlds on worlds have shown* (*The Good-Morrow* by John Donne)

mark VERB look at or notice ❑ Mark but this flea, and mark in this (The Flea by John Donne)

maroons NOUN A maroon is someone who has been left in a place which it is difficult for them to escape from, like a small island ❑ if schooners, islands, and maroons (Treasure Island by Robert Louis Stevenson)

mast NOUN here mast means the fruit of forest trees ❑ a quantity of acorns, dates, chestnuts, and other mast (Gulliver's Travels by Jonathan Swift)

mate VERB defeat ❑ Where Mars did mate the warlike Carthigens (Doctor Faustus Chorus by Christopher Marlowe)

mealy ADJ Mealy when used to describe a face meant palid, pale or colourless ❑ I only know two sorts of boys. Mealy boys, and beef-faced boys (Oliver Twist by Charles Dickens)

middling ADJ fairly or moderately ❑ she worked me middling hard for about an hour (The Adventures of Huckleberry Finn by Mark Twain)

mill NOUN a mill, or treadmill, was a device for hard labour or punishment in prison ❑ Was you never on the mill? (Oliver Twist by Charles Dickens)

milliner's shop NOUN a milliner's sold fabrics, clothing, lace and accessories; as time went on they specialized more and more in hats ❑ to pay their duty to their aunt and to a milliner's shop just over the way (Pride and Prejudice by Jane Austen)

minching un' munching phrase how people in the north of England used to describe the way people from the south speak ❑ Minching un' munching! (Wuthering Heights by Emily Brontë)

mine NOUN gold ❑ Whether both th'Indias of spice and mine (The Sun Rising by John Donne)

mire NOUN mud ❑ Tis my fate to be always ground into the mire under the iron heel of oppression (The Adventures of Huckleberry Finn by Mark Twain)

miscellany NOUN a miscellany is a collection of many different kinds of things ❑ under that, the miscellany began (Treasure Island by Robert Louis Stevenson)

mistarshers NOUN mistarshers means moustache, which is the hair that grows on a man's upper lip ❑ when he put his hand up to his mistarshers (Tess of the D'Urbervilles by Thomas Hardy)

morrow NOUN here good-morrow means tomorrow and a new and better life ❑ And now good-morrow to our waking souls (The Good-Morrow by John Donne)

mortification NOUN mortification is an old word for gangrene which is when part of the body decays or 'dies' because of disease ❑ Yes, it was a mortification – that was it (The Adventures of Huckleberry Finn by Mark Twain)

mought PARTICIPLE mought is an old spelling of might ❑ what you mought call me? You mought call me captain (Treasure Island by Robert Louis Stevenson)

move VERB move me not means do not make me angry ❑ Move me not, Faustus (Doctor Faustus 2.1 by Christopher Marlowe)

muffin-cap NOUN a muffin cap is a flat cap made from wool ❑ the old one, remained stationary in the muffin-cap and leathers (Oliver Twist by Charles Dickens)

mulatter NOUN a mulatter was another word for mulatto, which is a person with parents who are from different races ❑ a mulatter, most as white as a white man (The Adventures of Huckleberry Finn by Mark Twain)

mummery NOUN mummery is an old word that meant meaningless (or pretentious) ceremony ❑ When they were all gone, and when Trabb and his men – but not his boy: I looked for him – had crammed their mummery into bags, and were gone too, the house felt wholesomer. (*Great Expectations* by Charles Dickens)

nap NOUN the nap is the woolly surface on a new item of clothing. Here the surface has been worn away so it looks bare ❏ *like an old hat with the nap rubbed off* (*The Adventures of Huckleberry Finn* by Mark Twain)

natural ■ NOUN a natural is a person born with learning difficulties ❏ *though he had been left to his particular care by their deceased father, who thought him almost a natural.* (David Copperfield by Charles Dickens) ■ ADJ natural meant illegitimate ❏ *Harriet Smith was the natural daughter of somebody* (*Emma* by Jane Austen)

navigator NOUN a navigator was originally someone employed to dig canals. It is the origin of the word 'navvy' meaning a labourer ❏ *She ascertained from me in a few words what it was all about, comforted Dora, and gradually convinced her that I was not a labourer – from my manner of stating the case I believe Dora concluded that I was a navigator, and went balancing myself up and down a plank all day with a wheelbarrow – and so brought us together in peace.* (*David Copperfield* by Charles Dickens)

necromancy NOUN necromancy means a kind of magic where the magician speaks to spirits or ghosts to find out what will happen in the future ❏ *He surfeits upon cursed necromancy* (*Doctor Faustus chorus* by Christopher Marlowe)

negus NOUN a negus is a hot drink made from sweetened wine and water ❏ *He sat placidly perusing the newspaper, with his little head on one side, and a glass of warm sherry negus at his elbow.* (*David Copperfield* by Charles Dickens)

nice ADJ discriminating. Able to make good judgements or choices ❏

consequently a claim to be nice (*Emma* by Jane Austen)

nigh ADV nigh means near ❏ *He'll never know how nigh he come to getting lynched* (*The Adventures of Huckleberry Finn* by Mark Twain)

nimbleness NOUN nimbleness means being able to move very quickly or skillfully ❏ *and with incredible accuracy and nimbleness* (*Treasure Island* by Robert Louis Stevenson)

noggin NOUN a noggin is a small mug or a wooden cup ❏ *you'll bring me one noggin of rum* (*Treasure Island* by Robert Louis Stevenson)

none ADJ neither ❏ *none can die* (*The Good-Morrow* by John Donne)

notices NOUN observations ❏ *Arch are his notices* (*The Prelude* by William Wordsworth)

occiput NOUN occiput means the back of the head ❏ *saw off the occiput of each couple* (Gulliver's Travels by Jonathan Swift)

officiously ADJ kindly ❏ *the governess who attended Glumdalclitch very officiously lifted me up* (*Gulliver's Travels* by Jonathan Swift)

old salt phrase old salt is a slang term for an experienced sailor ❏ *a 'true sea-dog', and a 'real old salt'* (*Treasure Island* by Robert Louis Stevenson)

or ere phrase before ❏ *or ere the Hall was built* (*The Prelude* by William Wordsworth)

ostler NOUN one who looks after horses at an inn ❏ *The bill paid, and the waiter remembered, and the ostler not forgotten, and the chambermaid taken into consideration* (*Great Expectations* by Charles Dickens)

ostry NOUN an ostry is an old word for a pub or hotel ❏ *lest I send you into the ostry with a vengeance* (*Doctor Faustus 2.2* by Christopher Marlowe)

outrunning the constable phrase outrunning the constable meant spending more than you earn ❏ *but I shall by this means be able to* *check your bills and to pull you up if I find you outrunning the constable.* (*Great Expectations* by Charles Dickens)

over ADJ across ❏ *It is in length six yards, and in the thickest part at least three yards over* (*Gulliver's Travels* by Jonathan Swift)

over the broomstick phrase this is a phrase meaning 'getting married without a formal ceremony' ❏ *They both led tramping lives, and this woman in Gerrard-street here, had been married very young, over the broomstick (as we say), to a tramping man, and was a perfect fury in point of jealousy.* (*Great Expectations* by Charles Dickens)

own VERB own means to admit or to acknowledge ❏ *It's my old girl that advises. She has the head. But I never own to it before her. Discipline must be maintained* (*Bleak House* by Charles Dickens)

page NOUN here page means a boy employed to run errands ❏ *not my feigned page* (*On His Mistress* by John Donne)

paid pretty dear phrase paid pretty dear means paid a high price or suffered quite a lot ❏ *I paid pretty dear for my monthly fourpenny piece* (*Treasure Island* by Robert Louis Stevenson)

pannikins NOUN pannikins were small tin cups ❏ *of lifting light glasses and cups to his lips, as if they were clumsy pannikins* (*Great Expectations* by Charles Dickens)

pards NOUN pards are leopards ❏ *Not charioted by Bacchus and his pards* (*Ode on a Nightingale* by John Keats)

parlour boarder NOUN a pupil who lived with the family ❏ *and somebody had lately raised her from the condition of scholar to parlour boarder* (*Emma* by Jane Austen)

particular, a London phrase London in Victorian times and up to the 1950s was famous for having very dense fog – which was a combination of real fog and the

smog of pollution from factories ❏ *This is a London particular . . . A fog, miss'* (*Bleak House* by Charles Dickens)

patten NOUN pattens were wooden soles which were fixed to shoes by straps to protect the shoes in wet weather ❏ *carrying a basket like the Great Seal of England in plaited straw, a pair of pattens, a spare shawl, and an umbrella, though it was a fine bright day* (*Great Expectations* by Charles Dickens)

paviour NOUN a paviour was a labourer who worked on the street pavement ❏ *the paviour his pickaxe* (*Oliver Twist* by Charles Dickens)

peccant ADJ peccant means unhealthy ❏ *other peccant humours* (*Gulliver's Travels* by Jonathan Swift)

penetralium NOUN penetralium is a word used to describe the inner rooms of the house ❏ *and I had no desire to aggravate his impatience previous to inspecting the penetralium* (*Wuthering Heights* by Emily Brontë)

pensive ADV pensive means deep in thought or thinking seriously about something ❏ *and she was leaning pensive on a tomb-stone on her right elbow* (*The Adventures of Huckleberry Finn* by Mark Twain)

penury NOUN penury is the state of being extremely poor ❏ *Distress, if not penury, loomed in the distance* (*Tess of the D'Urbervilles* by Thomas Hardy)

perspective NOUN telescope ❏ *a pocket perspective* (*Gulliver's Travels* by Jonathan Swift)

phaeton NOUN a phaeton was an open carriage for four people ❏ *often condescends to drive by my humble abode in her little phaeton and ponies* (*Pride and Prejudice* by Jane Austen)

phantasm NOUN a phantasm is an illusion, something that is not real. It is sometimes used to mean ghost ❏ *Experience had bred no fancies in* *him that could raise the phantasm of appetite* (*Silas Marner* by George Eliot)

physic NOUN here physic means medicine ❑ *there I studied physic two years and seven months* (*Gulliver's Travels* by Jonathan Swift)

pinioned VERB to pinion is to hold both arms so that a person cannot move them ❑ *But the relentless Ghost pinioned him in both his arms, and forced him to observe what happened next.* (*A Christmas Carol* by Charles Dickens)

piquet NOUN piquet was a popular card game in the C18th ❑ *Mr Hurst and Mr Bingley were at piquet* (*Pride and Prejudice* by Jane Austen)

plaister NOUN a plaister is a piece of cloth on which an apothecary (or pharmacist) would spread ointment. The cloth is then applied to wounds or bruises to treat them ❑ *Then, she gave the knife a final smart wipe on the edge of the plaister, and then sawed a very thick round off the loaf: which she finally, before separating from the loaf, hewed into two halves, of which Joe got one, and I the other.* (*Great Expectations* by Charles Dickens)

plantations NOUN here plantations means colonies, which are countries controlled by a more powerful country ❑ *besides our plantations in America* (*Gulliver's Travels* by Jonathan Swift)

plastic ADV here plastic is an old term meaning shaping or a power that was forming ❑ *A plastic power abode with me* (*The Prelude* by William Wordsworth)

players NOUN actors ❑ *of players which upon the world's stage be* (*On His Mistress* by John Donne)

plump ADV all at once, suddenly ❑ *But it took a bit of time to get it well round, the change come so uncommon plump, didn't it?* (*Great Expectations* by Charles Dickens)

plundered VERB to plunder is to rob or steal from ❑ *These crosses stand*

for the names of ships or towns that they sank or plundered (*Treasure Island* by Robert Louis Stevenson)

pommel ■ VERB to pommel someone is to hit them repeatedly with your fists ❑ *hug him round the neck, pommel his back, and kick his legs in irrepressible affection!* (*A Christmas Carol* by Charles Dickens) ■ NOUN a pommel is the part of a saddle that rises up at the front ❑ *He had his gun across his pommel* (*The Adventures of Huckleberry Finn* by Mark Twain)

poor's rates NOUN poor's rates were property taxes which were used to support the poor ❑ *"Oh!" replied the undertaker; "why, you know, Mr. Bumble, I pay a good deal towards the poor's rates."* (*Oliver Twist* by Charles Dickens)

popular ADJ popular means ruled by the people, or Republican, rather than ruled by a monarch ❑ *With those of Greece compared and popular Rome* (*The Prelude* by William Wordsworth)

porringer NOUN a porringer is a small bowl ❑ *Of this festive composition each boy had one porringer, and no more* (*Oliver Twist* by Charles Dickens)

postboy NOUN a postboy was the driver of a horse-drawn carriage ❑ *He spoke to a postboy who was dozing under the gateway* (*Oliver Twist* by Charles Dickens)

post-chaise NOUN a fast carriage for two or four passengers ❑ *Looking round, he saw that it was a post-chaise, driven at great speed* (*Oliver Twist* by Charles Dickens)

postern NOUN a small gate usually at the back of a building ❑ *The little servant happening to be entering the fortress with two hot rolls, I passed through the postern and crossed the drawbridge, in her company* (*Great Expectations* by Charles Dickens)

pottle NOUN a pottle was a small basket ❑ *He had a paper-bag under each arm and a pottle of* *strawberries in one hand . . . (Great Expectations* by Charles Dickens)

pounce NOUN pounce is a fine powder used to prevent ink spreading on untreated paper ❏ *in that grim atmosphere of pounce and parchment, red-tape, dusty wafers, ink-jars, brief and draft paper, law reports, writs, declarations, and bills of costs (David Copperfield* by Charles Dickens)

pox NOUN pox means sexually transmitted diseases like syphilis ❏ *how the pox in all its consequences and denominations (Gulliver's Travels* by Jonathan Swift)

prelibation NOUN prelibation means a foretaste of or an example of something to come ❏ *A prelibation to the mower's scythe (The Prelude* by William Wordsworth)

prentice NOUN an apprentice ❏ *and Joe, sitting on an old gun, had told me that when I was 'prentice to him regularly bound, we would have such Larks there! (Great Expectations* by Charles Dickens)

presently ADV immediately ❏ *I presently knew what they meant (Gulliver's Travels* by Jonathan Swift)

pumpion NOUN pumpkin ❏ *for it was almost as large as a small pumpion (Gulliver's Travels* by Jonathan Swift)

punctual ADJ kept in one place ❏ *was not a punctual presence, but a spirit (The Prelude* by William Wordsworth)

quadrille ■ NOUN a quadrille is a dance invented in France which is usually performed by four couples ❏ *However, Mr Swiveller had Miss Sophy's hand for the first quadrille (country-dances being low, were utterly proscribed) (The Old Curiosity Shop* by Charles Dickens) ■ NOUN quadrille was a card game for four people ❏ *to make up her pool of quadrille in the evening (Pride and Prejudice* by Jane Austen)

quality NOUN gentry or upper-class people ❏ *if you are with the quality*

(The Adventures of Huckleberry Finn by Mark Twain)

quick parts phrase quick-witted ❏ *Mr Bennet was so odd a mixture of quick parts (Pride and Prejudice* by Jane Austen)

quid NOUN a quid is something chewed or kept in the mouth, like a piece of tobacco ❏ *rolling his quid (Treasure Island* by Robert Louis Stevenson)

quit VERB quit means to avenge or to make even ❏ *But Faustus's death shall quit my infamy (Doctor Faustus 4.3* by Christopher Marlowe)

rags NOUN divisions ❏ *Nor hours, days, months, which are the rags of time (The Sun Rising* by John Donne)

raiment NOUN raiment means clothing ❏ *the mountain shook off turf and flower, had only heath for raiment and crag for gem (Jane Eyre* by Charlotte Brontë)

rain cats and dogs phrase an expression meaning rain heavily. The origin of the expression is unclear ❏ *But it'll perhaps rain cats and dogs to-morrow (Silas Marner* by George Eliot)

raised Cain phrase raised Cain means caused a lot of trouble. Cain is a character in the Bible who killed his brother Abel ❏ *and every time he got drunk he raised Cain around town (The Adventures of Huckleberry Finn* by Mark Twain)

rambling ADJ rambling means confused and not very clear ❏ *my head began to be filled very early with rambling thoughts (Robinson Crusoe* by Daniel Defoe)

raree-show NOUN a raree-show is an old term for a peep-show or a fairground entertainment ❏ *A raree-show is here, with children gathered round (The Prelude* by William Wordsworth)

recusants NOUN people who resisted authority ❏ *hardy recusants (The Prelude* by William Wordsworth)

redounding VERB eddying. An eddy is a movement in water or air which goes round and round instead of flowing in one direction ❏ *mists and steam-like fogs redounding everywhere* (*The Prelude* by William Wordsworth)

redundant ADJ here redundant means overflowing but Wordsworth also uses it to mean excessively large or too big ❏ *A tempest, a redundant energy* (*The Prelude* by William Wordsworth)

reflex NOUN reflex is a shortened version of reflexion, which is an alternative spelling of reflection ❏ *To cut across the reflex of a star* (*The Prelude* by William Wordsworth)

Reformatory NOUN a prison for young offenders/criminals ❏ *Even when I was taken to have a new suit of clothes, the tailor had orders to make them like a kind of Reformatory, and on no account to let me have the free use of my limbs.* (*Great Expectations* by Charles Dickens)

remorse NOUN pity or compassion ❏ *by that remorse* (*On His Mistress* by John Donne)

render VERB in this context render means give. ❏ *and Sarah could render no reason that would be sanctioned by the feeling of the community.* (*Silas Marner* by George Eliot)

repeater NOUN a repeater was a watch that chimed the last hour when a button was pressed – as a result it was useful in the dark ❏ *And his watch is a gold repeater, and worth a hundred pound if it's worth a penny.* (*Great Expectations* by Charles Dickens)

repugnance NOUN repugnance means a strong dislike of something or someone ❏ *overcoming a strong repugnance* (*Treasure Island* by Robert Louis Stevenson)

reverence NOUN reverence means bow. When you bow to someone, you briefly bend your body towards

them as a formal way of showing them respect ❏ *made my reverence* (*Gulliver's Travels* by Jonathan Swift)

reverie NOUN a reverie is a day dream ❏ *I can guess the subject of your reverie* (*Pride and Prejudice* by Jane Austen)

revival NOUN a religious meeting held in public ❏ *well I'd ben a-running' a little temperance revival thar' bout a week* (*The Adventures of Huckleberry Finn* by Mark Twain)

revolt VERB revolt means turn back or stop your present course of action and go back to what you were doing before ❏ *Revolt, or I'll in piecemeal tear thy flesh* (*Doctor Faustus 5.1* by Christopher Marlowe)

rheumatics/rheumatism NOUN rheumatics [rheumatism] is an illness that makes your joints or muscles stiff and painful ❏ *a new cure for the rheumatics* (*Treasure Island* by Robert Louis Stevenson)

riddance NOUN riddance is usually used in the form good riddance which you say when you are pleased that something has gone or been left behind ❏ *I'd better go into the house, and die and be a riddance* (*David Copperfield* by Charles Dickens)

rimy ADJ rimy is an ADJective which means covered in ice or frost ❏ *It was a rimy morning, and very damp* (*Great Expectations* by Charles Dickens)

riper ADJ riper means more mature or older ❏ *At riper years to Wittenberg he went* (*Doctor Faustus chorus* by Christopher Marlowe)

rubber NOUN a set of games in whist or backgammon ❏ *her father was sure of his rubber* (*Emma* by Jane Austen)

ruffian NOUN a ruffian is a person who behaves violently ❏ *and when the ruffian had told him* (*Treasure Island* by Robert Louis Stevenson)

sadness NOUN sadness is an old term meaning seriousness ❏ *But I* *prithee tell me, in good sadness* (*Doctor Faustus* 2.2 by Christopher Marlowe)

sailed before the mast phrase this phrase meant someone who did not look like a sailor ❏ *he had none of the appearance of a man that sailed before the mast* (*Treasure Island* by Robert Louis Stevenson)

scabbard NOUN a scabbard is the covering for a sword or dagger ❏ *Girded round its middle was an antique scabbard; but no sword was in it, and the ancient sheath was eaten up with rust* (*A Christmas Carol* by Charles Dickens)

schooners NOUN A schooner is a fast, medium-sized sailing ship ❏ *if schooners, islands, and maroons* (*Treasure Island* by Robert Louis Stevenson)

science NOUN learning or knowledge ❏ *Even Science, too, at hand* (*The Prelude* by William Wordsworth)

scrouge VERB to scrouge means to squeeze or to crowd ❏ *to scrouge in and get a sight* (*The Adventures of Huckleberry Finn* by Mark Twain)

scrutore NOUN a scrutore, or escritoire, was a writing table ❏ *set me gently on my feet upon the scrutore* (*Gulliver's Travels* by Jonathan Swift)

scutcheon/ escutcheon NOUN an escutcheon is a shield with a coat of arms, or the symbols of a family name, engraved on it ❏ *On the scutcheon we'll have a bend* (*The Adventures of Huckleberry Finn* by Mark Twain)

sea-dog phrase sea-dog is a slang term for an experienced sailor or pirate ❏ *a 'true sea-dog', and a 'real old salt,'* (*Treasure Island* by Robert Louis Stevenson)

see the lions phrase to see the lions was to go and see the sights of London. Originally the phrase referred to the menagerie in the Tower of London and later in Regent's Park ❏ *We will go and see the lions for an hour or two – it's something to have a fresh fellow like you to show them to, Copperfield* (*David Copperfield* by Charles Dickens)

self-conceit NOUN self-conceit is an old term which means having too high an opinion of oneself, or deceiving yourself ❏ *Till swollen with cunning, of a self-conceit* (*Doctor Faustus chorus* by Christopher Marlowe)

seneschal NOUN a steward ❏ *where a grey-headed seneschal sings a funny chorus with a funnier body of vassals* (*Oliver Twist* by Charles Dickens)

sensible ADJ if you were sensible of something you are aware or conscious of something ❏ *If my children are silly I must hope to be always sensible of it* (*Pride and Prejudice* by Jane Austen)

sessions NOUN court cases were heard at specific times of the year called sessions ❏ *He lay in prison very ill, during the whole interval between his committal for trial, and the coming round of the Sessions.* (*Great Expectations* by Charles Dickens)

shabby ADJ shabby places look old and in bad condition ❏ *a little bit of a shabby village named Pikesville* (*The Adventures of Huckleberry Finn* by Mark Twain)

shay-cart NOUN a shay-cart was a small cart drawn by one horse ❏ *"I were at the Bargemen t'other night, Pip;" whenever he subsided into affection, he called me Pip, and whenever he relapsed into politeness he called me Sir; "when there come up in his shay-cart Pumblechook."* (*Great Expectations* by Charles Dickens)

shilling NOUN a shilling is an old unit of currency.There were twenty shillings in every British pound ❏ *"Ten shillings too much," said the gentleman in the white waistcoat.* (*Oliver Twist* by Charles Dickens)

shines NOUN tricks or games ❏ *well, it would make a cow laugh to see the* *shines that old idiot cut* (*The Adventures of Huckleberry Finn* by Mark Twain)

shirking VERB shirking means not doing what you are meant to be doing, or evading your duties ❑ *some of you shirking lubbers* (*Treasure Island* by Robert Louis Stevenson)

shiver my timbers phrase shiver my timbers is an expression which was used by sailors and pirates to express surprise ❑ *why, shiver my timbers, if I hadn't forgotten my score!* (*Treasure Island* by Robert Louis Stevenson)

shoe-roses NOUN shoe-roses were roses made from ribbons which were stuck on to shoes as decoration ❑ *the very shoe-roses for Netherfield were got by proxy* (*Pride and Prejudice* by Jane Austen)

singular ADJ singular means very great and remarkable or strange ❑ *"Singular dream," he says* (*The Adventures of Huckleberry Finn* by Mark Twain)

sire NOUN sire is an old word which means lord or master or elder ❑ *She also defied her sire* (*Little Women* by Louisa May Alcott)

sixpence NOUN a sixpence was half of a shilling ❑ *if she had only a shilling in the world, she would be very lilkely to give away sixpence of it* (*Emma* by Jane Austen)

slavey NOUN the word slavey was used when there was only one servant in a house or boarding-house – so she had to perform all the duties of a larger staff ❑ *Two distinct knocks, sir, will produce the slavey at any time* (*The Old Curiosity Shop* by Charles Dickens)

slender ADJ weak ❑ *In slender accents of sweet verse* (*The Prelude* by William Wordsworth)

slop-shops NOUN slop-shops were shops where cheap ready-made clothes were sold. They mainly sold clothes to sailors ❑ *Accordingly, I took the jacket off, that I might*

learn to do without it; and carrying it under my arm, began a tour of inspection of the various slop-shops. (*David Copperfield* by Charles Dickens)

sluggard NOUN a lazy person ❑ *"Stand up and repeat 'Tis the voice of the sluggard,'" said the Gryphon.* (*Alice's Adventures in Wonderland* by Lewis Carroll)

smallpox NOUN smallpox is a serious infectious disease ❑ *by telling the men we had smallpox aboard* (*The Adventures of Huckleberry Finn* by Mark Twain)

smalls NOUN smalls are short trousers ❑ *It is difficult for a large-headed, small-eyed youth, of lumbering make and heavy countenance, to look dignified under any circumstances; but it is more especially so, when superadded to these personal attractions are a red nose and yellow smalls* (*Oliver Twist* by Charles Dickens)

sneeze-box NOUN a box for snuff was called a sneeze-box because sniffing snuff makes the user sneeze ❑ *To think of Jack Dawkins – lummy Jack – the Dodger – the Artful Dodger – going abroad for a common twopenny-halfpenny sneeze-box!* (*Oliver Twist* by Charles Dickens)

snorted VERB slept ❑ *Or snorted we in the Seven Sleepers' den?* (*The Good-Morrow* by John Donne)

snuff NOUN snuff is tobacco in powder form which is taken by sniffing ❑ *as he thrust his thumb and forefinger into the proffered snuff-box of the undertaker: which was an ingenious little model of a patent coffin.* (*Oliver Twist* by Charles Dickens)

soliloquized VERB to soliloquize is when an actor in a play speaks to himself or herself rather than to another actor ❑ *"A new servitude! There is something in that," I soliloquized (mentally, be it understood; I did not talk aloud)* (*Jane Eyre* by Charlotte Brontë)

sough NOUN a sough is a drain or a ditch ❏ *as you may have noticed the sough that runs from the marshes* (*Wuthering Heights* by Emily Brontë)

spirits NOUN a spirit is the nonphysical part of a person which is believed to remain alive after their death ❏ *that I might raise up spirits when I please* (*Doctor Faustus 1.5* by Christopher Marlowe)

spleen ■ NOUN here spleen means a type of sadness or depression which was thought to only affect the wealthy ❏ *yet here I could plainly discover the true seeds of spleen* (*Gulliver's Travels* by Jonathan Swift) ■ NOUN irritability and low spirits ❏ *Adieu to disappointment and spleen* (*Pride and Prejudice* by Jane Austen)

spondulicks NOUN spondulicks is a slang word which means money ❏ *not for all his spondulicks and as much more on top of it* (*The Adventures of Huckleberry Finn* by Mark Twain)

stalled of VERB to be stalled of something is to be bored with it ❏ *I'm stalled of doing naught* (*Wuthering Heights* by Emily Brontë)

stanchion NOUN a stanchion is a pole or bar that stands upright and is used as a buidling support ❏ *and slid down a stanchion* (*The Adventures of Huckleberry Finn* by Mark Twain)

stang NOUN stang is another word for pole which was an old measurement ❏ *These fields were intermingled with woods of half a stang* (*Gulliver's Travels* by Jonathan Swift)

starlings NOUN a starling is a wall built around the pillars that support a bridge to protect the pillars ❏ *There were states of the tide when, having been down the river, I could not get back through the eddy-chafed arches and starlings of old London Bridge* (*Great Expectations* by Charles Dickens)

startlings NOUN twitching or night-time movements of the body ❏ *with midnight's startlings* (*On His Mistress* by John Donne)

stomacher NOUN a panel at the front of a dress ❏ *but send her aunt the pattern of a stomacher* (*Emma* by Jane Austen)

stoop VERB swoop ❏ *Once a kite hovering over the garden made a swoop at me* (*Gulliver's Travels* by Jonathan Swift)

succedaneum NOUN a succedaneum is a substitute ❏ *But as a succedaneum* (*The Prelude* by William Wordsworth)

suet NOUN a hard animal fat used in cooking ❏ *and your jaws are too weak For anything tougher than suet* (*Alice's Adventures in Wonderland* by Lewis Carroll)

sultry ADJ sultry weather is hot and damp. Here sultry means unpleasant or risky ❏ *for it was getting pretty sultry for us* (*The Adventures of Huckleberry Finn* by Mark Twain)

summerset NOUN summerset is an old spelling of somersault. If someone does a somersault, they turn over completely in the air ❏ *I have seen him do the summerset* (*Gulliver's Travels* by Jonathan Swift)

supper NOUN supper was a light meal taken late in the evening. The main meal was dinner which was eaten at four or five in the afternoon ❏ *and the supper table was all set out* (*Emma* by Jane Austen)

surfeits VERB to surfeit in something is to have far too much of it, or to overindulge in it to an unhealthy degree ❏ *He surfeits upon cursed necromancy* (*Doctor Faustus chorus* by Christopher Marlowe)

surtout NOUN a surtout is a long close-fitting overcoat ❏ *He wore a long black surtout reaching nearly to his ankles* (*The Old Curiosity Shop* by Charles Dickens)

swath NOUN swath is the width of corn cut by a scythe ❏ *while thy* *hook Spares the next swath (Ode to Autumn by John Keats)*

sylvan ADJ sylvan means belonging to the woods ❑ *Sylvan historian (Ode on a Grecian Urn by John Keats)*

taction NOUN taction means touch. This means that the people had to be touched on the mouth or the ears to get their attention ❑ *without being roused by some external taction upon the organs of speech and hearing (Gulliver's Travels by Jonathan Swift)*

Tag and Rag and Bobtail phrase the riff-raff, or lower classes. Used in an insulting way ❑ *"No," said he; "not till it got about that there was no protection on the premises, and it come to be considered dangerous, with convicts and Tag and Rag and Bobtail going up and down." (Great Expectations by Charles Dickens)*

tallow NOUN tallow is hard animal fat that is used to make candles and soap ❑ *and a lot of tallow candles (The Adventures of Huckleberry Finn by Mark Twain)*

tan VERB to tan means to beat or whip ❑ *and if I catch you about that school I'll tan you good (The Adventures of Huckleberry Finn by Mark Twain)*

tanyard NOUN the tanyard is part of a tannery, which is a place where leather is made from animal skins ❑ *hid in the old tanyard (The Adventures of Huckleberry Finn by Mark Twain)*

tarry ADJ tarry means the colour of tar or black ❑ *his tarry pig-tail (Treasure Island by Robert Louis Stevenson)*

thereof phrase from there ❑ *By all desires which thereof did ensue (On His Mistress by John Donne)*

thick with, be phrase if you are 'thick with someone' you are very close, sharing secrets – it is often used to describe people who are planning something secret ❑ *Hasn't he been thick with Mr*

Heathcliff lately? (Wuthering Heights by Emily Brontë)

thimble NOUN a thimble is a small cover used to protect the finger while sewing ❑ *The paper had been sealed in several places by a thimble (Treasure Island by Robert Louis Stevenson)*

thirtover ADJ thirtover is an old word which means obstinate or that someone is very determined to do want they want and can not be persuaded to do something in another way ❑ *I have been living on in a thirtover, lackadaisical way (Tess of the D'Urbervilles by Thomas Hardy)*

timbrel NOUN timbrel is a tambourine ❑ *What pipes and timbrels? (Ode on a Grecian Urn by John Keats)*

tin NOUN tin is slang for money/cash ❑ *Then the plain question is, an't it a pity that this state of things should continue, and how much better would it be for the old gentleman to hand over a reasonable amount of tin, and make it all right and comfortable (The Old Curiosity Shop by Charles Dickens)*

tincture NOUN a tincture is a medicine made with alcohol and a small amount of a drug ❑ *with ink composed of a cephalic tincture (Gulliver's Travels by Jonathan Swift)*

tithe NOUN a tithe is a tax paid to the church ❑ *and held farms which, speaking from a spiritual point of view, paid highly-desirable tithes (Silas Marner by George Eliot)*

towardly ADJ a towardly child is dutiful or obedient ❑ *and a towardly child (Gulliver's Travels by Jonathan Swift)*

toys NOUN trifles are things which are considered to have little importance, value, or significance ❑ *purchase my life from them bysome bracelets, glass rings, and other toys (Gulliver's Travels by Jonathan Swift)*

tract NOUN a tract is a religious pamphlet or leaflet ❑ *and Joe*

Harper got a hymn-book and a tract (*The Adventures of Huckleberry Finn* by Mark Twain)

train-oil NOUN train-oil is oil from whale blubber ❏ *The train-oil and gunpowder were shoved out of sight in a minute* (*Wuthering Heights* by Emily Brontë)

tribulation NOUN tribulation means the suffering or difficulty you experience in a particular situation ❏ *Amy was learning this distinction through much tribulation* (*Little Women* by Louisa May Alcott)

trivet NOUN a trivet is a three-legged stand for resting a pot or kettle ❏ *a pocket-knife in his right; and a pewter pot on the trivet* (*Oliver Twist* by Charles Dickens)

trot line NOUN a trot line is a fishing line to which a row of smaller fishing lines are attached ❏ *when he got along I was hard at it taking up a trot line* (*The Adventures of Huckleberry Finn* by Mark Twain)

troth NOUN oath or pledge ❏ *I wonder, by my troth* (*The Good-Morrow* by John Donne)

truckle NOUN a truckle bedstead is a bed that is on wheels and can be slid under another bed to save space ❏ *It rose under my hand, and the door yielded. Looking in, I saw a lighted candle on a table, a bench, and a mattress on a truckle bedstead.* (*Great Expectations* by Charles Dickens)

trump NOUN a trump is a good, reliable person wo can be trusted ❏ *This lad Hawkins is a trump, I perceive* (Treasure Island by Robert Louis Stevenson)

tucker NOUN a tucker is a frilly lace collar which is worn around the neck ❏ *Whereat Scrooge's niece's sister‾the plump one with the lace tucker: not the one with the roses‾blushed.* (*A Christmas Carol* by Charles Dickens)

tureen NOUN a large bowl with a lid from which soup or vegetables are served ❏ *Waiting in a hot tureen!*

(*Alice's Adventures in Wonderland* by Lewis Carroll)

turnkey NOUN a prison officer; jailer ❏ *As we came out of the prison through the lodge, I found that the great importance of my guardian was appreciated by the turnkeys, no less than by those whom they held in charge.* (*Great Expectations* by Charles Dickens)

turnpike NOUN the upkeep of many roads of the time was paid for by tolls (fees) collected at posts along the road. There was a gate to prevent people travelling further along the road until the toll had been paid. ❏ *Traddles, whom I have taken up by appointment at the turnpike, presents a dazzling combination of cream colour and light blue; and both he and Mr. Dick have a general effect about them of being all gloves.* (*David Copperfield* by Charles Dickens)

twas phrase it was ❏ *twas but a dream of thee* (*The Good-Morrow* by John Donne)

tyrannized VERB tyrannized means bullied or forced to do things against their will ❏ *for people would soon cease coming there to be tyrannized over and put down* (*Treasure Island* by Robert Louis Stevenson)

'un NOUN 'un is a slang term for one – usually used to refer to a person ❏ *She's been thinking the old 'un* (*David Copperfield* by Charles Dickens)

undistinguished ADJ undiscriminating or incapable of making a distinction between good and bad things ❏ *their undistinguished appetite to devour everything* (*Gulliver's Travels* by Jonathan Swift)

use NOUN habit ❏ *Though use make you apt to kill me* (*The Flea* by John Donne)

vacant ADJ vacant usually means empty, but here Wordsworth uses it to mean carefree ❏ *To vacant musing, unreproved neglect* (*The Prelude* by William Wordsworth)

valetudinarian NOUN one too concerned with his or her own health. ❏ *for having been a valetudinarian all his life* (*Emma* by Jane Austen)

vamp VERB vamp means to walk or tramp to somewhere ❏ *Well, vamp on to Marlott, will 'ee* (*Tess of the D'Urbervilles* by Thomas Hardy)

vapours NOUN the vapours is an old term which means unpleasant and strange thoughts, which make the person feel nervous and unhappy ❏ *and my head was full of vapours* (*Robinson Crusoe* by Daniel Defoe)

vegetables NOUN here vegetables means plants ❏ *the other vegetables are in the same proportion* (*Gulliver's Travels* by Jonathan Swift)

venturesome ADJ if you are venturesome you are willing to take risks ❏ *he must be either hopelessly stupid or a venturesome fool* (*Wuthering Heights* by Emily Brontë)

verily ADJ verily means really or truly ❏ *though I believe verily* (*Robinson Crusoe* by Daniel Defoe)

vicinage NOUN vicinage is an area or the residents of an area ❏ *and to his thought the whole vicinage was haunted by her.* (*Silas Marner* by George Eliot)

victuals NOUN victuals means food ❏ *grumble a little over the victuals* (*The Adventures of Huckleberry Finn* by Mark Twain)

vintage NOUN vintage in this context means wine ❏ *Oh, for a draught of vintage!* (*Ode on a Nightingale* by John Keats)

virtual ADJ here virtual means powerful or strong ❏ *had virtual faith* (*The Prelude* by William Wordsworth)

vittles NOUN vittles is a slang word which means food ❏ *There never was such a woman for givin' away vittles and drink* (*Little Women* by Louisa May Alcott)

voided straight phrase voided straight is an old expression which means emptied immediately ❏ *see the rooms be voided straight* (*Doctor Faustus 4.1* by Christopher Marlowe)

wainscot NOUN wainscot is wood panel lining in a room so wainscoted means a room lined with wooden panels ❏ *in the dark wainscoted parlor* (*Silas Marner* by George Eliot)

walking the plank phrase walking the plank was a punishment in which a prisoner would be made to walk along a plank on the side of the ship and fall into the sea, where they would be abandoned ❏ *about hanging, and walking the plank* (*Treasure Island* by Robert Louis Stevenson)

want VERB want means to be lacking or short of ❏ *The next thing wanted was to get the picture framed* (*Emma* by Jane Austen)

wanting ADJ wanting means lacking or missing ❏ *wanting two fingers of the left hand* (*Treasure Island* by Robert Louis Stevenson)

wanting, I was not phrase I was not wanting means I did not fail ❏ *I was not wanting to lay a foundation of religious knowledge in his mind* (*Robinson Crusoe* by Daniel Defoe)

ward NOUN a ward is, usually, a child who has been put under the protection of the court or a guardian for his or her protection ❏ *I call the Wards in Jarndcye. The are caged up with all the others.* (*Bleak House* by Charles Dickens)

waylay VERB to waylay someone is to lie in wait for them or to intercept them ❏ *I must go up the road and waylay him* (*The Adventures of Huckleberry Finn* by Mark Twain)

weazen NOUN weazen is a slang word for throat. It actually means shrivelled ❏ *You with a uncle too! Why, I knowed you at Gargery's when you was so small a wolf that I could have took your weazen betwixt this finger and thumb and chucked* *you away dead* (*Great Expectations* by Charles Dickens)

wery ■ ADV very ❑ *Be wery careful o' vidders all your life* (*Pickwick Papers* by Charles Dickens) ■ See wibrated

wherry NOUN wherry is a small swift rowing boat for one person ❑ *It was flood tide when Daniel Quilp sat himself down in the wherry to cross to the opposite shore.* (*The Old Curiosity Shop* by Charles Dickens)

whether prep whether means which of the two in this example ❑ *we came in full view of a great island or continent (for we knew not whether)* (*Gulliver's Travels* by Jonathan Swift)

whetstone NOUN a whetstone is a stone used to sharpen knives and other tools ❑ *I dropped pap's whetstone there too* (*The Adventures of Huckleberry Finn* by Mark Twain)

wibrated VERB in Dickens's use of the English language 'w' often replaces 'v' when he is reporting speech. So here 'wibrated' means 'vibrated'. In Pickwick Papers a judge asks Sam Weller (who constantly confuses the two letters) 'Do you spell is with a 'v' or a 'w'?' to which Weller replies 'That depends upon the taste and fancy of the speller, my Lord' ❑ *There are strings . . . in the human heart that had better not be wibrated*' (*Barnaby Rudge* by Charles Dickens)

wicket NOUN a wicket is a little door in a larger entrance ❑ *Having rested here, for a minute or so, to collect a good burst of sobs and an imposing show of tears and terror, he knocked loudly at the wicket;* (*Oliver Twist* by Charles Dickens)

without CONJ without means unless ❑ *You don't know about me, without you have read a book by the name of The Adventures of Tom Sawyer* (*The Adventures of Huckleberry Finn* by Mark Twain)

wittles ■ NOUN vittles is a slang word which means food ❑ *I live on broken wittles – and I sleep on the coals* (*David Copperfield* by Charles Dickens) ■ See wibrated

woo VERB courts or forms a proper relationship with ❑ *before it woo* (*The Flea* by John Donne)

words, to have phrase if you have words with someone you have a disagreement or an argument ❑ *I do not want to have words with a young thing like you.* (*Black Beauty* by Emily Brontë)

workhouse NOUN workhouses were places where the homeless were given food and a place to live in return for doing very hard work ❑ *And the Union workhouses?* demanded Scrooge. *Are they still in operation?* (*A Christmas Carol* by Charles Dickens)

yawl NOUN a yawl is a small boat kept on a bigger boat for short trips. Yawl is also the name for a small fishing boat ❑ *She sent out her yawl, and we went aboard* (*The Adventures of Huckleberry Finn* by Mark Twain)

yeomanry NOUN the yeomanry was a collective term for the middle classes involved in agriculture ❑ *The yeomanry are precisely the order of people with whom I feel I can have nothing to do* (*Emma* by Jane Austen)

yonder ADV yonder means over there ❑ *all in the same second we seem to hear low voices in yonder!* (*The Adventures of Huckleberry Finn* by Mark Twain)